PRAISE FOR
AND THE BLACK DAGG

"J. R. Ward's unique band of bro
series!"
—*New York Times* bestselling author Suzanne Brockmann

"Utterly absorbing and deliciously erotic."
—*New York Times* bestselling author Angela Knight

"J. R. Ward's urban fantasy romance series is so popular, I
don't think there's a reader today who hasn't at least heard
of the Black Dagger Brotherhood."   —*USA Today*

"Frighteningly addictive."   —*Publishers Weekly*

"Tautly written, wickedly sexy, and just plain fun."
—*New York Times* bestselling author Lisa Gardner

"A raw, gritty tour de force."   —*Booklist* (starred review)

"Ward's paranormal world is, among other things, colorful,
dangerous, and richly conceived."   —*RT Book Reviews*

"Delicious, erotic, and thrilling!"
—*New York Times* bestselling author Nicole Jordan

"Different, creative, dark, violent, and flat-out amazing."
—All About Romance

continued . . .

BY J. R. WARD

The Black Dagger Brotherhood Series

Dark Lover
Lover Eternal
Lover Awakened
Lover Revealed
Lover Unbound
Lover Enshrined
The Black Dagger Brotherhood: An Insider's Guide
Lover Avenged
Lover Mine
Lover Unleashed
Lover Reborn
Lover at Last
The King
The Shadows

Novels of the Fallen Angels

Covet
Crave
Envy
Rapture
Possession
Immortal

The Bourbon Kings

J. R. WARD

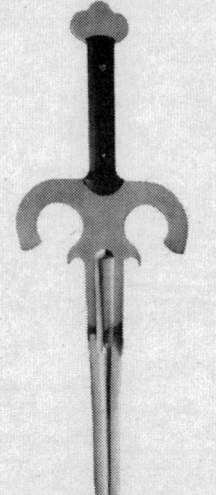

THE SHADOWS

A NOVEL OF THE BLACK DAGGER BROTHERHOOD

A SIGNET BOOK

SIGNET
Published by the Penguin Group
Penguin Group (USA) LLC, 375 Hudson Street,
New York, New York 10014

USA | Canada | UK | Ireland | Australia | New Zealand | India | South Africa | China
penguin.com
A Penguin Random House Company

Published by Signet, an imprint of New American Library, a division of Penguin
Group (USA) LLC. Previously published in a New American Library edition.

First Signet Printing, October 2015

 REGISTERED TRADEMARK—MARCA REGISTRADA

ISBN 978-0-451-41708-4

Printed in the United States of America
10   9   8   7   6   5   4   3   2   1

DEDICATED WITH LOVE TO:
THE BOTH OF YOU,
BECAUSE THERE IS NO WAY OF SEPARATING
ONE FROM THE OTHER.

ACKNOWLEDGMENTS

With immense gratitude to the readers of the Black Dagger Brotherhood!

Thank you so very much for all the support and guidance: Steven Axelrod, Kara Welsh, and Leslie Gelbman. Thank you also to everyone at New American Library—these books are truly a team effort.

With love to Team Waud—you know who you are. This simply could not happen without you.

None of this would be possible without: my loving husband, who is my adviser and caretaker and visionary; my wonderful mother, who has given me so much love I couldn't possibly ever repay her; my family (both those of blood and those by adoption); and my dearest friends.

Oh, and my WriterAssistant, Naamah.

GLOSSARY OF TERMS AND PROPER NOUNS

ahstrux nohtrum (n.) Private guard with license to kill who is granted his or her position by the King.

ahvenge (v.) Act of mortal retribution, carried out typically by a male loved one.

Black Dagger Brotherhood (pr. n.) Highly trained vampire warriors who protect their species against the Lessening Society. As a result of selective breeding within the Race, Brothers possess immense physical and mental strength, as well as rapid healing capabilities. They are not siblings for the most part, and are inducted into the Brotherhood upon nomination by the Brothers. Aggressive, self-reliant, and secretive by nature, they exist apart from civilians, having little contact with members of the other classes except when they need to feed. They are the subjects of legend and objects of reverence within the vampire world. They may be killed only by the most serious of wounds, e.g., a gunshot or stab to the heart, etc.

blood slave (n.) Male or female vampire who has been subjugated to serve the blood needs of another. The practice of keeping blood slaves has recently been outlawed.

the Chosen (pr. n.) Female vampires who have been bred to serve the Scribe Virgin. They are considered members of the aristocracy, and, in the past, they have been spiritually rather than temporally focused. They have recently been granted broad freedoms away from the Sanctuary, and are meeting the blood needs of certain Brothers. Some have the ability to prognosticate.

chrih (n.) Symbol of honorable death in the Old Language.

cohntehst (n.) Conflict between two males competing for the right to be a female's mate.

Dhunhd (pr. n.) Hell.

doggen (n.) Member of the servant class within the vampire world. *Doggen* have old, conservative traditions about service to their superiors, following a formal code of dress and behavior. They are able to go out during the day, but they age relatively quickly. Life expectancy is approximately five hundred years.

ehros (n.) A Chosen trained in the matter of sexual arts.

exhile dhoble (n.) The evil or cursed twin, the one born second.

the Fade (pr. n.) Nontemporal realm where the dead reunite with their loved ones and pass eternity.

First Family (pr. n.) The King and Queen of the vampires, and any children they may have.

ghardian (n.) Custodian of an individual. There are varying degrees of *ghardians*, with the most powerful being that of a *sehcluded* female.

glymera (n.) The social core of the aristocracy, roughly equivalent to Regency England's *ton*.

hellren (n.) Male vampire who has been mated to a female. Males may take more than one female as mate.

hyslop (n. or v.) Term referring to a lapse in judgment, typically resulting in the compromise of the mechanical operations of a vehicle or otherwise motorized conveyance of some kind. For example, leaving one's keys in one's car as it is parked outside the family home overnight.

leahdyre (n.) A person of power and influence.

leelan (n.) A term of endearment loosely translated as "dearest one."

Lessening Society (pr. n.) Order of slayers convened by the Omega for the purpose of eradicating the vampire species.

lesser (n.) De-souled human who targets vampires for extermination as a member of the Lessening Society. *Lessers* must be stabbed through the chest in order to be killed; otherwise they are ageless. They do not eat or drink and are impotent. Over time, their hair, skin, and irises lose pigmentation until they are blond, blushless, and pale eyed. They smell like baby powder. Inducted into the Society by the Omega, they retain a ceramic jar thereafter into which their heart was placed after it was removed.

lewlhen (n.) Gift.

lheage (n.) A term of respect used by a sexual submissive to refer to her dominant.

Lhenihan (pr. n.) A mythic beast renowned for its sexual prowess. In modern slang, refers to a male of preternatural size and sexual stamina.

lys (n.) Torture tool used to remove the eyes.

mahmen (n.) Mother. Used both as an identifier and a term of affection.

mhis (n.) The masking of a given physical environment; the creation of a field of illusion.

nalla (n., f.) or *nallum* (n., m.) Beloved.

needing period (n.) Female vampire's time of fertility, generally lasting for two days and accompanied by intense sexual cravings. Occurs approximately five years after a female's transition and then once a decade thereafter. All males respond to some degree if they are around a female in her need. It can be a dangerous time, with conflicts and fights breaking out between competing males, particularly if the female is not mated.

newling (n.) A virgin.

the Omega (pr. n.) Malevolent, mystical figure who has targeted the vampires for extinction out of resentment directed toward the Scribe Virgin. Exists in a nontemporal realm and has extensive powers, though not the power of creation.

phearsom (adj.) Term referring to the potency of a male's sexual organs. Literal translation something close to "worthy of entering a female."

princeps (n.) Highest level of the vampire aristocracy, second only to members of the First Family or the Scribe Virgin's Chosen. Must be born to the title; it may not be conferred.

pyrocant (n.) Refers to a critical weakness in an individual. The weakness can be internal, such as an addiction, or external, such as a lover.

rahlman (n.) Savior.

rythe (n.) Ritual manner of assuaging honor granted by one who has offended another. If accepted, the offended chooses a weapon and strikes the offender, who presents him- or herself without defenses.

the Scribe Virgin (pr. n.) Mystical force who is counselor to the King as well as the keeper of vampire archives and the dispenser of privileges. Exists in a nontemporal realm and has extensive powers. Capable of a single act of creation, which she expended to bring the vampires into existence.

sehclusion (n.) Status conferred by the King upon a female of the aristocracy as a result of a petition by the female's family. Places the female under the sole direction of her *ghardian*, typically the eldest male in her household. Her *ghardian* then has the legal right to determine all manner of her life, restricting at will any and all interactions she has with the world.

shellan (n.) Female vampire who has been mated to a male. Females generally do not take more than one mate due to the highly territorial nature of bonded males.

symphath (n.) Subspecies within the vampire race characterized by the ability and desire to manipulate emotions in others (for the purposes of an energy exchange), among other traits. Historically, *symphaths* have been discriminated against and, during certain eras, hunted by vampires. They are near extinction.

the Tomb (pr. n.) Sacred vault of the Black Dagger Brotherhood. Used as a ceremonial site as well as a storage facility for the jars of *lessers*. Ceremonies performed there include inductions, funerals, and disciplinary actions against Brothers. No one may enter except for members of the Brotherhood, the Scribe Virgin, or candidates for induction.

trahyner (n.) Word used between males of mutual respect and affection. Translated loosely as "beloved friend."

transition (n.) Critical moment in a vampire's life when he or she transforms into an adult. Thereafter, he or she must drink the blood of the opposite sex to survive and is unable to withstand sunlight. Occurs generally in the mid-twenties. Some vampires do not survive their transitions, males in particular. Prior to their transitions, vampires are physically weak, sexually unaware and unresponsive, and unable to dematerialize.

vampire (n.) Member of a species separate from that of

Homo sapiens. Vampires must drink the blood of the opposite sex to survive. Human blood will keep them alive, though the strength does not last long. Following their transitions, which occur in their mid-twenties, they are unable to go out into sunlight and must feed from the vein regularly. Vampires cannot "convert" humans through a bite or transfer of blood, though they are in rare cases able to breed with the other species. Vampires can dematerialize at will, though they must be able to calm themselves and concentrate to do so and may not carry anything heavy with them. They are able to strip the memories of humans, provided such memories are short-term. Some vampires are able to read minds. Life expectancy is upward of a thousand years, or in some cases even longer.

wahlker (n.) An individual who has died and returned to the living from the Fade. *Wahlkers* are accorded great respect and are revered for their travails.

whard (n.) Equivalent of a godfather or godmother to an individual.

PROLOGUE

The footprints he left on the white marble were red. Red as a Burmese ruby. Red as the core of a fire. Red as the anger in his marrow.

The blood was TrezLath's own, but he felt no pain.

The murder weapon he'd just used, a sterling silver paring knife about as long as his hand and as narrow as his forefinger, was still in his palm. It was dripping, but that was not the source of the stain he was leaving behind. He had been injured in the fight. His hip. His thigh. Maybe his shoulder, he wasn't sure.

The corridor was a mile long and sky-high, and he did not know what awaited him at its termination. A door, he prayed. There had to be a door of some kind—this was the way out of the palace, so there had to be . . . an exit. And when he came unto it? He had no idea how he was going to break out. But he'd also had no clue how to kill another living male, and he'd done that minutes ago.

Further, he had no plan for what was on the far side of the palace enclosure or how he was going to get over the Territory's retaining walls. No clue where to go, what to do. All he knew was that he couldn't be in that cell anymore. It was luxurious enough, with silken sheets on a feather bed, and a bath that had its own pool, and a private chef to feed him. He had books written by the Shadow Masters at his disposal, and a full team of care specialists, from healers, to bathers, to exercise commandants. As for his clothes? His now-torn vestments were studded with gems from the treasury, diamonds and emeralds and sapphires cascading down his robes.

And yet his body was regarded as far more valuable than the largesse it bore.

Trez was the sacred fatted calf, the prized breeding stallion, the male whose birth chart had proclaimed he was to sire the next generation of queens.

He had not yet been called into sexual service. That would come in time, when the Princess he was to mate had reached her astrological maturity.

Trez looked over his shoulder. No one was coming after him, but that would change as soon as the crumpled body of that guard he'd overpowered was found—and that wasn't going to be long. There was always someone watching.

If only he could—

Up in front of him, a door that was flush with the wall slid back, and a massive figure draped in black stepped directly into his path.

s'Ex, the Queen's executioner, had his chain-mail hooding in place, his features covered by the metal weave. But the sight of his face was unnecessary.

His voice, deep and evil, was pure menace. "You killed one of my males."

Trez shuffled to a halt, his dragging robes stilling on the floor. Glancing down at the knife in his hand, he knew that the flimsy "weapon" was going to get him nowhere against the Shadow he now faced. The silver blade had been designed to cut pears and apples, not even tenderloin meats.

And the executioner was not like that guard.

"You are trying to leave." s'Ex didn't take a step forward, but seemed closer anyway. "Which is not only unacceptable from my point of view, but against the law."

"Then kill me in punishment," Trez said in a tired voice. "Rip my body asunder and bury me in pieces outside of the Territory like the traitor I am."

"I would do just that. In retribution for your taking the life of my guard." s'Ex crossed his heavy arms over his thick chest. "But the very beating of your heart and breath within your lungs is divine. So that avenue is not open to me—or you."

Trez closed his eyes briefly. His parents had been thrilled with the news that one of their two fraternal sons had been born upon the perfect moment in time, a preordained, stars-aligned split second that would transform the family—a blessing for them, with attendant riches and social position; a curse for him that had robbed him of his life whilst ever still he lived.

"Do not even think about it," the executioner said.

As Trez lifted his lids, he found that he had put the knife to his own throat. His hand was trembling badly, but he was pushing the blade in enough to nick the skin over his artery.

His blood, warm and smooth, caressed over his clenched fist.

Trez's laughter sounded crazy to his own ears. "I've nothing to lose except a life sentence for the crime of being born."

"Oh, I think you do. No, don't look away—you're going to want to see this."

The executioner nodded at the open doorway and something was pushed out. . . .

"No!" *Trez yelled, his voice echoing up and down the corridor.* "No!"

"So you recognize him." *s'Ex uncoiled his arms and pulled up his sleeves, deliberately flashing bloody knuckles.* "In spite of my work. Then again, the pair of you have been together for how long?"

Trez's vision went in and out of focus as he sought his brother's eyes. There was no gaze to hold. iAm was not conscious, his head lolling to one side, his face beaten until it was so swollen the features were distorted. His body was bound in a worn leather sleeve that ran from below his knees all the way up to his shoulders and was secured by a brass buckle system. Stains, new and old, darkened the brown of the straps and dulled the glow of the metal pieces.

"Give him to me," *s'Ex commanded.*

As the executioner grabbed onto the back of the hold, he lifted iAm's limp body from the floor with no more effort than he might put into raising a flask of wine.

"Please . . ." *Trez begged.* "He is not of this . . . let him go. . . ."

For some reason, his brother's dangling lower legs registered with nauseating clarity. Only one of iAm's shoes was on still, the other having been lost in whatever abduction and torture had occurred. And both feet were pointing inward, the big toes touching, one tilted in unnaturally from a broken ankle.

"Now, Trez," s'Ex said, "did you think your decision wasn't going to affect him? I'm telling you to put the knife down. If you do not, I'm going to take this"—the executioner jogged iAm's limp body up and down—"and I'm going to wake it up. Do you know how I'm going to do that? I'm going to take this"—in his free hand he flashed a serrated knife—"and put it into its shoulder. Then I'm going to twist until it starts to scream."

Trez began to blink away tears. "Let him go. This has nothing to do with him."

"Put the knife down."

"Let him—"

"Shall I demonstrate?"

"No! Let him—"

s'Ex stabbed iAm's shoulder so hard, the blade cut through the leather and went into the flesh.

"Twist?" s'Ex barked over the scream. "Yes? Or are you dropping that butter knife?"

The clatter of the silver hitting the marble floor was overpowered by iAm's harsh, dragging breaths.

"That's what I thought." s'Ex jerked the knife out and iAm started to moan and cough, blood speckling the floor. "We're going back to your quarters."

"Let him go first."

"You are not in a position to make demands."

Guards came out of that hidden door in a swarm, all black-robed figures with chain-mail masks. They didn't touch him. They weren't allowed to. They surrounded him and began to walk, pushing him along with their bodies. Forcing him back to the place he had escaped.

Trez fought the tide, rising up on the balls of his feet, trying to see his brother.

"Don't kill him!" he shouted. "I'll go! I'll go—just don't hurt him!"

s'Ex stood where he was, that notched, bloodied blade catching the light as he held it aloft. As if he were considering major organs for the next stab.

"It's up to you, Trez. It's all up to—"

Something snapped.

Later, when the white light had faded from Trez's vision and the cresting wave receded, when the roar was silenced and a strange pain in his hands began to ride up his forearms, when he was no longer standing but on his knees, he would realize that the first guard he had killed that night was far from his last.

He would realize that he somehow murdered with his bare hands all who had surrounded him . . .

. . . and s'Ex was still standing there with his brother.

More than the deaths he caused, and the horror at iAm's imprisonment with him, more than the copper-scented blood that was so red and now not just marking his footprints, he would remember the soft laugh that percolated through the mesh links covering the executioner's face.

A soft laugh.

As if the executioner approved of the carnage.

Trez did not laugh. He began to sob, lifting bloody, torn hands to his face.

"The astrological charts did not lie," s'Ex said. "You are a force in this world, well suited for procreation."

Trez slumped to the side, landing in the blood, the jewels embedded in his robes digging into his flesh. "Please . . . let him go. . . ."

"Return to your quarters. Voluntarily and without hurting anyone else."

"And you'll let him go?"

"You're not the only one who can kill. And unlike yourself, I have been trained in the art of making living things suffer. Go back to your quarters and I will not make your brother wish, as you do, that he had never been born."

Trez looked at his hands. "I didn't ask for this."

"No one asks for life." *The executioner hiked iAm's body up higher.* "And sometimes they do not ask for death. You, however, are in the position to control the latter when it comes to this male. So what are you going to do. Fight against a destiny you can't change and sentence this innocent to a wretched, prolonged suffering? Or fulfill a sacred duty many before you have found great honor in providing our people?"

"Let us go. Let us both go."

"It is not up to me. Your chart is what your chart is. Your lot was determined by the contractions of your mother. You can no more fight this than you could fight them."

When Trez finally tried to stand up, he found the floor slippery. The blood. The blood he had spilled. And when he was on his feet, he had to scramble through the gruesome tangle of bodies, stepping over lives that he knew had not been his to take.

The footsteps he left on the marble were red. Red as a Burmese ruby. Red as the core of a fire.

And the ones he left now were parallel to his first set of tracks, heading away from the escape he had so desperately sought.

It would have heartened him to know that in some twenty years, three months, one week, and six days from this moment, he would get free and make it stick for quite some time.

And it would have shocked him to the numb core of his soul that he would, sometime after that, voluntarily return to the palace.

The executioner spoke the truth that night.

Destiny was as uncaring and influential as the wind to a flag, carrying the fabric of an individual's existence this way and that, subjecting that which it rocked to its whims without an inquiry as to what the banner may have desired.

Or may have prayed for.

ONE

There was no knock. The door to the office just flew open like someone had hit it with C4. Or a Chevy. Or a—

Trez "Latimer" looked up from the paperwork on his desk. "Big Rob?"

—cannonball.

As his security second in command stuttered and went into all kinds of hand flapping, Trez glanced over his shoulder at the twenty-by-ten-foot one-way mirror behind all his Captain Kirk, command central. Down below, his new club was poppin', humans milling around the converted warehouse's open floor space, each one of the poor sick bastards representing a couple hundred dollars of profit, depending on what their vice was and how much of it they needed to juice up.

It was opening night at shAdoWs, and he'd expected trouble.

Just not the kind that would make a veteran bouncer go twelve-year-old girl on him.

"What the fuck is going on?" he demanded as he got up and came around.

"I—you—I . . . the guy . . . he . . ."

Find your vocab fast, Trez thought. Or I'ma have to bitch-slap some words into you, my man.

Finally, the bouncer choked out, "Need to see this for yourself."

Trez followed Big Rob out and jogged down the stairs. His office was self-locking, not that he had any secrets shut in there. He did, however, have a couple of nice leather sofas, and some video-monitoring equip that could go the eBay route—plus he didn't like people in his spaces on principle.

"Silent Tom is containing the issue," Big Rob called out over the noise as they hit the ground floor.

"Like it's a chemical spill?"

"I don't know what it is."

T.I.'s "About the Money" was so pumped it formed a physical presence in the air, becoming something that Trez had to fight through as they made their way past the security guy guarding the entrance to the private lounges hallway.

As with his other club, The Iron Mask, there had to be little slices of Nobody Can See for his customers. It was tricky enough running a prostitution ring in Caldwell, New York, without having people flash their slappin' body parts out in the open.

"Back here," Big Rob said.

Silent Tom was a wall of human in front of the closed door of the third private room down. But Trez didn't need to have any reveal for him to put two and two together: His nose added that math up just fine.

The sickly sweet stench of a *lesser* permeated the hall, prevailing over the sweat and sex of the humans that were all around.

"Lemme have a look," he said grimly.

Silent Tom stepped aside. "Still moving. Whatever the hell it is."

Yeah, the slayer probably was. Those fuckers had to be killed in a specific way or they just kept on keepin' on—even if they were in pieces.

"We're going to have to call an ambulance," Big Rob said. "I did it. I didn't mean to—"

Trez held up his hand. "You're fine. And hold off on the nine-one-one."

Opening the door, he grimaced as the stench ramped up, and then stepped inside the ten-by-ten-foot room. The walls and floor were painted black, the ceiling mirrored, a single inset light glowing softly overhead. The slayer was curled up in the far corner under the built-in fuck bench, moaning and bleeding an oil slick that smelled like dead roadkill mixed with fresh-baked oatmeal cookies and Johnson & Johnson baby powder.

Nauseating. And once again, it put him off Mrs. Fields, which he did not appreciate—and children, which he didn't care about.

He checked his watch. Midnight. Xhex, his head of security, was enjoying a rare evening off with her mate, John Matthew—and Trez had had to force the female to take the break, because it was the only time that week her *hellren* was off his rotation with the Black Dagger Brotherhood.

He was going to have to deal with this himself.

Trez stepped back out into the hall. "Okay, so what happened?"

Big Rob discreetly flashed a handful of small cellophane packets with powder in them as well as a wad of bills. "We found him pushing this. He got mouthy. I popped him and then he fought back—he was a fucking demon, and when he pulled the knife, I realized I was in trouble. I did what I had to do."

Trez cursed as he recognized the symbol stamped on the heroin bags. It was nothing human—and the second time he'd seen it.

It was the vampiric Old Language—and the shit was on a *lesser* again? This time as a dealer?

He took the drugs and put them in his pocket. Let his bouncer keep the cash. "You were lucky you weren't killed."

"I'll talk to the police. Everything's on tape."

Trez shook his head. "We're not involving the CPD."

"We can't just leave him in there." Big Rob glanced at his mute partner. "He's going to die."

It was the work of a moment to overpower the humans' minds. Both of them. As a Shadow, Trez was like any other vampire, capable of barging into a cerebellum and rearranging thoughts and memories like they were armchairs and sofas in a living room.

Or maybe removing them from the house altogether.

Big Rob's body instantly relaxed and he nodded. "Oh, sure. We can hang here. No problem, boss—and don't worry, you don't want no one in there? You got it."

Trez clapped the man on the back. "I can always count on you."

Heading back to his office, he kept up with the cursing. He'd gone to the Brothers months ago, when he'd first found a slayer with this shit on him. And he'd meant to follow up even more with them. But life had gotten in the way, things like the s'Hisbe coming after him, and Selena and him. . . .

The mere thought of the Chosen female made him close his eyes and falter his feet on the stairs.

But then he threw off the sting. 'Cuz it was either that or go into a black-hole tailspin. The good news? He'd spent a lot of time over the last nine months trying to pull his mind, his emotions, his soul off the topic of Selena.

So he was used to this kind of power lifting.

Unfortunately, she remained a constant preoccupation, as if he had a low-level fever that dogged him no matter how much he slept and attempted to eat right.

And on some nights, it was a lot more than preoccupation—which was why he'd had to leave the Brotherhood mansion at times and crash back at his condo at the Commodore.

After all, bonded males could be dangerous, and the fact that he wasn't with her—and shouldn't be—meant absolutely nothing to that side of him. Especially when she was feeding fighters who could not, for whatever reason, take their mates' veins.

It was straight-up crazy.

She was a virtuous servant of the Scribe Virgin's, and he was a reformed sex addict with a life-in-prison-type sentence hanging over his head—and yet, according to his cock and balls, this was a recipe for true love.

Yup. There was some righteous math for you.

God, he was almost relieved he had a slayer leaking all over one of his sex rooms. At least it gave him a bomb to dismantle—which was better than staring out at that anonymous crowd of strangers who were feeding their own addictions thanks to the women and booze he supplied them with.

While he waited for the other shoe to drop back home.

At the s'Hisbe.

TWO

Rhage glared over the top of the *Caldwell Courier Journal*. From his vantage point on V and Butch's leather sofa, he had more view than he wanted of a shirtless Lassiter playing with himself.

Foosball, that was.

The fallen angel was working V's table like a pro, flashing back and forth between the two sides—and hurling insults at himself.

"Question," Rhage muttered, as he rearranged his injured leg. "Are either of your personalities aware that you're schizo-freakin'-phrenic?"

"Your mama's so stupid"—Lassiter dematerialized and re-formed on the far side, spinning the rods—"she thinks a California dime is something you dial a phone with."

V came over and took a load off. "That's multiple personality disorder, Hollywood. Not schizophrenia."

The Brother put a leather pouch of tobacco and a sheaf of rolling papers on the stack of *Sports Illustrated*s—just as Lassiter fired off a shout of triumph.

"Oh, look," V said under his breath. "The idiot is finally winning."

Rhage grunted as he tried to find a better position for his leg. He and V should both have been out fighting—except a *lesser* had gone Gordon Ramsay on him with a rusty knife and V had a gunshot wound through the left shoulder.

At least they'd both be back online in another twenty-four hours, largely thanks to Selena. Without her being so generous with her vein, they wouldn't be able to heal so fast—especially given that neither of their mates were capable of meeting their nutritional needs that way.

But, man, this sucked, sitting around like a couple of cripples.

And then there was the Lassiter factor.

The Pit was mostly as it always had been: full of gym bags, stereo and computer equipment, that Foosball table, and a TV the size of a city park. SportsCenter was on, talking about college football along with the NFL; there were dead-soldier Grey Goose bottles everywhere; and Butch's wardrobe was now spilling out into the hall. Oh, and yup, Schoolboy Q's "Hell of a Night" was bangin' on the speakers.

But it wasn't exclusively a bachelor pad anymore. Lingering in the air was Marissa's signature perfume—something Chanel?—and Doc Jane's medical bag was on the coffee table. Those vodka deadies? Only from this afternoon and tonight, and V was going to pull a tidy-up before he crashed. And then there were the *Journal of the American Medical Association* and the *People* magazines.

Oh, and the kitchen was clean, with fresh fruit in a bowl and a refrigerator full of things other than Arby's leftovers and soy sauce packets.

Rhage had dipped his toe into that Frigidaire pond as soon as he'd come in, snagging a half gallon of mint chocolate-chip ice cream. That was about a half hour ago, and he was feeling peckish again. Maybe it was time to head back to the main house—

As Jeezy's "Holy Ghost" broke in, Lassiter started rapping.

Rapping.

"Why did you invite him over?" Rhage asked—just as V extended his tongue to lick one of his hand-rolleds shut. "And Jesus, when the *hell* did you pierce *that*?"

"I didn't. He followed us across the courtyard. And a month ago."

"Why would you do that to yourself?"

V shot an evil smile across the sofa, his lids falling low over his diamond eyes. "Jane likes it."

Rhage went back to his newspaper. "TMI, my brother."

"Like you wouldn't do the same if Mary wanted it."

"Doc Jane *asked* for that? Like your goatee ain't enough shit going on with your piehole? Come on."

All he got was another of those smiles.

"Moving on . . ." He focused on the horoscopes. "Okay, so what sign are you, Lassiter?"

"I'm fabulous"—the fallen angel flashed to the other side—"with the sun rising in the Kiss My Ass quadrant. And before you keep asking, I was made, not born, so I don't have a birthday."

"I'll give you a funeral date," V cut in.

"How about a shirt." Rhage turned to the next page. "Just a shirt. Would it kill you to cover up, angel? No one needs to see that."

Lassiter gave things a pause . . . and then started pulling a Channing Tatum against the table, going all Magic Mike over the goal while he moaned like he was orgasming.

V covered his eyes. "Never thought I'd pray for blindness."

Rhage wadded up the paper and threw it at Lassiter. "Oh, come on, asshat! I wanna use that thing sometime—"

Rhage's phone threw off a seizure, vibrating against his ass until he leaned to the side and dug it out of the back pocket of his leathers. "Yeah," he said without looking at the number.

Trez's voice was low. "I got an issue."

"What's doing?"

"Incapacitated *lesser* in my club. I've done a scrub job on my bouncers—especially the one who fought him—but this ain't going to keep."

Rhage got to his feet. "Be there in five."

"Thanks, man."

Ending the call, Rhage nodded at V. "Come on, I know we're red-shirted, but this is not a fight situation."

"Don't need to ask me twice. Where are we going?"

Lassiter straightened from his grin. "Field trip!"

"No—"

"No—"

"I can be useful as well as decorative, you know."

V started to arm himself, grimacing as he strapped on his dagger holster and slipped in a pair of sharp-and-shinies, handles down. "Doubt we'll need a battering ram."

"Maybe we'd get lucky." Rhage headed for the door. "But I wouldn't bet on it."

"I don't want to stay here by myself—"

"And you ain't that decorative, angel."

Outside, the night was all about the fall, cold, crisp September air, making Rhage's sinuses hum and his beast surge under his skin as he walked across the courtyard to the great stone mansion's entrance.

Man, he couldn't wait for his Mary to get home from her work at Safe Place.

All that talk about tongues and females liking them in certain places—okay, it had only been about three sentences, but that had been more than enough—had gotten him tight.

Ten minutes, two forties, a pair of daggers, and a three-foot length of chain later, he dematerialized down to Caldwell's meatpacking district with V, both of them re-forming across the street from Trez's new joint. shAdoWs was located in a rehabbed warehouse, and as usual with any of the Shadow's places, there was a line snaking down the block, humans standing like cows about to go into a feeding shed. As music bumped, flashing lights and laser beams pierced the thousands of glass panes, making the place look like a three-story-tall psychedelic trip trapped under a tin roof.

As the pair of them walked around back, there were all kinds of turned heads, but whatever. Human women had a way of noticing vampires—maybe it was a hormonal thing; maybe it was the black leather.

Certainly wasn't that goatee. C'mon, now.

And yeah, there might have been a time in the past when he would have had to take advantage of the dubious wares, but no more. He had his Mary and that was more than enough for him. V was the same with his Jane.

Well, Jane plus a "healthy" dose of whips and chains.

Sicko.

The rear entrance of the club was a double-doored, triple-locked stretch of Staff Only, and it obvi had a security camera somewhere, because the instant they approached, a bouncer opened things up.

"Are you . . . ?"

"Yeah." V barged in. "Where's Trez at?"

"This way."

Dark halls. Dumb, drunk humans. DD working girls. And then there was Trez, standing outside a black door under a black light.

The Shadow made an impression, even from thirty dim feet away. He was tall and had an inverted triangle for a torso, big heavy shoulders dumping into a tight waist, with thick thighs and long legs holding the production off the floor. His skin was the color of the mansion's mahogany dining room table, his eyes black as midnight, his hair trimmed down to nothing but a pattern on his skull. All of that was just pretty window dressing, though.

The truth was that he was more dangerous a commodity than anything you could buy at a gun show.

Shadows were deadly, capable of tricks even members of the Brotherhood were impressed by—and their kind usually kept to themselves, sticking to the s'Hisbe's territory way outside of the city. Trez and his brother, iAm, were exceptions to that rule.

Something to do with Rehvenge. Not that Rhage had ever asked.

"Where is it?" V asked as he clapped hands with the Shadow.

"In here."

Rhage did the same, greeting the Shadow with a hard embrace. "How you doin'?"

"We got ourselves a complication." Trez stepped back and opened the door. "And not like you're thinking."

The "dead" slayer was moving on the floor, writhing its arms and legs slowly. Things were broken in various places, one foot pointing in the wrong direction, an elbow cocked at a wonked-up angle, and there was a good deal of leaking going on, the floor puddling with the Omega's oil-black blood.

"Nice work," Rhage said, taking a grape Tootsie Pop out of his jacket and popping the wrapper. "Bouncer did this?"

"Big Rob." Trez put his hand out. "And here is the complication."

In the center of his palm were a bunch of nothing-special packets of drugs—

Wait a minute.

V picked up the things with his gloved hand. "Just like the ones you gave to Butch, true?"

"Exactly."

"Yeah, this is dealing."

"Did anything come of this shit earlier?"

"Butch talked to Assail, and Assail denied, denied, denied he was doing business with them. And that was it. With nothing else to go on, we had other priorities, feel me?"

Rhage bit down to the chocolate center as he leaned in and did some WTF-ing of his own. The drugs were marked with a red stamp . . . of the Old Language symbol for death.

The *chrih*.

Assail was going to be in some serious ass-shit if he was using the enemy to get his product onto the streets.

V dragged his free hand through his black hair. "Now I know why you didn't just stab this thing back to the Omega."

"My bouncer said the slayer came in with the crowd and worked his way around, doing bit deals. He was asked to leave, argued, attacked, and then it was time for some lights-out when Big Rob took care of business. First time this particular *lesser*'s been around, but that's not saying much, because it's opening night. Bottom line, though, is I don't let people deal in my joints, human or otherwise. Don't want to be on the CPD's list of things to do any more than we already are . . ."

As the pair of them kept talking, Rhage sucked the white stick clean and found himself sizing up the Shadow.

Cutting into the convo, he demanded, "Why don't you come to Last Meal anymore."

V's diamond-hard glare swung around. "My brother, focus."

"No, I'm serious." He propped his hip on the black wall. "What's up, Trez. I mean, our food not good enough for you?"

Cue the throat clearing on the Shadow's side. "Oh, no, yeah, I'm just . . . busy, you know. Opening this . . ."

"And when was the last time you fed? You look like shit."

Vishous threw up his hands. "Hollywood, will you get in the game—"

"You know, I used Selena tonight and her blood is amazing—"

It all happened so fast. One minute V was jawing at him

while he was bringing up the very salient point that the Shadow needed to take a vein.

The next, Trez's racket-size palm was locked on his neck, cutting off all his air supply.

While the guy bared his teeth and snarled like Rhage was the enemy.

In the blink of an eye, and in spite of that nasty shoulder wound, Vishous counter-attacked the Shadow, tackling him in a total body slam as Rhage grabbed at that thick wrist to pull the grip free. Incredibly, it got them nowhere. Even with V's close to three hundred pounds trying to pry Trez off and all of Rhage's tensile strength getting thrown into the mix, the Shadow was brick-wall-going-nowhere, barely moving.

And then the three of them had something to really worry about.

Rhage blinked, and when he opened his eyes, brilliant light flooded the cramped, black space.

"Fuck," V gritted. "Let him fucking go, Trez! We got problems!"

Beneath Rhage's skin, his beast surged to life, awoken by the mortal threat.

"Trez! Let go!"

Something got through to the Shadow—whether it was all that light, or the fact that Rhage's features were already starting to morph—and he loosened his hold just a little.

V took it from there, throwing the Shadow to the slick floor and jumping on him, a black dagger flashing out and being put directly to the jugular.

On a sagging curse, Rhage coughed and breathed deep a couple of times. Shit. His beast had a hair trigger on a good night, when he was well-fed, well-fucked, and properly exercised. But when someone tried to kill him?

Even if there might have been a good goddamn reason for it?

Clearly, the Shadow had bonded with the Chosen. 'Cuz that reaction had male hormones all over it.

"I'm sorry," Trez mumbled. "I don't know what came over me. Swear on my brother's life."

"Why didn't you"—Rhage tripped over his own words—"tell us you bonded with her?"

There was a pause. Then Trez said, "I . . . shit."

V added a string of curse words. "You gonna stay put, Shadow, or am I slicing the front of your throat open?"

"I'm good. Swear."

A moment later, V came over. "Rhage . . . ? My brother?"

Rhage put his palms to his face and let himself slide off the vertical until he was ass-on-the-floor. Breathe in. Breathe out. Breathe in. Breathe out.

They already had a *lesser* in the club.

His beast was the last kind of patron they needed.

Breathe in.

Breathe out—

"What's going on with him?" Trez asked.

"Don't ever aggress on that motherfucker," was the last thing Rhage heard before the world receded like smoke in a draft.

THREE

In the most sacred hall of the s'Hisbe's Grand Palace, s'Ex stood on the far side of a door that had no knob, no handle, hardly any seam to distinguish the panel from the wall it was set into.

On the far side, he could hear the infant crying, and the sound, that plaintive entreaty for help, aid, succor, went into his ears and through to his soul. His hand shook as he put it to the cool expanse. His daughter. His offspring. The only one he would probably ever have.

The infant was not alone in the ceremonial room. There was the high priest, AnsLai; the Chief Astrologer; and the Tretary, a position charged with witnessing and recording events such as this.

The baby had been wrapped in a pure white blanket of woven wool by the nursemaid before being taken in there and left behind with those three males.

To cry for a father who would not come to save her.

s'Ex's heart pounded so violently the whites of his eyes registered the rhythmic pressure. He had not expected this reaction, but mayhap this precise fervor was why he had not been allowed to touch the child—or be alone with her. Ever since the Queen had given birth to her approximately six hours ago, he had been permitted to view her twice: once after she had been cleaned, and just now, as she had been rendered into that white marble room that had no windows and only one door . . . that locked from the inside.

The second of her birth had determined this, demanded

this. That was what custom dictated. The stars had aligned in such a way that his daughter was not to be the heir to the throne, and thus she had to be ...

Get in there! his heart screamed. *Stop this, stop this before—*

Silence.

Suddenly there was silence.

A sound like that of a wounded animal vibrated up his throat and out of his mouth, and s'Ex curled a fist, banging it into that door so hard, fissures formed in a star pattern, radiating outward from the point of impact.

Distraught and deadly, he knew he must needs retreat before he did something as unthinkable as what had just been done. Tripping over his black robing, he wheeled around and stumbled down the corridor. He was dimly aware of banging into the walls, his momentum bouncing him left and right, his shoulders slamming into the more slick white marble.

For some reason, he thought of a night many years before, at least two decades ago, when he had waited by the exit for TrezLath, the Anointed One, to come down and attempt to escape. Now he was doing what that male had done then.

Escaping.

Whilst in fact not freeing himself at all.

Unlike Trez, who had not been allowed to leave the palace, s'Ex, as the Queen's executioner, was permitted to. He was also the one who was responsible for monitoring all comings and goings.

There would be no delays for him.

And that would save lives this night.

That silence, that horrible, resonant silence, cannibalized his mind as he wound through the maze of halls, nearing the very exit Trez had sought. That male, too, had been condemned, the position of the stars the moment he was born more dispositive than nature or nurture.

Those constellations, so distant, so unknown at the time of birth and unknowable in maturity, determined everything. Your status. Your work. Your worth.

And his daughter, like Trez, had been born to a portent that had been a death sentence.

Nine months they had awaited her birth, society coming

to a kind of standstill with the Queen pregnant. Such fanfare, as there had been only one other pregnancy in the two centuries of the current monarch's reign—and that had yielded the Princess. Of course, the fact that the current conception had been by the Queen's executioner had been far less momentous and never publicly acknowledged. Better that it had been an aristocrat. A second cousin of royal blood. A male marked as significant by his birthing charts.

Or even better, some kind of immaculate miracle.

Alas, no. The sire had been he who had started as a servant and gained trust, access, and, much later, the sacred act of sex. But that was all largely insignificant in their matriarchal tradition; the male was as always a secondary afterthought. The result—the infant—and the mother were the most important.

There had been a chance, when the child had come out, that as a female, she might surpass the current heir to the throne, depending on the stars.

Although that would have resulted in another death, as there could be only one heir to the throne—the sitting Princess would have had to be ritually killed.

All had waited for news. With the time and date properly recorded, the Chief Astrologer had retreated to his observatory and completed his measuring of the night sky . . .

s'Ex had learned the fate of his infant before the general population, but after the courtiers: The birth would not be announced. The Queen would reaffirm her current daughter. All would continue as it had been.

And that was that, the personal tragedy for him buried under court protocol and reverence for royalty and longstanding astrological traditions.

He'd known all along that this was a possibility. But either through arrogance or ignorance, he had discounted the terrible reality.

This terrible reality.

When he finally burst out into the night, he drew breaths that he released in puffs. He had never expected an intersection between his personal history and this star-determining system that ruled everything.

Rather stupid of him, really.

Bracing his hands on his knees, he bent over and vomited into the cropped, dying grass.

The expulsion seemed to clear his head a little, to the point where he almost wanted to do it again. He needed to do something, anything . . . He couldn't go back into the palace—he was liable to kill the first Shadow he came to just to cleanse the pain.

His rescue, such as it was, came from duty. With this event, there was official business to be conducted, which, in his role as enforcer, he was required to discharge.

It was quite a while before he could calm his mind and emotions sufficiently to dematerialize, and when he was able to scatter his molecules, he proceeded out of the walls of the Territory with a strange sense of commiseration.

He was quite certain that the Queen was feeling nothing at this moment. As a result of that star chart, the innocent life that had been cut short had been devalued to the point of worthlessness, in spite of the fact that what had been born had come out of that royal womb.

The alignment of stars was more significant than the alignment of DNA.

That was the way it had always been. Would forever be.

In spite of the fact that it was but September, as he traveled toward downtown Caldwell, it was the coldest night he had e'er known.

FOUR

The Chosen Selena entered the training center through the back of the office's supply closet, and as she emerged, she jumped at the sight of the tremendous figure behind the desk.

Tohrment, son of Hharm, looked up from the computer. "Oh, hey, Selena. Surprise."

As her heart rate regulated, she put her hand to her chest. "I didn't expect to see anyone herein."

The Brother refocused on the blue glow of the screen. "Yeah, I'm back to work. We're going to open things up again."

"Open what?"

"The training center." Tohr leaned back in the ugliest green leather chair she had ever seen. And as he spoke, he stroked the arm as if it were a precious work of art. "Back before the raids, we had a good program set up here. But then so many members of the *glymera* were killed during the attacks, and those who did survive left Caldwell. Now, people are returning, and God knows we need the help. The Lessening Society is ramping up like rats to a warehouse."

"I wondered what all these facilities were for."

"You're going to see it firsthand."

"Maybe," she said. But only if they moved fast—

"Are you all right?" the Brother asked, jumping up.

With an abrupt spin, the world tilted around her, twirling her head on her spine—or was that the room itself? Either way, Tohrment caught her before she hit the floor, scooping her up in his arms.

"I'm okay, I'm all right . . . I'm fine," she said.

At least, she thought she spoke those words out loud. She wasn't sure, because Tohr's lips were moving and his eyes were locked on hers like he was talking to her, but she couldn't hear his voice. Her own. Anything.

Next thing she knew, she was in one of the examination rooms and Vishous's *shellan*, Doc Jane, was peering down at her, all dark green eyes, short blond hair and roaring concern.

The chandelier overhead was too bright, and Selena raised her palm to cover her face. "Please—this is unnecessary—"

All of a sudden, she realized she could hear herself, and the world, once dulled and diluted, came back in sharp detail.

"Honestly, I am fine."

Doc Jane put her hands on her hips and just stood there, as if she were a barometer making some kind of a reading.

For a moment, Selena was struck with fear. She didn't want them to know that—

"Did you just feed someone?" the Brotherhood's physician asked.

"About an hour ago. And I didn't eat. I forgot to eat." Which was not a lie.

"Do you have any medical conditions I need to know about?"

"No." Which was a lie. "I'm perfectly healthy."

"Here," Tohr said, pressing something cold into her hand. "Drink this."

She did as she was told and discovered it was Coke, in a red can that said, "Share with Buddy," on the side.

And actually, the stuff did revive her. "This is good."

"Your coloring is getting better." Doc Jane crossed her arms over her chest and leaned back against one of the stainless-steel cabinets. "Keep drinking. And maybe you should consider calling someone else in for—"

"No," she said sharply. "I will complete my duty."

The importance of coming here, and making her vein available to the Brothers and others who were not able to feed from their mates, was the only thing keeping her going. It was the connection to normal life, the grounding of a job that was of significance, the metronome of nights and days without which she would consume herself with a bad destiny over which she had no control.

The reality was that her time was running out—and she was never sure when her last moment was going to come, when the last time she did anything was going to happen. And that made being here in service absolutely critical.

As she continued to nurse the soda, many things were said, questions asked on the physician's part, answers given on hers. The vocabulary didn't matter—she would utter anything, any lie, partial truth, or false construction to get free of this tiled room and continue on to her last visit of the night.

"I shall complete my duty." She forced a casual smile onto her face. "And then I shall rest. Promise."

After a moment, Doc Jane nodded—and the skirmish, at last, was won.

The war, however, was a different beast entirely.

"I'm just fine," Selena said, hopping off the table. "Really and truly."

"Come and see me if it happens again, okay?"

"Absolutely." She smiled at the two of them. "I promise."

As she left the exam room, she supposed that the lie should have bothered her. But she didn't have the luxury of conscience anymore.

She was in a sprint against death, and nothing, not even the people she valued . . . or the male she loved . . . could get in her way.

For her, survival, such as it was, was a solo endeavor.

Back at shAdoWs, Trez had to take a moment to cough his larynx back into position before sitting up. One thing you could say about Vishous? The Brother did the dominating thing well.

Natch.

But whatever, shit was getting a little too real over there in the corner.

Across the dim space of the sex room, Rhage was curled into a ball, eyes shut, breath going in and out of his open mouth with such a measured rhythm he was either hypnotizing himself or in a fucking coma.

"What is he doing?" Trez asked.

"Trying not to turn into a monster."

Trez popped his eyebrows. "Literally."

"Godzilla. Only purple."

"Jesus . . . I thought that was just gossip."

"Nope."

V palmed a black dagger and lifted it over his shoulder. With a vicious—ha-ha—stab, the Brother obliterated the slayer's remains by nailing the thing in the empty chest, the second bright light of the night flaring blue-white as a blow-torch before disappearing and taking the majority of the stinking remains with it. The flash didn't take care of the grease spot, but Trez had outfitted these rooms with a drain in the center and a hose hookup discreetly mounted under the bench.

Humans could get messy, too.

"So you've bonded, huh," V said as he took a load off and watched over his Brother like a pack animal guarding a fallen wolf.

"I'm sorry, what?"

"Selena. You've bonded with her."

Trez cursed and scrubbed his face. "Ah, no. Not really."

"A very wise person once told me . . . lie to anybody you want, just never yourself."

"Look, I don't know—"

"So is that why you've been gone from the house so much?"

Trez considered staying on the blow-smoke train, but what was the use. He'd just attacked a male he respected, a male who, P.S., was totally and completely in love with his own fe-male, just because the guy had taken the vein—and nothing else—of a Chosen trained to be of service in that way.

If that didn't put the bonded-male stamp on his fore-head, he didn't know what would.

"I just . . ." Trez shook his head. "Fuck. Me. Fine, I've bonded—and I can't be around her feeding you all. I mean, I know it's a necessary service, and it stops at the vein, yada, yada, yada. But it's too dangerous. I'm liable to do that"— he nodded at Rhage—"at any moment."

"She won't have you? I know it can't be because of Phury. He respects the shit out of you."

Yeah, he and the Primale, who was responsible for all of the Chosen, were cool. Too bad that wasn't the issue. "It's just not going to work out."

"Why."

"Can we get back to why a *lesser* has Assail's drugs on him?"

"No offense, but I just cut you some huge slack by not turning your jugular into a sink drain. Think you can do me the honor of being honest?"

Trez looked down at his hands, and flexed the fingers out in a fan. "Even if I hadn't slept with a thousand human women, I'm not exactly a free man."

"Rehv said your debt to him is more than repaid."

"The tie that binds me is not to him."

"So who owns your leash."

"My Queen."

There was a long, low whistle. "In what way?"

Funny that he'd spent so much time with the Brotherhood and never told them anything about the anvil over his head. Then again, for so long all he'd done was try to pretend it wasn't there himself.

"I'm supposed to service the heir to the throne."

"When did this happen?"

"Birth. Mine, that is."

V frowned. "The Queen know where you are?"

"Yeah."

"You should have disclosed this to us before you moved in. Not saying we wouldn't have harbored you, but your people can be very particular about who they associate with. We got enough problems without a diplomatic issue with the s'Hisbe."

"There may be an extenuating circumstance, though." As his phone started to vibrate in his shirt pocket, he reached in and shut it off without looking at who the call was from. "I've been in neutral. With the possibility of either a head-on collision with a semi or a swerve that could save me."

"Selena know any of this?"

"She knows some of it."

The Brother inclined his head. "Well, it's your story to tell—at least with respect to the Chosen. As it impacts Wrath and our throne, though? All bets are off."

"Any night. I'll know any night—the Queen's due to give birth literally any moment."

"I keep nothing from my King."

Trez felt his phone go off again and he silenced it a second time. "Just tell him the dice are still rolling. We don't know what we got. Maybe the star chart will not match mine—and then I'll be free."

"Will pass that on."

There was a period of silence, and then Trez started to squirm. "Why are you looking at me like that?"

When there was no answer, he got to his feet, and brushed off his ass. And still those diamond eyes stared at him. "Hello? V—what the fuck."

"You're running out of time," the Brother said in a low voice. "On two fronts."

Trez's phone went off again, but he wouldn't have answered the damn thing even if he'd wanted to. "What are you talking about."

"There are two females. And in both cases, you're running out of time."

"I don't know what the fuck you're—"

"Yeah, you do. You know exactly what I'm talking about."

No, because there was only one ticking time bomb in his life, thank God. "Is Rhage going to wake up, or does he need a crash cart?"

"This is not about him."

"Well, it ain't about me either. Seriously, does he require medical help?"

"No. And that is not what we're talking about."

"Wrong pronoun, buddy. I'm not in this conversation."

Besides, who knew, maybe if the s'Hisbe shit went his way, he could work on the situation with Selena. After all, if he wasn't the Anointed One, he was free to be . . .

Shit, unless he gave up his work here, he'd still be a pimp. In recovery from his sex addiction. Who was going to need therapy to get over bad-destiny PTSD.

Yeah, wow. Bachelor of the year over here.

And hell, it wasn't like Selena seemed to miss him—and he didn't blame her. His past with all those human women, even though he'd stopped with the whoring as soon as he'd kissed her, was nothing romantic. It was downright disgusting.

The months of celibacy hardly made up for his efforts to deliberately stain his physical body—

"I'm having a vision of you." V rubbed his eyes.

"Look, unless you need me, I'ma—"

"For you, the statue will waltz."

As Trez's phone went off again, he found that the heebs had overtaken every square inch of his body. "With all due respect, I have no clue what you're talking about. Take care of that Brother for however long you need to, no one's going to disturb you here."

"Be present. Even when you think it will kill you."

"No offense, V, but I'm not hearing this. Later."

FIVE

In the training center's medical suite, Luchas, son of Lohstrong, lay on his back in a hospital bed with his torso and head propped up on pillows. His broken body was stretched out before him, rather like a landscape raked by bombs, scars and missing pieces transforming that which had previously functioned normally and well into a hodgepodge of painful, debilitating dysfunction.

His left leg was the biggest problem.

Ever since he had been rescued from that oil drum the *lessers* had imprisoned him in, he had been in a period of "rehabilitation."

Odd word for what was really going on for him. The official definition, as he had looked it up on a tablet, was to restore someone or something to its former state of normal functioning.

After so many months of physical and occupational therapy, however, he was confident in concluding that the nightly mental and bodily grind of movements both small and large was getting him no closer to his former self than it was successfully turning back time. The only things he knew for sure were: he was in pain; he still couldn't walk; and the four walls of this hospital room, which were all he had known since he had been locked in that cramped stasis, were driving him insane.

Not for the first time, he wondered how his life had come to this.

And that was stupid. He knew the facts oh, so well. The

night of the raids, the slayers had infiltrated his family's regal home, as they had so many others. They had slaughtered his father and his *mahmen*, and done the same to his sister. When they had come to him, they had decided to spare his life so that he could be used as a guinea pig, a test for whether a vampire could be turned into a *lesser*. Incapacitating him, they had packed him away in an oil drum at some location and had stored him in the Omega's blood.

There had been no experimentation, however. They had lost interest in him, or forgotten about him, or some other outcome had transpired.

Unable to get free, he had suffered in the black viscous void, living but barely alive, waiting for his doom to come, for what had felt like an eternity.

Unsure whether he had been in some way turned.

His mind, once a thing he had held with great pride for its scholarly achievement and capacity, had become as crippled as his body, twisting in on itself, once clear pathways of thought tangling into a dark nightmare of paranoia and terror.

And then his brother, the one he had never had time for, the one he'd looked down upon, the one he'd always felt so superior to . . . had arrived and become his savior. Qhuinn, the deviant with the blue eye and the green eye, the family embarrassment with the critical defect, the one who had been kicked out of the house and therefore not at home when the attack occurred, had turned out to be the only reason he had gotten free.

That male had also turned out to be the strongest member of the bloodline, living and working with the Black Dagger Brotherhood, fighting with honor, defending the Race against the enemy with distinction.

Whilst Luchas, the former golden boy, the heir to the mantle that no longer existed . . . was now the one with the defects.

Karma?

He lifted his now-mangled hand, staring at the stubs that were all that were left of four out of his five fingers.

Probably.

The knock upon the door was soft, and as he inhaled, he caught the scents on the other side. Bracing himself, he pulled the sheets up higher on his thin chest.

The Chosen Selena wasn't alone, as she had been last evening.

And he knew what this was about.

"Come in," he said in a voice he still didn't recognize. Ever since his ordeal, his speech had been huskier, deeper.

Qhuinn came in first, and for a moment, Luchas recoiled. Whenever he had seen his brother previously, the male had been in civilian garb. Not tonight. He'd clearly come fresh from the theater of conflict, black leather covering his powerful body, weapons strapped on his hips, his thighs . . . his chest.

Luchas frowned as he noticed two particular fighting implements: His brother had a pair of black daggers upon his sternum, the handles facing down.

Strange, he thought. It was his understanding that such blades were reserved only for members of the Black Dagger Brotherhood.

Mayhap they allowed their soldiers to wear them as well now?

"Hey," Qhuinn said.

Behind him, the Chosen Selena was silent as a ghost, her white robes floating around her slender body, her dark hair woven up high on her head in the traditional style of her sacred order.

"Greetings, sire," she said with an elegant bow.

Glancing down at his leg, Luchas wanted desperately to get out of bed and pay her the respect she was due. Not an option. The limb was, as always, wrapped up tight in white gauze from toe to knee, and underneath that sterile dressing? Flesh that would not heal, the heat of the infection simmering like a pot of water on the verge of breaking into a boil.

"So they tell me you've stopped feeding," Qhuinn said.

Luchas looked away, wishing there was a window so that he could feign distraction.

"Well?" Qhuinn demanded. "Is that true?"

"Chosen," Luchas murmured. "Will you kindly permit us a moment alone?"

"But of course. I shall await your summoning."

The door shut silently. And Luchas found that all of the oxygen in the room appeared to have departed with the female.

Qhuinn pulled a chair over to the bedside and sat down,

propping his elbows on his knees. His shoulders were so wide, the leather jacket he had on creaked in protest.

"What's going on, Luchas?" he asked.

"This could have waited. You shouldn't have come in from fighting."

"Not according to your vital signs."

"So the doctor called you in, did she?"

"She talked to me, yes."

Luchas closed his eyes. "I had a ..." He cleared his throat. "Before all of this, I'd had a vision of what I would be doing, what my future was going to be. I was ..."

"You were going to be like Father."

"Yes. I wanted ... all the things I had been taught defined a life as worth living." He lifted his lids and glared at his body. "This was not it. This ... I am as a young is. People tending to my needs, bringing me food, washing me, wiping me. I am a brain trapped in a broken vessel. I do nothing for myself—"

"Luchas—"

"No!" He slashed his mutilated hand through the air. "Do not placate me with promises of some future health. It's been nine months, brother mine. Preceded by a captivity in Hell that lasted a century. I'm done with being a prisoner. *Done* with it."

"You can't kill yourself."

"I know. Then I do not enter the Fade. But if I don't eat, and I don't feed, that"—he jabbed a finger at his leg—"will get the best of me and carry me off. Not suicide. Death by sepsis—isn't that what Doc Jane is so worried about?"

With a sharp motion, Qhuinn took off his jacket and let it land on the floor. "I don't want to lose you."

Luchas put his hands over his face. "How can you say that ... after all the cruelty in our household ..."

"Not your doing. That was the 'rents."

"I participated."

"You apologized."

At least that was one thing he'd done right. "Qhuinn, let me go. Please. Just let me ... go."

The silence lasted so long, Luchas began to breathe easier, thinking that his argument had been accepted.

"I know what it's like to not have hope," Qhuinn said roughly. "But destiny can surprise you."

Luchas dropped his arms and laughed bitterly. "Not in a good way, I'm afraid. Not in a good way—"

"You're wrong—"

"Stop—"

"Luchas. I'm telling you—"

"I'm a fucking cripple!"

"So was I." Qhuinn pointed to his eyes. "All my life."

Luchas turned away, staring at the cream-colored wall. "There's nothing you can say, Qhuinn. It's over. I'm tired of fighting for a life I don't want."

Another silence stretched out. Eventually, Qhuinn cursed under his breath. "You just need to feed and get your strength back—"

"I will e'er refuse her vein. You might as well accept this now and not waste any further time on arguments I find unpersuasive. I am done."

As Selena waited in the corridor, exhaustion cloaked her in heavy folds that were no less real for being invisible.

And yet she was antsy. Fidgeting with her robing, her hair, her hands.

She did not like time that was unconsumed by her duties. With nothing to occupy herself, her thoughts and fears became too loud to contain within her skull.

And yet she supposed there was a utility in this solitude. If she could stand to take advantage of it.

What she needed to do as she stood out here was practice her good-bye. She should try to compose the words she wanted to speak before she ran out of time. She should get up the courage that was going to be required to say aloud that which was in her heart.

She was going to follow through on the impulse to tell Trez good-bye.

Of the many people she would leave behind, the Primale and her Chosen sisters, the Brothers and their *shellans*, Trez was the one whom she mourned already. Even though she hadn't seen him in . . . many, many nights.

Even though she hadn't been alone with him in . . . many, many months.

In fact, after they had ended their . . . relationship, or whatever it was, he had all but moved out of the mansion. No matter what time she had come or gone, she had not seen him face-to-face, and only on occasion caught a glimpse of his big shoulders as he headed in an opposite direction from her.

That he was avoiding her had been a treacherous relief at first. It was going to be hardest leaving him, and harder still if they had continued their assignations. But lately, as her time grew shorter and shorter, she had come to decide that she needed to tell him. . . .

Dearest Virgin Scribe, what was she going to say?

Selena looked up and down the corridor, as if the perfect little monologue might obligingly march on by, at a pace leisurely enough so that she could memorize it.

For all she knew, he had forgotten their time together. By his own admission, he was well versed in finding female diversions of the human variety.

No doubt he had wiped the slate well clean.

And then there was the reality of him being promised to another.

She dropped her head into her hands. For her entire life, she had taken comfort and purpose from her sacred duty—so it was a shock to discover that as she drew closer and closer to her demise, the one thing she was driven to get right was her departure from a male who was not her own. With whom she had had an affair of the very shortest duration.

There had been many nights that she had spent in her bedroom up at the Great Camp, attempting to convince herself that what had happened with Trez was pure folly, but now, as time was running out? A strange clarity was focusing her. It mattered naught the why. Only that she accomplished the goal of telling him how she felt before she died.

She did not want to approach him too soon, however—rather embarrassing to pour out her soul to a potentially indifferent vessel and then linger for nights, weeks, months.

If only her expiration came with a date, as if she were a carton of milk—

Qhuinn emerged from the hospital room, and the tight expression on his harsh face cleared away her tangle of preoccupation.

"I'm so sorry," she murmured. "He is refusing again?"

"I can't get through to him."

"The will to live can be complicated." She reached out and put a hand on his shoulder. "Know that I am here for you both. If at any time he changes his mind, I shall come."

"You are a female of worth, you really are."

He gave her a quick, hard embrace and then stalked off down the corridor, as if he were leaving the facility. But then he paused in front of the closed door to Doc Jane's main examination room. After a moment, he pushed through.

As she prayed there was a solution for the two brothers, another wave of exhaustion, the bigger brother of the one that had swept her off-kilter in front of Tohrment, shambled through her body, making her throw out a hand to the wall lest she fall down.

Panic o'ertook her, her heart beating wildly in her chest, her head flooding with *do this, do that, run away*. What if this was an attack? What if this was her final—

"Hey, are you all right?"

Training her wild eyes toward the sound, she found that Tohrment was coming out of the exam room.

"I . . ."

All at once, the whirling sensation receded unexpectedly, as if she had been approached by a mugger who, having been confronted by the Brother, had reconsidered his attack.

Beneath her robing, she lifted one leg and then the other, finding none of the deadly resistance she was so terrified of.

"Selena?" he said as he strode toward her.

Leaning back against the wall, she went to brush over her chignon, and discovered that her forehead was damp with sweat.

"I believe I shall tender myself up to the Sanctuary." She blew out her breath. "I shall refresh myself there. It is needed."

"That is a great idea. But are you sure you'll be able to—"

"I'm just fine."

Closing her eyes, Selena concentrated and . . .

. . . with a twirl of the world and a spin of her molecules that her brain, rather than something in her body, initiated, she was relocated up to the Scribe Virgin's sacred, peaceful place.

Instantly, sure as if she had taken a vein, her body was

both eased and strengthened, but her mind did not follow suit—in spite of the lovely greens of the tree leaves and the blades of grass, the pastel colors of the tulips that were perpetually in bloom, the resplendent white marble of the dormitory, the Treasury, the Temple of the Sequestered Scribes, the Reflecting Pool, she felt pursued even though she was in arguable safety.

Then again, having a mortal disease of indeterminate duration made it difficult to tell the difference between symptoms that were on the "normal" spectrum, and ones that had greater portent.

She stayed where she arrived for quite some time, fearing that if she moved, she might trigger the expression of her disease. But eventually, she went upon a wander. The temperature of the still air was perfect, neither too hot nor too cold, and the sky overhead glowed a blue that was the color of a cornflower sapphire, and the baths gleamed under the strange ambient light . . . and she felt as though she were alone in a dark alley in downtown Caldwell.

How much time? she wondered. How many more promenades did she have left?

Shivering, she pulled her robing closer to her body as a familiar sense of sadness and impotence barged into her, crushing her chest, making it difficult to breathe. But she did not give in to tears. She had cried them all out some time ago, the why-me's, what-if's, and need-more-time's over now—proof that even boiling water could be gotten used to if you stayed within it long enough.

She had come to terms with the reality that not only had she not been granted a full life, she had not really lived much a'tall—and so, yes, of course she must tender a goodbye to Trez. He was the closest she had gotten to something that was hers, something private rather than prescribed, attained, for however briefly, rather than assigned.

In saying farewell to him, she was acknowledging that part of her life that had been her own.

She would approach him on the morrow.

To hell with pride . . .

After a while, she discovered that her feet had taken her to the cemetery, and given the direction of her thoughts, she was not surprised.

Chosen were essentially immortal, brought into existence long ago as part of the Scribe Virgin's breeding program where the strongest males were mated to the most intelligent females to ensure the survival of the species. In the beginning, the female breeding stock were quarantined up here, with the Primale serving as the sole male for insemination. As millennia passed, however, the role of the Chosen evolved such that they served the Scribe Virgin spiritually as well, recording the history of the Race as it unfolded upon the Earth, worshiping the Mother of the species, and serving as blood sources for unmated members of the Brotherhood—for whom some broke rank, and accepted mortality in exchange for love, freedom, the chance to bear young who would not be condemned to rigid roles.

And then the current Primale had come along and relaxed even further the roles.

Selena looked in through the graveyard's arched trellis; the marble statues of her sisters managed to loom o'er her in spite of the fact that they were quite some distance away and sequestered within their verdant bordering.

For all the good the ancient breeding program had done, there had been one treacherous result from it, one prison that, however modern-thinking this Primale was, he could not exempt Selena and her sisters from.

Deep in the cells of the Chosen, there lay dormant a critical weakness, a defect that came about precisely because of the limited pool of breeding that was supposed to make vampires invincible.

A sacrifice to the intention of strength. Proof that the Mother of the Race could, and would, be curtailed by Mother Nature.

The statues beyond filled her with terror. The elegant figures within the encircled acre were not actually made of stone—not in the sense that they had been carved from blocks. They were the frozen bodies of those who suffered from the same disease she had.

These were dead bodies of her sisters who had walked the path her own feet trod upon, frozen in poses that they had chosen, sealed in a fine mineral plaster that, coupled with the strange atmospheric properties of the Sanctuary, preserved them for eternity.

The trembling came over her anew as a wave—

—and once again, the quaking did not last.

This time, however, the cessation did not usher in a return to normalcy.

As if the sight of those frozen in the final stage had been some kind of inspiration for what ailed her, the large joints in her lower body locked tight, and then so did her spine, her elbows, her neck, her wrists. She became utterly fixed in place, immobile whilst fully aware, her heart continuing to beat, her eyes undimmed, her panicked mind hyper-aware.

With a shout, she attempted to shake herself free of it all, tried to pull her legs up, fought to move her feet, her arms, anything.

There was but a slight give on the left side, and that rendered her off balance. Upon a pitch and spin, she landed face-first on the ground, the fine filaments of grass getting into her nose, her mouth, her eyes.

Knowing she was in danger of suffocating, she put all the strength she had into wrenching her head to the side so that her air passages were clear.

And that would prove to be the last move she made.

From her vantage point, she was a camera overturned, the odd-angle view of the Sanctuary like something projected upon a screen: blades of grass close-up and big as trees, with the Reflecting Pool's temple far in the distance, nothing but the roof showing.

"Help . . ." she called out. "Help . . ."

Straining against her bones, she tried to remember the last time she'd seen any of her sisters up here. It had been . . .

Too many nights ago. And even then, no one came this far into the landscape, the cemetery being rarely visited at its peripheral site save for sacred remembrance rituals—that were not due to occur for months.

"Help!"

With a colossal pull, she fought against her body. But all that transpired was a twitch of her hand, the fingers dragging against the lawn.

That was it.

Tears flooded her eyes and her heart hammered and she wished absurdly that she had not e'er asked for an expiration date . . .

From out of the depths of her emotions, an image of Trez's face—his almond-shaped black eyes, his cropped black hair, his dark skin—came to the forefront of her mind.

She should have said her good-bye sooner.

"Trez . . ." she moaned against the grass.

As her consciousness receded, it was a door that shut softly, but solidly, blocking out the world around her . . .

. . . such that she was unaware, sometime later, when a small, silent figure approached her from behind, floating above the grass, a brilliant light spilling out from beneath flowing black robes.

SIX

With a curse, iAm ended the call that had just come through on his cell phone and braced his upper body on the counter in front of him. After a moment of arrhythmia, he yanked on his wool peacoat, the black one with the forty in a hidden pocket on the left side and an eight-inch hunting knife stitched into the lining on the right.

He might need the weapons.

"Chef? You okay?"

He glanced across the industrial kitchen at Antonio diSenza, his executive chef. "Sorry. Yeah. I gotta go—and I already started the *mise en place*." He picked his cell phone back up. "You can finish it tomorrow."

Antonio took off his toque and leaned a hip against the massive twelve-burner stovetop. All the equipment used for dinner service was cleaned up, the lingering steam from the dishwashers making the forty-by-twenty-foot kitchen seem like something out of the Amazon rain forest.

Too quiet, iAm thought. And the brightly lit place smelled like bleach instead of basil.

"Thank you, chef. Do you want me to stew the tomatoes before I leave?"

"It's late. Go home. Good service tonight."

Antonio wiped his face off with a blue-and-white dish towel. "Thanks to you, chef."

"Lock up for me?"

"Anything you want."

With a nod, iAm left the kitchen and cut through the tiled delivery hall to the back exit. Outside, two of his waiters were loitering around their cars and smoking, their tuxedo jackets off, their red bow ties loose and hanging from their open collars.

"Chef," one of them said, straightening.

The other immediately came to attention. "Chef."

Technically, he was more boss than chef here at Sal's, but he did do a lot of the cooking and recipe R & D himself, and the staff respected him for it. Hadn't always been that way. When he'd first stepped in to take over the Caldwell institution, he had not exactly been welcomed. Everyone from the waiters to the chefs to the busboys had assumed he was an African-American, and the deep pride and tradition of Italian ownership, cooking, and culture would have worked against anyone who didn't have Sicilian blood in his veins.

As a Shadow, he understood the deal better than they knew. His people didn't want anything to do with vampires or *symphaths*—and certainly never those rats-without-tails humans. And Sal's was one of the most famous restaurants in Caldwell, not just a throwback to the Rat Pack era of the fifties, but a place that had actually served the Chairman of the Board and his slick boys. With its flocked wallpaper, hostess stand, and formal everything, it was Sardi's north— and had always been owned and managed by Italians.

Over a year into his ownership, though, everything was all good. He had proved himself to everyone from the customers to the staff to the suppliers, not just stepping into Salvatore Guidette III's shoes, but filling them. Now? He was treated with respect that bordered on worship.

Wonder what they'd think of him if they knew he wasn't from Africa, he did not identify as American—and more to the point, he wasn't even human.

A Shadow was in their midst.

"I'll see you tomorrow," he told the two men.

"Yes, chef."

" 'Night, chef."

iAm nodded at them and strode around the far corner.

As soon as he was out of sight, he closed his eyes, concentrated, and dematerialized.

When he re-formed, it was on the eighteenth floor of the Commodore, on the terrace of the condo he owned with his brother. The glass slider was wide-open, the long white drapes billowing in and out of the dark interior like ghosts trying and failing to escape. There had been two possible destinations for him: here or shAdoWs, and he'd picked their bachelor pad because of what was waiting inside.

There was news from the s'Hisbe, and all things considered? iAm would rather be the messenger to Trez than the male they'd sent.

Putting his hand into his coat, he found the butt of his gun and stepped inside. "Where are you."

"Over here," came the deep, quiet response.

iAm pivoted to the left, toward the white leather couch that was against the far wall. His keen eyes adjusted in a heartbeat, and the enormous black shape of the Queen's executioner came into focus.

iAm frowned. "What's wrong?"

The sound of ice cubes in a club glass twinkled across the silence. "Where's your brother?"

"It's opening night at the club. He's busy."

"He needs to answer his phone," s'Ex said roughly.

"Has the Queen given birth?"

"Yes. She has."

Long silence. With nothing but the sound of those ice cubes to break it up.

iAm inhaled and caught the scent of bourbon—as well as an acrid sadness that was so great, he released his hold on his gun.

"s'Ex?"

The executioner burst up from the sofa and strode over to the bar, his robes swirling after him like shadows thrown in a great wind.

"Care to join me?" the male asked as he poured more into his glass.

"Depends. What's your news and how does it affect my twin?"

"You're going to need a drink."

Right. Great. Without further comment, iAm walked over and joined s'Ex at the bar. It didn't matter what went into which glass, whether there were ice cubes, if there was a splash of tonic. He drank what turned out to be vodka down and poured some more.

"So it wasn't the next Queen," he said. "The young that was born."

"No." s'Ex went back over to the couch. "They killed it."

"What."

"It was . . . decreed. In the"—he waved his glass around over his head—"stars. So they killed the infant. My . . . daughter."

iAm blinked. Drank some more. And then thought, Jesus, if the Queen could do that to an innocent young born of her own body, the s'Hisbe's leader was capable of anything.

"So," s'Ex said more evenly. "Your brother is once again Her Majesty's prime concern. There is a mandatory period of mourning and I shall depart to join in that. But following the Enclosure Ceremony and its attendant rituals, I will be sent to collect the Anointed One."

The Enclosure Ceremony was the formal entombing of the sacred dead, a right that was reserved for members of the royal family only. And the mourning would last a number of nights and days. After which . . . it appeared their reprieves had run out.

"Shit," iAm breathed.

"I am happy to inform your brother, but—"

"No, I'll do it."

"I thought so."

iAm sat down in the chair next to the executioner. Looking over, he traced the male's features. s'Ex had come from worse than the lower class; the male had been born of servant parents but, through his brawn and smarts, had risen to seduce the Queen. It was an unprecedented ascension through the strata of social levels.

"I'm sorry," iAm whispered.

"Whatever for."

"Your loss."

"It was decreed. In the stars."

The male's casual shrug was belied by the way his voice cracked.

Before iAm could say anything further, s'Ex leaned in. "Just so we're clear, I will not hesitate to do whatever is necessary to bring your brother home and provide him bodily to the purpose for which he was born."

"You've already said that." iAm likewise sat forward and locked eyes. "And get real, you don't actually believe that astrology bullshit, do you?"

"It is our way."

"And that means it's right?"

"You are a heretic. So is your brother."

"Lemme ask you something. Did you hear the infant scream? When they killed your kid, did you—"

The attack was not unexpected, the executioner launching at him with such force his chair was blown backward and the pair of them ended up on the floor, s'Ex straddling iAm while shaking with rage.

"I should kill you," the male growled.

"Get angry with me if you want," iAm shot back. "But be honest, at least with yourself. You're not quite so duty-proud anymore. Are you."

s'Ex shoved himself away and landed on his ass. Putting his head in his hands, he breathed hard, as if he were trying to pull a composure job—and losing the fight.

"I'm not going to help the pair of you anymore," the executioner said hoarsely. "Duty demands to be served."

iAm sat up and thought that the constellations under which his brother had been born were like a disease, something unvolunteered for, embedded in the life that was lived, a ticking time bomb waiting to go off.

Trez's detonation had been put off for oh, so long. It would not be denied any longer, however.

Not for the first time, iAm wished that he had been born before Trez. He would much rather have been the one cursed, the bearer of the burden. It wasn't that he wanted to be imprisoned for all his life, with nothing but repeatedly trying to impregnate the heir to the throne for a pastime, but he was different from Trez.

Or maybe he was fooling himself.

What he was clear on? He would do anything he had to in order to save his brother.

And he was prepared to get really damn creative.

By the time Trez came back to check the private lounge, Rhage had woken up from his coma, trance, nap, whatever it was. And although V's verbal diarrhea had been a real ball slapper, as the owner of the club and the guy who'd attacked first, Trez felt like he needed to make sure the Brother was okay.

"How we doing in here," he said as he reentered.

As Hollywood slowly sat up, it was clear he was trying to reenter reality, returning from some mental destination that had been far from the club.

"Hey, Sleeping Beauty," V muttered as he took out a hand-rolled and a lighter. "You back?"

"You can't smoke in here," Trez said.

Vishous cocked a brow. "What're you going to do? Kick me out?"

"Don't want to get shut down on my first night."

"You got bigger problems than the Department of Public Health."

Fuck you, V, Trez thought.

"You need something?" he asked Rhage. "I got all kinds of things that don't have alcohol in them."

"Nah, I'm all right." The Brother rubbed his face and then looked over. "So you've bonded with that Chosen, huh—"

"I even have food, if you want—"

"Come on, man." Rhage shook his head. "You just tried to eat my lunch."

Trez glanced at his watch. "Actually, it was over an hour ago."

"I mean, whatever—what's the problem? Why don't you get with her."

"You're still a little pale."

"Fine, fine. You wanna hit the mute button, that's your business."

Cue. Awkward. Silence.

OMG, this was the best fucking night, Trez thought. What next, a meteor hitting Caldwell?

Nah, probably just his club.

"Sooooo . . . I'll take the drugs," V said, pocketing the cellophane packets. "You get any more—"

The third goddamn flash in the room was bright enough to blind, and Trez put up an arm to cover his face as he fell back into a defensive stance.

"Oh, fuck!" one of the Brothers barked.

Bomb? Deadly slayer retaliation?

All that new electrical wiring failing on an epic scale?

Or maybe he shouldn't have given the universe a suggestion about the whole meteor thing.

As Trez blinked the spots in his vision clear, it turned out to be a case of None of the Above.

A figure was standing where the great burst of light had flared—a figure that was about as impressive as a garden gnome gone Goth: Whatever it was was four feet tall, covered from head to foot in black robing . . . and evidently the source of illumination: From beneath the hem, brilliant light glowed. Like maybe La Perla had gone Las Vegas strip under there.

Abruptly, Trez stopped breathing as he put the math together and came up with the impossible. Holy shit, that was the—

"Hello, Mother," Vishous said dryly.

—Scribe Virgin.

"I have come for a purpose." The female voice was hard as crystal and just as clear. "And it must be served."

"Really." V took a drag on his hand-rolled. "You gonna take candy from a baby? Or is it kick-a-puppy night?"

The figure turned Her back on the Brother. "You."

Trez recoiled, his head banging into the wall. "Excuse me?"

"You're not supposed to make inquiries of Her," V bit out. "Just FYI."

"Me?" Trez repeated. "What do you want me for?"

"You are summoned by one of mine own."

"You taking him to Disneyland?" V muttered. "Lucky you, Trez—but She's probably only tight with Maleficent, the Shadow Man, Cruella—"

"How do you know so much Disney shit?" Rhage cut in.

"Come with me," the Scribe Virgin said, extending her robed arm.

"Me?" Trez blurted a third time.

"You have been summoned."

"Selena . . . ?" he breathed.

Rhage shook his head. "Should I just get the marshmallows? 'Cuz you are about to get toasted for those questions, buddy."

That was the last thing Trez heard before a swirling vor-

tex of energy claimed him and carried him off to God only
knew . . .

. . . where.

As the sense of having been transported disappeared, he
steadied himself on his feet with a shout, both arms punching out from his torso, his head spinning so badly he figured
he was going to dreidel it to the ground.

A sudden awareness of his surroundings stopped all that.

Parkland. He'd been relocated to some kind of postcard-
perfect parkland, rolling green lawns interspersed with top-
heavy trees, blooming flower beds and, in the distance,
white marble buildings of Greco-Roman extraction. Except
the horizon struck him as all wrong. A forest boundary offered a verdant stretch of green off in the distance, but there
was an unnatural quality to it, the same trees seeming to
mark the acreage, as if nature were on a repeat pattern. And
overhead, the sky was likewise an all-wonky, its milky
brightness appearing to have no distinct source, like there
was just an enormous fluorescent light up there.

"Where am I?"

When there was no answer, he twisted around. The small
robed figure was gone.

Great. Now what did he do?

Later, he would wonder what exactly made him turn and
start walking . . . then running. A noise? His name? Some
instinct . . . ?

He found the body on the far side of a rise in the undulating ground. Whoever it was was facedown, in the traditional garb of a Chosen female, the soles of the sandals—

"Selena!" he shouted. "Selena . . . !"

Skidding to a halt, Trez dropped to his knees. "Selena?"

Her black hair was a mess, the traditional twist of her
chignon ratted and sloppy, falling over her face. As he lifted
the tangle, her skin was paper white.

"Selena . . ." He wasn't sure whether she was injured or
had collapsed, and with no medical training, he had no clue
what to do.

"Breathing, are you breathing?" He put his ear down on
her back. Then he leaned across her and took her arm to
check for a—

"Oh . . . God."

The limb was stiff, as if rigor mortis had set in. Except . . .

when he placed his two fingers on the inside of her wrist, there was a pulse.

Selena moaned and her foot twitched. Then her head jerked against the grass.

"Selena?" His heart pounded so hard, he could barely hear anything. "What happened?"

No reason to ask if she was okay. That was a resounding fucking no.

"Are you hurt?"

More moaning as she seemed to struggle against something.

"I'm going to roll you over."

Bracing himself, he took her arm and began to try to move her—but he had to stop. Her position did not change, her contoured limbs and stiffened torso were so rigid, it was as if he were dealing with a statue made of stone—

"Oh, shit!"

At the sound of Rhage's voice, Trez jerked his head up. V and Rhage had materialized out of nowhere, and while he had always liked the two of them, at the moment, he could have kissed the pair of warriors.

"You gotta help me," he barked. "I don't know what's wrong with her."

The Brothers knelt down, and Vishous went for that wrist, checking the pulse.

"She can't seem to move. But I don't know why?"

"She has a pulse," V murmured. "She's breathing. Shit, I need my stuff."

"Can we get her to . . . where the fuck are we?" Trez demanded.

"Yeah, I can transport her—"

"No one moves her but me," he heard himself growl.

The position paper was hardly a bene in this situation. The bonded male in him, however, didn't give a fuck.

Conversation rolled out between the Brothers, but damned if he heard any of it. His brain was tripping over itself, snippets of the past couple of months filtering through as he tried to look for signs that there had been something wrong with her.

There had been nothing that he'd seen, or heard of through the grapevine. If she'd only collapsed, it might have been the result of offering her vein too much, but that wouldn't explain the fact that her body had seized up in the way it had—she seemed to have literally turned to stone.

Someone tapped him on the shoulder. Rhage.

"Give me your hand."

Trez put his palm out and felt himself get lifted to his feet. Before they could talk at him, he said, "I have to carry her. She's mine—"

"We know." Rhage nodded. "Nobody's going to touch her without your permission. We need you to pick her up—then V will help you both back, okay? G'on now, gather your female."

Trez's arms were shaking so badly, he wondered whether he'd be able to hold her in his arms. But as soon as he bent down, a profound sense of purpose wiped away all the nerves and trembling: The goal of getting her to the training center's clinic gave him a physical power and a mental clarity that he had never known before.

He would die in the effort.

God, she weighed so little. Less than he remembered.

And beneath the robes he could feel her hard bones, as if she were wasting away.

Just before that whirlpool effect overtook him again, his eyes shifted to a thick row of stocky trees that were broken by a trellis. On the far side of the arch, there was a courtyard of some kind in which marble statues of females in various poses were set up on pillars.

Had she been on the way there?

For some reason, the sight of those statues terrified him to the core.

SEVEN

Standing in front of the long mirror in her bedroom, Layla tried to pull the supposedly loose coat around herself, but getting what seemed like its copious folds across her belly was like asking a throw blanket to cover a king-size bed.

Looking down, she could no longer see her feet, and for once in her life, her breasts were big enough to create some serious cleavage beneath her robing.

Given the breadth of her, it was hard to believe she still had months to go with the pregnancy.

Why couldn't vampires be more like humans? Those rats without tails took nine months to do this. Her species? Try eighteen.

Glancing over her shoulder, she checked herself out in the dresser's mirror across the way. According to the various human birthing shows she'd watched on TV, she was supposed to feel all aglow. Revel in her body's changes. Embrace the miracle that was conception, incubation, and impending expulsion.

Guess humans really were a different race.

The only positive thing she took from this experience—and arguably it was the only thing that mattered—was that her young was active and seemingly healthy. Regular checkups with Doc Jane had indicated that things were progressing with perfect order, milestones met and surpassed, stages entered and departed with grace.

That was it for the positives. The rest of the experience?

No, thank you kindly. She detested the way she had to heave herself to her feet. The big melons sitting on her chest made it hard to breathe. The swelling in her ankles and hands turned elegant limbs into tree trunks. And then there were the surging hormones. . . .

That made her want to do things she felt pregnant females really shouldn't do.

Especially given who she wanted to do them with—

"Stop it. Just stop it."

Dropping her head into her hands, she struggled with the piercing guilt that had been her shadow these past months, dogging her close as her own skin, heavy as a suit of chain mail.

Unlike the pregnancy, which had a termination date for all the discomfort and worry, there was no relief to be had with her other situation. No terminal event—at least not one that came with any joy.

She had made her bed, however. Now she must lie in it.

Going over to her door, she cracked the panels and listened for footsteps. Voices. The sound of vacuum cleaners. When there was nothing, she stepped out into the hall of statues and looked left and right. A quick check of her watch told her she had about an hour and a half before dawn would force her return to the Brotherhood mansion.

Stepping out, she wanted to jog, but she could barely manage a fast walk as she headed in the direction of the staff quarters.

Her route to the exit was preplanned and well-utilized, and she had the timing down to a science. Six minutes for her to get down the back stairs and out into the garage. Two minutes to the car that she'd been given to use and had told people she was taking out on a regular basis to "clear her head."

Sixteen-minute drive into the tracks of farmland east of town.

Two-minute walk up that field to the maple tree.

Where she would find—

"Layla?"

She tripped over her own feet as she wheeled around. Blay was at the head of the hall of statues and in his fighting dress, his leathers stained and his face exhausted.

"Ah—hello," she replied. "Have you come off the field?"

"Are you heading out?" Blay frowned. "It's awful late."

"Just for a short drive," she said smoothly. "To, you know, clear my head."

Dearest Virgin Scribe, she hated the lying.

"Well, I'm glad I caught you. Qhuinn's not doing so well."

Layla frowned and walked back toward the fighter. The father of her young was one of the most important people in her life, as was Blay. The mated pair were her family. "Why?"

"Luchas." Blay stripped his dagger holster off his chest. "He's refusing to feed, and Qhuinn's just hit the wall with it."

"It's been almost a month."

"Longer."

Ordinarily, if a healthy male vampire took the vein of a Chosen, he could easily go several months between feedings, depending on his activity level, stress, and general health. However, for someone who was as ill as Luchas? Much more than a week or two could quickly become a death sentence.

"Where is Qhuinn now?"

"Down in the billiards room. They called me off the streets early because . . ." Blay shook his head. "Yeah, he's not doing well."

Layla closed her eyes and put her hand on her belly. She had to go. She had to stay . . .

"I have to take a shower." Blay glanced over at the door to the room he and Qhuinn shared. "Is there any way you could sit with him until I get down there?"

"Oh, yes, of course."

Blay reached out and squeezed her shoulder. "You're going to need to help me with him. This is getting . . ."

"I know." She took off her coat and didn't bother putting it back in her room. She just tossed it on the floor in front of her own door. "I'll head down right now."

"Thank you. God, thank you."

They embraced for a split second and then she waddled off, heading for the grand staircase and the male who had given her the most priceless gift of this child she carried within her womb.

There was nothing she would not do for Qhuinn or his *hellren*.

She was, however, very aware of the male who was

waiting for her at this very moment, under that maple tree, out in that field.

Her conscience tortured her, especially as she passed by the open double doors of the King's study. Through the regal doorway, she saw the throne behind the great carved desk ... and was reminded of why she had struck the deal she had.

Selling her body to the head of the Band of Bastards had been done to keep all of them safe here at the mansion. The deal had not yet been consummated on account of her pregnancy, however—something that had surprised her at first. Xcor was a brutal warrior, one who not only had the reputation, but the actual character, for doing harm to others—and enjoying it. And yet with her, he seemed content to bide his time before he collected his due.

On a regular basis, they met beneath that tree and talked. Or sometimes simply sat in silence, his eyes roaming all over her as if ...

Well, sometimes she thought that he seemed to take strength from just staring at her, as if the visual connection was a kind of vein from which he needed to draw regularly.

Other times, she knew he was picturing her naked—and she told herself to be offended by that. Scared by that. Worried over that.

Lately, however, a strange curiosity about him had taken root under her fear, a curiosity tied to his powerful body, his narrowed eyes ... his lips, even though the upper one was ruined ...

She blamed it on her hormones—and tried not to dwell on the urges. The only thing she needed to keep in mind was that as long as she continued to meet with him, he had sworn on whatever honor he had that he would not raid the compound.

After all, the only reason he knew where they were was because of her. Indirectly, perhaps, but it felt like the security leak was solely her fault.

The whole thing was a deal with a devil, executed to keep those whom she cared for most safe. She hated the lies, the double life, the guilt ... and the fear that sooner or later she would have to live up to her end of the bargain.

But there was nothing she could do.

And tonight, her family had to come before her fraud.

*   *   *

Down in the training center's main exam room, Trez was having an out-of-body experience as the whirling transportation stopped and he once again had to recalibrate his location. Thank God they'd made it over in one piece. Now, if only there was help to be had here.

Cradling Selena's stiff, contorted body in his arms, he glanced over his shoulder. Doc Jane, V's *shellan*, was standing off to the side in full doctor garb: blue scrubs, green nitrile gloves, little booties on her feet.

She didn't approach Selena, however. She just stayed where she was, staring at them, for what seemed like forever.

Shit. Trez was no doctor type, but generally speaking, when someone with the big "DR." in front of their name had to take a TO when they first saw a patient?

Not a good sign.

Rhage and V were across the way, and they were likewise gawking at him and Selena, as if they also had no clue how to help.

Doc Jane cleared her throat. "Trez . . . ?"

"I'm sorry, what?"

"Will you let me look at her?"

Trez frowned. "Yeah—come on." When Doc Jane didn't move, he started to lose his temper. "What the hell's the problem—"

"Your fangs are bared and you're growling. That's the problem."

He pulled a quick self-check, and discovered—gee-whiz, he had in fact gone all Cujo on them, sinking his weight down into his thighs, flashing his hardware, and making a sound like an industrial mower in the back of his throat.

"Yeah, sorry." At that point, he noticed that he'd also backed into a corner and was holding Selena to his chest like someone was going to try to take her from him. "So I should put her down on the table."

"That would be a good place to start," V pointed out.

His body took its own sweet time as he gave it the command to move forward, and in the end, only the fact that she needed treatment by someone who had half a brain and a stethoscope got him anywhere close to the center of the room. Leaning down, he put her on the stretch of stainless

steel—and he shuddered because he might as well have
been handling a wooden chair: her body stayed in the exact
same position she had been in when he'd found her, legs
outstretched, torso twisted, arms curled up to her chest.
And almost worse? Her head remained at that bad angle,
wrenched around in the opposite direction of her shoulders
as if she were in great pain.

His hand shook as he brushed her hair from her face.
Her eyes were open, but he wasn't sure she was conscious.
She didn't seem to focus on anything, periodic slow blinks
the only indication she might be awake.

Might be still alive.

Trez put his face in her line of sight. "You're at the training center. They're going to . . ."

As his voice faltered, he ordered himself to get the fuck
away and let Doc Jane do her job.

Crossing his arms over his chest, he backed off until he
felt a heavy hand on his shoulder. It was Rhage. And Trez
was pretty sure that the gesture was part compassion, part
insurance in case the bonded male in him decided to grab
the reins again.

"Let them do their thing," Hollywood said as Ehlena,
who was Rehv's *shellan* and the nurse, burst through the
door. "Let's just see where she's at."

Trez nodded. "Okay. Yeah."

The good doctor leaned down and looked into Selena's
opaque eyes. Whatever she said was too soft to hear, but
Selena's pattern of blinking changed—although it was hard
to know whether that was a good or a bad thing.

Blood pressure. Pulse. Pupils. The first three checks went
quick, but Jane didn't waste time announcing what the results were. She and her nurse just kept working fast, taking
Selena's temperature, putting an IV into the back of her
hand because the crooks of her elbows were locked up.

"I want an EKG, but I can't get to her chest," Doc Jane
said. Then she glanced over her shoulder at her mate. "Do
you know any syndrome that causes this? It's like a full-
body seizure except her pupils are reactive."

"I don't. You want me to call Havers for a consult?"

"Yes. Please." As V stalked out of the room, Jane shook
her head. "I need to know what's happening in her brain,
but we don't have an MRI here or a CT scan."

"So we're taking her to Havers," Trez said.

"He doesn't have that technology, either."

"Fuck." As Rhage's hold tightened on him, Trez focused on Selena's face. "Is she in pain? I don't want her in pain."

"Honestly?" the doctor said. "I don't know. And until I get a handle on her neurological state, I don't want to give her any drugs that would depress function. But I'll move as fast as I can."

It seemed to take an eternity, time grinding to a halt as all he could do was watch the complicated medical dance going on around that table. And Rhage stayed right next to him, playing babysitter sentry while Trez straddled the extremes of Shitting in His Pants and Wanting to Blow His Brains Out with no grace whatsoever.

And then the Chosen Cormia burst through the door.

The instant the female saw Selena, she gasped and brought both hands up to cover her mouth. "Dearest Virgin Scribe . . ."

Doc Jane looked over from taking a blood draw from a vein on the back of Selena's other hand. "Cormia, do you know what could have—"

"She has the disease."

Everyone went still. Except for Cormia. The Chosen rushed to her sister's side and smoothed Selena's dark hair, murmuring to her in the Old Language.

"What disease?" Doc Jane asked.

"The Old Language translation is roughly 'the Arrest.'" The Chosen wiped at her eyes. "She has the Arrest."

Trez heard his voice cut into the silence. "What is that?"

"And is it communicable," Jane interjected.

EIGHT

As sunrise threatened in the East, Xcor, leader of the Band of Bastards, reassumed his form in front of a modest colonial. The house, which he and his soldiers had been using as a lair for nearly a year, was located on the far side of a boring cul-de-sac in a neighborhood full of middle-class humans halfway through their journey to the grave. Throe had secured the rental with an option to buy on the theory of hiding in plain sight, and the property had worked satisfactorily.

There were lights on in the interior, illumination bleeding out around the seams of the pulled drapes, and he imagined what his warriors were doing inside. Fresh from fighting *lessers* in the alleys of downtown Caldwell, they would be shedding their black blood-stained clothes and partaking of the victuals contained in the icebox and the cupboards of the kitchen. They would be drinking as well, although not blood to make them stronger, and not water to rehydrate them, but rather alcohol as an internal salve to treat fresh contusions, cuts, abrasions—

Abruptly, the nape of his neck began to tingle in warning, informing him, as if the burning of the exposed skin upon his hands did not, that he had little time to get safely indoors.

And yet he had no interest in going in there. Seeing his soldiers. Consuming food before he retired upstairs to that nauseating raspberry bedroom suite.

He had been denied that which he had counted down

the hours for, and the disappointment was like his body's response to the gathering dawn: His skin ached. His muscles twitched. His eyes strained.

His addiction had not been served.

Layla had not come this night.

With a curse, he took out his cellular device and dialed a number based on a pattern he had memorized on the numerical screen. Putting the phone up to his ear, he heard his heart pounding over the ringing.

There was no personalized voice-mail greeting activated on the account, so after six tones, an automated announcement detailing the number came over the connection. He did not leave a message.

Heading over to the door, he braced himself for an onslaught of noise and chaos. His bastards would inevitably be riding waves of adrenaline, the afterburn of their high-octane existence taking a while to dissipate.

Opening things up—

Xcor froze halfway across the threshold.

His five fighters were not, in fact, talking over one another as they passed around bottles of alcohol along with surgical tape and gauze for their wounds. Instead, they were seated on the available furniture that had been rented to them along with the home. There was no drink in any hand, and not even the metal-on-metal sound of guns being cleaned and daggers getting resharpened.

They were all there: Zypher, Syphon, Balthazar, Syn . . . and Throe, the one who hadn't belonged, but had become indispensable.

None of them were meeting his eyes.

No, that was not true.

Throe, his second in command, was the only male staring at him. Also the only of the group who was standing.

Ah, so he had been the one to organize this . . . whatever it was.

Xcor shut the door behind himself. And kept his weapons on.

"Have you something to say?" he inquired, staying by the door, meeting Throe's stare straight on.

His second in command cleared his throat, and when he spoke his accent was that not just of the upper class, but of the highest of vampire social orders: that of the *glymera*.

"We are concerned about your direction." The male glanced around. "Of late."

"Indeed."

Throe appeared to wait for something further in response. When none came, he uttered a curse of frustration. "Xcor, where has your ambition gone? The King has a single, half-breed heir and you suddenly forget about our collective quest for the throne? You put our goals aside as if a bowl now empty of its contents."

"Battling the Lessening Society is a full-time endeavor."

"Mayhap if you were in fact fighting."

"The slayers I killed tonight were of my imagination, then?"

"That is not all you do at night."

Xcor bared his fangs. "Be of care where thee tread the now."

Throe cocked his brow in challenge. "Shall I not say it in front of them?"

As he felt his males' eyes swing over to him, he wanted to hit something. He had thought his meetings with Layla had been unwitnessed. Clearly, that was a miscalculation.

And if he told Throe to stay silent? He might as well condemn himself to something worse than what he had been doing.

"I have nothing to hide," he growled.

"I beg to disagree. You spend too much of your time under that maple tree, like some lovesick—"

Xcor materialized in front of the male, such that a mere inch separated their faces. He did not touch Throe, but the soldier stepped back nonetheless.

His second in command did not back all the way down, however. "Do you wish to tell them who she is? Or shall I."

"She is irrelevant. And my ambitions are restrained by no one."

"Prove it."

"To whom." Xcor tilted his head and jutted out his jaw. "To them? Or is it you who has the problem."

"Prove that you are not going soft."

In the blink of an eye, Xcor withdrew his steel dagger and pressed it to the male's jugular. "Here? Now?"

As Throe gasped, the sharp tip nicked his flesh, a line of bright red blood gracing that oh, so shiny pale blade.

"Shall I prove myself on you," Xcor said darkly. "Would that suffice."

"You are distracted," Throe snapped. "By a *female*. You are weakened by her!"

"And you are deranged! I choose not to kill the rightfully elected King of the Race—and that is a crime over which you attempt to secure a mutiny among my fighters?"

"You were so close! We nearly had the throne! The dominoes were aligned, the *glymera* was going to do your bidding—"

Xcor pressed that dagger in again, ending the tirade. "Is this traitorous meeting about my ambition—or yours? Permit me to inquire precisely whose loss you are mourning."

"You are not leading us anymore."

"Let us ask them." Xcor broke off and stalked around the room, looking at the bent heads of his soldiers. "What say you all. Are you going with him or staying with me?" As curses broke out in the tense air, he pivoted to Throe. "Because that is what you're doing, is it not? Presenting them with a choice—either you or me. So, I say, let us proceed to the endgame with all due haste. Where dost thou stand, bastards mine?"

There was a long pause.

And then Zypher lifted his eyes. "Who is she?"

"That is not the question I posed to you."

"That's the question we want answered."

Xcor felt his temper rise. "She is none of your business."

There was no way in hell he was going to explain the liaisons with his Chosen.

Zypher's nostrils flared as he took a deep breath. "Jesus . . . you've bonded with her."

"I have not."

"I can smell it, too," someone said. "Who is she?"

"She is of no consequence."

Throe spoke up, loud and clear. "She is a Chosen. Who lives with the Brotherhood."

Annnnd herewith the chaos he had previously anticipated: The room erupted with male voices, all of them talking over one another, snippets of the Old Language mixing with English and German curse words.

Meanwhile, Throe took out a pristine handkerchief and pressed the white square to the wound at his throat. "I fail to understand why she meets with you—just what do you have over her? There must be some kind of inducement—money? Or is it a threat of some kind?"

Xcor let the insult stand, as it wasn't just close to the truth; the male had hit the nail on the head. The only reason the Chosen Layla met with him was that he knew the location of the Black Dagger Brotherhood's mansion, and she was terrified he was going to sack the property: There had been one night, nearly a year ago, when he had followed her blood trail and stumbled upon the great secret. And Throe was right—he had leveraged the discovery to his benefit.

She had promised him her body in exchange for his keeping the site sacrosanct.

And though he had yet to call upon her in a carnal way, out of respect for her pregnancy, her virtue, and her station . . . he would have her.

Eventually, he would take what was his and mark her as his own—

Shit, had he *bonded*?

Xcor refocused on Throe and his Bastards. "Let us concern ourselves with this mutiny and not anyone's imagination. So what say you. All of you." There was a long pause. "Any of you."

He supposed, as he awaited a response, the fact that Throe remained upright and breathing was proof that Xcor had, in fact, somewhat softened. Trained by the Bloodletter, he had not forgotten what he had learned in the war camp, but of late, he had come to realize that brute force and bloodshed were simply one means to an end—and there were others that could be more effective.

For example, Wrath had proven the point with the way he had handled the final assault against his throne. That king and his mate had shut down even the most foolproof attack against his rule—and they had done so not only without one life being lost, but with a castration so complete, the very powers of the *glymera* had been stripped away.

And Wrath, as a leader now chosen by his people, had unassailable power.

Throe broke the silence, addressing the fighters. "I believe I have made myself clear. I feel strongly that we should resume the quest for the throne. We shot Wrath once—we can get at him again. He might be democratically elected, but he cannot continue to rule if he isn't breathing. And then we need to remarshal support within the now-disenfranchised *glymera*. By coordinating a constitutional strategy with the former members of the Council, we can argue that Wrath overreached his powers and—"

"You are a fool," Xcor said quietly.

Throe spun around and pegged him with a hostile glare. "And you are a failure!"

Xcor shook his head. "The people have spoken. They chose to put Wrath on the throne he had previously inherited, and there is no fight to be won when there is not one front, but one thousand. Traditional laws and cultural norms are flimsy mantles of power and influence. Democracy, however, when it is truly exercised, is a stone fortress that cannot be surmounted, blown asunder, or burrowed under. What you fail to understand, second in command, is that there is nothing further to battle with—assuming that you are conducting this assault with any hope of prevailing."

Throe narrowed his eyes. "Tell me something, has your Chosen been educating you? I don't think I've ever heard anything close to that come out of your mouth before."

Xcor forced himself to stay quiet.

He and his fighters had been banded together long before Throe had come into the mix. But if those males could not see past this ill-fated ambition? Then Throe could have them all.

Xcor would bow to none herein.

In the silence that followed, Throe looked around at the fighters who had once shunned him for his dandy weakness, but had grown to respect him as a warrior over the last two centuries. "Manipulation is most successful when waged by one of the female sex. Think not that he speaks propaganda the now? Fed to him by precisely that which can most seduce his mind, his body, his emotions? You have smelled the bonding for yourself. Know that the soul follows the heart, and his is no longer with us, with our goals, with what we may accomplish. This is not strength that addresses you, but the sort of weakness he once deplored in others. See? Even now, he stays quiet!"

Xcor shrugged. "I have no taste for pontificating."

"Did you even know the definition of that word six months ago?" Throe countered.

"What say the lot of you?" Xcor glanced around with a sense of abiding boredom. "The choice is yours, but know this. Once it is made, like ink in the skin, it is indelible."

Zypher was the first to get to his feet. "I have but one allegiance."

With that, he went over to his gear and unsheathed his steel dagger. Slicing his own palm open, he approached Xcor and put out his hand.

Xcor shook what was proffered and found that he had to clear his throat. Balthazar was next, taking the same knife and cutting himself, putting forth his blood—and Syphon moved with equal efficiency, pledging himself.

Syn watched it all with lowered lids, staying still. He was, as always, the wild card—but even he rose and came across to Xcor. Taking the blade, he stabbed his palm and twisted, his upper lip curling up as if he liked the pain.

Xcor accepted the last of his soldiers' vows and then he looked over at Throe. Bringing his dripping red palm up, he bared his fangs and hissed, biting his own flesh and then licking the combined blood clean.

"As if this would go another way." He smiled cruelly. "You have never been one of us."

Throe's handsome face twisted into a nasty expression. "You forced me to join you. You did this to me."

"But you shall undo it, is that correct? Fine, I gave you your freedom a year ago. Let your ambition exercise your destiny if you wish, but once you walk out that door, it is a permanent closure. You are dead to us, your deeds your own and no one else's."

Throe nodded once. "So be it."

The male marched across and picked up his holsters and his coat; then he went to the door. Pivoting, he addressed the group. "He is wrong about much, but most especially the throne. A war with a thousand fronts? I think not. All that must needs be done is eliminate Wrath. Then the mantle shall be assumed by the strongest hand—and that male is no longer among this group."

The fighter closed the door behind himself with a clap.

Xcor ground his molars, knowing damn well Throe must have set up a contingency plan before he made his bid to them all—or he wouldn't have been so nonchalant about leaving mere minutes before dawn.

Throe had gambled and lost—except only when it came to the lot of them. Where would this take him next? Xcor had no idea.

But Wrath should well be worried.

There was some shuffling around. Throat clearing. And then, of course, commentary.

"So," Zypher blurted. "You gonna tells us what color her eyes are?"

"'Tis the least you could do," Balthazar interjected. "Paint us a picture."

"A Chosen?"

"How in the world did you—"

All at once, the house was back to normal, male voices crowding the air, drinks being summoned and poured, bandages coming out to wrap up those injured fighting hands.

Xcor exhaled in a relief he was shocked to feel—but he wasn't fooled. Though his fighters had stood by him, he now had a new enemy against whom to fight—and Throe, thanks to Xcor's very own training of the male, was dangerous indeed.

Taking out his phone, he glanced down . . . and found that his call had not been returned.

Given the state of Throe's defection? It was imperative that he get hold of his Chosen—and now he worried that mayhap Throe had gotten to her first and that was why there had been a no-show.

"So?" Zypher said. "Whatever is she like?"

Cue a sudden silence, which seemed to have crashed through the noise.

And he was shocked to find that he wanted to tell them. He had held this in for how long?

With halting words, he said, "She is . . . the moon in my night sky. And that is the beginning, middle, and end of it. There is no more to be told than that, and never shall I speak of her again."

As he departed and went o'er to the stairs, he could feel their eyes on him—and they were not regarding him with disdain. No, try as they might to hide it, there was pity flowing from them all—an acknowledgment of the ugliness of his face, and the mismatched nature of a romance for him with any female, much less one of Chosen status.

He paused with his hand on the balustrade. "By sunset

tomorrow, have all provisions and property packed up. We must needs leave this location and find another. This house is no longer secure."

Mounting the stairs, he heard the acquiescence of his fighters. And felt a stinging gratitude that they had picked him to continue to lead them.

In opposition to Throe's more obvious intelligence, breeding, background . . . and looks.

Let us hear it for the deformed, he thought as he shut himself in his bedroom. Though much had been lost to him over the centuries of his life, courtesy of his harelip and his coarseness, those soldiers below valued him.

And he valued them in return.

NINE

i Am returned to the Brotherhood's great stone mansion just before sunrise, jogging up the steps to the cathedral-like entrance, and pushing his way into the vestibule. Following protocol, he put his face into the security camera's eye and waited.

A moment later, the inner door opened and a cheery old puss greeted him—along with the rich scents of a well-cooked Last Meal.

"Good late evening, sire," Fritz, the butler, said with a bow. "How ever are you?"

"Hey, listen, have you seen my brother? I'm trying to find—"

"Yes, he's returned."

iAm nearly cursed with relief. "That's great. Just great."

At least the poor bastard was home safe and in a secure environment. But, Christ, Trez could at least have shot a text back that he was alive. How many times had that cell of his been unanswered—

From over on the left, a fast-moving shadow leaped up from the mosaic floor, going full-blown missile right at him.

iAm caught Goddamn Cat, also known as Boo, in his arms. He absolutely despised the animal—especially lately, as the fleabag had started sleeping with him during the day. All that cuddling. Purring.

Worse? He was getting used to the torture.

". . . clinic."

"Sorry?" iAm scratched the cat's throat and made Boo's eyeballs roll back. "I didn't hear a thing that you just said."

"My apologies." The butler bowed again even though it was not his fault. "The Chosen Selena has fallen ill and been taken unto the clinic. Trez is attending her as she is being treated—I believe the Primale and Cormia have gone down there as well? I'm sorry to say, but her condition appears to be quite serious."

"Damn it . . ." iAm closed his eyes and let his head fall back on his spine. They'd been waiting for the other shoe to drop, but that was supposed to have been about the s'Hisbe. Not the Chosen his brother had been so attracted to. "What's wrong with her?"

"I do not believe a diagnosis has been ascertained."

Shit. "Okay, thanks, man, I'll go—"

The Chosen Layla appeared in the archway of the billiards room, Qhuinn and Blay tight on her heels. "Forgive me, but did I just hear something about Selena?"

Letting the butler field that one, iAm headed off for the hidden door beneath the grand staircase—and he was not surprised when the others quickly fell in behind him.

Just as he punched in the code to open the sealed panels, a cell phone went off.

"Is that you again?" Qhuinn asked.

Layla silenced the ringer. "It's just a human misdialing."

"You want V to block the number?"

"Oh, there's no reason to bother him."

"Here, give it to me, and I'll see—"

Layla returned the phone to the folds of her robing. "They won't call again. Let's go."

After a subtle *beeeeep* sounded, iAm pulled things open and they descended a shallow staircase to a second locked door. On the far side of that was the underground tunnel that ran from the mansion to the training center, and farther still to the Pit, where V and Butch lived with their mates.

With each stride down the concrete-walled, short-ceilinged stretch of here-to-there, the tightness in iAm's shoulders increased, the muscles along his spine clamping up so hard that the pain reverberated all the way to his temples.

When they emerged into the office, Tohr looked up from the computer. "It's a convention down here tonight."

"Selena's sick," Qhuinn muttered.

The Brother got to his feet. "What? I just saw her like an hour ago. She was going to feed Luchas and . . ."

Which was how they ended up with five sets of shoes and shitkickers heading into the corridor.

The training center was a huge subterranean facility that included everything from an Olympic-size swimming pool, a target range, a weight room, a PT suite, and a full-size gym, to equipment rooms and a complement of classrooms that had been used for trainee teaching before the raids. There were also extensive medical facilities, with surgical suites and recovery rooms—and that was what they were gunning for.

The fact that people were clustered around the closed door of the examination room was not a good sign: Phury, Cormia, Rhage and Vishous were in anxious-wait mode, pacing, staring at the floor, twitching.

"Oh, thank God," Phury said as he saw iAm. "Trez is going to be glad you're here. We were trying to get hold of you."

Probably why his own phone had been going off—but he'd been ignoring the thing while leaving the condo and going to try to find Trez at shAdoWs.

"They're X-raying her," V said. "That's why we're out here. Trez isn't leaving her."

Layla frowned. "Why are they doing that? Did she break a—"

Cormia went over to the other Chosen and took Layla's hands. Soft words were exchanged and then Layla gasped and weaved on her feet. As Qhuinn steadied her, iAm decided that whatever it was, he needed to get in there.

"I'm not waiting," he said, putting the cat down and pushing the door wide.

At first, he couldn't figure out what he was looking at. As the heavy panel shut behind him soundlessly, he focused on what looked like table legs on the examination platform. Except . . . it was Selena. Her slender calves and thighs were bent, separated abnormally and held rigid at bad angles, as if she were in great pain—and it wasn't just her lower body that was affected. Her head position was all wrong, and her arms were twisted up against her chest, even her fingers cranked into claws.

She looked as if she were in some kind of seizure.

Doc Jane was moving a large piece of machinery into position over Selena's shoulder, and her nurse, Ehlena, was following behind so that the various cords didn't get tangled. Trez was by Selena's head, his trembling hands stroking that black hair.

He didn't even look up. Didn't seem to be aware that someone else had entered the room. Wasn't even breathing.

"Okay, Ehlena, the plate?" The doctor accepted something that was the size of an eight-and-a-half-by-eleven piece of paper, but had the thickness of a finger. Wires connected to one end of it led to a laptop that sat on a rolling table. "I'm going to try to get the elbow here."

The plate was slid under the joint, and then Doc Jane glanced at Trez. "Do you want to hold this one as well?"

He nodded and reached over, doing the duty. "I won't move this time."

"These are digital X-rays, so we can just do it over, okay?" The doctor gave Trez's arm a quick squeeze. "We're going to step behind the partition now."

Doc Jane looked up and jumped a little, as if she, too, were so intent on her patient, she hadn't known he'd come in, either. "Oh, iAm, good—but listen, you might want to leave while we—"

"I'm going nowhere."

"I can't . . ." Trez cursed. "I can't keep this steady."

Without a word, iAm went across the tiled floor and put his hand on his brother's, stopping the vibration. "Let me help."

Trez didn't jump. Didn't start. But his eyes shifted over, and oh, God, those eyes . . . they were black pits of sadness.

And that was when iAm knew that this was not bad, but BAD.

The male wasn't terrified.

He was already in mourning.

Trez wasn't immediately sure who his savior was. Didn't recognize the hand that joined his own, even though it looked almost exactly like his. Didn't track the new scent in the room. It wasn't until he looked up that he saw . . .

iAm, of course.

As if it would be anyone else.

The image of his brother got wavy. "iAm, she's . . ."

He couldn't say the words. His thought processes literally flatlined as if he'd had a stroke or something.

"Let's hold the plate," iAm said. "Together."

"You should be behind the lead thing."

"No."

Trez wasn't surprised iAm hung in, and he mouthed a thank-you, because he didn't think his voice was functioning any better than his brain or that hand of his was.

"Let's get as still as we can," Doc Jane said. Then there was a brief whirring sound from the machine and Doc Jane and Ehlena came back to the table.

iAm was the one who handed the plate over—and good thing, because Trez would have dropped it. Screw his hands; his whole body was shaking.

"Thank you," Doc Jane said. "I think we have enough now. Do you want to call the others in?"

Trez shook his head. "May I have a moment with her?"

"We need to stay in to look at the X-rays."

"Oh, yeah, I know. I just . . ." He glanced to the door, and knew those people had as much right to be in here as he did. Actually, they had more.

"Trez," Doc Jane said gently. "However you want it, that's how we'll do it."

But what did Selena want? he wondered, not for the first time.

"Look," Doc Jane murmured, "there doesn't seem to be an emergency issue right now. There will be time for the others to come in later—and if her condition changes? We'll make different choices depending on where we're at."

"Okay." He nodded toward his brother. "But iAm. I want him to stay."

His brother nodded and brought over a chair—but not for himself, as it turned out. He shoved it under the backs of Trez's knees, and functioning joints being what they were, a total collapse of the vertical happened but quick. As his ass smacked into the seat, he thought, yeah, he had been feeling a little light-headed. Probably a good idea to get off his feet.

With not a single word, iAm took a load off on the floor beside him, and it was incredible how just having the male in the room calmed him.

Trez refocused on Selena. She still had not moved from

the position he'd found her in, and all those hard angles of her body were a total nightmare.

In fact, this whole thing just seemed so . . . devastating.

From what Cormia had said, the Arrest was a disease that struck a tiny minority of Chosen females. In all of history, there had been only a dozen, maybe fewer, who had suffered from it—which meant the statistical chance of getting the disorder was very small. Unfortunately, the condition had been uniformly fatal.

Goddamn it, he didn't want any of those females to be sick, but why her?

Of all of them, in the entire history of the Race, why did Selena have to be one of the ones cut short like this?

And it was a horrible way to die. Frozen in your own body, unable to communicate, trapped in a fading prison until everything went dark and you . . .

He closed his eyes.

Shit, what if she didn't want him here? He had bonded, yes—and everyone else was treating him with the respect that a bonded male would have in this situation, even as they wondered how it had happened without them knowing.

The problem was, he and Selena weren't mated. In a relationship. Even dating.

Hell, they hadn't even spent two minutes together in months—

"Trez?"

With a jerk, he popped his lids. Doc Jane was in front of him, her forest-green eyes alert and grave. "I've looked at the X-rays."

He cleared his throat. "Maybe the others would like to be here for this?"

Shit, should he step aside so Cormia or someone could hold her hand? Would that be better? His body would hate that and so would his soul. But this was not about him.

A lot of people came in, more than there had been, and he nodded at Tohr, Qhuinn and Blay—and was glad that Layla was there, along with Cormia and Phury. Forcing himself to his feet, he went to step back, but the Primale came over and eased him down into that chair again.

"You stay where you are," Phury said, squeezing his shoulder. "You're right where you need to be."

Trez let out some kind of croak. It was the best he could do.

Doc Jane cleared her throat. "I've never seen anything like this." She called something up on the big computer screen by the desk. "It's as if the joints themselves have turned to solid bone."

The black-and-white image was of what appeared to be Selena's knee and Doc Jane indicated different areas with the head of a silver pen. "On X-ray, bones register white and pale gray, whereas connective tissue like ligaments and tendons don't offer that kind of contrast. Here"—she drew a circle around the joint—"there should be dark patches in between the cap and the socket. Instead it's just . . . solid bone. The same is true for the joints in her feet, her elbow, her . . ."

More of those images flashed up on the screen, one after another, and all he could do was shake his head. It was as if someone had poured cement into all the junctures.

"What's particularly worrisome is this." A new picture became visible. "This is her arm. Unlike the other joints, the bone growth appears to be spreading and invading into the musculature. If this continues, her entire body—"

"Stone," Trez whispered.

Oh, God, those marble statues in that place he'd found her.

That wasn't a courtyard—that was a cemetery. Full of the females who had suffered and died from this.

"The only thing I'm aware of that is remotely like this is a human disease called fibrodysplasia ossificans progressiva. It's an extremely rare genetic condition that causes bone to form where muscles, tendons, and ligaments are, and it results, over time, in a total restriction of movement—to the point where patients must choose the position they want to be locked into. The growth of the bone happens sporadically and can be triggered by trauma or viruses, or can be spontaneous. There are no treatments for the disease, and surgical removal of the growth just triggers further genesis. What Selena's going through is like that—only it seems to have occurred all over her body at once."

Trez twisted around to the two healthy Chosen in the room. "Has this ever been treated? At any time in the past, did someone try to find a way to stop it?"

Layla looked at Cormia and the latter spoke up. "We prayed ... that was all we could do. And still the attacks came."

"So this is ... an episode of some sort?" Doc Jane asked. "Not the terminus?"

"I don't know how many of these she's had." Cormia brushed a tear off her cheek. "Usually there is a period of them before the final one from which they do not recover."

Doc Jane frowned. "So the body unlocks? How?"

"I do not know."

Trez spoke up to the Chosen. "Did either of you have any idea she was sick?"

"No one did." Cormia leaned against her *hellren* as if she needed his support. "But considering the condition she's in now ... I believe she must be toward the end of the disease. It's my understanding that the early episodes affect only parts of the body. This is all of hers."

Trez deflated on his exhale, his strength expelling out of his mouth. The only thing that kept him from breaking down was the possibility that Selena might be aware of what was happening—and he wanted to appear to be strong for her.

Doc Jane leaned her hip against her desk and crossed her arms. "I can't imagine how the joints can recover from this kind of state."

Cormia shook her head. "The attacks, those few I've seen, come on fast and then ... I don't know what happens. Hours or a night later, they start to be able to move again. After a period of time, they regain mobility—but it always happens again. Always."

"They also choose a position," Layla said quietly as she, too, brushed at tears. "Like the humans you spoke of, our sisters always chose—they would tell us how they wanted to be and we would make sure ..."

There were more things said. Questions asked. Explanations given to the best of people's abilities. But he had stopped tracking.

Like a train gathering speed, his mind, his emotions, his sense of total impotence and all his regrets started to churn along a defined path, gathering speed and intensity.

He hated that her hair was a mess and he couldn't fix it.

He hated that there were grass stains on her robing, bright green smudges where her knees had hit the ground.

He hated that her shoes had fallen off.

He hated that he couldn't do one fucking thing to save her.

He hated the burden he carried with the s'Hisbe and everything it had made him do to his body—because maybe if his parents hadn't sold him to the Queen, he wouldn't have fucked all those humans, and maybe he would have been even slightly worthy of her. And then he wouldn't have missed all those months. And maybe he could have seen something, or done something, or—

Like the conversation around him, the thoughts continued to pelt their way through his brain, but he couldn't track them any more than he could whatever else was going on in the exam room. A violent roar had overtaken him, tsunamiing through him, wiping everything away except a rage that could not be held in.

Trez wasn't aware of moving. One minute he was holding on to Selena's hand carefully; the next he was at the door to the examination room—then he was through it, his body exploding forward, more momentum than coordination.

Running, running . . . going by the jerks in his vision and the passing walls of the concrete corridor, he was running . . .

And there was a lot of noise. The empty hall was echoing with some kind of tremendous noise, like the gear of a great machine had locked or was grinding—

Something tackled him from behind before he reached the exit into the parking garage, an iron bar hold locking around him.

iAm.

Of course.

"Drop it," came the shout in his ear. "Drop it . . . come on, now. Drop it—"

Trez shook his head. "What . . . ?"

"Drop the gun, Trez." iAm's voice cracked. "I need you to drop the gun."

Trez froze except for his panting breath, and tried to make sense of what his brother was saying.

"Oh, Jesus, Trez, please . . ."

Shaking his head, Trez ... gradually became aware that there was, in fact, someone's forty in his right hand. Probably his own. He always wore one in the club.

And what do you know, the muzzle was up against his own temple—and unlike back with those X-ray plates, his hand wasn't shaking at all.

"Drop it for me, Trez." With his finger on the trigger the way it was, his brother obviously didn't dare try to take control of the weapon for fear of causing a discharge. "You gotta put the gun down."

At that moment, everything became clear: him bursting up, bolting fast, breaking out of the exam room and into the corridor. Running down toward the parking garage as he palmed his weapon.

Intending to blow his brains out as soon as he was free of the training center.

He'd had the conception that maybe, if there was actually a Fade, he and Selena could meet on the other side and come together, in a way they never could down on Earth.

"Trez, she's still alive. Don't you do this. You want to kill yourself? Wait until her heart stops beating, but not before that. Not one fucking moment before that."

Trez pictured Selena back on that table, and thought, Shit ...

iAm, as always, was right.

The shaking returned as he began to lower his arm, and he moved slowly for fear of some twitch setting the forty off. But he didn't need to worry about that. As soon as that muzzle was out of the range of his gray matter, his brother took over, disarming him quick as a breath and putting the safety in place.

Trez stood there numbly as iAm patted him down and removed a couple more weapons, and then he allowed himself to be led back to that examination room and the group of people standing shocked and still around its door.

Not before she was gone, he told himself. Not while she was still here.

Unfortunately, he feared that was not likely to be very long at all.

TEN

Paradise, blooded daughter of Abalone, First Adviser to the King, frowned at the screen of her Apple lappy. She'd set herself up here in her father's library ever since he'd started working each night for Wrath, son of Wrath, because in the old rambling Tudor mansion, Wi-Fi was strongest at this desk. Not that a good signal was helping her at the moment. Her Hotmail account was full of unread messages, because, with iMessage on her phone and her Twitter, Instagram, and FB accounts, there was no reason to sign into it very often.

"So hold up, what was it called?" she said into her cell.

" 'New Trainee Class,' " Peyton, blooded son of Peythone, replied. "I forwarded it to you, like, an hour ago."

She sat forward in her father's chair. "There's just so much junk in here."

"Lemme resend—"

"Wait, I got it." She clicked and then clicked again on the attachment. "Wow. It's on official letterhead."

"Told you."

Paradise scanned the date, the personalized greeting to Peyton, the two paragraphs about the program, and the closing. "Holy . . . it's signed by a Brother."

"Tohrment, son of Hharm."

"Well, if it's a fake, someone's going to catch some serious—"

"But did you see in the second paragraph?"

She refocused on the words. "*Females*? Whoa, whoa . . . they're accepting *females*?"

"I know, right?" There was a bubbling noise and an exhale as Peyton took another hit. "It's unprecedented."

Paradise reread the letter, this time more carefully. Operative words leaped out at her: *Open tryouts for the training program. Females and civilians welcome to take physical performance test for entrance. Sessions taught by the Brotherhood themselves.* Tuition? *Nada.*

"What are they thinking?" Peyton muttered. "I mean, this is supposed to be for the *glymera* sons only."

"Not anymore, apparently."

As Peyton went off on a commentary about the fairer sex and traditional roles at home and in the field, Paradise sat back in the leather armchair. Next to her, logs set by the household's *doggen* crackled with orange flames in the marble-faced hearth, the warmth hitting one side of her face and half of her body. All around, her father's library glowed with yellow light and polished mahogany and the gold accents on the spines of his collection of first-edition books.

The mansion they lived in was one of Caldwell's grandest, with forty other rooms that were kitted out with equal luxury to this one, if not even greater: Beautiful silks hung from diamond-paned leaded windows. Fine Oriental rugs stretched out across polished floors. Oil paintings of ancestors were mounted up the stairwells and featured prominently over mantels and sideboards. Fine china was set at a formal table for every meal, food cooked and served by the extensive staff.

She had lived here with her father for years upon years, tutored by other ladies of the *glymera* in all the things that made an aristocratic female mateable: Clothing. Entertaining. Etiquette. Being the chatelaine of an estate.

And what was it all leading up to? Her presentation party, which had been delayed, as with the Brotherhood's training program, because of the raids two years ago.

Plans for her were likewise going to be reinstated, however. What was left of the aristocracy had moved back to Caldwell proper from their safe houses, and as she was of age, being at least four years out of her transition, it was time for her to find a mate.

God, how she dreaded all that—

"Hello?" Peyton said. "You still there?"

"Sorry, yes." She jerked the phone away from her ear at a loud crackling sound. "What are you doing?"

"Opening up a bag of Cape Cod potato chips." Crunch. Munch. "Oh, my hell, these are amazing. . . ."

"So what are you going to do?"

"I still have half an ounce left. So I'm going to finish it and a bag of chips. Then probably crash—"

"No, about the training center program."

"My father's already told me I'm going. It's fine, whatever. I haven't really been doing anything for three years now, and I would have matriculated in when they first opened the facility up, but . . . well, you remember what happened."

"Yeah, and you'd better stop smoking. They're not going to like that."

"What they don't know can't hurt them. Besides, I have First Amendment rights."

She rolled her eyes. "Okay, for one, you're not human, so their Constitution doesn't apply to you. And two, that's about freedom of speech, not freedom to light up."

"Whatever."

As Peyton took another hit, she pictured his handsome face, and his broad shoulders, and his very blue eyes. The two of them had known each other all their lives, their families having inter-married for generations, as all members of the aristocracy did.

It was the worst-kept secret in the *glymera* that his parents and her father had recently started talking about them getting mated—

The great bass sound of the front entrance's door knocker brought her head around.

"Who is that?" she said, getting to her feet and leaning forward so she could see out into the foyer.

Their butler, Fedrich, strode across the floor, and though her father never answered the door himself, he, too, came out of his private study across the way.

"Master?" the butler said. "Are you expecting anyone?"

Abalone pulled his suit jacket back into place. "A distant relative. I should have told you, my apologies."

"I gotta go," Paradise said. "Have a good sleep."

There was a pause. "Yeah, you, too, Parry. And you know, you can call me if you get the bad dreams, okay."

"Sure. Same for you. 'Day."

"'Day back at you."

As she hung up, she was glad her friend was still around. Ever since the raids had gone down and so many of their class had been slaughtered, the two of them had used the phone lines to pass the sometimes forever hours of daylight. The connection had been indispensable in the immediate aftermath of the raids, when she and her father had gone out to the Catskills, and she had rattled around that big barn of a Victorian for months.

Peyton was a good friend. As for the mating thing?

She didn't know how to feel about that.

Going around the desk, she jogged across to the foyer until her father caught sight of her and shook his head. "Out of sight, Paradise. Please."

Her brows popped. That was the code for her to take cover in the hidden tunnels of the house. "What's going on?"

"Please go."

"You said it was a relative?"

"Paradise."

Paradise ducked back into the library, but she stayed by the archway, listening.

The soft creak of the massive front door opening seemed very loud.

"It's you," her father said in a strange tone. "Fedricah, please excuse us, will you."

"But of course, master."

The butler walked off, crossing briefly over that part of the foyer Paradise could see. After a moment, the door into the back half of the house closed.

"Well?" a male said. "Are you going to invite me in?"

"I don't know."

"I'm going to die out here. In a matter of minutes."

Paradise fought the urge to put her head around the molding and see who it was. She didn't recognize the voice, but the precise pronunciation and haughty accent suggested it was someone from the aristocracy. Which made sense, considering he was a "relative."

"You are wearing the vestments of war," her father countered. "I do not abide them across my threshold."

"Is it my associations or my weapons that frighten you more?"

"I am not afeared of either. You were beaten, if you recall."

"But not defeated, I'm sorry to say." Clicking sounds suggested someone was handling things made of metal parts. And then there was a clattering, as if something hit the front stone stoop. "Here, then, I am naked before you. I am utterly unarmed, and my weapons are on your doorstep, not within your walls."

"I am not your cousin."

"You are my blood. We have many common ancestors—"

"Spare me. And whatever message your leader wishes to send to the King, have him do it through—"

"I am no longer affiliated with Xcor. In any way."

"I beg your pardon?"

"Ties have been cut." There was an exhausted sigh. "I have spent these months since the election that returned Wrath to the throne trying to convince Xcor and the Band of Bastards to disengage from their treason. Even after such entreaty and reasoning, such extended pleading for a smarter course, I am saddened that I cannot dissuade them from their folly. Finally, I just had to leave. I sneaked away from where they stay, and I now fear for my life. I have nowhere else to go, and when I spoke with Salliah back in the Old Country, she suggested that I pay you a visit."

Their distant cousin, Paradise thought. She recognized that name.

"Please," the male said. "Lock me in a room if you have to—"

"I am a loyal servant of the King's."

"Then do not turn away a tactical advantage."

"What are you suggesting?"

"In return for safety under your roof, I am prepared to tell you everything I know about the Band of Bastards. Where they spend the daylight hours. What their patterns are. Where they meet during the night. How they think and fight. Surely that is worth the use of a bed."

Paradise couldn't stand it. She had to see who it was.

Inching out, she curled her body around the archway and looked past her father's stiff shoulders. Her first thought was that the male's leathers and ragged button-down shirt did not match his intonation. Her second was that his eyes were bruised, they were so tired.

He did indeed appear to have come from the war's front lines, something sickly sweet staining the air that brushed by his body as it entered the house.

The male noticed her immediately, and his face registered something that he quickly hid.

Her father glanced over his shoulder and shot her a glare. "Paradise," he hissed.

"I can understand why you hesitate," the male said, his eyes never leaving hers. "Indeed, she is precious."

Her father turned back around. "You must go."

The male dropped down to one knee and bowed his head, putting one hand over his heart and lifting the other, open palmed, up to the heavens.

In the Old Language, he said softly, *"I hereby swear upon our common ancestry that I shall bring no harm to you, your blooded daughter, or any living thing within these walls—or may the Scribe Virgin cut my life off afore your very eyes."*

Her father looked back at her and slashed his arm through the air, an order for her to get out and stay gone.

She put her hands up and nodded, all, *Okay, okay, okaaaaay.*

Moving quickly, she went back into the library and across to the panels by the fireplace. Reaching under the third shelf from the floor to the hidden trigger point, she pressed the lever and was able to push the entire load of books out and over on the well-oiled track. With a quick slip, she emerged into the fully finished hallway that ran in a square around the first floor of the house, providing access, both visual and actual, to every room through hidden doors and viewpoints.

It was like something out of an Alfred Hitchcock movie.

Closing herself in, Paradise went to the shallow stairs that were all the way in the back, and as she ascended them, she wished she could hear what they were saying. As usual, though, she was in the dark; her father never told her anything about anything.

It was part of his old-school mind-set: Well-bred females didn't need to be bothered with things like mysterious, long-lost relatives who showed up unannounced and armed to the teeth. Or, say, where the head of the household was working, how much he was earning or what his net worth was. For example, when her father was appointed First Adviser to the King, that was all she was told. She had no idea what his job was like, what he did for the King and the Brotherhood—heck, she didn't even know where he went each night.

She believed he truly thought he was sparing her. But she hated being in the dark about so much.

At the top of the hidden staircase, she went forward about fifteen feet and stopped in front of an inset panel. The latch was to the left and she flicked it free.

Her bedroom was everything girlie and soft, from her frilly bed to the lace at the windows to the needlepoint rugs that were like slippers you didn't have to wear.

Going over, she turned the lock on her door, knowing it would be the first thing her father would check whenever he came upstairs—and if he didn't make it to the second floor because he was staying with their "guest"? He was going to make Fedricah come and do a test-turn of the knob.

At her bed, she sat down, kicked off her loafers, and flopped back on the duvet. Staring up at the canopy, she shook her head.

Locked in her room. Cut out from any action.

Immediately after the raids, it was the only place she had wanted to be, the only way to feel safe. But those nights of terror had turned into months of worry . . . which had transitioned into an uneasy normalcy . . . that had devolved into just plain life in general.

So that now she felt trapped. In this room. In this house. In this life.

Paradise glanced at her closed, locked door.

Who was that male? she wondered.

ELEVEN

Selena became slowly aware that she was no longer in the Sanctuary. She did not recognize where she was, however: Her brain was slow to process both the signals from her body and the cues from her environment, as if the attack had frozen not only her flesh, but her mind.

Gradually, however, it occurred to her that there was no more grass in her face. No trees or temples off in the distance. No soft sound of running water from the baths.

She tried to shift her head and groaned.

"Selena?"

The face that entered her vision brought tears to her eyes. It was Trez . . . it was *Trez.* . . .

Sure as if she had conjured him out of a dream, he was right before her, and she drank him in: his smooth dark skin, his almond-shaped black eyes, his tight-cut black hair, the looming presence of his heft and height.

Her first instinct was to reach out to him, but a blaze of pain stopped her, making her gasp.

"Doc Jane," he barked. "She's awake!"

Trez? she said. *Trez, wait, I need to tell you something—*

"Doc Jane!"

No, don't worry about that. I need to—

"She can't breathe!"

Things happened so fast. All at once, a mask was pushed onto her face, and something forced her lungs to inflate. Voices exploded around her. A shrill beeping sound suggested an alarm was going off—

Someone tried to straighten her out, and her joints roared in protest. Oh, wait, it was her trying to move—she was trying to sit up to see what was going on.

"She's moving!" That was Trez—she was sure of it. "Her arm moved!"

"She's in cardiac arrest. Can you flatten her chest?"

The pain that came next was so great, she screamed.

"I'm sorry," Trez said into her ear, his voice cracking. "I'm sorry, baby. I'm so sorry, but I've got to get you flat—"

Selena screamed again, but she didn't think it registered as sound. And then her vision blurred, starting with the peripheral and heading to the center, as if a fog were rolling in from all sides.

Suddenly, she was staring at the medical chandelier—which meant they'd somehow managed to get her on her back. Then came pressure on her shoulders, spine, arms. Her vision went in and out, that blurriness receding and returning as great waves of pain racked her.

"I don't want to break anything," Trez gritted out.

So it was his hands on her wrists, forcing her flat.

"I need to get in there. *Now*."

Doc Jane appeared on the opposite side of the table, and in her hands were palm-size blocks with curly cords hanging from the ends.

"Get her robing off." Doc Jane looked in another direction. "You males gotta leave or he's not going to let us get to her torso."

That alarm was so loud now, a solid continuous sound, no longer broken by intervals.

"Clear!" Doc Jane ordered.

A lightning strike hit Selena's chest, popping her torso up off the table, cracking each and every one of her vertebrae, busting her spine out of its hold.

As she slapped back down on the exam table's thin mattress, there was a brief, striking pause during which the three people around her—Doc Jane, the nurse, Ehlena, and Trez—all stared at her. She focused on Trez—and that was when she saw a fourth who was standing directly next to him, a big body turned away, a dark head tilted down and to the side.

iAm.

Oh, good, she was glad he was there for Trez.

Selena opened her mouth underneath the mask, looking directly into her Shadow's black eyes. If only she could tell him—

Chaos lit off around her once more, her lungs punching against her ribs, voices igniting, people shifting positions.

"Stop bagging her," Doc Jane shouted. "Clear!"

A second powerful current plowed through her, contorting her torso. This time there was no pause. That hard, powerful push into her lungs returned immediately and happened over and over.

"What do we do now?" Trez asked in a choked voice.

Oh, dearest Virgin Scribe, he was crying.

Trez, she thought at him. *I love you. . . .*

Trez was living and dying by the vital-sign machine that was about a foot behind the head of the exam table. A rope's worth of wiring connected Selena to its onboard computer, and the screen showed all kinds of info that didn't mean much to him. The one thing he did get, however, and get very goddamn clearly, was that the yellow line across the bottom was supposed to peak and valley at regular intervals as her heart beat.

It wasn't going up and down in a nice, steady pattern— even after the thing went haywire when Doc Jane put the paddles on the center and side of Selena's torso and sent all that electrical charge into the Chosen's chest.

Flat. It was flat again.

Ehlena kept bagging, her hands biting into a pale blue balloon that forced air into Selena's rib cage. And meanwhile, Trez stared at that yellow line, willing it to jump, willing it to respond to a beat of Selena's heart.

"Damn it, *beat* . . ."

Something brushed his face and he jumped back—only to find that Selena had actually reached up to him, her pale, slender hand extending in a series of jerks like the joint was rusty.

"*Selena*," he said, dropping down so she didn't have to strain. "Selena . . ."

He kissed her palm, her fingers, and then he let her brush his cheeks. Her eyes were incredibly blue, luminous, glowing. And for a moment, everything faded away so that it was just the two of them, the walls of the exam room, its equipment and personnel, even his beloved brother, disappearing from them.

Her lips started to move under the clear plastic mask.

"Okay, okay, okay." He had no idea what she was saying. "Can you stay with me? Please stay here—don't go."

She was moving, and that was good, right?

"Selena!" Shit, her eyes were rolling back. "Selena . . . !"

"We're losing her!"

There was no conscious thought involved for him. The instant Doc Jane barked those three horrible words again, he blew his form apart, and blanketed Selena's body with his molecules, his energy, his soul, surrounding her above, around, below. He threw himself into her, pushing through her skin, getting in deep, sharing everything he had in hopes that he could somehow do what the crash cart couldn't.

That he could somehow bring her back . . .

And then it happened.

Sure as if Selena reached out with her hands and grabbed what he had to give, a vital pull latched onto his essence, drawing him in, taking from him.

That's right, he thought. Use me—

"I have a heartbeat!" someone said.

"She's breathing!"

He heard the commentary not as sound, but as the thoughts of others—he didn't stop, though. Too early. Not enough had been given.

And yet all too soon, his strength started to fade, his energy draining in a flash, not anything that was gradual. As much as he wanted to keep helping her, he knew he had to get back into physical form or he was going to get stuck in vapor, and that was a death sentence.

Not until she was gone, he told himself.

And he could help her again, after he—

Trez landed on the tile floor like he'd been pushed down, all hard knocks and bad smacks. From his vantage point, he got a close look at Doc Jane's red Crocs, Ehlena's blue ones, and his brother's knees as the male immediately crouched down next to him.

iAm was all action, no delay, hooking a hold under Trez's pits, and dragging him back to Selena's head, lifting him up when he couldn't stand, kneel, or even hold his torso to the vertical.

No clue what Doc Jane and Ehlena were doing, the pair of them making their rounds of Selena's prostrated form with all kinds of medical equipment—

The door from the corridor burst open. Manny Manello, the human doctor who was Jane's medical partner, was in civilian clothes and a full hassle, like he'd been in a rush to get back to the training center.

Wrong gender. Considering Selena was naked.

Trez's lip curled up off his suddenly descended fangs, a growl percolating out of him.

"Traffic was a bitch!" Manny said. "I'm so sorry—"

"You need to leave," Doc Jane hollered as she looked up from checking Selena's eyes with a light. "Unless you want to get bitten."

As Manny shot him a look that was full of eyebrow, Trez could feel the strength coming back to him. And he wasn't the only one who noticed. iAm wrapped heavy arms around his chest.

"I'll be out in a second for a consult?" Doc Jane said to her partner.

"Roger that." Manny lifted a hand to Trez. "Sorry, man."

You had to respect his turnaround time, Trez thought as the guy disappeared.

"She has limited mobility in her arms, fingertips to shoulders," Ehlena announced as she went to the base of the table and took hold of Selena's leg. "Hip socket. Knee. Ankle. Same."

"Vitals are stable," Doc Jane reported. "I want another set of X-rays as soon as I'm sure she'll stay with us."

Jane glanced over at Trez. "You brought her back. You saved her life."

As if she heard the words and understood them, Selena looked over at him. Trez opened his mouth to respond, and didn't make it. Like someone had unplugged him from the world, everything faded to black and he went floating into unconsciousness.

The only thing he was aware of? Even after he passed the fuck out?

The steady *beep-beep-beep* of the machine marking Selena's heartbeat.

TWELVE

enzel got it right in *American Gangster.*
The best drug dealers were good businessmen.
And it didn't take nothing from Harvard to get
there.

Mr. C, *Forelesser* of the Lessening Society, weren't no
fucking suit with a bullshit piece of paper framed on his
wall. But he was born and bred on the streets and damn
good at moving product.

As sundown happened outside his broken office windows, he kept bundling his cash, the stacks of ragged twenties kept together with rubber bands he'd stolen from the
copier stations at the FedEx Office. Didn't look like much,
but that was something the movies usually got wrong.

Mr. C leaned down and handful'd another fist of crumpled, stained Andrew Jacksons out of the Hefty bag on the
floor. His men were required to empty their pockets every
dawn here in the headmaster's office, and even if it took
him all day, nobody helped him count.

At this point, after nearly a year of being in business, he
had roughly a hundred carriers working for him, the number floating up and down depending on how his recruiting
efforts kept up with the Black Dagger Brotherhood's killing efficiency. His idea for putting the Lessening Society all
in one place, in this defunct prep school, had been smart. He

could run the slayers like a military unit, housing them to-gether, keeping them on a schedule, monitoring every breath and each sale personally.

There was a fuckload of rebuilding to be done.

Soon after the Omega had come to him and elevated him to *Forelesser*, he'd realized the promotion was for shit. The Society had had no money. No real guns or ammo. No crib. No organization and no plan. All that was different now: An unusual, uneasy alliance had solved the first problem, and that was taking care of the second and third. The fourth was on him.

At this point, all he had to do was keep shit gaining. Make sure his men were in line. Track the cash coming and going. Start collecting some war toys. Once he was properly armed?

He was going to slaughter the Black Dagger Brotherhood, and go down in history as the one who'd finally gotten the motherfucking job done.

Mr. C finished the count just as the last threads of light were draining out of the now-night sky. Getting up, he strapped on a pair of forties and put the bundles of cash into a duffel bag. The total was four hundred thousand dollars.

Not bad for forty-eight hours of work.

As he left, there was no reason to lock up anything, be-cause access was everywhere. The headmaster's office had windows like sieves and doors that hung off their hinges, and on a larger scale, the decrepit grounds of the rotting boarding school were lined by an iron fence with more broken sections than ones that were upright.

What kept people out?

The slayers that roamed the property constantly, sentries whose sole job was to jack anyone who came too close.

Good news? The place was rumored to be haunted, so when those punk-ass fifteen-year-olds tried to come walkin', a couple of Omega tricks took care of that little problem. Bonus? His boys liked freakin' the fools out, and it was better than killing the bitches. Dead bodies were a pain in the ass, and he didn't want the human police involved.

After all, there was one and only one rule in the war against the vampires: No humans were welcome at the party.

Outside, Mr. C got into his black-on-black Lincoln Nav

and turned around on the unmowed, dead grass. In the twilight, he could sense his boys moving over the grounds even though he couldn't see them, the echo of the Omega's blood in them better than GPS chips shoved up their asses.

So, yeah, he knew one of his crew had been lost last night. He'd felt the death as a shock under his pasty white skin. Fucking Brotherhood. And the dumb-ass who'd been slaughtered had had cash and drugs on him, so that was a net loss of at least five grand.

On any given night, he had twenty to twenty-five dealers out on the streets at a time, each working in shifts of four hours. Shifts were critical. Anything longer than two hundred and forty minutes and the slayers had too much asset on them, too much to lose if they got picked up by the police, rolled, or killed by the Brotherhood. Too much to get a bright idea over.

He'd learned how to handle his business from back in the day, when he'd still been human and a bit player on the street, looking to get large.

And the no-bullshit truth? The Omega fucking needed him. Not the other way around.

The route he took to get to his supplier was different every time, and he was careful to track any cars behind him in case he was being followed by CPD or ATF. Likewise, there was no communication over the phone with his wholesaler—technological advances on the part of local and federal agents made that shit too risky. Plans were set or changed upon meeting, and if there was a no-show on either side, a contingency arrangement previously made meant they knew the when and where to reconnect.

None of his men knew the identity of his supplier, and he needed to keep it that way. He'd been where they were now—last thing he wanted was someone making a run at him.

And the fact that his wholesaler was a vampire?

Funny shit.

This week's exchange was scheduled for ninety minutes after sundown, out near, but not too close to, the quarry. It took him a good forty-five minutes to highway-travel it to the vicinity, and then it was a case of slow-as-you-go. The road into the thousand-acre parkland was a single-laner that was as well-traveled as an abandoned goat path, and maintained about as good as a crack house. Trees and underbrush choked the shoulder, turning the thing into a tunnel, and Wetlands warning signs glowed in his headlights.

He cut the illumination about two hundred yards in. As with his suppliers, he'd had the SUV modified to operate on blackout, and his eyes took only a second to adjust.

Thank you, Omega.

The turnoff he was looking for came a quarter of a mile up on the left, and he took the dirt path even slower. In the past, when he'd been a human and he'd pulled this exchange shit, his heart had always beat fast as he rolled up on it. Now, not only didn't he have any cardiac equipment left in his chest, but there was no getting juiced in the slightest. Thanks to his boss's modifications to his chassis and his brain chemistry, he could handle anything that went down, with or without conventional backup like guns and ammo.

So nah, he weren't worried. Even though nearly a million dollars was about to switch hands between two criminal elements.

When he finally got to the meeting place, his "partner's" Range Rover was already in the squat clearing, having crushed the saplings and bushes in a K-turn so it was headed out. As he pulled up driver's side to driver's side, they both put their windows down.

The vampire who ran the importing side of the business was straight-up Dracula: black hair brushed back, eyes that were like the laser sight on a Glock, mouth full of fangs, vibe like he enjoyed hurting people.

His brain functioned as Mr. C's did, however.

"Four hundred," Mr. C said, reaching over and snagging the duffel.

As he held it out the window, the vampire took it and traded an identical one. "Four hundred."

"Forty-eight?" Mr. C asked.

"Forty-eight. One forty-nine and forty?"

"Sundown. Ninety."

"Sundown. Ninety."

They put their windows up at the same time and the vampire hit the gas, heading off without any lights on.

Mr. C pulled the same efficient about-face and followed the way out; the second they came to the paved lane, the supplier went left and he went right.

No witnesses. No complications. Nothing out of sync.

For two confirmed enemies on opposite sides of the war, they got along damn good.

Abalone, son of Abalone, re-formed in front of a historic house in one of Caldwell's wealthiest zip codes.

This was the two hundred and seventy-first night he had come unto the beautiful manse.

It was daft to count, of course, but he couldn't help it. With his *shellan* having passed, and his daughter on the verge of being presented to the *glymera* for mating, this position of his as First Adviser to Wrath, son of Wrath, was the only anniversary he had to look forward to.

There was not a night when he did not take pride in living up to his father's legacy of service to the throne.

Or at least that was typically the case. For the first time, however, he felt as if he were letting both his sire and his King down.

Approaching the front door, he swallowed hard and fumbled with the copper key the Brotherhood had given him nearly a year ago. As he pushed his way into the mansion, he took a deep breath and smelled Murphy Oil Soap and beeswax and lemon.

It was the scent of wealth and distinction.

The King had yet to arrive, and Abalone took out his cell and checked to make sure he hadn't missed any callbacks. None. Those three times he had dialed Wrath and left voice mails had not resulted in any return communication from the King.

Unable to remain still, he went into the parlor on the left with its soft yellow decor, life-size painting of a French king, and the newly arranged stuffed chairs that lined the walls like it was a luxury doctor's waiting room. Signing into his computer at the desk by the archway, he could not sit down.

Wrath had reassumed the venerable tradition of taking audiences with civilians, and what had long been a vital connection between the rulers of the Race and their citizenry had evolved into a curious mix of the old and the new. Appointments were now arranged by text and e-mail. Confirmations were sent in the same manner. Inquiries were cataloged on an Excel spreadsheet that could be sorted by date, issue, family, or resolution. Old Law statutes were likewise searchable not in their ancient tome form, but as part of a database created thanks to Saxton.

The face-to-face interaction, however, remained unchanged and ancient, nothing but the subject and the King, communicating in privacy, reaffirming that important bond and strengthening the fabric of the Race.

Abalone had created, and was maintaining, the new modern record-keeping procedures, and the system was proving invaluable. With the volume of requests ever increasing, however—the number had more than quadrupled in the last three months alone—he was beginning to drown in the paperwork and the scheduling.

The delays were unacceptable, a disrespect to both Wrath and the petitioners.

Accordingly, it was becoming evident that he was going to need help. He had no idea where to find it, though.

Trust was an issue. He needed someone in whom he could place absolute faith.

The trouble was, he didn't know where to start the search—especially as the only people he knew were aristocrats and the *glymera* had not only been the source of the treasonous plots that had nearly taken Wrath off the throne, they were also disenfranchised from having had their political power stripped from them.

It would be folly to assume the dissenters had magically disappeared.

And that was just one of the reasons Throe's uninvited appearance on his doorstep at dawn had been so disquieting.

Forcing himself to focus, Abalone printed out the evening's dockets and then went into the makeshift throne room to check that all was as it should be. It was. The space that had been previously used for dining was now where audiences with Wrath were held—but, typical of the King, everything was low-key. There were no golden seats nor ermine robes nor velvet drapes nor carpets of grand majesty. Just a number of armchairs set facing each other in front of a fireplace that threw off cheerful flames in the autumn and winter, and sported fresh flowers from the garden during the spring and summer.

The logs were already set and he went over and lit them. The true throne, the one that Wrath's father had sat in, and his sire before that, and his sire before that, was back at the Brotherhood's mansion. Or at least that was what Abalone had heard. He had never been to the secret compound and had no interest in knowing its location or paying the facility a visit.

Some information was too dangerous to be worth knowing.

And in the end, that was the only reason he hadn't kicked out his cousin halfway through the day when it became obvious that the King was unreachable.

Even if Throe o'ertook Abalone? The male would learn nothing of consequence, nothing that could harm Wrath or the Brotherhood. This location was guarded by Brothers whenever Wrath was on the premises, and the Brother Vishous had insisted on installing bulletproof glass, flame-retardant siding, steel mesh around the dining room and kitchen, and other security measures that Abalone couldn't begin to guess at.

This residence was now as fortified as Fort Knox.

He was not afraid of the Band of Bastards here. Or the Lessening Society.

Besides, Throe had merely retired to a guest room and slept as if recovering from a vital injury. As aggression went, he had been no more trouble than any other guest could have been.

Yet.

As minutes continued to pass, Abalone paced around the audience room—

"You all right?"

Abalone wheeled around so fast, his Bally loafers squeaked on the polished floor. "My lord . . . !"

Wrath had somehow managed to make it not just into the house, but into the very room, without making a sound—and not for the first time, Abalone found himself in awe of the male. The King was nearly seven feet tall, and so broadly muscled, his warrior nature was a physical presence that made one want to put one's hands over one's head and submit just to get that out of the way. With his black hair falling from a widow's peak down to his hips, and black wraparounds hiding his blind eyes from everyone but his beloved Queen, he was both aristocratically handsome and brutally overbearing. And then there were the tangible representations of his exalted station: the black diamond ring on the middle finger of his dagger hand, and the dense tattoos of his lineage that ran up his inner forearms.

The male was always a bit of a shock, no matter how many hours Abalone spent in his presence. But that seemed especially true on a night like tonight.

The King bent down and released his Seeing Eye dog, George, from his halter, and then he looked over his shoulder. "Butch? Give me a minute in here, will ya?"

"You got it."

The Brother with the Boston accent pulled closed the sliding doors, and as the panels locked into place, Abalone could honestly say that he never thought he himself would seek an audience with his ruler.

Wrath's nostrils flared. "You got something on your mind."

For some reason, Abalone felt like getting down on his knees. "I attempted to reach you, my lord."

"Yeah, I know. I was having a rare day down in Manhattan with my *shellan*. I didn't get the messages until about five minutes ago. Figured whatever it was, we could do it face-to-face."

"Yes. Indeed."

"So what's doing?"

Dearest Virgin Scribe, this must be what it was like to be unfaithful to a mate, Abalone thought. "I . . ."

"Whatever it is, you can tell me. And we'll deal with it."

"I, ah, I received a visit this morning just before sunrise. From a cousin of mine."

"And that's not good news?"

"It is . . . Throe."

Instead of a recoil or a curse, the King laughed softly — rather like a great feline would purr when presented with the prospect of a meal. "Wheels within wheels. You didn't tell me he was a relation of yours."

"I did not know. I received a phone call from my third cousin once removed. I believe the tie is through marriage. If I had had any idea —"

"Don't worry about it. You can't help what's in your family tree." Again those nostrils flared. "Guess he wasn't welcome at your house, was he."

"No, my lord. I let him in only because he offered information on the Band of Bastards. He states that he has left them and is prepared to reveal their location, strategy, positions."

The King smiled, revealing fangs as long as daggers. "Then by all means, I want to meet with him."

Abalone gave in to his instinct, walked over and lowered himself onto the bald wooden floor. "My lord, you must know that—"

The King laid his hand on Abalone's shoulder, and that palm was so great, it seemed to engulf Abalone's entire torso. "Your loyalty is to me and me alone. I can smell it. I can feel it. Ditch the guilt. He at your house now?"

"Yes."

"Then I'll go to him."

"Would you not rather send an emissary?"

"I got nothing to hide, and I'm not scared of him or Xcor's little band of girls. They tried to kill me once, remember? Didn't work. Tried to dethrone me? Still here. They can't fucking touch me."

As if Wrath could read minds, he held out the black diamond, and Abalone clasped what was offered, pressing his lips to the sacred stone that had been warmed by the great male's flesh.

"Butch," Wrath called out. "Call the Brotherhood. We gotta make a social call."

The Brother hollered back on the far side of the door as the King moved his face downward as if he could look into Abalone's eyes. "Now, First Adviser, I want you to reschedule the first two hours of my audiences."

"Aye, my lord. Right away."

"And then we're going to your house."

"Whate'er you command, my lord. Whate'er you command."

THIRTEEN

Rez's savior from his captivity turned out not to be a person. It wasn't even an object, really.

His freedom, when it came, was courtesy of an unassuming vent located in the upper right corner of the vast suite he was imprisoned in.

Three nights before his eventual escape, he had been lying flat, contemplating absolutely nothing, when a flush of cool air hit the jewels on his robing and chilled his skin. Frowning, he looked up and saw the grate screwed into the smooth white wall.

First-generation security cameras watched his every move, so he knew better than to show any specific interest. But it got him thinking. Shadows could dematerialize, and they could also smoke out—which allowed you to travel vast distances, and stay invisible when you got wherever you were going.

He had tried both many times, and failed—and at first, he relegated any thought of ventilated escape to failure on that basis.

But the next night, for no particular reason, he looked down at what they had put on his body. The gems . . . the sparkling, precious gems that he had assumed were set in gold. The metal was silver in color. White gold, yes?

Unless . . . it was stainless steel. Which was the one thing vampires, even those of Shadow lineage, couldn't dematerialize through.

He had looked across the marble room to the bathing suite. Even when he was in the bath, when his body was ritually cleansed . . . they kept him festooned with sapphires and diamonds, collars of the gems set upon his neck and shoulders and wrists and ankles before he got into the water. As soon as he was out? The chain mail of jewels was locked upon his flesh yet again.

He closed his eyes. Why had he never considered this before?

It had taken him two further nights, two cycles of dawn and dusk, before he had developed a plan. The schedule of feedings, bathings, exercise, and study was never the same, as if purposely manipulated to a lack of pattern, and iAm's comings and goings were likewise random, for as he was not the Anointed One, he had certain freedoms of movement, certain allowances to go out into the palace for exercise or nutrition—although even that was not set in stone.

During his deliberations, Trez had been assiduous about changing nothing about his affect, his attitude, his habits, but internally his mind had been creating, crafting, testing theories for complications or potential failures.

He had anticipated tarrying for even longer, but the moment came unexpectedly, courtesy of a dropped meal tray. A maidservant had slipped on the freshly polished marble floor, and food and plates and silverware had gone everywhere. iAm, ever the helpful one, had volunteered to help deal with the mess, and he and the maidservant had left in search of cleaning aids out in the corridor's supply closets.

Click went the lock on the hidden cell door.

And that was that.

Moving fast, Trez had unclothed his body, tearing the fine mesh and the gemstones off of himself, ripping free the fasteners, popping all manner of buckles, belts, and securities. Then, naked and bleeding from the effort, he had closed his eyes and concentrated.

His anxiety had been so great, he had nearly failed, especially as he heard shouts outside of his door, the security cameras having reported his activities with alacrity and accuracy.

His conviction that this was his one and only chance had given him the grab to reach down and pull some greater strength out from his core.

Just before he went airborne, s'Ex had burst through the door, and they had locked eyes for a split second.

Then it was up and out through the air vent.

Poof!

He had followed the duct system by staying with the current that ran against him, figuring that the draft would show him the way to the great outdoors. He'd been right. Moments later, he had scrambled out into the night, expelling himself high above his previous confines, so shocked that he had gotten away with it that he had nearly re-formed and fallen to the roof of the palace.

A quick collection of his wits and he had been off, with no direction, no further plan, no supplies, no money.

But freedom was priceless . . . and would eventually lead him to cross paths with a vampire who had changed the direction of his life—

"Trez? Buddy?"

Trez exploded out of his sleep just as he had that venting system, and for a split second, he had no fucking clue where he was.

A heartbeat later, though, a pair of amethyst eyes directly in front of his face brought everything back: the training center, Selena, the present, not the past.

"Selena—"

Rehvenge put a hand out. "Whoa, easy. They're almost finished bathing her."

"Bathing her . . ." Trez rubbed his face and looked around, seeing a whole lot of concrete wall.

Christ, he was so exhausted, he'd crashed in the corridor outside of the examination room in the four-point-two seconds it had taken for him to sit his ass down and take a deep breath.

Rehvenge grunted as he used his cane to help himself down to the hard concrete floor. Stretching his legs out, he folded his full-length mink coat around his thighs, even though it was no colder than sixty-eight degrees.

"My Ehlena called me." Rehv gave Trez the once-over and, going by his tight expression, didn't like what he saw. "I would have been here sooner, but I was dealing with business up north."

"How're your colonists? Still psycho?"

"How are you?"

"I'm great, Your Highness."

"Don't try to fuck me, okay?"

"Sorry." Trez let his head fall back against the cool wall. "I'm not at my best."

Rehv glanced at the exam room's closed door. "Where's iAm?"

"Locker room. I think he went in there for a shower."

"Knew he'd be down here with you."

"Yeah."

There was a stretch of quiet. And then Rehv said, "How long have we known each other?"

"A million years."

The sin-eater laughed tightly. "Feels that way."

"Yeah."

"So why didn't you tell me?"

"About . . . ?" When Rehv just popped a brow, Trez took a shuddering breath. Of course the guy wanted to know about Selena and the bonding. "Look, I didn't even want myself to be aware of how I felt about her. I just . . . shit, you know what I was like with the whores. How the hell am I bringing that to the table with someone like a Chosen? But now this. For fuck's sake, all that wasted time. Not that we would have been together necessarily, but . . . maybe I could have helped. Or . . ."

Although, from what the other Chosen had had to say, it seemed like the disease or disorder, or whatever the fuck it was, was going to have its own course, regardless of what anyone did.

"I got some experience with that," Rehv murmured. "When I met Ehlena? She didn't know that I was half sin-eater, much less the heir to the throne of the *symphaths*. I sure as shit wasn't in a big hurry to tell her, but it wasn't like I could hide the tracks in my arms, or my impulses, or who I was. And remmy, I had the same night job you do now. Not exactly good news to bring on home to the little female. I fought it for as long as I could, and when the truth came out? I knew she was going to leave. Was convinced of it. For a while she did, and I had nothing but love for her anyway. In the end, though? Worked out."

Trez wished he could take some inspiration from that. "Selena's going to die."

"Maybe. Maybe not. Listen, I'm no fan of my subspecies, but we have know-how up north. Let me see what I can bring back for you."

Trez cranked his head around and stared at the guy. "You don't have to—"

"Stop it."

Trez had to look away. "Don't make me cry. I hate feeling like a pussy."

"You'd do the same for me."

"You've already saved me once."

"I like to think we saved each other."

Trez thought about the night the pair of them met. The how and the where, up in that cabin on the mountain, the one that was the first structure Trez had run into when he'd finally dropped himself out of the air . . . also the one where Rehv had had to do the duty with that nasty *symphath* Princess who'd been blackmailing him.

Trez had taken shelter when Rehv had arrived and fucked the bitch standing up a couple of times. Afterward, she had left him in a mess on the floor, the poison she'd put on her skin having leveled Rehvenge.

Caring for the guy had only seemed natural.

And in return? He and that purple-eyed bastard had become brothers of a sort. To the point where, when iAm had turned up on the outside, the three of them had fallen in together, Trez's loyalty and gratitude indenturing him and his kin to the sin-eater.

If he knew one and only one thing about Rehvenge after all these years, it was that he was a male of worth. In spite of being a pimp and a club owner, a degenerate and a reprobate, an evil-hearted, sadistic SOB . . . he was, and always would be, one of the finest males Trez had ever known.

"I'll get going then," Rehv said.

With another round of that grunting, the male got to his feet, and when he was on the vertical with that mink coat dusting the bald floor of the training center, he cleared his throat and didn't look at Trez. Not a surprise, and kind of a gift. Trez didn't deal well with big emotions either.

"Thank you," Trez said roughly.

"Save the gratitude for if I bring back something worth having."

"That's not what I'm talking about."

Rehv leaned down, offering his dagger hand. "Anything I got is yours."

Trez had to blink hard. Then pass his hand over his eyes.

"Your friendship's all I need, my man. 'Cuz it's pretty damn priceless."

As iAm walked out of the men's locker room, he checked to make sure the buttons on his shirt had been done up properly. The shower lasted only five minutes, tops, but the water had been ice-cold, and he guessed he felt a little more with it.

Hard to tell with all the brain fry he had going on.

He stopped as he looked up and saw Trez and Rehv linked by their palms. For some reason, the quiet moment between the males took him back to the night Trez had escaped.

So strange the paths that crossed when you least expected it.

Rehv glanced over as the pair released their grips. "Hey, iAm."

"Hey, man."

Like they were at some kind of funeral, the two of them met in the middle and did the backslapper embrace guys rocked when there were too many feels in the air. A moment later, Rehv left without a backward glance, striding down to the office, his floor-length mink billowing out behind him, his red cane plugging into the floor to keep his balance.

"Glad he showed," iAm said as he glanced at the shut door of the exam room. Guess they were still cleaning Selena up.

What a fucking night. Day. Whatever it was.

"Yeah."

iAm checked his watch. Well, whaddaya know. It was eight p.m. After sundown. They'd been here for, like, over twelve hours straight.

"So are you going to tell me what's on your mind?"

iAm dropped his arm and looked at his brother. "What are you talking about?"

"Come on, man." Trez let out an exhausted curse. "You think I can't read you? Really?"

iAm paced down a couple of yards. Came back. Went down again.

"More good news, huh," Trez muttered.

"Yeah."

"Get it off your chest. At least one of us will feel better."

"Doubt it."

"Like shit can get worse?"

"The Queen gave birth."

"And."

"Not it."

Trez closed his eyes and seemed to sag in his own skin. "Unbelievable timing."

"It's why s'Ex was calling you. He tracked me down when you didn't answer and, yeah, there you go."

Trez blew out his breath. "You know what my fantasy is? It ain't porn. It's good news. For once in my fucking life, I'd love to have some good news."

"They're in mourning." When Trez just shook his head, iAm felt like hell all over again. "We have a week, and then . . ."

"Then they're going to want their living, breathing dildo back, huh."

As Trez focused on the closed door of the exam room, he appeared to age before iAm's eyes, the skin of his face seeming to melt from the bone structure underneath, the corners of his eyes dragging down, his mouth going lax.

"Trez—"

"Tell s'Ex I want to meet with him. I can't leave now because of . . ."

"You're not actually thinking of going back, are you."

Trez's stare didn't leave that closed door.

"Trez. Answer me. You're not thinking about going back."

As the silence stretched out, iAm cursed. "Trez? Hello?"

"I've got to meet with s'Ex. But it has to be after . . ." Trez cleared his throat. "Yeah. Afterward."

iAm nodded because what else could he do? There was no blaming the guy for that kind of prioritization.

Unfortunately, the s'Hisbe was not going to be so understanding. But that was where iAm came in. No way anyone was muscling his brother while this shit with Selena was going on.

He didn't care what he had to do: Trez was going to be free to care for his female.

Fuck the Queen.

FOURTEEN

Qayla felt pursued as she kept a foot on the gas and both hands on the steering wheel of her pale blue Mercedes. Qhuinn had bought her the E350 4matic, whatever that meant, about three months ago. He'd wanted something flashier, bigger, faster, but in the end, the little sedan was what she'd felt most comfortable with. And she'd picked the color because it reminded her of the bathing pools up in the Sanctuary.

The farmland on Caldwell's outskirts rolled out over hill and dale, and she loved these gracious undulating fields that spiked up with corn in July and August, and were shorn down like a male's beard in the fallow months. She knew all of the landscape by heart now, this route well taken out to one specific rise, one particular meadow, one now-significant tree.

When she came to the base of the short hill, she cut her lights and let the car roll to a stop. She never felt good about coming here, but after seeing the state Selena was in and knowing what it meant, her heart was even heavier than usual.

Hefting herself out from behind the wheel, she put her hands on her lower back and arched her chest out, trying to loosen the muscles that seemed perpetually engaged—

"You're early."

With a gasp, she wheeled around. Xcor was standing mere feet from her rear bumper, and she could tell instantly that something was off about him. It wasn't that his harsh face looked any different; from the harelip that made him appear as if he were perpetually snarling, to his shrewd eyes and his heavy jaw, all the features were the same. And there wasn't a change in his skull-trimmed hair, or his long black leather duster, or even his leathers or his combat boots or all the weapons she knew he had on him, but which he always carefully hid from her.

She was unable to pinpoint exactly what the clue was. But her instincts did not lie, and they were never wrong.

"Are you unwell?" she asked.

"Are you?"

She put her hand on her belly. "I am not."

"What happened last night? Why didn't you come?"

An image of Qhuinn pacing around the billiards room as she and Blay sat on the sofas came to mind. And then she pictured the three of them down in the training center's exam room, standing to the side as Selena was assessed and more bad news was given.

"I had a family emergency," she said. "Well, two, actually."

"Of what sort?"

"Naught that concerns you."

"There is little of you that does not concern me."

Glancing up toward the tree that they usually sat under, Layla shivered. "I—"

"You are cold. We will get in your car."

In his usual way, Xcor took charge, opening her door and standing aside, a quiet demand. For a moment, she hesitated. In spite of the noble impetus to keep the King and the Brothers safe, she knew in her marrow that no one would ever approve of these meetings, these words, this time spent with the sworn enemy of the Brotherhood.

The one who had plotted Wrath's demise not once, but twice.

To sit with Xcor in the very car Qhuinn bought for her out of his own good heart was a violation of all the relationships she valued most.

Except she was protecting those she loved, she reminded herself.

"Get in," Xcor told her.

And she did.

Closing her door, Xcor walked around to the passenger side, and as he knocked on the window and she unlocked his door, she thought of the false human mythology of vampires, where what was supposedly undead had to be invited in before they could cross a threshold.

So far from reality.

Xcor's soldier-size body took up all the room in the sedan as he sat down in a seat that was overly big for her, even as pregnant as she was. As she inhaled to steady herself, she hated the fact that she liked the way he smelled—but she did. In fact, he always took pains to be clean whenever they met, his skin smelling of a spiced cologne that she desperately wanted to find unattractive.

This was all so much more palatable if she stayed focused on the fact that she was being coerced into the contact, the proximity, this closeness.

Because to be here with him upon freedom of will . . .

God, why was she so in her head tonight—

"Drive on," he said. "Please."

"What?" Her heart began to pound. "Why—"

"It's no longer safe here. We have to meet in another place."

"Why?" The reality of how little she knew and trusted him made her realize exactly how isolated they were. "What's changed?"

He looked over at her. "Please. For your safety. I shall never harm you—you must know that—and thus I say it is not safe for us here anymore."

She held his eyes for a long moment. "Where shall we go?"

"I have secured another location. Head west. Please."

When she didn't move, he put his hand over hers and squeezed. "This is not safe."

As he released his hold, his eyes never wavered from hers. And a moment later, she watched from a vast distance as she reached forward and hit the ignition button to start the engine. "All right."

As she put the car in drive, a subtle binging noise started up. "Your seat belt," she said. "You need to put it on."

He complied without comment, stretching the belt far, far out to extend over his massive chest, and then clicking it home.

"How far?" she asked, as a renewed spike of fear made her heart speed up again.

"Ten miles." Xcor put the window down a crack and breathed in as if trying to find a scent upon the air. "It's a secure location."

"Are you kidnapping me?"

He recoiled. "No. You are, as always, free to come and go."

"Okay."

She hoped he was telling the truth. Prayed he was. And didn't that shine a bright light on this deadly game she was playing.

This had to stop, she thought. There was a war going on with the *lessers*. He was a traitor to her King.

She was getting to be very pregnant.

The problem was, she didn't know how to disentangle the ropes that bound the two of them together.

Rhage was the last of the Brothers to materialize onto the lawn of an estate that was right out of a magazine for one percenters. As he looked up at the great looming house, he heard the narrator from the old *Batman* TV show: "Meanwhile, back at stately Wayne Manor . . ."

The Tudor-style mansion was set back on manicured lawns as if it were too good to fraternize with anything less than the White House, and lights were on in the interior, glowing with soft yellow luxury like maybe there were solid-gold shades on all those lamps. With quick efficiency, a butler could be seen crossing in front of a bank of diamond panes, his formal uniform something that Fritz would wear.

They probably had the same tailor.

"We ready for His Royal Highness?" V asked wryly.

There was a grumble of agreement among the five of them, and then Vishous disappeared into thin air. The plan was for him to join Butch in the cop's brand-new Range Rover, which was parked about four miles to the east with the King bitching about all the security measures from the shotgun seat. The two of them were going to drive Wrath over here—giving the group a number of ways to get the male out if shit went tits-up.

Rhage hated that they were bringing him here to meet with Throe, but Wrath refused to send a representative, and what were they going to do? Tie him to a fucking chair so he didn't come on his own?

"FYI." Rhage unsheathed one of his black daggers. "I give no guarantees I won't fillet this motherfucker."

"I'll hold him down for you," somebody tossed back.

A cold wind blew in from the north, scattering fallen leaves across his shitkickers, and Rhage looked over his shoulder. Nothing was moving over on the left. There was nobody in the bushes. No bad scents were on the air.

But he felt cagey as hell.

Well, duh. Anything that had to do with the Band of Bastards was hardly a night home on the sofa pretending he wasn't in fact watching *Scandal*.

Or *RHONJ*, if Lassiter had the frickin' remote.

Ten minutes later, the Range Rover rounded the corner of the drive and came over the rise, its headlights flashing across the face of the house as well as the bunch of them.

Butch piloted around the circle in front of the mansion so that the SUV was facing the escape route, and then Wrath opened his own door and emerged from the passenger seat. In his shitkickers, the male towered over the roof of the vehicle, and unlike the rest of them, he didn't have any coat or jacket on.

Just a black button-down. Under which was the mandatory Kevlar vest.

At least they had that.

Thank you, Beth.

Rhage fell into formation with the others and they shielded Wrath with their bodies as they moved forward. The instant they came to the front door, Abalone opened things up as if he had been staring out the windows to the lawn and waiting for their approach.

"My lord. The Brotherhood. Welcome to my home."

As the First Adviser bowed deeply, Rhage had to approve of the guy. Applebottom, as they called him, was one of the few aristocrats Rhage had ever tripped over who not only had half a brain, but a full heart, under the dandy act.

"If you all will proceed this way?" the guy said, indicating with his hand.

Part of the prearrangement for this was that the meeting would be in the library and one of the windows would be cracked in case Wrath had to ghost out. Throe, who would be waiting in a separate parlor, would be brought in by a Brother, and escorted out by one.

And there were a couple of other provisos.

Once inside the book-lined room, Rhage pulled a quick, but thorough, inspection of the joint, and said, "Let me go get the asshole."

"You sure?" V asked.

"I won't eat him. Yet."

He cut off any conversation by heading back out to where Abalone was hovering in the foyer, looking like he was stuck in an internal debate over whether to throw up on his shoes or try to make it to a bathroom before he ralphed.

"So where's your cousin?" Rhage shot the guy a reassuring smile. As if he were just gonna bubble-wrap the bastard and nothing more. "Over there?"

Abalone nodded toward the closed door across the way. "Yes. He is in the males' parlor."

Rhage put a hand on the First Adviser's shoulder. "Don't worry, Applebottom. This is gonna be a piece of cake."

You had to feel for the poor SOB as he exhaled in relief. "Yes, my lord. Thank you."

After another flash of the A-okays, Rhage slipped through the parlor door and closed things up behind himself.

Throe was standing across a paneled room, looking like the distinguished male he once was back in the Old Country—in spite of the fact that his clothes were common.

"Rhage?" the male said, coming forward.

"Yeah."

Throe had the chance to stick out his hand for a shake—and that was it. Rhage grabbed that wrist, spun him around like a ballerina, and shoved him face-first into the nearest wall.

"What are you—"

"Patting you down, asshole." Okay, so maybe "punching" him down was a little more accurate. "Spread 'em."

"You're hurting—"

"If I find a weapon, I'm going to use it on you. Clear?"

"Must you be so—"

"Front side." Rhage jerked the guy back by his waistband, twirled him like a top, and nailed him to the wall facing out. "Nope, head up."

He clapped a hand on the guy's chin and pushed that

handsome mug high. After giving a surprisingly thick chest a mammogram, Rhage slapped his way down and honked Throe's junk so hard, the guy sang a high C.

"I beg your pardon!"

"Nothing in there. Not a surprise."

Down the thighs. The calves. Back up to eye level.

"Here are the rules. If you make any move toward my King, in any fashion, that I don't like? You'll be dead before you hit the floor. Do we understand each other?"

"I've come here in peace. I'm through with fighting—"

"Do we have an understanding? If you so much as sneeze on him, try to shake his hand, or look twice at his fucking shitkickers? I'm going to put paid on your toe tag."

"Are you always so extreme?"

"This is calm, cool, and collected, you little bitch. You don't want to see me pissed off."

Rhage shoved the guy toward the door, opened the way out, and locked a hand on the back of Throe's neck.

"I can walk on my own," the male drawled.

"Can you? You sure about that?"

Rhage switched his grip around so that he crushed the male's face in his palm, leading Throe by that collection of eyes, nose, and mouth.

"This working better for you? No? Huh, guess you should have STFU'd."

As he deliberately kept Throe's balance off, he enjoyed the Fred Astaire routine as the guy tap-danced past Abalone and entered the library.

"Oh, this is going so well already," V muttered as he lit up a hand-rolled.

"At least there wasn't barbecue sauce involved," the cop tossed back.

"Yet." V exhaled. "The night is still young."

Rhage cleared his throat. "My lord and ruler, Wrath, son of Wrath, blooded father of Wrath, I present you with Throe, Piece of Shit."

On that note, he gave the male a good shove in the direction of the Oriental rug, and what do you know. Ass over teakettle and the motherfucker was where he belonged.

At the foot of the one true King.

FIFTEEN

"**N**o, I've got her, thanks."

As Trez spoke, he shot a smile at Ehlena because he didn't want the nurse to be offended as he shooed her away. But the truth was, he was beyond ready to be the one who got Selena out of the exam room. Away from the training center. Off to . . . somewhere, anywhere else.

Although that wasn't going to happen. Barely two hours ago she'd flatlined, been hit by two billion joules of electricity in the chesticular region, and then somehow managed to come back from the brink thanks to him pulling a living, breathing soul-blanket routine.

Oh, you know, just another day in the life.

Or was it night?

Who the fuck knew.

"You ready?" he asked Selena.

It seemed like something out of a dreamscape that she actually looked into his eyes and nodded. He would never have guessed the reconnection was possible—or the fact that her body actually bent as it was supposed to between the holds he put under her knees and at her shoulders.

"I'll be . . . gentle." As his voice cracked, he wanted to kick his own ass. "Nice and slow."

She nodded again, and then gasped as he lifted her off the examining table and moved her out from under the multi-light chandelier that had been pulled down close to her body.

"Which way?" he asked again, even though he'd already been told twice.

Ehlena, who was in charge of holding the IV bag, led the way to a door. "Here."

On the far side, the recovery room was nothing he wanted for his female. The bed was a hospital one with big handrails running down both sides, and blankets that were thin, and sheets that were plain and white. There was an IV pole set up to hang the bag and a lot of monitoring equipment. The pillows looked hard.

Then again, he could have been laying her on a handmade feather bed and even that would have been inadequate.

Selena shuddered as he put her down carefully. And then, when he went to try to get the covers out from under her, she closed her eyes and shook her head.

"A minute?" she groaned, like everything hurt.

"Yeah. Sure. Of course."

Annnnnnnnnnnnnd now he had nothing to do. Looking around, he spotted a chair and figured at least if his ass were in it, he wasn't crowding her.

As he sat down, and Ehlena left them to whatever small peace they could find, he thought, Shit, Selena was so still. But at least her joints were at seminormal angles, and she was breathing on her own. And she was conscious.

She was still very pale, though. Nearly the color of the sheets. And even though her hair had been smoothed, it had knots in the dark lengths.

"I'm . . . sorry. . . ."

"What?" He jacked forward. "What did you say?"

"Sorry . . ."

"About what? Jesus, like you volunteered for this?"

When she started to cry, he ditched the chair and went over to the bed, getting down on his knees next to her. Reaching up, he put the railing down and took the hand that was closest to him.

"Selena, don't cry." There was a Kleenex box on the bedside stand and he traded holds so he could snap one free and dry her cheeks. "Oh, no, not sorry. You can't be sorry for something like this."

Her inhale was ragged. "I didn't want you to know. I didn't want . . . worry."

"I wish you'd told me."

"Nothing to be done."

Okay, wasn't that a knife right between his fucking ribs. "We don't know that. Manny is going to talk to some of his human colleagues. Maybe—"

"I love you."

As her words hit him with all the slap of an open palm, Trez coughed, gasped, sputtered, and wheezed at the same time. Great response. Just really fucking masculine— reminding him, absurdly, of that synthesizer in *Ferris Bueller* when the little shit was on the phone with his classmates.

What the hell was his problem? The female he was in love with, the one he wanted above everything in the world, lays the Three Big Ones on him . . . and he turns into a giant bodily function.

So romantic.

Then again, at least he didn't let loose in his Levi's.

"I . . ." he stammered out.

Before he could go any further, she squeezed his hand and shook her head back and forth on the pillow. "Don't have to tell me back. Wanted you to know. Important . . . for you to know. No time left—"

"Don't say that." His voice grew strident. "I need you to not say that ever. There's time. There's always time—"

"No."

God, her pale blue eyes were ancient as she stared at him. Even in her perfectly unlined face, with her beauty shining through in spite of her condition, that exhausted stare of hers made her seem geriatric.

It was so unfair. Her in that bed, him kneeling fit and fine next to her—with no real way to share the health he had in abundance. Sure, when she'd been in cardiac arrest he'd been able to bring her back, but he didn't want to just drag her away from the brink. He wanted to cure her.

He wanted . . . years with her.

And yet, just as the thought hit him, he realized that was never going to happen: Even if her destiny changed, his wasn't going to.

"I love you . . ." she breathed.

For a moment, he felt himself hit his own brink, his heart and soul trembling on the edge of falling into her words, her eyes, her everything that made her female and mysterious and wondrous . . . but then he reminded himself that she had nearly died, was half-awake at best, and probably had no idea what she was saying.

Plus Doc Jane had announced that he'd saved her life. Which may or may not have been true—but given the drama, gratitude could make anyone feel something she wouldn't have ordinarily.

Or maybe fan the flames of affection into a temporary emotion that was much stronger.

"Don't have to say it back," she murmured. "Needed you to know."

"Selena, I—"

She held up her other hand, palm forward. "No need to go further."

There was a resonant silence, but only in the room. In his chrome dome? His brain was live-wire spastic, all kinds of thoughts and images pelting his consciousness like his gray matter had gone monkey and was throwing poo all over its cage.

Refocusing on her, he told himself to get a grip and try to help her.

"Would you like to feed?" He held up his free hand, flashing his wrist. "Please?"

When she nodded it was a total relief, and he scored his flesh with his fangs before stretching up, bringing his vein to her mouth. At first she barely latched on, doing little but swallowing. In time, though, she began to take some control, sucking at him, drawing what he had to give deep into her.

He got hard.

He couldn't help it. But it wasn't like he had any sexual drive. He was too distracted by worrying about her, wondering if, at any second, her body was going to give out again.

Stable, Doc Jane had told them. She was as stable as anyone could be a hundred and twenty minutes after total molecular collapse. But at least the second sets of X-rays had been nothing short of miraculous. Whereas in the first ones there had been all kinds of bone in what should have been the movable parts of her joints, now, according to both Doc Jane and Manny, things were more "anatomically appropriate."

No one knew where the bad stuff had gone. Or why it had left. Or when it would be back. What they did know for sure was that where there had once been no movement, now there was.

After quite a while, Selena's lips grew lax and her eyelids sank low. Retracting his arm, he licked the puncture wounds closed and then rested his forearm on the mattress and put his chin on it.

"How did you find me?" she asked in a sleepy voice. "I fell when I was up in the Sanctuary. . . ."

"Someone came and got me."

"Who . . . ?"

The Scribe Virgin, he thought to himself as she let out a soft snore.

"Selena?"

"Yes?" She tried to rouse herself, lifting her head and forcing her eyes wide-open. "Yes . . . ?"

"I want you to know something."

"Please."

"No matter what happens, I'm not going to leave you. If you want me around, no matter . . . where this goes, I'm going to be right by your side. If you want me to be, that is."

Her stare roamed around his face. "You don't know what you're saying—"

"The hell I don't."

"I'm going to die."

"So am I. But I don't know when and neither do you."

Her luminous eyes glowed with a complicated emotion. "Trez. I've watched my sisters go through this. I know what—"

"You don't know shit. With all due respect."

He got up and went to the base of the bed. Pulling the sheet and blankets out from between the mattresses, he looked under it at her feet.

"What are you doing?"

With a gentle hand, he tilted one of her ankles up so that he could look at the sole. "Nope."

"I'm sorry?"

"I don't see any expiration date stamped on here." He did the same with her other foot. "Not here, either."

He put the covers back down. Retucked them. Stared up her body at her—and tried to escape the fact that the very flesh he coveted could potentially be what separated them forever.

Except then he remembered the news iAm had given him out in the hall.

Shit, it wasn't like he didn't have his own set of road-blocks.

"I'm not leaving you," he vowed.

"Didn't want to tell you about all this." Her eyes watered up, the tears turning those blue irises into gemstones. "Didn't want you to know and feel sorry for me."

"I don't feel sorry for you."

"Don't do this to yourself, Trez. Just . . . just know that I love you and let me go."

He came back up to her. "Can I have your hand?"

When she turned stiffly on the bed and extended her arm, he took her palm and put it between his legs, on the rock-hard ridge that was punching out at his fly. The contact made him hiss, his fangs descending in a rush, his hips rolling.

"This feel like pity to you?" he gritted out.

Fuck, he had to step back. He'd pulled this crude move only to prove a point, but instead, he found himself ready to come, his body all zero-to-sixty in a nano.

"Trez . . ."

"I'm not saying we have to get sexual. Not at all. But I am not here because I feel sorry for you, okay?"

"I can't ask you to stay."

"You aren't. I get to pick this. I get to pick . . . you."

As he spoke the words, he realized, holy shit, that was true. For once in his life, he felt like he was choosing something—and in a weird way, that was good. Even though this was sad, sad stuff, it felt liberating to be all, This is mine.

This . . . situation . . . was something he was going to take ownership over for however long it lasted, wherever it took them both.

Assuming Selena wanted him here.

In the silence that followed, he looked around at the bare walls and knew he had to get her out of the hospital room. Sure, the place was close to the medical staff if she got into trouble, but it was hell on the mood, a depressing stretch of You Are Sick.

Trez refocused on her again. "Anything you need, I'm here for you, okay? If you want me."

After a moment, she croaked out, "I want you."

"Okay, then." He exhaled in a rush, and then held up his forefinger. "One thing. No expiration date, deal? We go into this like you're going to live forever."

Her expression shifted into disbelief, but he just shook his head. "Nope. That's my one rule."

He wasn't stupid. He'd listened to what those other Chosen had said, looked at the X-rays, watched over her contoured body. He had an internal conviction that he was going to lose her, and most likely sooner rather than later. But the gift that he could give her? The most important thing—hell, maybe the only thing—he could bring to this?

Hope.

And he didn't have to believe she was going to be cured to have it, to share it, or to live it.

Be present. Love her until the end. Never leave her side until the last breath.

That was how he was going to honor her with his heart and his soul, even though he wasn't worthy.

"No expiration date," he said. "We live each night as if we have a thousand of them ahead."

Selena blinked away another round of tears. On so many levels, she couldn't believe Trez was standing over her hospital bed, staring into her soul with a kind of purpose that suggested his will alone could keep her alive and healthy for as long as he wanted.

"I don't think we have a thousand nights, Trez," she said. "Do you know that? For certain?"

"No, but—"

"Then why waste a moment of the time we do have thinking like that? What's it going to get us? Seriously, how is it going to help—"

"Will you get in bed with me?"

He cleared his throat. "You sure about that?"

"Yes. Please."

She admired how smoothly he moved, getting up on the high mattress, shifting around, helping her make room for him. And as if he read her mind, he arranged her in his arms so that she was on her side and her head was on his chest.

Ragged. Sigh.

From the both of them.

"I'm relieved," she heard herself say. "I wanted you to know, but . . ."

"Shh. You need to sleep."

"Yes."

Closing her eyes, she could sense him on a different dimension now, his blood working its way into and through her system, strengthening her after the episode. In her mind, she calculated exactly when the last freeze had occurred. Thirteen nights. The one before that? Sixteen.

But maybe, if she wasn't offering her vein to anyone, she'd have even more of a reprieve. And maybe the strength he just gave her through his blood would help her fight off any episodes, too.

"I stayed away," she said, "because of all this. Not because of you. I don't care about your past. I just want you to know that."

Trez began to rub her back, his large palm circling. "Shh. Just try to rest."

Selena lifted her head. "You need to let me say this. You need to hear it and believe it. I know that you backed off because you thought that I . . . judged you or something. But I pulled away because of all this, not because you've been with a lot of . . . humans. And not because of your betrothal, either."

He closed his eyes in a wince. Then shook his head. "I gotta be honest with you. The last thing I want to think about right now is—"

"I don't think you're unclean, Trez."

"Please. *Stop*."

She took his hand and squeezed, trying to get through to him, feeling a pressure to say everything all at once, get it all on the table. His theory about a thousand nights was a good one for mental health purposes—and he'd come to the same conclusion she had: she didn't have a date and time stamped on her. But she had lived in this reality since the first episode those many decades ago, and her trajectory for survival was that of a car heading off the road and skidding into a ditch.

There was no living through this.

"I have to get this out, Trez. I've waited a long time to talk to you. I'm not losing my chance."

Dimly, she recognized that she was speaking with more emphasis, feeling more like herself, recovering even further thanks to the gift of his vein.

"You're a male of worth, and I think I fell in love with you the very first—"

Trez exploded out of the bed, and for a split second, she thought he was going to keep right on going, bursting out through the door and away from her and her dumb-ass illness. And for a moment, he paused in front of the exit.

But then he just started to stalk around the room.

"Why is it so hard for you to accept that?" she wondered out loud. "That you're a good male. That you're worth—"

"Selena, you don't know what you're talking about."

"You're prowling around this room like you're being hunted. So I'm pretty sure I'm onto something."

He stopped and shook his head. "Look, this is about you. This . . ." He waved his hand back and forth between them. "This is all about you. I'm here for you and your needs, whatever they are. We're going to keep me out of it, okay?"

Selena pushed herself up higher on the pillow. The strain on her elbows and shoulders made her grit her teeth, and she needed to catch her breath as the pain took its sweet time in fading.

But it was better than being frozen stiff.

When his eyes narrowed with concern, she said, "No, I don't need Doc Jane. Honest."

As he rubbed his face, she looked at him properly for the first time. He'd lost some weight lately, his cheeks hollowing out so his jaw seemed even more pronounced, his eyes sunken deeper, his lips appearing fuller. And yet even so, he remained an enormous male of the species, his shoulders three times the size of hers, his chest and abdomen carved with power, ropes of muscle running down his arms and his legs.

He was beautiful. From his dark skin to his black eyes, from the top of his shorn head to the soles of his booted feet.

"You are so very worthy," she murmured. "And you're going to have to accept that."

"Oh, really," he countered wryly. "I'm not so sure about—"

"Stop it."

Trez stared across at her and then frowned. "You know, I'm not sure why you're going on about this. No offense, but you nearly died in that other room. Like, how long ago? Feels like ten minutes. My shit is not important here."

Selena glanced down at her body. She was wearing a hospital johnny that was pale blue and had little darker blue spirals in a repeating pattern. The thing tied in the back, and she could feel the knots biting in where her bra strap would have been if she were wearing one, and down lower, at the small of her back.

It seemed strange to think that things in her body were functioning with relative normalcy now. And the reality that they wouldn't keep at it for much longer brought a stunning clarity.

"You know," she murmured, "I've never considered the fact that there might be a good part to having a mortal disease."

"And what's that," he asked tightly.

She swung her stare back to his. "It makes you unafraid to say the things you really mean. Honesty can be scary, unless you have something even more terrifying to measure it against—like the prospect of dying. So I'll tell you exactly why I think your 'shit,' as you put it, is important. Whatever is driving you, whatever is causing"—she motioned in a circular pattern, encompassing his entire body—"or caused that void that's inside of you? I think you used all those women to try to run away from it. I think you fucked those humans for all those years as a distraction—and the fact that you don't want to acknowledge this? It makes me worried that you're just going to use me as an even bigger, better way of avoiding yourself. What could be even more seductive or effective if you don't want to deal with your own issues than one specific female with a deadly disease?"

"Jesus Christ, Selena, I don't think like that. At all—"

"Well, maybe you should." She tilted her head, another conclusion hitting her like a ton of bricks. "And I'll tell you one more truth. Whether I have a thousand nights or two nights? I want them to be with you—but only in an honest way. I don't want to be your new excuse, Trez. I want you here, I want you with me, but I need it to be real between us. I don't have the energy or the time for anything less than that."

In the long silence that followed, she waited for his response. But no matter how awkward things got, she wasn't recanting a word.

She had said exactly what was on her mind.

Kind of liberating, actually.

SIXTEEN

Abalone was not accustomed to violence. Not in the outside world, and certainly not in the house where his daughter slept and practiced her singing lessons and ate with him.

As Rhage all but air-mailed Throe to the ground in front of Wrath, Abalone smothered a gasp with his palm. It was entirely unmanly to show any kind of shock in front of the Brotherhood, and he prayed that none of them noticed.

They certainly did not appear to. Their concentration was on the blond-haired, simply-dressed male who was, for all intents and purposes, naught but a throw rug before the shitkickers of the King.

Wrath smiled, baring fangs that seemed longer than Abalone's fingers. "Don't wait for me to help you up." As Throe began to pull himself up on his knees, the King tucked his arms over his chest. "And don't ask for the ring. I'll be tempted to crack you in the face with it."

Once he was on his feet, Throe brushed himself off and straightened his shoulders. He wasn't close to Wrath's size, but he was far from a lightweight, his body more a soldier's than the whip-thin figure that males from his class tended to favor.

"I have done nothing to deserve a presentation of your ring," he said in a low, grave voice.

"Well, what do you know, something we agree on." Wrath's wraparound sunglasses tilted toward the sound of

Throe's voice. "So, my boy Abalone says you have something on your mind."

"I have left Xcor and the Band of Bastards."

"You want a commemorative stamp," Butch muttered.

"Can I stamp him with the grille of my car?" Rhage tossed out.

Wrath's brows tightened over the bridge of those dark glasses, as if he didn't appreciate his males chiming in. "Change in direction for you, isn't it?"

"Xcor's goals are no longer my own."

"That right."

"It has been a long time coming." Throe glanced over his shoulder, and Abalone would have preferred not to be the object of his regard. "As my distant cousin recalls, I am not from soldier stock. Through circumstances beyond my control, I was forced to take advantage of Xcor's dubious kindness. He required me to repay him with a tenure of service. As you know, having found me bleeding in that alley many, many months ago, his methods for ensuring loyalty are not conversational in nature."

Ah, yes, that was right, Abalone remembered. Some time ago, Throe had been discovered by the Brotherhood, left for dead with a stab wound to the gut not inflicted by a *lesser*. In fact, from what Abalone had heard, the male had been injured by the Band of Bastards' own leader. Throe had been taken in by the Brotherhood who had sought to gather information from him, and then released back out into the world with a message for Xcor.

Word had it that Layla had fed the fighter whilst he had lingered on death's door, the Chosen offering her vein to one whom she had assumed to be a noble soldier instead of her King's enemy.

Quite a messy affair it all had been.

Wrath's nostrils flared as if he were testing the male's scent. "So what do you expect me to do with this little news flash? No offense, but where you're at and who you're affiliated with doesn't affect my world one way or the other."

"But learning the location of where the Band of Bastards sleeps would."

"And you're going to tell me," the King said in a bored voice.

"Do you think I'm lying?"

"Ever heard of the Trojan Motherfucker?" V spat. " 'Cuz I'm looking at him."

Wrath's jaw got tight. "Give us an address if you want. But just as with your political alliances, finding the B.o.B crib is not high on my list of shit to do."

"You're a fool then—"

All at once, the members of the Brotherhood jumped forward, and clearly Wrath's powerful shout was the only thing that kept Throe's skin still on his bones.

The King leaned forward and dropped his voice to a pseudo-whisper. "Do yourself a favor, asshole, and play it cool. This bunch of rabid cocksuckers has a serious hearing problem even when it comes to orders from me, and they don't like you any more than I do. You want to live long enough to see another nightfall? You'll dial back on that attitude."

"You should care about Xcor," Throe said, undeterred. "He is capable of anything, and the soldiers who fight under him suffer from the same single-minded devotion to him that your males show you."

Wrath chuckled a little, the sound somehow more evil and deadly than the naked aggression the Brothers had just shown. "Thanks for the tip. I'll be sure to keep that in mind. Abalone?"

Abalone let out a squeak and jumped forward. "Yes, my lord."

"Do you plan on letting this male stay with you? Relation to relation?"

"No, I told him he must leave this night."

"Don't kick him out on my account. It doesn't matter to me whether he stays or goes."

Abalone frowned—and had to wonder if he was getting a demotion. "My loyalty is to you and you alone. He is tainted in mine eyes no matter what he says his affiliations are."

Wrath made a noncommittal sound in the back of his throat, and realigned his face toward Throe. "You say Xcor's priorities are not your own."

"Aye."

"And you do not intend to pursue his goals."

"Nay, I do not. Very definitely, nay."

There was a pause where Wrath's nostrils flared as if he were testing the male's scent.

"Very well then." Wrath nodded at his private guard. "Let's get out of here. I have real work to do."

Nobody moved. Not the Brothers. Not Throe. Certainly not Abalone, who was feeling as though his loafers had been nailed to the floor.

"V," the King snapped. "Let's get out of here."

There was an awkward moment, and then the Brother Vishous and the Brother Butch stepped in beside the King. Standing close to his shoulders, they promenaded out with Wrath, Zsadist falling in behind the group.

The others stayed behind, clearly guarding Throe until the King was safely gone from the property.

"Abalone," Wrath said as he stopped at the front door.

At the sound of his name, Abalone scurried out of the library and across the foyer, his heart pounding. He had long been aware of how much he loved his King, but the idea that he would lose his vocation as well? Helping civilians meet with and find aid was—

"No, you're not fired," Wrath whispered. "For fuck's sake. What would I do without you?"

"Oh, my lord, I—"

"Listen up, Abalone. I want you to let him stay here for as long as he likes. I'm not buying any of this bullshit. He might well have left Xcor and the Bastards, but I don't trust him, and I'm a male who believes in keeping my enemies close."

"Of course, my lord. Yes, yes, of course." Abalone bowed even though a sudden unease shocked through his system. "I shall do anything and everything you wish."

As if the King once again read minds, Wrath said, "I know you're worried about your daughter. Until this sorts out, why don't you let her stay at my audience house? She can have a chaperone, and security is monitored twenty-four/seven there."

V stepped in close. "We got two different underground tunnels leading out from the basement suites, and we'll send our *doggen* over to take care of her. She'll be perfectly safe."

Oh, dearest Virgin Scribe, Abalone thought.

Except then he reflected that Paradise *was* getting antsy, and not because she was in love or anxious to be mated. She was a young, vibrant female with so much going for her, and yet as an aristocrat, her options were limited.

Perhaps getting her out of the house for a bit would be beneficial.

And he certainly didn't want her around Throe.

Torn between parental concern, a duty to his King, and sadness that his one offspring was in fact growing up, he found himself nodding through a surge of nausea. "Yes, please. I believe she will enjoy that."

"I'll personally make sure she's safe," Zsadist said, inclining his head once, as if he were taking a vow. "I got a daughter. I know where you're at."

Yes, Abalone thought. He had heard that the Brother Zsadist, in spite of his most fearsome affect, was in fact a settled family male with a beloved young of his own.

Suddenly, Abalone felt better, and bowed low to the scarred fighter. "Thank you, sire. She is my most precious love."

"Good. Settled." Abruptly Wrath's face changed positions, as if he were staring over Abalone's shoulder toward the library. "Xcor is predicable in his brutality, a real old-schooler right out of the Bloodletter's playbook. But the final salvo against my throne was a tactical one involving the law and my beloved half-breed Queen. That's the way an aristocrat fights. Xcor didn't pull that plan out of his ass—it had to have been something cooked up by Throe. Only explanation there is. So he may in fact be done with Xcor, but even though he wasn't lying in anything he said in there? We're not going to know where his allegiances truly lie for a while."

Abalone didn't mean to, but before he knew it, his hands were reaching forward and clasping Wrath's palm. Bringing the King's black diamond to his lips, he kissed the ring.

And thought once again, Thank the Scribe Virgin that the right male was on the throne.

"My loyalty is to you, my lord," he breathed. "And you alone."

Once Wrath was not just off the property, but out of the zip code, it was time to give Throe the middle finger and go Hardy Boys with the addy the bastard had given them.

Rhage was the last to leave the library, and just for shits and giggles, as he filed by Throe, he pulled a *Boo!* move that left the fucker jumping back and putting his arms up to shield his face.

Pussy.

Out on the lawn, he front-and-centered his phone and texted: *All well. Wrath et al ok. Off to secure 2ary local.* He paused. And then typed, *Wat r u wearing?*

He was putting the thing away again when he frowned and sent a second one to somebody else. *How r u? Need anything?*

"Okay, we ready?" Vishous asked.

Phury and Z nodded as Rhage disappeared his cell and cracked his knuckles. "I want the Bastards to be there. I need some good hand-to-hand. Need to get it in."

"Feel you," someone muttered.

One by one, they disappeared and traveled in jumbles of molecules, heading for a very different kind of neighborhood. When they re-formed, it was at the head of a cul-de-sac in a real estate development full of two- to three-hundred-thousand-dollar homes that were probably lived in by people who were popping out kids, working two white-collar jobs at the bottom of the corporate ladder, and desperately wanting to upgrade their three-series BMWs to fives.

Yuppies on the rise.

Spare him.

No one made a sound as they went from passively armed to palmed up but good. The approach to the house in question was multi-fronted, the four of them splitting up and coming at the darkened colonial from each of the compass points.

Putting up his black hood so that the blond hair wasn't such a screamer in the dark, Rhage took the back left corner, dematerializing through the woods, closing in while assuming cover behind trees. Sending his instincts out, he probed what might be under that roof, behind those solid walls, staying out of sight of the black windows.

Nothing alerted him to any presence. There were no flashes of light. No shadows moving inside. No sound, inside or out on the periphery.

Checking in with Z, who he could see out of his left eye,

and Phury, who he tracked out of his right, he motioned upward . . . then dematerialized onto the roof.

The asphalt shingles gave good traction and he stayed in a crouch, well aware of what a good target he was, silhouetted against the night sky. There wasn't a moon out, which was a bonus, but he was a goddamn sitting duck up here. Heading over to the chimney, he shouldered into the stack of bricks and mortar and listened.

No sounds again.

When the whistle came, it was from down below, and he closed his eyes and ghosted back to the ground.

Z, Vishous, and Phury were standing together in the rear.

"Nothing up there," Rhage whispered.

"I don't see anything inside," Phury agreed.

V stared at the house. "Then we have to assume that it's booby-trapped."

Yup. That was exactly what he was thinking.

"You have anything to disarm shit with?" Rhage asked.

V rolled his diamond eyes. "I'm a fucking Boy Scout. What do you think."

"What's the approach?"

They decided to enter through one of the windows in the kitchen. Doors were too obvious, as was the chimney, and anything through the garage.

Going around to the back porch, V removed his lead-lined glove, got out his black dagger, and went over to the window above the sink. Putting the tip of the weapon to the glass, he moved the blade in a circle; then placed his glowing fingers on the inside of the cutout and removed the section so that it didn't fall in.

Three. Two.

One—

Silence.

Rhage glanced around, listening for anything: footsteps in the undergrowth, the click of a safety being taken off a gun, a whisper of clothing.

Nothing.

V snaked his normal hand through the hole he'd made and clicked on his penlight. Inside, a nothing-special kitchen was illuminated in the thin beam: refrigerator, stove, cabinets. More to the point, there was nothing suspicious, no boxes or bags with wires coming out of them in the middle of the room, no beeping lights, not even an alarm panel that was obvious.

"Ready?" V asked.

Rhage breathed in deep, testing the air that was escaping from the house. The scents were of male sweat, booze, tobacco, gun cleaner . . . a pizza . . . cooked meat.

And it was all fresh.

"I'm going first," Rhage said. With his beast, he was the most likely to survive a bomb blast: any extremes of temperature, pain, or aggression, and his other side would be triggered in a split second, providing him with a set of scales that was better than any kind of Kevlar.

"Be careful, my brother," Phury said.

"Always. I got meals to look forward to."

Rhage ghosted in and took form on the linoleum. Cue the waiting. Again.

But there were no alarms going off. No ambushes. Nothing that screamed or even whispered "attack."

He took a step forward. Another. A third, waiting for a hidden mine to get triggered.

Under his shitkickers, floorboards creaked and groaned. That was it.

"Far enough, Hollywood," V ordered through the window's cutout. "Let me get in there."

Vishous joined him as the twins stayed outside to monitor the exterior. With quick, practiced moves, V put on a headset and looked around. Took out an aerosol spray can and hit the go nozzle, moving in a circle.

"It's clear, as far as I can see."

Rhage glanced to the back door. "So that's where the security pad is."

The ADT panel had no lights glowing on its face, no green means go. No red means armed.

"We have to go through the whole house," V said grimly.

Rhage nodded. "I'll take care of the first floor."

"We do it together."

With careful steps, they headed into the front of the house, V sporting his gogs, Rhage's skin prickling across his back as his beast joined the instinct parade.

The front room was clearly where the Bastards spent most of their time. There were a number of couches set at angles so they formed a circle, and the scents were the strongest in here—to the point that Rhage guessed the fighters had pulled the drapes and actually slept above-ground during daylight hours.

Detritus littered the floor: Empty ammo boxes that suggested they had both shotguns and forties. Dead-soldier bottles of Jack and Jim. Hannaford plastic bags filled with crushed protein-bar wrappers and Motrin bottles with the lids off and wads of surgical gauze marked with dried blood. An open Papa John's box had a single slice left in it—that was cold, but not moldy.

"They do not live here anymore," V said.

"And they up and left fast," Rhage muttered as he poked at another Hannaford bag with the steel tip of his shit kicker.

There wasn't a single backpack. Duffel. Piece of luggage. And although he wouldn't have counted the Band of Bastards as any kind of *Town & Country* types with the personal effects, there wasn't even a stray sock, backup set of combat boots, or a fucking comb left behind.

As Rhage came around to the base of the stairs, he felt his phone vibrate in the inside pocket of his leather jacket. No checking the thing, though. He wasn't about to get goat-fucked in this shell of a house, and the farther he and his brother went in, the greater the chances that they'd run into something that could cost them an arm. A leg.

Their lives.

That was the reality of their jobs, and something he accepted, because one, he wasn't about to let nobody push around his race or its King, whether it was a bunch of shitty-smelling slayers or Xcor's circle of douches. And two, it wasn't like he was suited to do anything else.

Well, other than eat and fuck, and God knew he took care of business on those two fronts very, very well during his time off.

Hell, even with all the high alert going on here, in the back of his mind, he was already counting down the hours until he could get his Mary really fucking naked.

Nights like tonight made him think fondly of going down on her for about seven hours straight.

Shaking himself back into focus, he approached the base of the stairs.

"I'm going up," he told his brother.

"Wait for me."

But of course, he didn't. He just headed on up, one foot after the other after the other. Probably a stupid move, but he'd never been good at waiting.

Just not part of his nature.

SEVENTEEN

As Trez stood in the corner of Selena's hospital room, he felt ... shit, totally cornered.

He didn't want to be angry with the female. For fuck's sake, she'd nearly died in front of him.

"What?" she said. "What's on your mind."

The good news was that he had watched, over the last twenty minutes or so, as her coloring had returned in full, how her eyes were now sharp as tacks, as her body, though still stiff, was so much closer to normal.

The bad news was that her little dissertation there about the nature of his sex addiction and him trying to do right by her was not anything he was going to hear. And he prayed to God she didn't keep pushing the subject.

"Selena, I think you need to rest."

"Don't tune me out, Trez."

He shoved his hand across his head. Wished he had some long-ass hair like Wrath's just so he had something to pull at. "Look, I don't want to argue with you."

"So tell me I'm wrong. Even though I don't believe that. But say something. Anything."

Trez grimaced and shook his head. "I'ma go now and—"

"Trez—"

"No, we're not going to do this."

"Why? If we have a thousand nights, what's one awkward conversation."

"This is a helluva lot more than awkward, sweetheart."

God, he could hear the sharpness in his own voice. Feel the ramp-up in his body. "Yeah, I think I'll come back—"

"It's still going to be here when you return." She motioned between them with her hand, and for a moment, he was so damned grateful for the movement, he forgot what they were talking about. "Distance is not going to help this."

His heart started to pound. Like he was afraid or some shit.

But that wasn't what was happening.

Really. It wasn't.

"What do you want me to say?" he muttered. "Give me the words and the inflection and I'll do it. Anything to make this go away."

"What aren't you telling me?"

"Nothing."

Long pause. "All right," she said with defeat.

Oh, great. That made him feel soooo much better.

How had they traveled the distance between relief at her survival to all this tension so fast?

He wasn't about to tell her the news from the s'Hisbe. She had more than enough to worry about on her own, and he didn't want her concerned that the Queen's executioner was going to put him in chains and drag him back to the Territory at any moment.

"Selena, listen . . ." He shook his head. "Am I embarrassed about what I did with all those humans? Absolutely. Do I have regrets? All the time. Do I believe that I'm tainted? According to my culture, I'm completely contaminated. But you need to know that sometimes a slut is just a slut. A whore is nothing more than a whore. I had a drive and I had nowhere else to go with it."

He looked away, tracing the floorboards with his eyes.

The silence grew louder than a scream.

"I think you're right," she said.

Trez exhaled in relief. Thank God she was buying it—

"You do need to go."

"What?"

"Until you can be honest? I think you need to stay away. Because either you're lying to yourself or you're lying to me. Either way, you need to—as the Brothers would say—get your shit together."

He shook his head. "Yeah. Wow. Not how I saw this going."

"Me neither."

"Okay. Then. So."

As she just stared over at him, the room ran out of its air supply. At least as far as he was concerned.

Trez cleared his throat. "Fuck . . . I'll go then."

He stalked out, using the door that led into the corridor rather than run the risk of running across Doc Jane and Ehlena in that examination room.

Yeah, 'cuz he really felt like having an audience right now.

Thank fuck iAm had left and gone to check in at shAdoWs, The Iron Mask and Sal's. His brother was the last person he wanted to be around at the moment.

Moving quickly, he stalked down the corridor and paused before stepping in front of the glass door of the office. When he didn't hear any voices, he peered around. Empty.

Score.

He made it through the supply closet and out into the tunnel without a hitch, and he even jogged down to the staircase. Codes were entered. Steps were mounted. The door under the stairs was opened quietly.

The sound of a vacuum cleaner running in the library was not a surprise. But the lack of any Brothers anywhere was. Usually, at this time of night, the ones who were off rotation were chilling in the billiards room, watching tube. Playing pool. Drinking.

He took advantage of the ghost-town routine and headed for the bar. As he came up to the top-shelf display, he paused for a moment to consider his options and then chose Woodford Reserve. And Grey Goose. And a bottle of chard that was sitting out, unchilled, on the granite counter.

Like he was really going to fucking care what he drank.

The grand staircase was a piece of cake, and he was not surprised to find the King's study empty as Wrath spent most of his nights out meeting with his civilians. Making the turn toward the hall of statues, he pared off before all that marble and opened the door to the stairs that took him up to the third floor.

The First Family's suite of rooms was hidden behind a bank vault, but his room and his brother's were right out in the open, just two normal doors close together.

In spite of the argument with Selena, he wasn't going to bolt to the Commodore. He wanted to be on site in case she . . .

Yeah.

Closing himself in, he put his three new best friends on the bedside table, and turned on the lamp. The velvet drapes were drawn, and he left them that way as he continued on to the bathroom, shedding his clothes. With a crank of the showerhead, he got the water rolling, and he was careful to leave the lights off.

No reason to meet his own eyes in the mirror.

He waited until things got steamy before stepping into the marble enclave. He'd had more than enough of things that were uncomfortable, thank you very much.

Soap—everywhere. Rinse—everywhere. Shampoo—on his head, followed by conditioner. Razor—on his jaw, his chin, his cheeks.

Then it was a case of out with the towel and naked into his bed.

He got under the covers from habit, his brain studiously checking out of absolutely all thought, only common practice driving him to a place and situation where he could get drunk horizontally.

Cracking the lid on the Grey Goose, he took a good pull and ground his molars as the burn fired down his throat and lit up his gut like Fenway Park.

As V would have said.

How in the hell had the night ended up like this.

iAm was not about to waste time with shAdoWs, The Iron Mask or Sal's. Screw that. There was more than enough competent staff at all three to take care of business. He'd just told his brother the lie because he didn't want Trez even more freaked out.

Materializing on the terrace of their condo, he glanced at his watch and then went inside. Pacing around, he turned on some lights, checked the refrigerator even though he knew there was nothing much in it, and poked around the cabinets.

He hadn't eaten since . . . Sal's the night before, actually. And he hadn't fed in . . . shit, he didn't know how long.

Probably needed to handle that, but as always, he had

little interest in the vein. Not that he didn't appreciate and respect the Chosen who served him and his brother. He just didn't like the whole business of sucking at someone's wrists when she was a stranger. Yeah, yeah, duty, whatever.

Guess he was far more Shadow-ish than his brother.

In their culture, anything physical like that was sacred. Which sucked, because biological necessity forced him to feed probably six times a year, and every time he did, it was an exercise in self-discipline—and not because he wanted to bang whoever it was.

He was, at his ripe old age, still a virgin.

He blamed the celibacy on the shit with Trez, and the teachings and traditions of his kind, which he sometimes felt like he took waaaaay too seriously—

Wow. He was so wound that he was talking to himself.

About shit he already knew.

Which wasn't even that interesting to begin with.

He paced around. Checked his watch again and then looked to the terrace. Where the fuck was—

"That you?"

iAm wheeled around at the male voice that came from the bedrooms. Striding forward to the hall, he palmed his forty, but given the inflection? Not much was going to be a problem.

And sure enough, as he rounded the corner into what had been his crib, he found s'Ex stretched out on the bed, the sheets wadded up around his naked body, a double-size bottle of Ciroc nestled in his arms like a baby.

"I thought you were in mourning," iAm said as he tucked his gun away.

"Am." s'Ex held up the half-empty bottle. "This is my Kleenex."

"Doesn't the Queen want you in the Territory"

"Not really." The male slashed his hand through the air. "Too embarrassing. I'm okay to fuck behind closed doors, but out in the open? No good. Course, all woulda been forgiven if the chart'd been right. But no."

iAm leaned against the doorjamb and crossed his arms. "How long have you been here?"

"Since you left—was it last night? You need more liquor up in here. When can you bring it? And I want some females."

iAm's first instinct was to tell the guy to go screw. Natch. But he needed something from the bastard.

"I can make that happen," he said.

s'Ex closed his eyes and rolled his hips under the sheets. "When."

"You gotta do something for me first."

Those lids lifted slowly, and the black eyes glittered. "It doesn't work like that."

"Actually, it does."

"Fuck you."

"Fuck *you*." iAm held that gaze steadily. "I need to get into the palace."

s'Ex shut his piehole. Then he shoved his tremendous torso upright, the covers falling down, pooling at his waist. In the light from the bathroom, the tattoos that covered every inch of his flesh glowed like they were fluorescent against his dark skin.

"Not what I thought you'd say," he murmured. "Without a gun to your head."

"What I need from you is a guaranteed out."

"So you're going to steal something."

"I just want access to the library."

"Lot of recreational reading out here in the human world."

"And I need to go now."

s'Ex stared at him for a while. And then he yawned like a lion, great fangs flashing as his jaw cracked from the strain.

"Now," iAm said.

"The palace is closed for mourning."

"You got out."

s'Ex made a noncommittal noise. "What kind of information are you looking for?"

"Not relevant for your purposes."

"The hell it isn't."

"Look, I need to go now, and I have to be back before dawn. This is an emergency. I'm not asking to stroke you."

s'Ex frowned. "Like I said, the palace is closed."

"So you're going to have to sneak me in."

"Why the fuck do you think I'm going to help you."

iAm smiled coldly. "Get me in and out, and you're fucking that Queen of yours."

"Ours. And if I want to screw her, all I have to do is slide into her bed."

"You think you can still stand to do that now?"

"Don't romanticize me," s'Ex said grimly.

iAm shrugged. "Whatever. Bottom line is, you're never going to get Trez at this point. I've got to try to help him."

If Selena died? Everybody was going to lose him. Shit, all iAm had to do was think of his brother bolting from that exam room, racing out into the corridor with a gun up to his temple, ready to pull the trig.

s'Ex stared up at him for the longest time. "What the hell is going on?"

"I'm giving it to you straight. Your interests and mine are aligned. I don't want my brother dead and neither do you. We'll fight over what happens to him at the end of this, but right now? You need me to get him through a certain crisis."

"Put a definition on 'crisis.' "

iAm looked away. "Someone who's close to him is sick."

"Not him, though?"

"No."

"You?"

"Do I look sick." iAm met the executioner's eyes again. "Look, you and I both have a management problem with him. You think I like trusting you? If there were any other option, I'd be getting it in. But like you know firsthand, you got to deal with what life gives you. And I need that goddamn library."

The s'Hisbe had a long and distinguished history as healers. And as Shadows were, like *symphaths*, an evolutionary offshoot of vampires, it would seem logical that this Arrest disease might have shown up at some point in his race's past—and if it had, it would be in that library.

If they were lucky, the healers might have some kind of treatment—at which point, stop number two was going to be the s'Hisbe's extensive pharmacology vault. The Shadows had been synthesizing drugs from plant and animal material for centuries, titrating all kinds of compounds to deal with diseases and disorders—and as with record keeping, the healers were meticulous about their trials and studies.

His people had brought rationalism into medicine long

before humans ushered out mysticism and embraced scientific thinking.

Maybe there was hope. He had to find out.

"I do not want to rely on you," iAm said roughly. "But I have to. Just like you are going to have to do this for me if you want any chance of getting Trez in line. He will be dead within the hour if that female dies."

"Female?" When iAm said nothing more, s'Ex cursed. "The two of you are a huge pain in my ass, you know that."

"I feel the same way about you and your Queen."

"Ours. You're a member of the s'Hisbe no matter where you choose to live."

It was, of course, total bullshit about Trez going back to the Territory and falling in line with that astrological chart of his. That was never going to happen. But iAm had to use whatever leverage there was, and s'Ex was probably drunk enough not to look too closely at the motivation involved here.

And what do you know, it worked.

With a curse, the huge male threw off the covers and got to his feet—and for a moment, iAm checked out those tattoos. Christ. The executioner's flesh was covered from throat to ankle, shoulder to wrist, with white markings, the only absent places his face and his cock and balls. Even iAm had to be impressed. The "ink" was actually a poison that discolored the skin. Most males prided themselves on withstanding the pain and sickness of a small symbol of their families on the shoulder or the name of a mate over the heart.

The fact that s'Ex had lived through all that was visible confirmation that he was a badass. Or a masochistic psycho.

Leaving the guy to get dressed, iAm went into the living area. As he approached the glass sliders, he looked out over the nightscape of Caldwell: the speckled illumination randomly spaced in the skyscrapers, the twin lanes of red taillights and white headlights wrapping around the curves of the Hudson River, a plane or two blinking high over the horizon.

In and out, he told himself. That was how this had to be.

And if there was a God, he'd be able to find something that would help Selena.

EIGHTEEN

"Turn here?" Layla asked as she leaned into her sedan's steering wheel.

"Yes. Here."

She put her directional signal on, and as the Mercedes let out a little *chck, chck, chck*, she remembered Qhuinn teaching her the where's and when's of all the driving business. Safe guess that he never would have thought she'd use the skills to take Xcor anywhere.

"Where are we going?" she asked. The headlights were showing little more than a narrow dirt lane with a lot of autumnal trees choked up tight against the "road." A short stone wall seemed to keep the arboreal aggression back, although what little shoulder there was was overgrown with brambles and long grass.

"Not far. 'Tis but a few kilometers now."

Was this it for her? she wondered. Was this the night when her paranoia turned well-founded, when Xcor took control of the situation in a way that not only harmed her, but her young and Qhuinn—who were both total innocents in all this?

Dearest Virgin Scribe, she needed to get out of—

The headlights swung around and what she saw made her heart stop and her foot pop off the accelerator.

It was a little cottage, which, in spite of the overgrown landscaping, was utterly charming. The front door was painted red, and with its two bay windows and pair of dormers on the second floor, the place seemed to be all wide-eyed and smiling. There was also a big fluffy tree to the left with golden leaves the color of sunrises she had seen only on TV or in books and magazines, as well as a slate walkway that led up to its welcoming visage.

"Do you like it?" he asked stiffly. As if he were afraid of the answer.

"Maybe this is naive," she whispered. "But it looks like nothing bad could ever happen in there."

"It is the caretaker cottage of the main house. The latter, which is down that lane there, has been abandoned, but an old *doggen* lived here up until a month ago." He glanced over at her. "Let us go inside."

She got out without turning the engine off, but Xcor took care of that, reaching over and silencing the purr as she walked in front of the headlights. As the illumination was cut off, she saw that there were candles glowing inside of the house—or at least that was what she assumed was creating the flickering golden light.

At the door, she touched the paint. It was well-weathered, cracked but not chipped. Candy-apple red, she thought. And no doubt, it had been a high gloss when it had first been applied.

"Open," he told her. "Please."

The latch was made of brass that was old and worn, but polished in the places where hands had gripped. A subtle creak was released as she pushed at the surprisingly heavy panels, but the sound was more a chipper greeting than anything sinister.

It wasn't candles. It was a fire.

The living space was open and paneled in a reddish wood, the hearth made from river stone of various sizes, shapes, and colors. The floor was bare, with wide panels that talked as she walked over them, chattering as if they had missed having company. Breathing in, she smelled the sweet smoke of the fire and an underlying clean, woodsy scent.

There was a slouchy couch off to the side of the hearth, positioned such that if you sat upon it, you could see out the bay window. The thing was slipcovered in a collection of quilts, the blankets laid one upon another, the swatches and colors so variable, the conglomeration formed its own unique pattern. There was also a big stuffed chair, some old-fashioned books in short shelves, and a circular braided rug that brought everything together.

"The kitchen is through here," Xcor said as he closed the front door.

She walked past him, his huge body too still, his eyes refusing to meet hers. The bathroom was modest and equipped with a stall shower, toilet, and a sink. The stairs up to the second floor were steep and narrow and carpeted with a worn runner. And the kitchen on the far side was filled with ancient appliances interspersed with stretches of countertop.

Layla pivoted around. "How long have you had this?"

"As I said, the caretaker died a month ago. She was a *doggen* who took care of us, with no kin of her own." He turned away and began to remove his heavy coat. "The family she looked after lived in the big house, but were killed in the raids. She stayed on the property because she had nowhere else to go. The *lessers* did not come back, so she lived."

Xcor turned away and began to disarm, his broad shoulders flexing as he removed the halter that kept his daggers in place upon his chest. Next, he unbuckled the holster at his hips, his elbows shifting around, the leather strap coming loose.

For some reason, she noticed the body under the clothes he wore, how his muscles bunched and released under that thin black cotton shirt, how his pants stretched across his thighs, his calves, his backside.

He was talking to her, slowly, in measured syllables, but she didn't hear what he was saying.

Xcor pivoted back around. Stared at her. Fell silent.

"Do you not wish to stay?" he said in a low voice.

"Why did you bring me here."

He cleared his throat. "I cannot abide your being pregnant out in the cold on the nights that we meet. Not when you are this far along."

From out of nowhere, she felt a flash of warmth. And she didn't think it was the fire.

"Come." He stepped back against the door, flattening himself. "It is warmer in here."

She walked up to him. And then kept going.

Taking a seat on the chair, she pulled down her robing. Wrapped her coat around herself. Looked into the flames.

Xcor stalked across the room, closing all the drapes before easing his body down on the sofa.

"Thank you," she heard herself say. "This is much more comfortable."

"Aye."

The silence stretched out between them. It was strange: In the field, with the vastness of the sky above and the rolling meadow around, she had not been so keenly aware of him. Within these four walls, however, his presence seemed to be amplified, any movement he made, whether it be breathing or blinking, registering a thousandfold.

There was a curious awkwardness between them, the fire's cheery conversation failing to relieve the growing heaviness in the house.

"Do you intend to consummate our arrangement," she blurted. "Is it . . . time?"

"It's a ghost town up here, true?"

As V called out from up in the colonial's attic, Rhage leaned into the bathroom of the master suite. "Nothing here, either. 'Cept a fuckload of pink."

Heading back into the bedroom, he got a second chance at the rose-colored stuff. The shit was everywhere, from the rug and the drapes, to the wallpaper and the sheets, and Xcor's scent was all over the place. Clearly, this was his private room—and there was some serious satisfaction that the fucker had had to crash in this estrogen-dominated nightmare.

Like sleeping in a goddamn womb.

Rhage shuddered as he walked out into the hall. "Wonder if he's been suffering from a phantom urge to wear high heels."

"There's a picture." V came out of the hole in the ceiling and down the folding stepladder. "Abandoned. They just ghosted off and left this place."

Nothing. There had been absolutely, positively nothing suspicious or threatening, no booby-traps to catch them, no bombs set to detonate, no alarms.

There had also been nothing personal left upstairs, either—like in the living room, there were piles of trash here and there, but no clothes, no weapons, no computers or cell phones.

Moving quickly, they went down the staircase, and back-tracked through the empty house. After dematerializing out through the open window in the kitchen, they rejoined Phury and Z.

"Nada," V said.

Rhage took out his phone for a quick look-see, and when there were no replies to either of his texts, he frowned and disappeared the thing again. Antsy, he went to the other side of his jacket and snagged a Tootsie Pop—then saw that it was orange, and traded that for a grape one. The purple wrapper slid off easily, like the suckah was ready to go to work, and he eased the sugar ball into his mouth.

"It's completely clean?" Phury asked. "That can't be right."

Rhage popped his mouth toy out. "Don't get me wrong—I think disarming bombs and booby traps is a bore, but I was ready to put the time in. I don't get it. They leave here because Throe's out and likely defecting? They must know that we're going to come as soon as we got the addy from that asshat."

V's white eyes shifted over the empty house. "They missed an obvious chance."

"Didn't think Xcor was that stupid—or lazy." Rhage shrugged. "Maybe they're hurting for money."

"Doubt that it's a lack of resources," Phury muttered. "They're well armed, going by their kills downtown."

There was some fast conversation and it was decided they'd go back and report to Wrath that Throe hadn't lied. Just before they dematerialized, however, Rhage spoke up around his lollipop.

"Listen, you boys mind if I take a little detour?"

"No problem, we'll start the debrief," V said.

"Thanks, my brothers. I just need ten minutes or so."

He clapped palms with his fellow fighters, and then one by one, they all disappeared ...

... but instead of re-forming in the backyard of Darius's old house, where Wrath held audiences with his subjects, Rhage materialized in front of a large, but far less opulent, home in the suburbs. A blue Volvo XC70 station wagon was parked in the driveway, and though the drapes were all pulled, lights were on in every single window all around the three-story house.

Rhage took out his phone, went into Favorites, and hit green-means-go. As the ringing started, he shifted his weight back and forth between his shitkickers.

"Hey," he said as the call was answered. "You okay?"

"Hey." His Mary, his perfectly beautiful and brilliant female, sounded all wrong. "How did you know."

Instantly, his beast surged under his skin, ready to tear into anything or anybody that threatened their mate. "What's going on?"

"We're having trouble with one of our moms."

Rhage's eyes sought out the windows. "Can I help?"

"Where are you?"

"Out on your lawn."

"I'm coming down."

Rhage hung up the phone and did a quick pass with the tidy-up, smoothing his hair, making sure his jacket was hanging right, pulling up his leathers.

Safe Place had been started by Marissa to meet the needs of victims of domestic violence within the Race. Although humans had a lot of programs and resources for their women and children, female vampires and their young had had absolutely nothing to turn to until Marissa had opened up this facility. Staffed with social workers trained thanks to the human world—night school or online—and nurses managed by Doc Jane and Ehlena, the residents were allowed to stay, without charge, for as long as they needed in order to get back on their feet and be safe.

Males were not permitted inside.

As far as he knew, there were at least twelve in the house at the moment, although that number fluctuated—and thanks to the Wellesandra Annex, built because of Tohr's gift in memory of his beloved first *shellan*, there was always plenty of room.

The front door opened and Mary slipped out, locking up behind her. Tucking her arms into her chest, she shivered as she ran over the lawn—and it took every ounce of his self-control not to be the one to cross the distance between them. But he had to respect the boundary of the property.

Opening his arms wide, he sank down into his knees so that when she got within range, he could hold her flush to him and lift her up off the ground. To him, she weighed nothing, but oh, God, she was vital, her body warm against his, her arms going around his neck and squeezing, her scent hitting him like a Xanax and a jolt of espresso at the same time.

"My Mary," he sighed. Deep inside him, his beast chuffed in satisfaction. "My Mary girl."

He'd started calling her that a while ago. No idea why. Probably because every time he did, she smiled.

Rhage eased her back down, but kept her against him. Brushing her cocoa-colored hair back, he didn't like how pale she was. "What the hell's happening?"

The sound she made was one of exasperation. Exhaustion. Sadness. "Do you remember that mother and child you rescued with Butch about two years ago? Maybe two and a half? Mom had been a victim for years, so had her child."

"Yeah, they were the first people in your program."

"Well, mom's not doing well. She didn't tell anyone that she was pregnant when she came here. She hid it so completely, none of us had any idea what was going on. Typical gestation is like eighteen months, but from what Havers told us, some babies can die in utero and just stay there—not possible with humans. However, Havers said he'd seen that before in rare cases."

"Wait. What? Are you saying she . . ."

"Yes. It's just terrible."

Rhage tried to imagine a female holding a dead young within her womb. "Jesus."

"She got sicker and weaker—until she lost consciousness and we called Doc Jane and Ehlena in. Jane took the baby out, but the mom . . ." Mary shook her head. "Mom isn't recovering. She's got a low-level infection that refuses to clear, and she just doesn't look right. And to make matters worse, she's refusing to have more treatment, and nothing is getting through to her."

Which meant Mary had been on the front lines.

Rhage tucked her in against his chest and felt like an asshole for coming on to her in text while she was dealing with life-and-death stuff. "Is there anything I can do?"

She eased back and looked up. "Actually, this little break is giving me a second wind. Your timing couldn't be more perfect."

He thought about what was going on back at the clinic

with Selena. The situation was weighing on him for some reason, even though he wasn't that close to Trez.

Good male, though. Real hard-ass with a good heart.

"Well, let me know." He brushed his mate's hair back again. "Anything you need, at any time."

As she lifted up onto her tiptoes, he met her more than halfway, kissing her lips once, twice, and again. She was, even more than his beating heart or his Brothers, the single most important thing in his life. From the instant she had first spoken to him, and he had closed his eyes and swayed at the sound of her voice, he had been lost in her.

Without her being his magnetic north? He would be worse than cursed.

"I love you," he whispered. "Now and forever."

"I'll try to come home at dawn, but I don't know how this is going to go."

"You do what you need to here. I'll check in and you'll update me when you can."

"You are always so understanding."

Like she knew that being separated from her during the day was a kind of hell for him.

"You do the same for me, Mary girl. And your work here is very important."

She tilted her head, her wide eyes grave. "Thank you. You know, that's . . . just really kind of you."

"It's the truth." He kissed her again. "Go on, now. Get back to your patient."

His Mary took his hand and squeezed. "I love you, too."

He stayed where he was, watching her run back to the front door, take out her key, and let herself back into the house. Just before she disappeared, she gave him a wave.

As the door shut, he imagined her turning the dead bolts, making sure everyone was safe. Working to improve the lives of the females and young inside.

After a moment, he took out his cell phone and checked again. Nope. Trez had still not gotten back to him.

That had been the second text he'd sent.

With a curse, he scattered his molecules over to Darius's old house—and as he traveled, the image of Trez bolting out the door of the exam room dogged him. Ate at him.

Shit, he hoped Selena was okay.

For some reason, that was of vital importance to him.

NINETEEN

cor's heart beat irregularly as he sat upon the sofa opposite Layla. She had chosen the chair in the corner to place herself in, and consequently, the light from the fire reached only up to her legs. He could picture all of her, however; every detail of her face, her throat, her body was known to him as well as his own.

The question she had asked was like a physical presence between them.

"Well?" she asked. "Has it . . . come time?"

The trepidation was obvious in that voice of hers, and he brought his palm up to rub his face. Unlike her, he was fully illuminated, and he didn't want her to be able to see him. If she was already anxious, the sight of him wasn't going to help.

"Xcor."

"I am not an animal."

"I'm sorry?"

"I would never . . . take you in your current condition. That would be beastly."

The deep breath she took was audible even over the fire's crackle. And not for the first time, he hated the position he'd put her in. He was actively lording what he'd discovered over her, forcing her to be here with him, keeping her engaged with him even though it was obviously not something she would choose freely and in spite of the fact that it put her in danger.

The Black Dagger Brotherhood did not forgive their

enemies any better than he did. And consorting with a known traitor was a capital offense according to the Old Laws.

Considering he and his Bastards had managed put a bullet into Wrath's throat last fall? That didn't put them on any ... what were they called, Boy Scotch?—lists.

"Nine months," she said.

"What?"

"Since we've been meeting."

He thought back to the beginning, when she had fed him from her wrist beneath that tree. And then later, when he had disarmed himself and gotten into that car with her. He had kissed her then—

"Are you aroused?" she said.

As he recoiled, his body shifted of its own accord, his hips punching up before he could stop the movement.

"Are you?" she whispered.

"Do you really want me to answer that."

"I asked, didn't I."

"Yes."

There was a long pause. "You are agreeing that I asked that?"

He dropped his hand and stared into the dim corner, giving her every chance to remember exactly whom she was talking to. "I think we need to change the subject."

"Answer me."

"I did."

Given the sound she made in her throat, he knew damn well she was swallowing hard, and he had no regrets that he made her feel awkward. After however many nights of meeting up—typically twice a week—he had never taken anything to the next level.

At least, not while she was in his presence.

When it was just him alone with his memories of her? All bets were off.

At this moment, however, he felt like the boundary he had every intention of crossing at some point shouldn't be approached at all. And he told himself it was because of the pregnancy.

Of course it was—

"I want to see."

Xcor went dead still, his breath freezing in his chest along with his heart. "Why? I can assure you I have the anatomy required of males—and in any event, I cannot fathom why its precise dimensions would be of any interest to you until the time, as you say, comes."

"Show me."

He frowned and glanced to the windows. He'd pulled the drapes. His bastards were out fighting, and they would not be returning to the property's main house until closer to dawn. But injuries in the field happened, and on occasion, required treatment away from the back alleys of down-town—

Wait a moment. He was *not* dropping his trousers. So this analysis was unnecessary.

Xcor got to his feet, and refused to look further than the fact that he did not want to expose himself to her. "We shall conclude this meeting now."

"Why? I should like to see you. It is a simple enough request."

Not even close, he thought. "Why would you want to do that."

"I thought you wanted to have sex with me. That's the whole point of all this, isn't it."

Xcor prowled over to her, his temper rising—along with the heat in his veins. Bracing his hands on the arms of the chair, he leaned over, forcing her back into the cushions.

"It is my intention," he snapped, "when the time comes, to spare you the visual. So I fail to see why a show would help you through what is going to be done to you."

The wave of anger that wafted up from her was a shock. She had shown him fear. Courtesy. A gracious restraint that made him respect her as much as he coveted her.

This was new.

"What ails you?" he asked. "What e'er has made you thus."

Without warning, and with surprising strength, she shoved him out of the way and burst up from the chair.

Layla paced around, making a tight circle in front of the fire, and her emotions were such that the air vibrated about her.

Eventually, she stopped before the flames, putting her hands on her hips as if arguing with them in her mind.

"My sister is dying," she blurted.

Xcor released his breath on a curse. "I am sorry."

"Her life is coming to an end." Layla's hands went to her swollen belly. "I have never really had a lover. In spite of this pregnancy, I feel like I am a virgin."

Xcor settled his weight upon the chair's padded arm. Or collapsed was more like it. For one, he hated thinking of the mechanics of how she had begotten the young. For two ...

He shook his head, tossing that thought right out. "The male has not mistreated you, has he?"

"Oh, no. And I do love Qhuinn. He is my family. But as I told you, the mating that occurred during my needing was solely for the purpose of having a young. I can barely remember what transpired." She looked over at him, the flickering glow making her seem impossibly beautiful. "My sister is dying. I am alive and I have not lived. That is why I say to you ... show me."

It was not supposed to be like this between them.

Layla hadn't meant to reveal this truth about herself to Xcor. Or to ask him to do what she had. But ever since she had walked into this little house, her brain had been functioning on two tracks: one here with him, the other back in that exam room at the training center.

Where she had stood over the contorted body of her sister, horrified to find out that yet another of them had been stricken with the Arrest.

Paranoia made her wonder if she had the disease; if she could pass it down to her young. There had been no episodes for her, but when had they started for Selena? Layla was younger than the other Chosen ... was it only a matter of time?

Of course, there was a good possibility that the mental wheel spin was tied to her hormones. She had noticed her thinking growing more convoluted and less accurate as the pregnancy had continued.

That did not, however, change the reality that, as all but a virgin who was in fact pregnant, she was scared of never knowing sex. Angry at what she had been denied by fate. Grateful for her young, and yet stifled by her body's natural progress.

And Xcor was the only one she could turn to. The Brothers were all mated, and besides, she didn't think of them sexually. Further, it wasn't as if she were going to come into contact with anyone else of the male persuasion anytime soon.

Xcor was her only avenue to express the toxic mix of fear and yearning.

He cleared his throat. "You need to consider this more thoroughly."

Lowering her eyes, she focused on his hips, at the straining length behind the fly of his combat pants. "I am."

His sharp inhale inflated that powerful chest and he dropped his hands to cover himself. The veins running down into his blunt fingers were yet another symbol of the power in his body, and abruptly, she wondered what his hands looked like on his sex.

"Leave the now," he said. "And consider—"

"No."

"I am not a toy, Layla. I am not something to be taken out and played with—and put away at will. Once certain doors are opened, they cannae be closed neatly. Do you understand? I have every intention of having you, but I shall endeavor to honor you and respect you for your station. This is against my nature, however, and if pushed too far, I shall revert. Especially when it comes to sex."

As his words drifted across the tense air, his eyes went down her body, making her feel naked even though she was fully clothed. And round with the pregnancy.

"I just want to watch you," she heard herself say. "I want to see what you look like when you pleasure yourself. I wish to start there."

Xcor closed his eyes and swayed. "Layla."

"Is my name leaving your lips like that a 'no'?"

"I shall not deny you," he groaned, lifting his lids. "But you must be sure you want this. Think on it o'er day."

At that, he gripped himself, closing a fist around his heavy arousal.

"Tomorrow night, then," she heard herself say.

But she already knew the delay was going to change naught—even though she understood on some level that he was right. There was a careening quality to all this, as if she had ricocheted from Selena's suffering to some kind of wild expression of an inner problem of her own.

"Tomorrow," he affirmed. "And now you need to go."

Walking over to the door, she glanced back at him. He was drawn in sharp lines, his shoulders tight and high, his forearms straining, his thighs twitching as if he were going to leap forward at any moment.

"Xcor—"

"Go," he barked. "Get out of here. Get the *hell* out of here."

Fumbling with the latch, she got the door open and burst out into the chilly night. In comparison to the cottage's warmth, the air was harsh and icy in her nose, and her coat offered little insulation. She paid no attention to the discomfort—

Xcor shut the door behind her, and as it slammed into place with a clap, she heard the *click!* of a locking mechanism.

She needed to go.

She had to go.

Instead, she stayed where she was, breath leaving her open mouth in puffs that rose up until they were consumed by the cold. Looking around, there were no indications that anybody else was on the property, no sounds of people walking or talking, no lights filtering through the trees.

She could not leave.

Stepping carefully so as to avoid hitting fallen sticks that might snap and give her presence away, she went to the bay window. A gap in the fall of the curtains on one side allowed her to see inside to the fireplace and the cozy room.

Where was he?

Abruptly, Xcor came into view, pacing like a caged animal, back and forth, back and forth. His face was twisted into a snarl, his fangs elongated, muscles straining up the thick column of his neck. Finally, he pivoted around to the hearth and punched out at the chimney, pitching his fist into the pattern of mortared stones.

She winced, but he didn't seem to notice any pain.

Splaying his palms out, he braced his weight against the mantle, his body bowing as he faced away from her toward the fire. Blood ran down the back of his hand and wrist from the wounds on his knuckles, twin dark streams uniting and seeping under the cuff of his black shirt.

A moment later, his bleeding hand dropped down. At

first, she thought he was shaking off the hurt. But then his pants moved, tugging left, tugging right.

His shoulders bunched up tight and his spine jerked.

He had gripped himself.

Layla bit down on her lower lip and leaned in closer, until her nose hit the cold glass. Spotlit against the fire's orange glow, Xcor's body cut a black silhouette as he widened his stance and let his head fall forward.

His elbow moved back and forth.

He was stroking himself.

Closing her eyes briefly, she sagged against the bay window. When she opened her lids again, he was working it faster. And faster.

Xcor turned his head to the side and bared his fangs. Sinking his sharp canines into his bulging shoulder muscle, he bit down through his shirt, his face wincing as if in erotic agony.

And then his hips punched forward toward the flames, over and over again as he climaxed.

Backing off, she—

—tripped over a root and fell into nothing but air. Between her big belly and her vital distraction, she tried to twist around and catch herself, throwing out her own hand to prevent herself from hitting the ground hard. Terrified for the safety of her young, she landed in a sprawl, her hip taking the brunt of the impact, her arm getting pinned.

The agony was instant and overwhelming, a sudden surge of nausea making her heave.

Groaning, she stayed perfectly still. "Okay, okay... you're okay...."

She really had to get out of here now.

Struggling to her feet, she weaved her way over to the car while holding her arm against her body. When it came time to open the driver's-side door, she had to brace the injury on the back window so she had a free hand, and she needed to catch her breath after she was behind the wheel.

Getting the Mercedes started and then turned around nearly made her faint, but she eventually made her way down the lane and out, out, out to the main road.

It was then that she realized that without Xcor's direction, she had no idea how to get home.

Tears of frustration pooled in her eyes and she envied Xcor's ability to punch something. If she could have, she would've.

But she'd already broken her arm.

Busted knuckles she did not need.

TWENTY

Am followed s'Ex's instructions to the letter, waiting a good hour and a half before dematerializing from the condo at the Commodore to the outskirts of the Territory of the s'Hisbe. When he resumed form in the forest, he tracked in about three hundred yards to the river that made a curl around a granite rock formation in the shape of that human president Lincoln's head.

He found the garb where the executioner had told him to expect it, tucked under the cleft chin of the makeshift face. As he shed his clothes and donned the traditional *farshi* dress of an unmated servant male from the lower classes, he was surprised to find he felt utterly vulnerable under the loose gray garment.

Of course he kept his dagger and his gun on his body: Relying on s'Ex was a had-to in this situation, but he didn't trust the motherfucker farther than he could throw the guy.

The Territory was north of Caldwell, on the transitional lands between the peaks of the Adirondack Park and the flat area around Plattsburg. Masquerading as an artists' colony, the two-thousand-square-acre property was bordered by a substantial concrete wall that was as tall and stout as an oak all the way around. The few humans in the communities around the parcel were long used to the presence of the "artists" and seemed to take a perverse pleasure in protecting the sanctity of the property and the "art" that was being done in their midst.

Which worked for the s'Hisbe.

The irony, of course, was that a mere twenty miles farther north, on the far side of a mountain? The *symphaths* had established their presence as well.

The proximity made sense. Neither subspecies was in a big hurry to fraternize with anyone else—the sin-eaters didn't respect humans or other vampires any more than the Shadows did, so the more isolated, the better. Accordingly, there had never been any envoys or diplomatic ties between the two nations. They were as separate as two strangers sitting side by side on a bus, asking nothing of each other except to be left alone.

He couldn't believe he was going back in.

Leaving his own clothes where the ones provided had been stashed, he strode off. The leather thongs on his feet were more like gloves than shoes, and as he traveled over the rough ground cover, he felt the nuances of fallen sticks, random rocks, and uneven earth. The advantage was silence: Except for the occasional snap and pop, he was as quiet as the moonlight that fell from the heavens.

It was not long before he came up to the retaining wall. Rising high, the vast construction was streaked with dirt stains and random vines, and here and there, fallen limbs were cocked at odd angles against its flank.

He wasn't fooled by the supposedly dilapidated appearance, however, and as he dematerialized up and over, he had forgotten how broad the thing was.

Re-forming, he took a moment to orient himself. It had been so long since he'd set foot on his people's land, but he shouldn't have worried that anything had changed: Unlike the face that was shown to the outside world, the bulkhead on the Shadow side was pristine, the concrete pale and sun-bleached and perennially washed, not even grass blades growing out of place around its base.

And no unruly forest. Absolutely not. The trees that were permitted to grow were spaced like chess pieces on a black-and-white board, each with their own delineated spot, even the branches clipped to stay within their boundaries. The lawn was likewise kept clean as a carpet. In spite of autumn ushering in a change of color and the inevitable leaf-from-limb departures, there was not a single fragment of anything marring the rolling expanse.

iAm had often thought the Territory was like a snow globe, a constructed version of reality existing in an artificial encapsulation.

The impression still stood.

Picking up his pace, he jogged over the brown grass. Soon, the first of the settlements appeared, the housing units little more than pup tents made of wood that were painted black and roofed with tin panels that were left silver. Like the trees, the shelters were placed in orderly rows, no lights glowing inside, no smells of cooking, no talk percolating out of them. This was where the servants of the palace resided, and they used the flimsy constructions as places to sleep and fornicate only. Otherwise, they were fed, clothed, and bathed in the staff wing of the Queen's grand enclave.

The walls to the palace appeared some distance thereafter, and they were even taller than the first barrier. Faced in white marble and polished to a high shine, they were maintained scrupulously on both sides, hand-scrubbed during the day by groundsmen on thirty-foot-high ladders.

Assuming things were still done like that. And come on, nothing changed here.

Falling in parallel to the wall, he continued along until he came to a sunken doorway marked with symbols.

Right one on the first try.

Checking his watch, he waited. Paced back and forth. Wondered where s'Ex was.

No one was around. This was the back of the palace, far from where the aristocrats and middle class lived out in the front of the Territory—then again, because of the mourning period, all citizens were expected to be indoors, on their knees, offering their respects to the night sky for the Queen's loss.

So even a frontal approach probably would have been fine.

The plan was for the executioner to open the door and sneak him through the maze of corridors to the library. As iAm was dressed in servant garb, there would be no questions asked. s'Ex had always had free run of the palace and the staff, thanks to his position as the Queen's primary henchman—

The blow came from the back and caught iAm on the

skull, ringing his bell so hard that shit went blackout in a split second.

He wasn't even aware of falling face-first to the ground. And there was no time to curse the fact that he'd made a mistake trusting that male or to try to go for one of his weapons.

Too late.

Back at the Brotherhood mansion, Selena emerged from the underground tunnel and had to take a breather to reorient herself in the grand foyer. It seemed like a hundred years since she had last been in the grand space.

How had things ended up like this? she thought as she went around the base of the ornate staircase.

On one level, she hadn't expected to be alive, much less mobile—or even partially mobile. On the other hand? She had gone from rushing to tell Trez how she felt about him ... to ripping his head off, as the Brothers would put it.

". . . First Meal the now. And following preparations, we shall . . ."

At the sound of Fritz, the butler's, voice, she started her ascent. Her legs were weak, her muscles straining to activate joints that remained stiff and painful. In order to maintain her balance, she had to grip the gold-leafed balustrade with one and then, as she got closer to the top, both hands. Her robing, which had been cleaned at some point, seemed to weigh a hundred pounds.

A surge of relief hit her as she got to the second floor without being spotted. It wasn't that she disliked Fritz or his staff or any of the Brotherhood; she just felt rather exposed. Part of what had helped her deal with her disease had been keeping it a secret. Then, when she was around others, she could pretend that she was just like them, with a long life expectancy, and priorities that involved normal things like work, and sleep, and food.

Now? Everyone was going to know.

There was no privacy in the mansion—and that was fine. The people were lovely and supported one another. It was just ... it had taken her years and years to come to terms with her illness.

The others were going to catch up with her reality quick, and she did not want to be pitied.

Going over to the head of the hall of statues, she paused at the discreet door to the left. Opening it with a shaking hand, she confronted yet another set of stairs, and had to wait a moment to gather her strength.

She ended up taking them slower than the main stairs. Then again, there was less of an imperative to run and hide. The only other people who used these were the First Family, who lived in a triple-locked and insulated space that no one but Fritz was allowed access to . . . and iAm and Trez.

iAm's bedroom door turned out to be wide-open, a lamp glowing in the far corner illuminating the tidy, empty space with its antiques and fine fabrics.

Trez's was shut.

Selena knocked, and then put her ear to the panels. When there was no response, she knocked again.

Maybe he hadn't come up here?

She knew he had dealings in the human world, but he'd seemed so exhausted as he'd left the clinic. It seemed only reasonable that—

"Yeah?"

Swallowing hard, she said, "It's me."

Long silence. So long that she wondered whether he'd cracked a window and dematerialized out of the room just to avoid her.

But eventually his voice came again: "Are you okay?"

"May I . . . ?"

"Hold on."

A minute later the door opened, and she had to step back. He was so big . . . and so very naked—although it wasn't like he was showing anything. He'd put a robe on, the bare, dark skin of his chest revealed in the V between the lapels.

It was impossible not to imagine what the rest of him looked like under there.

"Are you all right?" he repeated.

For some reason, she got frustrated by his concern. Which was insane. He was being polite and solicitous . . . it just made her feel like all she was was this disease inside of her.

"I, ah ..." She glanced around. "May we do this privately?"

In lieu of answering, he moved aside and indicated the way in with his arm. After she was over the threshold, she heard the door lock click into place.

"I want to apologize." She stopped at the windows and turned around. "I'm sorry. My emotions are raw right now, and my candor got away from me."

Trez crossed his arms over his chest and leaned back against the exit. His face was inscrutable, his dark eyes grave, his brows down.

As the silence stuck around, she cleared her throat. Shifted her weight back and forth. Filled the time looking at the messy bed. The black clothes draped over the chaise longue. The shoes that had been kicked off over by the closet. The towel hanging off the top of the open door into the marble bathroom.

"So ..." She cleared her throat. "That is what I came here to say."

Dearest Virgin Scribe, was this it between them?

"How long?" he asked roughly.

"I'm sorry?"

"How long do you have? Until the next ... whatever it is. When was the last one?"

Two weeks ... or actually thirteen days. "A month ago. Maybe longer."

His shoulders eased up. "I meant to ask that before."

Again he went quiet.

"Trez, I really am sorry—"

"There's nothing to apologize for. You're just where you're at. I'm not offended, and I'm not going to try to change your mind about how you feel."

"You seem offended."

"I'm not."

"Trez—"

"How are you doing?"

"Fine," she snapped. And then reeled in her temper. "I'm sorry. I just ... it's like you're freezing me out."

"I'm not."

"You're not talking to me."

"Then why are my lips moving."

"How is this happening again," she muttered as she mirrored his pose, crossing her arms over her own chest. "I just want things to be . . . normal between us."

"They are."

"Bullshit! You're standing over there like a statue—that's my job, okay? I'm the one who's supposed to be frozen. Why can't you be real, and tell me to screw off, or that I was a bitch, or—"

"You want me to be honest?"

"Yes! Damn it." God, she was sounding less and less like a Chosen. Cursing, using vernacular. Then again, she was feeling less and less like a Chosen. "Hello? You going to say something?"

"You sure?"

"For the love . . . look, do you just want me to go—"

"No. I want you on your back, in my bed, with your legs spread and my mouth all over you."

Selena stopped talking. Breathing. Thinking.

He cocked an eyebrow. "That honest enough for you? Or do you want me to go back to pretending I'm not thinking about sex right now. With you."

Okay, now she was the one being quiet. And he laughed harshly.

"Not what you had in mind, huh. I don't blame you." He turned the knob on the door and opened things up, repeating his "after you" gesture. "If you want to keep talking now, I suggest that you let me get dressed and meet up with you on neutral territory."

Selena looked down at his hips. She had known his body fully only once, when he had taken her virginity, and she was well aware that he was *phearsom*.

Was he hard now?

"Selena?" A flash of annoyance tightened his face. "Let me meet you downstairs. In the kitchen."

Without conscious thought, she brought her aching hands to the tie on her robe.

His eyes instantly tracked the movement.

"What are you doing?" he demanded.

She pulled the knot free and let the length of silk fall loose. With every breath she took, the robe parted a little further, until a path of flesh running from her throat to her sex was exposed. Trez's stare, that dark stare, dipped low, and all at once, the scent of him surged, filling the room with an erotic spice.

Selena eased the robe from her shoulders, letting the soft fabric drift to the floor. "Close the door, would you. I'd like some privacy."

TWENTY-ONE

Trez's cock had its own heartbeat. And that was before Selena went full-frontal at him. After that reveal? The damn thing had its own conscious thought pattern.

Mine.

When he heard the door shut, he wasn't sure whether some hand of his had reclosed it, or whether he'd simply willed the thing back into place.

"You sure about this?" he growled, already taking a step toward her. "Because I won't be able to stop."

"Yes." Her eyes did not rise to meet his. They stayed locked at his hips. "Oh, yes. Let me see you."

As he came to stand right in front of her, he said, "What about all those humans I was with."

"You're going to bring them up now?" She took the tie to his own robe with one of her hands. "Really?"

He stopped her from getting him naked. "Nothing has changed about me."

"That's your hang-up, not mine."

"In my tradition—"

"Which is not mine."

"—I am contaminated."

"Why are you still talking."

With that, she shook his hold free and uncovered him, loosening the tie, pulling the folds of black fabric from his body. His sex was fully erect, jutting out between them.

And that was the next thing she put her hands on.

Trez groaned and let his head fall back on his spine.

"You're hot," she breathed as she leaned in and kissed the skin over his heart. "And hard."

"Selena, I'm serious." He fumbled to stop her before she got to stroking. "I want to honor you—"

"You're wasting time."

With that she got on her knees and took over. As she was a tall female, her mouth was at the perfect height, and God save them both, she put it to use, extending her pink tongue to lick at the head of him. The velvet rasp left him shaking all over, and before he went the way of the robes and hit the fucking floor, he leaned forward and braced both hands on the nearest thing he could reach.

The bureau. Or it could have been the hood of a car. Santa's sleigh. A refrigerator.

Warm and wet, she drew him in, the suction and all the slick wiping out the world, bringing him instantly to the brink.

Gritting his teeth, he groaned, "I'm going to come—oh, fuck, I'm going to—"

He had some thought that he didn't want to disrespect her by orgasming in her—

Selena eased back, opened her mouth, and extended that magic tongue. Looking up at him, she started to pump hard at the same time she lazily licked at his tip.

Trez lasted, oh, maybe a second and a half. And as his release kicked out of him, she took it all, swallowing, sucking, easing back so he could cover her lips and her face. God help her, he kept orgasming, an endless sexual urge locking onto his body as he marked her, his scent blanketing her in an ownership that was primordial.

Defend. Protect. Love.

All of it was in this sacred space.

Mine.

When he finally stilled, she sat back on her heels and then, with a series of kill-me-slow moves, she licked around her mouth. Brought up her fingers, captured the slick trail on her chin, and sucked things clean. Looked down at her perfect breasts.

Cupping the full weights, she smiled at what had dripped down, making the swells and those tight nipples of hers glisten. "You got me messy."

"Where did you learn how to do that?" he choked out.

At least that was what he'd meant to say. The syllables came out a jumble of incoherent sound.

"What was that?" she whispered, before lifting one of her breasts up and bending her tongue down.

She lapped at herself.

The growl that came out of Trez's mouth was something that, if he were her, he would have been afraid of.

Selena wasn't. She just laughed throatily. "Is there something else you wish to mark?"

Freedom.

As Selena sat on her knees in front of Trez, with his taste in her mouth and his scent all over her skin, she reveled in the sense of sexual freedom that had overtaken her. The liberation seemed entirely at odds with the death sentence that she lived under, and yet her lack of time was what spared her any awkwardness or self-conscious worry. She was flying above the constraints that had long pinned her to the ground, her training as an *ehros* letting her soar on the currents of sex that ran, thick as tangible ropes, between their bodies.

With no idea how long she had, and under such frustration that she had wasted so much time, she was urgent in her personal expression, embracing any desires she had and acting on them.

All of which were with Trez.

And as if he were feeling the same, he leaned down and lifted her from the floor. Her joints protested at the change of position, but the complaints were nothing except murmurs against the roughshod lust she had for him.

She needed the penetration. By his body.

Trez took her over to the bed and laid her out on her stomach, his big, warm hands stroking her from shoulder blade to back of the thigh before lifting her up onto all fours and spreading her knees. Ducking her head, she wanted to see him—and she looked past the heavy, hanging swells of her breasts, watching him come up behind her, his sex bobbing as he moved into position to—

It was not his erection that brushed against her.

As his hands went to her hips, his thumbs dug into her butt and pulled away, until her sex split wider for him. And then he went in with his mouth, his lips finding her, stroking wet on wet, sucking, eating. With total domination, his tongue licked up and down, penetrated, flicked at the top of her sex until she jerked her way into an orgasm, each kick of pleasure pushing her into his face.

When he was finally finished, he jacked up, his fists punching into the sheets on either side of her.

"I'm going to fuck you now," he gritted out in her ear.

"Oh, God, please—"

Selena shouted loudly as he jabbed into her, stretching the inside of her nearly to the breaking point. The pain was the perfect bite—and then he started to pump. There was no slow-and-steady windup; hard, pistoning power made her see stars until she lost the strength to hold her upper body off the bed. Collapsing face-first into sheets that smelled of him, she struggled for breath and loved the suffocation as each thrust shoved her face-first into the pillows.

Bang! Bang! Bang!

The headboard was having the same rough ride she was, nailing into the wall, the sound reverberating along with a grunting from him that was all animal.

Craning her head around her shoulder, she strained to see him.

Trez was magnificent, his pectorals and shoulders seized up, his huge arms carved in muscle, his abdominals ribbed as his hips punched at her. As he orgasmed, his head fell back as it had when she had first taken hold of him, and he howled, his bright white fangs flashing long and deadly, his neck cording up on both sides, his hips slamming into her and locking in as he pumped, pumped, pumped....

He filled her up.

And her sex milked him, urging him on until she felt the wetness on the inside of her thighs.

He didn't so much disengage as fall over to the side, as if every ounce of strength had been spent from him. The headboard let out one last *bam!* as he landed and bounced, his hands and arms, his torso and legs going loose from all that straining effort.

His mouth moved, his dark eyes meeting hers and staying there.

She had no clue what he was saying to her. She didn't care. Her ass was still up in the air, her sex humming from the hard use, her body as satiated as his looked. Air currents, from the vent above, drifted down from the ceiling, brushing against everything that was exposed, tickling, cooling.

That had been the sex of her life. Hard and raw, the way she had been told and trained it could and should be.

Before Selena allowed herself to lie to the side and slip into her own sleep, she smiled so widely her cheeks hurt.

She had been, for the first time in her life, not just well and truly fucked, but marked by the male she loved.

Even with the future she had to face, it was hard not to feel blessed.

TWENTY-TWO

iAm regained consciousness, but kept his eyes closed. What woke him up was the shooting pain in the back of his head—that and the ice-cold floor his naked body was lying on. For a moment, he considered playing possum and trying to get an idea of where he was through his hearing, sense of smell, and instincts, but there was no reason to.

He knew exactly where they'd put him.

Fucking double-crossing bastard.

Opening his lids, he saw a whole lot of nothing much. Then again, he was on his stomach, one arm trapped under his torso like he'd been thrown in—

A door opened over in the corner behind him. And he knew that not by any hinge creaking, but by the sudden addition of voices and footsteps in the cell.

"Why would I check his marking?" a male asked. Not s'Ex.

"It is procedure."

Yup. Nothing had changed.

iAm reclosed his eyes and stayed perfectly still except for breathing shallowly as the footfalls came closer.

There was a gasp. And then fingers palpated the small of his back, as if they were stretching the skin where he had been marked, as all males were, when they were six years of age.

"That cannot be right."

The footsteps left in a hurry, and he assumed the panel was shut again.

Lifting his head, his vision blurred and came back into focus. There was no one else in the well-lit twenty-by-twenty cell, the glossy white walls so slick he could see his dark reflection in the panels of marble.

His head hurt so damned much, he was forced to lay it back down again, his cheek finding the exact spot on the stone that had been warmed to the temperature of his body while he'd been out of it. His arm was killing him, the limb both numb and painful at the same time, but he lacked the energy to move the thing free of his upper body's weight. Lying there, breathing, existing, he had no idea how long he'd been out, what they were going to do to him, or whether he was going to get out of this bright idea he'd had alive.

From out of nowhere, he had a mental image of him leaving Sal's the night before, stepping free of the restaurant he loved, talking to the waiters.

He found himself wanting to rewind time and go back to that incarnation of himself, his memories of the way the night had been cool on his face, and how the smoke from his waiters' cigarettes had curled up off of the lit tips, so clear that, for a moment, it seemed impossible that he could not return to that place in time . . . step into the shoes he had been wearing then . . . reassume his suit of skin just as he re-formed after dematerializing.

But of course, time didn't work like that. And memory was but a television show of your own life, a movie screen you could play witness to, but not interact with, change the course of, redirect.

Desperation for Trez, the great motivator in his life, had propelled him back into the heart of the enemy he and his brother shared.

And there was a very good chance this shit was going to get the best of him.

With a groan, he rolled himself onto his side and blinked a couple of times. His weapons, like the robing he had been wearing, were long gone. And there was nothing else in the cell—

The door opened, the panel sliding soundlessly into the wall. And what came in was robed from head to foot in black folds of cloth, the face covered, the feet covered, even the hands gloved.

Was it the Grim Reaper? he wondered. Had he passed out and was dreaming—

A subtle scent registered.

But not in his nose. Through his body.

Like a lick of electricity.

The door was shut behind the tall, robed figure. And as the male approached, iAm did his best to assume some kind of defensible position.

He didn't make it far at all with that one.

A gloved hand reached out; he was rolled back over; and then he felt a touch on the base of his spine.

"I will . . . kill you . . ." iAm mumbled. "Hurt you . . ."

How, he hadn't a clue. But he was going out fighting, that was for damn sure.

The figure stepped back. Tilted its head as if it were considering the method of death that would be used.

In the s'Hisbe, most prisoners were tortured first. Tenderizing, iAm had always thought. Then they were slaughtered and either buried or eaten by s'Ex and his guards, depending on the offense.

The latter was a proud tradition. Also took care of the whole what-to-do-with-the-body problem.

iAm curled up fists and braced himself for whatever came at him.

Except the figure simply regarded him for a long moment. And then backed over to the door and left.

Oh. Okay. They'd verified who he was, and there was no reason to kill him before they got Trez back here. That would be a waste of leverage.

Shit.

Relaxing his muscles, he tried to get himself to go loose and prayed that his body's natural healing abilities took care of the concussion quickly.

He was going to need to be able to back up his fighting words with more than an inert body and limbs made of lead.

Goddamn it, he should never have trusted s'Ex.

Back in Caldwell, Paradise sat on her bed, legs tucked under her, eyes on the night sky on the far side of her closed, locked windows.

"So you're going to do it?" she said into her cell phone.

Peyton laughed. "Hell, yeah, are you kidding me? I'm

dying to get out of here. Ever since the raids I've been on lockdown, and the fact that my parents are letting me go into that training program is a miracle."

She focused on the latches on her own bedroom door, which were, as a matter of fact, in the locked position.

"Wonder if my dad would let me," she murmured.

There was a pause. Then a laugh. "Oh, my God, Paradise. No. Uh-uh. No way."

"Yeah, you're probably right. He's really protective—"

"That program is *not* a place for females."

She frowned. "Excuse me. The letter from the Brotherhood said we were welcome to try out."

"Okay, number one, 'try out' does not mean 'accepted.' Have you ever even done a push-up?"

"Well, I'm sure I could if I—"

"Number two, you're not your average female. I mean, hello, you're a member of a Founding Family. Your father is First Adviser to the King. You need to be preserved to breed."

Paradise's mouth dropped open. "I cannot believe you just said that."

"What? It's true. Don't pretend the rules are the same for females like you. Like, if some scrub civilian who happens to wear a skirt wants to give it a shot, fine. That loss means nothing to the species. But, Parry, there aren't many of you left. For males like me? We don't want to get mated to anyone but you, and there are like, what, four or five of you left?"

"That is the most reductive reasoning I've ever heard. I gotta go."

"Aw, come on. Don't be like that."

"Fuck you. I'm more than just a pair of ovaries you can put a ring on."

She hung up and thought about throwing her phone across the room. When she couldn't manage to follow through on the impulse, she then got worried that all the manners that had been inbred and reinforced in her meant Peyton was right.

She was just a hothouse flower, good for nothing but tea parties and young and—

As the cell started ringing again, she tossed it onto her duvet, got down on her floor, and planted her palms flat on her needlepoint rug. Kicking out her legs, she balanced on the balls of her feet.

"Right," she said, gritting her teeth. "Up and down. Like a hundred times."

She got the down right on the first try, her arms more than willing to oblige. And as her nose came in contact with the depiction of a vase of flowers, she was in full-on beast mode, ready to punch it up and hit this hard.

Up was . . . only okay.

Down again to the carpet. Annnnnd up.

Sort of. The muscles in her upper arms started to tremble; her elbows wobbled; her shoulders ached.

She did three. Or, like, two and a half. Before she collapsed on the—

"What are you doing?"

With a yelp, Paradise flipped herself over. Her father was in the doorway to her bedroom, putting away the key he'd used to open things up—and his eyebrows had popped so high on his forehead, they were all the way to the base of his hairline.

"Push-ups," she said as she panted.

"Why-ever for?"

Ask him, she thought. Just come right out and say, I want to join the Brotherhood's training center program—

Her phone started to ring again.

"Do you need to get that?" her father asked.

"No. Father, I have a—"

"Something has arisen, dear one." He shut and relocked the door. "And I must be frank with you."

Paradise brought her legs up and circled her arms around them. "Have I done something wrong?"

"Oh, indeed no." He shook his head as he looked at her. "You are the very best daughter any male could e'er ask for."

As her phone went silent, she had to wonder how many of Peyton's views her father shared. And how many times Peyton was going to try to call her back.

"I need you to pack up some things," he said.

Paradise recoiled. "Why?"

"I'm going to ask you to leave the house for a couple of weeks."

A cold flush went through her. "What did I do?"

"Oh, love." He came over and knelt down. "Nothing. It is just, I think you might enjoy having a job."

Now she was the one with the mile-high eyebrows. "Really?"

She had broached the subject a number of months ago, when yet another night taking piano lessons and doing complicated, multistitched needlepoint had made her feel like she was losing her mind. But he had carefully denied her in the interest of her safety—a point she had both respected and been frustrated by.

It was hard to argue that the world wasn't a very dangerous place for vampires.

"What's changed?" Then she thought about their distant relation. "Wait, is that male going to continue to stay here?"

"It has naught to do with him. Rather, my work as First Adviser is growing more complicated and burdensome and I require someone I may trust with the King's business to help me. I can think of no one more appropriate than yourself."

"Really," she said, narrowing her eyes. "There isn't some other reason?"

"For truth. I promise you." He smiled. "So what do you say—would you like to work with me?"

With a sudden lunge of happiness, she tackled her father in a hug. "Oh, thank you! Yes! I'm so excited!"

He laughed. "Okay, but you'll have to move into the King's audience mansion. Worry not, you shall not be alone. You may take your maid *doggen*, and the Brotherhood have the building fully staffed—"

Paradise leaped up to her feet and ran to her walk-in closet. Throwing the doors open, she started pulling out pieces from her set of monogrammed Louis Vuitton luggage.

"I'll be ready in a half hour! Fifteen minutes!" She yanked out built-in drawers, fisting up underwear, bras, tank tops. "Oh, will you get Vuchie? She'll be so excited!"

Dimly, she heard her father chuckle. "As you wish, my lady. As you wish."

TWENTY-THREE

$\mathfrak{R}$hage re-formed on the lawn of Darius's former mansion and strode up to the front entrance. The second he came into the house, he heard a series of gasps, and glanced to the left. In the parlor, there were a number of civilians clustered in an awkward, standing group, like they didn't feel comfortable sitting on all the fancy silk-covered furniture—and their eyes were popped large at the sight of him.

Yeah, his reputation still preceded him.

Geez, you're a slut for a couple of centuries, and people just can't let that shit go after you get properly mated.

It was a PITA, and on an ordinary night, he would have gone over and introduced himself just to bring his Mary up in conversation.

Tonight, though, he headed to the closed doors of what had once been the dining room. Knocking twice, he said, "It's me."

Tohr opened things up with a "What's doin'," and Rhage stepped into the cavernous, mostly barren room: All they had in there were a bunch of armchairs, a desk with an office chair, and some ancillary seats in case an audience had a lot of guest ass to accommodate.

"No explosives," Wrath was saying from one of the armchairs. "No traps."

V was in the process of lighting up a hand-rolled, and as he exhaled, the scent of Turkish tobacco drifted over. "Hollywood and I went through the place with a fine-toothed comb. They had been there, clearly. Had just left as far as we could tell. But they hadn't bothered to try to fuck us."

With his dagger hand, Wrath stroked the boxy blond head of the golden retriever who helped him get around. George, ever adoring of his master, had his face turned to the King, his throat offered freely. "So Throe didn't lie."

"Not about that at least," V muttered.

"Interesting."

Rhage glanced around at the faces of his brothers. Z and Phury were standing together as they always did. Qhuinn was next to Z, and then Blay and John Matthew, even though the males weren't members, were beside him. Butch was opposite the King, propping his forearms on top of an armchair and leaning his weight in; V was behind him. Tohr stayed by the door.

"So what next," Rhage asked.

"We wait." Wrath bent down farther and scratched at the dog's ruff. "If he's got shit to stir, he'll hang himself. The aristocracy will have to be monitored—we need an inside source there. Any ideas?"

At that moment, there was another knock. Tohr put his ear to the panels and then cracked the door. "Ask and ye shall receive."

Abalone leaned in. "My lord? I'm sorry to intrude, but may I please make the presentation of mine blooded daughter prior to us getting started with tonight's audiences?"

Wrath gestured the male forward with his free hand. "Yeah. Bring her in."

Abalone ducked out and there was a hushed conversation. Then he reappeared, ushering in a sapling of a female. With her blond hair, slight build, and long legs, she was on the Arctic Princess spectrum of the fairer sex.

Pretty. Very pretty. Maybe even beautiful—although she didn't hold a candle to his Mary.

Abalone walked the girl forward, one hand at her elbow, his fatherly pride plumping up his chest. "My esteemed ruler, great King of all—"

"Yeah, yeah, enough with that," Wrath cut in. "Paradise, I understand you're moving into my *shellan*'s and her brother's house here. Welcome."

As the black diamond was offered, Paradise bent at the

waist, her hands shaking so badly they seemed to shimmer in the light from the chandelier.

"My lord," she whispered before kissing the stone.

Releasing his hand, she straightened and stared at the floor, her shoulders curling into her chest, her feet locked together.

"You want to meet my dog?" the King asked.

George, ever up for a good head rub, thumped his tail on the floor, the sound like someone was beating a rope into the hardwood.

"Pet him," Wrath said. "You're allowed."

The girl glanced around at the Brotherhood, her eyes sticking to the shitkicker level. And that was when Rhage felt sorry for her. A lot of the aristocracy sat on their females so hard, they were rarely around males they were not related to—so this was no doubt the first time she had been in the same room with so much testosterone.

"G'head, George. Go say hi."

At Wrath's urging, the dog padded forward and sat his fluffy butt down right in front of her, his ears pricking, that tail sweeping back and forth.

"Is . . . he a boy?" she asked softly as she lowered herself to the floor and reached up to all the fur.

"Yup." Wrath looked up. "All right, assholes, introduce yourselves, will ya? And keep it classy."

Cue the throat clearing. At least until Phury stepped forward and did the intros. Probably best—he was the closest to a gentlemale they had.

"Glad you're here," the Primale said. "I'm Phury—we love your dad, by the way. Good guy."

Annnnnd now Abalone was levitating right out of his Bally loafers.

She looked up into those yellow eyes and offered him a shy smile. "Hi."

"Over there is my twin." He indicated Z—and Zsadist, ever aware of what he looked like with that scar down his face, stayed way back, lifting his hand as Paradise recoiled. "Zsadist's mated and has a daughter named Nalla. She's gorgeous—here's a picture."

As Phury flashed his cell phone, the girl looked at the image. Glanced at Z. Went back to the snapshot.

"My baby girl," Z said in a deep voice. "She's two, and she got her *mahmen's* looks."

Instantly, the girl relaxed. Then Phury intro'd Vishous, who just nodded, and Butch, who gave her a Bostonian, "Hi, hawre ya!" John Matthew, Blay, and Qhuinn were up next, and then Phury indicated Rhage.

"And Brad Pitt over there is Hollywood."

He smiled. "Glad you're here."

Paradise's stare stayed on him, her eyes getting big, but not because she was scared. Far from it.

"Yeah, he's a looker," someone said. "Until you get to know him."

"Aww, come now," Rhage tossed back. "Don't hate."

Talk sprang up, with Wrath asking Paradise some questions to get her talking about herself. As the girl refocused on the King, Rhage thought back to before he'd met his Mary. No doubt he would have made a run at that innocent—and would have been successful. He'd had a zero failure rate as he'd controlled his beast by fucking anything and everything that had moved. Which had been good for him. Not so hot for females who'd wanted to keep their virtue.

And he had no doubt Paradise was one of those.

So yeah, he was glad he was meeting her now, when there was absolutely no chance of him getting with her. He had mated his Virgin, just as Vishous had said he would, and his life had been saved.

For some reason, a sick feeling came over him.

Shoving his hand in his pocket, he took out his cell phone. Checked his texts.

Trez, the poor bastard, still hadn't gotten back to him yet. It seemed stupid to bother the guy again, given everything that was on his plate, but it was hard not to reach out one more time.

Rhage wished there was more to be done to help the guy and his Chosen.

He truly did.

There was no doing any kind of turn signal.

As Layla drove her Mercedes back to the Brotherhood mansion, she had her injured arm propped on the middle console between the seats, a spare jacket wadded up to increase its height and provide some extra cushioning.

The pain was stunning, the kind of thing that was so bad, it registered in her gut.

So no, there was no signaling left or right.

At least there was nobody else out on the country roads this late at night.

It was hours, maybe years, before she made it to the turn-off to the compound's mountain, and the *mhis* was a nightmare. V's distortion of the landscape, a security measure to keep them safe, meant that everything was blurry, as if a fog had overtaken the forest. Exhaustion from fighting the urge to vomit, combined with her vision beginning to fail, meant that she felt utterly lost, and her instinct was to lean in and get closer to the windshield—not that that helped.

All that did was just piss her arm off even more.

When the glowing lights of the mansion finally came into view, she prayed, *prayed* that the Brothers were all out fighting and she could make it to her room without anybody seeing her. Pulling around the just-winterized fountain, she parked next to Rhage's purple GTO and Butch's new toy, a black Mercedes that looked like a bread box.

She had to reach around the wheel and push the gear lever in to get the engine into park—and discovered she had to stretch even more to hit the Stop/Start button to turn the sedan off. Then it was a case of breathing shallowly through her mouth as she recovered from the effort. Looking in the rearview mirror, she caught sight of the entrance to the mansion . . . and had no clue how she was going to get over there. Much less haul herself up to her room.

There was no other choice. Either she did it on her own, or she had to ask someone to lie for her: There was no hiding the injury, not as fresh as it was. And she couldn't let Qhuinn find out what had happened.

Or, even worse, what she'd really been doing when she'd fallen.

Damn it, this situation was the punishment for her double life—her two opposing realities slamming together, knocking her senseless, exposing her.

Potentially.

Time to go inside.

Layla got a fresh lesson in pain as she opened her door

and tried to straighten up from the leather seat, her arm letting out a scream as the broken bone ground against itself.

Recovery breath. A number of them.

And then somehow, she got herself out of the car.

Had the mansion always been so far from the parking area?

Walking around the fountain wasn't so much a case of putting one foot in front of the other, but shuffling over the cobblestones and trying not to pass out. When she got to the stone stairs that led up to the cathedral-size doors, she wanted to cry. Instead, she surmounted them one at a time.

Pulling open the vestibule's door, she realized she'd made two mistakes: She had left her car door unshut . . . and she was, in fact, going to have to interact with someone—there was no getting into the house this way without putting your face in the security camera and waiting for an answer.

Glancing back at the Mercedes, she didn't have the energy to go back there and close things up.

And trying to get around to the staff entrance by the garage was—

That was where things ended.

As her mind labored over her limited options, her body pulled its own plug out of the consciousness socket: Lights-out and gravity did their business on her, the stoop rushing up to greet her with a hard, hard embrace.

That she did not feel.

TWENTY-FOUR

It was four a.m. when Assail drove his bulletproof Range Rover out to the Hudson River's edge. The lane he was on was about as wide as a pencil and as smooth as an obstacle course. Beside him, Ehric was silent, the male's forty sitting out on his thigh, a twitchy trigger finger ready to squeeze rounds off at the drop of a hat.

A quick glance in the rearview showed him that Ehric's twin, Evale, was likewise on the alert and prepared for anything.

They had been working with the importers for how long now? Nine months? Longer? He couldn't remember. But only a fool let their guard down.

About twenty meters farther up on the "road," he was going to come to the shallow clearing on the shore. The procedure was the same every time: He would stop the SUV in the tree line and turn it around so that if anything untoward happened, he could get out fast with either his money or the drugs. Then he would wait with his males, typically about ten minutes, before the trolling boat putt-putt-putt'd into view.

His cousins were wearing bulletproof vests. He was not. They were sober. He was not.

Neither were a surprise. He never bothered with any kind of chest guard, and as for the second one? At this point, he would have to be unmedicated for several days to get the cocaine completely out of his system.

As he drove along, he found his mind drifting, the image

of another kind of shore, a different sort of body of water, presenting itself and refusing to leave.

He saw a beach. The ocean. Palm trees. All of it glowing in the moonlight.

He saw a lone female walking along the sea's lapping warmth, her arms locked over her chest, her head down, her aura that of a survivor who had regrets—

"Watch it!" Ehric barked.

Assail shook himself back into focus just before the Range Rover ate an oak tree for Last Meal—or more likely, it would be the other way around.

Fortunately, the trip was over minutes later, and he managed the K-turn just fine, crushing the dry underbrush until the SUV's prodigious front grille was pointed outward. There were no headlights to kill; the complete lack of running lights inside and out had been another of the modifications he'd ordered up along with the lead-deflection package.

The engine went quiet and his two passengers got out. Before he joined them, he palmed up a vial from the inside of his wool coat's pocket. Quick twist. Spoon up.

Sniff. Sniff.

And two for the other nostril.

After a quick huff to make sure everything stayed where it needed to be, he got out of the warm interior himself. Returning his stash to its safe place, he brought his coat around his body. The night air was very cold, and fallen leaves crunched under his boots as he joined his cousins.

There was no talking.

And yet their disapproval of his consumption rate was obvious in the grind of their lower jaws.

'Twas no matter to him, however. Whether they wasted breath on words, or simply glowered as they were the now, he had no intention of changing his usage.

The sound of a single-engine boat going at a slow speed came so quietly that, at first, one could not distinguish it from the ambient noises of the forest and the river. But soon enough, the troller came around the bend of the shore, flat and low to the water. There were two individuals sitting in its open hull, both dressed as nothing-doing fishermen in their caps and camo, only the black masks they wore hinting at anything nefarious. Fishing poles were likewise mounted on either side to promote the appearance of innocuous activity, the invisible lines trawling into the current, stretching out behind the stern.

The captain brought the humble craft in bow-first, toggling down on the engine so they landed with a kiss, not a punch.

The cousins closed in as Assail hung back, his own forty at the ready. The scents from the two human males identified them as different, but related, to the two that had come the last time. And the time before that. And so on.

"Where are the others?" Assail demanded.

The men stopped in the process of picking up three out of the five black duffels that had been hidden beneath a camo tarp.

Assail smiled thinly at their surprise. "Did you think I wouldn't know?"

"I am brother," the one on the left said in heavily accented English. "He is cousin."

Assail inclined his head, accepting the explanation. In truth, he did not care who delivered his product as long as they did so on a timely basis, for an agreed price and potency, and without interference from human law enforcement.

So far, so good with this pair.

Moments later, Ehric and his brother accepted the bags and walked off, one facing forward, the other backward so they provided each other cover.

"A moment," Assail drawled. "If you don't mind."

The human men stopped again, and he felt their anxiety sure as if it were a reverberation on the surface of a table, the transfer of energy traveling easily through the air that separated their bodies.

"What else is under there?" he said, pointing to the tarp. "There are two more duffels, are there not."

The smaller of the pair, the cousin, jerked the cover back into place and went around to the boat's controls.

"The schedule next month," the other said. "The same?"

"I'll be in touch with your bosses."

"Very good."

Just like that, they were on their way, *putt-putt-putt*ing against the sluggish current of the cold water—with someone else's merchandise along with them.

Frowning, Assail watched as they cut across the waterway, and proceeded parallel to the opposite shore.

A moment later, he returned to the Range Rover, and when he knocked on the front passenger-side window, Ehric put the thing down.

"Yes?" the male said.

"I'm going to follow them." Assail nodded in the direction of the boat. "They're dealing with somebody else. I want to find out who."

With a curt nod, Ehric dematerialized over into the driver's seat and put the SUV in gear. "I saw that, too. Call if you need aught."

As the Range Rover took off, Assail turned away and strode back to the water. Closing his eyes, he had to fight his cocaine buzz in order to calm himself, and it was a while before he could spirit himself away on the cold wind. When he re-formed some kilometers down the river, he waited until the boat came into view once more. The men were oblivious to his presence as he stood in stillness among the colorful trees and contrasting brown vegetation, watching as they progressed by.

Same engine speed. Same protocol for delivering the goods to him. The question was: who was their next client.

And what kind of drugs were they selling?

Their bosses had agreed to deal with him exclusively in this part of New York state. And whereas competition was good for capitalism, it was not welcome in his territory— also unnecessary to their income statement. His requirements were sufficiently large and established enough that he represented a book of business worthy of respect.

The bastards.

Indeed, it was necessary for there to be honor amongst lawbreakers. For everyone's good. And he had held up his end of the bargain, arriving consistently with the cash. Month after month after month.

He was prepared to fix this problem, however.

Readily.

Mortally.

Rhage, Tohr and V headed back to the mansion not long after meeting Applebottom's pride and joy, with Butch following in the Range Rover. As the three of them resumed their physical forms in the courtyard, a light shining among the lineup of cars got their attention.

Rhage strode over to the open door of the pale blue Mercedes. "Layla—?"

Except there was no one inside fiddling with her purse or bundling up before she headed across the courtyard for home.

He shut the door. "She's not—"

"Layla!" Tohr barked. "Oh, shit!"

Rhage looked up to the mansion's entrance. The heavy door into the vestibule was cracked open, a leg extending out at ground level, the ankle and foot propping the panels open.

The three of them bolted up the stairs. As Rhage cranked wide the tremendous weight, V, with his medical background, jumped over the Chosen's collapsed body and started checking vitals.

"Tohr," Rhage said. "Call—"

But his brother already had his cell phone up to his ear. "Yeah, Jane? We need you up here in the vestibule. Layla's collapsed—V, stats?"

As the brother put the phone in V's face, Vishous said to his mate, "Heart rate's steady, but slow. So is the breathing. No sign of trauma that I can see."

"You hear that?" Tohr said, resuming speaking. "Good. Thanks." As he ended the call, he immediately started dialing again. "She's bringing Manny and Ehlena." Back up to the ear. Waiting. Waiting.

He was obviously calling Qhuinn—

For some odd reason, the world went wonky on Rhage: One minute, he was staring down at Layla, and thinking there was nothing more terrifying than a pregnant female facedown on any kind of flooring. The next, the vestibule was spinning around him like a ball on the end of a string, his head the center point of the whizzing-by, his balance oddly uncompromised by the—

"He's going over!"

Huh. Guess he wasn't quite as steady as he thought.

When there was a bite on his upper arm, he looked down and saw Tohr's hand lock on his biceps and hold him up.

Wow. This was manly, Rhage thought.

A round of the Victorian vapors just because a female was—

"Layla!"

Qhuinn's panicked appearance right next to him gave him the wakey-wakey he needed, his mind clearing as the male shoved his way in to get to the female who was carrying his child. Blay, as always, was right behind him, ready to do whatever to support his mate.

"What the hell happened?" Qhuinn demanded.

V started talking. Doc Jane and her team arrived. Medical equipment was outted from a black, old-fashioned doctor's bag.

Turning to Tohr, who was still holding him up, Rhage heard a strange version of his voice say, "I'm having trouble breathing, my brother."

Tohr swung his head around. "What's wrong?"

"I don't know. I can't . . . seem to breathe." He massaged his chest with his free hand. "It's like there's a balloon in here. Taking up all the space."

As the medical peeps rolled Layla onto her back, there was cursing from the peanut gallery. Her arm was at an all-wrong angle, the part below the elbow showing a nasty break which must have happened when she fainted.

"Rhage?" someone said to him. "Hello?"

He glanced over at Tohrment. "What?"

Tohr leaned in. "You want some fresh air?"

"Aren't we outside?" To answer his own question, he looked up to the heavens. "Yeah, we're—"

"How 'bout we take a little walk."

"Want to help."

"Yeah, I get that. But I think going for a stroll's a really good idea. You're white as a sheet, and if you pull a lights-out, I can't guarantee you're not going to turn someone into a carpet underneath you and we don't need any other patients right now."

"Huh?"

"Come on."

As his brother pulled on his arm, Rhage kept rubbing his heart. "I don't know why I can't breathe. . . ."

The last image he had, as he was pulled away, was of Layla's face flopping to the side, her eyes wide-open, but unseeing.

"Is she dead?" he whispered. "Has she died—"

"Come on, my brother—"

"Is she?"

"No, she's not. She's alive."

Every time he blinked, he saw her blond hair on the marble tile like a liquid spilled, her lips as pale as her cheeks, those jade-green eyes opaque and unmoving.

"Mary? Yeah, Mary, I got a situation with your boy. Can you come home now?"

Who was that talking? Oh, yeah, Tohr. On his phone. The Brother had taken out his phone.

Rhage started shaking his head. "No, she can't come. The mother at Safe Place. She needs to stay—"

"Okay, thanks." Tohr ended the call. "She's heading back now."

"No, they need her—"

"My brother?" Tohr put his face into Rhage's. "I'm not sure you have any idea what you look like right now. Do me a solid and sit down here—yeah, right on the cobblestone. Good man, you're doin' good."

Rhage's knees were the ones following instructions, his brain too preoccupied with how much his *shellan* didn't need to waste her precious time on him. But it looked like that bus had left the station already.

Propping his head in his hands, Rhage leaned forward and wondered if he didn't have something wrong with his lungs. A fast-acting vampire flu. An infection. A poison in there.

The large hand of his brother made slow circles on his back, and beneath that heavy palm, the beast, in its tattoo form, surged and moved as if Rhage's little epi was making the thing nervous.

"Feel weird," Rhage said. "Can't . . . breathe . . ."

TWENTY-FIVE

For the first couple of miles, Assail was happy enough to dematerialize along with the boat. By the fourth time he re-formed, however, he'd become impatient for the destination to arrive, the exchange to be made, the identity of the third-party encroacher to be revealed.

And there was another reason to be disquieted. With the ever-increasing distance traveled, the two men were getting closer and closer to Caldwell proper—which was an idiotic idea.

Even though the hours were well into the night, downtown was not the suburbs and there were bound to be humans out and about—granted, rarely those credible with the police or others of their kind, but prying eyes were prying eyes, and every asshole rat without a tail had a cell phone these days.

He might be able to spirit away, but that pair in the boat could not pull off that trick—and he wanted to be the person to teach the lesson required here, not the CPD.

Disappearing once again, he was forced to re-form in the midst of the planted trees on the edge of one of Caldwell's shoreline public parks. And still the boat continued along.

Unbelievable.

As he waited to see whether they passed his newest position—and there was a good chance they would, because there was no further cover at the shore a'tall—that familiar itch started to twinkle at the base of his neck, triggering a need for more coke.

The urge was coming faster and faster of late. To the point where he was forced to acknowledge how fortunate he was to heal so quickly. If he were a mere human? He would have deviated his septum months ago.

Reaching into his pocket, he took his vial into his palm. Just the feel of the smooth glass container made him relax. And he wanted to pull it out and do his deed, but he couldn't run the risk of not being able to dematerialize. The problem with his addiction was that the need for more was coming before the buzz had even started to wear off, the worm in his gut turning, turning, demanding more and more even while his body and brain struggled to deal with the racing, bracing load of drugs.

And again, the last thing he wanted was to find himself in difficulty down here because he was too jittery to get himself gone.

God, to have this in common with the Homo sapiens he dealt to was just too demeaning for words—

"Oh, you can't be serious," he muttered as the boat finally made a beeline to a destination of sorts.

But it was not a safe one. Certainly not one he would ever have consented to.

The two piloted their craft toward an old Victorian boathouse. Granted, its windows were dark, but there were security lights shining on its shingled exterior, and no doubt a CPD patrol making regular rounds of the park behind the structure.

He had to go inside if they did, however.

And they did.

With no idea what the interior layout was, he settled for re-forming in the shadows between those annoying outside lights, his dark clothes blending him in against the boathouse's weathered flank. As the troller entered one of the slips, the sound of its pathetic engine echoed, sounding like an old man with the last dregs of a consumptive cough.

Twisting around to one of the windows, he focused his keen eyes through the bubbly glass. The inside was quite extensive, and as soon as he identified his spot, he dematerialized and gusted in through the very entrance the delivery boys used. He was careful as he reassumed his physical form, sticking to a tight nook in the far corner, between a stand of crew shells resting upon their bellies on racks and a forest of orange personal flotation devices strung upon hooks.

The engine was cut and the pair conversed softly in a foreign language. After they fell silent, the only sound was the water clapping and chortling underneath the boat and through the cribbing of the docks.

Assail hated the way the air smelled of old dead fish, decomposing flora, and damp canvas.

Dreadful.

After a measure of time passed, the approach of something outside got his attention—and then a flashing yellow light penetrated the interior. Locating a dusty window, he looked out to find a Caldwell Public Parks Department truck pulling up.

Well, now, this was about to get interesting.

Either the delivery was going to be intercepted and the police called . . . or some human working for the parks was looking to increase his monthly income and on the pickup.

It turned out he was wrong on both accounts.

The main door creaked as it was opened, and the instant a male figure appeared in between the jambs, cold air gusting in from behind him carried the scent of *lesser* into the boathouse.

It was the *Forelesser* with whom Assail did his business, entering with a duffel bag of his own.

Son of a bitch.

How *dare* that bastard do a runaround, Assail thought as his fangs bared of their own volition. And how in the hell had that slayer made contact with the importer?

Formulating a plan for his ambush, Assail outted both of his forties—and wished that he had bothered to put silencers on the guns. He hadn't expected to have to use them in downtown fucking Caldwell, for God's sakes.

"Let me see them," the *Forelesser* declared. "Unzip the bags and let me see them."

Assail took a step forward, thinking he could—

The deliverymen each unzipped a bag and tilted the contents forward.

Not. Drugs.

Not at all.

Instead of large blocks that had been sealed in layers upon layers of cellophane wrap, there were . . .

Guns. Long-muzzled guns that rubbed, metal upon metal, against one another in their duffel bags.

It was difficult, in the dimness, to determine exactly the specifications of the weapons, but there seemed to be a variety of either shotguns or rifles.

Assail's curled upper lip dropped back into place.

Although he had been prepared to intercede in the event of a drug/money exchange, he felt no such compulsion the now.

If the *Forelesser* wanted to use his profits to buy armaments, that was his business.

Leaving the boathouse the way he came in, Assail cast himself up river, toward his glass house upon its peninsula.

The only thing he cared about was whether that *lesser* continued to deliver product to the streets and clubs of Caldwell in a timely, reliable and honest fashion.

His responsibility started and ended there.

"No, no, I'm fine. Honest."

As Rhage spoke, he sat down at the rough-cut table in the Brotherhood mansion's kitchen. The rest of the household was gathering for an early Last Meal, *doggen* filing in and out of the flap door, delivering silver trays the size of tabletops stacked with all manner of freshly cooked meats and starches and vegetables.

Across the way, Mary leaned against the granite-topped center island, her arms crossed over her chest, her eyes trained on him like she was assessing one of her social-work patients.

Squirming, he wanted to go join his brothers and their *shellans*, but given her expression, that wasn't going to happen anytime soon.

"Fritz?" she said. "I'm going to fix him something, okay?"

The butler paused in the process of bringing a table setting over. "I was going to make up a plate in the other room and bring it—"

"I'm going to take care of my husband," she said gently, but firmly. "If you like, however—even though it goes against every self-sufficient bone in my body—I'll leave you the pan and dishes to clean up."

Fritz's old, wrinkled face assumed the expression of a

basset hound who was being denied chicken for the promise of beef later on: both worried and excited. "Is there not some manner in which I may render you aid?"

Three staff members in their gray-and-white uniforms came back empty-handed from the dining room, the trio heading for the final loads that were destined to be carried in and placed on the various sideboards in that huge, chandeliered space.

"Actually," his Mary murmured, "do you think he and I could have some privacy in here?"

"Oh, yes, mistress." Fritz brightened somewhat. "As soon as the presentation of the victuals has been made, I will direct my staff into the foyer. They will be most happy to tarry out there."

"Thank you." She gave his thin arm a squeeze, making him blush. "And just until it's time for dessert to be served. I know that you'll want free rein in here for that."

"Yes, mistress. Thank you, mistress. And I shall personally clean up after you both."

The butler bowed deeply, grabbed the last silver tray, and ushered everyone out. As the flap door stilled, Rhage's beloved *shellan* looked over at him.

"Eggs?" she said.

At the one word, Rhage's stomach let out a roar. "Oh, God, that sounds amazing."

Mary nodded and went over to the Sub-Zero. Taking out a fresh egg carton, she grabbed a gallon container of whole milk and a box of butter; then she hit the cupboards, snagging a frying pan, a big mixing bowl, and various and sundry utensils.

"So," she said as she broke the first of twelve eggs. "I'd really like to hear what happened out there."

Up until this moment, Rhage had been successful in ducking that question. Apparently, the reprieve was over.

"I'm fine, honest."

"Okay." She paused in mid-crack and smiled at him. "As your wife, though, how you are is really important to me. So if there's something bothering you, it makes me feel left out if I don't know what it is."

Ugh. Just . . . *ugh*.

As she began whisking the gallon of nascent scrambled egg, the sloshy sound reminded him of his own head.

Looking down at the pitted tabletop, he picked at one of the veins in the broad oak boards. "The truth is, I don't know what happened. I just felt really weird and had to sit down. I'm tight now, though. Probably just one of those random things."

"Mmm, well, tell me what your night was like."

"It was no big deal. I headed to the Band of Bastards' safe house and went through it — "

"Didn't you start down in the clinic, with Trez and Selena?"

"Oh, yeah. But that was, like, yesterday when she was . . . you know, taken there." He shook his head. "I don't want to think about that right now, if you don't mind."

"Okay, so tonight you went to the Band of Bastards' place?"

"Well, first we went to Abalone's. His cousin defected from Xcor's troops and told us where their hideout was. Anyway, me and V went through the place."

"What were you looking for?"

He shrugged. "Bombs. Booby traps. That kind of shit. No big deal."

She made another *mmmm* sound as she poured the contents of the bowl into a pan the size of the bucket seat in Qhuinn's Hummer. "Were you worried about getting hurt there?"

"No. Well . . . I worried about my brothers, sure. But that's just the job."

"Okay. And then where did you go?"

"I saw you. Then I went to D's old house. We reported in to Wrath and came back here. I was supposed to have a checkup with Manny to make sure my injury has healed properly. Same with V."

"Okay." She moved over to the six-slot toaster and filled the thing up with his favorite bleached-flour, totally processed, incredibly plastic-fantastic white bread. "So you got home, and what did you find?"

He blinked and saw Layla's foot sticking out of the vestibule. Then pictured Qhuinn's face as the Brother crouched down by the stricken female who was carrying his young.

"Oh, you know."

"Mmmm?" The scent of cooking eggs further tickled his Eat Now trigger. "What?"

"Well, you know what happened."

By the time Mary arrived, a stretcher had been brought up from the clinic and Layla was being loaded on, her body moved carefully by Qhuinn at her head and Blay at her feet.

Rhage fell silent and massaged his chest.

Pop! went his toast, and a moment later, a platter with everything done exactly the way he liked was in front of him.

Along with a mug of hot chocolate, a napkin, silverware . . . but most important, his lovely Mary.

"This is the best meal I have ever had," he said, just looking at the food.

"You always say that."

"Only when you cook for me."

It was funny. As a human, his Mary never had been able to understand the way a male vampire responded when the female he'd bonded with produced food with her own hands for him. That kind of thing was a sacred act, because it went against a male's core instinct to provide and meet his mate's needs first and foremost over those everything and everybody, including his own, his brothers', his King's, and those of any young they might have.

Rhage was hardwired to feed her first and then eat whatever was left. But before she'd ordered Fritz and the *doggen* out, she'd told him she was full, having grabbed a quick snack at Safe Place an hour ago.

"It's getting cold," she said, rubbing his forearm.

For some reason, his eyes got blurry and he had to blink things clear.

"Rhage?" she whispered. "Whatever it is, let it out."

With a quick jerk, he shook his head. "I'm fine. I just want to enjoy this feast."

He picked up his fork and started to alternate: one load of egg, one bite of toast, one load of egg, one bite of toast, sip, sip, sip of hot chocolate. And repeat until he had cleaned his plate.

"How is the female doing?" he asked, as he wiped his mouth and eased back in the wooden chair.

"I don't know." Mary shook her head. "I just don't know how this one is going to go."

"That bad?" When she shrugged, he said, "If there's anything I can do . . ."

"Well, actually . . ."

"Name it."

She reached out, took his hand, and turned it over so the palm was facing up. It was a while before she spoke, but as he was beginning to get worried, she said, "I want you to entertain, just for a moment, that it might have been upsetting for you to see Selena almost die and for you to witness Trez's pain. I want you to consider that it is not business as usual, for anyone, to have to go through some house they've never been in before, not knowing whether an explosion or an ambush is going to kill them or someone they cared about. I want you to reflect that going to Wrath and not being able to tell him that you'd found the Bastards or disarmed something or captured some kind of information might feel like a failure. And finally, I want you to understand that for you to come home and see Layla passed out, and know that she's pregnant, and care about her and Qhuinn and Blay, is yet another trauma. I think you've had a really hard twenty-four hours, and that your emotions have kind of tapped out on you."

"I didn't feel upset, though, my Mary. By any of it. I was just fine—"

"Until you had the panic attack in front of the house."

"I didn't have a panic attack."

"You said you couldn't breathe. That your hands and feet were tingling. That you were having trouble connecting to reality. Sounds like a classic panic attack to me."

He shook his head. "I don't think that was it."

"Okay."

Rhage took a deep breath and focused on his beloved's face. "You are the most beautiful female I have ever seen."

"I'm pretty sure that isn't—"

He captured her face in his hands, cradling her with care. As his eyes roamed around her familiar features, he couldn't get enough of them. God, it was never enough. Not a night, a month, a year, a decade . . . not the eternity the Scribe Virgin had miraculously given them both, was ever going to be enough for him.

"You are the most beautiful female I have ever seen." He brushed her lips with his own. "I don't know what I did to deserve a destiny with you, but I will never, ever take that for granted."

The smile he got in response was better than the sunrise he would never see, shaming even that great glowing fireball that was the sustainer of all life, including even those who could not bear its rays.

They were still sitting like that, staring into each other's eyes, when the *doggen* came in for dessert.

"You wanna go upstairs," he said in a dark, deep voice, his beast starting to surge under his skin. "I'm ready for dessert."

Her scent flared. "Are you."

"Mmm-hmm."

"You want me to get you some ice cream?"

He narrowed his stare on her mouth. "Not even close. I want to lick something else."

"Well, then," she whispered, putting her mouth to his. "Let's get you fed."

TWENTY-SIX

Cold sweat.

Trez woke up in an absolute cold sweat, every inch of his skin drenched, his core temperature all arctic, his heart going so fast it felt like someone had swapped the thing for a cake mixer. Bursting up off the pillows, he shouted—

Bedroom. Instead of something terrible and shocking . . . all he saw was a whole lot of his bedroom, and everything was on the normal-normal, from the lamp that was glowing next to him, to his clothes draped over the chaise lounge, to his shoes askew from where he'd kicked them off the other dawn.

For a moment, he was confused. Scribe Virgin. Some strange, mystical place. Selena in the grass, in the clinic, frozen, frozen—

A soft moan shattered the straddle between nightmare and reality.

Jerking around, he saw Selena lying in his bed, her naked shoulders showing above the sheets, her dark hair loose over his white pillowcase, her face and body turned away from him.

Closing his eyes, he sagged, and wished it had all just been a bad dream.

But then he refocused and got about his female, pulling the duvet up higher to keep her warm, discreetly leaning over and reassuring himself she was still breathing, wondering if he should go find some food for her.

As if she sensed his presence, she rolled over, her face tightening in her sleep like it hurt her to move.

Fuck. The sex had been out of control, raw, rough. Right after her body had been through so much.

Damn him, he thought as he dragged a palm down his face. How could he have done that to her? He should have jerked himself off until his cock had lost all sensation.

Worse? He wasn't sure they had actually worked things out between them. Shit knew, he still felt like an asshole.

Reaching across to the bedside table, he got his phone and checked the time. Five forty-four a.m.

There was going to be no more sleep for him. Sliding free of the sheets, he padded into the bathroom, shut the door, used the facilities, and took a quick shower. Then he was back out, picking up his pair of earbuds from the bedside table's drawer and putting them in place before he did a bed reinsertion.

Moving slowly, he was just as careful getting back in as he had been on his evac, maneuvering his nearly three-hundred-pound weight onto the pillow-top mattress without displacing her like she was on a trampoline.

When he was resettled, he pulled a quick check of his female and was relieved to find she was still sleeping. Which kind of terrified him. What if she were in a coma or—

As if she were searching for him, she patted around on the duvet.

"I'm right here," he whispered.

Instantly, she stilled her searching, and when he took her hand, her palm was warm, vital, just as it always had been.

He took a moment to study her fingers, bending them one by one, measuring the movement, checking for resistance. Which wasn't right, he thought.

It was unfair to try to solicit information from her body without her knowledge and awareness—and by way of apology, he stopped himself and smoothed the pink nail beds and the short white semi-circles she trimmed regularly.

As sleep reclaimed her, he felt . . . paralyzingly alone. Even though they were side by side, him propped up against the headboard, her nestled in close to his body, he couldn't seem to connect with her. He told himself it was simply a matter of asleep and awake. That was the divide—nothing scarier than the fact that her brain waves would read differently than his on a CAT scan.

It was bullshit, of course. And the harder he tried to force himself to believe the lie, the more trapped he felt—so to derail the internal fight, he turned on SiriusXM radio on his phone, jacked the plug of his earphones into the ass of his handset, and tried to get comfortable. Or somewhat comfortable.

Or . . . at least not consumed by the need to jump out of his own skin.

Naturally, because his luck sucked, the first thing he heard on the radio was more bad news.

"Are you kidding me?" he blurted out loud as Howard Stern's voice piped into his skull. "Eric the Actor is d—"

Selena's brows tightened like she was considering waking up and he closed his piehole. But he couldn't believe another wack packer had been lost. It just seemed cruel in light of everything he was going through.

Shit, it was as if bad news was making a concerted effort to come out of the shadows and find him.

Selena woke up slowly, and the scent of Trez's body was the first thing she noticed. The sound of his voice the next. The feel of his hand in hers the third.

Opening her lids, she found him sitting up next to her in his bed, his black eyes rapt on his phone, his brows down as if he'd received upsetting news through a text or—

"Is everything okay?" she asked.

When he didn't answer her, she saw that he had wires running from the phone to his ears like he was listening to something.

The instant she squeezed his hand, he jumped so high he popped the ear thingies free.

"Oh, my God! You're awake."

"I'm sorry, I didn't meant to—"

"Shit, no, don't be—are you all right? Do you need Doc Jane—"

"No, no . . ." She tried to get her brain working. "I'm fine. I just . . . you seem upset?"

As he looked at her, the only sound in the room was the hiss coming from what had been in his ears.

She pulled the covers up higher. "Is there something wrong with me?"

"Oh, God, no. I, ah, no—it's nothing." He glanced at his phone. "Just, someone who was on the Stern Show d—"

When he stopped, his eyes got wide, as if he had almost said something unforgivable.

"Died?" she finished for him.

"I, ah . . ."

"You can still say the word." She squeezed his hand again. "Honestly."

Trez cleared his throat and put the phone aside. "Are you hungry?"

"Not really."

"Thirsty?"

"No."

He fidgeted with the sheets. The duvet. "Warm enough?"

Frowning, she pushed herself upright and sat back against the pillows. Looking over at him, she smiled. "I'm glad I came up here. To talk to you and . . . do those other things."

"You are?" His eyes, those beautiful almond-shaped eyes, swung back to her. "Really? I feel like I was too hard on you when we . . ."

She smiled even wider. "I really, really lost my virginity now."

He blushed. Actually blushed, a red stain hitting his high cheekbones. "I worried I'd hurt you."

"Not at all. When can we do it again—"

Trez's coughing fit was sudden and loud, and she had to pound him on the back before he started breathing right again.

"You okay?" she said, still smiling.

"Ah, yeah. You just have a way of surprising me."

For a split second, she remembered him coming to her in the Sanctuary. Even though she had been in an Arrest at the time, she had known the instant he had arrived. It had been a miracle. But how had he known?

"How did you find me? Up in the Sanctuary?"

He shook his head slowly. "You wouldn't believe me if I told you."

"Try me."

"The Scribe Virgin. I was at my club and dealing with some stuff—Rhage and V were with me. All of a sudden this . . . figure appeared . . . black robes, light under the hem, voice that I heard inside here"—he tapped his head— "rather than through my ears. Next thing I know? I'm . . . well, anyway. I was with you."

Now she was the one fiddling with things. "I'm really sorry."

"About what?"

"About you seeing me like that. About . . . all of this."

"Fucking hell—like I said before, as if you'd volunteer to be sick?"

"I know, but still. I wish . . ." She tried to tilt her head back so she could look at the ceiling, but her neck was too painful.

"You're hurting."

"It's nothing unusual. This is how I always feel after I . . . well, anyhow."

Guess two could play at the avoidance game.

"This is so unnatural," she blurted.

"What is?"

She had to turn her torso so that she could look at him properly. And absently, she measured how good his dark skin looked against the white sheets, the contrast making both seem to glow.

Selena tried to find the words. "I feel like there's this huge . . . I don't know, divide or something . . . between us. It makes no sense. I mean, you're right here beside me—but there are words that we're tripping over, subjects we don't want to talk about. It's just . . . well, it sucks. Because right now? This is the good part. I mean, check me out."

She lifted her free hand and splayed her fingers wide; then wiggled them.

"Mobile and awake is so much better than where I was, right?" When he simply stared at her, she felt like a fool. "I'm sorry, I guess that sounds weird—"

Trez leaned in and kissed her quiet, his lips lingering. "No." He eased back. "It's . . . I know what you mean. It's not crazy, and you're right. Now is the good part—"

"You are so hot."

Trez let out another cough. "Damn, female. What are you like."

"I told you last night—or, jeez, what time is it? Anyway, I told you before, I'm all about honesty now."

His lids dropped low. "Being straight up suits me just fine. So lemme ask you, if I were to pick you up and carry you into the shower, would you—"

"Get on my knees again under the hot spray and see if you taste as good as I remember?"

The sound that came out of him was not a cough. But it wasn't a coherent statement, either. It was part growl, part groan, with a little moan thrown in for good measure, like he was getting ready to beg . . .

It was pretty much the sexiest thing she had ever heard.

"Is that a yes?" she drawled.

He kissed her again, harder this time. Longer, too. Then he pegged her with eyes that were boiling. "Shit, I'm dying over here—"

As Trez stopped himself again, she got thrown by that word herself. When it came to the two of them, one was, in fact, dying. It was her, not him, though.

"I'm sorry," he whispered. "I won't say that ever again."

"It's all right." She forced herself to smile. "Let's wash our cares away—"

"I'm going to find a cure for this," he said gravely. "I'm not going to let you lose the fight, Selena. I will literally move heaven and earth to keep you beside me—no divide, nothing but our naked skin . . . our souls."

Tears speared into her eyes, and she forced them back, willing them to get gone and stay that way. Reaching up to his handsome face, she brushed her fingertips over his features.

"I love you, Trez."

"God, I love you, too."

TWENTY-SEVEN

When Layla woke up, she was lying on her side on a much softer surface than the vestibule's floor. In a panic, she brought her hand to her belly.

Everything felt the same, the hard swelling, the size it had been—but dearest Virgin Scribe, had she injured the young? She could remember getting out of her car, struggling to walk over to the mansion's entrance, losing consciousness—

"Young," she mumbled. "Young okay? Young?"

Instantly, Qhuinn's blue-and-green stare was right in front of her. "You're all right—"

As if she cared about herself right now. "Young!"

With a curse, she thought, why had she ever complained about being pregnant? Maybe this was punishment for her having—

"Everything's okay." Qhuinn glanced across the room, focusing on someone she couldn't see. "Fine, just ... okay, yeah, fine."

The relief was so great, tears flooded her eyes. If she had lost their young because she was meeting with Xcor? Because she'd been staring at him while he ... did that to his sex?

She never would forgive herself.

With a curse, she wondered why she had asked that male to do those things. It was wrong on so many levels, adding to her guilt when she was already choking on the stuff.

After all, it was so much easier to take the high-road

victim role if you were not asking your blackmailer to jerk off.

"Oh, God," she moaned.

"Are you in pain? Shit, Jane—"

"I'm right here." The good doctor knelt down beside Qhuinn, looking tired, but alert. "Hi there. We're glad you're back. Just so you know, Manny reset your arm. It was broken clean through. We've put it in a cast and . . ."

There was some kind of conversation about her recovery time and when the plaster could come off, but she didn't pay attention to any of that. Doc Jane and Qhuinn were keeping something from her: Their smiles of reassurance were like photographs of the real thing—perfectly accurate, but flat.

"What aren't you telling me?" she cut in.

Silence.

As she struggled to sit up, Blay was the one who helped her, gently grasping her good arm and giving her something to push against.

"What," she demanded.

Doc Jane looked at Qhuinn. Qhuinn looked at Blay. And Blay . . . was the one who eventually met her eyes.

"There's something unexpected," the fighter said. "In the ultrasound."

"If you make me ask 'what' again," she gritted out, "I'm going to start throwing things, and to hell with my broken arm."

"Twins."

As if time and reality were a car that had suddenly had its brakes punched, there was a metaphoric screeching sound in her head.

Layla blinked. "I'm sorry . . . what?"

"Twins," Qhuinn repeated. "The ultrasound is showing that you are carrying twins."

"And they're both perfectly healthy," Doc Jane added. "One is significantly smaller, and its development has been delayed, but it appears viable. I didn't catch the second fetus during your previous ultrasounds because I understand— from a consult with Havers—that vampire pregnancies are different from humans'. There was apparently another fertilized egg that had implanted but did not enter a significant embryogenesis stage until much later—your last ultrasound was two months ago, for example, and I did not see anything at that time."

"Twins?" Layla choked out.

"Twins," one of the three replied.

For some reason, she thought back to the moment when she'd found out she had, in fact, conceived. Even though pregnancy had been the goal, and she and Qhuinn had done what they'd had to do to get there, the news that the needing had been successful had been the kind that stunned. It just seemed so miraculous, and overwhelming—a joyous gauntlet that she was not entirely sure wouldn't get the best of her.

This was the same.

Except without the joy.

She had known two of her sisters to carry twins, and one of the pregnancies had been lost. The other had resulted in only a single, living young.

Tears started to fall from her eyes.

This was not good news.

"Hey." Blay leaned down with a handkerchief. "This is not bad. It's not."

Qhuinn nodded, although his face remained a mask. "It's . . . unexpected. But not at all bad."

Layla put her hands to her stomach. Two. There were two young that she now had to get over the ultimate finish line safely.

Two.

Dearest Virgin Scribe, how had this happened? What was she going to do?

As the questions ran through her head, she realized . . . well, hell. Like so much of life, this was out of her hands. An impossibility had become manifest—her job now was to do what she could to help herself and the young get the rest, nutrition and medical care that was required.

That was the only thing she could directly affect. The rest of it?

Up to fate alone.

"Could there be others?" Layla asked.

Doc Jane shrugged. "I believe that is highly unlikely, but I'd like to send a sample of your blood off to Havers. He has much more experience than I do in this, and after having a look at a vampire-specific pregnancy hormone, he believes he can take a good guess as to where you're at. He did say, though, that triplets are virtually unheard-of, and yours is the typical course of multiples for females. If they are going to have twins, unless in the extremely rare case of identical twins such as Z and Phury, the second embryo will delay its development until the pregnancy is well along. Almost as if it is waiting to see whether things look good before deciding to join the party."

Layla glanced down at her distended belly—and vowed never, ever to complain about a goddamn thing. Not the swollen ankles, or the oversensitive, pendulous breasts, or the peeing every ten minutes. Not. One. More. Whinge.

Ever.

The fact that she'd somehow lost consciousness, fallen face-first on a marble floor, and still managed to have this young—

These young, she corrected with a shock.

—in her body safely was a reminder that the aches and discomforts were minor in comparison to the big picture, the big goal, the big concern.

Which was birthing them at the right time and having them survive.

"So do you consent?" Doc Jane asked.

"I'm sorry, what?"

"Is it okay to send a sample of your blood to Havers for analysis?"

"Oh, yes." She extended her good arm. "Do it now—"

"No, we took the vial already."

Ah. Which would explain the cotton ball taped to the inside of her elbow.

Her brain was not working right.

"Is that the reason she passed out?" Qhuinn asked. "The extra young?"

Doc Jane shrugged again. "Her vitals all look fine—and they've been stable for quite some time. When was the last time you fed, Layla?"

The problem was not whether she'd taken a vein lately. "I . . ."

"We'll deal with that right now," Qhuinn announced. "Blay and I will both give her our veins."

Doc Jane nodded. "It would be logical that, with the second baby beginning to require more nourishment, your caloric and blood needs may be much greater than you've realized. I think it's entirely possible you were pushing yourself and it caught up with you."

Layla felt utterly numb and had to force a smile. "I'll be more careful. And thank you. I really appreciate your caring for me."

"You're welcome." Doc Jane gave Layla's foot a squeeze through the light blankets. "Rest up. You're going to do great."

As the healer left, Layla thought about the strange sexual cravings that she'd been having lately, as well as the relatively sudden increase in her physical symptoms. Was it the second young—?

"Do you want something more comfortable than that?" Qhuinn asked.

She shook herself back into focus. "I'm sorry, more comfortable than . . . ?"

"That hospital johnny."

Glancing down at herself, she saw that she wasn't in her clothes anymore. "Oh. Well. Actually, it's a bit chilly down here. One of my robes would be nice, but I don't want to trouble you."

"No problem. I'll take your things back to your room and pick up a nightgown and a robe—meanwhile, Blay, you wanna offer her your vein?"

By way of answer, the soldier's wrist appeared right in front of her. "Take as much as you need."

In that moment, she had an overwhelming urge to tell them. Come clean. Wipe out the stress of the last year no matter the repercussions.

She just wanted to be free of the terrible burden that weighed her down. Scared her.

Tantalized her.

No doubt that would improve the chances of her carrying the young better—less stress was good for pregnant females, right? And now there were two lives at risk as well as her own.

"Layla?"

She swallowed hard. Looked up at the pair of them as they stood over her bed, concerned. She didn't want to betray the only family she had ever had. Besides, maybe if she told them about Xcor, they could . . . make the compound safer. Or move everyone. Or . . .

Layla cleared her throat and gripped the covers on the bed as if they were a roll bar and she was about to go into a hairpin turn. "Listen, I need to . . ."

When she didn't finish, Qhuinn jumped into the quiet. "You need to feed. That's what you need to do."

As if her fangs were listening, they punched out from the roof of her mouth, and she got in touch with the fact that, yes, she did need to take a vein.

And no, she really couldn't tell them. She just . . . it was no good. There was no good solution for her. They would hate her for endangering herself and the pregnancy—and meanwhile, Xcor would still know where they all lived because the Brotherhood was never going to leave the compound. This was their home and they would defend it when he attacked after she stopped seeing him.

People would be killed. People she loved.

Shit.

"Thank you," she said roughly to Blay.

"Anything for you," he replied, brushing her hair back.

She tried to strike as gently as she could, but Blay didn't even flinch. Then again, when he and Qhuinn made love, he was no doubt used to much, much harder bites.

Just as she began to draw against the familiar source, taking in the nutrition her body required and could get only from this gift by a male of her species, Qhuinn went over to where her clothes had been put on a chair in the corner. As he took them into his hands, he frowned and glanced down. Then rifled through the folds like he was searching for something.

A moment later, his mismatched stare shifted over to her and his body grew very still.

Ducking her eyes, she pretended to concentrate on what she was doing. She had no clue what he had found or why he was looking at her like that.

But given the way she was living, she had a lot to hide.

"When were you supposed to go?"

As Trez asked the question, Selena focused on the hot bowl of oatmeal he'd just made for her. As it was well after dawn, all of the household's *doggen* were taking their rest in their quarters, so she and Trez were alone in the enormous kitchen, sitting side by side at the oak table.

"Selena. What time is your checkup."

She should have watched her mouth. Two seconds ago, they'd been enjoying this Quaker Oats concoction, with its tributaries of heavy cream and meadows of brown sugar, the pair of them basking in the glow of what they had done in the shower, at peace and relaxed.

And now?

Not so much, as they say.

"First thing this morning."

Trez checked his phone. "Okay, that's okay. It's about eight. So even if we finish this, we can still be on time-ish."

"I don't want to go." She could feel him staring at her. "I don't. I'm not in a big hurry to go back there at all."

"Doc Jane said we had to X-ray your joints to monitor—"

"Well, I don't want to." She put a spoonful in her mouth and tasted nothing. It was just a texture. "I'm sorry, but I'm well right now. I don't want to go down there and get poked and prodded again."

Her reticence was grounded in the fact that now was the good part, and she didn't know how long it was going to last. Given that nothing could stop this, why did they need to bother with—

"It would mean a lot to me if you would see Jane."

She glanced up. Trez was staring at the windows behind her, even though the shutters were down and there was nothing to see in them.

His eyes were haunted. Like he knew she wasn't going to go to the clinic—and there was nothing he could do about it.

"Do you know what I'm most scared of?" she heard herself say.

His face turned toward hers. "What?"

She stirred her oatmeal. Took another taste, which still registered just as something warm. "I'm afraid of getting trapped."

"What do you mean?"

"I don't want to get trapped in here," she said with a catch in her voice. Then she patted her chest, her arms, her thighs beneath the table. "In my body. I'm scared of the episodes. I'm alive in there, you know, locked in and . . . when it happens, it's hard to hear and see, but things register. I knew you had come for me. It made all the difference. When you were with me, I wasn't . . . quite so trapped."

When he didn't say anything, she glanced at him again. He was back to staring at those windows that showed nothing of the day outside, not whether it was cloudy or sunny, or whether it was rainy, or if there was a wind whisking the autumn leaves along brown grass.

"Trez?" she prompted.

"Sorry." He shook himself. "Sorry, I got lost there for a second."

He pivoted in his chair, putting his feet in the rungs under the seat she was in. Then he took her hand, the one that didn't have the spoon, and he smoothed it flat against his palm.

"You have the most beautiful hands I have ever seen," he murmured.

She laughed. "I suspect you're biased, but I'll take the compliment."

He frowned, his brows going tight. "I can imagine how . . ." He did a long, slow inhale, exhale. "I can think of nothing more terrifying in the world than being locked in a place that you can't get out of— and to have your prison be your own body? That's inconceivable. That's a terrifying head fuck."

"Yes."

There was a long period of silence at that point, where he sat in front of his cooling bowl without touching the stuff, and she played with her oatmeal, making little S's with the tip of her spoon.

The argument they were having played out in the air between them, his please-go-for-your-own-good's at war with her not-until-I-absolutely-have-to's. There was no reason to actually say the words. She wasn't going to budge. And that meant his only option was to throw her over his shoulder and caveman her down to the training center.

Finally, Selena couldn't stand it, and had to change the subject.

"I sometimes wonder . . ." She shrugged. "I mean, what if everyone's lied about death? What if there is no Fade, but instead you're just stuck in your body forever, conscious but unable to move?"

Great. She'd wanted to try to lighten the mood.

Nice. Try.

"Well, bodies do . . ." He cleared his throat. "You know, rot."

"Hmm, good point."

"Although, as afterlife nightmares go, for me? I worry about the whole zombie-apocalypse thing." He picked up his spoon and started to eat, still holding on to her free hand. "That would suck. You kick it and then you roam the earth, stinking up the place on an Atkins diet that, like, never ends."

She put up her spoon to stop him. "Well, now, hold on a minute—see, you'd just be hungry, right? And if you found people to eat, then, you know, life is pretty good if you're a zombie."

"Not if the lower half of your face drops off. Without a jaw, how do you feed yourself? Then you're just hungry and you can't do anything about it. Total suckage."

"Straws."

"What?"

"You just need straws."

"Hard to fit a femur through a straw."

"And a blender. Straws and a blender. Then you're set."

With a bark of sound, Trez threw his head back and laughed so hard, it was a wonder he didn't wake half the mansion up.

"Oh, my God, that is so sick." He leaned in and kissed her. "So fucking sick."

Suddenly, she was smiling, too—so hard her cheeks hurt. "Totally sick. Is this what they call gallows humor?"

"Yup. Especially if we keep riffin'." Trez grew serious. "And okay, so you don't go."

"What? To the gallows? That is a relief."

"Down to see Jane. If you don't want to go, I'm not going to make you."

Selena exhaled in a rush. "Thank you. I really appreciate that."

"Don't thank me. It's not my call. It's yours." He ran his spoon around the inside of his bowl. "I think it's important that you have as much say as possible in any and every part of your life, especially the disease and the way it's managed. I'm guessing you feel like you have no choice about so much of this . . . fate . . . that's come to you, and that makes the opportunities to call the shots especially important." He glanced over at her. "I may have an opinion, and you can bet your ass I'll tell you what it is, but the last thing I want you to feel is pressure from me. You've got enough penning you in already. I'm not going to add to that."

"How do you know . . . God, it's like you know exactly what I'm thinking."

He shrugged and his eyes got a faraway look in them. Then he tapped the side of his head. "Good guess." He refocused on her. "So, the question is, where do you want to go?"

"Excuse me?"

"Where do you want to go? The clinic is not on the list . . . what is?"

Selena sat back in her chair. Now she was the one staring at the windows. "I like Rehvenge's Great Camp, if that's what you mean?"

"Be bolder. Think bigger. Come on, there has to be somewhere exciting. The Taj Mahal, Paris—"

"We can't go to Paris."

"Says who?"

"Ahh . . ."

"Never met Ahhh, don't know him, don't care how big he is—if he's standing in our way? I'ma murder the son of a bitch."

"You are so adorable." Selena bent in and kissed him on the mouth. Then sat back and tried to force her brain to cough up something, anything. "Isn't this just my luck. Finally get a free pass . . . and can't come up with—oh! I know."

"Tell me, and I'll make it happen."

"I want to go to Circle the World."

Trez sat back as well. "The restaurant?"

"Yup." She wiped her mouth with a napkin. "I want to go to Circle the World and have dinner."

"That's the one that goes around, that's on the top of—"

"The biggest building in Caldwell! I saw it on TV once when I was keeping Layla company in her room. You can sit right next to the glass and look out all over the city as you eat." She frowned as he seemed to swallow hard—and not because he'd taken a big spoonful of the oatmeal. "Are you okay?"

"Oh, yeah, absolutely." Trez nodded and puffed his chest out as he went all male on her. "I think it's a great idea. We'll have Fritz make the reservation for tonight—I've got some pull in this city so it won't be a problem. And they have dinner service until ten o'clock."

Selena started to smile, picturing herself in one of the Chosen robes, her hair done properly, her body normal . . . and Trez across the glossy black table they'd shown on the TV ad, with the napkins so white, the plates so square, the silver glinting in the candlelight.

Perfect.

Romantic.

And nothing to do with being sick.

"I am *so* excited," she said.

The next bite of oatmeal she put in her mouth was sweet and creamy and altogether the most perfect . . . what did humans call it? Brake feast?

That made no sense. But who cared.

"It's a date, isn't it," she realized. "Praise to the Virgin Scribe, I have a date!"

Trez laughed, the sound a rumble in his broad chest. "You'd better believe you do. And I'ma treat you like a queen. *My* queen."

As they both tucked in, she thought, wow, such a strange emotional landscape this all was, deep valleys of despair, followed by vast vistas that were so emotionally pure and beautiful, she felt honored to have them. It was almost as if her life, with its compressed time span, had been shoved together like a bolt of cloth, that which might have been smooth going and unremarkable, now undulating with great resonance.

She would have preferred the luxury of centuries. But in this moment, right now, she felt so very, deeply alive. In a way she couldn't say she had been before.

"Thank you," she said abruptly.

"For what?"

She stared down into her oatmeal, feeling a blush hit her cheeks. "For tonight. It's the best night I've ever had."

"We aren't there yet, my queen."

"It's still the best night"—she looked into his dark eyes—"of my entire life."

TWENTY-EIGHT

Am woke up to the smell of soup, and as his brain started firing again, there was no *Is this a dream?* bullshit going on for him. In spite of the fact that he'd been out cold from a concussion, not one second of what had landed him in this cell in the Queen's palace was lost on him: not the quick change of clothes in front of Almost Abraham Lincoln, not the back-end approach through the Territory, not the blow to the head followed by his brief wakey-wakey before.

The soup, though, was a surprise. It was something he remembered from his childhood, a blend of pumpkin and cream, spice and rice.

And there was another scent in the cell. The same one that filled his nose when that priest had come to double-check his markings.

Opening his eyes, he—

Recoiled.

A *maichen*, or maid, was kneeling before him, her body and head draped in the pale blue of her station, her face covered with a mesh mask that showed him absolutely nothing of her eyes or features. In her hands, a fine wooden tray held the bowl, a spoon, a carafe, and a glass, as well as a large torn-off piece of bread.

No priest. No one else was with them.

He inhaled again—and then realized that the female must have come in with the court official before and he just hadn't seen her.

He pushed against the floor. And that was when he discovered he was naked.

Whatever. He didn't want to make the *maichen* feel awkward, but if she didn't like the view, she could leave.

Not that she was looking at him. Her head was lowered in submission, as she had been trained.

s'Ex apparently was prepared to take some kind of care of him while he was in prison—or at least keep him alive for the time being. And for a moment, he pitied this poor female whose social rank was so low she was sent in, by herself, to possibly dangerous males without consideration for her safety or her sex.

Then again, in the hierarchy of things, she was considered to be essentially worthless.

Sad. But he had other problems to worry about.

Without acknowledging the *maichen* or his birthday-suit situation, he got to his feet and walked over to the screen in the far corner. The water facilities were behind it and he took advantage of them—getting another reminder he wasn't in Kansas anymore.

As he bent over a commoners' sink to wash his face, he had only a single crank to turn the faucet on, rather than separate ones for hot and cold.

It was not because he was a prisoner: The whole wait-for-hot-water issue was among the things he'd had to get used to outside of the Territory. Humans insisted on toggling some mix of opposites to a perfect temperature. Here at the s'Hisbe? All water was ninety-eight degrees. From drinking to washing to brushing your teeth, it was one single constant, neither hot nor cold.

Splashing his face, he picked up the black towel that hung on a wall rack and dried off. Soft. So soft. Nothing like human ones, and he was just a prisoner.

He retucked the damp length out of habit and stepped free of the screen. "Tell s'Ex I want to see him."

Prisoners were typically not afforded requests, but he didn't care. He also refused to speak in the Old Language or the Shadow dialect. Because of the predominance of human culture, English was taught in Shadow schools, and even staff were expected to have some rudimentary knowledge of the language.

"And I'm not eating that." He nodded at the tray. "So you can take it away."

God only knew what was in the shit, whether it was a drug or some kind of poison; he was very confident his treatment here wasn't going to stay so benign. They were, in most likelihood, going to pull his arms and legs out of his sockets at some point—although not until they notified Trez of his captivity.

Shit. He should never have trusted—

The *maichen* placed the tray on the floor. Then she extended her hand, picked up the spoon, dipped it in the soup, and brought it upward. With her free hand, she lifted the mesh far enough to expose her mouth and take a sample. Then she did the same for the bread, and the fermented apple cider that was in the carafe.

Allowing the mesh to fall back into place, she sat back on the soles of the leather slippers on her feet.

Unfortunately, the gesture did nothing for his suspicions. *maichens* were so far down the food chain, again, that even the word itself was paid little respect at the beginning of sentences. That she might be poisoned or compromised? No one would care.

His stomach, however, was seriously encouraged as she continued to breathe.

Before he could stop himself, he went over to her and the tray. The *maichen* did not look up, but then again, she was afraid of him—for good reason.

The scent of her fear mixed nicely with that spicy soup.

So did the scent of her skin.

Inhaling through his nose, he felt another shock go through his system, his muscles twitching—as did his cock.

Which made no sense. Here he was, stuck in shit up to his chin, and his sex decided to get interested? Really?

No wonder they called the damn thing a dumb handle.

Standing above her, he put his hands on his hips and watched for signs that she was going to hit the floor. When she remained upright, he waited a little longer. She was trembling, but she had been ever since he'd gotten to his feet.

iAm knelt down on the hard stone floor, mirroring her pose. Almost immediately his knees began to ache—another reminder of how long it had been since he'd been around his people. Such manner of sitting was a commonplace here in the Territory.

Handy if you're buck-ass naked, too. Didn't put your altogether on as full a display.

He ate fast, but not sloppily, and it was a good call. His brain needed the calories—his body, too, if he were going to bust out of here.

Which was the plan.

"s'Ex," he demanded when he'd finished. "Go get him."

With that, he pushed the tray toward the female. As was custom, she bent forward in supplication, her covered forehead nearly ending up in the empty white bowl.

She picked up the tray, straightened her torso, and gracefully got to her feet without wobbling or dropping any of the dishes. Backing out of the cell, she triggered the door by putting the sole of her shoe against a section of the wall. A moment later, because the exit was clearly monitored, someone opened things up remotely—either that, or the exit was footprinted somehow.

And out she went.

As the panel closed with a *Star Trek* sound, he knew it would have done him no good to overpower her and try to use her as a bargaining chip. s'Ex and his guards would be more likely to negotiate to save a dog.

Pacing around, he pictured his brother beside Selena as she lay on that examination table, under that bright light, her body all contorted, a frozen expression on her face.

God, he should never have done this. Talk about a no-win situation: Trez was going to want to come get him out, but leaving that female when she was ill was going to kill him.

Nothing like throwing gasoline on a fire. Along with about a hundred pounds of dynamite.

Trez had meant every word he'd said about Selena and her freedom of choice.

As he strode through the underground tunnel, heading for the training center's clinic, he was one hundred on pretty much one and only one thing—well, two, but the fact that he was in love with her was a rock-bottom given. The other thing he knew for sure was that Selena, and Selena alone, was going to decide how her condition was managed, and if anybody tried to strong-arm her in any way? He was going to butt-out them like you read about.

But that didn't mean he wasn't going to go see Doc Jane.

About his queen.

God, that pet name for Selena was so funny. The instant the sobriquet had come out of his mouth, it had locked in. As if his vocabulary had bonded to that word like his body had bonded to hers.

And she would be the only queen for him. No matter what happened to them, or where he ended up, she would be his reigning female, none other to supplant her place in his heart, his respect, or the utterance of that word.

Dragging his palm over his face, he forced his feet to stay at a walking stride even though a big part of him wanted to run at a full tilt to the clinic. There was no rush, however, at least as far as his female was concerned. Selena was up in his bedroom, naked in his tub, soaking her beautiful body in warm, scented water.

She was not completely pain-free. She hid the lingering stiffness and discomfort well, but the telltales were in the subtle winces of her face, and the jerky manner in which she moved her hands and arms. The bath and some OTC aspirin were going to help, though. And when she had had a good, long soak, she was going to get into his bed for a rest before their "date."

Her joy at the prospect of their dinner together was contagious. He literally felt warm inside his skeleton, as if her happiness held a kinetic magic that, through his bonding, magnified within his own flesh. Hell, all he had to do was think of her at that breakfast table, grinning over their bowls of oatmeal, or think of the sound of her voice getting all excited about where they were going . . . and he was sublimely at peace.

There had never been anything close to it for him. Not even the love and commitment he had for his brother came near to the feeling.

In a sick way, he supposed her illness had been good for both him and Selena. He could not fathom how they would have wiped away the bullshit between them so efficiently or completely without . . .

Hell of a trade-off though, wasn't it.

As he came up to the training center's access point, he

entered the proper codes, and then passed through the supply closet and into Tohr's office. The Brother was not behind the desk, which was a good thing, and not a surprise. It was around five p.m., and Tohr was no doubt waking up in his mated bed with his Autumn, about to get ready for the night ahead.

What had been a surprise was that Doc Jane was willing to see him at this odd time of day. With the hours she'd been pulling lately between injuries and illness and Qhuinn's brother, it seemed like she and Manny and Ehlena had been on shift constantly.

Made him respect the shit out of her.

Through the glass door. Down the concrete-block main corridor. Many doors down on the left.

Pushing his way into the examining room, he—

"Oh, shit!"

Leaping back out into the hall, he put the crook of his elbow up to his eyes, and prayed that what he'd just seen was not a permanent burn on his retinas.

There were some things that you didn't need to know about the people you lived with, no matter how much you loved them.

A split second later, V opened the door, and the *ziiiiiiiip!* as he did up the front of his leathers was loud.

"She'll see you now," he said matter-of-factly.

As if two seconds ago he hadn't been banging the ever-loving shit out of his *shellan* as she sat on her desk.

"I can come back?" Trez asked.

"Nope, she's ready. Selena okay?"

"I, ah . . . yes. She's moving, she's . . . well, I'm taking her out tonight."

V took out a hand-rolled. "No shit. Where to?"

In all his ruminations, Trez had been studiously avoiding thinking about their precise destination. The date idea was great, the food was going to rock . . . there was just one problem that he was going to have to suck up and deal with.

"That restaurant." He pointed to the ceiling. "You know the one downtown that, like, goes in circles?"

"Oh, yeah. Way up there." The Brother exhaled. "Helluva view."

Uh-huh. Fifty-plus stories. He'd gotten on the Web site to find out exactly how bad it was. "Yeah. Helluva view."

"Lemme know if there's anything I can do. For either of you."

V gave him a clap on the shoulder, and started to stride off.

"Vishous."

The Brother stopped, but did not turn around. And in the light above his head, the tendril of smoke from his hand-rolled struck an elegant swirl in the air.

"How much time do I have with her."

The Brother turned his head so that his powerful goateed profile cut a pale slice out of that illumination, the tattoos at his temple seeming more sinister than usual.

"How much," Trez repeated. "I know you saw it."

There was a subtle hiss as the Brother inhaled, the tip of the cigarette glowing a vital orange. "What I get is not that specific. Sorry."

"You're lying."

That dark brow popped up. "I'll forgive you that cheap shot. Once."

With that, the male resumed striding off, those massive shoulders shifting with his hips, his warrior's body not exactly the kind of thing anyone, even someone of Trez's size and with his Shadow skills, would voluntarily take on.

Especially with that glowing hand of his.

But there wouldn't be a brawl between the two of them. Not on this topic, at least.

They both knew he'd lied.

V was the Brother with the intelligence, the mystical visions, born directly of the Scribe Virgin's body. He was also incapable of bullshitting anyone about anything. It was just not part of his hardwiring, that incredible brain of his too busy to care about whether or not he offended or postured properly or couched things in ways that were palatable to the inquirer.

So when he had refused to turn around? When all he had done was show his profile?

He had answered the question well enough.

Vishous would never, ever voluntarily hurt or injure a male he respected. That was even more ingrained than the no-lying thing. And yes, Trez had heard that there was usually not a timeline on V's visions about death—but clearly it was different in this case.

Maybe because what had been seen was less about the Chosen's death, and more about what happened to Trez afterward.

There are two females. And in both cases, you're running out of time.

"... Trez?" Doc Jane said, as if she had been trying to get his attention. "Are you ready to talk with me?"

No, he thought, as V disappeared through the glass doors of the office. He was not.

TWENTY-NINE

"**D**id you think no one would know."

As *maichen* stepped out from the cell, she froze. The voice behind her was so deep, so low, that the words were more growled than spoken—and it was the last thing she had expected.

Footfalls, of a male twice her height and three times her weight, circled around her body, and through the mesh that covered her face, she looked up, up, up.

s'Ex's features were covered as well, but for the executioner, it was chain mail, not delicate links of silver, that hid his particulars, though not his identity.

Fear rang in her chest, a hollow strike that brought sweat out under her armpits and between her well-concealed breasts.

"And you were feeding him?"

When she neither confirmed nor denied the statement, the executioner threw his hands up in frustration—but he was careful not to touch her or anything that was indirectly touching her body, and that included the tray, everything on it, as well as her robing and even the large marble square that her feet had happened to land on.

It was forbidden for any male to come into contact with her, punishable by death, at s'Ex's hands—which would mean that he would be required to commit suicide, she supposed.

"Tell me," he demanded. "Did you poison him?"

"No! He has been without food for over twelve hours—"

"Do you normally concern yourself with my prisoners?"

"He is no normal prisoner." She lifted her chin. "And you have not taken care of him properly."

"There are a thousand others to look after such things."

"Am I not one of those thousands who live here?"

He leaned in. "Do *not* go in there again."

maichen removed her mesh so fast, he did not have a chance to look away in time. As he gasped and wrenched around, ducking his face under the folds of his sleeve, her voice matched the authority of his.

"You will not tell me where I can and cannot go."

"Drop your mask!" he barked.

"I will not. I do not take orders from you." She ripped the sleeve away from him so that he had naught to cover his eyes. "Are we clear?"

The executioner closed his eyes so hard, the features of his entire face distorted. "You're going to get us both killed—"

"No one is here. Now I command you to meet my stare."

Such was the turning of tables that he became the cowed one as he took his time opening those lids, as if his face did not want to obey the dictates of his mind.

When he finally looked at her properly, it was the first time in her life a male had ever seen her face—and for a split second, her heart got to beating so fast she grew light-headed. But the thought of that prisoner in there overrode the upset.

"He"—she jabbed her finger in the direction of the door to the cell—"is not to be harmed in any way. Do you understand me?"

"It is not your place to dictate—"

"He is an innocent. That is the Anointed One's brother, not he who must serve the throne. I know from the tattoo—"

"You looked at his body!" A series of words exploded out of s'Ex's mouth, unfamiliar ones that sounded like, "Jesus fucking Christ."

Whatever that meant. She knew English only formally.

s'Ex leaned into her and dropped his voice. "Listen up, you stay out of this. You don't know what's going on here."

"I know that it is unfair to hold an innocent responsible for something that does not concern him."

"I'm not going to lose my own life over you. Do we understand each other? And I will *not* alter my course just to please some moral streak you wish to indulge for a moment."

"Yes, you will." Now she leaned in—and in spite of his size, s'Ex jerked back. "You are well aware of the power I hold. You shall not cross me in this or any other desire I have—and when I bring him his next meal, you and your males will let me pass in there in peace. I don't trust you enough to feed him properly—or safely. And do *not* tell him who I am."

With that, she put her mesh back into place and started to walk off.

"What's your endgame," s'Ex demanded.

She paused. Looked over her shoulder. "What does that phrase mean?"

"What are you going to do? Keep him in there like a gerbil for the rest of his natural life?"

What was a gerbil?

maichen narrowed her eyes beneath the mesh. "That is none of your concern. The only worry you have is if anything happens to him. And bring him a proper bed."

At least he could be comfortable as she figured out a way to safely set the poor male free.

maichen made it around the corner and out of sight, before she began to shake . . . before she had to catch herself against the wall to stay standing.

Closing her eyes, all she could see was that imprisoned male, walking around the screen as he had reemerged from running the water.

His body had been . . . breathtaking, his naked form arresting her eyes, her thoughts, her breath. Broad of shoulder, thick of chest, long of torso, he had seemed to have been crafted by an artist, rather than born of a mortal.

And then there were the other parts of his body. Which had made her blush so fiercely, she worried the mesh would melt right off her face.

She told herself that she was just going to help him, and that was true. It was.

But it would be foolish to discount this burning curiosity. Mayhap even dangerous to.

Stars above, what was she doing?

*　　*　　*

When Trez jumped up on the examination table, his head nearly banged the chandelier, and while he ducked to create airspace, Doc Jane came over.

"Here, let me move my lights out of the way."

With that little problem solved, he gripped the thin mattress under his ass like he was about to go on a roller-coaster ride.

And he absolutely hated roller-coasters.

Doc Jane brought over a rolling stool and sat down, pulling the two halves of her white coat together and linking her hands on her knees. Staring up at him, she seemed prepared to wait for as long as it took him to get his thoughts together.

Clearing his throat, he announced, "She's not coming down here. She doesn't want to be fiddled with while she's feeling well."

"I can understand that."

He waited for more, and reminded himself to be civil because she was V's *shellan*.

When the good doctor didn't continue, he frowned. "That's it?"

"What do you want me to say? That Manny and I are going to make her come see us? I can't do that—I *won't* do that."

As he felt no relief at all at the statement, Trez realized that he had wanted Doc Jane to force Selena down here.

Hypocrite much? Not really a pro–free will stance, was it.

"How do I know she's going to make it through the night?" he said tightly.

"Without an Arrest episode?"

"Yeah."

"You don't." Doc Jane brushed her short blond hair back. "Even if I examined her now, I couldn't tell you when the next one is coming. I don't know much about the disease, but from what I've learned, that's part of the issue. There is no prodromal stage."

"What's that?"

"You have migraines, right?" When he nodded, she pointed to her eyes. "And you get an aura about twenty to thirty minutes before the pain hits, yeah? Well, sometimes sufferers get numbness and tingling in their arms or legs; others have sensory anomalies, like smelling things that aren't there or hearing things. With Selena's disease, there is no warning that an acute phase is about to happen. The freezing up seems to occur out of the blue."

"Have you spoken with that Havers fool?"

"Actually, he's never heard of such an illness. The closest he's come is dealing with arthritis-related symptoms." She shook her head. "It makes me wonder, if we were able to do genetic sampling from the Chosen, whether there would be a recessive gene in them somewhere. With a captive breeding population, such as they have been, you'd expect to find exactly this kind of a disease cluster." She shrugged. "But back to Selena, I wish I could tell you what was going to happen, or even what to look for. I can't, though. I've done a complete blood panel on her, and her white cell count is slightly elevated along with her inflammatory markers— but other than that? Normal. All I can say is that if she's up and moving around, her joints are by definition functioning well, and they will let us all know when they aren't."

He cracked his knuckles, one by one. "Is there nothing we can do for her?"

"Not that we can think of so far. One of the challenges is that we don't understand the mechanism of the disease. My suspicion is that after the bone growth is triggered by God only knows what, her immune system somehow rebounds and attacks the offending material, destroying it as if it's a virus or infection. And her body's defensive mechanism knows when to stop, as her original skeleton is intact afterward. There probably is something inherently different about the 'bone' growth, but I wouldn't know unless we did a biopsy."

"So why does she have to . . ." Shit, every time he blinked, he saw Selena lying on the table, her body in that god-awful contortion. "Why can't she just keep fighting things off and recovering?"

"My guess is, the immune system fails. When you think about it, it's an extraordinary series of events on the cellular level. When I saw the first set of X-rays, I would never have guessed her body could come back from that to any kind of functioning."

He fell quiet, and stared at the tile floor. "I want to take her out tonight. You know, for a date." When the doctor stayed silent, he glanced up. "Not a good idea, huh?"

Doc Jane crossed her arms over her chest, and pushed her chair back and forth on its little black wheels, the seated version of pacing.

Fuck. He should have had this conversation before he'd suggested an excursion—

"How frank do you want me to be?" Doc Jane asked.

Trez had an image of Vishous's goateed profile highlighted under that ceiling fixture outside in the corridor. "I need to know where we're at."

Even if it killed him.

It was a minute or two before Doc Jane answered, and he guessed she was running scenarios in her head. "The most conservative route is for her not to leave the compound, and for me to do a total work-up on her, one that involves multiple biopsies, a CAT scan, an MRI out in the human world, and consults with human doctors through Manny's contacts. And then we'd probably want to start her on an aggressive course of steroids—even though that's more a hunch than anything certain, I have to believe the inflammatory process has something to do with all this. There could be other drugs to try, maybe some procedures, but it's hard to guess at them with any certainty from where I'm sitting right now." She rubbed at her short hair until the stuff stuck straight up in blond spikes. "We'd have to get moving fast because we don't know how much time we have, and everything would be trial and error, with probably more of a prolonging goal than a cure. Although again, that's just a hunch, nothing concrete."

He closed his eyes and tried on for size telling his queen that instead of going to that restaurant she was so excited to eat at, they were going to—

"But that's not what I would do if I were her."

Trez popped his lids and looked over at the physician. "So there's another way."

Doc Jane shrugged. "You know, at the end of the day, I think you have to consider quality of life. I'm not sure how far we'd get in treating or understanding this disease even if we climbed all over her. I'm basing that on the fact that she is, to borrow an infectious disease term, 'patient zero' for us. Nobody has seen this even though a minority of her sisters have suffered for generations from it. There is a very complex series of things going on, and I just ... there's a lot to try to get a grip on. And for what? Do you want to ruin her last nights—"

"Nights?" he blurted. "Jesus Christ, is that all we have?"

"I don't know." She lifted her palms. "No one does, and that's the point. Would you—would *she*—rather spend whatever time she has living, or simply waiting to die? I'll tell you right now, if it were my choice, it would be the former. That's why I'm not going to make her come down here or try to have her feel bad because she's not in a big hurry to lie down on my table."

Trez blew out the breath he'd been unaware of holding. "Rehvenge went up North. To the colonies. To see if there was anything in the *symphath* tradition that would help."

"I know, Ehlena told me. We're hoping to hear something soon."

He could tell by the professional tone of the female's voice that she wasn't holding out much hope. "What happens if Selena gets into ... a situation ... and we're out to dinner?"

"Then you call us. Have I shown you Manny's new toy?"

"I'm sorry?"

She got to her feet and patted his knee. "Come with me."

Doc Jane led him out of the exam room, into the corridor, and then down, down, down, past the unused classrooms to the parking garage's heavy steel door. Opening the thing wide, she indicated through the jambs with her arm.

"Ta-da."

Trez stepped out into the cooler, damper air. The enormous ambulance was shiny as a penny, boxy as a LEGO, bigger than Qhuinn's Hummer. Bigger, actually, than the human ones he'd seen out and about in Caldwell.

It was a goddamn RV.

"That is some serious shit," he said.

"Yup. One of the things Manny and I have been worried about—"

The back doors of the vehicle burst open, and Doc Jane's human partner hopped out. "Thought I heard voices." The man grew grave as soon as he saw Trez. "Hey, man, how you holding up?"

The two shook hands and Trez nodded at the vehicle. "So this happened, huh."

"Come see inside."

Trez shoved his hands into the pockets of his jeans and walked around to the back. Through the open double doors, he saw ... a large center aisle with two gurneys, one after the other, surrounded by all kinds of medical equipment stored in glass-fronted, locked cabinets that lined the side walls like bookshelves on steroids.

"It's like a miniature operating room," Trez murmured.

Manny nodded and jumped back in. "That's the plan. We want to be able to treat serious, potentially mortal field injuries quickly. Sometimes, getting patients back here or to Havers's is too risky."

The doctor started opening up those cupboards and cabinets, showing an array of sterile dressings, sterile operating tools, even a microscope on an extending arm that could pivot around to either of the beds.

He patted the thing like it was a pet. "This baby is also a portable X-ray machine, and we have ultrasound technology. Oh, and as a bonus, the RV is bulletproof."

"That was my husband's contribution," Doc Jane added in.

"And V also did the computer systems in here."

"As he would say, true that." Doc Jane glanced at her partner. "So listen, Trez is taking Selena out for a date tonight."

"That's a great idea. Where you two headed?"

Trez made a circular motion with his forefinger. "The thing in the sky. That goes around and around."

"Oh, yeah, I know the one," the guy said. "At the hospital we called it Engagement Central, 'cuz that's where the doctors took their girlfriends when they were ready to put a ring on it. Very romantic."

"Yeah."

Trez stared at the expanse of the mobile OR, trying to decide whether it made him feel relieved or depressed as shit. The good news, he supposed, was that with the flashing lights over the cab of the vehicle and Manny's legendary lead foot, they could make it to downtown in about ten minutes. Especially with there being little traffic.

But what if that wasn't enough time? What if Selena needed—

"Trez?" the male doctor said.

He shook himself out of his ambient panic. "Yeah?"

"How 'bout I go with you—no, not as your chauffeur," he cut in as Trez recoiled. "I'll park in the rear of the building and just hang out in case you need us. This thing has counterfeit badges on the doors and the hood and the back, and I've got all kinds of forged papers. No one will bother me, and I'll bring a Brother with me in case I need to scrub any humans."

Trez blinked. "God, I can't ask you to do that—"

"You didn't. I volunteered."

Trez stared into the state-of-the-art ambulance. He couldn't believe the guy was prepared to—

"Trez?" Manny said. "Hey, Trez, look at me."

Trez swung his eyes back to the human. Manny was well built for a non-vampire, with an athlete's body that he continued to keep up after mating V's sister, Payne. But the strongest thing about him? His confidence. Trained in the human world, the former Chair of the Department of Surgery at St. Francis Hospital downtown radiated the kind of my-way-or-the-highway attitude that meant he fit right in with the Brothers.

"I got you," the guy said gravely. "I got you and her."

Manny extended his palm, and for a moment, all Trez could do was blink. But then he clasped that which had been offered him.

Trez's voice cracked. "I don't how I can repay you."

"You just go and enjoy your woman. That's all I care about."

As Doc Jane put her hand on his shoulder, Trez was humbled by the support. And hopeful, too, that maybe Rehvenge would come up with something from the *symphath* side of things.

After thanking both of them again, he went back into the training center, Doc Jane staying behind with her partner as if she knew he needed a minute to get his shit together.

God, his head was spinning.

And it was funny, he had no impulse to drink away the angst. At all. He didn't feel the need to go out and bang a hundred random chicks, either. He also didn't have any interest in checking in with Big Rob and Silent Tom about the club and its opening night, or following through about those packs of drugs they'd found on that *lesser*. He didn't even want to go upstairs to the mansion's third floor, wake up his brother, and give iAm an update.

He was curiously hollow. And that scared him.

Tonight was supposed to be a special one for his queen.

Had to be.

THIRTY

It was around six in the evening when Selena stepped out of the shower in Trez's bathroom. She had slept like a young all day long and into the night, aware only of Trez coming in and checking on her from time to time. As a result, she felt better than she had for . . .

Dearest Virgin Scribe, she didn't know how long.

Toweling herself off, she wrapped up her hair and put on Trez's black robe. The voluminous weight dwarfed her body, falling to the floor, the tie so long the ends nearly tangled in her feet. But it felt so good to have the thing on her, his scent wrapping around her as an embrace, the folds offering warmth.

Over at the double sinks, she picked up a hand towel and wiped free the condensation on the mirror. Under the lights, her skin was glowing, a flush to her cheeks and a blush to her mouth—all the result of the sex they'd shared.

And there would be more tonight. She knew that because every time Trez had entered the room, that dark spice of his had been an intense promise of what was to come.

Unraveling the towel on her head, she let her dark hair loose, the wet strands flopping down her back. She did the best she could to get the lengths pre-dried, rubbing the terry cloth over everything she could reach without straining too much. Then it was hair-dryer time—except . . .

No hair-dryer.

Looking around, she checked the cupboards under the sinks, but only found a whole load of backup toilet paper, soap, shampoo, and conditioner. Razors. Hand towels and bath towels. Moving over to the storage area on the wall, she found . . . more towels. Which smelled expensive and were as soft as fresh-baked bread, but would not get her where she needed to be.

Bone-dry was the ultimate goal. Ever so slightly damp was her second choice.

Okay, she could be in trouble here. The two of them were leaving at seven thirty and her hair, unaided, took about eight hundred hours to dry—

A knock on the outside door brought her head up. "Hello?"

"Is that a 'come in'?" a female voice asked from in the hall.

"Yes? Please?" Tucking Trez's robe in tighter, she went out into the bedroom proper—then stopped as the heavy panels opened. "Oh, hello . . . ah . . ."

Beth, the Queen, walked into Trez's room. And with her were Marissa . . . Autumn, Mary . . . Ehlena and Cormia. Bella. Payne. Also Xhex, who, with her short hair and her leathers, seemed a little out of place in the group.

Or maybe that was because of her awkward stance, as if she were unsure what she was doing with the pack of them.

"Is there something you needed?" she asked the Queen. The others.

Even though she had been aware of just Cormia and Layla coming to see her, it was a fair guess that everyone in the house had been told about her difficulties—she really hoped the females hadn't made the trip to offer condolences before she actually died.

Fortunately, Beth smiled—as opposed to breaking out the tissues. "We need you to let us do you up."

Selena popped her brows and looked at her feet. "I'm sorry. Am I down and don't know it?"

"Well, we heard through the grapevine—"

Marissa spoke up. "My *hellren* told me, actually. And he heard it through Vishous."

"That you're going on a date," Beth finished. "And we thought you might like some beautification."

Cormia put her palms out. "Not that you aren't beautiful enough."

At that point, there were lots of *oh, no*'s, *totally beauti-ful*'s, and *only if you wanna*'s—and all Selena could do was put her hands up to her cheeks. "I was just going to put on robing and do my hair as prescribed."

"Boring," Xhex said. As all the girls sent her looks, she threw up her hands. "I told you I'm not good at this stuff! God, why did you make me come up here?"

Beth turned back around. "Selena, you always look lovely, but we have some contemporary clothes for you to consider, ones that are maybe a little more—"

"You'll look like something other than a window drape." Xhex rolled her eyes. "I know, I know, I'll shut up from now on. But it's the truth."

"I look like a drapery?" Selena said, glancing over to the swaths by the windows that had just un-shuttered them-selves. "Is that bad?"

Beth came forward and took her hands, squeezing them. "Do you trust us?"

"Oh, of course, my Queen, it's just ... I don't know—I can't find a hair-dryer, and—"

Marissa stepped forward with a canvas tote full of ... every conceivable makeup and hairstyling whatever. "Worry not, I have you covered!"

And that was how Selena ended up sitting on a stool in the middle of Trez's bathroom with a bunch of females cir-cling her with hair-dryers, hairbrushes, something called mousse, and curling irons.

In the midst of the makeover, her eyes watered.

"Oh, am I too close," Autumn said over the din of the dryers.

Selena brought a hand up, hoping to hide her tears. The kindness was so unexpected; she literally felt as though the en-tire house was getting behind her and her male.

Xhex, the hard-ass, was the one who brought over the Kleenex box. And when Selena's hand was shaking so badly she dropped the tissue she took, Xhex was the one who did the duty, snapping another soft white square free and dab-bing under eyes that leaked.

Selena looked up into that gunmetal stare and mouthed, *Thank you.*

Xhex just nodded and kept discreetly mopping up, her

gentle touch at odds with that harsh face and masculine dress—and the gun she wore holstered at her waist in spite of the fact that they were all safe in the compound.

Selena had no thoughts in her head, only emotions too big to hold in her heart.

As the dryers were finally silenced, she knew it was time to pull herself together. All that sound and fury as her hair was blown around had offered a kind of buffering to hide behind, even if they had all seen her cry.

"Your hair is so lovely," Cormia said as she ran her fingers through the waves. "I think we should leave it down—"

"Thank you all," Selena blurted. "Thank you for this."

Beth knelt in front of her. "It's our pleasure."

A hand landed on Selena's shoulder. Another on her forearm. More on her back. And Xhex was right next to her with that Kleenex box.

Looking in the mirror, she saw herself surrounded by the females of the house, and none of them were pitying her—for which she was so very grateful. Instead, they were standing with her, doing what they could to show her that she mattered.

And for some reason, that seemed indescribably important.

Probably because it dawned on her, for the first time, that she would be remembered by these people after she was gone—and to be mourned by good folks was the best legacy anyone could leave behind.

"Down?" she heard herself say. "Really? You think I should wear my hair down?"

"Allow me to introduce my little friend." With that, Marissa held up a silver wand that was plugged into the wall via a black cord. "And now the warfare shall begin."

Selena had to laugh. Glancing up at Xhex, she said, "Have you ever—"

"Used one of those?" The female yanked at her short hair. "As if. But I think you should do what they say. You're looking at the species' brain trust here when it comes to being hot."

"Then submit I will." Selena found herself lightening up at the idea of a transformation. "Do with me what you wish."

Beth grinned. "You think this is gonna be good? Wait'll you see the dress."

* * *

"I'm sorry. I tried."

As Rehvenge apologized for nothing that was his fault—and nothing that was actually a surprise, Trez shook his head. The pair of them were standing in the grand foyer of the mansion, their feet planted on the mosaic depiction of an apple tree in bloom.

He put his hand on the male's fur-clad shoulder. "Seriously, Rehv. Thank you for giving it a shot."

Rehv plugged his red cane into the floor and walked around. "I looked everywhere in our records. Asked people—"

"Rehv, listen, I appreciate your going up to the colony. But honestly, I didn't expect some magical answer." Shit knew he was used to bad news at this point. "So don't beat yourself up about it."

That floor-length mink flared out behind the huge male as he continued to stride about. Eventually, he stopped dead. "Do you remember the night we met?"

"How could I forget."

"Always felt like that was supposed to happen." The male stared down at his ostrich-skin shoes. "I don't want . . . this for you. Especially considering what else is waiting for you."

Rehv was one of the few who knew about his being the Anointed One back in the s'Hisbe.

God, Trez thought. That mess at the Territory wasn't on his radar in the slightest. Selena was the great sanitizer of all his other concerns, not just wiping his slate clean, but scrubbing the shit raw.

"I'm going to see this through with Selena," he heard himself say. "I'm not going anywhere else while she's . . . you know."

"Anything you need, you got it." Rehv came over. "I just . . ."

It was unsettling to see such a great male, who was known for his brash arrogance, appear so defeated.

Trez had to cut off the commiseration or it was going to take him down. "Look, you don't have to say anything else. Frankly, I'd rather you didn't. Not for nothing, I gotta stay focused on where I'm at right now—Selena is going to come down those stairs and I can't be all up in my head for tonight."

"Understood. But I'm going to hug ya."

"Please don't—oh, no, come on, man—"

As he was enveloped in mink, he stiffened—and felt like an asshole. For fuck's sake, the guy was just being real, but damn, all Trez wanted to do was run into the billiards room. Maybe hit himself over the head with a cue stick.

Until the damn thing broke.

His head, not the stick.

"Wow, this stuff is soft," he said, stroking the coat.

Rehv stepped back. "I'm gonna go crash upstairs in the guest room. I'm whipped and Ehlena has been up all day with Luchas. I think we're going to go sleep for the whole night."

"Sounds like heaven to me."

Awkward. Moment.

"You gotta stop looking at me like that." Trez rubbed his face. "She's not dead yet."

"I know, I know. Sorry. I'll leave you alone."

Rehv clapped him on the back and then hit the grand staircase, ascending with the help of that cane. And as Trez stayed where he was, he realized why he had not hunted down his brother to talk about things. Usually, he and iAm would have spoken eight times already—and it was only seven o'clock in the evening.

But if Rehv being a good guy got under his skin, Trez really wouldn't be able to handle that shit with his blooded brother right now. He was barely holding on to himself— one look into iAm's black stare?

He was afraid he wouldn't be able to put things back together from the rubble.

Sometimes, the honesty was too much—

Oh, fuck him. Was he seriously quoting seventies Muzak now?

Pacing, pacing, pacing. He and Selena were set to leave at seven thirty, and he'd planned to help her down to the car. That had been a big-ass no-go, however: a good hour ago, he'd headed to the third floor to check on her, but Xhex had barred his entry and informed him he wasn't welcome in his own bedroom. Then the fighter had thrown one of his black suits at him, along with a black button-down, black tuxedo loafers and silk socks, and his black-on-black Audemars Piguet watch.

And slammed the door in his face.

Females. Honestly.

But he had changed into the clothes. Like a good boy. And come down here to wait.

As Rehv's draped figure disappeared up above, Trez took out his phone and checked his texts. He expected to find something from iAm, but, typical of his brother, the guy knew when he needed space and was giving it to him.

He fired off a quick update to the male, telling him that he was going out with Selena and that he'd touch base later on when they came back. Then he reached out to Big Rob and Silent Tom, and informed them to route everything that had to do with the clubs through Xhex—assuming she could get herself free of the extreme makeover stuff going down in his room. He was about to put the phone away, when he saw he'd missed a text.

From Rhage.

The Brother had reached out and—

"Hey, we ready to go? Where's your female?"

Speak of the Hollywood. The Brother in question came jogging down the main staircase, weapons jangling like human Christmas bells off various holsters that he had yet to strap on his body.

"Just got your text," Trez said. "Sorry I didn't respond."

"You got shit on your mind. It's cool."

The two clapped palms. Clinched up. Pounded shoulders. Stepped back.

"Check you out." Rhage did a walk around. "Lookin' fine."

Trez snapped out both of his French cuffs. "I can't embarrass the female."

"Lookin' like that, she'll be lucky to stand next to you." Rhage stopped in front of him. "See, this is what I'm telling my Mary. She wants me to add color to my wardrobe—it's been a thing, like, for the last couple of years."

As the Brother shuddered as if his *shellan* had suggested he wear women's panties under his leathers, Trez started to smile.

"You're into the black, Hollywood?" he said.

"She wants to match my eyes." Rhage pointed to his unbelievably teal peepers. "Like, seriously. I say, I've already got aqua on me all the time with these things. Why do we need redundancy."

"So how much color is in your closet?"

"I don't want to talk about it. Too depressing—"

Lassiter poked his head out of the billiards room. "Hey! Dragon boy—*Project Runway*'s on if you wanna come watch. Maybe pick up some pointers on your threads."

Rhage's stare narrowed, but he refused to look at the angel. "Isn't there a *Saved by the Bell* marathon you have to go watch?"

"Don't hate on Zack. He's like your little fucking brother, beauty queen." Lassiter wandered over, the gold he had on creating an aura around his blond-and-black head and his long body—or maybe the glow actually was an aura. "So, where are we off to? Your club, Shadow?"

"No."

"An embalmer's ball then? With all that black on, it's like you're getting into the funereal arts—"

Rhage moved so fast it was impossible to track. One moment, he was gritting his teeth beside Trez; the next, he was nose-to-nose with the angel, his hand locked on Lassiter's throat.

Words were spoken so softly, Trez couldn't track them, but a moment later the smart-ass drained out of the angel's face and attitude.

Rhage dropped the vise grip and stepped off. "So that happened," he muttered as he came back over and started strapping up. "Might as well get this shit on. I'm riding shotgun with Manny tonight."

"Oh, yeah." Trez took a deep breath. "Hey, thanks for doing—"

"But only because he promised me steak."

Trez popped a brow. "I'm sorry?"

"Steak? You know, cow? Meat? Heaven on a plate? I know you've had some before."

"I'm familiar with it, yes. But you're coming to help with—"

"The steak consumption. That's why I'm going."

There was an awkward pause. During which Rhage simply stared at him, as if making the statement that he was not going to be a drama zone.

And Jesus, that was probably the most helpful thing the Brother could have done. It was like a lifeline out of the emotional suck zone, and Trez grabbed on.

"Steak, huh. You going to order takeout from Circle the World?"

Rhage recoiled as if he'd been slapped. "So, okay, clearly you are not aware of this, which is a stunning lapse in your formal education, but the best steakhouse in Caldie, 518, is right across the street from the skyscraper your restaurant is in. My plan? While you and your girl are up there getting your jollies on and going around in circles, I'ma be down at the ground floor eating, like, a filet mignon, a roast beef end cut, a Kobe beef burger, a New York strip."

"Sounds good. Which one are you having? You decide yet?"

Rhage frowned. "All of them. With thirds on the mashed potatoes. See, you gotta get your mashed-to-meat proportion right. Makes all the difference. And then there are the rolls. I'ma get three baskets delivered out."

Trez put up his forefinger. "You know what you need? A meal at Sal's. You should come eat at my brother's joint."

"Is that Italian?"

"Yup. Talk about best in the city—"

"Shit, why haven't I—"

"Holy . . . mother*fucker* . . ."

At Lassiter's barked curse, Trez and Rhage glanced over at the angel. The PITA didn't notice them, however, his unusually colored eyes focused upward, as if the Second Coming had arrived at the top of the grand staircase.

Just then, a telltale scent reached Trez's nose and rocketed through his blood, the impact wrenching his head and his body around. . . .

Whereupon he lost all thought. All breath. And all of his soul.

Selena stood at the head of the bloodred-carpeted steps, her lovely hand resting on the gold-leafed balustrade, her body held stiffly, as if she weren't sure about her shoes, or her dress, or maybe even her hair.

There was absolutely nothing to worry about.

Unless she had a problem with being an H-bomb.

Her long dark hair was down around her shoulders, falling to the small of her back. Curled from tip to base, it was such a feminine glory, so overwhelming with its weight and its shine, that he fisted his hands and released them because he wanted to touch it, stroke it, smell it. But that wasn't the half of it. Her face was the only thing that could possibly have put the stuff to shame, her skin radiant, her eyes sparkling, her full lips red as blood.

And then there was the fucking dress.

Black. Simply cut. With a low-cut bodice and a skirt that ended north of mid-thigh.

Very north. Of mid-thigh.

Selena extended a foot, a delicately shod, high-heeled foot that was plugged into a teeny-tiny ankle and a perfectly curving calf that had him grinding his teeth.

He had to swallow hard as she started to descend slowly, each step she took bringing her closer to him being able to touch her, kiss her . . . take her.

Man, that dress was a total knockout, nothing but a sheath that followed the contours of her hips, her waist, and her breasts, with a gathering off to one side at her middle and a second at one of her shoulders. She wore no jewelry at all, but why would she? There was no diamond, no emerald, no ruby, no sapphire that could come near her devastating perfection.

As she reached the bottom of the stairs, she hesitated, glancing left and right, probably at Lassiter and Rhage—were they still in the foyer with him? Who knew. Who the fuck cared?

Selena smoothed the . . . was that silk? Wool? Taffeta? Tinfoil? Paper bag?

She reached up and pushed at her hair. Then grimaced. "You don't like it, do you. I can change. I was going to wear . . ."

Something knocked him in the side.

". . . traditional dress. But the girls thought . . ." She looked up over her shoulder to the females who stood at the top of the stairs. "I can change—"

Lassiter cursed. "Fuck no. Don't you dare. You look—"

Trez's upper lip curled off his descended fangs. Then he snapped his jaws in the direction of the fallen angel, like a German Shepherd. Or maybe a bull shark doing a test bite before he went chainsaw on his prey.

Lassiter put up his palms. "Whatever, man, I was going to say she looks like a charity case. A football referee. A Martha Stewart impersonator. You want me to keep going? I could break into dumb-ass Disney characters. There are so many of them."

That poke in his rib cage came again. Then Rhage leaned in. "Trez," the Brother hissed. "You gotta fucking say something here."

Trez cleared his throat. "I . . . I . . . I . . ."

He was dimly aware of the females on the second floor breaking into high fives and cheers of, "Nailed it." But his queen remained worried.

Okay, he needed to pull himself together—before Rhage's elbow nailed him in the liver again, and Selena bolted back to his bedroom. "You are . . . I am . . ."

He pulled at the collar of his silk shirt, even though the thing was wide-open.

"You like it?" she said.

All he could do was nod. He was literally nothing but hormones in a black suit. She was that beautiful to him.

"Really?"

More nodding. "Uh-huh. *Really*."

Selena started to smile. Then she glanced back at the females, who jumped up and down and gave her thumbs-up.

His queen turned back to him. Stepped in close. Took his hands and stretched up to whisper in his ear, "The only thing they didn't give me was underwear."

Naked.

She was n-n-n-n-nakey under that.

THIRTY-ONE

No sleep.

Paradise had gotten absolutely, positively no sleep whatsoever in the beautiful house. At first, it had been because she was so excited to have the run of the place that she'd gone through every parlor, bedroom, and bathroom, marveling at the art, the furnishings, the decor — twice. Then it had been a case of picking a bedroom underground (she'd chosen the one on the left) and unpack, unpack, unpack.

Her beloved *doggen*, Vuchie, had started to lay a pallet for herself out in the short, stone-walled corridor between the two subterranean suites, but Paradise had insisted her maid go across the way and stay in the other actual bedroom. This had led to a series of protests, whereupon her servant, trapped between a direct order and her discomfort at staying in such luxury, had nearly had a nervous breakdown.

In the end, though, and as usual, Paradise had gotten her way.

At which point, she'd retreated to "her" bedroom, changed into nightclothes and discovered the further good news that the Wi-Fi didn't require a password. Stretching out on the velvet duvet, she'd checked Twitter, Facebook, a couple of blogs, and the *New York Post* and *Daily News* — and continued to ignore texts from Peyton. When her eyelids had finally started to drop, she'd put her phone aside and dragged half the covers over on top of herself, her Syracuse b-ball sweatshirt and her yoga pants the kind of pj's she had slept in many, many times.

Annnnnd that was when the no-sleep thing had gotten its groove on.

Even as she'd closed her eyes, her mind had buzzed with what her father had told her she'd be doing at nightfall to help him with the King.

And then there was the fact that that long-lost cousin was alone with her father back at their house. What if he hurt her dad?

So, yup, she thought as she stepped in front of the mirror in the bathroom. No shut-eye . . . even when her lids had been down.

The good news was that the wait was over. And her father had texted her that his ETA was in about fifteen minutes—so clearly, he'd made it through the day okay, too.

Funny, she was shocked by how badly she needed to see him. After so many years of praying for some freedom, she had found the actual experience marked by a whole lot of homesick.

"But now I get to work."

Turning to the side, she straightened her navy-blue blazer. Tugged at her white blouse. Fiddled with her strand of pearls.

As she stepped back, she decided she looked like a 1960s stewardess for PanAm. Like the ones they'd had in *Catch Me If You Can.*

"Ah, come on." She yanked out the tie she'd pulled her hair back with, and fluffed things out. "Oh, yeah. That's *really* different."

Not.

Hair down so did not improve the situation. But she was out of time, and more to the point, who did she have to impress, anyway?

Okay, bad question to ask in any form if you were about to try to hold down your first job and it was not only for your father, but for the King of your entire race, and his personal guard of straight-up killers.

It was enough to get her praying to the Scribe Virgin.

Stepping out of her—

"Please, mistress. Allow me to make you some breakfast."

Vuchie was standing just inside the room, dressed in her perennial gray-and-white uniform, her weight going back and forth between her crepe shoes. The *doggen* had brown hair, brown eyes and skin the color of white bread, but she was lovely in her own way—and probably only fifty years older than Paradise. The two had known each other since Parry could remember—as with many daughters of aristocratic parents, the pair of them had been matched with the hopes of a lifelong mistress/servant relationship being formed. In a lot of cases, one's maid was the most important thing taken to your new home when you were mated to a male of similar privilege and breeding.

It was your tie to the past. Your sanity. And, a lot of times, the only person you could trust.

Boy, she much preferred this current relocation—that was because of a job, not some overbred *hellren* type.

"I'm fine, Vuchie." She tried to smile. "Are you hungry yourself?"

"Mistress, you did not have Last Meal, either."

Parry had no intention of coming clean with the truth—namely that if she had so much as half a nook or a quarter of a cranny, she was going to go golf sprinkler all over her stewardess-ness. That kind of candor was only going to lead to a fight over bed rest, and likely, Vuchie calling in her father for R&R reinforcement.

"You know what I would love?" Parry forced a smile. "If you could prepare something for me to eat at my desk." She went over and linked arms with Vuchie. "Come on, let's do this."

"But ... but ... but—"

"I'm so glad you agree. I just *love* it when we're on the same page like this."

Up at the top of the curving, rough-cut stone staircase, they stepped through a life-size portrait of a French royal into the parlor, where the receiving area was located.

"It's so quiet," Paradise said, stilling.

The room, like the rest of the house, was just so beautifully decorated, antiques everywhere, silks and satins on the walls and the floors, even the chairs people were to wait in covered in rich fabrics. It reminded her of articles she'd read in *Vogue* and *Vanity Fair* about Babe Paley and Slim Keith, the scale of the furnishings so perfect, the *objets d'art* little whimsies of jade and gold and brass, the colors restrained, but not weak.

"I guess Father isn't here, yet."

As if on cue, the automatic shutters rose from all the windows, the subtle whirring sound making her jump.

"I shall go attend to the kitchen," Vuchie said. "And prepare your First Meal."

As her maid walked off, Paradise nearly called the female back. But for God's sake, the *doggen* was not a security blanket.

Determined to get herself ready, even though she didn't know what she was going to be doing, she went over and sat down behind the desk and . . . played with the mouse, which got her to a password-protected screen she didn't bother trying to crack.

Wi-Fi underground was one thing. The computer here? Was going to be locked and then some.

One by one, she opened the drawers, finding nothing but stationery supplies, stationery supplies . . . and yeah, wow, more stationery stuff—

She heard the voices first. Deep. Low. Very masculine.

Then the front door opened. And there was the bass chorus of many, many heavy feet in boots crossing the threshold—

Paradise's first thought was to hide under the desk.

Members of the Black Dagger Brotherhood filed into the house, all of them dressed in black leather, each one of them armed with brutal-looking weapons.

They were bigger than she remembered from her introductions the previous night. And it wasn't like she'd filed the memory of them in the pipsqueak category, either.

". . . pump a couple of rounds off in their head," one of them said.

There was some laughter, and another added, "Or their ass. I ain't too proud."

Cue the proverbial tire squealing as they all stopped short and looked at her. Thank God she was sitting down. And the desk added a barrier of sorts between her and all that warrior.

"Hey," one of them said, the one with the Ben Affleck accent. "Your first night, huh?"

As she started to nod, her father flashed in through the open door.

"I am here, I am here!" Her dad pressed through the group. "Paradise, how fare you?"

As he came up to her, she got to her feet and hugged him hard. She could do this, she told herself. She could absolutely, positively do this.

Really.

Honest.

God, there were a lot of males in the house.

Twins. She was having *twins*.

As Layla lay in the hospital bed, she rubbed her belly with her free hand, the one that was not hanging out the end of the cast that ran up to above her right elbow. Her aches from her two falls had faded, and the bone break that Manny had taken care of was already knitted back together. The plaster or nylon or whatever it was was going to be cut off in a little bit.

Twins.

Even though she'd had all day to try to get used to the news, she was still stunned—and making things worse, she and Qhuinn hadn't really talked about it.

Or what he'd gotten so interested in when it came to those clothes she'd been wearing.

By the time he'd come back with a flannel nightie and her favorite pink robe, she'd been asleep. He'd been good enough to lay the robe over her and leave her be.

Was he mad at her? Had he guessed that she'd been lying about where her car trips had been taking her?

Goddamn, as the Brothers would say—

The knock on her door brought her head up. "Yes?"

Sure as if he'd read her mind, Qhuinn leaned his heavy upper body into the room. "Hey. I just wanted to check in with you before I left tonight. How're you feeling?"

Layla took a deep breath and tried to have nothing show in her face.

"I'm well. How are you?"

"Good."

Long pause. That got her heart beating hard.

"So, thank you for the robe." She stroked the fuzzy length. "I really appreciate it. I just woke up, but I'm going to put it on."

After a moment, he came in and eased the door shut. His

mismatched eyes went up and down her body, and for once, they were reserved.

"So how are you doing?" he said. "You know, with the twin thing."

"Fine. I mean, it's a shock ..." She shrugged. "But I'm adjusting. I'm happy. Two, what a blessing. I mean, yes."

"Good. Yeah. Uh-huh."

Silence. That was filled by him shoving his hands into the front pockets of his leathers, and her playing with the lapels of the damn robe.

As well as breaking out in a cold sweat under the hospital sheets.

"Is there anything you need to tell me?" Qhuinn asked.

The pounding in her ears was so loud, she was almost sure she answered him in a shout. "About what?"

"What you were doing last night?"

She forced herself to hold his stare. "I went for a drive."

"Why were your clothes covered with leaves?"

"I'm sorry?"

"Your clothes. Last night. When I took them upstairs, there were dirt and leaves on them. If you walked across the courtyard and fell in the vestibule, why were they like that?"

She dropped her eyes from his even though she knew that made her seem guilty. Then again, she *was* guilty.

"Layla?" He cursed softly. "Look, you're a grown female. Even though you're carrying my young, I don't have any right to know what's doing in your life except for pregnancy-related stuff. I just want to make sure you're safe. For your sake. For the young."

Shit.

Now was the time, she thought. Now ... had to be the time.

"I feel trapped," she heard herself say.

Between Xcor and the Brotherhood. Between danger and safety. Between desire and damnation.

"I kind of figured that." Qhuinn nodded. "The drives. You're going out a lot."

"I walk."

"Where?"

"Outside." In her head, she tried on a variety of come-clean confessions, swapping out nouns and verbs, trying to find a way for her to describe what she was doing without having him lose his shit all over the place. "Out . . . in the country."

Qhuinn walked across the room and straightened the already straight framed picture of a weeping willow. "People do that when they're working on something. In their head."

You got that right, she thought.

Dearest Virgin Scribe, she wanted to tell him. She really did . . . but the revelation was stuck in her throat.

For the first time, she started to get pissed off. At herself. At Xcor. At the whole goddamn thing.

"Did you trip and fall while you were walking?" he said.

"Yes." She took a deep breath. "I was stupid. I fell over a root."

So close to the truth. Just with all the salient parts left unspoken.

Man, this was killing her.

"Most females . . ." Qhuinn came over to the foot of her bed, put his hands on his lean hips and stared down at her feet. "Most females have a partner they can go through this with. I want to be that for you. So does Blay. We don't want to let you down."

Great, now she got teary that he might ever doubt how supportive he was. "You are incredible. Both of you are. You are utterly amazing. It's just . . . there's a lot going on."

At least that was not a lie.

"More now with twins." He shook his head. "Twins . . . can you believe it?"

"No." She rubbed her belly. "I don't know how they're going to fit. I already feel huge, and I have how many more months to go?"

"Listen, please know, I got you. I'm here for you, anything you need—"

As a shrill alarm started to sound next door, the two of them frowned at the same time and looked around for the source of the noise.

"Is that coming from Luchas's room?" she asked. "Oh, my God, is that . . . ?"

Shouting out in the hall. Running footsteps. Jane's voice barking out orders.

"Fuck, I gotta go see," Qhuinn said as he pivoted and lunged for the door. "I gotta go help ..."

As he bolted for his brother's room, Layla sat up. Got to her feet. Steadied herself.

Whatever was happening next door was bad news. And she was damned if Qhuinn was going to face it alone.

THIRTY-TWO

As Selena sat in the back of the giant Mercedes, the one that Fritz drove and was, in fact, driving, she was smiling so widely, her cheeks were numb and her jaw hurt.

Up ahead of the sedan, the skyscrapers of Caldwell glowed like the mythical sentries of some fantasy realm, and she leaned into her windshield, trying to see the particular one they were going to, the tallest of the giants, the pinnacle of them all.

"I can't *wait* to see what the view is like." She turned back to Trez. "I'm *so* excited."

When he didn't reply, but just kept staring at her, she smiled even harder. The male hadn't looked away from her since she'd come down the stairs, his eyes roaming, always roaming, over her lips, her breasts, her thighs and calves, back up to her hair, her face, her throat.

His arousal was straining the front of his black slacks. And even though he kept trying to put his jacket or his arm or a casual hand across his hips, she could sense his sex as clearly as if he were naked.

She leaned in, getting close. "Kiss me?"

"I don't trust myself."

"Sounds dire." Stretching up, she nipped the lobe of his ear. "Dangerous . . ."

The groan that vibrated out of his chest was the most erotic sound she'd ever heard.

"Maybe we should take care of this?" As she put her hand on his sex, he jumped and cursed. "Is that a 'yes'?"

While he braced himself against the seat and ground his hips into her hand, she glanced to the front of the car, which, due to the vehicle's size, seemed to be in another zip code. Fritz was focused on the road, his old, lined face preoccupied. Maybe they could—

Without taking those dark eyes off of her, Trez flopped his hand around his door. A split second later, there was a *whhhrrrrring* sound and an opaque partition went up, closing them off from their kind chauffeur.

"We don't have a lot of time," she said as she pushed his arm out of the way.

"Not gonna need it."

From out of a chest pocket, he pulled a white, folded handkerchief and, with a quick shake, freed it of its ironed rigor.

As she freed his erection.

She was of half a mind to lower her mouth to him, but he took her face between his bare palm and the one that was now covered with fine cloth and kissed her, his tongue shooting in deep, meeting her own.

He was hard and hot, velvety and thick, and she slid a grip around his shaft, pumping him. The more she stroked, the crazier the kiss got, until his pelvis was jerking up against her, and his chest was thrashing, and she was breathing as hard as he was.

When he orgasmed, he barked out her name and shoved the handkerchief onto himself—and she was so turned on, so giddy with the feel of his mouth on hers and the pump, pump, pump of her palm against his sex, that she felt a welling between her own thighs, an answer to what she was doing—which was so much less than what they both really wanted.

Her own release was a surprise, but she welcomed it, absorbing the sharp grabs of pleasure, making them stronger by squeezing her thighs together and rocking. Meanwhile, she continued her stroking rhythm, squeezing at his head, working his length.

When it was finally done, Trez fell back against the seat, his lids oh, so low, those lips of his parted, his head lolling to the side as if he didn't have the strength to hold the thing up.

"Was that a quickie?" she whispered as she pressed her breasts against his chest and kissed him.

Before he could answer, she ran her tongue along his lower lip, then sucked the flesh in. Easing back, she said, "Hmm? Was it?"

"Be careful, female, I'm liable to fuck you out of that dress you're wearing."

"Would that be a bad thing?"

"If any other male sees you naked, yes." He smiled and ran a fang over her lower lip. "I'm protective."

"You're still hard, too, aren't you."

With a quick grab of the back of her neck, he pulled her in tight and kissed the daylights out of her. Although she had been in control of the first part, now he took over, dominating her body, sweeping a hand between her knees and up, up, higher to her—

She orgasmed against his fingers as they sunk in deep, her core firing off round after round of pleasure.

"That's my queen," she heard him say from a vast distance. "Come for me . . ."

There was no knowing how many times he plied her with that talented touch of his, but eventually, she became aware of the car taking a fat turn that shifted her in the seat. Focusing her glazed eyes through the darkened window, she saw that they were getting off the highway, about to enter the complicated asphalt arteries that fed the countless skyscrapers.

"I ruined your lipstick," he said with satisfaction as he tidied himself up. "Did you bring more?"

Now she was the one with the case of the *huh-what's?* "Let me see if there's some in here." She fumbled with the slim black purse Marissa had given her. "Yup, they've got us covered."

As if the females had known exactly what kind of trouble she was likely to get into, there was a tiny packet of tissues, the lip liner they had taught her how to use, and the fabulous red lipstick they'd put on her.

"There's a mirror up there." Trez stretched out his long arm and popped something down from the ceiling. "And it's lighted."

She checked herself out and had to laugh. "Yup, I think you cleaned it all off."

A tissue took care of the smudging and then it was a case of carefully making a line around her mouth—while the car bumped over a road that was mostly, but not completely, even.

"Shoot," she said, going for another tissue as she ended up with a rose-colored streak headed into her nose. "Let me try—"

Trez took her hand and brought it down. As she looked over at him, his eyes, his soul-shattering, deep black eyes, seemed to be memorizing everything about her.

"You don't need it," he told her. "I like you better without it."

Selena smiled shyly. "Yes?"

"Yeah." His stare went down her body. And came back up. "This is wonderful. You look amazing. You're the most beautiful female in the city tonight, and when we get to that restaurant, waiters are going to be dropping their trays. But you need to know, my very favorite look on you?"

When he paused, she found herself having to swallow hard. "What?" she whispered.

"Your very best look, my queen, is the one you were born with. As far as I'm concerned, perfection can't be improved upon by either man nor God." Leaning in, he kissed her softly. "Just thought you'd want to know what your male's been thinking as I've been staring at you."

Selena started to smile, especially as she realized that sometimes "I love you" could be said without those particular three words lined up in a row.

"See?" she said softly. "I told you this was going to be the best night of my life."

Riding shotgun in Manny's RV ambulance, Rhage was eating Doritos out of the bag—and totally disagreeing with the doctor. "Nah, I'm not a Cool Ranch guy. Original only for me."

"You are missing out." Manny hit the directional signal to get off the highway. "I can't believe you, of all people, are so closed-minded when it comes to a snack food staple."

"But that's my point. Why improve on a gift from God?"

Tilting the bag, he looked inside and wanted to curse. He was coming to the end of the big chips, nothing but the broken parts and cosmic orange dust left. Which was not to say he wouldn't eat it all, and cap things off with a tip-up of the bottom above his gaping maw. But this was the unfun finger-dexterity part of the experience.

Munching along, he refocused on the ass of Fritz's third-world-dictator car. That Mercedes was so big, so black, and so completely tinted, it tended to get more attention as it drove by rather than less. And for shits and giggles, Rhage imagined what the humans would think if they knew there were vampires in the back.

And that the thing was being driven by a centuries-old butler with a foot that would make Jeff Gordon get a case of the jels.

"Do we turn right up here?" Rhage asked as they approached an intersection.

"That's a one-way."

"Like I said, do we turn?"

Manny looked over. "Not if we don't want to get arrested."

"We're in an ambulance."

"Yeah, but they're not."

Oh, right. Bummer. "You know, I really just want to hit the lights on this bitch."

Although the instant he said that, his rib cage shrunk around his lungs, and he ended up having to put the window down a little so he could get some air.

"Did you just leave nacho all over my door."

Rhage rubbed the bright orange spot away with his forearm. "Nope."

They kept to Fritz's bumper tight as a stamp on an envelope, turning left, heading away from the river, going right so they were in the heart of the financial district. No dirty alleys. No Dumpsters. No slush even during the wet months. And no nasty smells from the rotting remains of cheap restaurants.

This was the fancy part of town, where people wore suits and rushed around, channeled like cattle in chutes to their places of Urgent, Important Work.

The skyscraper that housed the restaurant they were gunning for had been completed only a couple of years before, its developers touting the enormous vertical rise as the tallest building in Caldwell. Jam-packed with the headquarters of big businesses, to him, it was nothing more than a filing cabinet for humans, each of them locked into their little slots.

Snooze.

"You okay?"

Rhage looked over at the doc. "Huh?"

"What's wrong."

"Nothing."

"Then why have you stopped eating. Bag's not empty."

Rhage glanced down. Sure enough, he'd left the detritus where it was—and he didn't have any impulse to finish. "Ahhh . . ."

"Watching your weight?"

"Yeah. That's it."

As he crushed the bag, he left orange prints all over the labels and marketing, until the thing looked like it had bruised that color from the rough handling.

Then he was stuck orange-handed. "Shit. I don't have anything to wipe off with."

"Are you kidding me?" Manny tossed a gauze roll at him. "We could do a buff and shine on half this city with what I got in here."

Rhage unraveled and cleaned up, then crammed everything into the wastepaper basket that was bolted to the floor between the bucket seats.

Manny slowed down as they came up to the glass building, and then he parked on the opposite side of the street as Fritz stopped completely at the flashy entrance, the taillights of the Merc glowing red.

A moment later, Trez got out and went around behind the sedan, the stiff wind catching his jacket before he did the buttons up, flashing the twin forties he had holstered under both of his arms.

With a gallant move, he opened the door for his female, and Selena emerged from the back, her incredible hair sweeping away from her body, a dark flag that teased this way and that.

"Good-looking couple," Manny said quietly.

"She doesn't even seem sick."

"I know."

Trez tucked her arm into his and escorted her up the gray granite steps, and as another couple came out of the revolving doors, both of the humans stopped and stared.

"Manny."

"Yeah?"

"You gotta do something, my man. You just have to figure this shit out for them."

Manny hit the gas and the souped-up RV's engine revved, taking them onward so they could go around the block to the back.

"You hear me?" Rhage demanded.

"Yeah, I did." Manny took a deep breath. "You know what the hardest thing to learn about medicine is?"

"Biochem."

"No."

"Human anatomy. 'Cuz it's gross."

The blinker made a *nuk-nuk-nuk* sound as the good doctor announced to the world, or at least this street, that they were taking another left around the skyscraper's footprint.

"It's that there are situations where there's nothing you can do."

Rhage rubbed his eyes. Something out of his subconscious was coming back to him, something he didn't want.

"Rhage?"

"Huh?"

"You made a funny noise there."

As Manny came up to the service bays, he pulled a neat little driver's-ed-style K-turn so that he was able to back that ass right against the building. Shutting things down, he turned in his seat.

"You sure you're all right?"

"Oh. Yeah. Uh-huh."

"You don't look right. And check out what I'm wearing. Scrubs. You know what that means."

"That you like having your pj's on all night?"

"That I'm a doctor and I know what I'm talking about."

"Don't get paranoid, big guy."

There was a heartbeat or twelve of silence. Then Manny said, "There is nothing I won't do to keep her with him. Nothing."

Now Rhage was the one pulling the pivot. "That's what I needed to hear, Doc."

"Just don't put your faith in miracles, Hollywood. That's a dangerous bet."

"It happened for me and Mary. When we needed one, we got one."

Manny stared out the front windshield—and didn't appear to see anything of the darkened street ahead. "I'm not God. And neither is Doc Jane."

Rhage resettled in his seat. "You need to have hope. They just have to have hope."

THIRTY-THREE

As the prison cell's door panel slid back into the wall, iAm wheeled around. But it still wasn't s'Ex. And it wasn't another bedding platform. And it wasn't more books he would not read or blankets he would not use or pillows he could give a rat's ass about.

It was that maid with another meal.

"Oh, come on," he spat, throwing up his hands. "Where the fuck is s'Ex!"

The female said nothing; she simply walked forward with that tray of hers as the door slid back into place, locking them in together.

As she lowered herself to her knees, he wanted to scream. So he did.

"I'm not fucking eating that! Jesus Christ, what is wrong with you people!"

The only thing that stopped him from marching over, picking up that frickin' food, and slinging it across the room was the fact that it wasn't the *maichen*'s fault. s'Ex blowing him off had nothing to do with her, and terrorizing the damn maid wasn't going to get him any closer to freedom and returning to Trez.

She was an innocent third party caught up in this bullshit just like he was.

Exhaling in a burst, he hung his head. It took him a couple of heartbeats before he was under any semblance of control. "I'm sorry."

At that, her head jerked up to level, and for a moment,

especially as that scent of hers reached him, he wished he could see her eyes.

What shape were they? What did her lashes look like? Were the irises as dark as his—

Why the fuck was he thinking like this?

Breaking off from her, he started walking around. "I gotta get out of here. Time is running out."

As her head tilted to the side in inquiry, he thought, no. Not gonna go there.

He nodded down at the tray. "If you want to leave the food, I'll flush it down the toilet so that you don't get in trouble for not feeding me."

And that was when she spoke: "It is not poisoned."

For absolutely no good reason, those four run-of-the-mill words stopped him dead. Her voice was deeper than he had expected; all her subservience seemed better paired with some high-octave, super-feminine tone. And there was a husky undertone . . . which made him think about sex.

Raw sex. The kind that left females hoarse from calling out the name of their lover.

iAm blinked.

All at once, he had the urge to cover his naked body. Which was kind of bullshit, wasn't it. He'd known she was a female all along and it wasn't like he'd ever had any clothes on in front of her.

Giving in to the impulse, he went over behind the screen, to the stack of towels that had been placed by the inset tub. As he wrapped one around his hips, he felt like apologizing for ever having aired his junk at all.

When he came back around, she was sampling the soup and the bread again.

"You can stop," he said. "I'm not going to eat."

"Why?"

Again, with that voice. Even on only one word this time.

"I gotta get out of here," he muttered. For a whole fucking lot of reasons. "I have to get out."

"Does something await you?"

He thought of Trez and Selena. "Just death. You know, no big fucking deal or anything."

"I beg your pardon?"

"Look, I gotta talk to s'Ex. That's what I need to do. Did you tell him?"

Although it wasn't as if she had any pull.

"Who is dying?"

"Nothing. No one. Nobody—"

"Who is passing? Not your brother?"

"Look, I need you to go. And not come back unless you're bringing s'Ex with you."

"Who."

Annnnnd he stopped again. Maids were never imperious, but that was what she sounded like. Then again, his emotions were running so goddamn high, he was capable of reading into just about anything right now—and jumping to the wrong conclusion.

"I came back here for help, okay." He threw up his hands. "s'Ex told me he would get me into the palace so I could look through the healers' texts."

"For whom?"

"My brother's mate."

The maid's head came up sharply. "He is to mate the Princess here, though, no? I heard that he is the Anointed One."

"He fell in love." iAm shrugged. "It happens. Or so I've heard."

"And she is the one who is dying?"

"She's not doing well."

As he resumed his prowling, he could feel the eyes behind that mesh track him. "So that's why I need to get out. My brother needs my help."

"He is in mourning. The executioner."

iAm glanced over, and then resumed stalking the cell. "Yeah. I know, but he had enough free rein to meet me on the outside. Shorter trip now that I'm in the palace itself."

"But that is the issue. He left and no one knew where he had gone. The palace wanted him to participate. The palace . . . insisted that he attend to the Queen. He is with her now."

Just his luck. "There are breaks in the rituals, though, aren't there? Can you catch him then?"

"Well . . . maybe I can take you to the texts?"

iAm cranked his head around slowly. "What did you say?"

Longest. Elevator. Ride. Of. His. Life.

As Trez stood next to Selena in a glass-walled torture

chamber, he was resolutely facing the closed doors—and praying for some kind of Dr. Who time warp thingy that had him stepping out of the goddamn thing rightfuckingnow.

Eyeballs locked on the glowing line of numbers above the chrome doors, he wanted to vomit.

L . . . 44, 45, 46, 47, 48, 49, 50.

"44" had yet to light up because they were in the screaming-fast, liver-in-your-loafer, express part of the joy-ride.

"Oh, you should look out here," Selena said, pivoting toward the all-access pass to vertigo. "This is so much fun!"

A quick glance over his shoulder and he nearly hurled. His beautiful queen had not just gone over to the glass, but put her palms on it and leaned into the ever-higher view.

Trez snapped back around. "Almost there. We're almost at the top."

"Can we go down and come up again? I wonder what the descent is like!"

Actually, maybe they should head back to the lobby. He was fairly sure he'd left his manhood there when this rocket ride had ignited.

"Trez!" Tap, tap, tap on his forearm. "Look at this."

"Oh, yeah, it's incredible. Yeah. Abso."

They were never getting to the four hundred and forty-fourth floor. Much less level fifteen thousand gabillion where the cocksucking restaurant was.

McDonald's, he thought. Why couldn't she have wanted Mickey D's. Or Pizza Hut. Taco Hell—

Beep!

At the sound, he braced himself for a *Die Hard* moment where some mastermind in a bespoke English suit blew up the rooftop.

Nope. *Beep!* Forty-five. *Beep!* Forty-six.

And more good news came as the bum rush to the heavens slowed.

"Trez?"

"Mmm?"

"Is there something wrong?"

"Just really psyched for dinner. Oh, my God, I can't *wait* to get there."

She tucked her arm through his and leaned her head against his triceps. "You really know how to treat a female."

Damn right he did. For example, he was very clear that it would be considered highly unromantic to go fetal and suck your thumb because you were nut-less when it came to heights.

Bing! And the doors opened.

Thank you, baby Jesus, to use a Butch phrase.

Now, he told himself, get your shit together, you sack-less wonder, and focus on your female.

Flashing his queen a Cary Grant plus fangs, he escorted Selena off the deathtrap and into a black marble lobby that for a split second took him back to his nightmare at the s'Hisbe: so much glossy black stone on the floors, walls, and ceiling, with lights inset up high—and nothing else.

"Trez?"

Shaking himself, he smiled down at her. "You ready for this?"

"Oh, yes."

A discreet black-on-black sign with an arrow indicated the way to the restaurant, but his keen senses of hearing and smell had already given him that information, thanks. As they started off, a human couple steamed toward them, the female's high heels like the F-word being used with every step she took.

". . . no reservation?" she hissed. "How could you not get us a reservation?"

The man next to her was staring straight ahead. Like you would if you were stuck next to a three-year-old on a bus.

"I can't believe you didn't get us a reservation. And we had to walk out like that. In front of all the other . . ."

As she continued to marching-band it to that theme song, the man's eyes locked on Selena—and the poor bastard recoiled in awe as if a living angel had appeared in front of him.

After Trez pointed out to his inner bonded male that an appropriate entrée didn't include Filet o'Fucktard, he realized that he, too, had failed to call ahead and lock down a time for a two-top. *Shit*. He'd totally forgotten to ask Fritz to make the damn call. And mind control worked on humans, including snotty *maître d's*, but what it couldn't fix was rank unavailability of empty seats.

Ahh . . .

"You know, I've heard the food isn't all that," he said numbly.

"That's okay. I'm really here for the view."

The entrance to Circle the World was not marked with any signage, like if you needed to ask, you didn't need to be there. All there was was a pair of smoky glass doors as wide and tall as a one-story house.

Getting a jump on the black handles, he pulled one half open and let Selena go ahead.

Total restraint.

That was the first impression of the place: Glossy black everywhere, from the tables and the geometric chairs to the square supports that held the ceiling up overhead. No flowers. No candles. Nothing fussy. And the dark night beyond all those windows? Black as well, so that it looked as if there was no divide between the sky and interior.

The only touch of whimsy? The curling LED lights that hung from that lofty ceiling on black wires, their twinkling illumination reflecting off of all the high-gloss.

Oh, and there was a soprano singing over in the corner, her dulcet voice piped in throughout the place.

"I've never seen anything like this," Selena whispered. "It's like there are stars everywhere."

He looked around. "Yeah."

Okay, where was the gent in the penguin suit who was in charge of turning people with good money away? There was no *maître d'* stand. Just thirty feet of black carpet that led to the first lineup of minimalist tables.

"They're looking at us."

On the whispered words, he frowned and focused on the diners. Well, what do you know. Every one of the humans at the tables seemed to have stopped eating and was looking in their direction—

From out of nowhere, a woman rushed over. Like the decor, she was all in black, and even her hair was a cap of stick-straight high-gloss.

"How do you do," she said with a broad smile. "Welcome to Circle the World."

And we will now self-destruct in three . . . two . . . "Yeah, I didn't call ahead—"

"Oh, Mr. Latimer, yes, you did. Your representative, Mr.

Perlmutter, let us know you would be gracing us with your presence. We are so pleased to accommodate you at the windows."

Fuuuuuck.

Thank you, thank you, Fritz, butler lifeboat supreme — who had clearly overheard something.

As his queen beamed, the woman indicated the way across the open room — and as they followed her, Trez realized that they had stepped onto a vast, slowly revolving plate: The entire restaurant moved around the center core of the elevator shaft and what must have been the kitchen space.

They went right to the edge. To a table for two that had one of its generous four sides directly against the glass.

Under which the entire city of Caldwell stretched out, about four hundred thousand feet below.

Time to sit, he thought, praying his sudden case of the wonks didn't wipe out his knees before he did his queen proper.

Helping Selena into her seat, he kept his eyes averted as he went over and fell down into a seat that was hard as rock.

The *maître d'* cast her pale hand over the table to the godforsaken windows. "This will be the spice to the courses of your meal."

No, that would be nausea, sweetheart.

She turned back to the rest of the place. "The interior is designed to be the night, the perfect background for savoring what the chef will provide for your pleasure."

When they were alone, Selena shifted herself toward the windows. "It's . . . incredible. The lights of the buildings. They're like fallen stars."

Trez wiped his sweaty palms on his napkin. Bracing himself, he glanced over and found that — well, yes, it was as bad as he had thought. Peering out the utterly clean glass, it was as if nothing separated him from a fall to the death, the lack of a ledge turning even a split second of eye contact into a terrifying swoop into the abyss.

Time to put the napkin to the brow.

"Trez?" She looked over at him. "Are you all right?"

Pulling it together, he reached out and took her hand.

"Have I told you how beautiful these are?" he murmured.

Her smile was radiant. "Yes, but I never get tired of hearing it."

"So beautiful." He smoothed his palm over hers. Then bent in and pressed a kiss to her skin. "Long and lovely. Strong, too."

When he finally looked up, it was into her eyes, and that was when things got better. One single heartbeat later, and he wasn't worried about his terror of heights, and he wasn't thinking about the humans around him, and he couldn't have given a shit that the twinkling view was subtly circling below them.

With her hand in his and that beautiful face of hers staring across at him, he was transported away from it all.

"I love you," he said, rubbing his thumb on the inside of her wrist. "No one could do this to me."

"Do what?"

"Make me forget all my fear."

She flushed. "I didn't want to bring it up, but why didn't you tell me you don't like heights? I thought you were going to jump out of your skin in just the elevator. We could have gone somewhere else."

"This was where you wanted to go. And like I wouldn't suck it up for you?"

"I want us to both enjoy tonight."

He lowered his lids. "I had fun in the car. Already looking forward to the trip home."

As her scent flared, she let out something that sounded like a purr.

Later, much later, he would remember this moment between them . . . the way it seemed to last forever, stretching into the divine infinite. All of the details would stay with him, too, from the sparkle in her eyes to the shine of her hair, from the way she smiled at him to the flush on her cheeks.

Memories were especially dear, when they were all you had left of a loved one to hold on to.

THIRTY-FOUR

"**W**hat's happening! What is . . . what's that alarm mean?"

Layla was right behind Qhuinn as he burst into his brother's hospital room and started talking. Over his shoulder, she saw Doc Jane standing by the bed, and Luchas down flat, his johnny ripped down to his waist, the covers shoved off his prone body, the pillows scattered on the floor.

Some piece of medical equipment had been rolled over and Ehlena was initiating something on its computer as Doc Jane grabbed a pair of handles that were connected by curlicue cords.

"Clear!" she barked, and then put metal paddles directly on Luchas's chest.

There was a juicing sound, and then a mini-explosion on the bed, his torso jerking upward.

And still the alarm sounded, a single note that was a mechanical kind of scream.

"Luchas!" Qhuinn yelled. "Luchas!"

Something told Layla to hold him back, and she wrapped her arms around his broad torso, pressing her belly into him. "Stay here," she said in a voice that croaked. "Let them do . . ."

"Clear!" Doc Jane called out.

The bed shook while Luchas's torso seized again, and as he flopped back down, Layla's own heart thundered. She couldn't believe she was seeing this once more. Yesterday, it was Selena, now it was—

Beep. Beep. Beep—

"I have a heartbeat." Doc Jane ditched what had been in her hands, throwing the paddles at the machine. "I need you to . . ."

Ehlena responded to the commands as fast as the physician gave them, providing medicine-filled syringes one after another before slipping an oxygen mask over Luchas's face and adjusting even more equipment.

About ten minutes—or it could have been ten hours—later, Doc Jane came over. "I need to speak with you." She nodded toward the hall beyond. "Out here, please."

As they all stepped from the room, Doc Jane rushed the door shut, even though it was trying to close on its own. "Qhuinn, I don't have time to sugarcoat this. I've barely got his blood pressure and heart rate stabilized, and he's not going to stay this way. If he's going to survive, I need to take that lower leg, and it's going to have to be now. The infection is killing him and that's the source of the problems. Hell, even if I do amputate below the knee, it may be too late. But if you want to give him a chance, that's what I've got to do."

Qhuinn didn't blink. Didn't curse. Didn't argue. "All right. Take the goddamn thing."

Layla closed her eyes and put her hand to the base of her throat.

"Okay. I want you to stay out here. You don't need to see this." As Qhuinn opened his mouth, the doctor cut him right off. "No. Not an option. If it comes to it, I'll let you say good-bye. Stay out here."

This time the door closed on its own, easing back into place.

Closing her eyes briefly, Layla could not imagine what they were doing in there. There had been plenty of surgical equipment with them, though—as if Doc Jane had been prepared for this.

And given Qhuinn's quick response, so had he.

"He's going to kill me," he said roughly. "If he survives."

"You don't have a choice."

"I could let him die."

"Could your conscience handle that?"

"No."

"So there's no choice." She put her palms to her face and

tried to get the image of Luchas on that bed out of her head. "God, how has it come to this?"

"Maybe I should tell her to stop it."

"And then what?"

"I don't know. I don't fucking know."

They were out in the hall forever, and Layla tried not to hear the sounds from the other side of that door, especially when there was a subtle *whrrrrring* that seemed really close to a miniature chainsaw firing up. Whereas she stayed still, Qhuinn paced back and forth, his head down, eyes on his boots, hands on his hips. After a while, he stopped and looked at her.

"Thank you. You know, for not leaving me here alone."

Stepping up to him, she held her arms wide and he came to her, leaning down, putting his head on her shoulder. As they waited together, she held him because that was all she could do.

It didn't feel like enough.

Approximately ten blocks over and fifty floors down from Circle the World, Xcor was standing flush against a sweaty brick wall.

The *lesser* he and Balthazar had been tracking was behind and to the left of where they stood, the stench of its body floating down on a breeze that carried a sting of industrial grit and grime along with it.

His body was itching for a fight, everything that had happened with Layla the night before making his inner demons ride him until he had been so nasty, all of his soldiers had left him underground alone during the daylight hours.

Better to face the risk of sunshine than deal with his mood.

At least he had a good killing to look forward to.

On his signal, Balthazar ghosted over the damp pavement, becoming one with the shadow of the building across the way. There was a clear night sky overhead, but the added moonlight was a largely irrelevant complication. Caldwell's downtown had enough ambient illumination that he could have read a novel even here in this narrow alley.

Assuming he were magically literate.

Staying in the shadows was not only part of the vampire myth, but a very prudent reality for them all.

With a practiced movement, he withdrew his scythe from its holster, freeing the weapon from the strap that ran across his back. Balthazar, on the other hand, preferred the more conventional double-dagger armaments, the pale blades flashing as he sank down on his thighs.

Footfalls came at them. Fast, multiple, but not at a run.

Two human males, hands in pockets, feet moving quickly, came down the alley. They paid no attention as they passed, and that probably saved their worthless little lives.

And then it was a waiting game.

A single set of footfalls now, at a much slower speed. Accompanied by the stench that preceded the undead.

As the *lesser* came into view, rounding a corner and hitting their straightaway, he, too, was paying no attention to them. He had cash in his hands, the sum of which he appeared to be obsessed with, counting, recounting, as he went by.

Xcor stepped out in his wake. "How much did you get for blowing them?"

The *lesser* wheeled around, shoving the money away into a baggy coat. Before it could respond, Balthazar sprang from his position, leaping high into the air and landing dagger-first. The slayer screamed as those blades penetrated his shoulder and throat, proving that though soulless and heartless, the bastards had central nervous systems that registered pain quite efficiently.

And that was when the bullets started flying.

Xcor was twisting around, prepared to swing his beloved scythe wide as soon as Balthazar rolled himself free, when a telltale popping sound echoed down at him. And then another.

And then a fury of them.

The discharging was too quick for even autoloaders.

The first hit he took was in the shoulder. Second was in the thigh. Third grazed his ear, leaving a burning that felt as if he had a bright red car blinker up there.

Balthazar was hit as well.

They had no choice but to run and pray. Was it humans? Unlikely, but not unheard-of. It could not be slayers; they were so pitifully armed, the heaviest firepower any of them brought into the alleys were nine-millimeters, and very few at that.

A quick dodge to the right and he and Balthazar were in a narrower lane, temporarily out of the onslaught. That would change as soon as the shooter or shooters got to the corner they had wheeled off around.

"Left!" Balthazar barked.

Sure enough, there was another opportunity in the maze of streets to pare off, and they ghosted down the next alley, ironically running past the pair of humans who had sauntered by previously. The two men were likewise going as fast as they could, having clearly heard the racket. Their speed was much slower, however.

So, as the machine gun came around the corner, they provided some vital cover.

Screams, deep throated and terror-filled, exploded as the next round of fire came down at them, the humans taking the brunt of the impacts.

"Left!" Xcor said, leaning into the turn.

His thigh was going numb, but he didn't waste time glancing down to measure any damage. That would come later, assuming he survived.

Another bullet came close, the sound as it whistled by his ear loud enough to overpower even his sawing breath and thunderous boots.

Balthazar was right beside him, that big body going at a dead run.

More discharges pinged off of a Dumpster as they passed it. Off the brick wall. Off the pavement. From time to time there were pauses, as if the gun or guns were being reloaded—or mayhap there were a pair of them working together, one handing off the ammo as the other shot.

Keep going. It was all they could do.

None of the alleys they were coming upon offered anywhere meaningful to hide; in fact, there were not even doors to break through.

It was strictly a question of outrunning the number of rounds the shooters had brought with them. Assuming he and his fighter didn't get gunned down first.

As the next rounds came at them, he knew without looking over his shoulder that it had to be the enemy and not humans in pursuit.

Only slayers could run this fast, this far . . . and appear to have energy stores sufficient to keep going.

It was possible, he noted in the back of his mind, that he and his soldier might be in trouble.

THIRTY-FIVE

"The check has been taken care of."

Trez paused in the process of taking his wallet out. "Excuse me?"

"It's been taken care of." The waiter smiled and bowed. "It has been our pleasure to serve you."

Jesus, if he hadn't known the guy was human, he'd have assumed one of Fritz's staff had followed them here. The service had been phenomenal all night.

"Enjoy your cappuccinos at your leisure."

Trez looked across at Selena. Her eyes were on the view again, but she was not smiling. Her perfect profile was cast in grave lines.

Reaching over, he took her hand in his, a spike of fear going through his chest. "You all right?"

Surreptitiously, he ducked into his coat and palmed up his cell phone.

"Oh, yes." Except she didn't look at him.

The soft patter of conversation around them dimmed down and the striding movements of the waiters disappeared from his periphery.

"Selena, what's going on?"

"I don't want it to be over."

"We can come here again."

"Yes." She squeezed his hand. "Of course."

As the restaurant continued to turn, turn, turn, the Commodore's flank came around into view again, the building's tall expanse speckled with random lights—including some in the penthouse.

Guess Rehv was in res.

Trez looked down at the coffee cup he hadn't touched. The steam rising up was spiced with cinnamon, which he'd never been a fan of. He'd ordered it only because his queen didn't seem to want to leave.

"It was so nice of them," she murmured. "To pay for dinner."

"I'ma take care of that when I get home."

"You should let them be kind."

Trez searched what he could see of her body, looking for signs that she was having problems that would require a quick call downstairs to Manny and Rhage.

"Selena?"

She shook herself and glanced over. "I'm sorry?"

"You want to order another dessert?"

"No." She gave his hand another squeeze before releasing her hold and folding her napkin and placing it on the table. "Shall we?"

He popped out of his chair to help her so fast, the four feet squeaked over the glossy floor. "Here, let me—"

But his queen rose to a stand on her own with an elegant shift, her body perfectly stable, perfectly at ease. At least physically, that was. He could sense the weight of her mood.

Escorting her out, he was aware of the eyes of the room on them once again, hushed comments being uttered behind the rims of wineglasses and the squares of napkins as the humans tried to place them upon the grid of celebrity. There was satisfaction to be had in the fact that the peanut gallery would never be able to.

At the great glass doors, he opened one of the panels for her, and as she stepped through, she paused and stared over her shoulder, as if she were worried she would forget some nuance of the way the place looked or smelled or sounded.

"We can always come back," he repeated.

"Oh, yes."

She flashed a smile at him and continued out into that minimalist open space where the elevators were. Going ahead, he hit the down button and then stood next to her, putting his hand on the small of her back.

"So where do you want to go next?" he asked.

"You mean tonight? I'm rather tired—"

"No. Tomorrow night."

She glanced over at him. "I . . ."

"Come on. Give me the next destination so I can get things ready for sundown tomorrow."

The elevator doors opened, and he urged her inside— and he was so focused on her, he barely noticed that hideous glass wall that was open to the lobby. Pressing the L button, he stroked Selena's shoulder.

"So . . . ?" When she didn't reply, he leaned in and kissed the side of her throat. "This is not the only night we're going to have."

"How do you know that." She met his eyes. "I don't want to ruin this, but how do you know?"

"Because I won't have it any other way."

Turning her to face him, he deliberately put his hips against her body and dropped his lips to hers. "Unless you're sick of me. Or seriously unimpressed by my being a vertical pussy."

Her eyes seemed very blue and very scared as they met his. "Boat."

He'd expected something else. "I'm sorry?"

"I, ah, I want to go on a boat ride on the river."

"Fast or slow?"

"Both?"

"You got it."

"Just like that?" she whispered. "Can you make everything happen?"

He put his mouth to her ear and whispered, "Come back to my room and I'll show you just how talented I am."

As her scent changed, he nuzzled her, kissing her neck, nipping over her vein. He wasn't playing fair, of course. He knew that she was likely to get distracted, and he wanted her to be. In fact, he couldn't guarantee her tomorrow night or even the coming dawn, but like forever memories, the illusion of them having all that time had to stand in for whatever fate had waiting for them.

Kissing her, holding her, feeling her body against his own, he discreetly took out his phone and brought it up behind her back. The text to Manny and Rhage was short and to the point: *Owh tx.*

On way home. Thank you.

The elevator reached the lobby just fine, and all the kissing helped him stay good and distracted, too. And then they were walking out of the building, into the cold, blustery fall night. Fritz was across the street in the Mercedes, and the *doggen* brought the car over the second he saw them.

There was no waiting for the butler to get out and do the duty with the door.

Trez wanted to be the one to wait on her.

Just as she was sliding into the warm interior, the last sound he ever wanted to hear when she was in his presence caught his attention:

Pop-pop-pop.

Gunfire.

Fuck.

Trez jumped into the sedan with her, and jacked up between the seats. "Get us out of here! U-ie now!"

Fritz didn't miss a beat. Throwing the S600 into reverse, he pounded the gas so hard Trez nearly ended up playing air freshener on the rearview. Recovering fast, he covered Selena with his body—so he could get to her seat belt. Yanking the band across her, he'd just gotten the catch home when centrifugal force threw him against the opposite side of the backseat, ringing his bell—but he didn't give a shit. Bracing his feet against the wheel wells and his palms against the roof and the door frame, he kept himself from battering Selena as they finished the spin that got them pointed in the right direction.

Make that the wrong way on the one-way they'd come in on.

"Let us proceed," Fritz shouted over the squealing tires.

The roar of the Mercedes-Benz engine and the explosion forward reminded Trez of an airplane takeoff. And as his body was sucked into the bucket seat, he looked over at Selena.

Her eyes were popping wide. "What's wrong? What happened?"

The buildings on either side of the three-lane road were steel and glass and pale concrete, and they started to flash by, faster, faster, faster. Glancing up in the front, Trez checked the road ahead, the grilles of the parked cars facing them like disapproving parents as they went in the wrong direction.

"Nothing's up!" he yelled over all the noise. "I'm just really excited to get you naked—"

Selena's brows rose even higher. "Trez, I heard something—"

"—'cuz I'm that desperate to have you!"

"—that sounded like a gun!"

They were both hollering over the engine, going back and forth as Fritz bat-out-of-hell'd it away from all the bullets.

And then the fun really began.

They'd gone about two blocks when the Caldwell police cars started showing up. And unlike the Benz? The blue-and-whites with their flashing lights were going the right way on the street.

"I shall have to go onto the sidewalk," Fritz called out. "Just a bit of a bump—"

That crazy bitch-ass butler yanked the steering wheel to the left and hopped the curb, capping a fire hydrant that promptly exploded in their wake, sending a gusher of water up into the air. And then, by the grace of God, the Benz landed like a gentleman, its superior shock absorbers cushioning what was no doubt a slam and a half.

Wrenching around, Trez looked out the back windshield. Cop cars were spinning around and breaking rank to follow them as Fritz hit a wall of newspaper dispensers, sending the red and yellow and green plastic boxes flying behind them. The flimsy things broke apart as they crashed on the sidewalk, sheets of papers fluttering off like doves released from cages.

As he turned back to Selena, he braced himself, trying to think of a way to reassure her—

Au contraire.

Selena was alive with excitement, her fangs flashing thanks to a huge smile, a giggling laugh bubbling out of her as she hung on to the door.

"Faster!" she yelled at Fritz. "Let's go even faster!"

"As you wish, mistress!"

A fresh roar from that massive piece of German engineering under the hood sent them careening not just down the sidewalk, but right up to the very edge of the laws of physics.

Selena looked over at him. "This is the best night ever!"

*   *   *

"Okay, time to pull out."

Rhage nodded at Manny. "I wonder what they had for dinner." He checked his phone again and wished he had actually gone to that steakhouse. He'd only flown that shit to put Trez at ease. "He said nothing about the entrée or dessert. I mean, come on, he could have given a few deets. We only got eight letters from the guy."

"Actually, it was five."

"That's what I said."

The Doritos had worn off an hour ago. Then again, sometimes he could say that about three-course meals.

Manny put the RV in drive and started off, the ambulance trundling over a pothole, then gathering speed. "I'd better get a move on. Fritz has a heavy foot."

"Like, did they have the roast beef? I saw a picture of the way they do it up there in a magazine—"

Boom!

Just as they came to a four-way juncture of alleys, something big flashed out in front of them and bounced off the hood. As Manny slammed on the brakes, the massive weight rolled off.

"Jesus Christ, was that a deer?" the doctor hollered.

"Try moose."

Rhage palmed both his guns and was about to jump out when the bullet shower started. High-pitched metallic pings ricocheted off the RV and spiderwebbed the thick glass.

"Oh, for fuck's sake," Manny bit out. Then he screamed through the windshield to the shooters, "I just got this thing!"

Rhage went for the door handle, but got nowhere with it. "Let me out!"

Ping-ping-ping. "No way, you'll get killed!"

"We're sitting ducks!"

"No, we're not!"

All at once, the RV settled about four inches and metal plating dropped down over every square inch of glass there was. Instantly, the sound of the gunfire was dulled to a distant snare drum.

Rhage glanced over in the relative silence. "You are a genius."

"Harold Ramis is."

"I'm sorry?"

"You ever see *Stripes*? My favorite movie of all time. I based this thing on Bill Murray's ride."

"I knew I liked you." Rhage quickly glanced at his phone. No Brothers were in the vicinity, and that was a good thing given the firepower. "Only one problem—we can't just sit here. The human police are going to be all over—"

An LED screen the size of a TV rose vertically from the dash, taking up most of the now-blocked windshield space. And on its flat surface was a green pictorial of the street-scape in HD—so they got a really good picture of the shooters as the pair of trigger-fingers ran into their head-lights. The two were both sporting long-nosed guns, AKs in his opinion, each discharge causing a bright flash from the muzzles as they kept those rounds pumping.

They didn't pause as they went by Manny's vehicle.

"Those are *lessers*," Rhage muttered. "They're going too fast for humans. Plus only slayers would be dumb enough to make this kind of racket. Let me the fuck out of here."

"You're not going after them—"

Rhage reached over and grabbed the front of the man's shirt, dragging him into the aisle between the seats. "Let. Me. Out."

Manny met his eyes. Cursed. "You're going to get your-self killed."

"No. I won't."

"How can you be so sure?"

"I got fun and games no one can handle." He nodded to the window. "Crack it and I can ghost out through the slats between your armed plates. Unless you have steel mesh in there somewhere."

Manny started muttering all kinds of vile things as he went for the requisite button and Rhage's little slice of see-through went down about two inches.

"As soon as I'm gone, hit the gas," Rhage demanded. "We need you on Trez's tail. No joke."

Closing his eyes, he concentrated and . . .

. . . dematerialized out of the interior, re-forming beside the RV and then pounding on the door. The shooters had gone past them, tracking their prey, which put him in a per-fect position. As the engine under all that metal plating revved up, and Manny's little portable clinic rambled off, he started to run. The scent in the air told him he'd been right; this was a pair of slayers with a very expensive set of toys— something they hadn't seen in how long?

Not since Lash, that bastard, had been *Forelesser*.

Thighs pumping, guns ready, he was closing the distance when the sirens came behind him. Suddenly, he was spotlit from the rear, and not in a good way. With two autoloaders in his palms, they were liable to think he was the goddamn problem, instead of the solution trying to catch up with his enemy.

Sure enough, a male voice projected out of a high-res speaker came down the alley. "CPD! Stop! Stop or we'll shoot!"

God. Damn. It.

Humans: Nature's remedy for an otherwise good time.

THIRTY-SIX

Back in his cell at the palace, iAm was busy wearing a track in the polished marble floor, going back and forth between that new bedding platform and the shelf of books.

The longer he was left by his little lonesome, the more he became convinced that the *maichen* had made the offer to get him to the healing texts out of an abundance of impotent compassion. But, hell, even if she had been serious and did show up again with some kind of plan, it wasn't like he was going to accept her help. There were so many people sucked into this mess already, and he wasn't sure she knew what she was volunteering for: He was a prisoner of the executioner's, which meant even though many could have access to him, there was only one son of a bitch who had the keys to his escape.

And it was not that lowly female.

If she did spring him? Even if it was not to the great outdoors, but the library? The monitoring systems would surely report them both—and then sudden death would be the best outcome she could hope for.

What was more likely was a long, suffering period of torture during which she would pray to be—

As that panel slid open, he made sure his sex was covered and wheeled around.

It was the maid, and she had bolts of cloth in her hands. As the door slid back into place, she tucked something next to the jamb to prevent it from closing all the way and rushed over to him.

"Put this on. We have no time—"

"Wait, what—"

"Put it on! The security staff is changing shift and they are required to have a mandatory prayer of sorrow and remembrance for the infant. We have to get you down the hallways now—"

"I can't let you do this—"

"You want help, right. For your brother's love, right."

iAm gritted his teeth. Rock, meet hard place. "Fuck!"

"I do not know what that means."

He grabbed whatever it was out of her hands, but kept up the arguing as he threw the folds over himself. "What about the trip back?"

"I'll create a diversion. You're going to need some time in the library—unless you know exactly what you're looking for?"

The heavy robing rushed down his legs. "What about in here?"

Without warning, the lights went out. "I activated the circadian system."

Ah, yes, the alternation of light and dark without which you couldn't sleep.

Click!

A tiny flashlight showed her the way to the bedding platform, and she quickly arranged the pillows and duvets such that it appeared there was someone in there. Then she ran back and put something up to his face.

Spritz!

He coughed as the heavy scent of lavender and something citrus-y shot into his nose. "What the hell—"

More with the spritzing. "That's a maid's uniform. No one will question if they happen upon the pair of us together, but your scent is too male. This should cover it up well enough for us to get by. Now crouch down—you're too tall for the robe. We can't have your feet showing or they'll know. Come *on*."

He followed her over to the panel, but before she could open things up, he grabbed her arm and spun her around. "You shouldn't be doing this."

"We don't have time—"

"It's going to get you killed."

"Your brother needs help. For his mate. Do you have another solution for getting out of here to see those texts?"

When she went to turn away, he pulled her back. "What's your name?"

"*maichen*."

"No, that's your station. What's your name?"

"That's it. Now, come—enough talk," she said urgently. "And don't forget to crouch."

Just like that, he was out of the cell and into the hallway. As he looked left and right, she jabbed him in the side with her elbow.

"Crouch," she hissed. "This way."

Bending his knees, he hunched his shoulders and followed in her wake, trying to mimic her spare movements. She was fast and decisive through the corridors, taking lefts and rights in a sequence that rendered him so turned around he was lost in the maze. Incredibly, they ran into no one, but that was the nature of mourning for the s'Hisbe. Lockdown for everybody.

Maybe she could just take him to a rear exit after this?

Yeah, but then what would happen to her?

"The security recording," he said.

"Shut up."

"When we're back, you need to take care of the monitoring video files or they'll know what you did if they ever review it."

She didn't answer him, just pressed on, leading him down the various corridors.

In keeping with the s'Hisbe tradition that simplicity elevated the soul, there was little signage anywhere in the palace, nothing but subtle plates up high on doorjambs to illustrate the covert entrances to various rooms and storage places and exits. Gradually, his years at the palace came back to him, and he was surprised to find he knew where they were: She was taking him the long way to the library, but it was smart. This was the rear of the palace, where if they did run into somebody, it was more likely to be a servant.

Which, considering he was masquerading as one, made the route all the better.

"Up here," she said, taking one last right and stopping on a black marble tile square, the vein of which ran counter to the prevailing direction of all the others. Putting her palm on the wall, she triggered the door, which slid open readily.

As they stepped into the darkness, motion-sensitive lights came on, illuminating stacks upon stacks of leather-bound volumes. The air was dry and vaguely dusty, but the library was neat as a pin, the floors polished to a mirror shine, the shelving gleaming. There were no chairs and no tables if you wanted to read anything—the expectation was that you'd take whatever you needed to your quarters and sit down with it there.

Shit, how were they going to find anything in here?

"The medical journals have been moved," she whispered, jogging forward.

He followed her once again, and didn't bother trying to shrink his stature anymore: No one around to see, and this part of the palace was not monitored.

The cataloging system, such that it was, was noted with black-on-black numerals on the flanks of the stacks. But again, it was vague, and presumed that you already knew where to find what you were looking for.

"Here," she said. "We go down here."

Eventually, she stopped and indicated a row of stacks. "This is where they have been relocated."

Frowning, he stepped in. The numbering system on the spines was no fucking help at all, so he pulled one of the volumes out and cracked the cover. When he finally got to some words in the Shadow dialect of the Old Language, he discovered he was about to read a treatise on setting broken bones.

Going down a row, he took out another random tome. Something on eyesight.

Farther on, he'd made it to pregnancy and childbirth.

"Diseases," he muttered. "I'm looking for diseases. Or congenital defects. Or . . . recessive genes . . ."

"I shall help." *maichen* began pulling out volumes. "What can you tell me about the sickness?"

"It's called the Arrest. They freeze—they get . . . it's like bone grows spontaneously . . . it's supposed to be fatal. . . ."

God, he didn't know enough about what he was talking about.

As the two of them worked their way down the stack, the categories and organization of the volumes became clearer and clearer. Like all vampires, Shadows didn't have to deal with human viruses or cancer, but there were plenty of other things that took them down—although not as many as the Homo sapiens had to battle against. With every book he slid out, he was aware that time was passing, and he was more worried about *maichen* getting caught than anything about himself.

Faster, faster with the reading, the returning, the picking another from the lineup.

There had to be something here, he thought. There just had to be.

Trez's entire body was rigid as he remained braced against the interior of the Benz. Fritz was still proceeding down the sidewalk—which would have been great if the *doggen* had been a pedestrian. Squeezing a sedan the size of an ocean-faring yacht into a concrete lane built for holding four or five people at a time?

Not so great—

Selena let out some kind of a yeeeee-haw! as they came up to another corner and sent a second set of *Caldwell Courier Journal* boxes airborne.

He was honestly glad she was enjoying herself.

He just really fucking wished they were watching this action movie instead of living it.

"Fritz," he yelled over the roaring engine. "Head down toward the river."

"As you wish, sire!"

Without warning, Fritz wrenched things left and sent them flying toward a pedestrian mall that skirted another of the skyscrapers. The Benz took to the stairs like a man wearing knee braces, the bumping, jostling, disjointed ascent the kind of thing that left your molars clapping and your kidneys begging for mercy. But then they were on the flat area that gave people all kinds of choices as to which of the four different entrance points to head through.

Fritz, naturally, choose the most direct route.

Through the fucking lobby.

Glass panes exploded as the S600 plowed into a wall of see-through, shards flying forward and to the sides before landing on the slick floor and coasting away like snow across the frozen surface of a lake.

Glancing out the side window, Trez got a good look at the night watchman jumping to his feet behind the bank of desks in the lobby. Seemed impolite not to acknowledge the poor uni'd bastard, so Trez popped a Queen Elizabeth and floated a wave as they roared through the interior and busted out the other side.

Smash!

Round two with the glass was just as trippin', the Benz's grille shattering through as they exploded back into the night.

"I believe we shall go airborne," Fritz called out. "Do secure yourselves."

Roger that, big guy.

Trez went rigid as they approached the lip of the set of stairs, and then—

Zero gravity, or as close as you could get to it without doing a U-ie at thirty thousand feet, happened as they soared, the ride getting super-smooth and relatively quiet, nothing but the sound of the throaty engine hitting the ear.

All that changed as they skipped over the sidewalk and landed on the paved road. The suspension absorbed as much of the impact as it could, but sparks flew out behind as some portion of the undercarriage got a dental file.

"Please forgive me," Fritz said, looking up in the rear-view.

"The terrain is hardly your fault," Trez hollered back. "But not sure about all that glass."

He glanced over to make sure Selena was still whoopin' it up across the way. Yup. She was smiling and laughing, eyes bright as Christmas lights.

When Trez glanced up front again, the butler was still looking into the rearview mirror and talking to him. "Sire, I'm terribly sorry, but I must needs return home—"

"Fritz! Focus on the road, buddy!"

"Oh, yes, sire—"

Screeeeeeeeeech as the butler course-corrected and narrowly avoided weed-whacking a lineup of parallel-parked cars.

"As I was saying, sire, I must needs return home," the butler continued without losing a beat. "Last Meal preparations have to be supervised."

Like this was just a video game you could put on pause? "Ah, Fritz—"

All at once the Mercedes went black inside and out, the

lights extinguished. And at that very moment, from high up in the sky, a blaring light pierced down to the road, flashing over them for a split second.

"Helicopter," Trez muttered. "Fantastic."

Twisting around, he checked out the rear window. Blue and white flashing lights were speeding along, but the cops were cutting across their path instead of following—which would give them a pass for only a block or two before the CPD pulled a recalibration of their own.

Shit, how were they going to get out of this?

Before he knew it, Fritz had them down by the river, but not on a road. Instead of taking one of the legal routes, he popped yet another curb and began to fly directly under the raised highway. Pylons the size of redwoods passed by the windows, the *doggen* playing dodge-'em car, jogging left and right like a runner in an obstacle course.

No one was behind them, but they could hardly keep this up indefinitely. The Northway, which was what was overhead, was going to rejoin the earth—

Sure enough, the descent from up above started to happen, and at such a velocity, Trez became convinced they were going to mash-potato themselves into the coming horizontal asphalt merger.

Except, no. Fritz jerked out from underneath, riding a ridge of pavement around to the roads that ran parallel to the Hudson. Somehow, he managed to get them in between a break in the guardrails and then, justlikethat, they were on an exit ramp that would take them onto the highway in the right direction.

Heading away from town.

Trez waited for a lineup of CPD units with their lights going all Fourth of July to fall in behind them.

Instead, he saw a fleet of those boys in blue tearing it up on the other side of the Northway, heading to the site of all the fun and games.

Fritz slowed down and put his lights back on. Pulled into the stream of traffic. Floated away at a modest seventy miles an hour.

"How the *hell* did you do that?" Trez said with H2G respect.

"Humans are rather easy to lose. They tend to track lights, rather like cats with a laser pointer. Without the illumination? It gives one a serious advantage—well, that and possessing twice their horsepower."

Trez turned to his queen. "You okay—"

Selena reached over and pulled his mouth in for a kiss. And another. "What a night! That was the most exciting thing that's ever happened to me!"

Adrenaline quickly transferred into lust as he kissed her back and pressed her into her seat. Licking his way into her mouth, he found one of her breasts with his hand.

"Should I tell him to gas it again?" Trez growled against her mouth. "'Cuz I don't think I can wait...."

"We'll be home soon," she murmured, smiling. "And I like anticipation. I've been hungry for you since the ride in."

Trez groaned deep in his throat as he reached for the button to raise the partition. "Fritz?"

"Yes, master?"

"A little faster, if you don't mind."

"My pleasure, sire!"

THIRTY-SEVEN

Shortly after Xcor and Balthazar made yet another running turn in the maze of alleys, Xcor was hit by something so big and so hard, he was totally stunned as he went airborne, the world spinning whilst he stayed steady—or, more likely, he was the one going 'round about.

In mid-air, he braced for a nasty impact—but for some absolutely stupid reason, he landed on his combat boots. It was a hole-in-one kind of thing—and not a blessing that would last, given his momentum. To keep from falling to the ground, he sprang forward, trying to continue his run.

Something was very wrong. His legs weren't working right a'tall.

Scrambling to stay upright, he was dimly aware of Balthazar shouting his name, and then suddenly, his soldier was right beside him, grabbing onto his arm and dragging him forth.

In the back of his mind, he sensed a presence departing the enormous vehicle in the manner of a vampire. And then the sound of the bullet impacts changed. High-pitched pings replaced the lower-register noises of lead burrowing into brick, asphalt, stone.

The *lessers* had come across that RV.

Which meant he and Balthazar had a second or two of greater coverage, and Balthazar took advantage of it. With a hard yank, Xcor felt his entire body get pulled off-track.

And then a moment later, he was behind some large structure.

No, a second vehicle—or something. Indeed, it was a gigantic square box with some kind of writing on the side.

P...O...D...S...

His overactive brain traced the shapes of the red letters, but the pattern they made meant nothing to him. What did register clearly?

They were about to get a clean shot.

He lifted his gun at the same time Balthazar did.

Forcing his lungs to cease their greedy gasping, he waited...waited...waited....

The shower of bullets grew louder and louder as the shooters proceeded toward them. And so caught up were the slayers in their noisemaking and their pursuit, neither of them bothered to slow down as they came up to the cover that worked so well—and continued forward.

With unspoken agreement, Xcor took the one on the left whilst Balthazar trained in on the right.

Two bullets. Not two thousand.

Two very well-placed forty-millimeter bullets square in the backs pitched both of the shooters forward, face-first into the dirty pavement.

"I have them," Balthazar barked, switching out his gun for his daggers.

Xcor would have argued, but he was beginning to feel the extent of his wounds.

Bali leaped out, his blades flashing. He hit the closest one first, a great explosion of light turning the alley into noontime. With nary a pause, he rolled off and stabbed the second shooter. Recoiling away during the second illumination, the soldier managed to reholster the daggers and grab both of the AKs before...

...that massive vehicle, the one that had hit Xcor, came barreling down the alley.

Balthazar ran back for cover, slamming his shoulders into the metal cube, and the two of them stared straight ahead, freezing in place as the thing left the area.

But the fun and games weren't over quite yet.

Calm down.

They needed to calm...

...down...

Dematerializing out of downtown was the only way they were going to get out of here: Sirens from the humans' po-

lice cars were growing louder and louder, and then headlights appeared down at the end of the alley, their brilliant
illumination making shadows out of everything.

"Go," Xcor ordered, knowing his soldier was in far better shape than he.

"Not on your life."

"To tarry here with me may be on yours."

"Then we shall die together."

As Xcor inhaled and exhaled deeply, trying to slow his
heart rate and ease off his blood pressure, the smell of
heated metal and gunpowder tingled in his nose along with
the diesel fumes from that vehicle and the lingering nasty
stench of the slayers' sweat and incinerations.

His legs were killing him, both of them. At this rate, the
pain was becoming such that he was going to have to sit
down—or pass out.

Shit.

The police cars zoomed by, going at breakneck speed,
one . . . two . . . three of them in quick succession, their noise
and strobing lights going on a fade as they passed.

There would be more. And the next wave would be
slower, in recon rather than pursuit mode.

"How badly are you hit?" Balthazar demanded.

He wanted to lie. "My legs are a problem. One is shot,
the other likely broken."

"When was the last time you fed. From a female, that is?"

Months and months. Since he had first met Layla. Her
ultra-pure blood had sustained him for a record amount of
time, and when the strength had finally begun to fade, he
had taken the veins of deer he hunted in the forest without
telling his males he had resorted to such.

But Bali knew. They all must have known.

"That long, indeed," his soldier grumbled.

Xcor looked around, not about to take the conversation
further. Across the way, there was a fire escape, but he
lacked the strength to drag himself up there at a sufficient
speed, and he would not be able to dematerialize.

"Go," he said to Balthazar.

"You can do this."

"I have not the strength to make it back to—"

Balthazar pointed up. "There. The roof. That is as far as
you must go."

Barking dogs. At least two of them. At the head of the alley.

Ah, yes, the humans had brought in noses worthy of a search. As opposed to the lame ones on their pitiful faces.

"You must," Balthazar said. "Just that far. And no farther."

Xcor traced the way up the fire escape, past the series of windows, up some fifteen floors. It could be worse, he supposed.

"Now."

Closing his eyes, he knew it wasn't going to work. "I want you to go. That is an order."

"I shall not—"

Xcor raised a tired arm and slapped his soldier across the face. In a weary voice, he said, "The others need organization and tending to. You are it. Go—and take those guns with you. They are valuable. *Go!* Someone must lead them!"

Balthazar was still swearing as he disappeared . . . and the dogs came ever closer to Xcor's position. With the fresh scent of his spilled and ever-welling blood, they would find him in a matter of seconds.

This time, as his lids lowered, it was from pure exhaustion, not from any kind of hope that he would dematerialize.

Except just before he was due to be captured, as he lifted his gun muzzle and knew that he was about to lose his life in a very bad gunfight . . .

The image of Layla came to him so clearly that it was as if she stood before him.

If he did not remove himself, he would die and ne'er set eyes upon her again.

As a profound sense of loss struck him in the center of the chest, it was then that he knew what he had been denying for some time.

Faced with the reality that he might be denied one last audience with that female, one final chance to hear her voice, catch her scent upon the night air, stand in witness to her physical presence . . . the bonded male in him screamed in rage at such a crime.

Just as a German shepherd rounded the corner of the metal container, its deputy on a short leash following suit, at the very instant when the human shouted something along the lines of, "Freeze," or some such drivel . . .

Xcor up and disappeared.

Only the drive to see his female again gave him the strength to cast himself upon the night air, scattering his battered, weakened body up to the roof that Balthazar had directed him to.

As the cop down below let out an exclamation of shock and another arrived to much ensuing conversation, Xcor fell out of thin air, landing hard on the gravel-topped flat roof of the building overhead.

"Thank you to the Scribe Virgin," he heard someone mutter.

Groaning, Xcor rolled over onto his back. Zypher was standing over him. Balthazar, too.

"He is injured quite badly."

That was the last thing he heard before blood loss and injury dragged him down into unconsciousness.

One block over, Rhage had his own list of problems thanks to all the damn humans who'd flooded the alleys. With his hands over his head, and his back to the approaching boys in blue, he was annoyed. And bored.

The real party, with those slayers, had gone ahead along with Bill Murray's—make that Manny Manello's—bullet-proof medevac thing. Meanwhile, he was stuck here with a six-pack of Caldie's finest.

"Don't move."

Just like in the movies, he thought while rolling his eyes. "Whatever you say, Officer."

His keen hearing meant he triangulated their positions with total accuracy. And there was nothing ahead of him in the alley. No cars, late-night pedestrians, or other cops.

God only knew where Manny was going to end up. Or what was happening with Trez and Selena.

He didn't have time for this.

"Officer?"

"Don't move."

"No offense, but I gotta blow."

Just like that, because the CPD didn't stress him in the slightest, he was up and out, dematerializing away.

He was smiling in his molecular state as he traveled off, imagining the OMFGs.

But he'd kinda done a no-no. There was one and only

one rule in the war with the Lessening Society: Thou shalt not tee up the idiot gallery. I.e., it was in everyone's best interests that humans didn't know that vampires were so much more than a Halloween myth, and the *Walking Dead* was actually not just a TV show.

Sometimes you didn't have a choice, however. And though he'd just given Frick and Frack, the handcuff brothers, and their other buddies, a helluva show, it was better than wasting time erasing their memories when Manny really needed him and Trez and Selena might possibly be needing him.

Blowing his way forward, he re-formed three blocks closer to the river on the roof of a delivery entrance's carport. Just as Manny sped down the alley in his armored tank, with his wedding train of CPD units behind him, Rhage flashed down into the light of those Xenon beams—and gave the good doctor a wave to keep going.

Then he calmly and very deliberately stepped into the ambulance's wake and opened fire on the markeds that were trailing the vehicle. He wasn't an asshole, though. His Mary had been human once—sort of still was except for her whole immortal thing. So he aimed at the front tires and the engine blocks on a first-come, first-served basis. The unit in the lead quickly lost control and went into a tailspin, which meant the second was harder to hit safely. But he rocked that shit, rendering them useless.

Buh-bye.

He caught up with Manny again by ghosting two more blocks down, and he materialized into the passenger seat in the same way he'd left the vehicle.

Manny gave a shout of alarm, but didn't lose his focus. He kept them moving and in the middle of the alley.

"We gotta get out of here," the good doctor said.

"Head to the river. I know exactly what to do."

"There are cops everywhere."

"I'll tell you when to turn." Rhage got out his phone and started texting. A block later, he barked, "Now! Right!"

Rhage hung on tight as Manny threw them into a ninety-degree and hit the gas again.

"They've got a helicopter on us," Manny announced.

Sure enough, the wide-screen was showing a lovely picture of a brilliant field of light pulling a heat lamp on them, the broad beam flashing around as the copter held them in view from the air.

"Two blocks up, take a left."

"They're going to close in on us from—"

"Do it!"

Annnnnd just like that they were under the highway, that spotlight extinguished.

"One more block," Rhage muttered, jacking forward, praying that—"There!"

Over on the right, a service bay was opening slowly, the panels rising to reveal a blackened garage space the size of a small house.

"That's us!"

"Holy shit, how'd you do that?"

"All hail to the V."

Just like that, Manny's RV, along with all its gauze and syringes and scalpels, and the two sorry sons a bitches in its front seat, was undercover and locked in tight as a tick in the delivery bay.

Manny canned the engine, but didn't take his grip off the wheel. Like he kinda expected to have to drive again. "What do we do now?"

Rhage put his window down further and listened to the sounds of the cop cars going by on the outside. "We chill—"

His cell rang and he answered it. "Nice work, my brother."

Vishous's voice was clear as a bell. "And you thought we'd never need it."

"Thank God for remote activation."

"Through my phone. Boom! You safe?"

"Yeah, but I think we're going to be here for a while unless someone comes and gets us."

"What the fuck is going on down there?"

"Pick us up and I'll tell you on the way home."

"Be there in twenty. Unless we have to worry about the CPD?"

"Oh, no." Rhage pulled a *pshaw* with his hand. "You'll be fine. No cops around."

As he hung up, Manny looked over at him. "Are you out of your mind? This zip code is crawling with the police."

"He needs the exercise."

With a curse, Manny banged his head against the back of

his seat a couple of times. "Damn it! I haven't even gotten a chance to use this bad boy yet, and it's all trashed."

"Well, least you got to play with some of the buttons. And this was a good beta test of the whole bulletproof thing." Rhage's phone went off as a text came through. "Oh, good news—Trez and Selena made it home safely. Guess they got out of town before the fun started."

"That is a relief." Manny took a deep breath, but then cursed. "How're we going to get this thing out of here? Every police station in town's going to have a description of it."

Rhage looked around the interior and shrugged. "Piece by piece, if we have to."

"Somehow that doesn't inspire confidence."

"You haven't seen your brother-in-law with a screwdriver. That motherfucker can take apart just about anything."

"How's he on the reassemble, though."

"Great."

"Are you lying to me just so I don't cry like a little girl?"

"Oh, no. Not at all."

Rhage twisted around in his seat and activated the flashlight app on his phone.

"Checking for hitchhikers?" Manny drawled.

"You got anything I can nosh on in here?"

"Not unless you like the taste of sterilization."

Rhage resettled in his seat and put the thing on recline. "Worse comes to worst—"

"No, you may not eat my RV."

"Are you off-limits, too?"

"Yes!"

Closing his eyes, he flipped off the doctor. "Party pooper."

THIRTY-EIGHT

In the palace's library, iAm slid out the last volume on the last shelf on the last row of healing texts. As he cracked the leather cover, the scream in his head was so loud, he couldn't focus to read the table of contents.

"Here," *maichen* said. "Allow me."

Even though it marked him as a pussy, he let himself fall back on his ass, the hard floor biting through the thin cover of the pale blue maid's uni.

He already knew what *maichen* was going to find. Or not.

The flaw in his reasoning, when he'd set out on this folly, was that he'd never heard of the disease. It wasn't like he was one of the s'Hisbe's healers, with an extensive knowledge of what ailed folks and how to fix it, but something like what Selena had? The Shadows would have viewed it as a defect to stay away from like the plague—so there would have been some common consciousness about it.

He should have known. But when it came to his brother, he was liable to do anything to save the SOB.

"Does he have a similar disease?" *maichen* asked.

"What?"

"You just said you would do anything to save your brother?"

Great, he was talking out loud now. "We'd better head back."

She closed the volume. "I am sorry we didn't find—"

"Come on, let's go."

iAm got to his feet and offered her his hand. In the process of reviewing that last book with all those worthless words, she, too, had seated herself on the floor.

Her masked face lifted upward as if she were staring at his palm.

"We need to go," he muttered, wishing she would just put the damn book back and head out with him.

When she finally extended her arm, the heavy sleeve slid down, exposing her thin wrist and her long, thin hand. Which trembled.

He loved the color of her skin. Darker than his.

"I'm not going to hurt you," he said roughly before he touched her.

"I know," she whispered.

As he made contact, his body jerked, electricity licking into him, traveling from the connection to his heart and making that vital rhythm-maker tick even faster. And he wasn't sure, but he thought that she felt the shock as well, the robing that covered her shifting sharply, as if she had jumped.

There wasn't time to think about any of that, though.

Taking the book from her free hand, he replaced it into the slot that had been created and started off for the long trek back to the exit. He'd gone about fifteen feet when he realized he hadn't dropped his hold on her yet.

He had to force himself to let her hand go.

When they came to the hidden door, he stepped aside and let her open things up in case there was some kind of tracer or security check in play.

Out in the hall, she said, "Crouch down, remember? You're very tall and very big."

iAm got with the program. "Thanks."

Letting her assume the lead, he found himself watching the way she walked, the shift of her body under the robing camouflaged nearly completely. What was she like under there? What was her face like?

As soon as the thoughts hit him, he dropped them. Now was hardly the time to waste even a split second on anything like that.

They had gone about twenty-five miles, as far as he could tell, when a set of prison guards came at them. From underneath the mesh that covered his face, iAm tracked their approach, bracing himself for a fight to get away. Typical of s'Ex's security team, they were in black, they were built like bouncers, and their weapons were obvious around their waists, the long-bladed daggers at their hips in ready reach. Their faces were uncovered, and he couldn't remember—did that mean that they were on the warpath?

Shit, had they been discovered?

Ahead of him, *maichen* didn't blink. She stopped, put both her hands in front of her heart in a steeple, and bowed her head in supplication. Staying in her lee, iAm copied her pose exactly, his thigh muscles tight as he forced his legs to remain at half-mast.

The guards looked the pair of them over, and iAm prayed that that lavender scenting trick did the job. If they caught a whiff of anything close to the aggression pumping through his veins . . .

But nope, they just nodded and kept going.

Thank fuck.

Another hundred yards or so later, she came to an abrupt halt—and he nearly plowed into her. "We're here," she said, looking up and down the hall.

He waited for her to trigger the door to his cell. When she didn't, he leaned into her and said softly, "It's not your fault. And thank you."

Her head lowered, and the voice that came out from behind her masking seemed choked. "I'm so sorry. About all of this."

"You don't worry about it. And I don't want you to come see me anymore. Trade off the duties, but don't get involved in this. We got enough people in this nightmare already."

That mesh panel shifted as she looked up at him. "I want to do more. Let me help you get free—"

"No."

"I don't want you to be a gerbil."

"What?"

"I don't want you to be kept in there forever."

"It won't be that long, I promise you." Although he did need to get out of here ASAP. "Now, will you *please* go?"

When she continued to hesitate, he was the one who triggered the prison door to open by taking her hand and placing it on the wall—

The lights were on inside, not off. And s'Ex was on the

bedding platform, his back against the headboard, his legs stretched out and crossed at the ankles.

In one hand, he had a whetstone. In the other, he had a dagger.

With slow, sure strokes, he was sharpening the blade.

He didn't bother to look up. "Imagine my surprise when I came to personally check on you."

iAm put his body in front of *maichen*'s, blocking her completely. "This is not her fault. I forced her."

"That is a lie." The executioner glanced up, his black eyes glittering. "But whether you did or didn't is the least of your problems."

As Fritz pulled up in front of the Brotherhood's mansion, Selena burst out of the back of the Mercedes before the car even rolled to a halt. The sudden lunge was an expression of her excitement, something she had been holding in, and it felt good to—

Except she was in high heels, and the landing went badly: As the tiny pinpoint back ends of her shoes skipped over the cobblestones, gravity grabbed hold of her and she threw out her arms, her weight shifting off-kilter—

Trez caught her in his arms with a powerful surge, capturing her before she could fall and sweeping her up against his massive chest.

He held her as if she didn't weigh a thing.

Putting her arms around his neck, she leaned back and smiled so widely, she probably looked like a lunatic. She didn't care.

"That was incredible!"

Trez grinned as he mounted the steps to the door to the vestibule. "It was something else, for sure."

Stretching around Trez's triceps, she called out to the butler, "Fritz, can we do that again tomorrow night?"

The butler followed in their wake. "But of course, mistress! Anything to be of service. I must comment, however, that the car shall require some attention prior to any further such excursions."

Probably right, and maybe that was why the *doggen* had parked it parallel to the front door instead of with the other vehicles on the far side of the fountain. Could the thing even reverse anymore?

There was a quick pause as they entered the vestibule, and then they were welcomed into the mansion's warm, lush interior by one of Fritz's staff.

"If you will excuse me," the butler said, "I must attend to Last Meal's preparations, as I indicated."

"Thanks for getting us back in one piece," Trez murmured.

"My pleasure indeed."

As the *doggen* went off through the dining room, Trez started for the stairs, his long strides crossing over the foyer's mosaic floor—and Selena started to smile for a different reason than pure adrenaline.

But he didn't take her up to his bedroom. Her male strode around the base of the grand staircase on the left, taking them to the ornate door of the bathroom.

"Open the door for me," he growled.

She glanced up and drank in the sight of his face. Pure sexual need gritted his jaw and narrowed his eyes, turning him into an animalistic version of himself.

His response to the car ride, she thought.

Reaching out her hand, she gripped the brass knob and released the lock, opening the way in.

Such a beautiful room, with its private stall for the toilet, and its sweet-smelling air, and especially its peach, red and pink veined marble that covered the walls and the floors. Red and peach satin fell from both sides of the mirror over the sink, as if the thing were a window to look out of, and the velvet skirting around the basin was bloodred with gold-tasseled fringe. Old-fashioned gas sconces burned incessantly all around the room, the mellow yellow light like that of candles.

"You're going to want to use that lock," he said, bending down so she could get to the thing. Slide it home. Give them some privacy.

There was a long, skirted bench on the far wall, and he brought her over to it, holding her with one hand as he shoved all kinds of silk and needlepoint pillows onto the floor. Stretching her out, he purred deep in his throat as he caressed her shoulders, her waist, her legs.

"I thought about this all night," he said.

Arching up, she felt the caress of her dress moving up over her thighs as he swept his palms higher and higher.

"Oh, God," he breathed as he looked at her sex.

"Did you forget already?" She smiled as she lowered her lids. "That they gave me everything but the panties?"

"Mmm, no, I remember."

He moved her around, pulling her forward so that he could split her legs around his hips. Leaning down over her, he put his mouth on the side of her neck and then drew his tongue up until he nipped at her earlobe.

"You know what the hardest thing is?"

He punctuated the question with a thrust of his pelvis, his arousal pushing into her bare sex through the fine fabric of his slacks. As she gasped, his fingers drifted over the bodice of the dress.

"Hmmm?" he murmured, nipping at her again as if to chastise her. "Do you?"

"I have a good idea," she moaned.

"It's not this." He pushed into her core again, stroking her with his erection. "Believe it or not."

"Wha-what . . . ?"

He put his mouth next to her ear. "It's not ripping your dress off with my teeth. I want to take you to Last Meal after this, and as much as I respect the Brothers . . ." Trez kissed his way down to her shoulder. "I'd have to kill them all if they saw you naked. And that's a lot of clean-up."

"So what are you going to do?"

"Sit up for me."

She was dizzy as she did what he asked, but it was from the passion, the heat . . . the need. "Now . . . what?"

"We very carefully get rid of this." Grasping the hem, he pulled the black wisp up over her waist . . . over her breasts. "Fuuuuuuuuuck."

As he tossed the silk to the floor, he just stared at what he had revealed. "Oh, that's what I want."

With his palms stroking up and down her thighs, he dropped his head to one of her nipples, sucking her in, nursing at her, his dark head contrasting with her paler skin. Letting her head fall back, she gave him the access he wanted, spreading her knees even further.

The sound he made was all male animal, and the hold he sank into her hips was rough as he jerked her forward.

"Gimme," he demanded. There was a quick *zip!* as he released himself, and then that growl was back. "All night. Thought about this all night."

He pushed into her with a thrust of his hips, and she grabbed onto his wrists, arching up again. With hard drives, he let himself go and she took everything he gave her, a powerful release gathering momentum immediately. So hot, so wild ... the culmination of the thoughtful dinner, the crazy ride home, the constant anticipation she'd had when she was around him.

Dragging him back down to her mouth, she clung to the power of him, seeking his lips and sucking his tongue inside of her until the rhythm of penetrations below made that impossible. Faster, harder, and then the orgasm hit her.

And it was just like careening through those panes of glass, a gathering speed and then a spectacular shattering.

Except it was her body coming apart.

In a wonderful way.

Just as she was beginning to float down, she found his wrist at her lips. "Take from me," he grunted. "I want to feel your teeth in my flesh."

Instantly, the heat rose again and she pushed his arm out of the way. As her fangs descended in a rush, she hissed and struck the side of his throat, right at the thick vein that ran up from his heart.

Trez cried out her name and clasped her to him, tilting his head and encouraging her to take more, take everything she needed—as his hips locked against her, his erection jerking as he came deep inside her body.

His release called another out of her, taking her to the edge again.

And all the while, she'd never felt safer or more loved.

THIRTY-NINE

As the cell door shut tightly behind him and *maichen*, iAm yanked the headdress off and tossed it. "Let her go."

s'Ex shifted his powerful legs off the bedding platform and got to his feet. "Do you know what my biggest failing is? I don't take orders well."

"She's not part of this. It's between you and me."

"Yeah, see, you're still getting it wrong. You and I are actually just bit players in the real drama, but that's beside the point."

The executioner walked forward, and iAm put his hands out, shielding *maichen*. "Stop."

"Or what."

"I'm going to kill you."

s'Ex halted right in front of him and stared down his nose. "Really."

"Yes." iAm curled his hands into fists and felt his fangs drop down. "If it's a question of you or her walking out of here alive, I will guarantee that she will be the one still on her feet when the door opens. And I don't care if I die in the process."

s'Ex frowned and glanced at the maid. Addressing her, he said, "Wrong brother. You know that, right?"

iAm leaned to the side and blocked the eye contact. "So arè we doing this?"

"You'd be a fool to fight me. Considering I came to get you out of here."

iAm refused to be distracted. "Are you throwing the first punch or am I."

"Did you hear what I said? I came here to take you to the fucking library—but I'm assuming that's where you two are coming back from? Or are we swinging by there on the way to the exit."

In the silence that followed, iAm ran the executioner's words back and forth, checking the syllables for meaning. Then he frowned. "I don't get it."

"If you don't mind, we need to do this now, because I have to be back at court in about twenty minutes."

What the fuck was this, iAm wondered.

s'Ex rolled his eyes. "I told you I'd get you in and out, didn't I?"

"You put me in here! You had me hit on the head—"

"No, asshole. One of my guards did that. I've been working behind the scenes to try and get you free—you're not supposed to be in this goddamn cell. That wasn't our agreement."

Blink.

"We have been to the library," *maichen* interjected. "We were unsuccessful. And I'm coming as well. I want to be sure he makes it out alive."

s'Ex and iAm both looked at her and barked, "No."

"See?" the executioner said as he walked around them to the door. "We can agree about something. Now, can we do this."

And the bastard wasn't talking about fighting.

Holy. Shit. It looked as though his trust hadn't been as misplaced as he'd thought.

iAm looked at *maichen*. In a soft voice, he whispered, "Don't follow us."

"You cannot tell her what to do," s'Ex said as he triggered the exit. "Now let us proceed—unless you want to rot in this cell?"

iAm shook his head at the maid. "Do not—"

"I'm waiting," s'Ex said.

"maichen—"

"I shall follow you if I wish," was all she said as she steamed by him and joined s'Ex in the hall.

iAm's hair was on fire as he followed, still wearing that maid uniform he'd sneaked around in. "I'm not going to have it on my conscience if you get yourself killed for a dumb-ass reason."

As they went down the corridor, she paid no attention to his bitching. Duh. She didn't seem to have a brain in her head.

Or maybe that was him . . . because he found himself not wanting to leave her.

Which was nuts.

s'Ex led them through the halls, taking a different path than *maichen* had. And all the way, iAm was prepared for an ambush, a confrontation, a sold-up-the-river outcome that was going to fuck him in the ass.

But fifteen or twenty minutes later, he was out of the palace, past the vacant servants' quarters . . . and standing in front of the wall that separated the Territory from the human world.

iAm looked over at the executioner. "You're just letting me go?" he whispered into the darkness.

"Like I said, that was our arrangement, wasn't it?" When iAm didn't reply, s'Ex shook his head. "Herewith lies the ending for the three of us. At least until after the mourning, when I have to come get your brother."

"Won't they notice I'm gone?"

"Why would anyone care? I dispatch delinquents regularly—and I have already erased the memory of your marking in any who had knowledge of it." s'Ex glanced at *maichen*. "Although all this would have been so much easier if you hadn't insisted on turning that cell into a furniture showroom."

iAm stuck out his palm. "I didn't expect you to be honest."

"Fuck you, too." s'Ex shook what was extended to him. "Now go."

Just like that, the way out was open to him. He didn't even have to dematerialize over the barrier.

iAm paused and glanced back at the maid.

In the silence that followed, s'Ex let out a vicious curse. "I do not approve of any of this between you two. But you know how to close things up after he leaves."

And on that note, the executioner stalked off, his black robes undulating behind him.

It was so strange, iAm thought as he was left alone with

the female. He was two feet from the escape he needed, but he couldn't seem to move.

"Can I see your face," he heard himself say. "Before I go."

When she didn't respond, he reached out and ran his hand down the fabric that covered her head and trailed down her shoulders. "I have to see what you look like or you're going to haunt my days."

He had a feeling she was going to do that anyway.

"I . . ." Her voice trembled. "I do not know."

iAm nodded and felt like an asshole. "I'm sorry, it's none of my business." He gave in to an impulse and bowed at the waist to her, as if she were so much more than a servant. "Thank you again."

Pivoting, he strode through the open doorway.

"Tomorrow night," she blurted. "Will you meet me?"

He froze, one foot in and one foot out of the Territory. "Where."

"I do not know. Somewhere. Some . . . how."

iAm frowned, and thought of where he'd found Trez on the mountain between the s'Hisbe and the *symphath* colony. That cabin still had to be there; the damn thing had been a hundred years old when Trez had taken shelter in it.

And shit knew Rehv wasn't using it anymore.

"Do you know Black Snake Mountain?"

"Yes," she whispered.

"Halfway up the east side, on the Lightning Strike trailhead, there's a cabin. I'll get there first and light a fire inside. You can dematerialize from here and find the light. Meet me there at midnight."

He could imagine her chewing on her lower lip as she hemmed and hawed.

"I will never hurt you," he vowed.

"I know."

"I have to go." He stared at her so hard, trying to see under those robes. "Think about it. I'll be there and I'll wait an hour. If you don't make it, I totally understand."

She wasn't "important" in the eyes of the s'Hisbe, but still, females were right to be cautious, no matter their station, when it came to leaving the Territory.

Especially if they had no relative power.

"Good-bye," he said before turning away and falling into a jog.

Moments later, when he dematerialized, he knew he was never going to see her again. And yet, even though that was all but a given, he was going to be at that place on the mountain tomorrow evening.

On time.

Guess even cynical virgins like him had romantic streaks.

When Trez and Selena finally made it out of the downstairs lavatory, it was a helluva lot later than midnight. In fact, as he checked his phone, he was surprised to find that it was three a.m. They'd blown a good three hours in there.

He couldn't think of a better way to pass the damn time.

People had obviously started to come home for the day, voices drifting out of the billiards room.

". . . rounds of bullets!" Hollywood was saying. "Like it was raining lead!"

"My poor mobile clinic." Manny's tone was less than enthusiastic. "Maiden voyage and look what happened to the goddamn thing."

Well, at least those two had gotten home safely. Jesus, he hadn't even thought about them, and how egocentric was that?

"And this asshole tells me there are no police," V cut in. "For the evac. Unbelievable—I walked into a convention of those badges."

Trez put his arm around Selena. "You want to join the party?"

"We need to tell our part!"

Kissing her on the forehead, he led her across the foyer and through the archway into the land of pool tables, sofas, and a wide-screen big enough to host a drive-in movie.

"Check it, we made CNN," someone said as that TV flared to life.

Sure enough, up on the tremendous screen, security cam footage of the Mercedes going *Die Hard* through that lobby was on an endless loop. Then came a statement from a police officer who was involved in the chase. And a witness from somewhere or another.

Trez nodded a hello to Rhage and Manny. Lifted his

palm to V and Butch. Sidled up with his female next to Z and Bella.

"Lot of coverage," somebody else said ruefully.

"Shit," someone else answered.

Even Selena's excitement got dialed down quickly, as if seeing for herself what everything looked like made it all very real.

When the vestibule's inner door was opened, Trez was dimly aware of a cold draft shooting into the room. And then a moment later, a hand landed on his shoulder.

As he twisted around, iAm was behind him.

"Oh, hey, man." He went to embrace his brother, only to recoil. "What the *fuck* is that smell?"

"New hand wash at work."

Trez followed through on the hug. "Get rid of it. Makes you smell like a little old lady—what is it? Lavender?"

"What happened to the Merc? The thing's banged to shit."

Trez pointed to the screen. "That happened."

iAm focused on Selena instead, tracing her profile and dress with surprise that he covered quickly.

"We went on a date," Trez blurted.

Selena glanced over, and when she saw who it was, she reached out her arms. "Hello," she said as she embraced his brother. "I think we broke downtown Caldwell."

Funny, iAm was the only male he didn't feel like killing if there was contact with his female. Guess his bonded male recognized that iAm would never, ever cross any lines in thought, much less deed.

iAm smiled a little. "Least I know why the Benz needs fifty grand worth of body work. You want a drink while I help myself?"

Trez shook his head. "No, I'm good."

Except as his brother went over to the bar, Trez excused himself and followed the guy. "Hey, listen, I just want to apologize for going radio silent—whoa!"

As the bottle iAm had picked up slid out of the male's grasp, Trez caught the thing before it hit the floor—and that was when he saw how badly his brother's hands were shaking.

"Jesus, iAm, are you all right?"

"Oh, yeah. Abso."

"Here," he said, giving the vodka back. "You sure you need to make your own drink?"

"Positive."

"Wait, lemme get you a glass." He came around the bar and got a short-and-squat off the shelf as iAm popped the cap off the square bottle. "Cranberry juice, right?"

"No."

"Neat? You don't usually drink vodka like that."

"Efficiency, my brother. It's all about efficiency tonight."

Trez held the glass out and watched as iAm poured a healthy measure of the see-through relax-o-matic in there. He kept expecting the level to stop rising, and when it didn't, he found himself studiously ignoring the shock he felt.

iAm was the moderate of the two of them.

He drank all this and his blood alcohol level was going to be in coma territory. Then again, it had been a very fucking long twenty-four hours.

"How's things at the restaurant?" Trez asked as he transferred ownership of the glass.

"Ah, good. Yeah. Fine."

"The clubs?"

"Same."

iAm drank the shit like it was water, downing the entire load in one long, open-throated sesh.

Trez cursed. "I'm so fucking sorry."

"Why?" iAm muttered.

"You know why."

The grunt that came in reply could have meant any number of things. "Listen, I have to go lie down. I'm done for."

"Yeah, I think we're going to do the same."

"How is she?"

Trez glanced over and intended to look right back at his brother, but his eyes refused to move. Tracing the graceful curve of Selena's back, he saw her naked in that loo, her legs spread, her heavy breasts bare to his mouth, his hands. Then he pictured her laughing wildly in the back of the Benz. Remembered her staring out at the night as they'd had dinner.

"She's amazing," he said hoarsely. "Absolutely amazing."

"That's good, brother. That's good." iAm recapped the CLIX and tucked it under his arm. "Listen, I gotta go lie down—but I'll be right next door if you need anything, 'kay?"

"Thanks."

As iAm turned away and didn't look back, it was hard not to feel every ounce of the burden Trez was to that male.

Someday, he vowed, he was going to find a way to make up for all of it.

FORTY

There was no getting away.

As Layla stood in the midst of the group in the billiards room, she was acutely aware that if she tried to sneak out and take her car for a little joyride, she was going to get hit with questions she couldn't easily answer. But more to the point, Luchas remained in stable, though serious, condition down in the clinic. Qhuinn was still with him, with Blay by his side, and she had come up here only to get something to eat.

Leaving the property was all wrong.

Especially to see the likes of Xcor.

And maybe this was for the best. She had been on the verge of crossing lines the night before, lines that would have taken her into territory that, after a lot of reflection, she knew she couldn't handle. Dearest Virgin Scribe, she couldn't imagine what she had been thinking, and this forced separation was a good thing—even though she didn't want Luchas to suffer.

On the huge TV screen over the fireplace, images of gunfire and screeching cars flickered like something out of a movie.

Unbelievable what had happened downtown. Thank God no one had been hurt.

"So where's your fancy RV now?" someone asked Manny.

"Still down by the river. We had to leave it in V's warehouse." The doctor rubbed his eyes like he had a screamer of a headache. "Bullet holes everywhere—and I hit something big with it."

"*Lesser?*" one of the Brothers said.

"No. When I got out and checked, there was red blood on the front headlights and grille. So it was either a human or one of you guys—and given the head count around here, and the communal lack of limps, it must have been the former."

"Or a Bastard."

"Maybe. Yeah. Whoever it was, I'm damn sure they were hurting afterward."

Layla frowned. "Someone was hit?"

"Not one of us, don't worry," somebody replied.

A strange premonition rattled through her.

Without saying anything further, she backed out of the room. After checking that no one had noticed her exit, she took her phone from the pocket of the fleece she'd borrowed from Doc Jane and sent a quick text. As soon as it went through, she erased the words and then made sure the cell was on vibrate before disappearing the device again.

Pacing by the front door, she kept her hand in her pocket on the slim body of the phone and waited for an answer. When nothing came through ten minutes later, she double-checked that she hadn't turned the thing off by mistake—

"Hey, there."

Pivoting around, she saw Qhuinn and Blay emerging from the tunnel's hidden door under the stairs.

Flushing, she said, "I was just coming back down."

"He's resting comfortably. Doc Jane says his vitals are improving. He's out of immediate danger."

Blay cut in, "So we're going to bed. Before we fall over."

Qhuinn yawned so hard his jaw popped. "Doc Jane is crashing herself down there. Guess she's been up for two days straight. She's going to call us immediately if anything changes."

"Let me know if you need me?" she said.

"I think we're okay for now. Thanks for everything. Really."

Hugs were exchanged along with good-days, and she must have done a pretty good job of playing normal, because moments later, they headed for the second floor together.

Unaware of her worry.

Layla glanced back toward the billiards room. Took her phone out and checked the time.

Three a.m.

Still no text in return.

Before she was clear on what she was doing, she slipped out through the dining room and the kitchen. The *doggen* were hard at work preparing Last Meal, and Fritz barely looked up with a deferential nod as she hightailed it past him.

Nobody noticed as she stepped through into the garage. Or rushed to the locked door on the far side. Once she entered the code on the keypad, there was a brief beeping sound as the dead bolt was released.

Moments later, she was behind the wheel of her car and speeding off.

As she proceeded down the mountain, the *mhis* slowed her, and the delay made her heart pound even harder. But she made it to the foot of the mountain, and as she turned onto the rural highway, she really hit the gas.

There was not a lot of time.

God, this had to be what an addiction felt like, she thought numbly as she gripped the steering wheel hard enough to make her knuckles burn.

The pull to the drug or drink ... or in her case, Xcor ... was irresistible. And there was no pleasure in giving in, just an aching guilt and a resonant self-loathing over the fact that you had once again overridden your better impulses and succumbed to what might very well kill you.

Or at the least, ruin your life.

But the Scribe Virgin save her soul, she was incapable of not going to make sure Xcor was okay.

At the King's audience house, Paradise smiled at the elderly male in front of her desk. "Oh, you're welcome. I'm glad that we got you in tonight."

"You have been most helpful." He bowed to her, his cap in hand. "Be of well hour unto the dawn."

"Yourself also."

As he walked out of the parlor, she sat back in her chair and closed her eyes. Last appointment of the night. Wrath had seen between two and four people an hour for eight hours, so that was at least sixteen, maybe up to thirty people. And for each of them, she had followed the protocol her father had set up: the check-in, the registration if they had never been to see the King before, the offer of food and drink before they were summoned. Then afterward, she had bid them good-day and entered into the database the notes her father gave her about the discussion and any decisions that had been made or permissions granted.

She wasn't just exhausted. She was wrung-out. So much to learn, so many names and issues, family trees and bloodlines, and there was no room for error.

Plus, she had had to be welcoming to everyone and engage them in conversation while they waited, especially if they came alone.

Not that that had been a requirement of the job set out by her father. But she had felt like it was important.

Maybe because of her stewardess outfit.

More likely because of her *glymera* training.

"Lot of empty chairs here."

Her lids popped open and she jumped. "Peyton! Jesus, can't you knock?"

"I did. And one of the Brothers let me in—which nearly made me lose bladder control." He glanced back at the open archway. "And you don't have a door in front of your desk or I woulda done the knuckle thing. Sorry I scared you."

Jogging her mouse to the side, she cleared the computer screen of multicolored, transparent bubbles. "What do you want."

"You haven't answered any of my texts. Or calls."

"I'm pissed off at you."

"Parry, come on. Don't be like this."

"I've got a question for you." She shifted her glare from the Excel spreadsheet she'd been working on to his blue eyes. "How'd you like it if you were denied making a choice because you have blond hair."

He threw up his hands. "Whatever, we're not talking about hair color—"

"I'm serious. Stop arguing with me and answer the question."

"I would go to CVS and buy some black hair dye."

Shaking her head, Paradise picked up the notebook with

her punch list on it and checked off a couple of things she'd already done.

"I don't understand why it's such a big deal," Peyton muttered. "Why do you want to be in the war anyway? Aristocrats are going to get killed out there, too, you know. Why don't you want to be safe—"

"Behind a desk, right? Or more likely in a dress in a big house. Right?"

"It's not wrong to look out for the fairer sex."

"Don't you have to get back to your bong."

She could feel him glaring at her from his greater height. "Don't you remember the raids, Parry? Don't you remember what that was like? People were slaughtered in their own homes. They had pieces of their bodies hacked off of them while they were alive. They found Lash's parents sitting around their dining room table, the dead bodies arranged so they were upright in those chairs like they were having dinner. Why do you want to be a part of that?"

Paradise met that hard stare again. "I don't!"

"So why are we having this fight!"

"Because *I* want to choose. I want to be able to assume the risk if I want—and don't hit me with the recap on those deaths like I don't recall every single thing that happened. Members of my bloodline were murdered, too. Am I not allowed to want revenge? Or is that a dick-only thing as well?"

He planted his hands on the desk and leaned into her. "Males can't give birth."

She stood up out of her chair and met him jaw-to-jaw. "You got that right. I'd like to see even one of you try to go through that experience. You'd be crying like a little bitch in ten minutes."

Peyton's stare dropped to her mouth for a split second, and the distraction surprised her.

In all the years of friendship, that was something that had never happened.

It hadn't even been approached, actually.

"Fine," he said grimly. "Put your money where your mouth is."

"Excuse me?"

"Join the program." He swept his hand over the desk. "Come out from behind here, put your application in, and try to pass the physical test."

"Maybe I will—"

At that moment, her father walked in. "Oh, hello, Peyton. How are you, son?"

Immediately, Peyton disengaged. "Sir, I'm well, sir. Thank you."

As the two shook hands, she was pretty sure her father was clueless as to the undercurrents in the parlor—and very sure Peyton was not. His shoulders were still set tightly, as if he were arguing with her in his head.

". . . kind of you to come and support Paradise." Her father smiled at her. "Especially on this first night. I must say, you have exceeded my expectations, my dearest one. This is going to be a wonderful way for you to keep busy before your presentation."

"Thank you, Father," she said, bowing.

"Well, I must needs depart. Peyton, perhaps you will keep her company until the dawn?"

Those sharp blues shot back over to her. "You're not at home anymore?"

"Do not be alarmed," her father interjected smoothly. "She is fully accompanied and properly chaperoned. Now, if you will excuse me, I must depart."

To check on their "visitor," no doubt.

"The Brothers have escorted the King off the property," her father said as he came around the desk and embraced her. "The *doggen* shall be cleaning for an hour, at least. Call upon me if you need aught?"

"I will."

And then he was gone.

"I can't believe he's letting you stay here," Peyton said.

"It's not necessarily his choice."

"What's that mean?"

"Nothing." She pulled a hand through her hair, shaking out the waves. "You don't have to stay. As a matter of fact, I wish you wouldn't."

She could feel him staring at her, and when he didn't reply, she glared at him. "What."

Those eyes of his were heavy lidded in a way she'd never seen before. "You've never been so . . ."

"Obnoxious?"

"No," he muttered. "Not that."

"Well, what, then." When he didn't answer her, she shook

her head. "Go home, Peyton. Just go home and light up and get ready to big-man all over the campus at the training center. It's the role you were born to play."

With that, she walked around him and left the parlor. She didn't care what he did, whether he left . . . or kept standing there at her desk until the *doggen* Swiffered him out with the dust bunnies.

She was done.

For the night. And with males, in general.

FORTY-ONE

"No. Here. Put him by the fire—"

Xcor broke himself loose of the holds upon his arms.

"I am not an invalid."

As he limped across the shallow room of the cottage he had bought for Layla, he kept to himself the fact that he was cold to the bone, and he did, in fact, appreciate the warmth of the flames that boiled around the logs at the hearth.

"Your leg is broken," Zypher said.

Whilst he settled himself upon the sofa, a sharp nausea threatened to empty his stomach, but he buried that response as well, swallowing down the risen bile. "It shall mend."

"There are victuals here."

He didn't know who said that. Did not care. "Where is the liquor?"

"Here."

As a bottle of God only knew what appeared before him, he took what was proffered, shucked the cap, and brought the open mouth to his lips. Vodka it was, the white bite burning the back of his throat and lighting a second set of flames in his gut.

It had been a very, very long trip home, with him dematerializing mile by mile because they had no motorized conveyances at their disposal. And now, all he wanted was to be left alone—and he feared, given that all of them were here and worrying over him, it was going to take more energy than he had to get his soldiers to go in peace.

"You were nearly killed," Balthazar said from by the door.

He drank more of the spirit. "Yourself as well—"

"Someone is here," Syphon said by the bay window. "A car."

Immediately, all guns were unholstered and trained upon the glass—except for his. Beneath his thin jacket, his arm was hanging limp, the joint most likely dislocated.

And he was not putting down the vodka.

"Who is it," he demanded, thinking it was likely the *doggen* he had sought to hire.

" 'Tis a female," someone breathed. "And not of the servant class."

Instantly, Xcor wrenched around and bared his fangs. But he didn't need visual confirmation. There was only one female who knew about this place, and who would come in a car.

"Leave us," he commanded. "Now."

When his Band of Bastards just stood in a semi-circle, transfixed by what was out that fucking window, he released a lion's growl. "Leave us!"

Zypher cleared his throat. "She is bonny, indeed, Xcor—"

"And she shall be the last sight e'er you behold if you don't get out of here!"

One by one, the soldiers grudgingly dematerialized . . . such that, when his female knocked upon the door, he was by himself.

Seeking further fortification from the bottle, he drank hard; then rousted himself off the couch, walked over and opened the panels wide.

The second Layla looked at him, she exclaimed, "You're hurt!"

The shock in her face was such that he glanced down at himself and his bloodstained clothes. "Yes, it would appear I am." Funny, now that she was before him, he felt no more pain. "Won't you come and warm yourself by the fire."

As if there were nothing wrong. As if she hadn't blown him off when they were supposed to have met at midnight—so she could give him her decision.

He knew her answer, however. Her previous absence was all the reply required—she had clearly come to her senses.

Layla stepped inside, her eyes going up and down his body. "Xcor, what happened?"

"Nothing." He closed them in. "I thought you indicated you could not get away."

"I saw what happened downtown. And I had to ..."

"Had to what? Come here to see if I had died and thus set you free of your obligation?" When she didn't answer, he chuckled and returned to the couch. "Pardon me, but I need to sit."

He was acutely aware of that stare of hers tracking him. And no doubt her keen ears caught the groan that he did his best to hide.

"You should go to a doctor."

Xcor laughed and took another drink from the bottle. "You think this warrants attention? The Black Dagger Brotherhood must have a different standard for injury than we do. I have had much, much worse happen upon me in the course of centuries. This is naught of consequence, nothing that shall not be cured upon the night's fall."

"When was the last time you fed?"

Abruptly, his body stilled. "Are you offering."

As she got busy looking everywhere in the cottage but at him, he laughed softly again. "I'll take that as a no. Besides, you already aided and abetted the enemy once, and we all know how well that turned out."

"Why are you baiting me?"

He drank anew, swallowing hard. "Because I feel like it. And I'm a bastard, remember? A bastard who has forced you to come unto my presence night after night whilst you become heavy with another male's young."

"You are in pain."

"Actually, now that you are here, I am no longer."

That quieted her for a moment.

And then he was shocked when she took steps forward, approaching the couch ... because as she came forth, she pushed up the sleeve on her right arm.

"What are you doing?" he demanded.

"I am going to give you my vein." She stopped before him. Close enough to grab. Near enough so that if he wanted, he could have yanked her into his lap. Found her breasts with his hands, his mouth. "You are worse off than you think."

"Oh, aye," he said harshly. "You are right. But not about my injuries."

She put her wrist to him. "You were hit by a vehicle of the Brotherhood's, weren't you."

"So you feel you owe me this? Interesting change in affiliation."

"You do not deny it, then."

"I cannot fathom where you are going with this, female. You had no comfort being treasonous before. What has changed?"

"You didn't attack them tonight, did you. You had a chance when the fighters happened to go after members of the Brotherhood, but instead of ordering your soldiers to target Manny and Rhage, or the other Brothers who were down there, you left the theater without hurting any of them."

Aye, he thought. He had gathered that the RV was the Brothers'.

He had caught that scent dematerializing out of it—and no other vampire group could afford such a luxury.

Xcor cracked a hard laugh. "Have you not heard of self-preservation? If I was injured as badly as you think I am, I left to save myself."

"Bullshit. I know your reputation. You had an opportunity tonight and you didn't take it. Matter of fact, you've had the chance to attack our compound for almost a year and you've done nothing."

"Must I remind you of the nature of our arrangement here?" he asked in a bored tone. "You show up and indulge mine eyes, and I don't slaughter them all."

"A vow given to a female would never stop you. You are the Bloodletter's son."

Oh, but a vow to you would, he thought to himself.

Her voice grew strong. "You are not going to agress on them, are you. Not tonight. Not tomorrow night. Not a year from now. And not because I'm coming here to see you—otherwise, you would have killed one or more of them in the alleys this eve. That would be outside the scope of our agreement, would it not?"

As he stared up at her, her eyes were so shrewd that he felt diminished in stature—and not because he was sitting down and she was standing over him.

"For whatever reason, they are no longer a target for you, are they," she said. "Are they."

As Layla stood above Xcor, she spoke aloud the realization that had formulated in her head during the drive from the Brotherhood compound here to the cottage.

It was as if she had been walking at a steep incline and had suddenly reached a clearing in the brush that showed her the vista that she had been a part of, and yet unaware of.

"Answer me," she demanded.

He cocked a brow. "You said I am a male of no honor, that the vow to a female would not curtail my actions. Why do you want me to give you any reply when it cannot be trusted."

"What's changed? I know it has nothing to do with me, but something has shifted."

"Since you are so good at filling in my responses, I believe I shall just sit back and allow you to hold both sides of this conversation."

As he continued to stare up at her, his face as calm and composed as a mask, she knew he was going to give her nothing further. And perhaps he was right: She could not trust what he said.

She would, however, put faith in his actions.

"Take from me," she said, extending her wrist. "And heal."

"You are a perverse female. What about your young?"

"Females can safely feed a male, provided they do not take overmuch."

She had fed Qhuinn and Blay up until about a month ago, when they had switched to Selena out of an overabundance of caution. And anyway, she herself had taken a vein a mere twelve hours ago, so she was at her very strongest.

And he was not.

"You have not fed properly since you took my vein, have you."

His eyes flicked away to the fire. "Of course I have."

"You lie."

"Please make use of that car of yours and spirit yourself back to the Brotherhood."

"No."

His eyes narrowed to a glare as he looked back at her. "You are trying my patience."

"Because I'm right about all of this—"

Just like that, he was up on his feet, and even though he had a limp, he still managed to press himself against her, forcing her to take a step back or fall off her heels. And another. And another.

Until she was up against the wall.

And held there by his body.

"You might want to rethink your conclusion, Chosen."

Layla found it difficult to breathe, but not because he was putting any direct pressure on her chest. "I know something else."

"And what might that be."

She thought back to overhearing what Blay and Qhuinn had said about the night before, about how Rhage, V, and the twins had gone out to where the Band of Bastards had stayed.

"I know that you had yet another chance to kill them. I know they went to the house you had been living in, and you didn't leave anything behind that could hurt them. You could have either ambushed them there, or set up some kind of offensive, and you did not."

At that, he broke off from her.

It was painful to watch him limp around, see his blood-stained, torn clothes, witness the exhaustion.

Grimly, she said, "So I'm not exactly feeding the enemy anymore, am I?"

Eventually, he stopped before the fire. Putting one hand upon his hip, he stared down at the flames and seemed curiously defeated.

"Just go," he said.

"Why would you choose to hide what for me is good news?" The idea that he might not be trying to kill the Brotherhood or Wrath anymore would be a tremendous relief. "Why?"

"If we did not have our arrangement, would you come and see me."

Layla felt a strange warmth come over her, and she was dimly aware that they were, once again, approaching some kind of divide.

All of their nights thus far had been a dance defined by the role of manipulator and victim.

And there had been a perverse safety for her in the position she took.

It meant she could hide behind doing a duty for the Brotherhood.

It meant she could pretend that she was forced into this.

The truth . . .was far more complicated than that.

An image of him from the night before, standing where he was now before the hearth, made her want to take off her fleece; if she had been hot before, she was now afire.

Xcor looked over his shoulder. As the flickering light filtered over his features, his facial deformity seemed even more prominent. And yet though he might have been ugly to some . . . he was not to her.

She tried to picture him without his clothes on.

"So," he taunted. "Would you still come here? And do not worry about hurting my feelings. The very female who birthed me did not want me. I am well familiar with feminine disregard."

After further silence, he slashed his arm through the air. "I believe that is your answer, then—"

"I would," she said forcefully. "I would come to see you."

She found herself putting her hands to her swollen belly, and wishing she could spare her unborn young this reality.

His eyes flared in shock. Then narrowed. "Why."

His voice was strident, a demand that challenged her to speak some other truth.

"I don't know why." She shrugged. "But reasoning doesn't change the fact, does it."

There was another long silence.

When Xcor spoke next, it was so softly that she was unsure what he said. But it sounded like, "I wasn't looking to be transformed."

She didn't bother to ask him to repeat whatever it was. No doubt, if he had intended her to hear the words, he would have made things louder.

"Take my vein."

In issuing the order, she knew there was no going back. Having crossed into this realm that lacked pretense and was all about choice, she was very aware that her destiny was changing. But at least it wasn't through some random and irrelevant decision to go left or right.

This was conscious. So conscious that it was as if the cozy room in this picturesque little cottage had been bolded with color and infused with scents more vivid than her nose could handle. Her hearing, too, was acute to the point of pain, every crackle from the fire or breath from her mouth or his resonating into some great canyon's echo.

This time, when he came over to her, it was not fast and it was not with aggression.

His eyes were on her, but they were wary, as if the predator was now in fear of his prey.

Stepping in beside her, Xcor offered his forearm. When she just looked at it, he said, "I saw them once do this. A gentlemale to a female of worth?"

"Yes," she said roughly. "It is done thusly."

After she slipped her own arm into his, he led her over to the sofa and sat her down on the worn cushions. Then he turned around and left the room.

"Where are you going?" she called out.

FORTY-TWO

"**Y**ou have the most beautiful hands."

As Trez lay in his bed with Selena beside him, they were both naked and totally exposed. The sex had been so heavy-duty, the covers were on the floor, their hot skin only now beginning to cool in the subtle air currents of the dark room.

"You've mentioned that before," she said with a smile.

He made an *mmmm-hmmmm* in the back of this throat. "I like them on me. I like to look at them. I like the feel of them."

Smoothing his palm over hers, he felt the contact all over his body. So peaceful, he thought. This was so peaceful.

"I like to see the stars," she said, after a while. "Through the window over there."

"Yeah."

As it was just before five a.m., the shutters were about to come down for the day. With fall getting a grip on not just the weather, but the sunlight, dawn wasn't arriving until later these days.

"You know, I've never had this before," he heard himself say.

She turned over on her side, propping her head up on the hand he'd been attending to. And like she knew he missed the contact, she gave him her other one to play with.

"Had what?" she asked.

"This kind of quiet."

During all those years of empty orgasms, he wished he'd

known such profound communion was waiting for him. It would have made that nutrition-less gorging totally unnecessary.

"Do you want some music or something?" he asked abruptly, in case he was the only one enjoying the quiet.

"No, this is . . . perfect."

At that, he had to twist around and kiss her on the mouth. Then it was a case of resettling back against the pillows and resuming this new kind of hand job . . . where he traced each of her fingers with his, stretching them up and pulling them out, before playing with the strong, blunt tips.

"I love the stars," she said as if she were speaking to herself.

"I have an idea about tonight."

"Do you?"

He threw out another *mmmmm-hmmmm*. "It's a surprise. You're going to need to put off our boat ride, though."

And he was probably going to want a valium. But she was going to love it.

"Trez?"

"Yeah?"

"I want you to do something for me."

He smiled in the darkness. "Does this involve my tongue, by any chance? Just name the body part, my queen."

"No."

The change in her voice stopped him. And for a split second he wanted to say, *Please, no. We can talk about it at nightfall. Let's leave the day hours for the fantasy of forever.*

But as always, he could deny her nothing. "What is it?"

Selena took a while to answer, and that probably meant she was choosing her words carefully.

He tried to stay calm. "Take your time."

"My sisters." She hesitated. "The ones who have passed . . . they're put up in a cemetery. You know, right where you found me?"

That hedgerow, he thought. The one that he had looked through to see those marble statues . . . which now he feared weren't made of marble at all.

"Yes, I remember."

"Don't let them take me up there." She took her hand away from him and sat up. As she stared down at him, her long, beautiful black hair poured over her shoulders, cover-

ing one of her breasts, touching the skin of her thighs.
"They're going to want to. You're supposed to pick a position . . . you know, when the time comes, they can put you in
any position you want. Then they plaster over your hair and
your face and your body. It's a ritual. That's why they're all
different up there—in different poses, I mean."

Trez rubbed his face. Which did nothing to relieve the
lancing pain in his chest. "Selena, let's not talk about this—"

She grabbed his arm. Hard. "Promise me. I won't be able
to advocate for myself when that time comes. I need you to
do that for me."

Again, he could deny her nothing—and as a bonded
male, that not only seemed right, but healthy. Except with
this request? It broke him in half to nod.

"All right." He cleared his throat. "Okay, I'll make sure
of it."

At once, her body relaxed and she let out an exhale.
Then, as she resettled beside him, she shook her head. "I
know this is against everything I've been taught and all the
traditions of my service . . . but a part of me is paranoid that
they're stuck in there."

"I'm sorry—what? You mean, your sisters?"

She nodded. "How do we know for a fact that the Fade
is real? What if everything we've been told is true is actually
not? As with everyone else in the Sanctuary, I have always
tried to avoid that cemetery—I hate the silence and the
stillness inside, and, God, those poor females, some of
whom I knew and shared meals with and worked alongside
in service to the Scribe Virgin." She cursed softly. "They're
stuck in that cemetery, not just frozen in their bodies, but
forgotten by the rest of us because we can't stand how we
feel when we're with them. What if they can see us? What if
they can hear us? What if time just stretches out into forever with them imprisoned . . ." Selena shuddered. "I don't
want that. When I go, I want to be free."

Her eyes returned to the window, to the twinkling stars
so high above.

"Every species has a version of an afterlife," he said.
"Humans have Heaven. Vampires the Fade. For Shadows, it
is the Eternal. We can't all be wrong—and each one is a
version of the same. So it would seem to make sense that
there's something after all this."

"But there's no guarantee—and you won't know until it's too late." She seemed to retreat into herself. "You know, when I'm in the Arrest, I can hear things . . . when I'm in that place where my body is just . . . out of my control, I can hear and smell, I can see. My awareness is with me, I am there, but I can't do anything. As I've said before, there's no greater panic than what you feel when your brain is functioning and nothing else is."

Don't lose it, he told himself. Don't you dare lose it.

You pull your shit together and you be there for her. Right here, right now.

As she grew quiet, he put himself in that place she had described, aware of everything, but unable to respond or speak or react.

Reaching over, he stroked her long hair back. And then he was kissing her, softly, slowly. A moment later, he rolled on top of her and found her sex with his own. As the penetration happened, as that familiar yet ever shocking tightness of her gripped him, he gave her his vow through the physical act.

Sometimes, the evil you fought wasn't anything you could hit or shoot or dismember. Sometimes you couldn't even hurt it.

And that was really fucking awful.

As his hips rocked and she wrapped her arms around him, he kept the rhythm sweet and careful so that he could kiss her the entire time.

Halfway through, he caught the rainwater scent of tears.

They were both crying.

Down in the training center's gym, Rhage was running like he was being chased by his own beast.

The treadmill was not feeling it. He was pretty sure that the scream coming from the belt—which was loud enough that he could hear it over the T.I. he was pumping into his ears like the shit was heroin—meant the machine was going to check out at any moment. But he didn't want to break stride long enough to move to the one next door.

When the thing began to smell like a *lesser*, however, he knew the decision had been made for him. Jumping to the side rails, he pulled out the red Stop card and the slowdown was pretty instantaneous. Either that or he had timed his get-off with the machine's functional demise.

Catching his breath, he mopped his face with one of the scratchy white quarter towels. The things were pretty much sandpaper, but they all preferred 'em that way. Fritz had tried, from time to time, to switch the old schools out to something softer, but he and his brothers always protested. These were gym towels. They were supposed to be thin and mean, the terry-cloth equivalent of coyotes.

When you were sweating like a pig and couldn't feel the bottoms of your feet from exertion, you didn't want to pat yourself down with a Pomeranian.

Had he really done twenty-four miles?

Shit, how long had he been down here?

Popping off his Beats, he realized that not only had his high-steppers gone numb, but his groin muscles were on fire, and that shoulder he'd injured a good five nights ago was cranked off.

He ended up parking it on one of the wooden benches that ran down the far side of the room. As his breath gradually came back to him, he felt as if he were surrounded by his brothers even though he was alone: Whether it was the bench press that was still set to the six-hundred-pound load Butch had put it at yesterday or the barbell that Z had been doing curls with or the chin bar that Tohr had been crunching up and down on, he could picture each of the fighters with him, hear their voices, see them walk by, feel their eyes on him as they talked.

And all that should have made him feel more connected, instead of less so.

But the reality was, even if the forty-by-sixty-foot space had been crammed tight with all those big bodies, he would still have felt isolated.

Passing that towel over his face again, he closed his eyes and was transported to a different place, a different time . . . to a memory that he knew now was what he had been trying to put behind him ever since it had threatened to resurface.

Bella's white farmhouse. That porch of hers, the wraparound one that was so New England cozy you wanted to either vomit . . . or cop a squat and eat some apple pie on the bitch. Him walking out that front door, head hanging like he had been decapitated and only the gristle of his neck was keeping his basketball still on.

His beloved Mary upstairs in that bedroom, having just told him to fuck off.

Although, of course, she hadn't been so crude.

His life had been over as he'd left that house. Even though he'd been ostensibly alive, he had been a dead male walking . . .

. . . until suddenly she had exploded out of that doorway in her bare feet.

I'm not okay, Rhage. I'm not okay. . . .

"Why are you thinking like this, buddy." He rubbed that hard towel over his face once more. "Just drop that shit . . . come on, think about something else. . . ."

Except his brain wouldn't be rerouted. And the next memory was even worse.

A hospital room, but not one here at the compound, or even at Havers's clinic. A human hospital room, and his Mary was in the bed.

Shit, he could still remember the color of her skin. Wrong, all wrong. Not just pale, but beginning to go gray.

To save her, he had done the only thing he could think of, thrown the only Hail Mary he had: He had sought out the Scribe Virgin. Had left that human hospital and gone home to his room, and lowered himself down on cut diamonds until his knees had run red with blood.

He had prayed for a miracle.

With a curse, he stretched out on the bench, leaning his torso back on the unforgiving wood while keeping both feet on the floor on either side.

His Mary wasn't coming home today. She was staying at Safe Place.

The mother of that child had been taken back to Havers's. After slipping into a coma.

The staff had decided to keep the young at the house for the day, and Mary wanted to be with the girl.

God, he remembered that anguish of daylight when Mary had been sick in the hospital. It hadn't been safe for him to be with her during the sunshine hours, and he had been terrified she would die when he couldn't get to her.

Guess they could drive that young over to see her *mahmen* if shit came to that. As a pretrans, she could go out even at high noon.

Staring up at the ceiling, he thought of Trez and Selena.

Their date. Their escape from downtown. The fun they'd had evading the human police.

That was so worth fighting for. All of it.

His Mary wasn't coming home today, and he didn't know how he was going to make it through the next twelve hours until he saw her in person again. And that was even knowing he could call or text, or Skype with her at any moment for as long as he liked.

That little girl was probably going to lose her *mahmen*.

And Trez was probably going to lose Selena.

Rhage was pretty sure all of them were praying for a miracle just as he had. And maybe that was what he was having problems with.

Why had he gotten lucky? Tohr hadn't. Well, yes, the brother had found Autumn, and that was a blessing beyond measure. But as much as he loved that female, his losing Wellsie had nearly killed him.

He just didn't get it. Unless the Scribe Virgin stepped in again, or someone found a cure . . .

Why had he and Mary been spared?

As his brain began to cramp up on that one, he had to shut the thoughts down. He didn't want to go mad down here all by himself.

Yeah, he thought wryly. 'Cuz it was so much better to share that with your loved ones.

Scary times. Scary times.

If deaths came in threes . . . he thought numbly. Who was going to be the third one?

FORTY-THREE

As Xcor walked away from the cottage's main room, Layla was prepared to follow him outside and make him feed on what passed for a lawn if she had to. But just as she was about to heft herself off the sofa, she heard the sound of . . . the shower.

Continuing through on the vertical impulse, she went across and around the corner to stand in front of the closed door of the bathroom.

". . . fuck . . ." he muttered on the far side.

"Xcor?"

"Leave me be. I shall return in a moment."

As another curse floated out through the gaps around the doorjamb, she took hold of the latch, and pulled things open.

Xcor was standing before the sink, his shirt half on and half off, his torso turned at a wrong angle as he tried to get the button down over his head—without hurting the bullet wound in his side.

"What are you doing?" he demanded through the folds of black fabric.

For a moment, all she could do was stare at his ribbed abdomen, the muscles striated across his belly and cut so deeply they threw shadows. But then there were his hips, hollow and jutting out from under his skin, his combat pants hanging so low only the huge muscles of his thighs were keeping them on.

He was unbelievably powerful. But also too thin.

Shaking herself into focus, she said, "I'm going to help you get that off."

"I can handle it, just—" As he twisted again, he let out a groan of pain.

Ignoring him, she shut the door so what little heat was boiling up from the shower stayed in the bath. "Stop. You're just going to hurt yourself."

"I'm fine," he snapped.

The instant she put her hand on his arm, he went dead still.

"Let me help you," she whispered.

The good news was that he'd gotten the bulk of the shirt up over his head. So there was no way he saw her hands shake as she took hold and gently pulled upward, inching it up his arms, revealing to her eyes the fans of muscle that ran down the sides of his torso and then the massive bulges of his pectorals.

His breath panted in and out of him, his chest rising and falling in a pump that got faster as she carried the shirt over his arms.

Heavy arms. Thick arms that narrowed at the elbow and then at the wrist, but plumped up everywhere else.

As what had covered him came loose, all she could think of was that he was a killer. A straight-up killer whose body reflected the work that he did.

"Wait for me out there." He refused to meet her eyes. "I shall not take from you when I am unclean."

"That's a bad gash there."

When she touched the warm, pale skin under the angry red stripe on his side, he flinched. But his voice remained strong. "It shall be healed by nightfall."

"Only if you feed."

The grunt she got in response was a dismissal if she'd ever heard one. And he followed it up with, "If you do not leave, you're going to see a lot more than my chest."

"You're injured worse on your leg." She eyed the ever-growing blood spot on those combats.

His hands went to the zipper of his fly. "Well?"

As if he were giving her one last chance.

"Well?" She shrugged. "Do you honestly think I'm going to let you get under that hot water without help? You're white as a sheet. Your blood pressure is obviously low. You're liable to pass out."

"Oh, for the love of . . ."

Now he looked at her. And, with quick efficiency, released the fastening at his waist. The top part of the pants fell away. The bottom stuck in place over those thighs.

But something was revealed.

And it was . . . erect.

Xcor cocked a brow. "You can stop staring. I find it hard to believe you are enjoying the view."

She tried to look away. She did. But her eyes had a mind of their own.

"You are so big," she breathed.

He recoiled. As if that was the last thing in the world he'd expected her to say. And when he spoke next, his voice had changed.

Now, he begged. "Layla . . . Chosen Layla . . . you need to leave."

As Xcor stood all but completely naked in front of the female, he couldn't move. And not just because his combats had wedged themselves above his knees and turned into a hobble.

Layla's green eyes were impossibly wide as they focused on his sex—and stayed there.

Could this evening go any farther off the rails, he wondered.

Wait—mayhap he should not offer that kind of opening to the Fates.

Meanwhile, his cock was loving the attention. The damn thing kicked as if to suggest she should shake and make friends.

He covered the rigid length up with both his palms, stretching it flat over his lower abdomen. "Layla."

Instead of doing the reasonable thing and backing away from him in horror and disgust, she bent and grasped the waistband of his combats. Before he could shove her off, his pants were down his thighs and pooling around his ankles.

"Come, let's get you under the spray."

She didn't give him a chance to protest. And a second later, his battered and bruised body was under the warm falling water, aching bones and healing scars both scream-ing and sighing at the impact. With a snap of the curtain, she gave him the privacy he wanted—except the *klonk* over by the toilet suggested she hadn't departed, but rather had shut the lid and sat down.

There was no reason not to follow through with the soap and the shampoo, and he tried to be quick about it. Unfor-tunately, the bullet that had narrowly missed his lung was stinging sure as if there were battery acid upon his flesh. And the soap did not help that.

The other reason to be fast was that he was acutely aware of both his nakedness and his arousal. The more effi-cient he was, the sooner he could get dressed.

No clothes, though. He had no clean clothes.

Closing his eyes in defeat, he rinsed the suds out of his hair, tilting his head back. Which was a mistake. The water's rush hit his cock, and damned if it didn't feel like hands, her hands.

Or maybe her mouth—

The release was not unexpected. It was, however, un-wanted. As his erection kicked and his orgasm rolled through him, he gritted his teeth—

"You don't have to hide it," she said in a husky voice. "I can see the shadow of you."

"So look away," he groaned as his hips rolled into his ejaculations.

"I can't."

Sagging against the tile, he knew he had lost whatever upper hand he had believed he had in the situation. That female had guessed the terrible truth about him. She knew his aims had changed. And she seemed unwilling to keep whatever relationship this was on terms that gave both of them some honor and dignity.

But at least she didn't know it was all based on her.

That his life . . . pathetic as it was . . . was based on her now.

If that came to light, it would be his ruination.

Xcor twisted the faucet off with a crank, determined to put an end to all of this and send her away just so he could get his defenses properly back in place. Just as he was going to rip the curtain down and put it around himself, the heavy weight of a towel was tossed over the pole.

"For your modesty," she said.

Was she laughing at him?

Not bothering to dry himself off, he covered his lower body and pushed the curtain back. She was indeed on the loo, the fleece she wore camouflaging her changed shape from the pregnancy.

Without a word, she pulled her sleeve back again and put out her arm.

There was a challenge in her eyes.

"Fine," he snapped, angry at himself. At her. At this new territory they had entered.

Lowering himself to his knees—because she was right, he was awfully dizzy—he put his fangs to her flesh.

Starved. He was starved for her.

And yet he struck as gently as he could.

At the first taste, he moaned, his body swaying, its weight knocking into the cabinet into which the sink had been mounted. Her blood was a dark wine that made him thirsty instead of satiating his dry throat, and between his legs, his cock kicked again and again.

He was orgasming into the towel, the pleasure coursing through his veins, his bones, his flesh—

Mine.

From out of the depths of him, the urge to take her rose so violently that he started to act on it, his body on the verge of leaping up and dragging her to the floor so he could mount her.

Pregnancy or not, he was going to get at her sex and leave his mark inside of her—

Breaking off the contact, he pushed himself away from her, bracing his feet against that cabinet, the cold porcelain of the tub behind him biting into his shoulders as he went rigid in an attempt to control himself.

"What's wrong—"

"Go!" he shouted.

Within him, his sexual beast was prowling and ready to have her—and coupled with his blood lust, he knew he could not handle the pair of instincts together. He was liable to chew her wrist off at the same time he fucked her raw.

"Xcor, you have not had much at all—"

Gritting his teeth, he closed his eyes and strained. "Get the fuck out of here! If you want your young to live—leave! I will attack you! *Go!*"

That got her attention.

As, no doubt, did the fact that he was still orgasming all over himself, the towel now lost, the jets kicking out and marking his own thighs and belly as his leg muscles trembled at the force he was exerting—to make sure he didn't jump on her.

"Go!"

A split second later, she was out of the bathroom; one moment after that she was out of the cottage. And she was in such a hurry, she left both of the doors open, so he saw the headlights of her car come on and watched them circle the scruffy lawn in front before streaking off down the lane.

It wasn't until he could neither see her red taillights nor hear the crackle of her tires that he eased up even a little on the bracing.

Gripping his cock, he began to stroke his shaft as he pictured her eyes on him, and heard anew the strange tone she'd used as she had pronounced him sizable.

He had no interest in masturbating.

But what he really didn't want was his rational side to completely desert him—such that he went after her through the night, stopping her somewhere unsafe just so he could do what he did not want to do to her.

No, this way he would stay put.

Oh, God . . . the way she had looked at him, he thought as he started to come again.

FORTY-FOUR

"**H**e said I needed a parka."

The following evening, as darkness settled over the compound and the shutters rose for the night, Selena looked back and forth between the two coats Fritz was holding up to her. One was red, the other black; both were wool and relatively long.

"Oh, I'm sorry, mistress." He turned back to the closet in the mud room by the garage. "How about either of these?"

This time, he offered her a choice between a puffy waist-length jacket that looked like it was made of dinner rolls, and one that was much longer. Both were black and had little tags that read, PATAGONIA.

"It's a relatively mild night," Fritz pointed out. "Perhaps the shorter of the two?"

"Yes, I think you're right."

Slipping the thing on, she was amazed at how light it was, and after zipping it up, she tested out the two pockets.

"This is fantastic."

The butler beamed. "My pleasure. Gloves?"

"I think I'll just keep my hands in here."

"As you wish, mistress."

Heading out into the kitchen, she felt as buoyant as a bubble. Trez had refused to tell her anything about where they were going, and the unknown was like a heady wine, making her head buzz and her body float.

She hesitated at the flap door into the dining room. The sounds and smells of First Meal were obvious and friendly, the voices ones she knew well, the scents making her stomach rumble. And yet she turned around and headed out the other exit of the kitchen, the one that opened up by the flank of the grand stairway.

Everyone had been so kind the night before, all the females lavishing such incredible attention and support on her.

She didn't want to bother them again and didn't really want the extra regard.

She was feeling a little tired and wanted to save all her strength for the date.

As she came into the foyer, she saw Trez and Manny standing close together on the far side of the mosaic apple tree in the floor. They were talking intently, each one grave.

Her heart stopped. Was the physician insisting she stay in? Or was he going to make her go down to the clinic first?

She glanced behind her and considered bolting. It wasn't going to be underground, though—

"You need to take care of her," Manny warned.

"I will. I swear on my brother's life."

Oh . . . shoot—

Manny took something out of his pocket. A key fob of some sort.

Dangling it in front of Trez's face, he said, "She's never been driven by anyone else."

"Then why are you giving her to me?"

"Because you need to go in style. You're taking your woman out, you don't need to be in some BMW."

"You are a car snob."

Selena frowned. Car? They were talking about—

Trez whipped around as if he had noticed her scent on the air, and the instant he saw her, he started to smile. "Hey, there, you ready, my queen?"

Stepping across the vast space, she smiled in return. She'd left her hair down again, because she knew by the way he stared at it, played with it, stroked it that he preferred it that way. And actually, she was not just getting used the style, but coming to like it best as well.

That formal chignon the Chosen were supposed to wear could give you one heck of a headache after a couple of hours.

Rising up to her tiptoes, she kissed his mouth and then

tucked herself in against his side, fitting perfectly under his arm. "I am *so* ready."

Manny clapped palms with Trez, and then said under his breath, "We gotchu."

"Thanks, man."

Then the doctor gave her a wink and headed to the dining room and all the people in it.

"What does that mean?" Selena asked as Trez opened the door out into the vestibule. "That 'gotchu'?"

"Nothing."

Leaning ahead, he pulled the second door free, and the cold of the night rushed in, making her nose tingle and her cheeks flush.

"Too much?" he asked.

"What?"

"Too cold? You shivered."

"I love it."

"Good, I want to put the top down."

Parked right in front of the stone steps was a vicious-looking black car, with black wheels and some kind of tail on the back.

"Dearest Virgin Scribe, what is that?" she said.

"It's called a Porsche nine-eleven turbo."

"Oh . . . my."

Going down to the steps, she approached the machine, taking one hand out of her pocket and running her fingertips down its flank. Smooth, shiny, ice-cold.

"But it has a roof, no?" she said.

"It does tricks."

Opening the door, he settled her in the passenger seat. "It's Manny's new baby. He got it a week ago—it's the same make and model of his last one, but the interior is different? That's what he says, at any rate."

Inside, she smelled leather and the human's cologne and Payne's scent.

Trez got in behind the wheel and shut his door. When he turned a key, a great growl started up, a subtle vibration emanating through the interior.

"Check this out." He hit another button. "Look up."

Like magic, everything that was overhead unlatched and lifted away, retracting in an orderly series of folds into a rear compartment.

"I figured you'd like to see the stars." He smiled and got the heater going. "It's got a screen, so we don't have to worry about backdraft."

Leaning back, she saw . . . the velvet heavens with its twinkling lights.

Letting out a shout of joy, she threw her arms around him and pulled him in for a kiss. "This is incredible!"

He laughed. "I can't believe you've never seen a convertible before."

"I never travel by car. Unless I'm with you."

"Well, get your belt on. This bitch is going to fly."

As he hit the gas, the car leaped forward like a horse out of the gate, and she couldn't help but look up to the night sky and smile so hard her cheeks hurt.

Even with the *mhis*, he went so fast, firing down the mountain until they got to the road at the bottom. He took a left.

"Where are we going?" she said as he punched the accelerator again, and she was sucked into the contours of her seat as the engine roared.

"You'll see." He glanced over. "Warm enough?"

"Perfectly so!"

It was loud and exhilarating, cold air whirling around her head, hot air blasting on her feet, the car growling and leaning into the curves of the road. Before she knew it, her heart was beating fast and her stomach doing flip-flops and she felt octane in her veins.

"I hope it's a long trip!" she shouted.

"What?"

"Never mind!"

She lost track of the minutes and the miles, but gradually she became aware that the forest landscape had grown dotted with human settlements. Soon, stores, neighborhoods of houses, a park, and stacks of apartment buildings appeared.

"Where are we?" she asked as he slowed to a stop at a red light.

"On the outskirts of Caldie."

"Are we going downtown again?"

"Nope." He smiled at her. "But we're almost at our destination."

A small car that was low to the ground and the color of a banana pulled up next to them, and she felt the driver glance over. Music was thumping inside of the other vehicle, and its engine revved up.

"Is he having some kind of spasm?" she asked. "Of the foot?"

"No, it's happening in another location," Trez muttered.

When the light overhead turned green, the little car exploded forward, its tires squealing, an unpleasant burning smell left in its wake.

"What was that all about?" she wondered.

"Wait for it."

Sure enough, a car with blue and white lights popped out of a parking lot and fell into pursuit. But not of Trez and herself.

Trez shook his head. "The little shit should know you never drag on this street. Besides, he's crazy to take this car on." He reached over and gave her hand a squeeze. "You ready?"

"Oh, yes." She looked around and saw nothing but a stretch of single-story businesses linked together by a common roof and a parking lot. "Are we here?"

"Almost."

Actually, they went quite a bit farther on, past another bunch of stores with the word *outlet* tacked onto every name. And then there was a shallow stretch of woods and a little hill, followed by . . .

Parking lots. Vacant parking lots big as the lawns of the Sanctuary.

Except then she looked out the other side of the car. "What . . . is *that*?"

"Welcome to Storytown."

Selena sat forward. On the far end of the biggest of the parking lots was a set of lit entrance signs so high and wide they defied comprehension. But what came after them? Was even more astounding. Vast mechanisms reaching high into the sky were lit up like rainbows, all flashing lights and spinning tops as if they were toys made for giants.

Trez turned Manny's car onto all the asphalt and roared across the acreage, heading for a gate in the fencing over to the left of what looked like the check-in area. As he stopped before the side entry, they had to wait for but a moment before a human in a navy-blue uniform triggered something and waved them through.

"Hey, Mr. Latimer."

Trez reached out and offered his hand. "Call me Trez."

"I'm Ted." They shook and the man nodded at Selena. "We're going to take great care of you guys tonight. Head through there."

"Roger that. Thanks, man."

"No problem."

As he hit the gas, Selena was overwhelmed by all of the neon lights. "What is this place. This is . . . magical."

"And it's all ours. No one else is here, just you and me."

"How is that . . . possible?"

"One of my security guys is the brother of the head of security over here. They spoke to the owners and they're doing me a little favor."

When they came up to a second guard, Trez stopped the car and cut off the engine. "You liked that crazy ride last night through downtown, right?"

"Oh, yes—yes, so much."

He leaned in and kissed her. "Wait'll you go upside down, my queen."

iAm watched from a security tower high in the center of the amusement park as Trez piloted the Porsche through the gate and came to a stop at the second security point.

"You want binocs?"

He glanced over his shoulder at Big Rob. "Nope. I'm good."

The bouncer from shAdoWs whistled as he put the handset back up to his peepers. "You have awesome eyes to see that far."

iAm just shrugged and took another draw from his Thermos mug. The coffee inside was strong and hot enough to pizza your tongue. Just the way he liked it.

He'd been not just asleep, but practically in a coma, when his brother had woken him up with this bright idea around ten this morning. The plan was nuts, of course. Who the hell rented out an entire park for three hours?

Especially when the damn thing had closed for the season the week before?

Trez did. That was who.

And iAm helped the guy get it done.

Making this all happen for Selena had taken an unbelievable amount of money, and some candid phone calls that had been hard to get through. But thanks to Big Rob back there, and his brother, Jim, a.k.a. Jimbo, and the wife of the owner who had just lost her father to cancer the summer before, they'd gotten it all set up: Staff had been called back from post-season retirement, and machines that were in the process of being winterized had been called into service again. They even had the concession stands working— thanks to the waiters at Sal's.

The joy on Selena's face, and the pride on his brother's puss—obvious even from up here in the tower—had made it all worth it.

And you know, it was impossible to have disdain for humans tonight.

For chrissakes, the owners weren't even keeping the money left over after the staff were paid. They were giving it to the American Cancer Society.

Sometimes people rallied, he thought. They really did.

"So who is she?" Big Rob asked. "I mean, I heard he had a girlfriend, but I didn't know she was . . . you know, sick. They been together long?"

"Long enough."

There was a thick silence. "He's not coming back to work, is he."

"Not for a while."

"Are you guys going to sell us?"

"I don't know. We haven't gotten that far."

And wasn't that true on a variety of levels.

iAm checked his watch again. Eight thirty. Perfectly on time with a departure set for eleven thirty. Manny's fancy-ass mobile surgery center was stuck downtown, the area still too hot from the party the night before to move the thing, but they had a good contingency plan for Selena. Manny had his old refurbed regular ambulance still and the thing was on standby, the amusement park's management more than happy to accommodate the medical wait-and-see and the good doctor on their property.

"I can understand why he didn't say anything," Big Rob murmured as he dropped the binocs. "And not for nothing, but wow, she's out of this world looking."

"She's also really good people."

"Does she know what he does . . . you know. Classy woman like that, I mean . . ."

"To be honest, I think that shit's the last thing on their minds."

"Yeah. Sure. I mean, yeah."

iAm glanced over at the guy. "Don't worry, I got 'em. You can head over to the club."

The human nodded. "I should go."

As the man hesitated, iAm put out his palm. "And as for future plans with the businesses, we'll take care of everybody, I promise. No matter what happens."

Big Rob shook. "Thanks, man. But I gotta say, we really like working for you. Besides, I don't know if Silent Tom has another interview process in him. Nearly killed him five years ago when we applied with Trez."

"Yeah, I think he's said all of twelve words the entire time I've known him. Drive safe out there."

"Thanks. Call me if you need anything."

Big Rob put the binocs down on the desk and paused for one last moment, looking out to where Trez and Selena were strolling between the bumper cars and a children's teacup ride. Shaking his head, he went to the exit, and closed the door behind him as he left.

iAm checked his watch again.

Three hours.

And then what. What the hell was he going to do about *maichen*?

What if Trez and Selena needed him . . . and he was out meeting with that female?

Jesus, after a lifetime of celibacy, it was a shocker to find that he'd made an arrangement to be alone with a member of the opposite sex. And it was not to talk.

No, he was not in a talking kind of mood.

Rubbing his eyes, he pictured the female draped in all those pale blue robes and the urge to get under all that masking took on an obsessional edge. Hell, if it hadn't been for a molecular exhaustion, he probably would have spent the entire day staring at the ceiling over his bed thinking about what he was going to do to her. As it was, he'd crashed with a hard-on and woken up with one, too.

He'd done nothing about either erection.

If he jerked off, it somehow felt too real.

And for the same reason, he'd told his brother nothing

about the trip into the s'Hisbe or the female he'd met or the "date" he'd made.

Compared to what Trez was facing, all that was such small potatoes. And there was also a dreamscape to it all, which he was surprised to discover he wanted to keep in place.

Maybe because it made things less intimidating?

But come on, he didn't think he was going to go. How could he leave . . . ?

No, he wasn't going. For the first time in his life, he didn't think he could trust himself not to go straight-up animal on some poor female. And hell, she was probably having second thoughts, too. Meeting an unknown male in the middle of nowhere? She'd be insane to do something like that.

Especially because she had to know what was on his mind.

No, he told himself. Neither of them was going to show up at that cabin at midnight. And that was better for everybody.

Really.

It was.

FORTY-FIVE

"It's dead! Fates, it is gone—will you stop!"

No, Xcor thought. He would not.

As he continued stabbing the *lesser*, black blood speckled his face, his chest, his forearm. Black blood pooled on the cold asphalt of the alley. Black blood got into his eyes.

And still he kept with the assault, his shoulder driving the blade into the torso everywhere but the hollow chest as Zypher yelled at him, pulled at him, cursed at him.

That was all for naught. Unhinged, he was a beast without a leash, his mind floating above the exertion, driving him ever onward to kill, kill, *kill*—

The yank that finally pulled him free of his prey was that of a tow truck, the force enough to separate him from the mangled, oozing carcass.

He did not take the unconsented-to relocation well. Swinging around, he slashed his dagger through the air, narrowly missing Zypher's throat. And as the soldier leaped out of range, Zypher unholstered his own weapon, prepared to fight.

Caught in between a lunge and a relenting, Xcor panted, great clouds coming out of his mouth. He had left the deserted farmhouse without any of them, bursting out and heading to the theater of conflict half-naked and fully crazed.

And it had been for his soldiers' own good.

"What is wrong with you!" Zypher demanded. "What ails you!"

Xcor bared his teeth. "Leave me alone."

"So you can get yourself killed?"

"Leave me!"

The echo of his shout rebounded up and out of the alley, the words bouncing back and forth between the brick walls of the buildings before careening into darkness like bats released from a cave.

Zypher's face was pure fury. "They have guns, remember? Or is last night too dim a memory for you!"

"They have always had guns!"

"Not like those!"

Xcor looked down at the slayer. Even mostly dismembered, it was still moving, arms grasping at thin air in slow motion, legs sawing in a stew of innards and black oil.

Snarling at the thing, he let out a shout and then stabbed it into oblivion. The light was so bright he was blinded by the flash, his retinas revolting at the glare. But the readjustment came quickly, each blink clearing his vision further.

He just needed more. He needed to find more—and he needed something else, too.

"Get me a whore," he barked.

Zypher recoiled. "What?"

"You heard me. Find me one. Bring her to the cottage."

"Human or vampire?"

"It matters not. Just make sure she's paid enough to be willing."

He expected questions. There were none.

Zypher merely inclined his head. "As you wish."

Xcor wheeled away, prepared to hunt and fight and kill. And before jogging off, he glared over his shoulder. "Blonde. I want a blonde. And she must have long hair."

"I know who to call."

With a nod, Xcor ran down the alley, his combats thundering over the rough pavement. Sniffing the breeze, his brain filtered through the smells of diesel fumes and cheap restaurants, and humans that were homeless and unbathed, and rotting fish in the river.

His rage at himself sharpened every sense he had—

"Hey, man, you looking for a taste?"

Pulling his body up short, he turned around, but knew from the scent coming at him on the gusts that it was no human who stood in the shadows.

The enemy he was looking for had found him, the *lesser* as yet unaware of who it was speaking to.

"Aye," he said. "I would like a taste."

"Foreign motherfucker," the slayer said. "What do you want?"

"Whate'er do you have?"

"I got the good stuff. Pure Columbian white powder H, not that Mexican black tar—"

Xcor did not allow the sales pitch to continue to a completion. With a vicious lunge, he leapt forward and swung his dagger in an arc, clipping the slayer right across the front of the face at eye level. Instantly, the undead brought up his hands, bending in half, howling in pain—and Xcor took advantage of that, hauling back his right boot and spinning it around, kicking the skull like it was a soccer ball, sending the undead flying off its feet to the side.

Leaping high into the air, he landed on the *lesser*, rolled it over, and trapped its hands over its head in one of his palms. The stench was rancid milk and fetid sweat, and that sweet smell triggered his kill reflex.

The rage he had been unable to contain since Layla had left came out once more. Holstering his dagger, he curled up a fist with his dominant hand and drove it into the pale face of the *lesser* over and over and over again, until the features all but liquefied under the beating, bones crushing in, jaw hanging free. With each inhale he drew his arm up; with every exhale he slammed his fist down, his steady pace of respiration driving the impacts.

Zypher had better work fast.

He needed to fuck his way out of this mood as well.

Sitting on the edge of her bed, Layla's hands trembled as she held her phone in both palms. She had already read what had been sent to her, and not just once. In fact, she had been reading the words ever since she had been awoken at dusk to the sound of her cell vibrating on her bedside table.

Do not come to see me again. I shall not be ever at the cottage nor the farmhouse again nor consent to be in your presence. I am uninterested in anything you have to offer.

Xcor must have dictated it into his iPhone. He had never sent her anything via text before, and she had always suspected that he could not read or write.

Of all the ways she had seen their relationship ending for them, of all the ways she could have imagined them parting, it was not like this. Not because she had ended up getting him naked and trying to force him to feed from her.

". . . hello?"

She jumped, the phone flying out of her hands and landing on the short-napped carpet. As Qhuinn stepped over to pick the thing up, she panicked and scrambled off the bed to get there first. Or tried to scramble.

With her belly, she couldn't get far very fast and she caught her breath as his lean hand scooped up the cell phone.

"Are you okay?" he said. "You look pale."

Don't look at it. Don't look at the screen—

"Oh, my God, are you crying?"

"No." She held out her hand. "I'm not."

Give me the phone, give me—

Qhuinn came over to her and tilted her face up. "What's going on?"

As his thumb brushed across her cheek, he put the goddamn fucking cell phone back where it had been, on the bedside. Face down.

"I knocked and no one answered," he said. "I got worried."

With a shudder, she closed her eyes, her raw nerves still vibrating at the near-miss. "Just reading a sad story online. Guess I'm more emotional than I thought."

He sat down next to her. "Lot of shit going on the last few days—"

Before she knew it, she burst into tears and leaned into his big chest.

Circling her with his heavy arms, he held her gently and let her cry it all out—and the fact that he mistakenly assumed the tears were only because she was pregnant and having twins and overly hormonal made her cry even harder.

She cried for the months and months of lying and deception; she cried for all the trips to that meadow; for her sneaking in and out of the house; for using the car Qhuinn had bought her to do it.

And most of all, worst of all, she cried for a sense of loss so powerful it was as if someone had died before her and there had been naught she could do to save them.

Images of Xcor bombarded her, from his attempts to make himself comely and see to it that he had been always clean even fresh from fighting . . . to the way he looked in that shower, silhouetted as his body climaxed behind the curtain . . . to the defeat that had hung his head as he had stared into the fire like some vital part of him had been exposed and was bleeding him, weakening him, changing him.

She tried to tell herself it was for the best. No more double life. No more falsity. No more hiding her phone or worrying about whether her whereabouts were discovered.

No more Xcor—

"I'll call Doc Jane," Qhuinn said urgently as he went for the house phone.

"What? No, I'm—"

"How bad are your chest pains?"

"What?" she said through the sniffles. "What are you—"

He pointed to her sternum. Looking down, she found that she had grabbed onto the front of her flannel nightgown, the soft fabric bunching up under her tight fist.

It was the origin of the tears, she thought.

They were coming from her heart.

"Honestly," she whispered. "I'm all right. I just had to get it out—I'm so sorry."

Qhuinn's hand hovered over the receiver. And even when he finally retracted his arm, she was very clear that he was not convinced.

"I think I need to eat something," she said.

It was the farthest thing from the truth, but he immediately went into order mode, calling Fritz instead of the medical types, asking for all kinds of food.

His worry about her well-being and his attentiveness only made her cry all over again.

Dearest Virgin Scribe . . . she was in mourning, wasn't she.

FORTY-SIX

"Okay, so we get in this."

Selena grabbed onto the hand that Trez offered her and stepped over the lip of the first capsule in a lineup of six. The little pod-like constructions were set upon a pair of tracks, and had two seats side by side with a bar that was raised over the shallow hood. After Trez joined her, a uniformed operator gave them a nod from a control panel at the far end of the platform.

"It goes that way?" she asked, pointing ahead to a mountain rise. "We go up that?"

Trez had to clear his throat. Twice. "Ah, yeah. We do."

"Oh, my God, that's so high!"

"I, ah, yeah. It is."

She turned to him as the bar came down over the top of their legs. "Trez, seriously, you're going to hate this—"

There was a jerk and then they were moving forward on the track, a little *chk-chk-chk* created as the wheels began to turn with increasing speed.

"You, however, are going to love it," he said, kissing her. "You may want to hold on."

As they began an ascent that was nearly vertical, her back pressed into the padded seat and her hands gripped the cold metal bar. For a moment, she wished she'd taken the gloves that had been offered back at the house, but then she forgot all about the discomfort.

Higher, higher, higher . . . impossibly high.

Craning over the side, she grinned. "Oh, my God, we're so high up!"

And they were only halfway to the top.

The *chk-chk-chk* became very loud, and the jerking got stronger, until she felt as if someone were pushing at her shoulders. The breeze grew cooler and more brisk, too, her hair whipping off to the side, her parka challenged to keep the warmth of her torso intact.

"The view is incredible," she breathed.

It wasn't as high as they'd been the night before, but with no buffer between her and the expanse below, no panes of glass to insulate her from the drop, nothing but the track ahead and the ever-increasing distance to the ground, she felt as if she were soaring.

And the park's lights were magnificent. Multicolored and flashing, they were everywhere she looked down below, marking the contours of the various rides, reflecting off the mirrors and the red and yellow and blue tops of the concession stands.

"It's as if the sky has been inverted and the stars are down here!"

"Yeah. Oh, uh-huh … yeah. I guess we're at the top … oh, yeah, wow. Uh-huh."

Abruptly, they leveled off and everything got quiet except for the wind that muffled in her ears, the ride becoming smooth and gentle as they rounded an easy corner.

A quick glance at her male, and she saw that, despite his dark skin, he was pale as a ghost.

She let go with one of her hands and covered his. "Trez, how about we stay on the ground after this, okay?"

"Oh, no, it's fine—I'm tight, I'm good."

Uh-huh. Right. His jaw was set so hard she worried about his back teeth, and his neck was rigid above the collar of his black leather jacket. Matter of fact, the only thing that was moving on his entire body was his right knee. It was bouncing up and down, up and down, upanddown, upanddownandupanddown—

"Here we go," he muttered. Like he was bracing himself for a body punch.

She whipped her head forward just in time to see absolutely nothing in front of them. It was only open air, as if the track had fallen away.

"Where does it—"

Whoooooooooooosh!

All at once they were at breakneck speed, weightless and flying, pitching headlong down, down, down.

Selena laughed like she was crazy, releasing her hold and throwing her arms up. "*Yesssssssssssss!*"

So fast, the air ripping at her hair, slapping her in the face, pinning her against the seat; then it was hard right, hard left, zoom-zoom-zoom, up another giant rise when the *chk-chk-chk* came back and then ...

"Oh, my God!" Trez hollered.

Up and around, so that the world tilted and went upside down before righting itself again. And another looping over and done, and then one that veered them off to the side.

It was like the ride home the night before, only even more vivid and reckless and wonderful.

"I could do this forever!" she screamed as another sequence approached. "Forever!"

"Oh, Christ, not again!"

Four times.

In a row.

And Trez had been the one insisting.

As their little cart of horrors came back to the platform once again, he was prepared to keep the torture up.

Selena was ecstatic and that made it all worth it—even the intestinal loops in the middle of the roller-coaster ride.

Which turned his own guts into a fizzy mess.

"Let's do it one more time," he said, trying to fly the flag. Even though at this point someone was going to have to surgically remove his hands from the bar.

"No, I think we've had enough."

"Are you kidding? I love this shit—"

"We're finished," she called out to the attendant.

"I got your pictures," the human male said as he pulled a crank down and an engine that was out of sight came to a rambling halt. "They're just printing."

Okaaaay, time to get out. Yup.

"Trez?"

Prying his grip off the bar, he watched his metal savior rise up and clink into place overhead. "Yup. I'm coming." Right now. "Here I go."

As Selena got to her feet and balanced herself on the roll bar, he was ready to follow her out. Walk her over to the attendant. Get those pictures he'd been unaware that someone had been taking of them.

Instead, he just sat there breathing in a shallow pump. Come on, though, he wasn't a pussy. Forcing himself to try to stand up, he found that his legs were numb from mid-thigh down—but on a messy stumble, he somehow managed to get out of the cart and onto the platform without completely embarrassing himself.

Although the fact that Selena had to steady him was not exactly a vote of confidence in his verticality.

"Oh, thank you," he heard her say to the attendant. Then she glanced at him. "Here, let's walk over to that bench and look at the pictures."

Before he knew it, he was sitting on a stretch of wrought-iron hard-and-cold, and staring at photographs of Selena having a party and him looking like someone had his nuts in a vise. Meanwhile, her hand was stroking his back, riding over the leather of his jacket in a slow circle.

"Here you go, ma'am."

"Thank you so much." She held something out to him. "Why don't you take a quick drink?"

He was too wrung-out to throw out a "S'all good." He just took whatever it was, put it to his mouth, and did what he was told.

"Oh, that's good," he breathed when he finally lowered the soda bottle.

"Ginger ale. I learned about it from Doc Jane."

About ten minutes later, he was able to properly focus on what he was supposedly looking at. "You are so beautiful," he said as he stared at the image of the two of them together.

"I'm not sure about that, but I'll tell you one thing—that is the time of my life right there. How you feeling?"

He rubbed his thumb over the picture of her face. "You are so alive. Look at you, your eyes are amazing."

One by one, he studied each of the photographs. They'd been taken during the big drop after the second ascent, where you went all but weightless and the wind roared and you were not entirely convinced shit was going to end well when you got to the bottom.

He could practically feel the thrill coursing through Selena's body, the excitement, the pleasure, the vibrating force of life transforming her into a contained lightning bolt of joy.

On his side? He'd never seen himself looking pale before, his dark skin pasty as shit—which was evidently possible.

Who knew.

"We should make a calendar of these," he announced. "One half of them, at any rate."

"You look so much better now. Less green. You were kind of green."

"I would go on that motherfucker a million times more if that's what you wanted."

She leaned in, turned his face toward her, and kissed him. "You know what you just proved?"

"What? That even real males need airsick bags sometimes?"

"No." She kissed him again. "That somebody can say 'I love you' without speaking."

His chest puffed up. He couldn't help it. "Check me out. A Casanova—who'da thought."

Finishing the ginger ale, he tossed the empty into the trash bin five feet away, and put the pictures in the inside pocket of his jacket.

Getting to his feet, he offered her his arm. "How would you like a nutritionally deficient, but totally satisfying meal? We're talking real chemicals and complete over-processing. The kind of stuff humans traditionally enjoy in this setting and later get home and have to take TUMS for?"

"Sounds delightful." She took hold of what he offered. "I look forward to whatever is served."

Trez gave the attendant a wave—and then considered maybe throwing in a couple of bodybuilding poses just to get his guy card restamped.

The concession stands were behind and to the right, and as they walked around the foot of that roller-coaster, he glanced up, way up, at the metal scaffolding that held the track in the air. Man, he was glad he hadn't seen this view from the base before heading up there.

The more he thought about it, the more his case of the vapors threatened a return, sweat breaking out on his palms

and across his upper lip, but good news came in the form of
the distraction of the hot-dog stand that had been opened
just for them.

Stepping up to the counter, he held Selena tight to his
side, catching her scent as well as that of the shampoo and
the soap she'd used before they'd left the house.

A human female with a round body and a nice smile
came over, putting aside her copy of *People* magazine.
"What can I get you guys?"

"Good heavens, so many choices," Selena said.

The menu was all lit-up red panels with yellow lettering,
offering the kinds of things that were guaranteed to taste
great going down and cause trouble once they were in you.
But like he'd told her, that was what antacids were for.

"What are you having?" she asked him.

"I'm going with the Coney Island special," he announced. "With a high-test Coke, extra ice."

"You got it," the server said. "Ma'am, you know what
you want?"

Selena frowned. "I really want a hamburger. But am I
missing out if I don't do the hot dog?"

"You can have some of mine."

"Great, I'd like a hamburger with cheese and some
French fries."

"No problem." The woman pointed at another section of
the menu. "You want something on them?"

"I'm sorry?"

"On your fries. Like chili, cheese, jalapeños—the list is
over here."

As Selena considered round two of her options, Trez
took the opportunity to study his queen's stunning profile.
Those lips of hers were nearly irresistible, and the more he
stared at them, the more the residual burn of all that adrenaline overload shifted from fight or flight to pure, undiluted
lust.

With a discreet move, he had to rearrange himself.

He couldn't wait to get her home. Get her naked.

His eyes drifted down to her breasts. The Pata-Gucci
jacket she had on had obligingly customized itself to those
curves he loved so much—

"Trez?"

"Huh?"

"Do you have any money? I didn't think to bring human—"

He cut her off. "You're not paying for nothing." Taking his wallet out, he said to the lady, "How much do I owe you?"

"It's on the house."

"Let me give you something, then."

"Oh, that's okay. I know why you're—"

Trez jumped in, putting a hundred down on the Formica and sliding it forward. "Take it. For being so kind to us."

The woman's eyes popped. "Are you sure?"

"Positive."

For one, he didn't want her to keep going and make Selena feel like some kind of charity case. For another, the human had come out on a cold night for only a couple of hours of work. Holidays were coming for her kind. No doubt she could use the extra cash.

"Wow. Thanks."

As the woman got to work on the food, he could feel Selena looking at him with respect, and didn't that make him go all puffed up again in the chestral region.

Talk about getting his guy card stamped—fuck posing like Ahnold. The way she stared up at him? He felt big as a mountain.

A couple of minutes later, they were heading over to a picnic table painted a screaming blue color and sitting down side by side.

The air was cold, the food was steaming hot, the sodas were frothy and sweet. Handling the overstuffed buns was tricky stuff, with both of them going tilted heads and mop-up napkins, but that was even its own sort of fun. And the conversation, when they could manage it, was about the taste and the spice and the tongue burning . . . the roller-coaster ride . . . what they were going to do next . . . whether they were going to have cotton candy or hot-fudge sundaes for dessert.

It was magnificently, beautifully, resonantly normal.

And as he sat with his female, and maybe wiped off the corner of her mouth with his napkin, or shared his soda with her, or laughed when she said they'd better do the carousel next because it was only two feet off the ground, he soaked in the memories until they permeated his mind, body, and soul with a glow he had never felt before.

Just to be with her. Doing nothing special. In the middle of an amusement park.

Was a miracle.

A blessing beyond measure.

Frowning, he realized that if it weren't for the reality lurking around the corner of this perfect moment, sneaking up behind them like some evil shadow . . . he might well be wasting this time with her by having half his brain worrying over the opening of shAdoWs, or wondering what was going on at the s'Hisbe, or fixating on whatever happened to be tickling his ass with a feather at that point in time.

He would have squandered this, as a rich male would let diamonds fall from his pockets simply because he had bowls of them back home.

Rarity went hand in hand with reverence.

"I could sit here forever," he said as he swallowed his last bite. "This is my heaven."

Selena glanced over and smiled. "Mine, too."

FORTY-SEVEN

Just before the first civilian arrived for their appointment with the King, Paradise presented a folder to her father with no small amount of pride. "I've reorganized the appointment sheet. I think you'll find it makes things easier for you and the King."

Her father smiled as he opened the cover and saw the spreadsheet listing each civilian's name, family lineage, current issue, and any past concerns that Wrath had dealt with.

"This is . . . so helpful," he said, as he ran his forefinger down the columns.

"I thought I could improve on the way it was done."

He looked up. "You have."

"What comes next"—she pulled the second of many sheets free—"is a dossier for each subject that goes into greater detail."

Abalone frowned as he reviewed her notes, and then riffled through the reports. "How did you find all this out?"

"I have my sources." She grinned. "Okay, so some of it comes off of people's Facebook pages, and other stuff is from friends of mine."

"This is . . . I didn't know he'd been mated." Her father tilted the folder toward her. "Him?"

"Last year. It was a low-key thing." Paradise dropped her voice even though they were alone. "They say she was with young."

"Ah. So now he wants the mating validated."

"She's about to give birth. If I were Wrath, I'd spare the

poor male the indignity of asking too many questions about
the due date, and just give him the respect he wants to provide his young—"

"Trying to take your father's job?" Wrath's voice interjected.

As the Blind King himself appeared in the parlor's archway, Paradise jumped. "I didn't mean, oh, no, I—"

The King smiled. "I'm impressed with your thinking.
Keep up the good work, Paradise."

With that, he and his blond dog went across to the dining
room.

"I can't feel my feet," she mumbled.

Her father embraced her. "You are exceeding any expectation I had for this."

She pulled back and pushed her hair over her shoulder.
"I like this. I really do."

"You're making me quite proud."

To hide her flush, she sat down behind the computer that
she already felt was hers. "How're things at home? With—"

"Just fine. I am very well, although you are missed."

"I could come back."

"No, no, it's best you stay here." He tucked the folder
under his arm. "Did you and Peyton enjoy yourselves last
evening?"

"He left right after you did."

Abalone frowned. "I hope you didn't quarrel?"

"He's got an antiquated way of looking at things."

"He does come from a traditional family."

She picked up one of the Montblanc pens she'd found in
the desk. Tapping it on her palm, she pulled her navy-blue
skirt down further on her knees. "Ah . . . Father."

"Yes?"

Drawing in a deep breath, she pulled open the top side
drawer and took out the application to the training center's
program. "Father, would you ever let me do something like
this?"

As she handed the paperwork to him and his eyes traced
the wording, she hurried on. "I'm not saying I want to go
into combat or anything. It's just, they're accepting females,
and I—"

"Fighting? This is . . . this is to *fight*."

"I know. But see"—she reached up and pointed to a part in the preamble—"they're saying they can train females—"

"Paradise."

Annnnd his viewpoint was all pretty much summed up in the way he said her name: a combination of be-serious and don't-break-my-heart.

"You're not cut out for this," he said.

"Because I'm a female, right," she countered bitterly. "Which means desks and papers at the most—and only until I'm mated—"

"This is *war*. Do you understand what that really is?" He jogged the application. "This is death waiting to happen. It's not a Hollywood movie or a romantic fantasy."

She kicked up her chin. "I know that."

"Do you?"

"I'm not as sheltered as you think I am. The family you lost in the raids was my blood, too, Father. Friends of mine died. I know what this is about."

"No, Paradise. I will not allow it." He leaned down and put the application in the trash. "This is not for you."

Without another word, he turned on his heel and strode off, somehow managing to close the hidden panel doors in her face, even as the panels stayed in their pockets in the walls.

Throe materialized about a half mile from the house Abalone went to every night.

The GPS locator Throe had put into the outer chest pocket of the male's camel-hair coat had worked like a dream. And one had to admire the wealthy neighborhood.

Not bad, not bad a'tall.

Falling into a casual stroll, he checked out the houses as he zeroed in on the signal his cell phone was directing him to. Actually, the proper term for the residences would be mansions. These places were far too large to count as mere houses: multi-storied, sprawling, set back from the road, they all had dramatic landscape lighting on their exteriors, as if the wealthy humans living inside couldn't bear to think their position would be ignored during the night hours.

As he proceeded, he had to control his frustration. He missed the fighting more than he'd thought he would. In fact, the lack of bloodshed—of any variety—was a shocking dissatisfaction. When he had started with the Band of Bastards, he'd been horrified by the aggression and gore. After several centuries, however, the warfare had become what he thought of as normal.

The stone manse that came next was an effeminate, mod-con'd version of the medieval pile of rock the Band of Bastards had all lived in back in the Old Country, and he stopped in front of the sprawling expanse. Figures moved inside, crossing windows that were framed by heavy swaths of fabric as lights inside picked up glints of gold and silver on the walls.

And abruptly, he wasn't thinking of Xcor's former lair.

He was recalling where he had come from, his true origin of privilege and wealth.

In seeking revenge for his sister, he had sold himself to the devil. Now, on the far side of that bargain, he was poor and alone and without prospects.

His only hearth was his ambition.

At least there was plenty afire in it to warm him over the coming winter months.

Throe pressed on, the cold biting through the leather coat he wore, the one that was still stained with the kills he had wrought from nights ago.

Before all had changed.

The house that was his target turned out to be on the left, on the opposite side of the street. It was grand and historic, a white Federal manse with the bone structure of a true beauty and the attended-to upkeep that only the very wealthy could bring to an old estate: No peeling paint for her. No scruffy bushes. No sagging rooflines or porches.

Unlike with the others, there was no way to see inside.

The drapes were all pulled and so heavy he could see no light through them. There were no cars in the driveway, but as he waited, taking cover behind a shrub, he caught sight of two individuals approaching the front door . . . even though they had not arrived at the property by any motorized conveyance.

Because they were vampires who had dematerialized to the place.

Ten minutes later, another visitor arrived. Fifteen minutes after that, two more.

They were discreet, and not everyone used the front door—no doubt to avoid suspicion.

Throe checked his phone, in spite of the fact that he knew he had the location correct. Yes, Abalone was in there.

Keeping to the shadows, he stayed longer, not because he had any particular plans to infiltrate, but rather, because he had yet to formulate them. His ambition, strong as it might be, was not as yet an engine in drive—he had recon to do, weaknesses to discover, strategies to define.

A car turned the corner and came down the street.

As it passed under the streetlight across the way, he saw that it was a Rolls-Royce, a dark one with a trademark pale hood.

And here he was without a motorcar.

Indeed, his lack of prospects was a problem.

How was he going to marshal any resources? he wondered. How was he to support himself whilst he built a coalition?

The answer, when it came, was so obvious, it was as if destiny had spotlit a path through darkness for him. Yes, he thought, that was the way . . .

A moment later, he returned to Abalone's most generous accommodations with a smile on his face.

FORTY-EIGHT

On his hospital bed, Luchas was in and out of consciousness, waves of pain rolling through him, battering him senseless. When he simply could not take it anymore, he fumbled around with the hand that still had fingers. Finding the call button, he pressed with his thumb until his hearing registered a beep.

The door burst open, and Doc Jane came in. "Luchas?"

"My leg," he moaned. "Hurts . . ."

She came over, checked machines, IVs, God only knew what. "I'll get you something for the—"

"The infection . . ." he babbled, turning his head from side to side. "My leg . . ."

He'd had this plan to waste away, but instead, this felt like he'd decided to kill himself by stepping into a fire pit feetfirst—leading with his bad ankle and calf.

On a crazy surge of strength, he sat up and started pulling at the sheets. Doc Jane grasped his shoulders and tried to get him to flatten out—while at the same time, someone else entered the room. Qhuinn—it was his brother.

"Luchas, *Luchas*, stop—"

That was Qhuinn, coming in close, trying to capture his hands, and get him to lie back. It was not a fair fight. He was weak, so weak, and then he went on a ride, a sudden floating feeling replacing the burning sensation down below.

Glancing to the side, he saw Doc Jane retracting a syringe from the clear plastic tubing that ran into his arm.

Qhuinn's face appeared above his own, those mismatched eyes intense. "Luchas, relax. We got you."

"My leg ..."

The drug was working magic, soothing him sure as if his body had been sunk into a warm bath. The pain was still there; he just didn't care as much about it.

"It's getting worse," he heard himself say. "The infection ... thought I would be dead by now."

"Luchas ..."

Something about his brother's affect registered, something about his tone of voice, and the tightness in his mouth and eyes.

"What," Luchas said. "What?"

Qhuinn looked at Doc Jane like he was hoping for a proverbial airlift out of a danger zone.

"Luchas," his brother said, "I had to save you."

Save him? But that was the whole point of all this. He wanted out. "What?"

"I told her she could take the leg. To save your life."

Luchas fell silent. Surely he must have gotten that wrong, the proper translation of what had been spoken misappropriated by the painkillers they'd just given him.

"It was the only option. We were losing you."

"What did you do to me," he said slowly. "What did you—"

"Calm down."

Luchas sat back up off the pillows, an indescribable horror draining the blood from his head. Looking down at his lower body, he found that the thin sheets revealed the contours of the thigh, knee, calf, and foot of his left leg ... but only the thigh and knee of his right one.

With a shout, he reached for what should have been there, jerking at the flat sheets, pulling at them as if they were somehow hiding what was in fact no longer there.

"What did you do!" He turned on his brother, grabbing at his shirt, yanking, pulling with the set of fingers he had left. "What the fuck did you do!"

"You were dying—"

"Because I wanted to! How could you!"

He batted at Qhuinn, ineffectual fist flying, his ruined hand slapping.

Qhuinn did not defend himself. He just allowed the beating, such as it was, to happen—not that there was much to the attack. And Luchas didn't last long. Energy soon spent, he collapsed back against the pillow, his hollow chest pumping up and down, blood running up his IV line, vision flaring in and out of clarity.

And still the limb that wasn't there hurt.

"Get out," he said numbly. "I don't want to see you again."

Turning his face to the wall, he heard quiet conversation and then the door opened and closed softly.

"How is your pain level now?" Doc Jane asked.

"Why does it hurt . . . ?" he mumbled. "You took it away."

God, he was even more mangled now; still more of who and what he had been was gone.

"It's called phantom-limb pain. But the sensation is very real."

"Did you take . . . were you the one who cut it off?"

"I was."

"Then get out of here, too. I didn't consent to this—"

"You were dying—"

"I'm not listening. Get out."

There was a pause, and he detested the way she looked down at him, all kind, concerned, caring.

"In time, Luchas, when you feel better—"

He ripped his head around. "You denied me my death. You butchered my body without my permission. So you'll have to excuse me, but I'm completely uninterested in *anything* you have to say."

The doctor closed her eyes briefly. "I'll send Ehlena in with some food."

"Don't bother. You've just delayed the inevitable. I intend to finish the job myself now."

Luchas went for the IV that ran into his arm, pulling at it until the thing sprang loose, clear liquid and red blood going everywhere—

People came through every door there was, racing in with panic, grabbing at him, talking loudly. He fought against them, writhing and shoving, struggling to stay upright because of his missing calf and foot. . . .

Someone must have given him another shot, because all

of a sudden his body went lax. Even though his brain was ordering all kinds of movement, nothing was responding.

As his eyes rolled around, he caught dim sight of Qhuinn standing in the doorway, his big, healthy, strong body blocking the way out.

It might as well have been the door unto the Fade the male was in the way of.

"I hate you!" Luchas screamed. "I hate you!"

Back at the King's audience house, Rhage was in the dining room, standing with his back to the shut doors, his arms crossed over his chest. Most of the Brotherhood was in the room, milling around with too much kinetic energy.

Wrath was sitting in his armchair, his legs crossed ankle to knee, his dog's head in his lap. "He's late. That motherfucker is late."

Rehv nodded from where he was standing in front of the fire and fanning his hands out as if they were cold. "He'll be here."

"I got people to see."

Hollywood checked his watch. "You want me to go pick him up? I can throw a lasso on him and drag him here by his dick—"

The doorbell went off with a chime, and V opened one half of the drapes at the window across the way. "Speak of the dealer."

"Let me go welcome him," Rhage muttered as he slipped out.

"He's not alone," V barked.

"Neither am I."

Closing the door, he went across to the parlor. "Paradise?" As the girl looked up from the desk, he smiled at her. "I'ma shut your room up for a sec. Do me a favor and stay in here until I come get you?"

Her wide, pretty eyes got even wider. "Is everything okay?"

"Yup. But I want you to hang here."

"Okay. Of course."

He winked at her. "Good girl. And lock it up behind me, 'kay?"

"Sure."

Shutting her in, he waited until he heard the copper lock

turn on her side, and then he went to the front door. Opening things up, he gave Assail the once-over. The guy was dressed right out of Butch's closet, everything tailored and matched, fitting like the shit had been drawn on his body. Behind him, a pair of identical thugs stood side by side. The fact that they were in loose-fitting black was a well, duh.

He could just imagine the firepower that was hiding under those coats.

"Thought you were coming alone," he said.

"Your King wanted to meet my crew. Here they are, my cousins."

Rhage leaned in. "That ain't your whole crew, is it."

"I can assure you, these are the only two I use."

Rhage stepped back and nodded for them to enter the foyer. "I gotta search you."

"We're fully armed."

"No shit."

As the three filed in, Rhage pointed to a huge silver tray on the table under a gilt mirror. "Drop 'em there. And make sure it's all your metal. I find something on you, it's going to put my panties in a wad."

Clink. Clink . . . clink . . . clank, clank . . . rattle, rattle, rattle.

Rhage didn't want to be impressed, but he had to give them some credit. Good-looking guns and a lot of sharp knives.

"You first," he said to one of the twins.

The other one stepped forward. "Do me. My brother's a little jumpy."

"Excuse me? Did I miss the memo where you were put in charge, douche bag?" He motioned for Mr. Antsy to come forward and patted him down. "There, now, you want a lollipop 'cuz that was so hard? Now you, with the list of demands, get over here."

He discharged number two, and then stepped over to Assail, who had been watching the show like a snake.

"Nice cologne," Hollywood muttered as he threw the guy's arms out and banged down a surprisingly muscled torso. "Where'd you get it, CVS?"

"Are you always this rude," Assail said in a bored tone.

"You're the second person to ask me something like that in the last forty-eight hours." He kicked the guy's fancy Italian loafers wide. "You got a problem with me, file a claim with human resources."

"How corporate of you."

Rhage straightened after he'd checked out that lower body. "FYI, Vishous, son of the Bloodletter, is our personnel contact. He prefers complaints that are made in person. Have fun with that."

Done with the three of them, he walked over to the audience room's closed doors, knowing they would follow. Opening things wide, he stood to the side and glared at the SOBs as they filed in, one by one.

"Assail," Wrath drawled. "We're meeting again."

"And this time no bullets," the drug dealer replied.

"Not yet," one of the brothers muttered.

Assail's eyes traveled over the assembled masses. "Quite a bit of protection you have here."

Wrath shrugged. "I had a choice of collecting them or Hummel figurines. It was a toss-up."

"To what do I owe the honor of a command appearance."

"Rehv? Do the deed, since you know what you're talking about."

The sin-eater stepped away from the hearth and smiled like he was about to eat something. "We have reason to believe you're participating in the drug market in Caldwell."

Assail didn't flinch. "I have never hid my business."

"Ever see this before?"

When Rehv tossed a packet into the air, Assail caught the thing and looked it over. "Heroin."

"The symbol is yours, isn't it."

"Says who."

Rhage spoke up. "We found a number of those on a slayer at a club that happens to be owned by a friend of ours."

Wrath smiled coldly as he reached down to stroke his guide dog's blond coat. "So you can see how this puts us all in an awkward sitch. You're using the enemy to disseminate product. Aren't you."

Again, Assail showed no reaction at all. "If I am, what's the issue?"

"You're funneling money into their pockets."

"And . . . ? So?"

"Don't be fucking naive. How the fuck do you think they're going to spend it."

"Last night," Rhage said, "we got caught in some cross fire between the Band of Bastards and some slayers. Guess what the undead were squeezing off? AK-forty-sevens. It's the first major gun power we've seen in this city since the raids."

Assail shrugged and put up his palms. "How does this have anything to do with me? I'm a businessman—"

Wrath jacked forward in the chair. "Your *business* is making it more dangerous for my boys. And that fucking cranks my shit, asshole. So your *business* is now mine."

"You have no right to stop me."

"If the three of you don't make it out of here alive, I think that'll be game-over, don't you."

On a oner, every single brother in the room outted a dagger.

Rhage braced himself for an explosion of some sort, but Assail remained cool as a cucumber. He didn't fidget, didn't blink, didn't hem and haw.

Maybe the motherfucker had no central nervous system.

"What did you think was going to happen," Wrath said, "when I found out. Did you think I was just going to let this really big fucking conflict of interest ride?"

There was a long period of silence.

Finally, Assail bowed his head. "Fine. I'll stop selling to them."

Wrath's nostrils flared as he tested the male's scent. A moment later, he said, "Good, now get the fuck out of here. But know if I find any of that shit on even one slayer, I'm going to come after you and not for the conversation."

Rhage frowned, but as Wrath nodded to the exit, he opened the door and watched from the jamb as the three of them walked out, went for their potpourri of pistols and knives, and rectified their collective iron deficiency. Then they were out the door, and on the way off the property.

"He lied," Wrath said grimly.

"Knew it was too easy," Rhage muttered. "Why'd you let him go?"

"I want you to follow him." Wrath nodded to Rhage and V. "The pair of you. If we kill Assail now, we can't find his supplier and make sure that the Lessening Society loses all access to product. Follow that motherfucker, find out where he gets his shit, and then make it so the enemy doesn't have anything else to sell in Caldwell." The King shifted forward in his armchair. "And then put a bullet through the chest of each one of those three."

"No problem, my lord." Rhage glanced over at V, who nodded back. "Consider it done."

FORTY-NINE

$\mathfrak{M}$oving quickly, but not too quickly, *maichen* whispered along the empty hallways of the palace, heading for the Queen's ritual chamber. From time to time, she passed guards, other maids, even a Prime or two. None paid any attention to her.

Because she was hiding in the guise of her humble alter ego.

If any had known who was beneath the pale blue robing, a great commotion would have ensued.

Instead, when she came upon her destination, the guards standing to the left and right barely looked at her. They were exhausted at the end of their shifts, and that was why this was such very good timing.

"Clean-up for the Queen," she said with a dutiful bow.

They opened the door for her, and she slipped inside.

The sacred space was all black marble from floor to ceiling, and there was nothing to diminish the mind-bending effects of being surrounded by all that glossy *noir*: no rugs, no furniture, only a few inset cabinets in the corner where food was stashed and replenished. Illumination came from lamps that had open flames on wicks, the special oils being consumed giving off a whitish-green flicker.

She didn't look around. She had long since learned not to.

There was something terrifying about the room, especially if you spent any appreciable time in it. The longer you sat within its confines, the more you began to lose your sense of orientation, until you weren't sure whether the four walls and everything below and above had disappeared and placed you in the midst of the great night sky, suspended without gravity, in another dimension that you were not sure would ever release you.

She hated the room.

But she'd been compelled to come here.

Her mother, the Queen, sat in the center of it all, facing the north, black robes that had a sheen to them falling to the floor all around her, falling from her covered head, falling to become one with the marble.

Until it seemed as if the stone had gone liquid and was seeking to consume her.

Her mother was stock-still, not even breathing.

She was in the thick of the mourning meditation.

This was good news.

maichen padded over to the corner and opened the hatch on the cabinet without making a sound. None of the food that had been left there earlier had been touched. Another positive sign.

In less than an hour, at midnight, the high priest, AnsLai, would come filing in along with the Chief Astrologer and rituals would be performed, fragments of meteorites being crushed and consumed in sacred teas as a way to commune with the stars that determined everything for the Shadows. Then there would be a bloodletting and ritual sex. After which the Queen would be left again to drift away from the earth and find solace from her grief.

Or "grief" was more apt.

It was difficult to believe that female actually felt anything for those she birthed.

Now assured that the ritual was in fact still progressing, *maichen* backed toward the door. Before she passed through it, she glanced at her mother. She had seen the female only at formal occasions all her life, when *maichen* had been brought out at court in full noble robing, rather as one would tease the display of a prized vase or work of art. Save for those viewings, which were for the benefit of the Territory, she lived in sacred quarters that were surrounded by guards.

She had never been visited by the female who, immediately after birthing her, had given her into the care of specially trained staff in that suite of rooms that was a prison.

Such was the life of the Princess of the s'Hisbe.

She had found a way out, however.

And had been drifting around the palace under the guise of a maid, a low priest, even an astrologer, ever since.

maichen slipped out and briskly walked away.

Nothing like discovering s'Ex, her mother's favorite lover, having a tryst with two human females, whom he had evidently smuggled in — likely through the rear entrance. *maichen* hadn't meant to find out his secret, but she had discovered that there was a grate up high on the wall, and learned that, if she dematerialized into it, she could travel along the system of heating and air-conditioning ducts.

For quite some time, it had been nothing but a game with which to pass the time, and she had learned nothing of note from her spying. That had changed one night, however, as she had, in her Shadow form, looked down through one of the slats, and gotten her first and only sight of the mating act.

Although . . . well, there had been a lot of body parts.

So she wasn't sure what she had seen exactly.

She must have made a sound or something, because s'Ex had frozen and looked up, meeting her eyes even while the humans kept moving and grinding against him . . .

s'Ex had come to her cell immediately thereafter, and they had struck their little deal. In exchange for keeping what she had seen private and no longer using the venting system, she was allowed to leave her quarters provided she stayed within the palace and kept herself duly camouflaged.

s'Ex's indiscretion could well have been the death of him: Shadows believed that mating was a sacred act. And the Queen would have been infuriated to know that certain body parts of hers had essentially been . . . exposed . . . to the body parts of *humans* by virtue of s'Ex's exploits.

That male was supposed to be hers and hers alone. Everyone knew this.

And those human women? He might as well have had sheep in that bed of his.

As *maichen* padded along, moving through the corridors, her stomach began doing flip-flops. As she had gained age, she had been granted some privacy, such that she could send all attendants away from her quarters — and she had exercised that privilege once again this evening: Before going to check that her mother was, in fact, in full mourning, she had told her servants to depart from her quarters, as she was exhausted from stress and desirous of some privacy as she exercised the rituals required of her.

None had questioned her. And no one would be back until after dawn.

It would be easy to use the grate system and escape out into the world.

Meet up with her betrothed's brother.

And . . .

Well, she didn't know what.

Stars above, was she really going to do this? She wasn't even exactly sure where the cabin he had spoken of was.

No, this was foolhardy. Stupid. Reckless—

An image of iAm standing naked before her cut off all thought.

As her body began to warm from the inside out, she realized that, in spite of all her mind might be telling her, her flesh was going to drive her to him.

She would go. Heaven help her . . . she was going to go.

And deal with the consequences, whatever they may be, later.

FIFTY

Trez just needed to cop to shit: When it came to Story-town, he was only good at the kiddie rides. Stuff like the Teacups, and the Dragon Tail—which was a swoosh that didn't leave the ground and barely gave you a breeze in the face—and the f-in' carousel with its elevator Muzak and those hard-seated, impaled horses and unicorns going up and down.

Speaking of poles and up and down . . .

"You ready to go home?" he asked.

Selena looked up at him. "I am. This has been so much fun."

"I know, right? Best night of my life."

She leaned into his body, giving him a squeeze. "That's not totally true, though. I thought you were going to lose it on the roller-coaster."

He stopped. Pivoted her around. Swept her hair back from her face. "I was with you. So it was perfect."

The kiss was supposed to be one of those I'm-making-a-point ones, a quick affirmation that he meant what he'd said. But he'd been wanting to get it on with her all night, and before he knew it, he had her flush against him, her breasts pushing into his chest, her hips locked in his palms, his tongue stroking hers.

"You wanna get out of here," he growled again.

"Yes," she said against his mouth.

It was probably time anyway, he thought with a quick glance at his watch—yup, eleven fifteen.

Even though his cock was in a hurry to get gone, he didn't want to miss the stroll back to where the car was parked. With his arm around her shoulders, and their left-rights in step, they walked the paths that took them by all the rides they'd gone on, past the blue picnic table where they'd done the dog and burger, around the cotton-candy concession where they'd gotten a big cone of Marge Simpson hair and torn off pieces to feed each other.

"I didn't get you a stuffed animal," he said.

"Buy me one? Oh, I don't need—"

"No, win you one. At like a six-gun shooting range."

She sent him a look from under her lids. "I know how you can make it up to me. Remember eating that cotton candy?"

"Yeah . . ."

"Your tongue was very good at it."

As all kinds of hallelujah images of her naked with her thighs wide hit him, he had to wonder if there wasn't a hotel on the way home.

"God, I wish this were summer," he groaned.

"Oh?"

"I could push you into a dark corner and take those pants down."

"You could do that now, you know."

He stopped. "It's too cold."

"Is it?" She took his hands and pulled on them. "Look over here. There are no lights. It's sheltered."

Sure enough, the visitors' center, which was lights-out closed because it was just them, was a star-shaped facility, multiple entrances jutting out from its central body, creating pockets of dense, private darkness.

"No one will see," she whispered against his throat.

Without any exterior lights, the juncture she drew him into was pitch-black, and his sex hit the go button before his brain did. Turning her to face him, he kissed her hard and pressed her back against the painted siding, his hands sneaking into her parka and finding her breasts. Her nipples were tight and he pinched at them through her bra and blouse, tweaking and then thumbing them as he eased his thigh in between her legs.

"Fuck, I've wanted to do this all night," he said before taking her lips again.

She was hot and fluid under his hands and against his

body, ready, so fucking ready, so with him. He wanted to get her totally naked—there was something really frickin' hot about the idea of her like that and him fully clothed; plus then he'd be able to get to her nipples with his mouth. It was way too cold for that action, however, and besides, he was down for a quickie in this hidden place, but he was not feeling the idea that anyone would see her in that state, all gloriously undone and hot as hell.

The bonded male in him was liable to tear some poor Good Samaritan human apart with his fangs.

Not the romantic end to the evening he was looking for.

His hands went down to the waistband of her slacks and it was a case of unclip, unzip, and down-you-go. They were boot-cut, thank fuck, and one side slid off from her shoe just like a dream.

"Do you want my panties off?" she asked between heaving breaths.

"No, I'm going to fuck you with them on."

And he did. He grabbed her perfect ass and hopped her off the ground and around his waist. Reaching in from behind, he stroked at her, feeling how ready she was, how hot she was, how desperate she was.

He wanted to spend all night there. Instead, he shoved the silk aside, and—

"Oh, God, *Selena*," he hissed.

Slick and hot, tight and vital, the penetration rocked him and kept him standing at the same time. As he began to move, he held on to her ass and rocked her back and forth. Her hair was in his face; her scent was in his nose; she was an overwhelming tide that made him want to drown.

Faster. Harder.

She came first and he loved that, her rhythmic grips juicing him even further. And then he jumped on the one roller-coaster he was willing to ride for infinity, his cock kicking inside of her, the orgasm bringing them soul-close.

When it was over, he panted against her until he worried he was crushing her. "I'm sorry—"

"Mmmm." She went for his mouth, sucking his lower lip in and nipping at it. "More."

Instantly, he was ready to go again, but even as his hips started to pump, he had to stop. "Home," he grunted. "We need to do this at home."

"Still concerned about the cold?" she drawled, running a fang down his jaw to his jugular. "And here I am, feeling so hot."

Trez moaned and wobbled in his boots. "I'm greedy. I want more access to you than I can get here."

Her laugh was like a caress over his bare flesh. "Then by all means, take me to your bed."

It was treacherous getting her fully back into those slacks. Particularly as he bent down to the ground and went eye-to-eye with her sex.

Gritting his teeth, he somehow managed to get her dressed and have him restuffed into his fly without going caveman on her. And then it was a case of nonchalantly strolling out of the shadows, all nothing-doing as he pulled her back in close to his side.

"That was so amazing," she whispered. "I can still feel you inside of me."

Trez started to walk funny. It was either that or break something you couldn't put a cast on.

By the time they made it to the car, he was calculating the exact ETA for his bedroom—assuming he was going a hundred and fifty miles an hour.

Hey, it was a Porsche, right?

Opening her door for her, he sat her down and closed her in, and then all but wide-receivered it around to the driver's side. The second his ass hit that bucket seat, he fired up the engine.

"Oh! Cold!" she shouted.

The heater had been going when he'd shut things down, and now that powerful blower was kicking out arctic everything. They both reached forward, slapping at various buttons and knobs—

Music exploded out of the Burmester sound system, thanks to the Sirius dial, and before he could turn the stuff off, DJ Khaled's "Hold You Down" came on.

"Wait," he said. "No, leave it on."

Getting out, he hopped around to her side again, opened the door, and offered her his hand. "Dance with me."

"What?"

"Dance with me, my queen."

Sweeping her out of her seat, he led her to the front of the Porsche, into the headlights, pulling her close. Together they moved, bodies shifting, fingers intertwining, the beat transforming the parking place and the wide-open amusement park into a private dance hall.

"Forever . . ." he murmured against her. "I'll hold you down . . ."

Trez curled his head onto her shoulder so that his much larger body was all around her, encompassing her, protecting and loving her.

Together, they danced in and out of the headlights.

Up in the security tower, iAm watched his brother take Selena back out of the car and bring her around to the front grille. There was no knowing what song was playing, and it wasn't like it mattered. Just watching the two of them come together and move as one, shifting to the music, holding each other close, was enough.

iAm found himself having to brush at both of his eyes to clear them.

It was too damned hard to look at.

Turning away, he paced around the tight space and thought of how much Trez would hate being so high up in the air, nothing but the wide-angle view and the drop to the ground to focus on. The male had always hated heights, to the point where it had been a miracle to get him to agree to a place on the eighteenth floor of the Commodore.

He was staring at the roller-coaster when, a few minutes later, his phone let off a wiggle in the pocket of his leather jacket. He took the thing out.

Time to go, was all the text said.

Almost immediately a second one came in from his brother. *Thank you so much.*

Trez never spelled out words in text. So he must have really meant it.

iAm hesitated with his response. Then he sent: *Glad to help. Will c u home.*

He went to put the thing back into his jacket when he hesitated. *Thn ima go to check on thgs.*

It was a text he'd sent a million times over the last couple of years. And in fact, he meant it. He was going to go see about the restaurant and the clubs—how they were functioning, if anyone needed anything.

That was exactly what he needed to do next. And exactly what would keep him from going to that damn cabin.

Time to head out.

With no one else around to play witness, he was free to dematerialize down to where he'd parked the BMW X5 that he and his brother had been sharing. A moment later, the Porsche was released through the side gate and he followed the leader at a discreet distance across the two-acre empty parking lot—as did Manny, in a conventional ambulance.

The entire way back to the Brotherhood compound, iAm had that picture of his brother and Selena in his mind, the pair of them dancing in the headlights like a pair of teenagers.

Too bad they were in a John Green novel.

How many more nights did they have, he wondered.

Shit, he felt morbid thinking like that, but there was a clock running here. With every hour that passed, it was more likely instead of less that Selena was going to collapse again.

And then what the fuck was he going to do with his brother?

Jesus Christ, Trez was going to be unmanageable.

With happy thoughts like that running through his head, he lost track of time, and before he was aware of having covered any distance at all, they were mounting the *mhis*-covered rise up to the mansion, Manny having broken off to head in the back way with the ambulance.

Hopefully, Selena was never going to know the precautions they were taking on her behalf.

It would have been a buzz kill. How could it not be.

iAm was careful to keep his distance as the last turn before the mansion approached, giving Trez time to get her inside. When he finally did pull into the courtyard, he went around the fountain and parked next to Rhage's GTO.

Which wasn't going to be out there much longer. The Brother always moved it into the garage during the winter months.

Manny's Porsche was at the base of the stairs, its top up, its key no doubt making its way back to the doctor so he could bring it to the training center's underground lot, too.

iAm shut the BMW off. Got out and locked it even though he didn't need to.

And stalled out.

Staring up at the sky, he watched the breath leaving his mouth drift off and disappear. That image of Trez and Selena dancing was like a dog with its fangs in his gray matter, the memory refusing to budge—and not, he was ashamed to admit, because he was thinking of everything his brother was in danger of losing or because he was stressing about how to peel the sad bastard off the pavement when things came to a bad conclusion.

Instead, he was wondering . . .

Shit, he was wondering what that felt like. To hold a female close to your body. Have her scent in your nose and your hands on her shoulders, her waist, her hips. He wanted to know what it was like to turn her face up to yours and—

Okay, he needed to pull back from all that.

Because none of it was happening for him. Not now. Not in a half hour if he went to that cabin. Not in a week or a month or a year from now—

As if on cue, a cold breeze came barreling by. Like the universe wanted to underscore all the cold and lonely he had going on.

The sound of the vestibule's outside door opening snapped him to attention. He liked Manny, but he didn't need the guy coming out to play musical cars and finding him—

It wasn't the good doctor.

Trez was coming out of the house. Jogging down the stone steps. Heading across the courtyard.

Shit.

iAm put his hand on his phone in case he needed to call . . . whoever the fuck. "Hey, is she all—"

He didn't get the "right" out.

His brother wrapped him up in a bear hug. "Thank you so much for tonight."

At first, iAm didn't know how to respond. He and his brother weren't huggers.

"I was so glad you were there. It meant everything to me."

iAm had to clear his throat. "I, ah . . ."

Trez just squeezed harder.

Cautiously, iAm put his arms around Trez. The movement felt all weird, but when he finally embraced the guy in return, he felt his brother shudder.

I'm sorry, man, he said in his head. *I don't want any of this for you.*

The cold wind continued to blow, and after a long moment, they stepped back.

Trez had ditched his jacket and he shoved his hands into the pockets of his slacks. "I got your text. I feel bad that I've just dumped everything on you."

"It's okay."

"It's not."

"Trez, you need to be with her and take care of your female. That's the most important thing. The rest of it is just conversation."

Those dark eyes focused on something above iAm's left shoulder. Or maybe whatever it was was above his ear.

"I seriously do not know why you're out here wasting time with me," iAm muttered.

"I want more for you than this."

"I happen to like my job at Sal's just fine."

His brother's stare locked on his. "That is not what I'm talking about, and you know it."

iAm joined the club with the fist-in-the-pocket routine. "Enough with the talk. Go to your female."

Trez was a hardheaded son of a bitch, capable of tremendous acts of hell-no. But iAm, as usual, got through to him.

The male turned around, but made it only halfway to the mansion's entrance before he stopped and looked over his shoulder.

"Don't waste all your life on me, okay." Trez shook his head. "I'm not worth it, and you're worth more than that."

iAm rolled his eyes. "Stop thinking. Start walking again."

"Ask yourself what's going to be left for you after I'm gone. If you're honest, I don't think you're going to like the answer any more than I do. And spare me the everything's-gonna-be-fines. Neither one of us is that naive."

"Why are you distracting yourself with this. Seriously, Trez."

"It's not a distraction. It's the kind of shit that eats you alive when you love someone."

On that note, Trez kept going, heading up the stone steps and disappearing through the vestibule's door.

iAm closed his eyes and sagged against the SUV. He didn't need that little monologue of his brother's in his head right now. He really didn't.

FIFTY-ONE

Selena's hands were stiff.

Standing at the counter in the Brotherhood's kitchen, she tried to open a can of Coke and found that her fingers refused to grip the tab right. Instead of pulling the metal lip free, they skipped over the top.

As all kinds of warnings went off in her head, she reined in the panic, and reminded herself that she'd spent three hours in the cold without any gloves on.

Making a couple of loose fists, she blew into them; then shook her arms. Cracked her knuckles. Tried not to start looking for other problems elsewhere in her body.

People who had her disease could still get minor-league frostbite.

She faced off at the can again, her heart pounding as she watched from a great distance while she approached the pop-top once more. She viewed her hands and fingers with dispassion, as if they were attached to someone else's wrists, moved by somebody else's brain.

Crack! Fizz!

She exhaled and had to steady herself on the granite.

"You okay?"

Covering up the relief, she smiled as Trez came in from the dining room. "Just getting some soda. I'm thirsty."

"How's your stomach?"

"Very well. How's yours?"

As he came up to her, she had the sense that he was hiding something from her as well. And it was a shock to discover that in spite of her big living-the-truth speech after she'd come out of the latest Arrest, she wanted him to keep his secret, just like she wanted to keep hers: They'd had such a wonderful night; the last thing she needed was to ruin it with heavy conversation that would just expose problems that couldn't be solved, and questions that weren't going to be answered until it was too late.

"Tum's just fine."

She forced another smile. "Would you like to head up-stairs?"

"That'd be great."

Picking up her soda, she took the palm he offered her and went out with him through the dining room and into the foyer. The house was essentially empty, the Brothers off working, Wrath seeing civilians, Beth and Marissa and Mary at Safe Place, Bella babysitting L.W. and Nalla up in the new nursery suite, the *doggen* attending to their duties.

All of this was going to continue, she thought, when she was gone. All of the doors opening and shutting, menus planned and consumed, people living their lives.

Dearest Virgin Scribe, she wanted to stay with them. She didn't want to go on to what might well be absolute noth-ingness, an utter unplugging of who she was and what mat-tered to her and how she thought and felt.

Gone. Nothing left.

She had been trained—no, programmed, really—to be-lieve in the afterlife, and serve the Mother of the Race, and adhere to traditions she had neither established herself nor volunteered for. And she had done all of that without ques-tion.

Coming to the end of her life, she wished she had asked and challenged and had a voice.

So much wasted time.

As she started up the stairs with Trez, she found herself wondering why, if there was a Fade and people continued up there...why had the Scribe Virgin demanded that everything on Earth be recorded in the Sanctuary? Why all of those volumes and volumes of lives lived...if after death, the people still existed only in a different form?

You had to preserve only that which could be lost.

Her heart started to pound, a sudden terror taking hold—

"Oh, shit," Trez breathed.

Clearly, he'd read her mind. "I don't know what I'm thinking. It's probably just nonsense—"

He threw out his free hand for the banister and weaved.

"Trez! What's wrong?"

"Shit. Fuck." He looked over at her, but his eyes were unfocused. "Can you help me to the room? I can't see—"

"Dearest Virgin Scribe, let me get Doc Jane!"

"No, no, it's just a migraine." He steadied himself with help from her. "I don't have a lot of time. I have to get upstairs to a dark room and lie down."

"Let me call Doc Jane—"

"No, as you remember, I've gotten these all my life. I know what's coming. It's going to be hell for eight hours, but it can't really hurt me."

Selena tried to take as much of his weight as she could while they hobbled up to the second-story landing and then crossed over to the door to the third floor. His big body moved slowly, and at some point, he just gave up on his vision entirely, those eyes of his shutting.

Somehow, she got him up to his room and down on the bed.

"Dark is going to help," he said, putting his forearm over his face. "And could you bring a wastepaper basket over?"

Hustling around, she turned off all the lights except the one in the bathroom and made sure there was a receptacle right next to his head. "Do you want me to take your clothes off?"

"Okay. Yeah."

It was not exactly the experience she'd been banking on, but then again, her mood had gotten ruined even before this. And as she did the deed, she was oh, so careful with him, helping him with his jacket, then shucking his boots and socks, and doing away with his slacks.

"I'ma keep the shirt on. I just don't have the energy for it." He captured her hand and tugged her into a sit by his hip. "Not the way I'd planned on ending tonight."

She kissed his palm. "What else can I do for you?"

"Just let me lie here for the next six to eight hours. And don't worry, like I said, all of this, from the headache to the nausea, is normal. Unfortunately."

"What causes this?"

"Stress."

"Do you want me to call iAm?"

"Shit, no. He has too much on his plate already. Actually, I think he's why I got it."

"Is there something wrong with him?"

As Trez fell silent, she wanted to press, but he was ill.

"You don't have to go," he said.

"I don't want to disturb you."

"You won't." He rubbed her hand with his own, and his lips, which were the only part of his face showing, broke into a smile. "I love your hands. I've told you that, right? They're so smooth and soft . . . long fingers . . ."

As she stayed with him and he ran his fingertips from the inside of her wrist to the base of her fingers, she felt her panic melt away. Nothing felt strange in those joints anymore. So it definitely had been the cold.

A little later he let out a soft moan, his mouth flattening, his body tensing up. And then he began to swallow.

"I need you to go," he mumbled. "I'm sorry—I don't want you to see this. . . ."

"Are you sure—"

"Please. *Now*."

It was the last thing she wanted to do, but she got to her feet. "I'm in the house, okay? I'm not leaving. Call me if you—"

He jerked over onto his side and reached for the bucket. Pausing over the thing, he opened his eyes and pegged her with a frazzled stare. "You need to leave now."

"I love you," she said, rushing for the door. "I wish I could help."

She wasn't sure he'd even heard her as she slipped out, and just as she shut the door, the sounds of him retching made her wince.

For a split second, she thought she might camp out in the hall beyond his room. But then, as she debated where she was going to sit on the floor, she realized that she couldn't get her grip off the doorknob.

Her palm had frozen on the brass.

"Of course I am not quitting. Don't be daft."

As Assail addressed his cousins in the kitchen of his glass house, he was in a vicious mood—and sinking even deeper into anger upon Ehric's inquiry.

"But the King—"

"Has no right to interfere in matters of commerce flowing to humans." He conveniently avoided thinking or commenting upon the conflict-of-interest issue. "And I have no intention of complying with that order of his."

"So how do we proceed?"

"He will have us followed. That is what I would do were I he. I want the two of you to go activate the warning to my colleague. We'll suspend operations briefly and reconnoiter."

"Aye."

After the pair of them left, he stayed in his kitchen so that whatever Brothers had been stationed around his house would have him in plain view. Taking out his vial of cocaine, he discovered it was, once again, nearly empty, but at least there was enough to tide him over.

When he finished partaking, he went into his study on the other side of his home. It too had glass windows, and he turned on the desk lamp so that they could keep a good eye on him. Sitting down, he looked at the piles of papers he'd made. Investment accounts. Brokerage accounts. Monies in the U.S. and abroad.

Growing, growing, growing.

The fortune at his disposal had turned another corner about a month ago, the laundered money from the Caymans transferred into more legal accounts in the U.K. and Switzerland.

So much, and all of it accumulating interest, dividends, and appreciation.

When he had started in the business of drug dealing, shortly after he had come to America from the Old Country about a year ago, he had already been doing very well for himself even by his standards. Now, there was double that amount in his various accounts.

Picking up a random sheaf of papers, he looked at his month-end report. The daily one in his computer was even more recent.

In spite of his largesse, the idea that Wrath was getting in the way of his pursuits infuriated him to his marrow.

Just not for a reason he would admit to anyone.

Without this . . . he had nothing.

What had started as an extension of his European businesses had grown into his *raison d'être*, the sole purpose he had in his life, the only drive that got him out of bed in the evening, and dressed, and out the door.

To be fair, he'd always enjoyed making money.

But ever since last winter . . .

Cursing, he leaned back in his leather chair and put his head in his hand. Then without looking, he reached into the inner pocket of his suit jacket and took out his phone.

He had memorized Sola's number long ago.

But he hadn't called it. Not since she had moved away from Caldwell to Miami with her grandmother. Not since she had left here to get out of exactly the kind of criminal life he was leading.

Going into his phone, he went to the numerical dial pad. As he had so many times before, he punched in the sequence of ten numbers, one after another, his fingertip finding and following the pattern he knew by heart.

No, he hadn't called her. But on a regular basis he did this: ten numbers that were anything but random to him, punched into his phone . . . and cleared away without him having hit "send."

If the King took his livelihood away? Then he was going to have fucking nothing to do but stew in the fact that the one woman he wanted was utterly unobtainable.

Woman. Not female.

She was human, not vampire. Hell, she didn't even know that vampires existed.

And therein lay the catch. Even if he broke out of the drug dealing? It wasn't like he could go down to Miami, show up on her doorstep, and be all like, Hey! Let's pick up where we were!

Not going to happen—because sooner or later, his species was going to come out and then where were they going to be?

For some reason, the stillness and silence of his glass house sank in, reminding him exactly how alone he was—and would be if he stopped his drugging. Hell, his cousins were not going to be content with sitting around and mourning a female they were not in love with—he would lose them, too.

God, he was rather pathetic, wasn't he.

More to the point, what was he going to do?

With the cocaine sizzling in his veins, his brain made a sudden A + B = C calculation that was based on a totally . . . preposterous idea.

Which nonetheless offered him a rather stunning solution to all this.

Straightening in his seat, he frowned and looked around the room, his eyes going on a wander as his brain pick, pick, picked apart the plan. When he could find no fault, he cleared Sola's digits from the screen of his phone and dialed Ehric. When he got voice mail, he figured they were probably still dematerialized.

A second later, his phone rang and he answered, not bothering with a greeting. "Have you left the symbol for him yet?"

Ehric's reply was muffled by the wind down by the river. "We've just arrived."

"Wait for him. Do not reveal yourself."

Assail continued to give instructions, and at the end of it all, Ehric's response was perfect: "As you wish."

Assail ended the call and sank back into the chair. Taking a deep breath, he cursed. This was going to be a lot of work. But it was the only solution he seemed to have.

Plus, the fact that this would consume him for the appreciable future? Was exactly what he wanted. And if it didn't work? Well, then he'd be dead and he wouldn't care about anything anymore.

Not even the woman he longed for with every inch of his body and all of his black, misbegotten heart.

Her mother had gotten it right with that name of hers.

Marisol had indeed stolen his soul.

FIFTY-TWO

iAm had not intended for Trez's words to sink in any more than the cold breeze had when they'd been standing in the courtyard. He had planned to go inside, eat something fast, and forget that whole interaction had occurred. Go about his night. Head over to the clubs and the restaurant. Push papers, take control, make some decisions that were concrete and solid.

Instead, he was stuck in the foyer, staring up at the three-story-high ceiling that had been painted by some great artist. The subject matter was, he supposed, inspirational: heroes on venerable steeds, fighting in the clouds, heavenly warriors who were brave and strong and on the side of the righteous.

But all that glory wasn't why he'd gone into pause mode.

Trez's destiny was a house of cards, a delicate, tricky thing that had had to be managed all of both their lives. Every move iAm took had to be careful, deliberate, and calculated with the goal of survival.

His brother's.

He was a centuries-old virgin because of it.

Hell, he hadn't even looked at a female, like, ever.

Whether Trez had been banging them in the clubs, or throwing porn up on the TV, or talking about what he'd done all over his desk, in the back of his car, outside in the fucking parking lot, iAm had never had any interest in any of it.

He'd been a flatline motherfucker.

Mother-*not*-fucker, as it were.

And yeah, he'd tried on the whole gay thing for size, wondering if maybe he was attracted to men and males.

Nope.

It had gotten to the point where, if it weren't for the fact that he washed them every night, he'd have wondered whether or not he had any balls.

Ask yourself what's going to be left for you after I'm gone. If you're honest, I don't think you're going to like the answer any more than I do.

Without being aware of having come to a decision, iAm turned on his heel and went out through the vestibule. On the front stoop of the massive gray mansion, he stood in the wind ...

... and then took flight.

On the journey to his destination, flashes of the past battered at him: Trez escaping from the palace. iAm being held until he promised to bring the male back—which had been the last thing he'd actually intended on doing. The mad hunt.

The cabin on Black Snake Mountain.

As iAm resumed his form, he had a moment of straight-up nausea as he took in the ragged, weathered structure with its rough vertical siding and its cedar shingles and that rock chimney which extruded from the roofline like a bad tooth. It was ... exactly the same. Not even kind of the same, with different windows or shrubbery growing or trees that had fallen or overgrown.

No, for a split second he wasn't sure whether this was years ago or right now.

Shaking himself, he walked to the front door. The hinges creaked as he opened things up, and at least he was better prepared for what he saw.

Precisely the same. From the placement of the no-frills furniture, to the old-fire smell, to the drafts that wheedled their way through the walls.

He closed the door behind him and walked around, his boots making the rough-cut floorboards clap and groan. Over by the river-rock hearth, he found a generous supply of wood—guess the last hunters who had used the place had been good little helpers and ready to pay shit forward.

His hands shook as he laid logs on the andirons and

shoved pine needles underneath. Taking out the lighter he kept on him thanks to having worked with a lot of temperamental gas cooktops, he lit things, fanned them, got the flames up and rolling.

He told himself it was a waste of time and heat. She wasn't going to come. There was no way she was going to come.

He was just going to hang here for a half hour or so, play witness to his brain sinking into some dark, dangerous territory, and then put out the fire and head back to Caldie.

The clubs. He would go to the clubs first, and then—

The sound of that creaky door opening made him stiffen. *maichen*'s scent flooded the interior.

Cranking his head around, he lifted his eyes. There in the doorway, she stood in the flesh, her robes flapping in the cold wind rushing in from behind her.

She was both a ghost . . . and soul-shatteringly vital.

And as he looked at her, he knew exactly why they had both come.

FIFTY-THREE

Selena took the long underground tunnel to the training center slowly. It was a case of one foot after the other, from the base of the short stairs that led into the subterranean passageway to the door that opened into the office closet. Every time she had to enter a passcode or push her way through a jamb, she waited for the reconsideration to hit her. The turnaround to happen. The back-upstairs to be made manifest.

Instead, she ended up not just emerging into Tohr's work space, but going through its glass door and coming out into the concrete corridor beyond.

The clinic was about thirty yards down, that collection of doors coming after all kinds of alternate destinations presented themselves: weight rooms, gyms, locker rooms.

Her feet didn't stop at any of those.

No, they took her right to the one place she had resolved never to return to voluntarily.

Her knock was quiet, an opportunity for a no-reply either because nobody was there (score!) or they were busy helping someone else (sad, but a relief, too) or so engrossed in work they didn't hear her (which was like leaving a voice mail for someone you didn't really want to speak with anyway).

Doc Jane opened up. And did a whoa-hey! recoil. "Selena, hi."

She lifted her palm up lamely. "Hi."

There was a pause. And then the doctor said, "Is this a social thing or do you need . . ."

"You're probably pretty busy, right."

"Actually, after having been slammed for about three days straight, I've just been catching up on medical records." The female eased back. "Come on in if you like."

Selena braced herself. Stepped over the threshold. Tried desperately not to look at that exam table.

Meanwhile, Doc Jane went over and sat down on a rolling stool, folding her white coat around herself and crossing her legs. The scrubs she had on underneath were blue. Her Crocs were red.

Her eyes were forest green. And grave.

Selena started to walk around, but everywhere she looked, all she saw were glass-fronted stainless-steel cabinets with torture instruments in them. Rattled, she eyed the door to the corridor, which was shutting slowly, silently, on its own.

Like the lid of a coffin.

"Hey," Doc Jane said, "I was just going to go stretch my legs. You want to join me for a couple of laps around the gym?"

"Oh, God, yes. Thank you."

The pair of them went out together, heading down past a number of doors and many, many yards of corridor. When they got to their destination, Doc Jane opened the heavy steel panel and turned on the caged ceiling lights.

"I know it's weird, but I love this place," Jane said. "The wood with that beautiful honey-yellow color and everything smells like floor cleaner. Which is kinda nuts, because I hate chemicals in the air or on things."

As the doctor started them walking around the far edge of the basketball courts, Selena was pretty sure that the pace was kept slow on purpose.

They'd made it down the short side, under the hoop, and through the left turn to head along the bleachers before Selena said anything.

"I think . . ." Tears came to her eyes and she realized she was terrified.

"We have all the time you need," Doc Jane said softly.

Selena wiped under both eyes. "I'm afraid to talk about it. Like if I do . . ."

"Are you having some symptoms?"

She couldn't speak. But found herself nodding. "I think . . . yes."

Doc Jane made an *mmm-hmmm* sound. "Do you want to tell me what they are?"

Selena put out her hand, the one that had gotten frozen on the doorknob, and flared her fingers wide. As she flexed things open and closed, her mind went on a wild ride of *Are they worse? Are they better? Are they the same?*

"Your hands?" When all she did was nod again, Doc Jane asked, "Anywhere else?"

At least this time she could shake her head.

"Do you remember," the doctor said, "when an attack came before, whether or not you had any prodromals?"

"What does that mean?"

"Any sort of advance warning?"

Selena brushed at her eyes again and wiped her hands on the pants Trez had taken off her body no more than a half hour before. With a surge of agony, she wanted to go back to that moment, back to the time before her disease had started talking again.

"I don't know. I don't remember ever noticing anything. But before . . . I used to ignore it as much as I could. I didn't want to think about it." She glanced over at the doctor. "I'm sorry that I didn't come back down to see you, you know, after I . . ."

Doc Jane batted at the air. "God, girl, don't worry about it. There are no hard-and-fast rules, and you have to do what feels right. People need to direct their own lives."

"Is there anything we can do for me? Anything . . . we should do?"

The healer took her time in answering. "I'm going to be straight with you, okay?"

Ah, yes. Nothing was available. "I'd appreciate it."

"For the last forty-eight hours, there have been a lot of people searching for solutions. Manny's reached out to his human contacts. I've talked with Havers. Rehv headed up to the *symphath* territory—and I got a text from iAm saying that he went to the s'Hisbe."

"Nothing?"

"Havers is only aware of patients who struggle with local-ized episodes, like arthritis flare-ups that hit hands or knees, hips or shoulders. Nothing with the systemic symptoms as severe as you present with. He treats the patients with anti-inflammatories and painkillers—even though he's tried some human drugs, he hasn't had any breakthroughs of note when it comes to prevention or cure. And neither the *symphaths* nor the Shadows have any familiarity with the issue."

Management. That was the best she could hope for.

"Can you tell me how much time I have?"

Doc Jane shook her head. "I can check your inflammatory markers. But I don't really have anything to compare them to—and the attacks come on fast, from what I understand. That suggests a sudden surge, like an earthquake."

They kept going around the gym, heading down, down, down to the distant end, where there was a door marked, EQUIPMENT ROOM AND PT.

"I guess we should go back and check my . . . you know." Selena circled the air next to her with her hand. "Inflammation things."

"We can if you want. I think the important thing is that you do whatever makes you feel supported and calmer."

"Okay. All right."

A moment later, she felt Doc Jane take her hand and squeeze. And as she looked over, she was shocked to see the emotion on the healer's face. Such stark sadness, a pain that went deep.

Selena tugged the other female to a halt. "This is not your fault."

Those forest-green eyes went around the cavernous expanse of the gym, not landing anywhere. "I just . . . I want to help. I want to give you the rest of the many, many years you're due. I want you to live. And the fact that I can't find a solution . . . I'm so sorry, Selena. I'm so sorry—and I'm going to keep fighting. I'm going to keep trying, looking. . . ."

It seemed liked the most natural thing in the world to put her arms around the woman and hold on.

"I'm so sorry," Doc Jane choked out.

Later, Selena would realize . . .

. . . it was the first of her good-byes.

maichen had struggled to find the cabin. Black Snake Mountain was easy enough. East side of the peak was also not a problem. And the scent of the fire should have been simple because even when she was in molecular form, her sense of smell was strong, and there was nothing clearer than smoke on a fall night. Even so, it had been difficult. She had traveled through the air, searching, searching. . . .

She had been on the verge of turning around and going back, an aching sadness taking hold within her—but then that smoke had come upon the breeze and she had criss-crossed over its trail, tracking the strength of the scent, ze-roing in on its source.

And there was the cabin he had spoken of.

She had Shadowed up to the thing, staying in her energy form, shooting over the scruffy ground, going around the small, simple structure—reassuring herself that it was, in fact, him and him alone.

Taking form, she approached the door and knocked. When he didn't answer, she opened the way in.

He was by the fire, crouched down, tending to the flames.

Instantly, his big body rose to a stand, the flickering light behind him creating an aura.

As she stepped inside, the wind caught the door and flipped it closed, the slam making her jump.

"It's cold in here," he said roughly. "I'm trying to get it warmer."

Seeing him was enough to make her completely unaware of her surroundings. She could have been in a desert, on the ocean, off to the polar ice caps and nothing would have registered.

"Come closer." He beckoned her with his hand. "To the fire."

Her body obeyed him without hesitation, although it was to him she went, not the flames. And as she stepped beside him, he moved back as if he didn't want to crowd her.

"Let me get you something to sit on."

Before she could tell him not to bother himself, he went over to a bedding platform and pulled the soft pad off the top along with some rough blankets. With sure hands, he arranged everything and then once again moved away.

The sex rolling off of him was irresistible.

As cool as he was trying to be, as respectful as he was being, she could sense the need in him.

And yes, she realized . . . this was indeed why she had risked so much to come here.

She wanted him, too. Even though it was going to create a crisis. Even though it was irresponsible. Even though it made no sense.

She had followed the rules all her life. But there was no responsibility or duty that was even half as captivating as he was—and her time for what relative freedom she had was running out.

Lowering herself onto the bedding, she crossed her legs under her heavy robing. "Please. Sit with me?"

"You sure you want me to." He loomed over her, his dark face absorbing that playful light.

"Yes," she breathed.

He lowered himself to his knees, his heavy-lidded eyes moving over the robing that covered her from crown of head to sole of foot.

"Will you let me see you," he said in a deep voice.

maichen swallowed hard. Then she lifted her hands to the mesh that covered her face—but it was to hold the masking in place. "I am afraid."

"Of what?"

What if he didn't like what he saw?

"I already know you're beautiful," he said, as if he read her mind.

"How?"

He touched the center of his large chest. "I see you in here. I know you . . . in here. You are very beautiful to me, no matter what you look like."

Acutely aware of everything that she hadn't told him about herself, she whispered, "We do not know each other."

"Does that matter to you?"

"No."

"Me, neither." He frowned and looked into the fire. "The last couple of nights, with everything going on with my brother—it's been an eye-opener. I don't want to waste any more time. I want to get on with living, instead of keep going in this neutral-zone nightmare, waiting for the ax to fall."

"Is your brother . . . is he going to come back to the Territory ever? They say . . . he refuses his duty, even though the Queen has decreed after the mourning . . ."

She had to stop. The anxiety was too great.

She was supposed to come unto her mate untouched.

That was not going to happen.

But what could the Anointed One do to her? They were both being forced into the mating, and tradition dictated that he was essentially her property.

A protest from him would be like a chair making an argument against being sat upon.

iAm shook his head. "After Trez loses Selena, all bets are off—and frankly, that Princess? She isn't going to want what's left of him, not unless she's into necrophilia. He's going to be dead whether he's walking or in a grave."

maichen hung her head. She had never not known about the mating that awaited her. It had been part of her rearing, the expectation that the Anointed One was destined by the stars to be her impregnating mate—and that with him, through him, she would ensure her mother's bloodline continued to rule over the s'Hisbe.

Preordained. Written in the sacred stars.

She had accepted what was her due the same way she had accepted everything about her life, from her station to her loneliness to the perennial sense that she was missing out on so much through no fault or choice of her own.

She cleared her throat. "I would imagine that the Princess would let him go, if she could. She would not want anyone to suffer, most especially one who had lost a female of worth."

"Do you know her?"

"I have attended her."

"What's she like?" Before she could answer, he put up his hand. "Actually, I don't need to know."

"I think she would say that she is as trapped as your brother. I think . . . she is in a jail of destiny, too."

He rubbed his face. "That actually makes me hate her less. I guess I never thought about what it's been like for her."

"She was told of her destiny just as he was. She has not chosen any of this."

iAm gave a short laugh. "Maybe they can tell the Queen to go screw. If both of them refuse to play the game, it could be all over. Not that it's going to save my brother from losing his love."

"But the stars have revealed their destinies."

That dark stare swung back to her. "Do you believe

that? I mean, do you actually think that the alignment of a bunch of disinterested planets a million light-years away should be used as a map for people's lives? I don't."

"It has been the way for generations," she said in a hollow voice.

"Doesn't make it right. In fact, that makes it even more offensive. Think of how much has been ruined."

maichen's chest got tight as he spoke out loud things that she had been thinking about . . . ever since she had learned many years ago that the male she was to mate had found his fate so distasteful that he had escaped the Territory under threat of death and upon punishment of expulsion.

"Enough with this talk," he said. "It isn't what we came here for. Is it."

Her eyes shifted to his under her mesh. "No, it is not."

His stare went to her robing, as if in his mind, he was getting her naked already.

Her heart started to hammer again, her palms growing sweaty. "I must have you know that I haven't . . . I am not . . ."

"Neither have I."

She recoiled. She couldn't help it. He was just so masculine, so beautiful of form, so . . .

"Change your mind?" he clipped out. "Not sexy, is it—"

"How is that possible," she blurted. "You're so *phearsom*."

There was a pause. And then without warning, he threw back his head and laughed. The sound was so unexpected and . . . captivating . . . she nearly pulled back in surprise again.

When he leveled his eyes on her once more, he smiled for the first time. And he took her breath away.

"That is the nicest compliment I have ever received."

She felt herself break into a smile under the mesh—but then as he grew serious once more, she did, too.

There would be no going back, she thought. If she didn't leave now, before he took her hood off . . . she was not going to go until the deed was done.

maichen's hands lifted to her masking, her decision made.

Gripping the bottom of the mesh, she began to raise it.

Anxiety made her heart skip beats, but she didn't slow; she didn't stop.

Planets should not rule the choices of the quick or the legacies of the dead, she thought as the cooler air hit her throat, her jaw . . . her mouth.

She was choosing this.

She was choosing him.

FIFTY-FOUR

Am felt like he was suspended in time as *maichen's* face was revealed inch by inch. Her lips were full and deep red, her skin smooth and slightly darker than his, her cheeks wide and high—

He stopped being able to form a thought as her eyes were uncovered.

Deeply set and with heavy lashes, they were a brilliant peridot green. But then again, she was in high emotion and that was a sign of it, something that the stares of Shadows did.

Maybe his were that way, too.

And then there was her hair. Tightly waved, it flowed from the crown of her head and covered her shoulders and beyond. It was so long that he couldn't see where it ended.

She was, quite simply, the most extraordinary thing he had ever seen.

She was both exotic, because he had been living among humans for so long and had missed the features of his people—and completely normal, because her beauty and her coloring were so much like his own.

"It is a crime to keep you covered," he breathed.

The blush that ran up from her throat made his fangs descend, and his hands curled from the need to touch her.

"In truth?" she whispered.

"On my blood."

As if his regard gave her courage, she put the mesh aside, and continued with her uncovering, releasing the simple brass clasp at her collarbone and letting the first layer of robes fall from her shoulders.

She was delicately built, but she was all female, and as much as he tried not to linger on what her body looked like, his eyes refused to go anywhere else.

That flickering pulse at the side of her neck was an invitation to bite.

The swell of her breasts was an entreaty to touch.

The scent of her sex was a call to be answered.

iAm swallowed the curse that wanted to escape from his mouth. She was too much, too beautiful, too alive. His heart was pounding and his cock was hard as marble behind his fly.

He wished he'd had a drink before he'd come here.

Or six.

"You're hungry," she whispered.

"Yes."

"Would you care to take my . . ."

He couldn't believe where she was going with that. "Your vein?"

"If you should care for it."

Oh, fuck him, *yes*. "I would beg for such. . . ."

"There is no need for that."

He expected her to offer him her wrist, but as she lifted her chin and exposed her throat, he was rendered really fucking stoopid.

iAm knew he should ask if she was sure, press her to think this through. This was going to move very fast if he struck her with his fangs.

Instead, he groaned, "Please tell me your name."

"It is *maichen*. I told you. That is the only name I feel is mine."

He ground his molars. "*maichen*, you need to know . . . I don't think I can stop. If I get in there."

"I know. That is why I want you at my throat. No going back."

His eyes rolled and his torso swayed. "But don't you have a father back home? Someone who will care that you're . . ."

He knew the standards were different for members of the servant class—females were not expected to be virgins, as they were required to be of service in whatever way was demanded of them. But still.

"Are you certain of this?" he said.

His erection was screaming for him to STFU, but his conscience was even stronger than that roaring drive.

"I am."

Those peridot eyes of hers were steady, strong, certain.

Time to stop talking.

iAm went for her, lunging forward, grabbing onto the nape of her neck, bending her backward, holding her in his arms and putting his mouth to her flesh. He had never taken from a female this way, and he didn't immediately strike. He was overcome by the scent of her, by the soft skin under his lips as he extended his tongue and licked up her vein.

He intended to nuzzle at her further, but as her hands took hold of his shoulders and she arched into him, he couldn't wait any longer. He hissed and penetrated her skin.

At the bite, she cried out, but instead of pushing him away, she pulled him even closer.

Her blood was a blast in his mouth, tasting of dark wine and promising an intoxication that started to take hold the instant he swallowed. Sucking at her, he swept his hand down her body, finding the curve of her waist and the flare of her hip. More, he took more as his pelvis pushed forward, seeking that vital juncture of hers that was still under folds of fabric.

Dizzy and hyper-focused at the same time, he laid her out flat and straddled her body, as a wild animal might protect its prey. But he wanted to give to her as well. Moving one of his arms up, he put his wrist over her mouth, rubbing at her lips.

Taking the cue, she struck as well, taking his vein as he took hers, completing a circle that exploded the heat between them.

Before he knew what he was doing, he went to work on her robes, pulling up, higher and higher, the hem, the folds, the weight. Her thighs were smooth and supple, and they opened for him, giving him access to what he wanted most.

No panties. Shadows didn't wear them.

When he swept his hand over her sex, she moaned and pulled harder on what he was providing her—and he wanted her to drain him dry. But not the other way around. Forcing himself to release her vein, he licked the puncture wounds closed and then found himself drawing his lips downward, crossing over the graceful wing of her collarbone. Heading for her breasts, he gripped the top of her robing with his fangs and ripped it apart, the fabric giving way until—

"Oh, sweet Jesus," he gasped.

Her breasts were high and tight and tipped with little nipples that he didn't spend a lot of time looking at. No, he went for them with his mouth, worshiping them while she continued to take from his wrist.

And still, he wanted more of her.

Just as he was getting greedy to head lower—even though he had no idea what he was doing—she released his vein and freed him up. Without giving her a chance to seal where she had struck, he reared up over her and took both sides of what he had begun to tear in his hands.

Riiiiiiiiiiiiiiiiiiiiiiip.

With that, the under robing was in two halves, and she was naked before him.

Writhing dark skin was bathed in firelight, and her body was marked with smudges of his red blood—and didn't that make him want to put other things of his on her.

So that all would know she was his.

Dimly, in the back of his addled brain, he was astounded that the stories he had heard and assumed were fiction—those tales of males being around a given female and bonding instantly—were in fact totally and absolutely true.

He had seen her face but moments ago, and now he had gone down the wormhole, lost and found by turns, overwhelmed and starved for more at the same time.

"Mine," he growled.

Bared to her lover's eyes, *maichen* had expected to feel self-conscious or embarrassed. Only her female bathers had ever seen what iAm was looking at.

Instead?

She kicked the robing free from her hands and brought her palms up to cup her breasts. "Yours," she heard herself say. Then she moved down and touched her exposed sex. "Yours."

His upper lip curled back and he let out a growl that was both reverent and a little evil.

Then he took off his coat, his shirt. His shoes and pants.

Firelight moved over his skin, casting shadows under the cuts of muscle that ribbed his arms, his chest, his abdomen.

His arousal was enormous.

It was all so out-of-control, this extraordinary series of events—and the culmination was yet to come. What next, she wondered? She had been nominally instructed in sex in preparation for her mating, the healer giving her an anatomical overview of how things were going to go—and there had been what she had seen of s'Ex and those humans. But neither of those awkward exchanges had done anything to explain how electric it was going to be. How much she was going to want the joining. How desperate she would feel.

Planting his hands on either side of her, iAm suspended himself above her body and slowly brought his lips to hers. The contact was featherlight and fleeting, leaving her wanting more—but then he gradually laid himself on top of her, his weight impossibly erotic, his hard contours cutting into her.

His hard sex brushing at her core.

She began to arch under him, sawing her legs, searching for something although she did not know what.

"I gotchu," he said. "I'll take care of it."

But he didn't. He just kissed her and made it all worse, leisurely licking at her mouth, rocking against her breasts, her inner thighs—all without joining them.

"Why do you wait," she moaned.

"I need to make sure you're ready—or it's going to hurt."

Her eyes flipped open. "There will be no pain. Will there?"

"How much do you ... ah, know about ...?"

Her mouth started moving, and she supposed she was speaking—and he was nodding, saying something in return. But she had no idea what was being said on either side.

Except then his hand was moving down, going between them, brushing at her sex, delving in. The pleasure he brought out of her was like the firelight, hot and all over her body, taking her to some different consciousness.

Then there was pressure at her core, but nothing painful. Just a pushing, a gentle pushing that made her give way internally.

When his hand reappeared by her side, she realized it was his arousal going into her, not his fingers.

Shifting her hips to accommodate him further, she was aware of a pinching shock, a barrier breaking away—and then the joining was so deep, she felt as though he had entered her all over her body. Good, so good—she reveled in how close he was, their skin-to-skin contact warming her inside and out, a lifetime of hands-off treatment wiped away.

And then he began to move. Slow at first, with growing momentum, she was transported along with him to a rising, shimmering pleasure.

Sweeping her hands down his surging back, she loved the power of him, and the knowledge that this particular male was the one who had been the first within her body.

And then a dam broke and everything became so much more vivid, a cresting rush pushing her up against that body of his.

Her mouth opened and she cried out, but not in pain.

He shouted as well, and there was a pulsing inside her core.

But that was not the end. He didn't stop. He just kept going, pumping against her, in her, over her.

The healer had not told her it would be this good.

Not at all.

FIFTY-FIVE

He came into her life wearing a Syracuse ball cap and blue jeans that had holes in them.

Paradise was at her desk, making entries in the system, fielding inquires on e-mail, settling visitors in the chairs, when yet another cold breeze shot through the parlor. By now, she was used to the shafts of frigid air—there was one every time the front door opened and shut as a new arrival came in.

So she didn't actually look up until she sensed a large presence at her desk.

As she lifted her eyes, she had her professional smile in place—but promptly lost the expression.

Standing in front of her was a male about six feet, seven inches tall, with shoulders as wide as a doorway, and a jaw that was straight as an arrow. He had some kind of windbreaker on, even though it was cold enough for a proper coat, and no gloves.

And then there was the Orange ball cap and those jeans.

"May I help you?" she asked.

The brim of that hat was so low, she couldn't see his eyes, but she could feel the impact of them.

"I'm here about the training program."

His voice was very deep and surprisingly quiet. Given his physical size, she would have expected something much louder.

"The training program?"

"For the Black Dagger Brotherhood's soldiers."

"Oh, yes. I know, but it's not—I mean, it's not here. At this house."

As he looked around, she tried to catch sight of his eyes. "I know," he said. "I mean, I need an application, and I thought there might be one here."

"There was an e-mail that went out. Would you like me to forward it to you?"

"I, ah . . ." He glanced around again. Shoved his hands into the pockets of those jeans. "Do you have an application that's printed out?"

"I can just send you the whole thing right now—what's your e-mail address?"

As he seemed to focus on the wall behind her head, she decided that his hair was dark. Dark and very short.

"I don't have an e-mail address," he said softly.

Paradise blinked. "Hotmail is free."

"It's okay," the male said, taking a step back. "I'll find another way to get one."

"Wait." She opened up the desk drawer. "Here. Take mine—I mean, this one."

He hesitated. Reached a long arm over. Accepted what she had previously taken out of the wastepaper basket.

"Thanks." He glanced down and frowned—at least, she thought he was frowning. "This one is already filled in at the top?"

As he passed it back to her, she cursed. "Sorry. I . . . let me print you out a fresh one."

Clicking through with her mouse, she signed into her e-mail, got Peyton the Jerk's forward, opened the attachment, hit print.

As the machine behind the desk woke up and started whirring, the male put the application down on her desk. "You're going into the program?"

Great. Like she needed to get The Lecture from a complete stranger.

She snatched the paperwork back. "Females are allowed to join, you know. It's in the e-mail. We can join—"

"I think you should. Even if you choose not to fight, I think females should be trained—you don't know when or under what circumstances you might have to protect yourself. It's only logical."

Paradise just stared up at him. "I ..." She cleared her throat. "I happen to agree with you."

As the printer fell quiet, she pivoted in her chair and took the warm pages off the top of the HP. There was no real need to paper-clip, staple, or otherwise tie them together, but she made work out of pulling open another drawer and rifling around for something from OfficeMax.

"You can bring them back here," she said when she handed them over. "Once you've filled them out, I can give them to the Brothers."

He folded the application once and put it inside his thin windbreaker. "Thank you."

And then he took his ball cap off and bowed to her.

As he straightened, she got a better look at him, and file that under OMG.

Make that OMFG.

His eyes were a perfect sky blue, deeply set, with dark brows and lashes. His face was hollow-cheeked, because he was a little too lean, but that just set off the masculine bone structure. And his mouth was ...

If he'd gotten her attention before, he pretty much knocked her on her ass now.

Thank God for her chair.

"What's your name?" she blurted as he turned away.

He put his ball cap back on. "Craeg."

She got to her feet and stuck out her hand. "I'm Paradise—well, you probably know that already, because you read the thing I'd filled in."

Great, she was babbling.

"Nice to meet you, Craeg," she prompted when he made no move toward her.

He nodded once, and then walked out, leaving her palm hanging there in the breeze.

Flushing, she sat back down—and realized that ooooooh, about five people had witnessed that whole exchange. And were now busy thumbing through issues of *People* and *Time* magazine, trying to look busy. One of the older males even picked up an entire *Caldwell Courier Journal* and put it up to his face.

Well, she could play at the pretend-to-be-busy thing, too.

Making all kinds of tapping noises on her keyboard, she tried to camo the full-body fluster she had going on.

She'd never seen him before. Like, ever. So maybe he had just come over from the Old Country—except what were the chances of that? The vast majority of the population had been in and around Caldwell for how long? Plus no accent. So he must be . . . well, a stranger, obviously. But he had to be a member of the aristocracy if he'd heard about the training program, right?

Glancing over at the archway he'd come through, she found herself wishing he would hand-deliver that application back.

Who was he—

"Paradise?"

She jumped. And focused on her father, who'd come out of nowhere. "Yes?" Realizing her voice sounded too close to normal, and she was supposed to still be angry at him, she cleared her throat. "What may I do for you?"

Like he was simply another person she was taking care of.

"I just wanted to inquire how you were doing?"

His affect was nothing aggressive. Instead, he seemed so worried—damn it. She wanted to keep being angry at him.

She sighed. "I'm fine, Father."

"You're doing such a marvelous job. Truly. Everything is running so smoothly. The King is so pleased—I am so proud."

See, this was just like him. It was impossible to be pissy when you were confronted by this . . . this earnest, his-version-of-an-apology stuff.

"May I bring you something to eat or drink?"

"You're not a *doggen*, Father."

"Perhaps you need a break?"

"No." She rolled her eyes. Got to her feet. Walked around to him. "You drive me nuts."

She gave him a hug because that was what he was looking for. Then she stepped back. "Oster, son of Sanye, is next."

As she indicated the gentlemale in question, and the civilian got to his feet, her father gave her hand a squeeze and then reassumed his official duties.

Following his example, she sat down again. Looked at the computer in front of her. And still felt caged.

But what was she going to do? Even though he technically couldn't stop her—she was of age, and there had been no specification on the application that a female had to get a male elder to approve the submission—she nonetheless found herself paralyzed.

It was hard to rebel against your parents when there was only one left.

And he was all you had in this world.

Selena hated pretty much everything about the exam, the blood draw, the X-ray process. And she felt bad about that. It wasn't that Doc Jane was anything less than perfectly gentle and very kind. But to be in one of those hospital johnnies, getting poked and prodded, twisted and pictured, was like having the countdown to some kind of detonation happen right in front of you.

Plus, she hated the fake-lemon antiseptic they had to use on everything.

And the fact that she was cold even after they put a blanket over her legs.

And then there was that bright light hanging over her head.

Mostly, though, it wasn't the external environment that was hard to put up with. It was the internal screaming that she found she had to hold in through force of will.

"Okay, I think that's our last X-ray," Doc Jane said from over by the desk.

On the computer screen, a ghostly image of Selena's knee was front and center, but she refused to look at it.

She had to stay lying down until Doc Jane came back over and moved the X-ray arm out of the way. And as she sat up, the doctor took the plate from underneath her leg and put it aside.

"So . . . what now?" Selena asked.

She was numb. She was cold. She was sweaty.

But mostly she was feeling stiff. And not just in her hands.

"Let me take a good look at the X-rays with Manny. And then we'll come talk to you."

Selena shifted her legs off and looked over the lip of the table at her feet. She flexed one and then the other, her brain going into a tailspin of *Better? Worse? The same?*

"When?" she said roughly.

"Why don't we meet around dawn? Trez could come down here with you if you like—"

The crash came from outside of the room, and both of them looked to the door across the way. When the sound repeated itself, Doc Jane raced over—and so did Selena.

After all, she wasn't frozen stiff yet, and it seemed like a good time to remind herself of that fact.

The pair of them rushed out into the corridor and listened. The training center was otherwise silent, what with the Brothers getting their workouts in the field, and there being, fortunately, no one with injuries in the clinic rooms—

The clatter came again, and they took off, heading two doors down.

Doc Jane opened things wide.

The healer had to duck as something came flying out of the room. A tray. It was a meal tray, and it skipped along the concrete floor like the thing was really glad to be free of there—and looking to put a little extra distance in.

Inside, Luchas was out of control on the bed. Half of him appeared to be tied down, but one hand and arm were free and he was using them to destroy anything he could reach—he'd knocked over some monitoring equipment along with his IV pole, did the same duty with the rolling table that had had some sort of meal on it—and was now reaching for the back of the headboard like he wanted to tear the bed apart.

"Luchas," Doc Jane said, with admirable calmness. "What's going—"

"Fuck you!"

Selena recoiled. She'd been here to feed Qhuinn's brother over the last several months, and he'd always been nothing short of a gentlemale.

"Luchas—"

"Fuck this!" He gave up on the headboard and grabbed onto the side table, shoving it so hard the thing went down, its drawers exploding out like that was its way to bleed. "Fuck you!"

Doc Jane backed out and muttered, "I've got to go get a sedative. Don't go in there."

As the doctor took off at a run, Selena stayed in the doorway.

"What are you looking at?" he screamed at her. "What the fuck do you want!"

There was a red stain on the bed. The sheeting, on one side, a little more than halfway down, was stained—he was bleeding. From some kind of wound—

"Your leg," she breathed, well aware of the infection that had been plaguing him. "Be careful of your leg—"

"I wanted to die!" he spat. "I was trying to die!"

His face was a twisted facsimile of the features she knew well, his too-white skin stretched nearly to the breaking point over a bone structure that had no doubt been enviable before he'd been tortured by the Lessening Society.

"They took my fucking leg to save me!" He pulled the sheets off. "To save me!"

The stump was wrapped carefully in layers of surgical gauze, but underneath wasn't doing well—blood was seeping out, everywhere.

He started to claw for what was left and that was when she had to get involved.

Marching across the room, she grabbed his flailing hands and pinned them to the bed by his head.

Luchas. Went. Wild.

Screaming, twisting, cursing at her.

All she did was shake her head and let him exhaust himself—which didn't take long at all.

When he stopped fighting, she said, "You are so lucky. So damned lucky."

That shut him up. Probably in a way that a direct confrontation wouldn't have.

"What?" he stammered.

"I'm dying," she said plainly. "And if someone could take part of my leg to save me? So I could stay here to be with the person I love? I'd do it in a heartbeat. So, yeah, I think you're very lucky."

He was still breathing hard, but the tension in his body left him. "Dying?"

"'Fraid so." She released her hold and stepped back. "Don't waste this time you have. I know you're hurting, and I don't doubt you're angry at where you are. But personally, I'd trade places with you in a heartbeat."

Doc Jane came back—and stopped when she saw that the place wasn't on fire or something.

"I'm going to go get dressed," Selena said as she headed

for the door. "I'm cold in this gown. Do you need help cleaning up?"

Doc Jane looked back and forth between them, clearly wondering what had been said or done to turn things around. "Ah, no, let me take care of it."

"Okay." Selena nodded at the doctor, and then glanced back at Luchas. "Take care of yourself."

She could feel his eyes on her as she stepped out into the corridor. Could feel them still as she went back to change.

When she reentered the tunnel, she began to get paranoid that she'd have an attack halfway back to the main house, and get stuck dying under the fluorescent lights. Or maybe if it happened on the stairwell up to the foyer . . . or —

Okay, she'd better stop this.

She had enough to worry about without looking for more trouble.

FIFTY-SIX

He couldn't stop looking at her.

As iAm lay naked in front of the dying fire, his body was entwined with *maichen*'s, their legs one among another, their hips still locked together, their sexes close, but no longer joined. She had her head on her folded arm; his was propped up.

"I want to see you again," he whispered.

He wanted to tell her how much he needed more of this special time, this complete break from all the shit he couldn't shift and couldn't make a difference with back in Caldwell. In coming here, it was as if he had briefly stepped to the side, changed his track, taken a breather. It wasn't a permanent relocation, and he didn't want it to be—there was no way he was abandoning his brother.

But it was enough to give him a second wind.

"It is hard for me to get away." She kissed his fingertips. "I have only a few more days when it will be this easy. After the mourning, it will be more difficult."

"Tomorrow night, then. Midnight."

maichen nodded. "I will be here."

He glanced around at the decrepit cabin. "No, come to Caldwell. Meet me in town."

As she hesitated, he said, "I have a place there. It's private. No one will know—and I can make you more comfortable."

He wanted her in a bed. In the shower. Maybe on the kitchen counter.

In order to persuade her, iAm dipped down and took her mouth, stroking her lips with his own, licking his way inside. "Follow the signal of my blood and you'll find me."

The sound she made in the back of her throat was all about surrender—and before he knew it, he was rolling her onto her back and mounting her again. The fact that they had actually had sex was so monumental that he couldn't think about it while he was with her now.

It was just too huge a milestone.

Guiding himself in, he groaned and ducked his head into her neck. With great arching surges, he rode her, finding that rhythm, driving harder and harder. His body knew exactly what to do, and it was a shock, as he orgasmed, to find that he was glad he had waited for this one particular female.

It was also crazy to think that a part of him was starting to plan a way to get her free of the s'Hisbe.

So now he had two on that list.

Her nails bit into his back, and her thighs squeezed around his hips as she found her own release, the subtle milking on him kicking off another sharp spear of pleasure as he came again.

Afterward, he collapsed against her.

"Sorry," he mumbled, trying to find the strength to do anything but breathe. "Heavy."

"No, I like the weight." She stroked over his skin. "You feel as powerful as you are."

"I don't want to go."

"Neither do I."

Eventually, he was in no-choice land. For one, the fire had died and it was getting cold, but more importantly, he didn't want her to get in trouble for missing her duties.

At least he didn't have to worry about her and the approaching dawn.

He'd be psychotic.

Pushing free of her, he slipped out of her sex and realized, shit, she was covered in his scent.

"What's wrong?" she asked, those peridot eyes staring up at him.

"We should wash you." But the damn cabin had no running water. "Next time, we do this in Caldwell."

"I'll be careful. There is a hot spring on the edge of the Territory. I can wash there."

"What about your robing?" As he handed the load of fabric to her, he cursed. The shit was wrinkled. Ripped. Smudged with dust. "Damn it."

He should have hung her things up. What the hell had he been thinking?

Getting to his feet, he helped her get dressed, arranging the under-robe, clipping the top layer with that brass fastener, shaking out her hood and mesh.

"Let me do this," he said as he went to cover her hair and face up.

He hated masking her, his stomach rolling, his mouth going dry: It made the fact that he was sending her back to the Territory unprotected all the more stark. And then he took a step back and looked at what had been so pressed and pristine when she had arrived—and was now a hot mess.

He kind of felt as though he'd taken something that was not his to own, and ruined her in the process.

"I should go back with you," he said. "Make sure you—"

"That will be harder for me. I shall be all right. I've become quite facile at hiding myself after all these years."

And then there was nothing much else to say, no combination of words that could be spoken that would make him feel better about any of this.

With a curse, iAm took her arm and escorted her to the door. "Be careful. That is a dangerous place."

"I will."

When she went to bow to him, he stopped her. "No. Don't do that. We're equal, you and I."

For a moment, she just stared at him. He could feel it through the mesh that hid her eyes. "We are not," she said. "Sadly, we are not."

With that, she was out the door and gone before he could stop her. And as the cold air racked his naked body, he hurt all over—but it wasn't physical.

After pulling his clothes back on, he went to check that the fire was totally extinguished and then he left the cabin. As he closed things up and stepped away, he thought it was completely bizarre how so much of his life had happened in this one random place: finding his brother, meeting Rehv . . . now tonight.

Dematerializing, he returned in a scramble to the Brotherhood mansion, resuming form in the courtyard. As he stared up at the great stone manse, with its Gothic gargoyles perched on turrets, and its diamond-paned windows, and all the shadows that lurked in the corners, he realized he was testing it out for security and defensible position.

So, yeah, he was thinking of bringing *maichen* here.

Except what kind of life would she have? He was still all up in his head about Trez and Selena. And what was going to happen if the only way to keep his brother free from the s'Hisbe was the pair of them disappearing around the globe, never to light in one place for any length of time again?

Was she going to be into that life of a fugitive? And what if the s'Hisbe found her with them?

She'd be dead faster than a breath.

And yet he wanted her, to distraction . . .

Another no-win situation.

Just what he needed.

Rhage's ass was numb.

Then again, he'd been sitting on a rock, staring through the forest into Assail's glass house for how long? Hours. And all the guy had been doing was masturbating a bunch of paperwork on his desk.

At least that drug dealer had a nice chair to sit in.

Rhage checked his watch. Dawn was going to come sooner rather than later. "Running out of time here, people."

Just as he was about to front-and-center his phone, and find out how V was doing tracking the dealer's two cousins, the Brother materialized next to him—and the Range Rover the pair of dealers had left in came down the peninsula's drive to the house.

"Where'd they go?" Rhage asked.

"Downtown. They went to this boathouse down on the river. No one showed up to meet them as far as I saw. It's entirely possible one of them dematerialized out of there for a short period of time and went somewhere else. I don't fucking know."

As V rubbed his eyes like they were full of sand, Rhage asked, "My brother, when was the last time you slept?"

V dropped his arm and got thought up, like he was re-membering *pi* to a thousand decimals. "It was . . . ah . . . I mean, yeah, it was . . ."

Rhage glanced back at the garage door, which was trundling shut. "They're in for the day. Let's ghost."

"What did Assail do?"

"Other than a lot of blow?"

"He didn't leave, then."

"Nope. Other than playing with his papers, and making two phone calls that lasted no longer than thirty seconds apiece, he had his thumb up his ass." He clapped V on the shoulder. "We'll get 'em tomorrow night."

V was still cursing as they took off and traveled home through the cold night air. As they arrived at the courtyard in front of the mansion, they found iAm staring up at the house's facade like he was expecting Godzilla to clubfoot it over the roof and do a clean sweep with that barbed tail.

"Hey, man, you okay?" Rhage asked.

iAm jumped. "Oh, shit."

As the wind changed direction and carried the male's scent over, Rhage popped his brows. The Shadow was covered with the smell of a female—and not as in store-bought perfume.

"Oh, shit" was right.

In all the time they'd known the guy, iAm had never paid any particular attention to the females. Or the males. Personally, Rhage had always thought the poor bastard was suffering from Phury Syndrome—a condition whereupon one brother was so fucked-up that the other fell into a black hole trying to save him.

Unfortunately, it didn't look like Trez was going to come out of his tailspin anytime soon. But clearly, iAm had done something for himself.

By doing someone else.

Good for him, Rhage thought. About time the male had a break.

"So," V drawled as he lit up a hand-rolled. "How was your night, Shadow."

Clearly, he'd noticed the scent, too.

"Fine," iAm said.

"Mm-hmm." V exhaled. "Do anything in particular?"

"No. You?"

"Nada," Rhage replied as the three of them started for the vestibule. "Business as use."

Actually, the night with Assail had been straight-up

frustrating, but more than that, he'd kept waiting for word from his Mary about the female who'd been taken to Havers's in a coma. Nothing. He'd heard nothing. Was she alive? Dead?

Goddamn, he'd met that *mahmen* only once—on the horrific night when they'd rescued her and her young from that abusive male. But the situation was bothering his Mary, weighing on her—and that meant it was really on his radar, too.

Plus, his *shellan* hadn't been home now in two nights.

And he was beginning to get desperate.

Cell phones were no substitute for contact.

Not the kind he needed from her, at any rate.

As they filed into the vestibule, Rhage put his puss into the security camera's lens. A second later, the lock was thrown and they went into the foyer. Last Meal was getting its groove on, *doggen* busy bringing food into the dining room, people gathering in the archway, more members of the household coming down the stairs.

iAm looked like he was ready to bolt, his eyes locking on the red carpet that ran up the stairs to the second floor—as if, in his mind, he was already halfway to his bedroom. Out of sight.

No doubt fast on his way to the shower.

Even though he'd just looked at his phone and the thing was on vibrate, Rhage took his cell out again, and rechecked to see if he'd missed anything—

Lassiter came out of the billiards room, his blond-and-black hair braided into a thick rope that came down over his pecs. He had a Yoo-hoo box in one hand and a sleeve of Starburst in the other and enough gold on him to give his body a karat weight of its own.

"Anyone else catch *Real Housewives of New Jersey*?"

People turned and stared at the guy.

"How are you still a guest in this house?" someone asked. "Haven't you left yet?"

"I'll call him a cab," somebody else muttered. "Or maybe we can just airmail him off the mountain."

"I got a potato launcher," Butch said. "Small bore, but we can force him into the thing."

"Oh, I ain't leaving." Lassiter smiled. "Come on, like I'd miss all this great free food and cable—wait a minute."

Those strange-colored glittering eyes narrowed on iAm . . . and then he shouted, "Holy shit, you got laid!"

In the frozen silence that followed, Rhage smacked himself in the head. "Angel, your tact meter is even more broken than mine, buddy."

FIFTY-SEVEN

"So what's on your mind, First Adviser?"

Abalone bowed as Wrath addressed him. "Thank you, my lord." Stepping into the audience room, he closed the sliding door behind him. "Thank you very much."

"Must be serious for you to shut us in together," the King murmured.

"My lord . . ." He cleared his throat. "I seek always to serve you. In all ways."

"Stipulated. So what's doing?"

Not for the first time, Abalone wished he could see the male's eyes. Then again, maybe it was better that those wraparounds hid so much. He preferred having proper control over his colon.

The presences of Phury and Zsadist registered, as did the reality of the time. They had no more than five or ten minutes left before they would have to return Wrath to the compound. But this couldn't wait.

"My lord, I appreciate your allowing Paradise to stay here. It is most generous of you—"

"But you want her back home with you and you don't like Throe being there."

Abalone closed his eyes. "Yes, my lord. She is . . . the separation is more difficult than I anticipated. And please know it is not that I feel she is unsafe here. She is probably more safe—"

"I put you in a really shitty situation, didn't I," Wrath cut in. "It's not fair to ask you to play babysitter for some asshole like that at the expense of your own personal life. I apologize."

Abalone blinked. Of all the ways he had thought this would go, Wrath expressing regret had not been even close to the list. "My lord, please, I am the one failing you—"

"You want us to help you get him out?"

Phury spoke up. "Rhage would volunteer for that in a heartbeat."

"My lord, you are so—"

Wrath ignored him and focused on the fighters. "So what's our plan here? Are you two going over there with him now and doing the evac?"

Zsadist's eyes changed from yellow to black. "Let's do it—"

"Wait, wait." Abalone put his palms out. "I shall speak with him."

Wrath shook his head. "Not alone, you won't. You're too valuable to me. Tell Paradise to stay here one more night while we get the coast clear."

And that was how, some ten minutes later, he ended up dematerializing to his home flanked by a pair of the King's personal guards.

As he re-formed in front of his Tudor's heavy front door, he looked at the glowing windows and wondered where Throe was, what he was doing—what he was finding. The staff had said the male had slept around the clock that first night, and that was not likely to happen two times in a row. Accordingly, Abalone had taken care to lock a whole lot of doors before he'd left, and there were plenty of *doggen* with watchful eyes around.

Squaring his shoulders, he glanced over at the Brothers who stood on either side of him, like a set of Sun Tzu's bookends.

"I should like to be the one to speak with him."

Phury nodded. "It's your house. You should do the disinviting."

Abalone opened the copper lock with his key, and he felt none of his usual comfort upon crossing the threshold, no easing as his beloved butler came forth from the parlor to take his coat.

"Master," the *doggen* said, bowing deeply. "May I serve your guests as well for Last Meal?"

"They shall not be staying. Where is Throe, may I ask?"

"He has been in his bedroom. I have been checking—the door has been closed and he has not come down even for meals. The one time I knocked, early in the evening, he replied that he was resting."

Abalone did not hesitate. He took to the stairs, keeping the copper key in his hand. When he reached the top, he continued forward, passing doors until he got to the second-best guest room.

It had seemed an undeserved honor to put the male in the best guest room—even if Throe was none the wiser.

"Throe," Abalone said sharply. "A word if I may."

When there was no answer, he rapped on the closed panels with his knuckles—

The door opened of its own volition, revealing a dimly lit interior. He was about to lean in when a heavy hand landed on his shoulder and held him back.

"Allow my brother," Phury said gently. "You do not know what you will find."

Z walked in with a gun down by his thigh. A moment later, after those heavy footfalls traveled around the room, he said, "Clear."

Abalone rushed forth. Indeed, the room was vacated—the bed had even been made. There was no sign that anyone had been there.

Except for the slightly open window across the way.

Verily, one of the multipaned panels with their steel mesh overlays had been cracked and left ajar.

"He was not a prisoner here," Abalone said as he went over and reclosed the thing. "Why escape?"

"The more important question," Phury said, "was how can we be sure he's actually gone? This is a big house. Lots of hiding places—"

"Maybe this will explain things." Z went over to the desk in the corner and held up a sealed envelope. "It's got your name on it."

The Brother brought the thing over and handed it to Abalone.

With shaking hands, Abalone opened the back flap and took out the single sheet of paper that had been folded twice. The stationery was his own, with an engraving of a line drawing of the house at the top:

Dearest Abalone, son of Abalone,

Forgive me for not relating my thanks to you in person. Your hospitality has been much appreciated and very generous. In recognition of the difficult position my presence must undoubtedly place upon you, I am going to seek refuge with another.

I very much anticipate our paths crossing once again, cousin mine.

Until then, thank you once more for opening your home to me, and until then, I remain,

Your Blooded Relation,
Throe

"What does it say?" Phury asked.

As the automatic shutters began to come down for the day, Abalone handed the letter over. "Nothing of consequence. I agree. I need to search the house, but I fear that shall take too long for you to safely return to your compound."

"Then we'll stay the day with you," Phury said as his eyes traveled over the script. "But until we know you and your staff are all right? We're going nowhere."

Abalone exhaled. "Blessed am I for your presence."

Z laughed tightly. "You think we want to go back and tell Wrath you got your throat slit because we didn't do our job? Not the kind of report I want to make to the King."

Phury gave the letter back and put his hand on Abalone's shoulder once again. "And let us do the dirty work — it's safer for everyone that way. Where's your bedroom?"

"Down that way."

"Come on, we'll take you there and then get your staff secured. After that, we're going to fine-tooth-comb this house until we know there's nothing but that letter left behind."

Abalone found himself nodding. "Thank you, sires. Thank you so very much."

"I am most pleased that you called upon me. And I am sorry that I kept you waiting."

Throe smiled at the female addressing him and indicated the comfortable sofa he'd been sitting on since he arrived on her property. "It has been no hardship. I've been warm and dry. Already, you have been as gracious as any hostess could possibly be."

The aristocratic female smiled, flashing teeth that were as white as the diamonds at her throat. Her wrists. Upon her fingers and earlobes. Standing just inside the modest caretaker's residence on her huge estate, she looked like a model who'd walked into the wrong photoshoot.

"My mate is unwell," she said gravely. "I had to attend to him."

Dressed as she was in a skintight leopard-print cocktail dress, one had to wonder exactly what kind of needs her elderly *hellren* had.

Hardly the sort of thing a *shellan* would wear to tuck an older gentlemale into bed.

More likely, Throe thought, she had dressed to meet him.

"Yes, I recall he was ailing," he said smoothly. "I'm very sorry."

"It grieves me so."

"How could it not."

"I shall be a widow soon."

As he nodded in solemn sympathy, he deliberately allowed his eyes to drift down from her black straight hair to her dainty feet.

The last time he'd seen her, it had been here, but there had been far fewer clothes involved—for both of them, as well as his fellow Bastards. She had been lying before the hearth, and he and the soldiers had swarmed over her naked flesh, feeding, fucking. That had been about a month ago, only the most recent of the sessions that had been ongoing for the previous year at regular intervals.

"Is it only you then tonight?" she asked in a husky way.

"Yes, and I must have you know that I am afraid we have parted ways, Xcor and myself. I'm getting out of the fighting."

"Are you," she purred. "And where are you staying?"

"I am between residences at this moment."

"Really."

"Indeed."

She came forward, crossing the shallow room to stand within arm's reach of him. "Dawn is coming soon."

He sent his stare down her body again. "Is it. Well, then I shall have to go."

"So soon," she pouted.

" 'Tis only safe." Idly, he trailed his fingertips up her hip, across her lower belly . . . down to the juncture of her thighs. Pressing in through the dress, he gave her cleft a little stroke. "So I'm afraid I must end things here—"

"Perhaps you and I may come to an arrangement," she said.

"Oh?" he said.

"My *hellren* is far older than I. He is my true love, of course."

"Of course."

"But because of his advancing age, there are certain needs of mine that he is not capable of fulfilling regularly."

"I believe you are familiar with my abilities in that regard."

The female smiled in a feral fashion. "Yes. I am."

"And it would seem only fair that, were you to offer me room and board, you be compensated in a manner which you deem appropriate."

The female put one of her stiletto-clad feet on the arm of the sofa and lifted the hem of her dress up to her waist, exposing her bare sex to him. "Perhaps you shall refresh my memory as to your talents first."

Throe purred in the back of his throat and leaned into her, extending his tongue, licking his way into her slit. As her hips tilted toward him, and her head fell back, he sucked at her clit—

And then stopped. Sat back. "I have one problem."

"Yes?" she grunted, pulling her head back to level.

"I cannae stay here at this cottage. Not if the Band of Bastards are going to pay you . . . homage. Surely, on an estate as large as this, there must be other accommodations available?"

She frowned. "You are of the Bluerme bloodline, are you not?"

"I am. Through my *mahmen*'s people."

"You are a distant relation of my *hellren*'s, then, and it would therefore be rude of us not to offer you shelter. Of course, if you are going to be in the main house, we shall have to purchase you clothing."

Throe smiled at her. It was just so perfect.

After all, she and her mate had supported the political

coup against Wrath—and there was no way they were rejoicing the King's subsequent disbanding of The Council.

He had his in, as well as his base of operations.

"That would be most acceptable," he said, slipping his hands around her hips and drawing her back to his mouth.

Against her sex, he murmured, "Now, allow me to demonstrate my affection for your generous nature."

FIFTY-EIGHT

"**I** work alone," the whore was saying as she went over to her clothes. "I don't have a pimp. If you want me again, you know where to find me."

Xcor stared across the cottage's living area, watching the female dress with an efficiency that was only a second slower than the speed of sound.

The blonde departed without any good-bye, her duty having been discharged, his payment of two thousand dollars having been accepted. As the door shut behind her, he shifted his eyes to the dying fire. He had paid to fuck her any way and anywhere he wanted and he had done so. Repeatedly. He had also taken from her vein.

For which the second thousand had been recompense.

Thanks to his keen hearing, he heard her outside, walking through the leaves. And then her voice drifted through the thin walls of the structure that he had bought for another.

"Yeah, I'm leaving now. Yeah. He was ugly, but he fucks like an animal—"

That was the last he heard, so she must have dematerialized.

His body was naked as he sat on the floor before the hearth, knees up, elbows plugged in, arms dangling. The sweat was cooling on his skin, his fangs still descended from the feeding, his sex flaccid and shrunken and red from the beating it had taken.

The scent of everything he had done lingered in the air,

every draw in through his nose a reminder of what his body had wrought.

And with whom.

Hanging his head, he rubbed at his too-long hair, numbly thinking that he should get it cut.

Images played through his mind of him getting that female on all fours and mounting her like a dog. His balls had slapped against her sex as he took her in the ass and he had come so many times, he had left her dripping.

He had tried to make it as dirty as possible—and he had even kissed the female. Everywhere.

He had wanted to stain his very skin with the experience. Change his body. Alter his mind.

Wipe the slate clean.

Instead, as he sat on the hard floor by himself, he found that he had done the opposite. Layla was the only thing he thought of now: her lovely, shy face; those pale green eyes so smart and kind; that body of which he had had only hints. The session with the whore had merely served to dim him down, such that the illumination offered by the one he loved burned all the brighter for the contrast.

As a strategy, this had been a total failure.

So he would have to find another. Or try this again—yes, he would try again with another or the same or three or four. Money was scarce, but Balthazar and Zypher were so seductive, Xcor was quite sure they could successfully advocate on his behalf.

And then there was always alcohol to help him.

And fighting, which could be an excellent energy drain.

What he would not do was give in to the nearly choking urge to phone Layla and hear her voice, and beg her to see him in spite of what he had told her.

That would only be a further death for him.

The Bloodletter had taught him that part of strength was the elimination of weakness, and over time, with repeated exposure to that Chosen, his emotions had castrated him: He was making choices and finding distractions in things that compromised the integrity of his warrior self.

And somehow she had figured it all out and called him on his truth.

Her knowledge of all he sacrificed for her had been the wake-up call, and only a fool did not abide by that kind of trailhead; he needed to alter this destination she had become for him, turn away from that untenable situation with her, proceed with alacrity back to the clarity he had once possessed.

Because what was their future? Further clandestine meetings here? Such that eventually a Brother followed her due to some infinitesimal slip-up she made or some suspicion she was unaware of garnering for herself? His soldiers and he needed a safe place to rest and recharge during the daylight hours, and he could not compromise that.

What had he been thinking? Bringing her here?

He and his Bastards had not the money to move once again so soon, the lease on the property being a burden upon their meager coffers now that Throe had departed.

At least Xcor sensed he could trust her. She had had nine months to give up the location of the meadow they had always met at, and he still knew where the Brotherhood compound was. It was a mutual *détente*—if she divulged this place, she had to know his next move would be to marshal a full-scale attack on the Brotherhood's sacred mansion.

Where, if the gossip was true, the King's firstborn slept in his crib.

No, she would say nothing—

Bing!

The sound of his phone going off cranked his head around. The cellular device was on the floor by the door, in the tangle of his pants.

Jumping across the space, his hands were sloppy as they clawed through the folds, fought against the pocket's hold, got the glass-fronted plate out.

He had heard nothing back from her concerning the message he had voice-recorded into a text.

Entering a four-digit touch pattern on the number pad, he unlocked the device and went into the text messages. His illiteracy was so pervasive he had to use a text-to-audio translator application in order to receive communications from his soldiers and from her.

But he knew enough to see that whatever had been received was not from the Chosen.

He put the phone away without listening to whatever it was.

The fact that he stalled out, and stood there at the front door as if he were lost, pissed him off.

He could not—he would not—allow this castration to continue. There had been many things in his life that had been more destructive than leaving a female who had not been his to begin with: his mother had been disgusted at his appearance and abandoned him because of his harelip; he had endured unimaginable, sustained abuse at the Bloodletter's camp; and then there were the centuries of depravity in this war, his unhinged hatred of the world defining him, driving him.

This issue with Layla was not going to break him.

Forcing his feet forward, he went into the bathroom and turned the shower on. The blood the whore had given him was providing him with a physical strength he had not felt since . . .

No, he couldn't think of Layla anymore.

He had to shut her out. Shut his emotions down.

It was like a death, he told himself. And Fates knew he was all too familiar with and accomplished in that most definitive currency.

Stepping under the cold spray, he picked up the soap to begin to wash his skin—but then he stopped himself.

No, he needed to keep the stank on his flesh.

The purpose of this shower was solely to wake him out of the post-feeding lethargy that was fuzzing up his brain. After this, he was going to go address his soldiers.

It was time to refocus and renew their efforts in the war.

And resume the natural course of his life.

FIFTY-NINE

Trez replugged into the world on a buzzy, trippy high that was the only arguably positive thing about having a migraine: Following the great storm of pain and nausea, there was always a floaty, post-agony period when you were so fucking grateful not to have an invisible ax buried in half your gray matter anymore that you just wanted to hug the world.

Opening his eyes, he blinked a couple of times and looked at the open door to the bathroom. Where was—

"Are you awake?"

At the sound of Selena's voice behind him, he shoved his torso up off the mattress and cranked around. "Hey."

She was over on the chaise longue, reading from a Kindle, the glow from the screen casting her features in soft light.

"How are you feeling?" She put the thing aside and came over.

"Better." Kinda. Now he was worried about her again. "How are you?"

Had anything changed while he'd been out of it? How long had he—

"No, nothing's changed. And you've been out for about eight hours."

Ah, so he'd spoken all that.

He took her hand and tried to be subtle about the way he tested how she gripped his palm back, how she sat down on the mattress beside him.

"Is there any particular reason you won't look me in the eye?" he asked.

"Are you hungry?"

"No, especially not when you're dodging that question."

He was being way too direct, but social pleasantries and bullshitting were not his core competencies on a good night.

"I, ah, I went to see Doc Jane."

Now his blood ran cold as ice. "Why?"

"I just wanted to check in with her."

"And?"

"She did some tests and . . ."

At that point, his hearing punched its time card and went on break. "I'm sorry, say that again?"

Maybe if she repeated the words, things would somehow sink in through the alarm bells that were DEFCON 1'ing it in his skull.

". . . when we're ready to see her."

Trez sat all the way up. Rubbed his face. Looked over at her—while she stared at the carpet. "Go down to the clinic, you mean?"

"And meet with them both. Manny will be there, too."

"Okay. Yeah." He glanced at the bathroom. "I need a shower first."

"There's no hurry."

Right, that was not how he felt at all. Pushing himself around her, he got off the bed and padded into the loo, where he turned on the water, used the toilet, and got under the spray. Fast hands with the shampoo and the soap and he didn't bother shaving.

Out. Drying off. Heading back into the bedroom with a towel around his waist.

She was still sitting where she had been.

As he passed by at a near run to the walk-in closet, her hand snapped out and grabbed onto his wrist.

When she finally looked up at him, her stare was rock-steady, but intense enough to burn a hole through the back of his head. And for some reason, the combination terrified him.

"I need to talk to you first," she said.

Closing his eyes briefly, Trez sank down to his knees in front of her, and in the back of his mind, he thought, *No, no, I don't want to hear it. Whatever this is, I don't want—*

Her hands, those beautiful hands, reached up to his face and traced his brows, his cheeks, his jaw. As one of her thumbs brushed over his lower lip, he kissed it.

"Luchas lost it tonight."

Trez frowned and shook his head. "I'm sorry—what?"

"Down at the clinic. He just . . . lost it. They took part of his leg to save him—I think he's going to live. But he isn't happy about it."

"Oh. Okay. Yeah."

Even though it was cruel, all he could think was, So what?

"He wanted to die. He was so angry that they didn't let him."

What does this have to do with us, he screamed in his head. Who gives a shit—

"I don't want to go," she said. "I don't want to leave you. On some level, I don't even know how to—I mean, when my time comes, I literally can't imagine it."

Trez swallowed through a throat that was tight as a vise.

Before he could respond, she whispered, "I'm terrified."

"Oh, my queen—"

"About you." As Trez recoiled—'cuz that was the last thing he expected her to say—she cupped his face. "Seeing that anger in Luchas, that hatred for the world and everybody in it . . . I'm worried that after I go, that's where you're going to be."

Forcing himself to be calm, he said, "Listen, I—"

"Don't lie to me or yourself. Whatever you say here, it has to be honest."

Well, didn't that shut him up good.

"Having you be that angry scares me more than anything that's going to happen to my body or my soul. Whether there's life eternal or nothing at all at the end, what I'm really concerned about is you." Her eyes bored into his. "I want you to promise me—I want you to swear on your heart and mine—that you'll keep going. That you'll stay here with iAm and the Brothers and let them take care of you. That you won't let the grief destroy you. I can't . . . I won't be able to help you, so you're going to have to let them be there for you."

"Selena, first of all, you're not going anywhere—"

"My hands are beginning to feel stiff. My feet and ankles, too. I don't think we have a lot of time left, Trez."

As Selena spoke, she smoothed Trez's eyebrows when they threatened to clench up tight. She had practiced the words for hours in her head, trying to find the right combination so he wouldn't reject the message.

This was very important. She had to say these things and he had to hear them.

"It is going to be so much harder on me to go through this if I'm worried about you."

She could feel the emotions coursing through him, and wasn't surprised as his black eyes flashed brilliant green in his dark face—and she wished like hell she could spare him this, but she couldn't.

"I need you to swear to me," she said, "here and now, that you won't close yourself off from the world, that you'll—"

Trez burst up to his feet and walked around, hands on his hips, head down, like he was trying to get some control over himself.

"Trez, I want you to keep living after I'm gone." As he started shaking his head, she cut in, "Because that is the only thing that's going to make any of this okay for me."

He threw his hands up. "All right, fine. I'll keep living. Now, can I get dressed so we can go down to the clinic—"

"Trez. Don't lie to me."

He stopped and pivoted toward her, his magnificent body full of tension, the muscles in his thighs and his shoulders twitching under his smooth, hairless skin. "What do you want me to say?"

"That you'll let people help you. You're going to need it—I would need it if you—"

"And I will! Fine! I'll even see Mary—I'll wear a fucking sign around my chest that reads, 'Processing Grief,' for fuck's sake. Happy? Now can we fucking stop talking about this."

As he barked at her, she closed her eyes in exhaustion. "Trez—"

"You say you can't imagine leaving me, right? Well, I can't even think about it. I don't think about—I *refuse* to even construct in my mind"—he jabbed his forefinger into his head—"a reality where you're not here. So not only can I not project what the fuck I'm going to feel like, but I sure as hell can't swear to a hypothetical."

"You'd better start thinking about it," she said roughly. "You'd better begin to prepare. I'm telling you right now that the endgame is coming."

He seemed to deflate in front of her, even as he stayed his same height and weight. "Don't talk like that."

"And I want you to find another female, sometime far off in the future. I want you to . . ." At this, her voice cracked from a pain so great she could have sworn it was going to leave a bloodstain in the center of her shirt. "I don't want you to spend another nine hundred years sleeping alone."

As she fell silent, the devastation in him was so great, he stumbled backward and all but fell into the chaise longue.

"I thought you loved me," he said in a voice that didn't sound like his.

"I do. With all my—"

He rubbed his sternum. "Then what's this all about. Why do you want me to go and find some other female—"

"Trez, listen to me." But he was gone, having retreated to somewhere in his head that she couldn't reach. "Trez, I do love you, and that's the point—"

"Then why would you ever tell me you want me to be with anyone but you?" His eyes were crushed as they swung around to her. "Why would you want that? Ever? It's a violation of everything I thought we felt for each other."

"Trez—"

"I've bonded with you. You know this. Why would you ever tell a bonded male that he has to go out and have sex with someone else?"

"You're missing the point."

Shit, it wasn't supposed to go like this. He was supposed to give her his vow—and take her permission to heart so that, a million years from now, when he'd moved on from her and everything they'd meant to each other wasn't so raw, he wouldn't feel guilty about finding someone else to be happy with.

It was the right thing for her to do.

"Maybe you should just go," he said in a dull voice.

"What?"

He brushed at his eyes. "Just leave. Just get out of here." He nodded at the door. "I was prepared to go through absolutely anything with you, but not this. You don't want my love, that's fine. I get it. This has been a crazy couple of nights for you, and high emotion has a way of contaminating everything and making things seem more important than they really are. But you can't be here with me anymore."

She shook her head, like maybe that would help make his words make sense. "What are you talking about."

"I don't blame you. Doc Jane told you I saved your life, so there's a lot of gratitude you must be feeling—that can be confused for love. I get it—"

"Wait, what—I don't understand what you're saying."

"But I can't be around you. You say you don't want me to destroy myself? Fine, then a good place to start is with you leaving now."

A weird flickering panic made her nape tighten up. "Trez, you haven't listened to what I've been saying. You're taking this in a completely different direction—a wrong one. I love you—"

"Don't say that," he snapped at her. "Don't you say that to me—"

"I'll say anything I like," she snapped back. "It's your hearing that I'd be worried about if I were you."

"Oh, my ears are working fine, sweetheart. I just had the female I love and worship more than anything in the entire world tell me she wants me to go out and fuck someone else. Maybe before you die, you should write Hallmark and suggest that shit for a Valentine's Day card, it's really fucking romantic."

Now she was the one springing to her feet. "I don't want that! I don't want any of this!" Her voice rose to a hysterical level, but she couldn't help it. "Do you think I'm *happy* about saying these things, thinking these things! I have God only knows how many nights left and I've wasted this one sitting on that fucking chair right there staring at some bullshit book I haven't been reading, imagining you hanging yourself in a bathroom after I die! Or getting drunk and running your car into a tree! Or going on another fucking spree that lasts not a decade but a century!"

She circled a finger next to her head. "These thoughts—

I don't want them! You think I *want* to tell you this? Jesus Christ, Trez, I love you! I don't want you to ever be with another female, like *ever*! I want you to sit in a corner and mourn me until you die—I don't want you to see the sun or the moon, or enjoy another meal, or have a good day's sleep! I want to haunt you for the rest of your life, until everywhere you go and anyone you talk to, all you can see is the ghost of me—because then I know you won't forget me!"

He put his hands out. "Selena, I—"

"You want to know what death is! I'll tell you what it is—death is the living forgetting you! What you smell like and look like, what your voice sounds like, how you laugh! Even if there is an afterlife, my death is going to be you going on without me until you can't remember what color my eyes are or how long my hair is—"

It turned out she was the one who went Luchas.

Suddenly, her vision went all white and she had no control over the way she lunged for the nearest lamp, yanked it off its side table, and hurled it across the room at the bank of windows, throwing the thing so hard its silk shade went flying and hit the chandelier hanging in the middle of the ceiling.

Cue the shattering. Everything broke, glass splintering into shimmers that went everywhere, such that Trez had to lift his arm to protect his eyes.

She burst into tears. "I don't want you to go on without me."

As her soul split in half, he jumped up and came over. When he tried to hug her, she flailed at him, beat him with her fists.

"You're going to find someone else," she moaned. "You're going to fall in love with someone else and she's going to be able to give you young and hold you when you have daymares and make you dinner." The tears came so hard and heavy, she couldn't take a breath. "And she's going to be better than me because she's going to . . ." Selena collapsed against him. ". . . she's going to be lucky enough to be alive."

Trez held her to his heart and stroked her back.

There it was. The truth was out. The evil she had been trying to package and pretty-bow up revealed because she had wanted to be a female of worth instead of the pathetic, clingy curse she actually was.

And yet, he was still with her. Standing soul-to-soul, flesh-to-flesh, undaunted, utterly determined to love her through it all.

Eventually, she became aware of the beat of his heart.

Thump. Thump. Thump.

So steady and strong.

Taking a shuddering breath, she eased back. As he brushed under her eyes with his thumbs, she said hoarsely, "Wow, that went well, huh?"

SIXTY

As Selena spoke up, Trez broke out a laugh. And she smiled.

They were both total hot messes, her face swollen and beet red from the screaming and the crying, his forearm bleeding from the glass that had hit him, their bodies shaky as they stood together.

"Did you practice all that?" he asked, brushing her hair back.

"Oh, yeah. For, like, hours."

He led her over to the bed and sat them both down—before they fell over onto the broken glass that littered the carpet. "And in your head, how did it go?"

Selena leaned to the side for the Kleenex box next to the alarm clock. She offered him a tissue, and then took one for herself.

After they'd both blown their noses, she took another deep breath. "It went so well. You were touched at my magnanimity. Humbled by the purity of my love. And when I got teary, it was all *Sleepless in Seattle* dewy—not like this."

As she indicated her face, he tilted her to him and kissed her. "You're even more beautiful to me than ever."

She rolled her eyes. "Come on, get real. I just told you I want you to be celibate for the rest of your life."

"And nothing could possibly make me happier."

"Trez, be real. That is a total bitch move on my part."

"Do you think I'd be any different?" He shrugged. "Man, if I were to die? I wouldn't want you to look at another male—forget being naked with him." He couldn't hide the recoil of disgust as he tried that nightmare on for size. "Oh, shit, nope. No way. Uh-huh."

"Really?"

"Straight one hundred. Serious."

As she looked down at the rug, the most beautiful smile hit her face.

Man, it felt good to be on the same page.

But then her expression faded.

They were quiet for an awfully long time. And he had a feeling he knew where she'd gone in her head.

"Life can be very long," she said. As if she were imagining the time he had before him—and how things could change.

"Yes, it can." He felt as though they had lived three lifetimes in the last two nights. "But my memory is stronger than time. When it comes to you, my memory will be the immortal part of me."

"If it does come to pass." She cleared her throat. "If you do find someone, I want you to know . . . I would never hold that against you. I love you too much to blame you for that."

"Not going to happen."

Selena snapped free another tissue, but she didn't use it. She just folded the fragile square in half. And then halved it again. And a third time.

"I don't want you frozen in a cemetery of your own making," she said finally. "I guess that's the point I'm trying to make. My big fear about being trapped in my body forever? Locked in? I fear that for you in your grief, too. Yes, sure, there is a part of me that wants you to duck your head and let the years pass you by, but an even bigger part of me doesn't want that kind of prison for you. I guess . . . what I'm trying to say is that if you ever feel bad, you know, at some point, because something happens and you think it's funny or you do eat a meal you enjoy or . . . if there's a movie you want to see or you're happy about a present somebody gives you, just please know I love you in that moment. Maybe you could even pretend that they're gifts from me from the other side." She smiled sadly. "A kiss from me to you."

Oh, shit, now he felt like losing it again.

"Can you promise me that, Trez? That you'll let the good things in even after I'm gone?" She ran her fingers down his face. "Even if those things happen because there's another female by your side? The only thing worse than me dying is both of us going away, in spite of the fact that that big strong heart of yours continues to beat in your chest."

He closed his eyes. "I don't want to think about this."

"Neither do I."

In the silence that followed, he was once again confronted by the reality that there was nothing to fight, no one to scream at, nobody he could stab with a dagger to stop any of this.

"You want to go down to Doc Jane's now?" he said.

"I'd rather you answer the question."

Trez gathered up her hands in his own. "If it will give you peace of mind, then yes, fine. I promise that . . ." Okay, he couldn't actually say it. "I'll keep going."

Relief loosened up her face, her shoulders, her entire body. "Thank you. That really helps. You won't ever know how much that really helps me right now."

He kissed her softly, and then got up and went into the closet. He had no clue what he put on himself, but he covered up the naughty bits and even remembered to put on deodorant. When he came out, his stomach felt like it had been dredged.

"You ready to go to the clinic?"

She glanced around the room as if searching for something. Or maybe she just wanted to put off the inevitable a little longer.

"I'm so sorry about your window," she blurted.

"That's okay. The shutter is still in place, so that'll cut the breeze and the cold."

"And the lamp."

"Like I care."

She nodded and stood up. She was wearing black skinny jeans and a loose white blouse—and he was struck by how good she looked in normal clothes, not all that Chosen formality. And it was funny, her language was loosening up too, becoming more vernacular.

Goddamn, he thought . . . he would really love to have had children with her.

*   *   *

The trip down to the clinic felt endless, and Selena wasn't sure whether that was a bad or a good thing. On the one hand, she was ready to have the news just so she could deal with whatever it was. On the other, she would have been content to live in the no-know zone a little longer.

Trez held her hand all the way to the training center, not letting her go even when he put the various passcodes in or when they had to go one after the other through the supply closet. Walking down the corridor to Doc Jane's, she thought about all the doors they could have entered instead of the one they were destined for.

As they came to the examination room, she looked up at him. "I couldn't do this without you."

He leaned down and brushed her mouth with his. "The good news is that you won't have to."

Together, they entered the clinical space. Instantly, Selena had trouble breathing, that chemical scent and all the shiny-shiny getting to her once again. And the choking sensation got worse as Doc Jane and Manny straightened from the computer screen over at the desk and put on identical, professional smiles.

"Bad news, huh," she said. As both doctors started to prevaricate, she cut them off. "Please. Respect me and my time enough not to waste words trying to sugarcoat all this. Tell me what my body told you."

"We see some change in the joints." Doc Jane stepped back. "Everywhere we X-rayed."

Well ... didn't that take the starch out of her. Even though she had expected that very answer.

The two doctors were taking turns explaining things, and Trez was nodding like he was tracking the conversation. She, however, was focused on the computer screen's side-by-side comparison of two images, one that had been taken after the last episode had happened ... and the other that had been taken hours ago. Separated by a mere two days ... the joints now had a gray haze in the spaces between the bones.

"It's as if it is kindling," Doc Jane said. "Maybe your body is holding it at bay?"

"For how long?" Trez asked.

"We have no idea." Manny reached forward and adjusted and readjusted the contrast of the moniter, as if searching for something. "We would like to suggest that you come in for more imaging every six hours for the next day. That way we can see if things are continuing to change."

"Are you in pain right now?" Doc Jane asked.

"No."

"Because we can give you relief if you need it."

Trez spoke up. "Are there any medications we can try?"

Dearest Virgin Scribe, her brain seemed to have shut down.

"Well, we've talked it over." Manny glanced at Jane. "And we're stuck."

Doc Jane took the lead. "One of the things we've been considering is anti-inflammatories. Oral steroids would be problematic, because they suppress the immune system and it's unclear to what extent an episode is being held off precisely by your body's own defenses."

"Your white blood cell count is very high," Manny cut in. "So there's definitely something happening right now."

"And steroid injections into the joints, even if we stuck with only the largest ones in your body, would be but a partial solution." Jane drew a hand through her short hair. "It would seem logical to start you on some NSAIDs—think prescription-strength Motrin."

"Not a lot of negative side effects," Manny chimed in.

"They would ease any pain up to a point, but also work as anti-inflammatories that wouldn't affect your immune system."

Selena closed her eyes and wished she could be anywhere else. Wished that she could be anyone else.

To think that the entire compound was filled with people who had no fear of whether they were going to wake up at dusk.

It wasn't that she begrudged them that blessing. Not at all.

She just wanted to be a member of that club.

More conversation happened, but her brain had left the clinic and the clinical discussion. Instead, it was back up in Trez's bedroom, reliving the knock-down, drag-out that had ultimately brought them even closer.

Trez was right. They had lived a lifetime over these last forty-eight hours.

". . . you think?" he said to her.

"I'm sorry?" she mumbled.

"So what do you think? Would you like to try the pills?" When she stayed silent, he leaned down. "You okay? You need some time?"

"I need to make you dinner," she blurted. Then shook herself. "I'm sorry, yes, sure, I'll try whatever you want to give me. But after I get the pills . . . I want to make you dinner after sundown. At the Great Camp. With no one else around."

Trez smiled a little. "Okay. You want to plan tonight's date, you got it, my queen."

She took a deep breath and nodded at the doctors. "That is what I want to do. And then I want to go for my boat ride."

Both of the healers said all the right, caring things, reaching out and touching her hands, her shoulders—and she really appreciated the contact. It made her feel as if she weren't some machine they were fixing from a distance, but someone they loved and cared about. A few minutes later, an orange bottle with a white lid was pressed into her palm and instructions she didn't track were given.

More nodding. More thanking. Then she and Trez were leaving.

She waited until the door shut behind them. "Did any of that register for you? Like what I'm supposed to do with these?" The pills inside rattled against the plastic as she looked down. "Oh, there's a label."

"I remember everything," he said, putting his arm around her shoulders. "Come on."

He led her back to the office. Back out through the closet. Back into the damp-smelling, went-on-forever tunnel.

"Can I tell you something?"

She glanced up at him. "Of course. And I promise I won't throw any more lamps—well, not like there are any around at the moment, but still."

"You can throw anything you want." He stopped and turned her to face him, brushing her hair back. "You are the bravest person I know."

She laughed in a burst. "Okay, stop humoring the dead person, all right?"

"I'm serious. And don't say that."

"You live with the Brotherhood. They are the bravest people in the race."

"No," he whispered.

As he stared down at her, the admiration on his face was . . . simply stunning. But it was all wrong. "Trez, I'm terrified about everything." She held up the pills. "I'm scared to take these. I'm scared to go to sleep—"

"You're very brave—"

"I'm scared to cook you dinner." She held up her forefinger. "And FYI, you should be, too. I can't even make toast. Which is bread. In a toaster. How hard is that—and yet I have burned up loaves of the stuff."

He shook his head. "Courage doesn't mean you aren't scared." He dropped his mouth to hers and kissed her. "God, I love you so much. I love you so deeply. I love you forever."

Putting her arms around him, she held on hard—and maybe wiped some tears on his shirt. "Fine, you think I'm brave . . . well, you're the most romantic male I've ever known, seen, or heard about."

Now he was laughing, and the deep rumble sounded so good against her ear. "Yeah. Uh-huh. Right."

Melding her body to his, she said, "There is nothing more romantic on the planet than loving someone with your full heart, even though you know they're leaving."

He went still. "How else could a male love a female of worth like you but wholly. Completely. And without a single regret."

As they stood there in that tunnel, halfway from the compound and halfway to the main house, she thought it was apt that what was on either side of them seemed to go off into infinity. They had but this middle point of the here and now, and they had to make it count.

"I don't need to mate you in a ceremony," she said.

"No?"

"We're living the vows right now."

"So you're saying you won't mate me."

"Are you asking?" she teased.

"You want me to one-knee it?"

Sinking down to the floor, he took her hands. "Selena, will you be my *shellan*? My one and only? I don't have a ring, but we can go get you one—it's what the humans do.

Plus, I don't know, I kind of want to buy you something expensive."

Her first instinct was the one she had been trained to have—a demure deferral of the attention, the fuss, the pleasure.

But, in the words of her male, Fuck. That.

"I would love that. I would love everything, a ceremony, a ring, a party, the whole thing." Opening her heart wide, she let the love in. "Everything!"

"That's my queen," he murmured. "That's what I'm talking about."

And that was how she ended up . . . engaged.

As she bent down to kiss him, it seemed utterly bizarre that the pair of them kept ricocheting back and forth between such incredibly opposite emotions. But this situation seemed to amplify the highs and lows, funneling feelings and experiences through a bullhorn until everything was too big to contain.

"So, a ring?" she said against his mouth.

"Yup, a ring."

He ran his hands around the back of her thighs and stroked up and down. "And maybe a little sumthin'-sumthin' you can't get at a store."

"And what might that be?" she drawled.

"Oh, you know. I'll just have to show you upstairs. . . ."

SIXTY-ONE

"**Y**eah, I heard you arguing during the day."

As iAm spoke, he glanced into the mirror over his bathroom sink. His brother was standing behind him, in the doorway to his bedroom, and the guy was dressed in all black, looking like he was right out of a magazine.

Clearly ready to take his female out again for the night.

"Sounded heavy," iAm tacked on.

"It was bad for a little while." Trez came in and sat down on the lip of the Jacuzzi. "But we got through it. I asked her to mate me."

"Congratulations."

"Thanks."

Picking up the can of Barbasol, iAm hit the go button and then patted down his cheeks and chin. "How's she doing?"

"Okay."

iAm knew the male was lying. The tells were all over the place, but mostly in the way his brother didn't meet his eyes.

"What's on your mind, Trez."

Trez cracked his knuckles one by one. "She doesn't want her remains to be . . . like, where her sisters are up there." He pointed to the ceiling, but meant the heavens above. "So, you know, when the time comes, I'm thinking of disposing of—"

As that deep voice cracked and couldn't keep going,

iAm forgot about his razor and went over, tightening the towel that was around his waist and sitting down beside his brother. "Shit."

Trez rubbed his face. "Yeah, that about covers it. Anyway, I'm thinking I'll build a pyre for her. Rehv's people do that. That way, she'll be . . ." He cleared his throat. "She'll be free. She wants to be free at the end. You know."

iAm shook his head. "I hate this for you."

"Me, too. Guess I was born under the wrong star in a major way."

"What can I do?"

"Nothing. Just listen to me and forgive me if I say the wrong thing or get pissy. The stress is fucking crazy."

They sat side by side in silence—because sometimes that was all you could do for someone you loved: There were paths that had to be walked alone. And that just sucked.

He wanted to ask how long. But that was the question of the hour, the one that nobody could answer.

"Are you going to have a ceremony?" iAm asked.

"I don't think she wants that. I'm not sure what the Chosen do for funerals—"

"I was talking about the mating."

"Oh, yeah. Ah, yeah, I guess." Trez slapped his knees and got to his feet. "I gotta head out. I'm going to take her out tonight and get her a ring. I want to put a star from the heavens on her finger. Then she's going to cook me dinner up north at Rehv's."

"Sounds good." iAm looked at the guy. "Listen, this is none of my business—"

"Everything is your business. You're my blooded brother."

"Does Selena know about what's doing with the s'Hisbe? About your . . . situation with the Princess?"

Trez shrugged. "I told her. A while ago. But I'm not thinking about all that right now."

God, they were down to only a couple of nights left in the mourning period. And then . . .

One nightmare at a time, iAm thought. His brother was right.

"Listen," iAm said. "I'm just a phone call away. You need anything, you hit me."

"Thanks, my man."

They clapped palms, and Trez offered a dead smile. "You look like Santa Claus."

On that note, his brother left.

iAm sat there for a while, the uneven rim of the tub and the marble ledge making his butt feel like someone was hitting it with a two-by-four over and over again.

It was the saddest commentary that Trez was more focused on the funeral than the mating ceremony.

For a moment, he considered canceling his own . . . date. Or whatever it was with *maichen*. But he could just as easily wait by the phone in her company.

Naked company.

As he stood up and went to the sinks, he grabbed his Gillette eight hundred–bladed whatever and started de-Santa'ing himself. The guilt that he felt about heading off for a couple of hours of sex while his brother was suffering like this was enough to make him want to throw up.

His entire life had been in service to the male, and thinking of himself and what he wanted for his own shit was like exercising a limb that had been in a cast for decades: It seemed uncomfortable, unsure, unlikely to sustain weight.

But he felt kind of like Trez did . . . as if there was a limited time to enjoy what he had before everything changed and not for the better.

Trez might not want to think about it. But his time for reckoning with the s'Hisbe was going to come whether he acknowledged it or not. Their parents had been stripped of their station and their ill-gotten gains for essentially selling Trez to the Queen. There were no other levers to pull on that front—even if their mother and father were tortured and killed? Which had been brought up nine months ago? It had been no motivator for Trez or himself. And the s'Hisbe must have realized that because that was the last either of them had heard of that line of threats.

Impossible to get emotional about two people who had allowed you to be jailed your entire life—just so they could rise to be Primaries at court.

One thing he knew for certain? As the time for the ritual mating came due, the Queen was going to take things to a higher level. Which meant both he and Trez were going to have to watch their backs.

Probably a good idea to encourage any dating scenarios

to stick close to home. Or, preferably, in the compound it-self.

Shit, Trez was going to hate that.

"Hmmmm."

As Trez let out a purr, Selena pivoted around in the closet. He had materialized behind her, his arms crossed over his chest, his body tilted against the jamb.

"Well, hello," she said.

"I *love* what you're wearing."

"I don't have anything on."

"Exactly."

He came forward, turning her to face him and drawing her closer. "Gimme."

His kiss was forceful, his hips thrusting into her, his arousal a very good indicator that they were in danger of being late.

She laughed and pushed at his solid chest. "Aren't we supposed to be at the jeweler's in a half hour?"

"Who cares."

As if she were going to say no?

Wrapping her arms around his neck, she let herself get loose. Or . . . as loose as she could become. Even with the pills that she'd taken two doses of, her joints were aching all over, her body's battle reaching the point where her mind was being brought into the fight, the sensations no longer a figment of paranoia, but an actual, dogged drag.

The good news? The lust she felt was so loud and perva-sive it overrode everything else.

Trez picked her up and carried her back to the bed. Lay-ing her out flat, he kissed her deeply, his hands caressing her breasts and thumbing at her nipples, his pelvis pushing and retreating. When she was writhing underneath his weight, he broke off from her lips and began a slow descent down her body, lingering to lick and suck, heading for her sex.

She called out his name as contact was made, spreading herself wide for him, drinking in the sensations of his wet mouth on her core. The orgasm was a beautiful series of contractions, pleasure vibrating through her, filling her up on the inside.

And all the while, he watched her, his eyes looking up from where he was, his hands cupping her breasts.

She was expecting him to stop so that she had time to dress.

No. He kept going, licking up to the top of her sex, lolling his tongue around, giving her every opportunity to see what he was doing to her, showing off as he flicked at her, his pink flesh moving quickly. . . .

Punching at the pillows, she stretched herself against the heat and the thrill of it.

And still he continued.

Somewhere in the back of her mind, it registered that he was doing this not just to pleasure her, but to bank the memories in his mind: His eyes never left her, his peridot stare capturing her face, her throat, her breasts, her belly.

"Trez . . ." she moaned, arching up.

When he finally released her core, he reared over her body and all but ripped off his clothes. As his shirt went fluttering to the floor and his pants were treated with no concern at all as he yanked them off, she smiled.

She was so ready for him.

He brought her knees up with his dark hands, bending her legs and moving them out to the sides gently. And then he gripped his erection and brought the head of it to the center of her need. Stroking her, he went up and down, glossing himself as he stared at where the two of them were about to be joined.

Pressing inside, he retreated and came at her again, his palm doing the work more than his hips. And each time he popped free, he bit down on his lower lip, his fangs compressing the flesh that had worshiped her.

For some reason, she thought about all her training as an *ehros*. She had been prepared to do her duty, had even been curious about the act, but these experiences with him, the choice to have him, the joy at giving herself not out of some trained obligation, but because she loved him and only him, was so much grander and more glorious than anything her station might have prepared her for.

Eventually, his control snapped and he groaned, sinking into her to the hilt. Propping himself up on his hands, he moved above her, his eyes traveling around her face until he dropped his head and kissed her.

Soon, his pumping became hard and fast, and she stretched her arms out, stroking his lower back, his buttocks, his hips.

As he started to climax, she fell still and felt him orgasm.

It went on for the longest time, his gasping breath, his groans, the sound of her name being wrenched from him as if his soul were being torn apart. And still his hips moved and his sex stroked, and then once again she was coming along with him.

When he collapsed on top of her, she wrapped her arms around him. He was so big, she could barely make it up onto his back, much less have her hands meet at his spine.

He was panting into her hair. Into her throat.

"I love you so much," was all he said.

SIXTY-TWO

maichen sneaked into the ritual chamber and checked on her mother before she tried to leave the palace once again. The Queen was still sitting in her mourning pose, her robes now red after having been changed by staff from those she had had on the night before.

All appeared well for another escape.

Tiptoeing across the marble, she headed for the cupboard in the corner, opening the door and—

"*Did you think I would not know it was you,*" came the words in the Shadow dialect.

maichen froze.

"*You have fooled them all, but not me. I know my own flesh.*"

Shutting the cupboard door, *maichen* fell into the posture of greeting, placing both hands on her shoulders so her arms crossed over her chest, and then lowering herself to her knees and prostrating her torso.

"*My Queen.*"

"*I have allowed you your freedom around the palace.*"

"*Thank you, my Queen,*" she said to the marble floor.

"*Do not abuse my good nature.*"

"*I shall not, my Queen.*"

"*I believe you already have.*"

"*My devotion, as my service, is to you and you alone.*"

"*I can have another of you if I wish. You are as replaceable as anything else in this world of mine. Never forget that*

I am the sun around which this galaxy spins, and I can alter your destiny with the blink of an eye."

Her mother's head turned toward her, the red robing twisting around as if she were some kind of evil creature. And then AnsLai, the high priest, and the Chief Astrologer stepped into the room from a hidden door across the way.

Beneath her robes, *maichen* began to shake, and for self-preservation, she blocked her mind by repeating the word *maichen* over and over again in her head. If her mother or those two advisers got into her thoughts and recent memories, she feared not only for her own life, but for iAm's.

How had her mother known?

"I shall excuse myself and go worship, Your Holiness," she said, as she would have if she were but a servant.

"You do that. And you might contemplate the fragility of life whilst you are in your state of reverence."

maichen ran out of the sacred room and escaped through the halls to her own cell. As she closed herself in, she was breathing hard, her lungs burning, her hands shaking as she tore the hood from her head.

She had been spared, she realized, only because her mother found the appearance of propriety more valuable than punishing a daughter who had gone on a wander: if it got out that the Princess had been compromised by interacting with commoners, or even Primaries, it would not reflect well on the Queen.

For a moment, *maichen* contemplated staying in her rooms, but she wasn't going to get many other nights like this. The mourning was ending soon with a s'Hisbe-wide ceremony where the Primaries and the general population would join in the Queen's up-until-now private "pain."

After that? Especially given that her mother was aware of her forays around the palace and the fact that she was to be mated? Leaving the Territory was going to become impossible.

Likely, she would find it difficult to even leave her suite of rooms.

She had to see iAm, especially if it was one last time.

Extinguishing the lighting overhead, she took off the jewelry at her throat and upon her wrists and left it on her bedding platform. As the with the prior night, she had informed her staff she needed privacy and would summon them at her leisure.

So she had some time.

Closing her eyes, she ...

... spirited away, finding the ventilation shafts and using them to gain access to the great outdoors.

She was not unfamiliar with where Caldwell was. She had seen maps. But the reality of finding the city and locating one particular housing unit within it struck her as craziness.

Except then she homed in on the echo of her own self, her own blood. It was so much louder than she'd expected, a veritable beacon that led her into the dense buildings of the metropolis, those high spires of glass and steel that were as a man-made forest amid a landscape of asphalt and brick and restricted greenery.

Following the signal, she found herself zeroing in on a certain terrace among many others on one of the taller constructions—and upon her arrival, she did not reassume her form. She remained as a Shadow, pooling on a shallow porch-like function before a wall of glass.

Inside the living space beyond, iAm looked up as if instantaneously aware of her presence. Coming forth, he opened one of the massive panes by sliding it off to the side.

"You came," he said.

Rising up from a loose collection of molecules, she became corporeal. It was only then that the frigid breeze from off the river down below penetrated her robes, flipping them to and fro as it chilled her to the bone.

"Inside," he told her. "Let's get you warm."

She didn't know what to say as she stepped over the threshold and the gusts were extinguished as he closed them in together.

"What's wrong?" he asked.

How he could read her so well with her mesh in place, she did not know.

And indeed ... she had to tell him her truth. Even though it was going to spoil everything between them—how could it not? She had seduced him, and he had been the one to take her first, not his brother. She was also the female who, by his own admission, he had hated for so long, the reason for the ruination of his brother's life.

"maichen?"

She studied him for the longest time, trying to find the words. How did she start? And why had she wasted the daylight hours fantasizing about him, when she should have been preparing to reveal herself?

She needed a moment further to think.

"There is naught," she said, keeping her voice level as she started to walk around. "How lovely this is."

At least the latter was not a lie. Everything was honey gold upon the floors and white everywhere else, the furniture understated in the great open space, the view expansive and spectacular.

"Are you hungry?" he asked her—from very close.

Jumping, she looked over her shoulder. He was looming behind her, his body seemingly poised for something.

For sex.

But no, she told herself. They needed to talk. She had to reveal herself to him; otherwise the passion, on his side, was a disingenuous manipulation of which she was guilty.

"Are you," he growled softly as he stepped in against her body. "Hungry?"

Beneath her headdress, she licked her lips.

His hips rolled against her robing, what was no doubt a very hard, very thick erection pushing into the fabric that separated their bodies.

There would be time afterward, she told herself. She would tell him afterward.

The guilt was strong. The lust was stronger.

"I am," she breathed. "But not for food."

As if he read her mind, the lighting which rained down from the ceiling went out, effectively eclipsing them from any external viewers.

"I'm going to take that off," he gritted, as if he hated her hood.

Abruptly, she was freer to breathe, see, smell.

The purr that percolated up out of his chest was that of an animal, but his hands were not harsh as he reached for her over-robe. Up and off her head the weight went, and then the lighter sheath beneath disappeared.

And she was naked before him.

His hands worshiped her as he ran them over her shoulders and down to her breasts. Bringing them together and up, he tasted one nipple and then the other, lapping, sucking—and oh, it was too good. Her legs went loose, and as if sensing this, he swung her up off her feet and carried her out of the light and airy room, down a hallway, and into a bedroom with a large raised mattress platform that proved to be as soft as a cloud.

"This is how I wanted it last night," he said as he laid her out.

There was a light on in some small room, perhaps one with water facilities, and thanks to the dim illumination, she could revel in the obsessional nature of his expression: He regarded her with such rapt focus, she felt beautiful without his having to utter a word to that effect.

His broad palms swept down her legs. "I want to know all of you."

"I offer my body to you," she said hoarsely. "Do as you wish with me."

Rhage was halfway across the Hudson River, heading for the other side of Caldwell in his GTO, when that feeling of being suffocated and light-headed hit him like a ton of bricks.

Swallowing a shot of bile, he cracked his window and turned off the heater. Didn't help. About a mile later, he nearly pulled off to the side of the road.

"Get it together, ass-wipe."

Fucking pussy. What the hell was his problem? He was uninjured, looking forward to cracking the case with Assail and his mirror-image cousins, and on the way to see his beloved *shellan* in his very favorite car. Life was as good as it could get.

He just needed to get a grip.

On that note, he tightened his hold on the steering wheel and started tapping his free shitkicker, the one that was not on the gas.

So close now. He was so close.

Maybe he just needed to hold his Mary for a little bit.

Havers's clinic had been moved to this new, state-of-the-art location, and Rhage had been to visit only a couple of times: Once when he'd gotten an abdominal wound that wasn't going to wait to head all the way back to the Brotherhood compound. Another when Mary had needed a pickup after attending to a female and her young son. Maybe a third time. He couldn't remember.

When he finally got to the turnoff, he cursed at the breathlessness. At the rate he was going? He was going to need treatment.

Maybe he had a virus. Vampires didn't get human ones, or cancer—thank God—but they could get taken down by colds and flu that affected members of the species.

Yeah, that was probably it.

Had to be.

As the GTO's headlights finally splashed across a dull, unassuming little concrete-block structure, he felt the whatever-it-was ease off a bit, which was a welcome surprise. At least he wouldn't have to see his Mary with him lookin' all wall-eyed weird.

Getting out, he went around to the trunk and sprang the deep purple panel.

The sight of Mary's duffel bag, which he himself had packed, brought back the symptoms: His head swam and his palms got sweaty—like he wasn't standing in the cold wind with nothing but leathers and a muscle shirt on.

"Enough with this bullcrap." He picked up the handles and lifted the bag out, then reshut things. "You've *got* to get your shit together."

Approaching the low-slung building, he went into a nothing-special anteroom and checked in. A moment later, the elevator came up its shaft and opened for him. Like a lot of things that had to operate in the daylight by necessity, Havers's newest facility was completely subterranean, the upper part nothing but a prop to weed out valid visitors from potential problems.

Like humans. Slayers.

Down into the earth. Out into the waiting room. As he emerged into the reception area, he wondered how he was going to find her—

"Oh, God, you're here."

His Mary came at him like she was being chased, and as she jumped into his arms, he dropped the damn bag, closed his eyes and held her so hard it was a wonder she could still breathe. But, like she said, *oh, God* . . .

Her scent, her feel, her body, the way her arms wrapped around his neck and squeezed the ever-loving shit out of him—it was all like water in a desert, filling him up, soaking him with a nourishment that he had sorely missed, giving him back his strength and power.

"I've missed you so much," she said in his ear. "So, so, so much."

Not wanting to put her down, he bent and picked up her bag; then carried her and the duffel full of clothes to the far corner, away from the eyes of the receptionist.

Which were focused on them like the female was writing romantic dialogue in her head.

Whatever, he wasn't going to get pissy about it, but he didn't exactly want to broadcast his reunion to the world, either.

Settling his Mary in his lap, he ran his hands down her arms and then went in for a kiss, fusing his mouth with hers as a way to solidify the reconnection. He didn't trust himself, though—so he broke shit off fast.

Too much lip-to-lip and he was liable to mount her in public.

Oh, heeeeeey, Havers, how you doin'?

His Mary smiled and ran her fingers through his hair. "I feel like I haven't seen you in a year."

"Me, too, only it was a decade on my end."

Yeah, so what if he was a panting dog for her. Fuck ya.

"Are you okay?" she asked.

"No, I'm wasting away to normal. I haven't eaten, I can't sleep, and I feel like someone has put itching powder in my jock strap."

She laughed. "That bad? Jeez, I shouldn't feel complimented, should I?"

Leaning in, he said softly, "And I've got carpal tunnel in my left wrist."

"From doing what?" she drawled.

"What do you think?" He nuzzled at her neck. Nipped her vein. "I've had to do something to keep busy in our mated bed. And the shower. And once in the pantry."

"In the pantry? Downstairs?"

"We baby new potatoes for Last Meal. They reminded me of you naked."

More of that laughter and he closed his eyes, letting the joy resonate in his hollow skull.

"How is that possible?" she asked.

"They look like breasts."

"They do not!"

"I didn't say they looked like *good* breasts." He kissed down to her collarbone. "Or your breasts, which, parenthetically, are the most perfect ones I will ever see. In my life. Or my afterlife. Or whatever comes after that."

"You're that desperate that you're triggered by carbohydrates."

"Aren't they a starch? And I jerked off twice in the pantry, actually. Because after I took care of things the first time, I realized I was standing next to the canned peaches." He surreptitiously inched his hand up her thigh. "And you can imagine what that got me thinking about."

Ohhhhh, yeah, he thought as her scent changed, her arousal super-charging the air around them.

Abruptly, he eased back. "Hey, you got a minute?"

She cleared her throat like she was trying to refocus. "Yes, sure. Is there anything wrong?"

"I just have to show you something out in my car."

"You took the GTO?"

"I had to bring your stuff, so I figured I'd take it for a drive."

"How nice." Getting to her feet, she stretched in a way that made him want to palm her breasts. "Actually, I'd love to get some real air for a second. I could use the break."

As they went past reception, he put the duffel on the counter. "Okay if we leave this here for about ten minutes?"

As the receptionist nodded, it appeared that something had gotten the better of her voice. And her sense of balance apparently, because as she went to sit back down, she nearly yard-saled it by falling off the side of her chair.

Over at the elevators, Mary whispered, "I think she likes you."

"Who?"

"The receptionist?"

Leaning down, he said back, "She might as well be a vacuum cleaner for all I care. And I mean that with all due respect."

As the doors opened, that small, secret smile on his Mary's face was a gift from God as far as he was concerned.

Up, up, up they went, and then they were outside and he

was sheltering her with his body as he put his arm around her and led her over to the GTO. By some stroke of complete luck, he'd parked the car in a darkened patch, away from the security lights—and that was just perfect.

Opening the driver's-side door, he put the seat forward and indicated the way into the back.

Mary frowned, but bent down and shuffled into the backseat. As he joined her, he shut them in, and was really glad the glass had been recently tinted.

"What is it?" she asked. "What's going on—"

Taking her hand, he put it on his rigid arousal. "This."

"Rhage!" She laughed some more. "You brought me out here just to—"

He started kissing her mouth and putting his hands around her waist. "Outcome engineer. You knew it when you mated me."

As she kissed him back, he and his Beast were all about the thank-fuck, and he moved fast, because he didn't want them to get caught—not because he had anything against sex in semi-public places, but rather because he didn't want to have to tear the throat out of some innocent son of a bitch who had come for a Band-Aid and ended up with an eyeful or an earful of what they were doing.

Talk about your boo-boos.

He got her loose pants off one of her legs and her in his lap before pulling a fly-away in front of his hips.

And then it was go time.

When he thrust up hard, Mary let out a curse—as her head bonked into the roof of the car.

"Oh, shit, sorry," he groaned.

"Like I care?" she said, taking his mouth with her own. "I need you so badly."

SIXTY-THREE

rez pulled Manny's Porsche up in front of Marcus Reinhardt's jewelry store. The oldest jeweler in town, the place had been featured in things like the *New York Times*, and even the *Robb Report*, for its extensive inventory.

And by extensive, that was carat weight.

Glancing over at Selena, he said, "You ready?"

"I have never had a ring of my own."

"Really?"

She shook her head. "There were jewels in the Treasury—" She stopped. "*Are* jewels in the Treasury, but as Chosen, we were unadorned except for our pearl—and that was not really ours."

Unlatching his door, he said over his shoulder, "Yet another pity as far as I'm concerned."

But he was going to rectify that tonight. Walking in front, he opened her door, and as her beautiful hand extended, he caught hold and gave in to the urge to bend down and kiss the back of it. Then he pulled her carefully to her feet and offered her his elbow.

As she took it, he had a feeling that both of them were ignoring how the gesture was not just that of a polite gentlemale, but something that was needed.

She wasn't walking as well as she had been.

Before they got to the door, the iron-barred thing opened wide. "Mr. Latimer, greetings."

The man was dressed in a formal suit and had a neat

head of hair and a precisely cropped beard. Along with his patrician accent, and the fact that he had a three-point pocket square, he was pretty much central casting for what you'd blue-sky as a guy who specializes in six- to seven-figure engagement rings.

"Thanks for opening things up for us," Trez said as they shook hands. "This is my fiancée, Selena."

"My pleasure. Madam."

Okay, you had to approve of that bow.

Inside, everything was set up for a private showing, and Trez suddenly felt really fucking good about all this. The cases with their fillings of precious gems twinkled under the special lights, as if they were applauding Selena's and his arrival. Champagne was cooling in a silver bucket, and a pair of crystal flutes had been set out.

"May I offer you some Veuve Clicquot?" they were asked.

"I think I'm good," he said. "Selena?"

She tilted up her chin as if she were determined to enjoy herself. "I would like some, please."

"Make that two," Trez amended.

Pop! Fizz! Pour and hand over.

He clinked their glasses. "Let's do this."

Mr. Reinhardt took them into a private room that had a video camera mounted in the corner on the ceiling. "Mr. Perlmutter gave me your specifications, and I took the liberty of preparing you a tray for consideration."

Annnnnnnd out came the ice.

In black velvet slots, diamond rings sat up like good little children panting to get picked to answer a question.

Selena's inhale was like a pat on the back for him.

"See anything you like?" Trez asked.

She tried on every single one, putting the rings on any finger that fit and turning her wrist this way and that under the light. The *coup de grâce* was her sliding on alllll of them, her ten fingers stacked with about twenty spectacular baubles.

"How much money is all that?" he asked idly as he sipped his champagne.

"Several million," Mr. Reinhardt said.

At that, Selena blanched and put her hands down. "What?"

"Several million," the jeweler repeated.

"How much are these things?" she demanded. And then, when informed what the square on her pinkie was worth, she exclaimed, "Dearest Virgin Scribe!"

There was an awkward moment as Trez wished he'd STFU'd. "Selena, I'm not thinking about the price—"

"You should be!" She started taking the rings off at a furious pace. "I haven't spent a lot of time on this side, but I've learned a thing or two about human money—"

"Will you give us a moment?" Trez said smoothly. "And you can take these away if you're worried about the security."

"Your credentials have been well verified, Mr. Latimer." The man got to his polished shoes. "Take your time."

The second the door closed behind the man, Selena turned to him. "Trez, I don't want you spending this kind of money on me."

"Why not?"

"It's a waste. I'm not going to wear the thing for centuries."

He exhaled like someone had kicked him in the chest. "Yeah, wow. You're really missing the point here if you think I'm looking for some kind of time value on the cash." He gathered her hands. "I want to do you right. I want . . . I just want this experience with you, okay? This time, right here"—he motioned around the desk—"this is our infinity. It's happening right here, right now. So let's get you the biggest fucking ring in this place and a pair of earrings to match. Let's just say fuck-you to dying, all right?"

She blinked fast. "Oh, Trez . . ."

He picked up one of the rings she had thrown back on the velvet tray and put it over the nail of her ring finger. "Come on, say it with me."

"Say what?"

" 'Fuck you, death.' "

"Trez. Don't be ridiculous—"

"Hey, on the outside chance the Grim Reaper is listening, I think he needs to know how much we hate his ass. Come on, my queen, say it with me. 'Fuck you, death.' "

She put her free hand up to hide an off-kilter smile. "You're crazy."

"Tell me something I don't know—and stop ducking this.

'Fuck you, death!'" When she just mumbled the words, he shook his head. "Nope. Louder. 'Fuck you, death!'"

Selena started to laugh. "This isn't funny."

"Couldn't agree more." He smiled and nodded at her, still poised with the ring at the top of her finger. "All together—like he can hear you."

"Fuck you, death!" she hollered. Then she smiled broadly. *"Fuck you, death!"*

He slid the ring home and sat back, staring at the sparkler. "You know, I really like that one, actually."

Selena peered over her hand and regarded the grape-size, pear-shaped rock. "Oh . . . boy. It's so big."

"That's what she said."

As they both started to laugh, he pulled her in by the back of the neck and kissed her. "You want to keep trying on some more?"

She shook her head. "No, this is perfect. I want this one."

Putting her beautiful hand out, she did that thing females did with rings, pursing her lips and smiling to herself.

God, I love you, he thought, you perfect, perfect female of worth.

"Are you sure it's not too expensive?" she said.

"No matter the cost"—he kissed her again—"it's yours."

iAm got naked really damn fast. As soon as he was birthday-suit ready, he wanted to go down on *maichen*—even though he had no idea what to do to a female below the waist, he was three hundred ready to find the hell out.

Didn't happen.

The wrench in the works was when he got within range of her, his sex brushing up against hers as he positioned himself on top—

That was pretty much it.

"I need you," he groaned as she ran her hands up his back and down his sides.

"Then take me."

iAm forced himself to stop. "Are you okay, though? After last night?"

God, he couldn't get enough of her almond-shaped eyes, and that black curling hair of hers all over the white pillow-case, and her resplendent skin. She was a constant revelation, one that shocked in a good way every time he looked at her.

"I am well," she said. "And I am of strength, thanks to your generous vein."

He really loved her accent, the dialect that was spoken in the Territory tinting her English with the sounds of home—

No, not home, he reminded himself. Caldwell was home.

Reaching between them, he angled his cock and drove in slowly with his hips, wanting to make sure he didn't force anything.

In response, her nails bit into his skin, and she arched up, her breasts all tight tips. "iAm . . ."

His hips took over, driving in and out, the friction going to his head like he'd been drinking all night. Harder, faster—until she came, jerking up against him, straining under him, one of her hands slapping down on the bed and twisting the duvet up hard.

He just kept going, coming over and over again. And then he pulled out of her and stroked himself, orgasming over her sex, her belly, her breasts.

Even as he was all in with what he was doing, a part of him refused to recognize the significance.

He wasn't marking this female.

He just . . . nope, he wasn't.

Because if he was marking her, if this was anything more than just an intense session with a female he happened to be really fucking attracted to?

Then it could put him in a very difficult situation. Especially as his brother was going to refuse to return and do his duty at the Territory, and iAm was then going to have to go on the lam to avoid an ax falling on the head of the only blood relation who mattered to him.

But again, he told himself as he collapsed against her naked body, he wasn't marking anything like that.

Nope.

Not at all.

SIXTY-FOUR

They held hands all the way home.

As Trez drove the Porsche back to the compound, he kept contact with his queen, thumbing her palm, playing with her new ring, bringing her hand up for a kiss.

"Everyone has been so kind," she murmured, her head back against the seat rest, the flaring lights from the streetlamps at the highway junctions giving him blue-tinted hints of her face.

"Yeah. Good people."

He thought of his brother. Rhage. Rehvenge. He'd even gotten a text from Tohr—who had walked a different version of this path. And then there was Doc Jane. Manny. Ehlena.

"All of them trying so hard to help," she said.

"Yeah."

"Doc Jane and Manny have been working around the clock, attempting to find solutions."

"Yeah." He kissed her hand again. "They have."

"And Rehvenge went up to his people."

"He did."

"And iAm went to the Territory—"

Trez ripped his head around. "*What*?"

She turned her head to him, her eyes half-lidded and sleepy. "iAm went to the Shadows—" Abruptly she frowned. "Ow, you're hurting me."

Shaking himself, he let up on his grip. "Sorry. I—what did you say?"

As she repeated it for a third frickin' time, his heart started to pound. Keeping his voice deliberately calm, he asked, "Do you know when he went?"

"No, Doc Jane just mentioned it when I went to see her. You were having your migraine. Trez, what's wrong?"

"Nothing." He brought up her hand for yet another kiss. "Nothing at all."

The rest of the trip home was a *Sybil* experience, one part of him connected with Selena, the other half hunting down iAm and screaming in the male's face something along the lines of, *What the fuck were you thinking, you asshat motherfucker, putting yourself in danger like that!?!*

Or something to that effect.

". . . changed before we go up there?"

"I'm sorry?" He took the right-hander that led up the mountain. "What did you say?"

"I'd like to get changed. This cooking thing is going to get messy."

"You could do it naked. I'm just saying—cleanup would be a breeze, because I could take you directly into the shower. Plus I could lick off cake batter if it landed . . . you know, anywhere."

She laughed. "Might be cold."

"Then I could keep my hands on you the whole time."

"I won't get any cooking done."

"Don't underestimate the power of takeout." He leaned in and kissed her shoulder. "But that's fine. Whatever you want."

When the great gray mansion came into view, he parked the car in front of the steps as Manny requested, and then went around to open his female's door. As she reached her hand out, the diamond caught the light from the house's security lamps and flashed a rainbow.

"I love it so much," she said.

"Good. That was the plan."

Once inside, he took Selena up to their bedroom. Fritz and the *doggen* had moved clothes into his closet for her, and he had to admit he loved all her shit mixed in with his.

Thank God she needed to change, he thought as he acted as nonchalant as he could.

"So listen, I'm just going to go next door," he said, keeping his voice level. "For a second. You know, to check on iAm."

"All right," she said, smiling.

The instant he was out of her sight, he bared his fangs and ditched the all-cool act. At his brother's door he didn't bother to knock; he just whipped the thing open.

"iAm!" he barked, even though he doubted the guy was there.

Not waiting for an answer, he took out his phone and hit the guy up. One ring, two rings . . .

"Yeah? Trez? What's wrong—"

"What the *fuck* were you thinking?"

There was a pause. "Excuse me?"

"You went to the fucking Territory?" He tried to keep his voice down. "Are you out of your fucking mind!"

"Trez—"

"What the fuck are you doing!"

"I am not discussing this with you over the phone."

"Then get your fucking ass home now."

He hung up and marched around. Then, snapping himself out of it, he masked up and went back to his room. "Hey, Selena?"

"Yes?" she said from the closet.

"I've got to hang here for a little bit. Not long. If you want, you can head on up and I'll be there quick?"

He knew in the back of his mind that he wasn't thinking right—she shouldn't be alone—but he was seeing red, his brain locked on his brother's idiot move.

Sticking her head out, she smiled and said something that didn't sink in. Going by her nod, though, she was going to leave. He went over and kissed her, and then shut himself into iAm's bedroom.

It felt like it was an hour until his brother showed up, but it was probably five or ten minutes. And as the guy walked into the room, a strange scent on him dimly registered: It was female. But whatever.

"What the *hell*, iAm?" he demanded. "Like I don't have enough problems?"

"You need to back off. I went there because I wanted to see if there was any record of the Arrest in the healing journals. It was just a trip in and out—"

"How. Who did you make a deal with."

"Myself."

"Bullshit."

"Trez, no offense, but why are you wasting time with this? I got out—"

"Was it s'Ex? Did you use s'Ex?" When iAm didn't reply, he threw up his hands. "Oh, come on! Are you kidding—"

"Calm down—"

"Calm down! You don't think that it might be seriously fucking nuts for you to turn yourself over to the Queen's executioner? Who I've spent the last nine months buying off with a supply of prostitutes? That doesn't strike you as irresponsible, considering they want me to go back there?"

"You know what? I'm not doing this with you. I'm not—"

"The fuck you're not! You exposed us both going there! They could have used you as leverage—"

"They didn't—"

"—to get me back there to service that fucking Princess! You told me I had 'til the end of the mourning period— that's only three days and I've got shit I need to deal with here! I don't need you wild-carding—"

"Trez, I know you're caught up with Selena. I get it. But you're outta line here—"

"Out of line? What if they'd kept you? What if AnsLai had come to me and been all like, 'I got your brother, time for your mating'? Did you think for even a second what kind of position that would put me in? Either you and a life of imprisoned fucking for me—or not being here for Selena at the end of her life! What the fuck—"

For some reason, iAm's abrupt change in affect registered: The male had frozen in place and was staring over Trez's shoulder, his expression instantly going blank.

Trez clamped his mouth shut and closed his lids. Even before he turned around, he knew what he was going to find in the doorway to the bedroom.

Yup. Selena had opened the way in and was standing between the jambs, pale as a ghost.

"You're to be mated?" she said in a thin voice. "In three days?"

iAm cursed under his breath. Just exactly how this didn't need to come out.

And worse, as Selena came forward, her gait was off, like her knees or maybe her hips were giving her bother.

"What are you . . ." She stopped in front of Trez. "Are you going to mate that female in three days?"

Time to go, iAm thought. This was definitely something the two of them—

"No," Selena said as he went to head by her. "Stay."

Like she wanted him available to fill things in if she felt her male wasn't being straight with her.

"What's going on?" she demanded.

Even though Trez had been rip-shit only moments before, the guy looked as composed as an inanimate object: "It's not important."

"That's not what I just heard. And before you accuse me of eavesdropping, the two of you were yelling so loudly, I could hear it next door."

Trez rubbed his short-cropped hair and walked around. "Selena—"

"Are you going to be mated?"

"This doesn't affect us."

"It most certainly does."

When there was a tight silence, iAm decided, Fuck it. "He was sold by our parents when we were infants to the Queen of the Territory—as a mate for the heir to the throne. It was decreed by his astrological chart. He's done everything possible to escape from it, and the reason he's pissed at me is because I'm his Achilles's heel. He's just freaking out at a close call, probably because the real thing he's worried about is you and he can't do anything about that."

As they both looked at him, he shrugged. "Whatever. I've been watching *Dr. Phil* with Lass downstairs when I can't sleep."

"Is this true?" Selena asked.

"Yeah." Trez went over and sat on the bed. "I didn't talk to you about it because, honestly, like he said, no matter what they do in three days, I'm not going to mate some female I don't know and don't care about and give her the second in line for the throne. It's just not going to happen— and that's true whether or not you're in my life, and whether or not you live a hundred more days or a thousand more years."

He clapped his hands together as if he were closing a door. "And that's that."

Selena was quiet for a time. "You should have told me."

"I don't like to think about it."

iAm rolled his eyes. "Truth."

"And, Selena, I'm serious. I'm not going to do it in seventy-two hours or seven million." Trez glanced over. "Did you see our parents while you were there?"

iAm shook his head. "I was only in the palace." In a cell. "And they've lost their station so they were on the other side of those walls. I sure as shit didn't look them up. They're dead to me. I couldn't give a fuck about them."

"Me, too." Trez looked back at Selena. "This is my life here. *Here* is my life—these people, this place, my businesses . . . you most of all. I'm not going to let anyone take it away from me, especially not because some astrologist looked at the stars in the heavens and decided they meant something."

Selena wrapped her arms around herself. "I really wish you'd told me."

"I would have if it meant anything to me."

"And these businesses . . . do you still sell females through them?"

iAm stared at the door. Started inching his way to it.

"They sell themselves," Trez countered. "I give them a venue to do so, but they are in charge of themselves. They choose who, how much, how often. My job is to keep them safe."

"While you earn money off of them."

"They pay the club. Not me."

"But you own the club."

"iAm," Trez said sharply. "I want you to stay."

He closed his eyes. "That's not what I'm thinking."

"No," Selena spoke up. "If he has nothing to hide, let him say it in front of an audience."

Great. Just what he was looking for. A job as mediator. Not.

And *maichen* was still at the condo.

"Actually, I really do have to go." iAm glanced back and forth between the two of them. "I've never been in a relationship before, so I don't have any advice for the pair of you. But, Selena, I think you should be aware of two things. One, his entire life has been defined by rebelling against the s'Hisbe and our parents. And two, he has not been with a single female since he got with you last year. He has been faithful to you even when you two weren't together. So don't crucify him because you think that the human women who work for him are somehow with him. I'm out."

He didn't give them a chance to reel him back into their drama. He had enough of his own. He'd left *maichen* buck-ass naked in his bed and he was worried she was going to take off without his getting back.

Rushing down to the foyer, he bolted through the vestibule, broke out into the night, and dematerialized to the Commodore.

As he assumed form on the terrace, he yanked back the glass door and rushed across to the corridor that led to the bedrooms.

"*maichen*," he called out.

Just as he rounded the door to his bedroom, she said, "Yes?"

He took a deep breath as he saw her reclining against the pillows, her bare shoulders emerging from the cover of the duvet.

"Oh, thank fuck," he said.

"Are you all right?" She sat up. "iAm?"

Kicking off his shoes, he didn't answer her. He couldn't. There was too much to say about things he couldn't change and hated.

Instead, he pulled back the sheets and got in fully clothed. Her body was warm and naked and yielding as he brought them heart-to-heart.

As her arms came around him, and she stroked the back of his head, he shuddered—and realized that in all the years he'd had on the planet, this was the first time he'd had somewhere to go when he felt like the world was a shitty place and time was nothing more than torture to be endured.

It was so much better than even the sex.

This moment where he sought and was given haven? It made him understand why the Brothers lit up every time their *shellans* came into the room, and why those males would lay down their lives for those females.

"Thank you," he heard himself say.

"For what?" *maichen* whispered.

"Being here."

"Is Selena unwell?" she asked. Because he'd told her why he'd needed to go.

"Not acutely so. But she and my brother got into it."

"Why?"

"There's nothing like your fiancée finding out you're betrothed to another while she's dying. That is just *such* an awesome conversation to have."

maichen stilled. "This has to end."

"The shit with Trez and that fucking Princess? I agree—if you come up with any bright ideas . . . let me know," he said starkly.

SIXTY-FIVE

It was very easy to escape from his own house.

Assail simply cracked the window on the upper floor and departed his premises with all the fuss and circumstance of a draft escaping into the night.

He had been tracking the movements of the Brothers in his woods with his night-vision cameras, the huge shapes of the males moving like T. Rexes through his property, their presences sticking to the trees.

Following the sun's disappearance, he had kept the illusion blinds in place, effectively preserving the daytime, vacant appearance of his interior. It would give the Brothers something to do as they contemplated the where and when of his and his cousins' nocturnal reappearance aboveground.

Which would not be until he had completed a specific endeavor.

With alacrity, he traveled to the east, to a prearranged location at an abandoned strip mall approximately five miles outside of the downtown area.

The Hertz rental car was parked grille-out against the rear wall of a building that had a faded BLUEBELL'S BIRTHDAY BOUTIQUE, DELIVERIES ONLY sign hanging cockeyed from above a paint-chipped reinforced door.

Ehric put the driver's-side window down as Assail reformed. "Are you driving?"

"Yes, I am."

As his cousin got out and Assail assumed the male's

place behind the wheel, Evale spoke up from the backseat. "What do you want us to do?"

"Nothing."

He put the engine in gear and headed off, moving swiftly, but obeying all traffic laws. He'd gone but a couple of miles when the cocaine that he'd taken about two hours earlier began to wear off in earnest.

But he was not going to reload. He needed to be focused enough to dematerialize if need be.

He took the three of them and the pedestrian Ford Taurus through the sprawling suburbs and out farther from the metro hub, into the farmland that formed a skirting around the Adirondack Mountains. As he went along, the roads became narrower, the yellow line in the middle and the white lines at the shoulders growing so faint, the headlights failed to pick them out. And still he continued onward, no one behind him, no cars or trucks coming toward him.

Some miles later, he arrived at the dairy farm he was looking for. Like Bluebell's Birthday Boutique, it, too, was abandoned, and the sedan bumped along as he transitioned off the asphalt onto a dirt lane that went out into the overgrown fields. Crossing through the bramble and cornstalk tangle, he drove all the way to the forest's edge and found shelter among the birch trees and maples that retained few of their leaves. With quick circles of the wheel, he turned the rental around so they were facing out and waited, leaving the car running. He hated that the headlights remained aglow, but there was naught to be done about that.

The Brothers' presence had made taking his Range Rover impossible.

"He's late," Ehric said a little later.

"He'll be here." There was too much at stake for the *Forelesser* not to show. "He shall not fail us."

And sure enough, moments later, a dark shape came forward through the field, following their path. No running lights. So he knew it was the one for whom they were waiting.

"You know where to go," he said softly as he cracked one of the back windows an inch.

Just like that, the cousins dematerialized out of the backseat . . . and the *Forelesser* arrived, coming to a stop. As usual, Assail and his business associate both put their windows down at the same time.

"Where's your Range Rover, vampire?"

"In the shop."

"Be fucking real. Have you been trailed?"

"In a manner of speaking."

The slayer frowned, his dark brows falling down over his dark eyes. For a moment, Assail mourned the Old Country, where you knew the bastards not just from their stench, but because they had been in the Lessening Society long enough for their coloring to pale out. Not in the New World. No, here, in the disposable culture of American humans, the undead did not last long enough to have their pigments fade.

"ATF?" the slayer demanded. "Or CPD."

As if during his years as a human he had often found inconvenience from those two organizations.

"By the Black Dagger Brotherhood. And the Blind King, Wrath."

The undead threw his head back and laughed. "Whatever, my man, that's on you."

"No, I'm afraid that shall be on you, mate."

Without warning, Assail lunged out of his window and stabbed the slayer in the eye, using the dagger he had discreetly placed upon his thigh. As the *Forelesser* screamed, Assail wrenched the blade free and slashed across the front of the throat. Gurgling sounds and copious amounts of black blood filled the interior of the slayer's SUV, and Assail was forced to awkwardly extract his upper body or be drenched in the mess.

Ehric rematerialized with his cousin and made quick work of searching the vehicle as Assail looked around, ensuring that there were still no witnesses. As the slayer choked and clawed at the second mouth that had been made in his neck, Ehric emerged with three AKs and many rounds of ammunition. Without conversation, the weapons and lead were placed in the trunk of the Taurus, and the cousins opened both rear doors and got back into that vehicle.

Assail reached through the window and pulled one of the *Forelesser*'s arms out. Finding an unstained section of sleeve, he wiped off his dagger, reholstered the thing . . . and extracted a serrated hunting knife from his belt.

Quick work to sever the head completely.

He left the body where it was, behind the wheel of the SUV, its hands and feet as yet moving, the right hand even flopping up and gripping the wheel.

Going to be rather difficult to drive, considering there was no brain and no vision to direct things.

No, he had the CPU by the hair.

Walking around to the front passenger's-side door, he opened things up and placed the still-blinking, still-mobile head into the cardboard Amazon.com box that had been lined with Hefty bags.

Then he went across and got back behind the wheel of the Taurus. Before the interior lights extinguished themselves, he peered over the lip of the box and met the rolling, shocked eyes.

"You were a fine partner," Assail murmured. "Such a shame we must needs part association."

With that, he put the sedan in drive and headed off.

SIXTY-SIX

Trez let himself fall back on his brother's bed, his arms flopping out to the sides, his eyes focusing on the ceiling above. Goddamn it, that frickin' curse of his was never going to stop haunting him. Here he was, trying to do right by the one female who had ever mattered to him . . . and that s'Hisbe shit was, as ever, a noose around his neck.

"You have been . . . without a female?" Selena asked. "Since . . ."

He lifted his head and stared across the empty bedroom at her. "Why would I have been with one? Ever since I had you? Nobody's been of interest."

There was a long pause. "Really?"

"Really."

She put her hands to her face. "That is . . ." She shook her head. "Pretty fantastic, actually."

Pushing against the mattress, he sat up on his elbows and regarded her. "Do you remember what you said? After you . . . well, you know, when we were down in the clinic the first time? That you were worried you were just another obsession for me to sink into?"

"Yes."

"Well, if you are? I sank into you before we even hooked up. You probably don't remember this, but . . ." He shook his head. "I used to wait for you in the foyer every night."

"What?"

"Yeah, pathetic. I know. But see, you'd come here to feed V or Rhage, or Luchas, and I'd linger by the front door just in case you came up from the training center—or went down to it from somewhere else in the house. One night—shit, I can remember it clear as anything—you finally made an appearance. I rushed down the big staircase—you were, like, in the foyer when I caught your attention. I stared at you, and thought . . . this is the most amazing female I have ever seen." He shrugged and sat all the way up. "You got me then and there, my queen. I've been obsessed with you, for good or not, so good since waaaaaay before I knew you were sick."

She smiled a little. "I had no idea. I mean, I knew, when we were up at Rehv's together and you . . . well, I knew that . . . um, you liked me."

He blinked and saw her naked in that bed of hers at the Great Camp. "Yeah, I was into you then. Way into you." Grimacing, he said, "Look, I haven't handled everything well. I should have told you about the particulars of the s'Hisbe stuff, but I was worried it was going to freak you out and make you want to have nothing to do with me. I've lost years of my life imprisoned in that palace, and I've ruined iAm's entire existence—I was not going to lose a shot at you because of that crap on top of all of that. And as for my businesses? They're not legal according to human laws, but I've always believed people have a right to make their living in any way they want, as long as they don't hurt anyone. That's why, unlike Rehv, I don't allow drugs to be sold on my premises. The human women are protected when they're under my roof, they practice safe sex, and they keep ninety percent of what they make. The ten percent I take goes to my electric bills and my bouncers. So, yeah . . . that's where I'm at with that."

She took a deep breath. "I'm really glad you're being honest."

"Is there anything else you want to know? As I told you before, I don't talk about my parents because they're nothing but biology to me and iAm. They've never cared about our welfare. They've never been there for us. All along, it's been iAm and me together, and that's been enough for both of us. And that's why they don't come up."

Selena came forward haltingly, and sank to her knees beside him on the floor. "Thank you."

Her eyes were so clear, so blue as they stared up at him.

"For what," he said hoarsely. "I don't like showing you weakness. I hate it."

"It just makes me love you more." She smiled. "In fact, this honesty right now? Is the single most attractive thing about you."

Aw, shit. She was going to make him go Kleenex over here.

"I love you so much." When his voice broke, he cleared it. "More than even my brother."

"That's some kind of pledge."

"Yeah, it is."

They stayed like that for the longest time, him staring down, her looking up, and in the silence, he realized they had reached the very realest part of who they were as individuals and what they were together. It was the base core of them both, their faults, perceived and actual, on the table, nothing hidden—not her illness, not everything he hadn't wanted her to know . . . and their eternity was still intact.

Their love had only been strengthened.

"You have been," she whispered, "the very best part of my life. You're such a miracle, it almost makes up for my illness."

"I'm not that big a blessing."

"Yes, you are."

He caressed her cheek with his knuckles. Brushed her lips with his. "So . . . you wanna go cook me dinner?"

She nodded, and when he offered his palm to help her to her feet, she put her hand in his, the one with the diamond on it.

Her beautiful hand, with its long tapering fingers and its little wrist.

At first, he didn't understand why, when he stood up and went to pull, his grip slipped free. "Oh, sorry, sloppy—"

She wasn't moving.

Selena was exactly in the position of having placed her hand in his, her forearm up, her head tilted so she could meet his eyes, her body on her knees.

The only thing that had changed was the terror in her eyes.

"Oh, no . . ." he said. "No, no, not now . . ."

He knelt beside her, but she didn't turn her head to him.

Instead, her body began to list to the side as if it were solid, falling, falling ...

"*No!*" he screamed.

The next thing Trez knew, he was in the clinic.

He had no idea how he'd gotten there with Selena in his arms, but somehow he must have picked her up from the floor in iAm's bedroom and made it down all the stairs and through the tunnel and out of the supply closet.

He was vaguely aware of people in his wake. Lassiter, who had probably come out of the billiards room. Tohr, who'd been behind the desk in the office. Another Brother who was limping.

But none of that mattered.

Giving his back to the door into the exam room, he barged in without knocking, his heart thundering, his hearing shot, his brain jammed up with that one word he kept repeating over and over again to himself.

Nonononononononononononononononono—

This couldn't be happening now, after they'd had that transcendent moment. Not now, when they were supposed to go and have her dance naked around Rehv's kitchen together. Not now, without him having taken her for that boat ride.

It was too soon, too soon. . . .

Suddenly, it dawned on him that Doc Jane was standing in front of him, her forest-green eyes locked on his, her mouth moving.

"Can't hear you," he told her. Or at least, he thought that was what he said.

Goddamn it, this ringing in his ears wasn't helping.

When the physician pointed at the exam table, he thought, Right, okay. He would put Selena there.

Moving across the tile floor, he approached the place he needed to get to and bent down, intending to lay her flat. Except, no—her body didn't shift to accommodate the repositioning.

It nearly killed him to ease her onto her side.

Crouching down so she could see him, he took her hand, the one that was as yet extended to him, the one with his ring on it. "It's okay, my queen. It's all right—you got out of this last time, you're going to do it again. You're going to come out of this."

He never looked away from her panicky eyes. Not when machines were hooked up to her, and IVs started, and X-rays taken. Not while the two doctors and Ehlena worked feverishly, administering drugs and taking her pulse and blood pressure. Not as she began to tear up, the crystal drops forming and dropping off the bridge of her nose and the side of her face.

"I got you, my queen. I'm not going anywhere. Stay with me. You've come out of this many times before, and the same thing's going to happen tonight. Believe with me, come on . . . you've got to believe with me. . . ."

He had to open his mouth, because he was breathing so hard his nose couldn't keep up with the demands. And he kept having to swallow—it was either that or run the risk of needing to tilt to the side and throw up on the tile.

This can't be it, he thought.

I'm not ready.

I can't say good-bye.

I can't let her go tonight.

This can't be it . . .

SIXTY-SEVEN

As Rhage stared up at Assail's glass house, he knew in his gut something was in all-wrong territory. Ever since he and V had arrived, nothing had changed. The interiors, whether it was the kitchen, that football field–size living room, or the office, were each exactly right—except there was no one moving through them.

"Maybe Assail's doing his toenails underground," Rhage muttered. "A lilac, perhaps. Or a cherry red."

"Sooner or later," V bitched, "if he's going to stay in business, he'll have to leave by car. You can't transport the kind of money or drugs he deals in while ghosting."

"Unless they all overdosed together."

They both had to assume Assail and his boys had been drafting in and out since nightfall, and there was nothing they could do to stop that. V had, however, set up tiny cameras before they'd left the dawn before, and there had been no activity during the daylight hours—no duffels left out for pickup, nothing dropped off. So, as V said, there was no way they were moving any product—

Like they were being choreographed, he and his brother went for their phones at the same time.

AH911.

From Phury.

Without hesitation, they both dematerialized, traveling back across the river and re-forming at the rear door of the audience house. V entered the code and they burst into the kitchen, startling the *doggen* who was at the stove.

The fact that Paradise's maid, Vuchie, didn't seem alarmed was a good sign. There was also no loud beeping of an alarm having been triggered in the air.

Nonetheless, they outted their guns and jogged for the dining room, punching through the flap door in the back corner—

Just in time to see Assail pull a head out of a cardboard box by the hair.

"Thought you'd like to join the party," Phury whispered out of the corner of his mouth. "He just showed up."

"I should like to introduce you," Assail was saying, "to my partner. My *former* partner."

The undead's brown eyes lolled around the room, the black bloodstained lips gaping slowly like a fish's would if it had landed on the bottom of a boat in the sun.

The various Brothers standing around the room cursed.

And as George growled next to Wrath's chair, the King reached down and soothed the dog. "How do we know that's not just some slayer off the streets?"

"Because I'm telling you."

"Your credibility is not something anyone should fall on a sword for."

"But I will." Assail disappeared the head and put the box down on the floor. "I know where all the *lessers* are staying."

Everyone went silent.

Wrath sat forward in his armchair, his wraparounds trained in the drug dealer's direction. "Do you."

"Aye."

Wrath's nostrils flared as he tested the male's scent. "He's telling the truth, boys."

Annoyance tightened the drug dealer's arched brows. "Of course I am. You informed me I was not to do business with the Lessening Society. I have obeyed your command. If the Brotherhood goes and eradicates them where they stay, I shall no longer have to prove that I have complied with your orders whilst I continue my pursuits. Our interests are therefore aligned, and if you need strong backs to fight alongside, I hereby volunteer myself and my cousins."

"I am touched by your magnanimity."

"It has naught to do with you. As I have told you, I am a businessman. There is nothing I will not do to protect my endeavors and it is very clear to me that you and the assembled herein are capable of shutting that which is precious to me down. Therefore, I have taken the necessary steps to ensure I may continue—even though it is coming at great inconvenience and my revenue stream will suffer as I am forced to reestablish my network on the streets."

As the air in the room began to hum, Rhage glanced around at his brothers. He was so fucking ready for a full-on war, for a chance to pay those undead bastards back for what they did during the raids.

This was an unexpected boon.

"It is my understanding"—Assail pointed to the box— "that that is the *Forelesser*. I attacked him in private and deliberately did not send him back to his Maker. There will be a short period of time during which his absence will be tolerated."

V spoke up. "So where is this den of iniquity."

"The Brownswick School for Girls. Its campus has been abandoned for some time and they are living in the dorms."

"And trying to learn long division," someone muttered.

"Or writing the slayer version of *Our Bodies, Ourselves*," somebody else said.

Assail cut through the chatter. "I learned of their location many, many months ago. After all, it is important that one know the particulars of one's business partner's life. My cousins have investigated the grounds this night and have confirmed that they are still in place. I imagine you will wish to scout the property as well prior to any coordinated siege."

Immediately, all the Brothers started speaking up, volunteering to go—but Wrath put a hand out, silencing them.

"Will you let us keep that," he asked, nodding in the direction of the box. "Or is that a souvenir you want to put on your mantel."

"As with the information I have provided, it is yours to do with as you wish."

"Where's the rest of the body."

"Out on Route 149. There's an abandoned dairy farm. Go into the south pasture to the woods, you'll find the rest of the body and his SUV there."

Wrath sat back and crossed his long legs knee to ankle. "This is a much better outcome than us having to kill you."

"I am not pleased with this."

"It's better than a coffin," Rhage said.

The drug dealer glanced over. "That is correct." With that, Assail turned on his heel and headed for the door. "You know where to find me if you have further inquiries or require assistance with a raid."

Butch let the male out, escorting him to the house's front door.

It wasn't until the Brother was back and had reshut them all in together that anyone said a thing.

"If that is the *Forelesser*," Wrath said, "the Omega will know instantly."

"But he changes them every fifteen minutes," V said. "And one of us didn't kill him. Maybe he'll just anoint the next one and move along."

"Maybe." Wrath nodded to the cardboard box. "Get rid of that when you go to confirm the corpse."

"I can go," Butch offered. "And take him out of the game permanently."

V shook his head. "You can't dematerialize. Too danger-ous—"

All at once, everyone's phone went off, the collective *ping*s, *bong*s, and whistles like someone had cranked up a *Sesame Street* epi.

As everyone went for their pockets, Rhage wondered what the hell it could be about. Tohr was off rotation at home. Rehv hated phones. And Lassiter had been forced to give up group-texting after V had disabled the function on the idiot's Samsung—besides, it would have been a chorus of Denis Leary's "I'm an Asshole," which everyone had put as the angel's ringtone.

"Oh, shit," someone said.

Rhage had to read twice what had been sent. Then he let his arm fall down to his side and closed his eyes.

"Somebody had better fucking tell me what the mourn-ing is all about," Wrath said roughly.

"It's Selena," Rhage heard himself reply. "She's gone down."

Sitting on the rumpled bed at his place at the Commodore, iAm found himself checking *maichen*'s robing, looking for anything that was out of place, wrinkled, cockeyed. He was not sending her back to the Territory looking as if she had been sexed but good.

Even if she had, in fact, been.

"Tomorrow night," he said.

"Yes."

"Good." Shit, he wasn't sure whether he could wait that long. "That's tight."

Motioning her closer, he arranged the hood in his hands so that, as he put it over her head, the mesh was in the right place. He hated covering her features once again. It was as if he were imprisoning her even though she was free to come or go as she pleased.

Relatively free, that was.

"Until the morrow," she said, her beautiful voice muffled.

He reached out and took her hand. He intended to squeeze it and let her go, but he found himself not able to release the grip.

"*maichen.*" He took a deep breath. "What would you say if I offered you a place here? Here in Caldwell, I mean. If I took care of you and kept you safe here in the city."

It definitely wouldn't be in this condo; that was for sure—s'Ex was no doubt going to resume using the four walls and a roof as a fuck palace as soon as the mourning was over—

Oh, wait. That was when they were going to want Trez.

Whatever.

It would be somewhere else.

As she hesitated, he said, "You wouldn't have to serve anyone. You could be free."

You could be with me, he thought.

Which was, yeah, nuts, but time was feeling really damn short lately, and he just didn't want to wait about anything. Especially anything that was on the feel-good instead of the get-you-in-the-nuts scale.

"You'd be safe," he repeated. "On my life, I would keep you safe. And there's a whole world out here, things for you to do and places to explore, schools to attend. The humans are mostly idiots, but they'd leave you alone."

In a flash, the fantasy spun out like a gold thread, images of him cooking for her at Sal's, introducing her with pride to his waiters, maybe bringing her to the compound for a meal.

He studiously ignored the whole run-from-the-s'Hisbe thing.

"iAm," she whispered.

Shit. That tone of hers said it all.

And he wasn't going to hear it. "You could have a real life out here. You're so much better than just a maid for other people. You could really live."

With me, he finished to himself.

Oh, God, he was so done-for with her. And whereas he might have chalked it up to his finally getting laid, it was so much more than that. In his soul, he somehow *knew* her.

Over on the side table, his phone went off with a text.

"Think about it," he said. "I know it's a lot—so don't give me any kind of answer right now. Head home, and be safe—I'll see you tomorrow."

Getting to his feet, he escorted her out to the living area and over to the glass sliders. A moment later, she was gone as if she had never been—and for a moment, he wondered if he wasn't imagining all this.

It just seemed surreal.

Was he really falling in love here?

Closing things up, he intended to go back to his room and make the bed—mostly so that if s'Ex showed up, there wouldn't be a lot of awkward convo. Instead, he just stayed at the sliders, staring out into the night, his brain chewing on what-ifs and how-'bouts.

The sound of his phone ringing back in the bedroom got him refocused, and he strode to the thing, going down the hall and through the doorway, heading over to the bedside table, reaching out for the glowing screen.

Picking it up, he accepted the call. "Rhage? Everything okay—"

"Trez needs you. Right now."

"Is it—"

"Yeah. She's in the clinic."

iAm closed his eyes. "Tell him I'm on the way."

As he hung up, he fucked off the messy bed and ran for the glass doors. Once out in the cold air, he tried to dematerialize, but his pounding heart and scattered emotions got in the way of his focus.

It was only by picturing Trez having to deal with a tragedy alone that he was able to pull his shit together, and a moment later, he was on the front steps of the Brotherhood mansion. Bursting into the vestibule, it took for-flippin'-ever for a *doggen* to answer the door, and iAm barely said two words to the male as he broke into a run.

It was a case of full-tilt down to the training center, and when he finally leapt out of the supply closet and careened through the office—

iAm skidded to a halt in the corridor.

There must have been . . . forty people outside the exam room, some sitting on the hard floor, others walking around. V was smoking while Butch was tapping one foot like someone had plugged his ankle into a socket. Phury was pacing like crazy; Z was stock-still. Bella was rocking Nalla in her arms. Payne was shuffling cards incessantly. John Matthew was holding hands with Xhex. Qhuinn had his arm around Blay. Autumn was holding Tohr around his waist as if she were the only thing keeping him off the concrete floor. Rhage was alone, standing far from the others. Even Wrath was there with Beth and L.W. and George.

All of the Chosen were present. Every single one of them, including Amalya.

And Rehvenge was closest to the door into the clinical space.

iAm closed his eyes. He couldn't believe they had all shown up.

When he started walking forward, people embraced him, reached for his hands, squeezed his shoulders. He did his best to thank them and respond, but his head was spinning. When he got to Rehv, he just shook his head.

"What happened?"

"She collapsed—or whatever you want to call it—about twenty minutes ago. They're working her up. He's been asking for you."

Those amethyst eyes had a sheen of red in them.

iAm could have used a minute to collect himself, but he'd already missed how much? God only knew what was going on in there, and there was only one way to find out.

Pushing his way inside, he recoiled. Selena was on the table once again, but seeing her all contorted was a stab in the heart.

Trez was right by her head, his eyes staring into hers. His lips were moving as he talked to her softly against a backdrop of beeping medical equipment and wires and tubes and cuffs. The clothes she'd been wearing had been cut off, and a thin white blanket had been spread over her.

Nodding at Ehlena, Jane, and Manny, iAm went over and crouched down. Trez jumped and then looked around as if he'd forgotten there was anyone else in the room.

"You're here," the male said.

"Yeah, I am."

Trez turned back to Selena. "Look who's here, it's iAm."

That normally strong voice was reedy and choked, as if being funneled through a synthesizer.

"Hey, Selena," iAm said.

As her eyes shifted over to his, he forced himself to smile against a tide of sorrow and fear. She was terrified. Utterly terrified.

Why wouldn't she be.

Trez began to murmur again and iAm glanced over at Manny, cocking an eyebrow in inquiry. The healer slowly shook his head.

Shit.

SIXTY-EIGHT

Trez waited for a miracle.

For the next six to eight hours, he waited and he prayed and he talked until he lost his voice. He even blanketed his beloved with his energy not once, but twice. And still she remained where she was, trapped inside her frozen body, her vitals slowly fading . . . her eyes beginning to shut from time to time.

Only to have them pop open and her gasp through her ever-paling lips.

Later, he would remember the moment when they reached the point of no return.

It was when the medical staff turned off the alarms that had at first been beeping with warning every now and again, but which had subsequently begun to go off constantly.

"Is it—" As his voice cracked, he cleared his throat. "Time for more X-rays?"

Jane came around to him and spoke quietly. "Trez, I think we'd like to speak with you."

Manny nodded. "Maybe out in the hall."

"No, I'm not going to leave her." He smoothed his beloved's hair back and was relieved when her eyes focused on his. "I'm not leaving you, my queen."

iAm bent in and said into his ear, "You want them to talk to me?"

It was a while before Trez answered. He didn't want to hear what they were going to say. Even though in his heart, he knew ... he knew that things were not changing this time ... he didn't want the words out in the air.

But the cycle of gasping and fright that kept happening to her was wearing on him.

"Yes, please," he said politely. "Thank you."

The bunch of them, including Ehlena, went into the room next door.

And it dawned on him that he and Selena were alone with each other. Leaning into her, he stroked her hair and brushed her mouth with his.

Shit, her lips were so cold.

He wanted to close his eyes, but he was terrified he'd miss something. Instead, he let a couple of heartbeats go by.

I want to be free. The thing that scares me most is getting trapped in my body.

"Selena," he said in a voice that was as thin as his skin. "Selena, can you focus on me? Can you hear me?"

She blinked twice, which was the code he'd established with her for "yes."

"I need to know ..." He swallowed hard. "I need to know if you want to go ... do you want to go?"

In response, her eyes ... her magnificent blue eyes ... welled with tears, and he began to cry, too. With a sense of profound pain, he reached up with his free hand and brushed the wetness from her nose and her cheeks. He left his tears where they were.

"My queen, is it time for you to go? Tell me if it is."

Her stare never left his.

She blinked once. And then ... again.

Oh, God.

"Do I understand you correctly?" he said. "Do you want this ... to end?"

They were both crying in earnest now. And she didn't have to blink it out again, because he knew in his heart and soul what she wanted—and yet, he waited for the signal one more time. This was one of those moments when he had to get it right.

Or he would never be able to live with himself.

"Is it time?" he whispered.

She blinked once ... and then again.

Now he shut his lids and found his body swaying as if a

tremendous weight had been set upon his shoulders, and not balanced well.

When he opened his eyes, iAm and the physicians were back in the room. One look into his brother's stark face and he knew that whatever had been said had not been marked by much if any optimism.

As iAm came over, the male was careful to acknowledge and smile at Selena—which Trez really appreciated. Then he leaned in and whispered, "There's nothing they can do. The anti-inflammatories aren't working, and the last set of X-rays exhibited a change that the first episode didn't have. The joints—or what should be the joints—are showing bright white on the films, with the kind of intensity metal would have. That wasn't the case before. Her vitals are not good and getting worse, even though they've given her things to help with her slow respiration and heart rate. Their sense is . . . this is the end."

Trez nodded, and then took a moment to tend to Selena's face. "She's ready to go," he choked out. "She told me so. Is there . . . something . . . we can . . ."

Manny stepped over. "We can help her along. If she's sure."

"She is."

iAm leaned in close again and whispered something else.

Trez took a deep breath. "Selena, do you want to see your sisters? Phury? The Directrix? They're all here. They're right outside."

In response, she closed her eyes. Once. And then kept them that way until he felt a fresh needle of panic go through him.

But she opened them again. She was still with him.

Now, her tears were coming faster and faster, and he wished he could concentrate enough to try to get in her mind, but he couldn't. He was too wrung-out, too emotional, too filled with grief. And he understood what she wanted anyway.

"You don't want them to see you this way." Blink. "You love them, though, and you want them to know you're going to miss them." Blink. Blink. "You want me to say good-bye for you."

Blink. Blink.

"Okay, my queen."

Then there was this weird pause.

Later, when he obsessively reviewed every single thing that happened, every hour that passed during the crisis, every nuance of the room and the people, every twitch of her face and each word he spoke to her, he would dwell on that moment. It was, he would suppose, rather like staring down the muzzle of a gun just before you got shot.

"I love you," he said. "I love you forever."

Tenderly, he stroked her face and prayed she could feel his touch. He didn't know whether she could or not; there was an alarming gray cast seeping into her skin.

Switching hands, so that his right one was grabbing hers, he patted around thin air, searching for—

iAm, as always, was right there, grabbing onto his palm with strength, steadying him.

He was not going to make it through this unless his brother was holding him up off the floor.

"Okay," Trez said to whoever was listening, "we're ready."

Manny went over to the IV line, a syringe filled with fluid in his hand. "The first shot is a sedative."

Trez sat forward on the chair he had been given. Putting his mouth right next to her ear, he said, "I'll love you forever. . . ."

He repeated the words until he wasn't sure how many times he'd said them. He just wanted them to be the last thing she heard.

"This is the final shot," someone said. Maybe it was Manny, maybe not.

Trez started saying his words faster. And faster.

"I love youforeverIloveyouforever. . . ."

Moments later, he stopped.

He wasn't sure how he knew it exactly.

But she was gone.

Sitting back, he looked into her still-open eyes. They were as beautiful as they had always been . . . there was no life in them, however.

That mystical spark that had animated her had gone out.

And her soul, no longer possessing a viable home, had left with it.

The silence and stillness of death was a void in and of

itself, a black hole that sucked everyone and everything around it in; and so powerful was the pull, the lives of others were halted, too, momentarily crippled by the tremendous, contagious force.

Trez put his face down on the exam table and released the two hands that had sustained him, hers and his brother's. Then he wrapped his arms around his love, and he wept over her with such grief that glass exploded all around the room, the doors of the steel cabinets splintering and falling free of their frames, even the screen on the computer and the segments of the medical chandelier above cracking into shards.

He had been preparing himself for this terrible moment ever since he had found her outside of the Sanctuary's cemetery, subconsciously bracing himself, trying on the grief as one would test how hot a stove burner was or how toxic a smell.

The reality was indescribably worse than he had predicted even in his most pessimistic moments.

In reality, he was just another piece of glass in the room.

Utterly shattered, beyond repair.

SIXTY-NINE

Well, now he knew what it was like to see someone you love get mowed down by a car, iAm thought as he watched his brother sob.

Trez's emotions had put the clinic into a deep freeze, the air so cold, breath came out of everyone's mouths in puffs and stripped whatever clothing they had on to metaphorical shreds. Glancing up, iAm noted that the three medical professionals were likewise *in extremis*, Manny rubbing his eyes with his thumbs, Ehlena taking a tissue out of the shirt pocket of her scrubs, Jane wiping her face with her palms.

iAm sat up on his knees and massaged his brother's back. He wasn't sure whether the contact was annoying or helping—more likely, it was a neither-here-nor-there that wasn't even noticed.

Eventually, Trez took a shuddering breath and eased back.

There was a table stand within iAm's reach, and on it, there was a stack of folded white and blue towels. Snagging one, he put it up toward his brother.

Trez was outside of any Kleenex capability at this point.

The guy scrubbed his face and took a number of deep breaths. Then he sat back in the chair he'd been using and stared ahead.

"I want to go through the preparations," he said hoarsely.

"You got it," iAm replied. As the medical staff gave a collective brows-up, he said to them, "I have everything he needs. I put it in the locker room a couple of days ago."

It had been something he'd done before he'd left to go to the Territory, just in case he didn't make it back.

Although that had been kind of stupid. If he'd been captured and held there, he wouldn't have been able to tell anyone where to find the shit.

"Is it okay for him to use this room?" iAm asked, even though it wasn't really a request.

"Absolutely," Jane said. "He can be assured of privacy."

"Thank you." iAm patted his brother's knee. "I'll be right back, okay. I'm going to go get the supplies."

"Thanks, man," Trez said dully.

iAm got to his feet, and as his knees cracked, he realized he'd spent quite a while crouched on the tile floor.

He couldn't bear to look at Selena. It was just too damn hard.

Going over to Manny, he hugged the guy in a manly way, and then gave Jane and Ehlena something gentler.

"Thanks for taking such good care of them."

Manny just shook his head. "Outcome would have been different if we'd been able to do that."

"Some things . . ." iAm shrugged. "There's nothing you can do."

Heading for the door, he pushed on the panel . . . and frowned as paint chips came off in his hands. Jesus, the steel had warped, the fit in the frame no longer right.

Outside, there wasn't, as the saying went, a dry eye in the house.

"What can we do?" the King asked, stepping forward and putting his palm out into thin air.

Approaching Wrath, iAm gave what was offered a shake, and then was surprised to find himself yanked in against that incredibly huge chest. For a moment, he allowed himself to sag into all the strength of the King's body, to the point where he was quite certain Wrath was holding him up off the floor.

But then he needed to pull it together. There were practicalities that had to be dealt with.

As he stepped back, the group of Chosen in their robes registered, and he felt a special kinship to them as a sibling himself.

"Trez is going to tell you later," he said, "but she wanted you to know she loved you so much. It was hard, at the end . . . she couldn't really communicate. The love for you all was there, though." He focused on Phury's yellow eyes. "And you, too."

"She was a female of great worth," the Primale said in the Old Language. *"A credit to her tradition and duties, and also an individual who mattered for her own special gifts. There is a place in the Fade open to her this night and e'ermore."*

iAm nodded, because he just couldn't bear to think that the female's life was just over. That one moment a person was in her body and then . . . *poof!* . . . she was gone as if she had never been, nothing but the translucent, ever-fading memories of others to testify that she had, in fact, been born and had lived.

"I have to get something for him. In the locker room." God, he felt like he was talking through molasses. "It's for our way of tending to . . ."

He left the rest of that one just dangling in the breeze.

As he passed by Tohr, he stopped. The male was white as a sheet and shaking in his shitkickers, his dark blue eyes pools of suffering.

"I'm so sorry," iAm found himself whispering.

"Jesus, why would you say that?" the Brother choked out.

"I don't know. I have no idea."

He hugged the male hard, and felt a deeper connection with him. Then he pulled back, squeezed Autumn's shoulder, and thought, Man, it was going to be a long couple of nights for the pair of them as Tohr processed his PTSD.

The Brother knew exactly where Trez was in this moment.

Rhage was the last of the lineup, and strangely, he seemed to be in the worst shape. At least his Mary was by his side.

"It's going to be okay," iAm lied.

The truth was, he didn't know what the fuck was going to happen next.

"You gotta give me something to do," Hollywood said around his gritted teeth. "I gotta . . . I gotta do something."

"You're here. That's enough."

iAm embraced the guy and then kept going to the entrance to the locker room. Pushing his way inside, he stilled and just breathed for a couple of moments. Then he proceeded to the lockers immediately on the right.

There were four Nike bags in four separate units, and he took them out one after another. Strapping two on either side, he hefted the heavy weights and squeezed back out through the door.

In the tradition of the Shadows, remains were cleansed with sacred minerals and purified water over and over again while a litany of prayers was said forward and backward. Then there was a wrapping process with fragrant cloth, followed by wax that had to be melted on.

He was about to pass by Rhage again when he stopped and frowned.

Looking at the Brother, he said, "What time is it?"

Rhage checked his phone. "Five in the morning."

"Actually, there is something you can do," he murmured. "At nightfall."

SEVENTY

As soon as the sun was safely under the horizon, Rhage was the first one out of the mansion. Leaving through the library's French doors, he stalked across the empty terrace, its iron furniture having been put in storage for winter. The pool had likewise been drained and covered, the umbrellas stored away, even the flower beds and the fruit trees had been battened down for the coming snow.

It seemed appropriate. Like the compound was in mourning along with the rest of them.

At his side, a Husqvarna 460 Rancher chain saw hung from his dagger hand, all ready and waiting.

The daylight hours had been torture, the strange neutral aftermath of the death coupled with everyone having to stay indoors turning the house into zombie land.

The good news was that he was finally free and he was going to get to cut things.

Striding down to the trees at the far edge of the lawn, he penetrated the line and proceeded to the twenty-foot-tall retaining wall that ran around the compound. There was a reinforced door about twenty yards over, and he went to the thing, entered a security code on a keypad, and waited for the chunking slide that meant the internal bar had retracted.

Pushing the weight open, he stepped out and left the door wide for his brothers as well as Beth, Xhex, Payne, and all the others.

The trees beyond were mostly pines, and in the moonlight, he assessed the sizes of the trunks. He was going to avoid the old growth and stick to the young'uns.

Firing up the saw, he smelled gas and oil, and he reveled in the power as he approached a conifer that was about a foot in diameter. The blade went through the bark and into the meat of the thing like a dagger through flesh, the cut as fast and clean as a surgical strike. And as the fluffy-headed pine landed with a bounce, he moved on to the next, revving up, slicing through, monitoring the landing so no one got hurt.

In his wake, Tohr picked up the first twenty-foot-long section and dragged it off to the opening in the retaining wall. Beth was next. Z. Payne. Butch. John Matthew and Xhex. Blay and Qhuinn. On and on they went, working like an assembly line, nobody saying a word.

None of them had bothered with coats or even work gloves.

The blood that was spilled on those trunks as palms were scratched was part of their tribute.

On the autumn night air, the sweet pine pitch smelled like incense.

Rehvenge had helped him with the planning during the day. In the *symphath* tradition, funeral pyres had two parts: a triangular base of nine nine-foot vertical posts that was topped by a sturdy platform made of nine six-foot lengths, and an upper portion that was constructed out of ninety-six logs, of which ninety were nine feet long and six were six feet long. For the top part, each of the nine-footers was set nine *zemuhs* apart—which was roughly nine inches—and the succeeding layers were set across the one below perpendicularly.

The goal was to ensure plenty of airflow and a bright fire.

So that was the way they were going to do it—because none of them knew any other alternative, and although neither Trez nor Selena was a *symphath*, everybody figured it was best to go with something that had been proven to work rather than run the risk of a homegrown solution that failed.

Upshot was, Rhage was going to fell about sixy-five twenty-foot-plus trees. Then they were going to strip the branches and the bark using a combination of daggers, saws, and other tools, and set the whole thing up on the flat stretch of lawn to the west of the house.

As he worked, with the saw jumping at each and every cut like it was a wild animal barely leashed, he kept going back to his own past with his Mary.

He had been there, right there, where Trez had sat at the bedside of his beloved. He had known that frigid fear and disbelief that life, with all its endless permutations, had come to such a point. He had gone home and undressed and knelt on diamonds that had cut into his knees ... and he had bowed his head to the only deity he had known and begged and pleaded for Mary to be saved.

And the Scribe Virgin had come unto him and provided him what he had asked for—but at a tremendous cost.

His Mary would be saved, but in exchange for the gift, she could not be with him. That was the payment for the incredible blessing, the balance to the miracle.

That pain had been a galaxy that had opened in his chest, an infinite wound that was so deep and of such a mortal nature, he had been surprised he had not started to bleed ...

Rhage watched as another tree fell to the side in a dead faint to the cold ground.

He knew exactly what Trez was feeling right now.

The difference? At his nightfall, some two years ago, after he had sworn to give her up so she could be saved from her disease ... his Mary had burst through his bedroom door alive and well, cured and saved, restored to health.

And able to unite with him.

It was the only sunshine he had known as an adult: Sure as if the roof above him had disappeared and the sun had risen just for him, warmth and light had shone down upon them both as he had held on to his female.

They had both been restored by the Scribe Virgin's mercy in that moment.

Later, he had learned that because Mary had been rendered infertile due to her earlier cancer treatments, the Scribe Virgin had decided that that was enough to balance the gift of everlife.

And so Mary and he were together to this day.

Trez had not been granted such a miracle.

Selena had not been saved.

It was Tohr and Wellsie all over again.

Even though Rhage wouldn't have admitted it to anyone, he didn't understand why he and his *shellan* had been spared. Especially given how the Scribe Virgin had cursed him with his beast earlier in his life for being so out of control.

And yet she had then seen fit to return his beloved to him.

Thanks to the mother of the race, his Mary was now free to exist without death until she chose differently—which would be when he went unto the Fade.

The fact that they had been spared ... seemed just as random as why Tohr and Trez had been condemned.

At least his brother had managed to go on.

He could only hope the same for that Shadow.

"Take this," iAm said to Fritz, "to my condo at the Commodore. Place it on the outside of the glass slider on the terrace."

"My pleasure, sire," the butler replied. Except then the *doggen*'s brows went up. "Is there aught else?"

"No."

As Fritz just stood there outside the exam room, looking confused, iAm couldn't figure out—

Oh. Right. He wasn't letting go of the note.

Forcing his hand to release its hold, he stepped back. "Thanks, man."

"If there is aught else you or your brother require, please call upon me. I would do anything to be of service, especially now."

The butler bowed low and then headed down the corridor, disappearing through the office's glass door.

iAm looked around even though he was still alone. His eyes just needed something to do, and in that regard, he understood why Rhage and the Brothers had been begging for a duty—also why the females of the house who were not out working in the forest had gone upstairs to help prepare a meal of ceremonial dishes traditionally served at mourning meals. And why the Chosen and the Primale had shut themselves into the gym to perform ancient rituals, the perfumed smoke from the sacred candles they were burning permeating the training center with a fragrance that was both dark and sweet.

It was such a hodgepodge of belief systems and traditions, all intermingling around the nucleus of grief.

His brother.

And so iAm waited here.

Sometime in the next three hours, the male was going to emerge, naked and dripping in his own blood.

The marking of a male mourner's chest and abdomen was the very last part of the preparation ritual for a departed female mate.

And as the next of kin to the sufferer, iAm was the one who was going to seal the wounds with salt, making them a forever-in-the-flesh kind of thing.

He jogged the heavy black velvet bag that was full of Morton's best in his hand. It was tied with a golden rope, and the weight was substantial.

In the back of his mind, he couldn't help looking to the other side of all of this. To nightfall on the following eve.

To the end of the s'Hisbe's mourning period.

For quite some time, he'd been mulling over that solution which involved a lifetime of travel. Any debt that had once been owed to Rehvenge had been discharged, and with Selena's death, Trez was arguably free to cash out of his businesses here in Caldwell and hit the road.

The Shadow Queen could not claim what she could not catch.

And that option was the smartest thing to do.

The problem now . . . was his thing with *maichen*.

iAm refocused on the closed door, imagining his brother wrapping up his beloved—and for a moment, he tried to picture Trez being in any shape to hit the road.

Probably not going to happen.

Shit. It was entirely possible that Trez was going to solve the situation for all of them.

By putting a gun to his head.

SEVENTY-ONE

Trez had no memory of being born.

But as he approached the door of the exam room, he felt as though the experience was coming back to him firsthand. After hours upon hours of nothing but pain, dogged by an exhaustion that was existential, he put his palm upon the cracked surface of the panel and realized that, even if there had been no tangible barrier between him and what was on the other side, stepping out was going to require a pushing, a forcing, a constriction that popped him free of the dense time capsule he'd been in.

Lifetimes separated the male he had been when he had come down here with Selena in his arms . . . and where he was now.

Lifetimes.

And similar to the womb, he couldn't stay here anymore.

There was one last duty he had to fulfill; not that he had had the strength for any of this.

"Selena," he whispered.

Her name spoken out of his dry lips was the key that unlocked the exodus . . . and out he arrived, into a world that was as new to him as it must have been when he had been birthed.

He was no more capable than he had been as a babe.

And similar to his birth . . . iAm was waiting for him.

His brother looked up so fast, the male knocked his head into the concrete wall he was leaning against. "Hey . . ."

Those dark eyes did a vertical sweep, and Trez glanced

down at himself. His black slacks were stained with his blood as well as candle wax and gauze fibers from the wrapping. His chest was a raw pattern of wounds. His free hand was matted with what was on those pants.

"Salt," Trez said. "Salt, we need . . ."

His voice was like a clarinet with a bad reed in the mouthpiece. Then again, he'd been talking to his queen for how many hours straight? So many prayers, and the odd thing had been the way they had come back to him . . . even though he had neither spoken nor heard the verses or the Shadow dialect in—

What was he doing out here again?

As iAm held up a black velvet bag, he thought, Oh, right.

It was so damn easy to let his Bojangles body fall to the floor, his knees absorbing an impact that must have been hard, but was something that didn't register.

Leaning his head back, he arched his sternum forward, the pattern of cuts that he'd dug into himself pulling wider, reopening so that the wounds began to weep blood anew.

"Are you ready?" iAm asked over him.

He made some sound that even to his ears could have been a yes or a no or . . . something else. But his ready position clearly spoke for itself.

Breath exploded out of his raw throat as the salt hissed out of the neck of that bag and hit him on the collarbones. The flow carried with it a stinging pain that was so great his heart skipped in his ribs and his lungs spasmed up—and yet he bore the sensations willingly, telling himself that it was in service to Selena.

After this, he would be forever marked for her.

It was, he supposed, what happened in a mating ceremony—only in his case, his female was no longer with him. And with that sacred joining ritual flipped on its head, it made sense that instead of great joy, he knew only crushing sorrow; instead of becoming one with her, he was marking his solitude without her.

When there was no more salt left in the bag, he stayed where he was, out of choice and necessity. The necessity part was that the muscles in his back and shoulders had seized up on him, maybe in solidarity with his female, more likely because he'd been bent over for the last ten—or was it fifteen?—hours straight. And as for the choice part? As much as he hated the rituals because they were like a loud, screaming *she's dead* in his head, he didn't want them to be over.

Each moment that passed, every minute under his belt in this new reality was a step away from her. And these small increments, with enough of them strung together, soon would turn into nights, which would become weeks and months . . . and that passage of time was the measure of his loss.

It was taking him away from her.

While he'd been caretaking her in the final way, part of his mind had been obsessively playing back everything. From that black-robed figure coming and finding him at his club, to him picking Selena up from the bright green grass of that other place, to them fighting for her life that first time she was here. And then the collapse upstairs in iAm's bedroom.

The first thing he was going to do, after the final part of all this was done, was race upstairs to see exactly where her knees had been on the carpet.

"Tell Fritz not to vacuum," he blurted.

"What?"

He forced his head level and opened his lids. "Tell Fritz—he can't vacuum your room."

"Okay." The word was said with the kind of calm-down someone would use to a jumper on a ledge. "All right."

Trez looked down at his chest. There were granules all over him, some white, some pink or red from his blood.

He prayed that the *doggen* hadn't been efficient about cleaning tonight. He just needed to remember exactly where it had happened. He needed to . . . remember the trip down to the clinic, and where the chair beside the exam table had been, and what he'd said to her. What the needle with the shots had looked like. How . . . everything had happened.

It wasn't out of some morbid fascination. It was more the conviction that he didn't want to lose anything of her.

Not one memory.

Struggling to his feet, he mumbled, "Need to build a—"

"It's done."

Trez shook his head and motioned with his hand. "No, no, listen. I need an ax . . . or saw . . ."

"Trez. Listen to me."

". . . and some gasoline or kerosene . . ."

"Here, why don't you give me that."

"What?" As his right wrist was gently captured by his brother, he frowned and looked down. He still had his dagger in his hand. "Oh."

He ordered his fist to release.

When nothing moved, he tried harder. "I can't let go."

"Turn your hand over." iAm pried the fingers loose one by one. "There you go."

As the male tucked the weapon into his belt at an angle, Trez tried to get his brain to work. "But I might need that for—"

"The Brothers and their females have taken care of the pyre."

Trez blinked. "They have?"

"They've been building it for the last three hours. It's all ready."

Swaying in his loafers, he closed his eyes and whispered, "How will I ever repay them."

"Here, put this jacket on, you must be freezing."

Rhage looked down at his Mary. "I'm sorry? What did you say?"

She held up a parka. "Rhage, it's thirty-two degrees out here. All you're wearing is a muscle shirt."

It wasn't that he doubted her, but he glanced at his bare arms. "Oh. Guess you're right."

"Let me put this on you."

He was very aware that she was treating him like he was a child, but somehow that was okay. And when she threaded one of his arms through a sleeve, and then wrapped the body of the coat around him, he let her do as she wished.

Coat. No coat.

Didn't matter to him.

His eyes drifted over to the pyre. It was higher than he'd anticipated, rising up like a small house off the flat section of lawn beyond the gardens and the pool. They'd had to construct a stair-like rise so that the top level could be reached, and after a discussion and following Rehvenge's advice, they had doused the base in gasoline.

Along with everyone else, he was standing upwind of things.

Quite a crowd, he reflected. Everyone who lived in the house. All of the servants. Also all of the Chosen.

"And I brought you some gloves," his Mary said.

As she reached for his hand, he shook his head. "I'll just bleed into the insides of them."

"It doesn't matter. You may already have frostbite."

"Is it that cold?" Wait, hadn't she already told him what temperature it was?

"Yes," she whispered. "It's unseasonably cold."

"Seems right. I don't think it should be warm . . . that wouldn't be . . . I think we should hurt, too."

Which was why he really would have preferred to be without the parka. But he was incapable of denying his *shellan*—

From out of the corner of his eye, he caught a flash of white.

As he twisted around, his breath caught in his throat. Trez had emerged from the same door they had all been using in the library; iAm was behind him.

And so the final walk began.

Carrying that which was so precious to him, the Shadow took step after step down the lawn, closing in on what they had been laboring over. Without any conversation, but through some kind of group-think, everybody who was assembled formed two lines, providing him with an aisle.

Trez was transformed, and not in a good way. Like someone who had been on a monthlong trek with insufficient food and water, he was a shrunken, exhausted echo of himself, his face hollow, his aura that of illness, even though he was not sick in a disease sort of way.

As he passed, Rhage shivered.

The makeshift stairs they'd built creaked as Trez went up them, but Rhage wasn't worried that the steps were going to fall apart. He and Tohr had tested them together a number of times.

And hold they did.

Silhouetted against the moonlit sky, Trez's dark shape blocked the stars that had come out for the evening, cutting a swath from the galaxy sure as if some god had taken a pair of scissors to the fabric of the universe.

Bending down, he placed her in the center. Then he stayed up top for a while, and Rhage could imagine he was arranging things. Saying a final good-bye.

It was good that that kind of stuff was out of sight, out of hearing. Some things, even in a supportive environment, were best left to privacy.

The torch they were going to use to light it all had come from the Tomb. V had flashed over to the *sanctum sanctorum* and taken one from the many that lined the great hall—which was yet another way to honor the Shadow and his loss. Tohr set the thing afire when Trez finally stretched up to his full height and backed down the slats, the flames leaping to life on its head, ready to spread further, undaunted by the cold wind that was blowing.

At the foot of the pyre, Trez accepted the torch and the two males spoke. In the flickering light, it was clear that Trez's chest had been brutally cut and sealed, and there was salt and blood and wax all down the front of his slacks.

Funny how the passage of time could be noted on something other than a clock or a calendar: The condition of that clothing and that flesh spoke about the hours the male had spent tending to his dead.

And then Tohr was falling back in line beside Autumn.

Trez stared at the pyre. Looked up to its top.

After a long moment, he went around to one of the points of the triangular base, leaned in and—

The fire took off as if it were a wild animal freed from a cage, racing over the gasoline pathways, finding its version of nutrition and commencing its meal.

Trez took a step back, the torch falling to his side as if he'd forgotten it still burned.

With a quick lunge, iAm stepped in and removed the thing, and just as he turned away, Trez began to shout.

As chalky wood smoke and orange sparks and fingers of fire cascaded into the night sky, Trez screamed in fury, his torso jutting forward on his hips, his legs sinking down as if he were about to throw himself into the heat.

Before he could think, Rhage jumped out of line and ran to the guy; iAm certainly couldn't, what with the torch in his hand. Locking his arms around the Shadow's pelvis, he picked Trez up and backed him away about ten feet.

Even with the wind still coming from behind them and carrying things off, the heat was tremendous.

Trez didn't seem to notice—not the fact that he had been

relocated, nor the reality that if the gusts shifted, he could still be incinerated.

He was just roaring at the pyre, his neck muscles sticking out, his chest pumping up and down, his body jacked forward against the iron bar of Rhage's hold.

There was no tracking the precise words, but there probably weren't any.

Sometimes language couldn't go far enough.

All you could do was scream.

SEVENTY-TWO

"**A**ctually ... I think I'd rather stay here."

As Paradise spoke, she looked up from her desk. Her father was standing in front of her, the report she'd just given him lowering down to his side as if he were stunned.

"But surely you should wish to return home."

There was no one in the waiting room—for that matter, there wasn't anybody in the house except for Vuchie and the other staff. Something had happened at the Brotherhood compound, and Wrath had canceled all appointments for the following several nights as he and the Brothers went into mourning. She knew no details, but whatever it was had happened suddenly.

She prayed it wasn't somebody dying in the war.

"I'm really ... happy here." That wasn't exactly true, but it was close enough. "I like having my own space."

Her father glanced around, and then brought over a chair. "Paradise."

Ah, yes. His "be serious, darling" voice. And usually, when he started off like that, she got sucked back into whatever seat she was sitting in, as if his *pater familias* tone held a centrifugal force enough to beat gravity.

Not tonight. "No," she said. "I'm not coming home."

Oh ... great. It turned out there was something even worse: the pain that flared in his eyes now.

She put her hands up to her face. "Please don't."

"I just ... I do not understand."

No, she imagined he didn't. "Father, I need something that's mine—and I'm not talking about a mate and young and a big house somewhere."

"There is no shame in having a family."

"And there should be no shame if a female wants a life of her own, either."

"Perhaps if you meet the right—"

She dropped her hands down onto the desktop, hitting the edge of her keyboard and making it jump. "I'm not interested in getting mated. Ever."

At that, he paled. Sure as if she'd told him she wanted to run out naked at noontime.

"Your presentation season is approaching."

"I have a job now."

There was a long period of silence, in which he measured her and she didn't waver. "Is this because we argued?" he asked.

"No."

"So what . . . has changed, Paradise?"

"I have."

Defeat curved her father's shoulders, and that was when she realized that as much as he was her *ghardian* according to the Old Laws, in fact, he couldn't force her to do anything.

Sadly, this was probably long overdue.

"Is it about the training center program?" he asked.

"Yes and no. It's about me making choices in my own life, instead of having things forced on me. I just . . . I want to be free."

Her father shook his head. "I suppose I am from a different generation."

Crossing her arms on the desk, she leaned into them and thought about what that civilian male had said, the one who'd come for the application—and told her his name, but refused to shake her hand.

The one she found herself looking for every time that front door opened.

"It's about safety, Father."

"I'm sorry?"

"Me wanting to take the training course. I think I would like to know how to defend myself. It doesn't mean that I'll end up downtown, fighting slayers. It does mean, though, that if something were to happen to me, I'd be a heck of a lot more prepared to deal with it."

"You are totally protected. Whether you are here or at home—"

"But what if I want to go other places?"

As the next wave of quiet hit, she knew where he was in his mind. Although he rarely said it out loud, it had always been clear to her that, among the many things the male missed about the passing of his beloved *shellan*, he wished that her *mahmen* could have partaken in awkward conversations like this. He seemed to assume that having a female intercede would yield more harmonious outcomes—a conclusion that was always available to him because it could never be vetted.

Maybe her *mahmen* would have helped him in moments like this. Maybe not.

There was a lot rolled into that sigh of his.

Beside her, the phone rang, and she went for the receiver on the first ring, because whatever was on the line would be easier to deal with than these kinds of family dynamics.

"Good evening," she said.

There was a slight pause, and then a male voice with a strange accent said in the Old Language, "*This is the audience house of Wrath, son of Wrath.*"

She frowned, and answered in the same way. "*Yes, it is. How may I help you?*"

"*It is located at eight sixteen Wallace Avenue.*"

As the male gave her the address, she looked at her father. "*How may I help you?*"

"*You may carry unto your King a message of import. If he does not surrender custody of the Shadow Anointed One, TrezLath, upon midnight on the morrow at the boundaries of the Territory, Her Most Sacred Soul, Queen Rashth, ruler of the s'Hisbe, shall construe the harboring of said male as a declaration of war against our people. She intends for the sacred mating to occur with the heir to the Shadow throne on the first night following her period of mourning. Compliance will spare all vampires much bloodshed. Failure to comply will ensure a scourge against your already beleaguered populace.*"

Click.

Removing the receiver from her ear, Paradise could only stare at the black plastic grip with its two square heads.

"Paradise?" her father said. "Whate'er was it?"

"Assuming that wasn't a hoax . . ." She lifted her eyes to his. "The Shadows are declaring war . . . on us."

SEVENTY-THREE

Sometime later, Trez became aware that he was no longer outside.

In fact, he was sitting on his bed up on the mansion's third floor, his palms on his knees, his body somehow still in motion, even though he was not moving.

After he'd stayed by the pyre until it had collapsed in on itself and the flames had died out, someone must have brought him up here.

Was that the sound of a shower?

iAm appeared in the doorway to the bathroom. "Let me help you."

"Isn't that what you always do," Trez mumbled.

"If the roles were reversed . . ."

As his brother approached, all Trez could do was stare up at the male as if iAm were a giant.

Emotions bubbled up through his exhaustion.

"You are," Trez said softly, "the very best male I have ever known."

iAm stopped short. Cleared his throat. "Ah . . . let's get those pants off you, okay? And before you say it, yes, I know you're not hungry, but I got you some food and, yes, some alcohol."

When iAm reached out a hand, Trez blinked and saw Selena's frozen in space, perpetually waiting for him to grab hold and save her.

Except he hadn't been able to.

Bowing his head, he was too tired to tear up, and the

sense that he was going to feel this bad for the rest of his natural life was like a suit of steel with spikes on the inside.

"Come on," iAm said in a voice that broke.

Trez took what had been offered to him out of reflex, neither caring about his dirty body nor his dirty pants nor the food.

But the booze ... now, that might help.

At the very least, he could pass out from it.

As they headed into the bath, his cell phone began to ring on the bedside table, and for a moment, he paused and thought, How strange.

Except that was normal, wasn't it. People called people when they wanted something, when they needed something, when they had news to share or just wanted to check in.

Remember, he said to himself. That was how it worked ...

The next time he had a conscious thought, it was as he was stepping naked under the shower.

Ow.

That was all he had.

Just ... *ow.* As all that water got into the wounds on his chest.

iAm was the one who leaned in and washed his hair and his body, even though the guy's shirt got soaking wet down the front and along the sleeves.

And then they were getting out and it was towel time.

At his next check-in, he was sitting up in bed with the covers folded at his waist and a lap tray of food next to him. iAm was on the edge of the mattress, his mouth moving.

With an odd displacement, Trez watched his brother from a distance, observing his elegant hand motions, his worried expression, his smart eyes.

"I'm going to be okay," Trez said as a lull presented itself.

He had no clue what his brother had been talking at, but he was pretty sure his welfare had been the topic.

"Will you do me a favor?" Trez asked as he glanced at the door across the way. "Will you thank ... everybody? For me? For what they did? I was so tired ... I didn't know how I was going to build it."

No reason to add a noun there. iAm knew what he was talking about.

"I will. Sure."

"And I want you to take a break."

"I'm sorry?"

"I'm not going anywhere. Not tonight." He flexed his hands and felt the soreness in his forearms, his shoulders. Wrapping all those bandages had required an exertion he'd been unaware of throwing into the job. "I'm too ... everything. I'm just too fucking everything."

iAm hit him with a pair of laser beams. "Are you sure? I was going to sleep in here with you."

"Thanks, but I could use the time alone. And before you say it, no, I'm not going to do anything stupid. You can take all my weapons."

"Would you believe I already have?"

An image of himself with that gun to his head the night Selena had first gotten sick came to mind. "Yes, I would."

Except there was at least one forty the guy wouldn't have found. Not unless he took apart the Jacuzzi.

iAm started to talk again and Trez watched him go, nodding at different places just because he didn't want to be rude. His mind had drifted off again, and before he knew it, his eyes were following that lead, rolling back in his head.

Next thing he knew, he was lying down flat.

iAm's voice came from up above, like God's or maybe a movie theater announcer's: "I'm leaving the light on."

As if he were four years old.

"Thank ..."

iAm stood over his brother as Trez passed out cold halfway through a thank-you. As a soft snore percolated out of the guy, he shook his head.

His brother was going to be like that for a while.

Glancing to the foot of the bed, he saw the pants that he'd removed on the floor, and he went over and picked them up. It was probably best that they weren't the first thing the male saw when he woke up—and iAm would have preferred to throw them away. The idea that they might be an important symbol of the death stopped him, however, and he settled for folding them up and putting them on a shelf in the closet.

He checked on Trez one more time. But short of pulling up a chair and watching the guy breathe for the next four or six or ten hours, there wasn't anything for him to do here.

Backing out of the room, he paused again in the doorway . . . and saw nothing that gave him any concern other than the fact that Trez looked dead already.

Yup. Nothing amiss.

Same ol' same-ol'.

God, he wanted to vomit.

Heading down to the second floor, he went over to the open doors of Wrath's study. All the Brothers and fighters were in there, some sitting, others pacing, a few leaning against walls.

They stopped talking and looked over at him.

He raised a hand in greeting. "Sorry to bother you all. Figured you'd want to know that he's crashed upstairs. He's so grateful for everything you did, and he asked me to let you know that."

There was some murmuring—but something was off. Way off.

"What's going on?" he said slowly.

Wrath spoke up from the ornate throne behind the ornate desk. "You mind coming in here for a minute and shutting the doors?"

So they'd been waiting for him.

"Ah, yeah. No problem."

When he'd closed them all in, he crossed his arms over his chest. "Tell me. And don't bullshit around whatever it is. I haven't the patience or the energy."

Wrath leveled those black sunglasses at him. "We received a phone call about a half an hour ago at the audience house."

"Okay."

"The individual did not identify themselves. They were, however, evidently from the s'Hisbe. Bottom line, either I turn over your brother at midnight tomorrow or the Queen is declaring war on not just myself and the Brothers, but vampires at large."

iAm closed his eyes.

He should have seen this coming. He really should have.

He just really could have used, like, ten minutes before the next drama bomb landed in front of him.

Letting out his breath, he muttered, "Son of a bitch—"

"But we're not giving him up."

iAm's lids popped wide. *"What?"*

Wrath braced his powerful arms on the desk and leaned in, baring his fangs. "I don't respond to threats. And we are prepared to go to war if that's what it comes down to—but whatever the outcome, I will *not* deliver that male anywhere. Period."

As a low growl vibrated through the air, iAm looked around.

He hadn't cried since the moment Selena had passed, not even when he'd walked out of the back of the house behind his brother to the pyre. It was as if, when the Chosen died, the electrical fuse to that part of him blew under the load that it was having to carry, the center of his chest going lights-out.

Now, though, as he met the steady, aggressive stares of the males in the room, the tears started to roll down his cheeks.

It appeared, after decades of being without a tribe, that he and his brother had found theirs.

These proud warriors, and their females, had adopted two orphans who had been out in the world on their own . . . and they were prepared to fight to the death to protect what was theirs.

Taking a shuddering breath, he pulled his shit together and shook his head at Wrath, even though the male couldn't see him. "I'm sorry, I can't let you do that—"

"Excuse me?" the King bit out. "I know you aren't trying to tell me my business."

"But Shadows are capable of . . ." He cleared his throat, not wanting to insult them. "You don't understand what my people can do."

They had tricks that regular vampires did not.

Wrath smiled with a blood thirst. "Maybe you haven't met my ally?" As the King swept his hand to the side, he pointed at Rehvenge. "Do I need to make introductions?"

Rehvenge's amethyst eyes were cold. "As the leader of my people, I am not without resources to call upon—and I assure you, we are more than capable of countering any attack that Queen brings."

The *symphaths*, iAm thought. Jesus . . .

Wrath glanced around the room. "She wants a war? I'll give her one—and I guarantee that a scorched-earth policy is going to look like a Sunday fucking dinner compared to what I'm prepared to do to her if she tries to take our boy."

At that, all iAm could do was stand there and blink like a dummy.

God. Damn.

It was enough to almost make him feel sorry for that female.

SEVENTY-FOUR

When iAm materialized on the terrace of the condo at the Commodore about twenty minutes later, he found that the note he'd told Fritz to bring over was still Scotch-taped to the glass. He peeled the thing off, saw that it had been opened and read, and put it away inside his leather jacket.

Then he opened things up, and turned on some lights with his mind.

As the illumination flared, he blinked until his eyes adjusted properly. The cold gusts coming in fluttered the drapes, and even tipped a throw pillow over on the sofa. He did not shut the slider behind himself as he entered.

Taking off his jacket, he paced around.

His conscience was not at peace. Not at all. To have found his tribe, only to have them go to war for him and his brother? That was too much to live with. Yeah, sure, the Brothers were all big boys, and specially trained, and armored up the ass—and they had the *symphaths* backing them.

But people were going to die.

That was the nature of weaponized conflict.

Whatever the other solution was, he had to find it. Fast—

"iAm?"

As *maichen's* voice registered, he wheeled around. "Oh, God, you're here."

Without giving the poor female so much as a hi-how're-ya, he went over and dragged her against him, holding her hard. Even through all the robing, he felt her body, her warmth, her soul, and he drank that in, taking from it the energy he needed.

Pulling back, he removed her hood and clasped her head, bringing her in for a kiss. "Thank God."

"iAm, what has happened?"

He took her hands urgently. "I need you to listen to me, and listen to me carefully. I want to take you somewhere safe."

"iAm, I can't go with you."

"The Territory is not safe."

She stilled. Frowned. "Whate'er do you speak of?"

Fucking hell, the last thing he needed was the reality that if he didn't take care of the no-win situation with the Queen properly, *maichen* was likely to get injured or killed: Nobody was going to be spared if there was a war with the s'Hisbe—and after talking to Wrath and Rehv, he knew both of those leaders were prepared to attack the Shadows where they lived.

At midnight tomorrow.

"Things are happening at very high levels. The palace isn't going to be secure enough—"

"Are we to be attacked? By whom?"

"I don't want to go into it."

She stepped back sharply. "What is wrong."

At that moment, a figure came in from the hallway, a massive figure robed in black.

"Well, well, this is a surprise," s'Ex drawled. *"Princess."*

After a moment of confusion, iAm glanced over his shoulder at the open slider, wondering if a fourth person had entered the condo. Considering the way the drama had been running lately? Yeah, the Queen's daughter absolutely could have shown up here for no good reason.

Things were *that* out-of-control.

"Have you not properly introduced yourself yet?" s'Ex said. "Would you like me to do the honors, Your Serene Highness?"

As iAm shook his head, he decided maybe there was another explanation: s'Ex had clearly lost his ever-fucking mind. "What the hell are you talking about?"

"You mean she hasn't told you?"

iAm looked back at *maichen*. "Told me what? She is a maid who took care of me."

"She is your brother's betrothed." The Queen's executioner came farther into the room, stalking them both. "And under palace law, I am now required to kill you, because you've seen her face." The male leaned in and dropped his voice to a stage whisper. "Although I'm thinking, considering the way you greeted her . . . that you've probably seen a lot more than that. Haven't you. Unless you want me to believe that she's meeting you here solely to pretend to do your laundry?"

Cold. Cold over his head, on his shoulders, across his chest, down to his feet.

iAm went instantly cold.

s'Ex was a lot of things, but one thing he rarely ever was . . . was angry. And the male was rip-shit pissed-off at the female who stood across the way from him, as if she'd put all of them into a situation that none of them were going to be able to handle.

If she'd actually been a maid? He wouldn't have cared. The servant class was not valued above their ability to perform functions—s'Ex might have ordered her back to the Territory and sent her for some punishment, but he wouldn't be this incensed.

Turning to *maichen*, iAm leveled his stare at her. In a perfectly calm voice, he said, "I am going to ask you once, and only once—and you are never going to get another chance to be honest with me. So take your goddamn time to think about what your answer to this question is going to be. Who. Are. You."

As he waited for her reply, he thought back to one particular thing she'd said. At the time he'd taken the meaning in an opposite way. Now? He feared she'd been hinting at her truth; he just hadn't realized it.

We're equal, you and I.

No, she'd said, *sadly we are not.*

Princess Catra vin SuLaneh etl MuLanen deh FonLerahn stared into iAm's eyes. Although his voice had been even to the point of relaxed, he was anything but. Fury seethed under his skin as he came to his own conclusion—and was obviously just waiting to see if she had the guts to reveal herself.

"Give us a moment," she said to the executioner.

"I don't think so, Princess."

"You will depart this room and wait out there"—she pointed to the open door—"until I call you back in here."

s'Ex's eyes narrowed, a flare of hatred glittering out at her. "Don't flex muscles you do not have, female."

"And I advise you not to test me. You will *not* enjoy the outcome—or survive it."

As she pegged him with a hard stare, s'Ex's upper lip curled back, but she did not care. He was a killer and a very potent male, but he was, and always would be, ruled by the traditions of the s'Hisbe. That was what was not understood about him—he had never once killed or maimed without provocation. And she had long suspected that he gave himself unto her mother not out of love, but to provide a stabilizing effect politically.

Few would guess the true role he played behind the scenes—but she knew it, because she had eavesdropped for all those years.

And yet in spite of the sway he held and the influence he had at the palace, he had never tried to overthrow or even diminish her mother in any fashion.

Instead, he had always upheld their ways. Protected them. Nurtured them.

"Go," she snapped.

With a curse, s'Ex turned and walked off. When he reached the slider, he muttered, "You have no idea what you're dealing with, iAm. Have fun."

Stepping out, he closed the door. And stayed exactly where she had ordered him to remain.

Closing her eyes, she tried to find the right words. She hadn't slept at all during the day, but had wrestled with her conscience for hours. And when she had come here earlier, she had been resolved: She was totally and completely in love with iAm.

And knew that it had been a terrible mistake to take things as far as she had.

It was time to tell him . . . before he touched her. After that, she would likely to be too lost once again.

Clearing her throat, she said, "I am—"

"Actually," iAm interrupted, "don't bother. That little act you just pulled with him is as much explanation as I need." He broke off and began to pace, dragging his hands over his head. "What the fuck were you thinking—"

"I did not mean for this to happen."

"Oh, come on, Princess, like you slipped and fell on my dick? We both know that's not what went down."

She frowned. "I do not quite understand that phrase, but given your tone, I must ask whether such crudeness is required—"

"Are you kidding me?" He threw his hands up. "You're *betrothed*. To my *brother*. And not only did you lie to me, you *fucked* me!"

Catra crossed her arms and glared at him. "Perhaps you would like to rephrase that to reflect the truth."

"So you're delusional as well as a liar? Great. Fabulous. What exactly are you disputing? Your lying or our fucking?"

"If I remember correctly, you were hardly taken advantage of by me. And that's what you're making it sound like." She jutted forward on her hips. "Indeed, I recall exactly how your voice sounded in my ear as you said my name."

He recoiled. Blinked a couple of times. Then he leaned in as well. "But that wasn't your name, was it. As far as I knew, I was laying with a maid, not the heir to the goddamn throne!"

"You *were* laying with me!" She struck her own chest. "I'm who you were with!"

"Bullshit! You don't think for a fucking moment that I would have made different choices if I'd known who you really were? Or are you so fucking selfish and stuck-up, Your Serene Highness, that you can't comprehend or care, for even a minute and a half, that there are repercussions when you lie about your identity and lose your virginity to the wrong fucking brother!"

"I didn't mean for it to go as far as it did!"

"That I believe," he countered grimly.

"iAm—"

"No." He put out both his palms. "Just—no. I'm not going to rehash this bullshit with you. I don't have the time or the interest."

"I was going to tell you. I know that I've put you in a horrible position—"

"My brother just lost his *shellan*," he snapped. "*That* is a problem. She died in front of him, and he spent most of the day and some of the night preparing her body for a goddamn funeral pyre. Then he got to watch her burn until there was nothing left but ashes on the cold ground. *That* shit is real. But, wait, the fun and games ain't over! To top it all off, I just learned that your mother, bitch that she is, is prepared to attack the only people who have *ever* tried to take care of me and Trez if he isn't delivered like an overnight package on her doorstep tomorrow at midnight. All so that he can have the very dubious honor and privilege of getting mated to the likes of you." As Catra gasped, he bit out, "So the fact that I had sex with you is so far down my list of priorities, it's not even on my radar screen. You just aren't that big a deal, Princess."

She was not going to cry.

No, she was not.

Even though her chest was screaming in pain, she would not crumble in front of him. She had brought this upon them both—and beyond the private strife, it appeared that real dangers for her people were imminent.

"I wanted to live," she heard herself say hoarsely. "For once, I wanted to live. And I was not going to get a second chance. You . . . you were the only opportunity I was going to get, and I was going to tell you tonight. I knew it wasn't fair. I'm very sorry."

Turning away from him, she went to the sliding glass door and opened things up.

"Time for me to come and join the lovebirds?" s'Ex muttered.

"Were you aware that my mother has issued a declaration of war against Wrath, son of Wrath? Over the Anointed One and our mating?"

The executioner grew very still, his robes flapping around him in the gusts. Meeting her eye, he shook his head gravely. "If that is true, that would not be advised."

SEVENTY-FIVE

Annnnnnnnd this was why people shouldn't get married in Vegas after knowing a person for only twenty-four hours, iAm thought.

As the female he'd assumed was just a maid, but had turned out to be the heir to the fucking throne, confronted her mother's executioner, he wanted to take the bridge. The only possible saving grace in the whole mess was that even though he'd managed to be the first lover of his brother's betrothed, at least Trez wasn't likely to be shattered.

Not because of that, at any rate.

Small comfort.

Wasn't life grand.

The good news? He wasn't going to have to be worried about any of this female shit again for a long while. After this experience? He was going back into the land of the left hand. Celibacy had worked for him thus far, and he was ready to re-embrace himself, so to speak.

s'Ex came in properly and shut the door behind him. "What is this about war?"

iAm rolled his eyes. "Don't try to tell me that the Queen has made the threat without you. You're the general of her army. Her enforcer. Give me a fucking break."

"I can assure you," s'Ex muttered as he whipped off his hood, "I would have told her no. We are capable warriors, especially my guards, and we have armaments that no one is aware of. That does not mean it is advisable to court the wrath of Wrath. His reputation over the centuries precedes him."

iAm looked at the guy. Under other circumstances, he would have been convinced that s'Ex was talking truth, but after having just been snowed by *maichen*—the Princess, rather—he was not as arrogant about his powers of perception anymore.

"They're not turning my brother over to your people," he said. Then he glanced at the Princess. "And they have the backing of the *symphaths*. It doesn't matter what you threaten or what you do, where you go or who you try to strong-arm, Wrath and the Brothers are *not* going to give him to you."

"You make it sound as if I want him." Her voice grew hoarse. "I do not. I shall take no male unto my body or my heart."

He shrugged. "That would be poetic. If you hadn't already proven how great a liar you can be."

The flare of pain in her eyes was something he refused to dwell on. Hell, for all he knew, she was just disappointed she'd gotten caught.

Jesus, if she had mated his brother, would she have expected these little rolls in bed to continue—

Stop it. Just cut the crap, he told his brain. Given the number of things he could legitimately beat himself over the head with, he really shouldn't be adding hypotheticals to the list.

"How did you find out about this?" s'Ex asked. "This declaration?"

iAm looked over at the male. "A call came in to the audience house. It was from an unidentified number on an untraceable line, but more to the point, as no one else in Caldwell knows about my brother's situation with the s'Hisbe—or the mourning period of the Queen—it had to be legit. There was too much inside information, and as for how they got the number? It's no big secret."

Interesting how he'd used the *they* there.

Yeah, he was beginning to feel vampire, not Shadow, regardless of his DNA. Then again, Wrath and the Brotherhood had offered him and his brother food, shelter, friendship, loyalty.

The s'Hisbe had only been full of demands and jails.

"When you go back there," iAm said, "you can tell them my brother and I aren't staying with the vampires anymore, and Wrath and the Brothers have no knowledge of where we have gone. We are going to disappear, and none of you"—he glared at the Princess—"will be able to find us."

Another bene of this royal reveal of hers?

The one thing that might have torn him up at the idea of leaving, the one tie he might have had to here, was now gone.

Leaving Caldwell, leaving the United States, getting good and gone and staying that way was probably going to be healthy for him.

Shit knew they had enough money to go for a century even if they never earned another penny. And although he would be sad to see the last of the King and the Brotherhood and that whole household, if it avoided war, he was prepared to leave them.

He and Trez were out of here.

For good.

As iAm went over to the sliding glass door, Catra had to yell at herself not to run after him. It all seemed like such a nightmare, everything about the evening.

He did not look back at her as he left.

And even though she could not blame him, she wanted to cry out.

Closing her eyes, she bowed her head and breathed into her palms.

"Do not tell me you fell in love with him," s'Ex said grimly.

Forcing herself to drop her hands and address the executioner, she met his eye. "Why were you here? You couldn't have been following me. I was careful."

He looked away. "I am not unfamiliar with this place."

"You have been here before?"

"You are not the only one who wishes to be free from time to time. Those two brothers owed me certain . . . favors, shall we say."

When he stopped there, she sensed there was pain in him. Deep pain. And she wondered if perhaps he had not been mourning his infant in this private place, mourning the loss that had been decreed by the stars.

Staring at the proud male, she found herself forming a kinship of sorts with him. She would ne'er have guessed he was unhappy or unfulfilled in his lot, and perhaps he was not. But he had had to sacrifice his own flesh and blood for the traditions . . . and for her mother.

Or been forced to, because of the stars.

"I am sorry," she said.

"Whate'er for?"

"You are well aware of what."

It was rare that a male such as he would duck eyes to avoid a stare, but he did that now. "I am unaware of what you speak."

Refocusing, she knew they had to leave, and for several reasons. She was very clear, however, that this would be the last time she stepped foot in this place that held such memories for her. Though she had known iAm for mere nights, it had been . . . a lifetime.

Departing from here was like closing the door on the one bright spark she had e'er had.

"Let us proceed," s'Ex said, as if he read her mind, sensed her emotions.

Without further conversation, they donned their hoods, went to the door, and stepped out. The wind was so strong and cold that it stole her breath away, and for a moment, she couldn't concentrate and dematerialize. Soon enough, however, she was off along with s'Ex, traveling to the Territory.

When they re-formed, it was in the forest to the rear of the retaining wall. In her maid's disguise, she would never have been allowed through the front entrance—

Something was wrong.

Several guards were clustered around the back entrance, talking with animation.

"Stay here," s'Ex ordered. "And don't argue with me."

"They won't know who I am."

"Unless someone figured out you left."

She had been careful, she thought.

Except . . . her mother was onto her, wasn't she.

s'Ex took a step forward. Stopped. Pivoted around and indicated to the left. "There's a secret panel about a quarter of a mile that way. I'll meet you there as soon as I can."

Catra frowned, and was curious when she had a sudden protective urge over s'Ex. The Queen's executioner was more than able to take care of himself, however.

Unless, of course, he was somehow found sneaking her back in. Then he was in mortal danger.

"I regret the position I have placed you in," she said.

"Regret is not a luxury you and I can afford. Go that way. I'll get you to your quarters somehow."

With that he strode off, not bothering to hide his footsteps. And at the sound of cracking sticks, the guards drew weapons, prepared to attack.

"'Tis I," s'Ex announced.

The fact that the guards did not relax made her worried.

"You are wanted," one of them said suspiciously. "The Princess is gone."

"I know. I have been out looking for her."

"AnsLai has been in search of you," another added.

"Then I shall go to him now and make my report." He dropped his voice to a threat. "Unless you are of a mind to attempt to prevent me access."

"The Princess is not in her quarters," a third repeated.

Catra swallowed hard. They still had not put their weapons away.

"Did you not hear that I have gone looking for her in the forest? She has been dressing as a maid. She could easily have gone out this way for a nocturnal stroll."

With subtle movements, s'Ex reached behind his back, his hand finding a flap in his robing and ducking inside. When he casually retracted his arm, the biggest serrated knife she had ever seen emerged with it.

And yet his voice continued calmly. "She has no food, no shelter, no weapons, and she is not capable of existing on her own. Where exactly do you think she would go? It is far more likely that she is within the Territory, or even in the palace itself."

"They said you helped her escape."

"Who says?"

"AnsLai."

Ah, yes, the high priest that was her mother's other right hand.

Could this be an attempted coup against the executioner?

"Who exactly do you think ordered me to go look for the Princess?" s'Ex asked. "Or are you telling me that the

Queen's command is not as powerful as a priest's? Is that what you would like me to carry back to your ruler? Because I will, along with your dead bodies."

Instantly, everything changed, the situation defused, the guards resheathing their weapons, s'Ex tucking his blade into the folds of his robe at his thigh.

A moment later, he was inside the walls.

Standing alone in the darkness, Catra wrapped her arms about herself and shivered. As the cold night enveloped her, and the enormity of what was happening sank in, all she heard was iAm's voice in her head:

My brother just lost his shellan.

She died in front of him, and he spent most of the day and some of the night preparing her body for a goddamn funeral pyre.

Then he got to watch her burn until there was nothing left but ashes on the cold ground.

I just learned that your mother is prepared to attack the only people who have ever tried to take care of me and Trez if he isn't delivered on her doorstep tomorrow at midnight.

For so long she had been in the shadows, a peripheral player to the true power of her people. As the heir to the throne, she was supposed to have no present influence.

That time had passed.

She had always respected the traditional ways. But having experienced heartbreak and loss personally? She couldn't let this continue.

iAm's hurt and anger had transformed her in a meaningful way. She had injured him, compromised him, lied to him. He was right; she had been selfish.

There had to be a way to stop all this. Stop the war. Allow Trez and iAm to be free. Let herself be ...

Well, if not free, then at least not a poison that infected others and ruined their lives—all because of some astrological record that didn't for one moment take into account personal choice, personal emotions, personal lives.

Walking off in the direction s'Ex had told her to go, she tried to be silent and stick to the thickest parts of the forest.

She wasn't sure exactly where the hidden panel was.

And had no idea what she was going to do if s'Ex didn't

show up. Or ... if he had a change of heart and, either through self-interest or self-survival, turned her over to her mother.

But after a lifetime of being proper, she was going down fighting.

SEVENTY-SIX

There were plans to be made.

As iAm took form in the back parking lot of Sal's Restaurant, he was all about the parachute. Checking his watch, he took note of the time—he had about twelve hours to get everything arranged before he and Trez could leave. Tickets he would get online. The SUV was already gassed up. Banks and lawyers opened at nine—although he'd been keeping things in good order on those fronts so he was going to be able to get seriously liquid very fast.

Xhex could take over shAdoWs and The Iron Mask if she wanted. If she didn't, they could leave those to Big Rob and Silent Tom. God knew those two bastards were co-owners by virtue of sweat equity alone. And Sal's?

Well, that was going to go to his head chef, Antonio diSenza. The guy was on the ball, good with the front of the house and the back. And he would treat the rest of the staff well.

All those transfers were what the lawyers were going to be for. At least he'd been smart enough to get Trez's power of attorney years ago, so he was going to be able to sign over everything without having to bother the guy.

And as for Trez himself?

The male was sound asleep; the text from Fritz had come through about ten minutes ago. The plan was to let the poor bastard rest for as long as possible. Then tell him they were going on a trip around the world.

If the way Trez had been in that bedroom of his was any

indication? He wasn't going to put up much fight. He'd been so out-of-it, iAm could have done open-heart surgery on him without putting him on a bypass machine.

Sooner or later that bubble of exhaustion and shock was going to wear off, and there was going to be some hard-core shit on the other side for sure. But they could cross that divide when they got there: First order of business was to secure the path out of Caldwell. Second was to get Trez moving. Third was to stay ghost.

As for the Brothers and the King? He was going to sign off to them all via text and leave his phone behind.

The Shadows could read minds if the situation called for it. If he left no trace and no way of being contacted? Then when Wrath told s'Ex or AnsLai or whomever from the s'Hisbe that he didn't know where they were and didn't help them escape? The truth was going to be verifiable and obvious.

That way the Brotherhood and the vampires would be safe.

Walking forward, he passed by the cars of the people he'd been working with for the last two years. Even though they were human, he was going to miss them—although not because he necessarily had deep personal relationships with them. It was more because he had enjoyed this stretch of his life. The cooking, the pretend stress, the demands.

Compared to what was really on his shoulders, it had been a nice relief, like going to see a movie when you needed a break.

Besides, here at Sal's? If there was shit wrong, he could always manage to fix it.

Opening up the rear door, he stopped. The urgent voices, the clattering, the heat, the smells . . . for a moment, he had to blink quickly.

"Chef!" someone said. "You're back!"

Instantly, people were coming at him, clapping his palms, talking at him, asking him questions.

God, I want to stay here, he thought.

As with so many nights, he changed train tracks in his head, stepping away from the Trez stuff to the things he wished he were free to think about all the time. The place was hopping during the after-hours cleanup, reports that their dining rooms had been full, and that a critic from *Food*

& Wine had come in for a four-top, being told to him over and over.

He wasn't going to inform them all about the change in ownership. He was just going to set it up and mail the papers in. And he was going to take care of the tax implications, too, so the title was free and clear.

Going over to the stove, he popped the top of the marinara pot and sniffed. Then he picked up the oregano container and added some. "I told you last week," he said to the sous-chef. "You need to watch the balance here."

"Yes, chef."

As he replaced the lid, he thought about how he'd imagined bringing *maichen* here. How in a rose-colored moment, when he'd pictured her settling in Caldwell and being with him, he'd seen them sitting in this kitchen on a Monday night, when the restaurant was closed, at a two-top over there where the *mise en place* stations were.

He'd gone so far as to plan the menu.

In a way, he and Trez were walking similar paths. He hadn't literally had his beloved die . . . but the female he'd fallen in love with wasn't on the planet anymore.

God, that really hurt.

And actually, maybe he needed to add one more thing to his pre-departure to-do list. After he checked on the two clubs, maybe it'd be a good idea to have a drink.

Yup. When it was time to go back to the mansion, what better way to spend what remained of the night than cozied up to a bottle of bourbon. It was probably the last time for a while that he was going to be able to unplug.

Plus he never got hangovers. So he'd be fresh as a daisy in the a.m.

It was the only benefit to being a Shadow that he'd ever found.

A quarter mile.

s'Ex had told her to go a quarter mile. Catra had no idea what that meant, but it had to be a long way. Or . . . not?

As she proceeded along, she went from tree to tree, taking cover behind trunks—which, she supposed, was rather stupid, and testament to s'Ex's point that she couldn't really take care of herself: An attack could very well come from the back, and even as she listened as hard as she could, the pounding of her heart was a loud snare drum that dulled her senses.

It would have been far better to spirit along the ground, assuming a Shadow state, but she was too scattered for that—and she didn't want to stop and waste time trying to concentrate—

Weeeeeeeeeeeeeeeeeeeeee-ooooooooooooooooooooooh.

Freezing at the high-pitched sound, she looked in a panic to the direction it had come from. A moment later, a figure stepped out into a shallow clearing.

It was a male servant.

A male servant who ... happened to be as extraordinarily tall and broad as s'Ex was.

Weeeeeeeeeeeeeeeeeeeee-ooooooooooooooooooooooooh.

As he made the sound again, she proceeded forward, lifting her skirts up. Breaking free of the thickest branches of pine, she prayed he was still on her side.

"Pardon the outfit," he muttered from under the gray hood of his *farshi* dress. "But I figured it's worked for you for how long?"

She was out of breath even though she had not run any distance at all. "Whate'er is happening?"

"It's not safe for you. There are guards everywhere, searching. Your mother knows you've left not just the palace, but the Territory, and she's ordered a public cleansing for you."

Catra closed her eyes. She had seen that horrific torture, a special acid introduced into the blood such that the "treated" writhed in pain and vomited for nights until they had rid themselves of whate'er impurities they had supposedly been contaminated with.

"You will not survive it," s'Ex said grimly. "Your only hope is to go back to Caldwell. We can find a place for you to stay—"

"No," she barked.

"Do not try to be a hero here. You're only going to lose."

"If I run, they're just going to make Trez mate someone else. The Queen will try for more young, and eventually she will have one. It doesn't save him."

s'Ex shook his head. "You don't need to worry about that male right now. Your life is over if you go anywhere near that palace. At least if you run, you've got a shot."

"But they'll find me. They'll never stop looking for me, you know that." She squared her shoulders. "There has to be another solution."

"No, there doesn't. Look, I'll help you. I'll do what I can—"

"Do not be a fool. You told those guards that the Queen sent you out looking for me. That was a lie. Sooner or later she finds out everything in the palace—she'll know that you were away from the Territory on the very night I disappeared. Even if you try to lie and say you weren't involved with my escape, she'll know. She'll have you tortured and killed for the treason of aiding and abetting me, and she'll dishonor your name."

s'Ex started talking, but Catra didn't hear anything of it. Her mind was churning, churning . . . churning.

Without warning, like something surfacing from the depths of dark waters, she remembered something the Queen had said:

I can have another of you if I wish. You are as replaceable as anything else in this world of mine. Never forget that I am the sun around which this galaxy spins, and I can alter your destiny with the blink of an eye.

Alter. Destiny.

A sudden horror grabbed her around the throat. "s'Ex . . . you must take me to the astrology room."

"*What?* Are you out of your mind? The idea is to stay away from AnsLai and the Chief Astrologer, not head directly for them."

She shook her head slowly. "No, they'll be in mourning with her. It's the last night. They've got to be with her to complete the rituals." She looked up at him. "I would go alone, but I might need to defend myself—I need your help to do that."

"What the hell do you think you're going to find in there?"

"Just take me there. *Please.*"

He cursed under his breath. "The palace is full of guards."

"Yes."

"It's not like we can just wander right into the most sacred part of your mother's compound."

"If it takes a minute or an hour or the rest of the night, it does not matter—so long as you get me there."

An eternity passed as he stared down at her. "You're going to get us killed."

She met his eyes through the mesh that covered her face. Shaking her head, she said, "We're already dead. And you know it."

SEVENTY-SEVEN

When Trez came awake, his face and his pillow were wet. Wiping his cheeks, he splayed his fingers out and looked at them glistening in the lamplight.

So.

This was the other side of it all.

Letting his arms flop back to the bed, he stared up at the ceiling. On some level, he couldn't believe he was still here. Physically and mentally.

Had his room always been so quiet?

Jesus, every time he took a deep breath, his chest hurt like he'd broken all his ribs. Twice apiece.

And then there was the movie reel of torture: With each blink of his lids, another part of the loss played across his retinas—and he had to wonder if maybe this was what had been going on in his sleep and why he'd woken up as he had.

Part of him wanted the incessant processing to stop. Another part was terrified that if it did, it would mean that that forgetting thing he was so worried about was already starting.

How long had he been asleep?

He stayed where he was for a minute or two—or maybe it was hours? Or nights?—and then he threw out an arm and patted around for his phone. When he called up the screen to read the time, there were tons of notifications about texts and missed calls and voice mails, but he didn't have the strength to go through them all.

Putting the cell back down, he realized the second he let go of the thing that the time hadn't registered.

Where was Selena? he wondered.

Addressing the ceiling, he said, "Are you up there?"

What had she seen? Was there a Fade?

Funny, he hadn't anticipated the fear he had now, but he probably should have. The idea that he didn't know whether she was okay or not after death was something he was going to have to live with.

Until he passed himself, he guessed. And then if it was just a big black void? Well, then he wouldn't exist to care.

Happy thought.

When he finally went to sit up, he gasped as pain exploded all over his body—sure as if the emotional agony in his soul had manifested itself in his flesh, his muscles stiff, his bones aching.

It was from the preparation ritual.

Maybe it would fade in a day or two.

He got up and used the bathroom. Brushed his teeth. Checked in with his stomach.

No, food was not a priority.

Drink might be good.

Yet even as those internal thoughts registered, it was from a distance, as if they were being yelled at him from across a football field.

Heading back out into his bedroom, he went over to the closet and opened the double doors. As the lights came on, he recoiled.

He could still smell her.

And two of her robes hung among his clothes.

Walking forward, he reached out to them, but ultimately hesitated to touch the folds of white fabric, especially as the raw wound behind his sternum flared up in pain again.

It was, he decided, kind of like a cut on your finger, one that didn't hurt until you flexed your thumb—and then the thing really stung. Except on a much grander scale, of course.

Was this what it was going to be like? Him going through his nights and days bumping into random things and getting jolted back into the depths of his grief?

"I don't know how to do this," he said to her clothes, "without you."

And he wasn't just talking about getting dressed.

When there was no reply—but come on, like he expected her ghost to answer?—he took the nearest pants and shirt that he got to, threw them on his body, and walked out. For a good ten minutes, he stood in the center of the room and entertained the temptation to trash everything around him. But his body didn't have the strength or the coordination, and his emotions couldn't sustain the boil of the anger he felt.

He looked over at the window Selena had broken. She had been magnificent in her fury, so alive, so . . .

Holy shit, he was going to drive himself insane.

On his way to the door, he picked up his cell phone out of habit and then stopped in front of the exit to his room. He was pretty sure he wasn't ready for pitying looks or prying questions. But he thought he'd seen that the shutters were still down?

Yup.

So hopefully the whole Last Meal thing would have been long cleaned up and the *doggen* retired for their brief rest before the daytime cleaning started up.

He thought he'd seen a seven in the time.

Yeah. Seven something o'clock in the morning, the numbers had said.

Grasping the brass doorknob, he felt like he was back downstairs at the clinic, when he'd gone to leave the examination room after all that time with Selena's body: this was another portal he was going to have to push himself through.

With a twist of the wrist, he released the mechanism and put some weight into the—

On the bald floor across from his bedroom, iAm was horizontal and out cold in the hallway, his head on the curl of his arm, a half-consumed, fully capped bourbon bottle cozied up to his chest like a loyal dog, his brows down like even in his sleep he was dealing with shit.

Trez took a deep breath.

It was good to know the male was still with him.

But he was not waking the guy up.

Stepping with care so he didn't disturb his brother, he found himself wanting to take this first trip out into the world on his own.

Down at the bottom of the shallow stairs, he did another

brace-yourself with a door latch—and wondered how long it was going to take to get himself over that habit—then he pushed things open.

". . . you bunch of photophobic freaks."

Shaking himself, he frowned.

Lassiter, the fallen angel, was in the doorway to Wrath's study, hands on his hips, blond-and-black hair pulled back in a braid. "You'd better show some fucking respect or I'm not going to say one damn thing about what I found out on my little trip to the Territory."

From inside the room, there were all kinds of muttering.

"No," Lassiter said, "I want you to say you're sorry, Vishous."

It was so weird. Like a camera lens that was suddenly focusing, Trez came back online, his senses sharpening, some shadow of his former self returning.

"I'm waiting." There was a pause. "Good enough. And I want the remote for the next week—days *and* nights."

Incredible grousing, and someone threw something at the guy, the coaster landing on the carpet outside the room.

"Well, if you're going to get nasty again—"

Following an instinct, Trez dematerialized—at the very instant Lassiter dropped the asshole act and shot a shrewd glance in the direction of where Trez had been standing.

His presence had been sensed.

But he would not allow that to happen again.

Shadowing along the carpet, he seeped into the study as Lassiter stepped inside, closed the doors and addressed the Brotherhood.

"We got a map?" the angel said.

Being careful to stay out of the way of anyone's feet, lest they tweak to his altered state, Trez pooled in the corner farthest away from Wrath's dog. Fortunately, George was sound asleep by his master's throne.

The Brotherhood clustered around Wrath's desk as Butch flipped a blue-and-green, three-foot-by-three-foot square of paper out of its folds.

"Here," the angel said, pointing with his forefinger. "This is where I found it. There's a retaining wall that runs around the entire property. Dwellings are here and here. The palace . . . right here. Security is tight, and from what I was able to see, they are gathering their forces."

Gathering forces? Trez thought.

"We need to get to them first," Wrath muttered. "First strike is critical. We don't want them coming into Caldwell."

What the *hell* was going on?

". . . can't find this house. No one can find this house," V said. "But yeah, I'll stay behind. I don't like it, but someone needs to be here on a just-in-case."

Lassiter looked across the desk at the Brother and proved that he could get serious if he had to: "I gotchu. I'll be here, too."

There was a split second where the males stared into each other's eyes. "Good," V said. "That's good."

"Where's iAm?" Wrath asked.

"Last I saw of him," Rhage answered, "he was heading upstairs to check on Trez and crash."

"We need to make sure he keeps Trez under this roof. I don't want that Shadow getting kidnapped in the middle of this. I'm happy to fight—shit, I'm looking forward to it—but I don't want them getting a hold of the poor bastard. That's a complication I don't want to have to worry about."

What the fuck?

This was all about *him*?

Trez stayed in that French study, with those Brothers and fighters, until he learned everything he needed to know—and then he had to get gone before Rehvenge arrived from having readied his people up north in the *symphath* colony.

His old friend the sin-eater would have known he was in there.

When it was time to go, he didn't take a chance. He shadowed out under the door and continued on down the grand staircase, across the foyer's mosaic floor . . . and out farther, passing through the minuscule gaps in the jambs of the vestibule's entrance and exit.

Outside, the sun was rising over the autumnal landscape, golden and pink rays hitting the yellow and orange and red leaves as well as the bristly dark green pine boughs and spiky cedar branches.

He did not reassume form until he was some distance away from the house, although the security cameras would no doubt register the appearance of his presence anyway. The good news, if you could call it that, was that the Brothers were all talking about the upcoming battle, so they weren't going to be going ADT on shit. And if one of the *doggen* happened to see him out here? They would just assume he was out for a walk to clear his head.

He hadn't put on a jacket, and he was glad.

The cold slapped him even further awake.

Even though it had been sinking in for a good hour, he still couldn't believe any of it: the Queen declaring war on Wrath and the Brotherhood. Their refusing to turn him over. The sin-eaters joining in on the side of the vampires.

He couldn't believe that there were so many prepared to rally to his cause.

"Selena?" he said, letting his head fall back so that he was looking at the heavens.

No stars because of the daylight.

No clouds, for that matter.

Nothing but pale blue.

Trez thought about that time he had tried to escape the palace and had ended up slaughtering all those guards in front of s'Ex. So much bloodshed.

Only back then, it had been strangers to him.

If he thought that had been bad, shit was going to be so much worse if the Brotherhood went into the Territory. They would ultimately prevail, with the sin-eaters at their backs ... but there would be death. Maiming.

More lives ruined.

Turning around, he looked up at the great gray mansion.

However dour the exterior of the manse was, the interior was full of life and love and family.

If this war went forward, where he was in his mourning, this terrible stretch of pain, was going to rain down upon this house and the people in it.

He would not put someone he hated in his shoes, living with this loneliness and heartache.

He could not put those he loved where he was.

Not if there were a way to stop it.

At the very moment he made his decision, a ray of sunlight broke across the rooftop, that incredible light spilling down over the orderly rows of slate.

Selena had made him swear he would live without her, and he had given her that vow, but only because she'd forced him to.

It wasn't as if he'd believed what he'd told her.

Now, though, as he imagined all the lives he could save, how he could protect these males and females and their young?

"This is as close as I can come, my queen," he said to the sky.

SEVENTY-EIGHT

It took them forever to get to the sacred astrology chamber.

Or at least it seemed that way to Catra. Then again, with every corner they turned, and each straightaway traveled down, she expected to get jumped, arrested, sent to a prison cell.

Along the way, s'Ex revealed to her hidden rooms and passageways she'd had no clue about—and proved himself to be capable beyond measure: sure of foot, fleet of mind, both careful and aggressive.

Finally, however, they not only gained access to the palace and its grounds, but the innermost restricted areas of her mother's compound where few were allowed and security was at its highest. They had one advantage, at least: The guards who were in search of her were preoccupied with looking on the exterior, convinced they had searched the Queen's domain sufficiently—and the rest of s'Ex's males were gathering in the center courtyard and preparing to fight.

It was a grim affair. The lot of it.

But they were able to move faster and with, thus far, no notice.

Part of her wanted to check to make sure her mother was following the rituals so that they would not be chanced upon in the astrology chamber, but there could be no risking a reveal of her presence.

They had one and only one chance to get to the records.

"Here," s'Ex whispered as he stopped abruptly.

She frowned under her hood. "The entrance to the chamber is up farther ahead, is it not."

"No, our entry is here."

Freeing his hand from his robing's voluminous sleeve, he placed his palm against the wall. Instantaneously, a pocket door slid open, disappearing into its slot.

The moment she smelled the incense, she knew they were close, and yet the space revealed was pitch-black.

She stepped in without hesitation, and felt s'Ex's looming weight come in behind her. When the door shut itself, she might as well have been blindfolded.

Keeping his voice down, s'Ex said, "Reach out ahead of you."

As she followed the command, she felt something rough.

"Walk to the left," he commanded. "Keep your hand on the wall to guide you."

When she did, she slammed right into his chest. "Sorry."

He turned her around. "Your other left."

Shuffling along, she could barely breathe. They must be going parallel to the corridor outside, she thought, this inner space a shadow of the outer, public one.

"I built these passages," he whispered. "I know them by heart."

"Very smart of you—"

"Stop."

Obeying him, she dropped her hand. "Now what."

"Look to your right."

At first, when she did, she saw nothing save more blackness. Except . . . no. There were tiny fissures of glowing red in the wall, as if some ghostly hand had drawn a pattern of dots with a mystical pen.

Tiles, she thought with awe. They were on the opposite side of a tiled partition.

Reaching her hand back out, she touched them.

"Let me go first," he said. "And do not come out until I say so."

Stepping aside so that he could trade places with her, she watched as his tremendous palm cut a swath into the subtle cubic pattern. . . .

When he pushed, the tiles broke apart on a seam that was uneven. Except nothing cracked or crumbled; there was no structural damage. It had been built to accommodate such access.

And beyond was a strange, overwhelming light source.

s'Ex walked forward into the circular chamber beyond with that serrated blade up in front of him, ready to attack.

"Clear," he hissed.

Taking a deep breath, she left the darkness for that amazing light.

Except it wasn't anything magical. It was normal candle-light, housed in a room of magnificent red marble.

Wait, no, the illumination wasn't from wicks. It was the sun, pouring through an immense, curved sheet of glass in the ceiling. And when it was nighttime, she reflected, one would be able to keenly observe and monitor the stars from the transparent oculus.

They moved in silence across the space, their soft-soled shoes lending themselves to muffled footfalls over the red marble flooring. In the center of the room, there was a circle cut in the floor, perhaps for a dais that lifted up like the one in the reception area at the palace? There was no furniture, no wall hangings, nothing that would impede one's devoted concentration.

More importantly, there was nobody else around.

Three doors. There were three doors . . . one that opened to the concourse. One that was probably the private resi-dence of the Chief Astrologer. And the other . . .

"The record room is through there," s'Ex said, pointing at that third door.

Denoted by its gold jamb, and the inscribed words above it, the sacred place could not be mistaken, and she felt a shimmer of awe even with the pressures of time and cir-cumstance dampening all her emotions.

Striding forward, she put her hand out—

"No. Your palm won't work."

s'Ex placed his on the correct spot on the smooth, un-marked panel and . . .

Nothing happened.

He tried again. "They've removed me from the com-puter. And chances are I've just set off an alarm." Turning to her, he said, "We have to get out of here. Now."

"No! I need to see—"

"We don't have time to argue." Grabbing her hand, he

began to drag her back across to the secret passageway. "I don't want your death on my conscience."

Yanking against his far superior strength, she blurted, "I think my mother has engineered the birth records!"

s'Ex froze. "What?"

Catra kept pulling against his hold and got nowhere. She might as well have been tied to a tree. "I can't be certain until I get in there. But I believe she may have deliberately altered birthing records to her own ends. I need to get in there to be sure. *Please.*"

s'Ex reached up and removed his headdress, and as he let it fall to the smooth red floor, his eyes narrowed and flashed peridot.

"How sure," he demanded.

"Willing to put my life on it. And yours."

His decision was announced as he looked at the locked door—and then, without making any fuss, he took two leaps toward it . . . and buried that serrated blade right into what turned out to be a seam.

Either that, or he simply made one.

Placing both hands on the knife's hilt, he put his tremendous weight to the side and *crack!* He made an entry into the small gold room.

"Make it fast," he said grimly.

Catra wasted no time. Running over the chips of stones, she jumped inside and slid on the gold floor, throwing her arms out to balance herself.

Numbers. She saw a thousand gold drawers marked by numbers.

It was all arranged by birth date, not name.

Closing her eyes, she cursed. She had no idea when Trez had been born.

Except, wait—up high on the right, there were two drawers that were not gold. They were white.

Heart pounding, hands shaking, she rose up on her tiptoes and pulled out the top one. The drawer was as deep as her arm, and she had to catch the back of it lest the contents spill out.

No, it had a lid.

Putting the thing down to the floor and opening the top, she found four rolled sheets of parchment, each tied with a ribbon of silk and sealed with red wax that bore the Queen's star. Other than that they were not labeled. One was smaller than the others.

She took out the first she came to and broke its seal, unrolling the document on the floor. It was so old, the parchment cracked in places and so resented the flattening, she needed to put a lip of the thing under the drawer and kneel on the other end to keep it flat so she could look the chart over.

Sacred symbols and writing in black pen were interspersed with countless red and gold dots that, when she leaned back, formed a constellation.

It was her mother's birth chart.

She let the thing curl up on itself and put it aside. The next ... was her chart, and it, too, resisted an awakening from its slumber. The third ...

The third unfurled itself as she released the bow and broke the seal, and as she leaned over to read it, she smelled the sweet scent of the fresh ink and paint that had been applied to the parchment. This brand-new chart was the infant's, and the ritual death was marked in each corner with black stars—showing that the soul had been returned to the heavens. Or at least that was her interpretation.

After a moment of sadness, she set the thing aside.

The fourth one, the smaller one, had to be Trez's. And indeed, when she unfolded it, she was right. For one, in the scribing, there were notations that it was a male, and born with a twin—it was this momentous birthing occasion that had first sparked interest in Trez and iAm. Catra could remember all her life palace staff remarking about the unusual and special occurrence.

His chart was not as big as the other three because he was not a royal, but in the corners of the parchment there were golden stars, showing an ascension to the heights of the Shadow court.

Sitting back on her heels, she read through its notations and symbols.

Then shook her head.

She had been so sure ... and yet nothing seemed amiss.

"Stand down," she heard s'Ex say out in the circular room. "Or, as much as it pains me, I shall have to kill you all."

Wrenching around, Catra looked through the messy portal s'Ex had made for her.

Three guards, dressed in black, had surrounded the executioner, and they had their knives out.

Oh, stars above . . . what had she done?

She had made a terrible mistake coming here. What arrogance to think she had ascertained some secret that would save them all.

And now, there was nowhere to run. No way to win against what was surely just the first squadron of many that had been sent for them.

She did not want to die.

Reaching forward, she picked up the long, thin, heavy drawer. It was the only weapon she had—

For some reason—and later she would wonder exactly why—as Trez's chart rolled up on itself, resuming the shape it had been trained to prefer, she looked down at the thing.

The floor had been perfectly clean as she had entered, no dust marring its surface, no scuffs, no scratches.

But now there were chips of . . . paint . . . and little flakes . . . around where the chart had rolled itself up.

Frowning, she put the drawer aside and flattened the parchment back out.

As the sounds of fighting commenced in the gazing room, folds of robes flapping, grunts and groans sounding so very loud and close, she leaned over the sacred writing.

In the center of the chart, a portion of the paint had chipped off.

Revealing . . .

The exhale that left her mouth was the result of her ribs seizing up.

And to make sure she was not imagining things, she re-read what she thought she was seeing.

Then she took her fingernail and flicked it under the cover-up that had been executed.

"Oh . . . Fates . . ." she breathed.

Scrambling to her feet, she raced over to the boxes where the charts of the subjects of the s'Hisbe were kept. Her eyes bounced around, searching for the right birth number, and when she found that drawer, she slid it out, put it on the floor, and lifted the lid.

The civilian records were tied with strings that had little tags on them, and they were in no particular order, some twenty different scrolls shoved in together. With her breath panting out of her mouth, and her hands shaking, she rifled through them as quickly as she could.

When she found the one she was looking for, she rushed back to the doctored document.

Putting them side by side, with the drawer at the very top, she stretched them out.

Sure enough, there was a patch in the center of the second one, the area of cover-up painted in with such care that the doctoring wouldn't have been noticed at the time. It had, however, aged badly over the course of the years.

Chipping it free, she found . . . that in fact . . . the Anointed One was not Trez.

Of the pair of twins, he had been born second, not first.

It was iAm who was the sacred male.

In spite of the mortal danger outside, she slumped over the records, putting her hands to her face.

Why had they switched them? Why—

"Princess," s'Ex barked. "We need to get out of here—"

"She switched the records."

"What?"

Catra looked at him over her shoulder, and recoiled at the amount of blood on his sleeves, his robes, his face, and hands. But there was no time to get rattled. "The Queen switched the records of the infants, of Trez and iAm. I don't know why, though." She pointed to the doctored parts of the charts. "It's right here. The Chief Astrologer is the one who prepares the most sacred charts for royalty, not the Tretary. So he must have done this, and AnsLai had to have known. But what's the benefit—

"Behind you!" she screamed.

Just as the guard who had appeared at s'Ex's back raised a knife over his head, the executioner wheeled around— with his own blade at throat height. Within the blink of an eye, s'Ex overpowered the guard by slitting the male's jugular open, red blood splashing out.

Horrified by the sight of the death, Catra could feel her mind departing, sure as a spectator might retreat at a fighting contest that had turned too violent.

But, as with what s'Ex said about regrets, she didn't have that kind of luxury.

Rolling up the charts, she put Trez's and iAm's in with

hers and her mother's in the box. s'Ex's infant daughter's was still on the floor—and she nearly left it behind.

At the last minute, however, she reached over and began to roll it up—and that was when she felt an odd cool spot. In the center.

Why would parchment be cool?

She flattened the chart out again . . . and ran her fingertips over the surface. When she got to the middle, there was a subtle change of temperature.

Because a thickened area of paint was still drying.

That was the source of the sweet smell.

They had doctored the infant's as well.

"Time's up, Princess," s'Ex said with urgency. "We—"

"Give me your knife."

"What?"

"Clean it off and give me your knife," she commanded, putting out her hand.

SEVENTY-NINE

The last thing Trez did before dematerializing away from the Brotherhood mansion was take out his phone. He texted his brother just four words.

I am at peace.

And then he walked back over to the front steps and placed the cell down on the cold stone.

A moment later, he was gone. He didn't look back at the house ... didn't hesitate ... didn't have any misgiving.

The fight was over. The long stretch of struggle that had defined his life had reached its conclusion.

When he re-formed, it was before the great gates of the s'Hisbe.

Walking forward, he knew that he would be instantly spotted on the security cameras, and he was right. Without his having to make any announcement at the check-in telephone that was for the benefit of humans, there was a clinking and a break in the center of the entrance's two solid panels.

For the first time in so many years, he put his feet back on the soil of his people, striding over the divide that he was prepared to never resurface from.

The guards gasped as they recognized him, and he was immediately surrounded by a circle of black-robed males. They didn't touch him, though. They were prohibited from coming into contact with his sacred body.

And, indeed, there was no need to strong-arm him. He was here of his own free will.

He was but a false gift to the traditions, however.

His body was no more capable of mating with a female than was a eunuch's. He was dead from the waist down in that regard, so whatever dynastic hopes the Queen might have were not going to go well for her.

He did not care. They could do to him as they wished.

What he was coming to realize was that Selena had taken him with her. His soul had left sure as hers had—the only difference being that his body had yet to lie down and stop its functioning.

But maybe the Queen would take care of that for him.

When it became obvious that he was unable to perform, she probably was going to have him killed.

Whatever.

All he knew, all he cared about, was that his brother was now free of the burdens that had long weighed him down, and the Brotherhood and their families were safe.

That was all that mattered.

Along the way to the palace, he found himself removing his clothing, unbuttoning his shirt and letting it fall to the ground. Kicking off his shoes. Shedding his pants.

He was naked in the cold autumn sunlight as they came up to the palace doors.

AnsLai, the high priest, was waiting for him. And although the male's head was hooded, he wore no mesh over his face, so his satisfaction was evident.

"What a fine decision you have come to," the male intoned, bowing at his waist. "I commend you for your level head and your devotion, although perhaps late in its manifest, to your duty."

At that, the great white marble-faced entrance split in half and revealed a white corridor that, as Trez stared down it, seemed to go on for eternity.

For a moment, he thought of Selena and him embracing in the training center's underground tunnel, holding on to each other.

That infinity he had spoken of, that he'd had with her, was still in him.

And it was going to have to sustain him through whatever came next.

The guards in front of him parted and he went forward, placing bare foot after bare foot upon the shallow steps.

As he came up to AnsLai, the high priest bowed again. "And now we must proceed unto your cleansing."

"Take this one instead, you'll have better luck with it."

Instead of giving Catra the knife she'd asked for, the executioner handed over to her a smaller one, with a smooth blade.

Leaning back down over the infant's chart, she worked quickly, taking the razor-sharp point and trying to find a fissure or a seam under the added paint.

"We need to do this somewhere else, Princess," he said. "We need—shit, stay here."

She barely noticed as he left, her concentration consumed by the delicate operation she was performing. If she went too quickly or dug too much, she was liable to wreck what was underneath....

At last, she got the patch loosened, and then off altogether.

Fortunately, the ink that had been used first had stained the parchment, sinking into the very fiber of the paper.

Closing her eyes, she swayed.

They had doctored the infant's as well.

The newborn had been the rightful heir to the throne according to the stars.

As the implications sank in, Catra opened her lids and looked over her shoulder. s'Ex had his back to her and was struggling with someone—or, rather, someone was struggling against the executioner's hold.

When s'Ex turned around, the Chief Astrologer, in his red robing, was up against that enormous body, locked in a grip that was so tight, she could hear the labored breathing under that ceremonial hood.

With a hard yank, s'Ex ripped off what covered the male's head. Beneath the folds, the Astrologer was terrified—and the fear got even worse as he put two and two together and clearly concluded he was looking at a female no one was supposed to see.

"Yes, I have to kill you now that you've seen the Princess," s'Ex said. "But first, some answers."

Catra glanced back down at the charts and thought ... what she had found here was something her mother's adviser should be even more scared of.

As soon as s'Ex found out . . .

"Shall we tell him what you've discovered," s'Ex said, dragging the smaller male with him. "Shall we ask him why the charts have been altered?"

Catra stared up at the executioner.

Something in her face must have betrayed her emotions, because s'Ex frowned. "Why are you looking at me like that?"

Absently, she noted that the executioner's gray disguise was stained with even more blood. He had not hesitated to do away with any of the males who had sought to attack, in spite of the fact that he had trained them, worked with them, no doubt found a kinship with them.

If she revealed this part of what she'd found?

Well, if she did, then, in addition to this Chief Astrologer and no doubt AnsLai, the Queen . . . Catra's mother . . . the female responsible for leading the s'Hisbe . . . was going to die.

And Catra felt . . .

She actually felt nothing.

Then again, the female was her leader, not her parent — and the Queen had violated the traditions to her own ends.

It was the only explanation, especially given what the female had said in the ritual chamber.

Catra spoke up to the Chief Astrologer. "These charts have been doctored. I assume you did it."

The male had turned his head away so as not to see her, but s'Ex was having none of that. He bit his serrated blade, holding the weapon between his teeth, and clapped his now-free palm on that skull, wrenched the thing around by the jaw.

Then he spoke around the steel. "The Princess asked you a question. I suggest you answer it."

When there was only a gaping mouth and no words, s'Ex looked at her. "Shut your eyes."

She shook her head. "Do what you must. I shall be fine."

s'Ex cursed, but then he gripped the Astrologer's gloved hand and squeezed it so hard the male moaned . . . and then jerked and screamed as bones were broken.

Then s'Ex took the dagger from his lips and placed it back against that throat. "Now, answer the question—"

"Yes! I changed the charts!" the male shouted. "I

changed the charts! I did not desire to do so, but the Queen demanded it of me! I was sworn to secrecy!"

"Does AnsLai know?" Catra asked.

"No! He does not! No one knows!"

The explosion of speech seemed as much due to the threats he was facing as the purging of a conscience that had long been troubled.

"I did not wish for this!" The male began to weep. "It is a violation of my sacred position, but she told me she would kill all of my bloodline—she said she would kill my mate, my young . . . my parents. . . ."

"Why switch the charts for TrezLath and his brother? I don't understand why it was necessary to change one for another."

"The true Anointed One, the infant born first of its mother's womb, iAm, was sickly. He was not expected to live past the night, much less survive into adulthood. The Queen wanted one of the sacred twins for you, Your Holiness, so she ordered me to change the chart to the second son, who was hearty and strong. That was the reason."

Catra took a deep breath.

In the silence that followed, she knew that what she said next was going to change everything. Violently.

She swung her eyes back to s'Ex's. The executioner was preternaturally still, his huge body exuding a calm that she had a feeling was like that before a storm.

In an utterly level voice, he said, "Tell me."

As if he might already know.

She turned back to the chart, rolled it up, and placed it in the heavy gold box with the others. Then she got to her feet and approached the executioner and the male.

"Give me the knife," she said again to s'Ex. For a different reason this time.

"Why."

"Because we need him alive."

She expected him to argue, and was shocked when s'Ex flipped the weapon around and handed it to her hilt-first without comment.

It weighed almost as much as the box.

"Now let him go. You have to let him go," she said. "He's not going to run off, because I am the only one who can save his life. Release him, s'Ex. I am commanding you to do so."

When the executioner complied with the order, the Chief Astrologer dropped to the ground as if he were no more than a bolt of cloth. And he was smart. He dragged himself a number of feet away.

Locking eyes with s'Ex, she said loudly and clearly, "Now, Astrologer, tell him why his daughter's chart was changed."

EIGHTY

The phone was ringing.

As Paradise sat up against the giant bed's head-board, she shifted her eyes over to the subtle chiming sound across the way on the desk.

At least answering it would give her something to do, other than sit here in this subterranean suite and stew over what might be happening at nightfall.

Her father had been absolutely livid that she had still refused to go home with him, even in light of the threat against all vampires by the s'Hisbe. But she'd felt like she had to stand up for herself, in spite of the change of circumstance. If she caved? It was like running the clock of her life backward.

And she'd stuck to her guns even when he had reminded her, not that it was necessary, that he'd already lost her *mahmen* and did not want to have her go over unto death's cold embrace, too.

As she had uttered her last and final "Not going," he had stared at her as if she were a stranger.

And perhaps she was.

Riiiiiiing.

Maybe it was her father. She couldn't imagine he had found any rest, either. Although he would probably have tried to text or call her cell.

Shifting her legs off the edge of the mattress, she jumped down and jogged to the phone.

Picking up the receiver, she said, "Good morning, how may I help you?"

It was a male voice, but not that of her blooded sire. It was the one who had called before from the s'Hisbe, the one who had issued the decree of war in that strangely accented tone: *"I have a message for your King, Wrath, son of Wrath. The Queen wishes to thank him for the swift return of the Anointed One. Wrath's compliance is that of a wise leader and statesmale, and it is my pleasure to reassure him that no military action shall be taken by us and that there is accord, once more, between our peoples."*

Click.

Paradise looked at the phone.

Had she gotten that right?

Punching her finger into the two buttons on the cradle, she cleared the line, and when the dial tone came back on, she tapped out her father's number on the buttons. Or tried to. She was shaking so badly, she couldn't get the sequence of digits right.

When things finally rang through, she found herself breathing hard.

"Hello—"

"Father!" she cut in. "Father, they called again—"

"Paradise! Are you safe—"

"Yes, yes, you have to listen to me! They called again, the s'Hisbe—they said Wrath returned the . . ." What was it? ". . . the Anointed One? They said everything was okay—I mean, they called off the war!"

Stupid way of putting it, she thought in the back of her head. Like the thing had been a birthday party canceled because of bad weather?

"Whate'er speak you of?" her father said slowly. "Wrath was not going to give Trez up."

"He must have changed his mind?"

"I spoke with him at dawn. The Brotherhood had sent out a day-faring emissary to gather intelligence on the Territory. Whate'er has . . . I shall have to call him at once."

"Will you try to let me know what happens?"

"I shall."

"I love you," she blurted.

"Oh, Paradise, I love you, too. Stay underground."

"I promise."

As she hung up the phone, she found herself praying she got the chance to apologize in person to him. Although she supposed that impulse was just her inner four-year-old wanting to be a good girl.

No matter the outcome of the conflict with the Shadows, she had to stand firm.

The threat of war was a good reminder that you only had one life to live.

So you'd better make it count.

As s'Ex met the unwavering stare of the Princess, he decided she was very smart to disarm him and get the Chief Astrologer away from his reach before he got the answer she had prompted from the male.

But the explanation was unnecessary; he knew the "why" of the chart's alteration.

The Astrologer stumbled through his words. "The infant was the rightful heir, supplanting you, Princess. But the Queen did not want a commoner's bloodline on the throne. She knew that her executioner was the sire. She forced me to change the time of birth by four minutes, thirty-two seconds—which would place the young under a disadvantageous positioning of the sixth planet from the sun."

At once, the sound of his daughter's plaintive cry ran through s'Ex's mind . . . and then entered his bloodstream.

His chest began to pump with hard breath.

His fists curled up.

His heart skipped a beat . . . and then settled into the slow, steady beat of a killer.

The Princess held out his blade to him. Her eyes were full of sorrow, but they were also very, very clear. In a voice that shook, but had strength in it, she spoke four words.

"Do what you must."

She knew she had just sentenced her mother to death. By this truth coming to light, he would not hesitate to avenge the murder of his blood.

With his war hand, he accepted the serrated blade—and tilted the tip toward his face. With two quick streaks down the hollows of his cheeks, he marked himself.

Once for his daughter whom he would never know.

Once for the wrong he was going to rectify.

As he turned for the break in the tiled partition, he was single-minded—and yet he stopped.

Cranking his head over his shoulder, he pegged the

Chief Astrologer with his stare. As the male shrank back in mortal terror, s'Ex said, "If my daughter was to be the heir, who succeeds the Queen now?"

"Sh-sh-sh-she d-d-d-does." The male pointed to the Princess. "She has rightful claim to the throne. Her records have not been altered. She would have been second in line after your daughter, and with the death, she is the legitimate heir—"

"The *murder*," he cut in, "of my daughter, you mean."

He glanced at the Princess.

She didn't seem to care about the repercussions of what had just been said. She didn't even appear to have heard the words that she was about to become Queen. Instead, she was cradling that long, thin gold box to the chest of her maid's disguise, her head bowed.

Tears hit the brilliant yellow metal, falling from her eyes.

"You must rule," s'Ex announced. "You must take the reins of this community and rule it properly. Do you hear me? Snap out of this emotion, and get ready for what is about to happen."

Her stare shifted up to his. "She was my sister. They killed . . . my sister."

For a moment, s'Ex recoiled. It was the last thing in the world he expected her to say.

And abruptly, the reality that his grief was shared hit him, and he was strangely touched.

Walking over to the Princess, he cupped her face and lifted it unto his own. After wiping away her cheeks, he bent down and pressed his lips to her forehead.

"Thank you for that," he whispered.

"What?"

He just shook his head and stepped back. "You." He pointed to the Chief Astrologer. "You need to take care of her. You believe in your traditions, you hated your lies? Prove it by making sure she survives—in about ten minutes she is going to be your Queen."

Instantly, the male shuffled around on the floor, prostrating himself and putting his forehead to the bloodied red marble at the female's feet. *"By all that is written in the stars, I shall serve Queen Catra vin SuLaneh etl MuLanen deh FonLerahn until the final beat of my heart and the last breath of my lungs."*

s'Ex sensed the sincerity, and knew that the new Queen was going to be safe. "You have the ceremonial garb in here, do you not?"

The Chief Astrologer answered at the floor. "I do."

"Get her dressed. In twenty minutes, her mother's head is going to be at the foot of the throne. Bring Catra there so that the change-of-power ceremony can be completed."

"What about you?" Catra said. "You'll be there, too? Please tell me you'll be there."

"Worry about yourself, my Queen. You are so much more important than any one individual in this room, this palace, this land."

With that, he turned and disappeared into the hidden passageway.

EIGHTY-ONE

The cleaning and preservation of a warrior's weapons were a sacred duty, a way of honoring the connection between the fighter and his tools.

As Rhage sat with his head bent over the second of his two favorite forties, the sweet scent of metallurgical detergent was as familiar as the sound of his own voice.

Across the bedroom, he could feel his Mary's tension. But she did not say a word.

"I'll be careful," he told her, putting the spray can back in his gun cleaning box. "I promise . . . I'll be really careful."

He gave the vow even though he knew that personal discretion was only part of surviving a battle. Being aware of your surroundings, watching your back, having your brothers watch out for you as well—all of that helped, sure. There would always be the element of luck, however.

Or destiny.

Fate.

Whatever you wanted to call it.

"I know you will," she said tightly.

He brought the chamois square up one side of the barrel and down the other. "If I don't . . . come home, though."

He stopped there. She was going to know the question he was asking. He'd given her enough to go on.

"I'll find you," she choked out. "I'll find you somehow."

He nodded—and thought he probably should go over to her, but he couldn't handle the closeness. As it was, he was on the thin edge of falling apart, and with a flat-out war waiting for him at nightfall, he just couldn't afford the emotion.

"I simply can't bear the thought of you getting hurt," she said as she blew her nose with a tissue and blotted at her eyes. "That bothers me almost more than the dying."

Well, yeah, because they had been granted that miracle—which would pay dividends when death tried to separate them.

He thought of Trez and wanted to vomit.

God . . . the sight of that male mounting that fucking funeral pyre was a tattoo on his brain.

Abruptly, he dropped his gun and his cloth to his knees. "I'm a horrible person. I'm a really horrible fucking asshole."

Across the way, Mary sniffled again. "What are you talking about?"

He forced himself to resume cleaning, mostly because if he looked her in the eye, he wasn't going to say it.

Hell, maybe he shouldn't say it—although he never could keep things from her.

"I, ah . . . I hated what Trez and Selena went through. The same with Tohr."

From out of nowhere, he remembered sitting in Manny's fancy-ass clinical RV and demanding that the doctor save the Chosen.

Like if he just ordered the guy to find a cure, it would happen.

Then he had a snapshot of Layla, bundled up outside as the flames had roared into the sky. Pregnant Layla, who was carrying Qhuinn's twins, for fuck's sake.

Who had looked as if she were going to expire from the mourning of her sister's passing—to the point where Rhage wasn't the only one worried about her pregnancy, her life, the young.

"I'm an asshole," he whispered.

"Talk to me, Rhage."

"I'm glad that wasn't us," he choked out. "As much as I love all of them, and I mourn with them . . . I'm so fucking glad I didn't lose you. . . ."

Tears came to his eyes.

And his *shellan* came over to him.

As she took his gun and put it aside, and then wrapped

her arms around him, murmuring support into his ear, he felt even worse.

It just reminded him of what Trez was never going to have again—

Boom! Boom! Boom!

"Rhage," V barked from out in the hall. "Trez turned himself in."

Rhage straightened up and scraped his tears away. *"What?"*

Moving Mary out of the way, he jumped across to the door and ripped it open. "What the *fuck* are you talking about?"

"You heard me—meeting in Wrath's. *Now.*"

As the Brother went to run off, Rhage grabbed V's arm. "Are you sure?"

"The call just came in from the s'Hisbe."

"Does iAm know?"

That stopped the Brother, and he looked up to the ceiling. "Shit."

"Are you sure Trez isn't in the house?"

"No, he's gone. I checked the security camera feeds. He left his cell phone on the stone steps and disappeared about an hour ago."

"Holy . . . *shit.* Okay, all right . . ." Except he wasn't sure if that was true. Maybe there was no war . . . but what about the Shadows?

Their two Shadows?

"Let me go up and tell iAm," he heard himself say as he glanced back at Mary.

"Do you want me to come with you?" she said.

"Yeah, I do."

iAm came awake to two pairs of shoes at eye level. One was a set of shitkickers, big as recliners. The others were Coach sneakers, with the logo in gray and black, and Velcro straps instead of laces.

As he lifted his head, he looked up at Rhage and Mary. "What time is it?"

Mary knelt down, and that was his first clue that whatever message they were delivering was bad, bad news.

Rhage was the one who spoke up, though. "iAm . . . we got reason to believe your brother has turned himself in."

The words filtered through his mind on a series of clunks and mis-hits, the combination of nouns and verbs and other things making no sense.

"I'm sorry, what did you say?"

As he sat up, the bottle he'd been nursing rolled away, knocking into Rhage's boots.

"We received word from the Territory that the Queen is no longer going to attack because Trez has voluntarily returned to the s'Hisbe—"

"Jesus *Christ*!"

Jumping to his feet, he shoved through the pair of them and burst into his brother's room. The bed was messy, and the closet doors were open ... and there was absolutely, positively no sign of Trez.

"No—no, we're supposed to leave!" he shouted at nothing and nobody. "I'm arranging everything! We're going to leave!"

When he wheeled around, the two were standing in the doorway.

Mary's voice grew strident, as if she knew damn well he was liable not to follow what she was saying otherwise. "We know you're going to want to go after him, iAm. But before you do—"

He headed out of the room, prepared to mow them down if he had to, as much as he appreciated their concern.

But Rhage caught his arm and yanked him back. "Let me get you armed first. And Lassiter is going with you. He can be out in the sunshine."

iAm was about to argue when he thought, Well, duh.

"We're still prepared to back you up, my man," the Brother said grimly. "You're not in this alone."

For a moment, iAm couldn't figure out what the guy was saying—and then he realized, Shit. If he went back in there and got Trez out ... the Queen was likely to attack Caldwell in retaliation.

And then these people would be under siege.

"Why did he do it?" iAm moaned. "Oh, God, why did he do it?"

Mary took his hand. "He must have found out about the threat. Somehow he must have heard something in the house."

iAm closed his eyes. "This has to stop. This whole goddamn thing has to stop."

Because assuming Trez had finally fallen on that sword he'd been cursed with? The guy was going to mate and have sex with the only female iAm had ever loved.

'Cuz he and his brother were lucky like that. Yup.

"Come on," Rhage said. "Let's get some weapons on you. Lassiter is already waiting."

What happened next was all a dizzy haze. Down to the second floor. Holsters belted onto his hips, wrapped around his shoulders. Guns. Knives. A long black leather trench coat that covered the lot of it.

Then it was down to the foyer, where the fallen angel was similarly adorned, and not making jokes at all.

Just before the pair of them left, Rehvenge stepped up and embraced him. "I have to stay here. In case the Shadows attack Caldwell, I need to be able to command my sin-eaters to defend during the daylight hours."

Fuck. He and his brother's private misery had become so many's.

"I'm so sorry," iAm said, glancing around at the Brothers. Wrath. The rest of the household. "I can't believe it's coming to this."

Rhage shook his head. "We gotchu. We do what we have to, to take care of our own."

And then the talking was over and iAm and Lassiter were out through the vestibule and on the front steps of the mansion.

The fallen angel reached out and grabbed his arm. "Get ready to ride."

Frowning, iAm looked over at the black-and-blond-haired male. "What are you talking about—"

In an instant, he was consumed by a sun ray, up and out of there without any control or thought or will of his own . . .

. . . heading for the home he hated and the destiny he was still fighting against.

EIGHTY-TWO

The gems were cold and heavy.

As the Chief Astrologer draped Catra with mesh after mesh of platinum-set diamonds and sapphires and emeralds and rubies, she was less and less able to breathe right.

Although that was probably more because the enormity of what was happening was sinking in, rather than the weight of the ceremonial robes.

The final part of the Queen's dress was a thin veil that drifted down over her face like a breeze.

"It is done," the Astrologer said.

In ordinary circumstances, the garb would have been delivered to the Queen's quarters and cleaned and prepared for the wearer by a fleet of maids. But this was not ordinary.

Was the Queen dead now?

How would the death happen?

As those questions played through her head over and over again, she —

". . . has arrived! He has arrived!"

Out in the hall, the sound of voices shouting the same thing permeated the dense quiet of the chamber.

Frowning, she picked up the skirting and walked forth — only to remember she couldn't activate the door to the corridor.

"Will you please open this up?"

"At once, Your Highness."

The Chief Astrologer rushed forward, placed his palm on the wall, and the panel obligingly retracted.

"...Anointed One has arrived!"

It was mad chaos outside, people running and jumping with joy, a celebration breaking out. For a split second, she stood in the doorway, taking it all in—before remembering there was carnage in the circular room behind her.

"Come out here," she hissed to the Astrologer.

Just as he walked through, the door shut automatically, her presence registered to the multitudes racing up and down the corridor.

Everyone stopped. Dropped to the floor. Prostrated themselves.

As the citizens began to murmur the required greeting to royalty, they clearly assumed she was the current Queen.

While that dawned on her, so did another thought. "Cleansing..." She wrenched around and forced herself to keep her voice down. "Oh, stars above, they're going to cleanse him—quick, we must go unto the high priest!"

The Astrologer didn't ask any questions. He just followed her as she ran through the palace. Fortunately for them, her presence carried with it a wave of genuflections, what would have been a congested trip freed up by the fact that everybody, from courtier to Primary to servant, hit the floor as soon as they saw her.

AnsLai's sacred chamber was not far from the ceremonial hall, and when she came to it, she went to put her hand on the wall—but the Astrologer ducked in first and found the spot with his palm.

As the panel slid back, she got a look at a large naked male form stretched out on a black slab of marble, his arms down at his sides, his feet together.

AnsLai was across the way, standing before a fire pit, both palms up to the heavens as he whispered an incantation.

"Stop!" she said. "I command you to stop!"

The high priest wrenched around—and promptly dropped to his knees. "Your Highness, I thought you were still in the ritual room?"

Catra rushed over to the male who was lying with his eyes closed. "Tell me you haven't cleansed him—"

"I have just administered the solution unto his veins—"

"Oh, no, no, no," she said. "No!"

"Whate'er do you speak of, Your Highness?" the high priest said, straightening. "He has been on the outside for decades. He is impure to mate with your daughter—"

"He's not the Anointed One."

At that, the male they were discussing turned his head slowly toward her.

And that was how she finally met, after all those years, TrezLath.

"I'm so sorry," she breathed to him, bending down and clasping his hand. "I didn't make it in time—I'm so sorry. . . ."

As Trez lay on the table, he could feel a burning on the inside of his forearm from where they had injected him using a surprisingly modern, human-world needle.

He would have assumed, given how ancient the ritual was, that they would have preferred some kind of reed or hand-fashioned ancient metal syringe.

But no. It was actually precisely the same kind that his Selena had been injected with.

Instantly, he had felt the poison in his veins, and, rather like the venom of a snake's bite, it wasted no time in spreading, multiplying, taking over.

Weakened as he was from grief and exertion, he realized there was a good chance he wouldn't survive this.

And that made him focus on the ceiling above him. Funny, whenever he'd pictured this ritual, it had always been with him tied down.

Strange where you ended up. Now, he welcomed the coming pain—because it might just be his ticket back to Selena. Gossip held that you didn't get into the Fade if you committed suicide, but if you were killed?

Not your fault.

There was, of course, an existential issue to be reconciled: namely how the pair of them, coming from different traditions, could in fact find each other on the other side of life. If there was another side.

But if faith had any power, he was going to believe they would.

He might as well go out on that note.

Gradually, he became aware of two other presences in

the room with him and AnsLai. And one of them sparkled from head to foot in a rainbow of colors.

The Queen.

She began speaking to AnsLai after the high priest bowed down to her. And then AnsLai was straightening, talking, looking alarmed ... then panicked.

The Queen approached Trez—and after a lifetime of hating the female, he thought idly of reaching up and trying to strangle her.

He didn't have the strength, however. Especially not as the pain intensified even further.

He hadn't intended to move, but he began to writhe, his body trying to escape the poison.

And then suddenly his entire suit of flesh was on fire on the inside.

The last thing he remembered was more people racing into the room, and they did not drop to the floor. They stared at the Queen in confusion.

And then the Chief Astrologer in his red robes addressed them all.

A moment later, they did hit the floor before the female.

Oh, what did it matter, Trez thought.

What did any of this, even the monumental pain, matter ...

EIGHTY-THREE

That fallen angel got them to the Territory.

And as iAm re-formed, he realized it was a good thing that Lassiter had taken control of the flight. With his brother in the clutches of the Queen, he doubted he would have been able to concentrate enough to dematerialize.

"I'll take it from here," iAm said.

"Got your back."

With a nod of gratitude, iAm strode over to the front entrance of the s'Hisbe. Among the things the Brotherhood had given him as parting gifts were a couple of pounds of C4 plastic explosive. All he had to do was set a serving or two of it up at the huge gates and—

As if the entrance to the s'Hisbe wanted to avoid bodily harm, the giant halves split and opened before the pair of them.

But it wasn't a fortuitous departure of someone on the far side.

s'Ex stood tall and proud, the perfect guard to the Queen's lands.

Except . . . something was all wrong. The male was wearing the kind of *farshi* servant dress he'd given to iAm before, and it was dripping with blood.

There was also a red-stained, serrated dagger in his hand that was as long as a male's forearm.

"We don't have a lot of time, come on," the male said urgently.

Ordinarily, iAm would have thought twice about going anywhere with a Grim Reaper like that. But he'd already trusted the male once—and it was clear there was a coup in play.

Falling into a jog, he and Lassiter followed the executioner to the palace complex and entered the compound through a hidden door. Once inside, s'Ex led them through corridors that were utterly empty.

No servants. No courtiers.

And s'Ex had no apparent concern that they would be detained, questioned . . . threatened.

The male had either lost his mind or . . .

"What the hell is going on here?" iAm demanded.

"You're the Anointed One, not your brother."

iAm stopped so fast that Lassiter had jump to the side or mow him down. *"What."*

"No time. Your brother's being cleansed—he's on death's door. If you want to say good-bye to him, you'd better hurry up."

As iAm just stood there, like someone had unplugged him, Lassiter and s'Ex grabbed him under the arms, jacked his feet off the ground, and carried him off.

A second later, he came to and forced his way out of their holds, taking control of his own feet. "It's not possible," he shouted over the pounding of their footfalls.

"The Queen forged the charts. You were the one all along—but you weren't supposed to live for long after the birth. Trez was the better bet—for the Queen and for your parents."

All at once, they burst into the main audience hall, and iAm found his feet faltering again.

Up on the dais . . . his *maichen*—the Princess—Christ, whoever the hell she was—was having the crown of the Territory placed upon her dark hair.

As about two thousand Shadows fell to their knees on woven silk mats, their heads bowing in supplication.

"She figured it out," s'Ex said. "She figured it all out— even though it nearly cost her her life."

"Where is the former Queen?"

"At the feet of the daughter."

That was when he saw the severed head off to the side, black eyes staring out at the crowd, but seeing nothing.

"I believe in fate," the executioner said. "I believe in the stars. This is the way it was meant to be."

iAm shook himself. This was all really too much, and nothing that really concerned him. Trez, on the other hand. "My brother . . ."

"This way."

When iAm finally burst into the room where Trez was, he lost his breath. His brother, his blood, was on a marble table, that big body twisted up in pain.

His first thought was that it reminded him of Selena, the way she had contorted.

iAm rushed over without acknowledging the other people who were standing around. Clasping Trez's hand, he fell to his knees. "Trez . . . Trez . . . ?"

But there was no reaching his brother. He was gone, alive but transported somewhere else, as if his body had issued a temporary vacate order.

"No," he heard himself say. "Not after all this . . . Trez, you're free . . . you can stay with me, we're free. . . ."

Well, sort of free if he himself was the Anointed One. But he couldn't worry about that right now.

Fuck.

"Don't leave me, my brother."

". . . antidote. We shall have to see."

iAm looked up and saw AnsLai, the high priest, standing on the other side of the table. "What?"

"I gave him the antidote . . . as soon as I knew." The male glanced at s'Ex. "But it may be too late. He was in a weakened state when he came here."

iAm started talking, blathering about . . . shit, he didn't know what.

It was all he could do.

As his brother twisted and turned, arms and legs sawing against a pain that iAm couldn't even imagine, iAm was helpless. So helpless.

". . . see you?" AnsLai asked him sometime later.

"What?" he said in a voice that was hoarse. Guess he hadn't stopped talking.

"Your blooded parents. They have heard that you are both within the Territory—that you are rightfully the Anointed One, and they would like to—"

iAm bared his fangs and glared into the high priest's worried eyes. "You tell those two that if they want to live they will never, ever approach me or my brother again. Do you understand? Tell them that the only thing that could distract me from Trez right now is murdering them both where they stand."

The high priest blanched. "Yes. But of course."

iAm refocused on his brother.

And resumed talking nonsense. Just as Trez had done to Selena as she was in the grips of passing.

Sometime later, he was dimly aware that a female came into the room. And he knew who it was by the echo of his own blood, but he did not acknowledge her.

He was too consumed by trying to keep Trez on the planet when, undoubtedly, the male was busy working to make his way to the far side.

EIGHTY-FOUR

Trez got his wish.

In the course of his dying from the cleansing, he learned that, in fact, there was a Fade. And yes, people of different traditions and faiths all went to the same place.

At some point, the pain became too much and his body gave out—and the abrupt lack of any sensation was a shock. Yet he welcomed the numbness.

And the sense of flight.

Soaring, he was soaring . . . until he found himself in a vast white landscape, a foggy landscape that, as he walked along, made him feel both weightless and grounded.

Soon enough, a door was presented to him. A door with a knob that he instinctively knew if he turned, would allow him to step into what was beyond and thereby never, ever go back to Earth.

And that was when he saw Selena.

Her face and form appeared to him not on the door, but in it, as if even closed, the panel contained three-dimensional space.

Instant. Joy. And it was the same for her, her smile radiating through the distance between them, their eye contact translating to a caress he felt throughout his body.

She was healthy. She was strong. She was whole.

"My queen!" he shouted, reaching for her.

But she put her palm out, stopping him. "Trez, you need to stay."

He recoiled. "No. I need to be with you—this is the way it's supposed to be—"

"No. You have more to do. You have things you need to do, people you have to meet. Your journey's not done."

"It sure as shit is." Check him out with the cursing. Way to do the whole reunited-in-Heaven fantasy. "You're dead and I want to be with you."

"I'm going to be here, waiting for you." She smiled again, and warmed him anew. "It's wonderful where I am—I flew because of what you did, the way you freed me. I found flight and I am free and I am going to wait for you until your journey's done."

"No," he moaned. "Don't send me back."

"I don't have that power. But you do. Make the choice to stay down there—you have to take care of iAm. You need to pay him back for all the years he's been there for you. It's not fair for you to leave him alone. He will never be at peace, and he's earned it."

Well, hell. That was probably the only argument she could have made that had a chance of getting through to him.

Shit.

"What about us," he moaned. Even though that was selfish. Childish. "What about me . . . I'm nothing without you."

"I'll come to you in the night sky. Look for me there."

"Let me touch you—"

"Make the right choice, Trez. You have to make the right choice. You have a debt to repay to the one you have loved all your life."

"But I love you," he choked out, beginning to cry.

"And I love you, too—for eternity." Her smile resonated through him. "Infinity and back, remember? I'll be here waiting for you and for whoever else you love. That's what the other side is. It's just love."

"Don't leave. Oh, God, don't leave me again—"

"I'm not. We're separated, but not lost or truly apart. Do not mourn me, my love. I have not died. . . ."

"Selena!"

As iAm heard the shout, he jerked up from the base of the slab. Shit, some savior he was. He'd fallen a-fucking-sleep holding his brother's—

"Trez?" he said, as he realized the guy had, by some miracle, almost twenty-four hours after the cleanse, come back to consciousness.

His brother was crying, tears spilling from his eyes, rolling down his cheeks.

"Trez? Are you back?" iAm jumped to his feet and leaned over the guy. "Trez?"

Those sunken black eyes shifted to his, and there was a long moment in which Trez seemed to struggle with what was and was not real.

"Trez?" iAm whispered, suddenly worried that the poison had eaten that brain up. "Are you—"

All at once those long, strong arms wrapped around him and jerked him off his feet.

And his brother was holding him.

And speaking.

"I'm here, I'm here, I'm here . . . for you, I am here. . . ."

At first the words didn't register, but then . . .

"I'm not leaving you," Trez said in a rough, scratchy voice. "I'm here and I'm not leaving you."

Oh . . . shit.

They were the words iAm had said to the male in so many different variations throughout their lives together . . . words that had been represented by the deeds he had done, and days he had stayed up worrying, and years he had spent just praying they were going to make it through another night.

iAm collapsed on his brother's now-scarred chest, his knees suddenly going out from under him.

In his fantasies, he had wondered what it would be like to be free of the curse of worrying about his brother.

He'd had a variety of iterations.

None came close to the real thing.

EIGHTY-FIVE

It was around noontime when Mary left the Brotherhood mansion . . . and the Shadow brothers returned.

Rhage had just sent his *shellan* off to Havers, after telling her that no, really, he was totally fine, when the security checkpoint at the main entrance went off.

Excusing himself from the restless cohort of his brothers in the billiards room, he beat Fritz to the monitor, and the instant he saw those two dark faces, he shouted.

"Who is it?" Butch asked.

"Who we've been waiting for!"

Releasing the locks, he positioned himself right at the inner doors—and there they were, looking like shit, both haggard and worn shadows of their former selves.

Har-har, hardy-har-har.

But they were alive. They were together. And the sight of them upright, walking and talking, relieved a little bit of the pressure that had been riding his chest for nights now.

"Hey, my man," he said, embracing the nearer one, and then going to the other.

Trez's voice was thin, but strong enough. "Hey, thanks for everything."

"Thank you so much for—"

"Trez, buddy, good to see you—"

"Jesus Christ—what a story—"

"iAm, welcome back—"

And so it went, the Brotherhood filing out of the bil-

liards room along with the females of the house, the greetings and exchanges like those of war survivors.

Or almost-war survivors . . .

"Oh, my God, you two made it back in time for Steve
Wilkos!"

Everyone halted and looked at Lassiter, who was standing in the archway, naked to the waist in nothing but black
leathers, that I'M HORNY baseball cap with its silver lamé
protrusion sticking out the front of his head—and a pair of
giant fuzzy slippers on his feet which, if you put them together, formed a complete Dalmatian.

The angel had returned twelve hours ago, saying that the
pair of them were safe, but there was no telling whether
Trez was going to make it. And for once, the asshat had
seemed utterly and completely devastated by something. To
the point where he'd been inconsolable.

In the silence following that happy TV announcement,
Trez stared across the foyer . . . and then burst out laughing.

The poor bastard laughed so hard, he had to wrap his
arms around his middle and wipe tears from his eyes.

As everybody joined in, the Shadow tilted his head up to
the ceiling and said, "Thank you, my queen. I needed this."

Then he walked over to the fallen angel and embraced
the guy. Words were said, serious ones that made Lassiter
duck his eyes.

Because he seemed to be tearing up.

But then the jackass broke rank and said, "Now take
your hands off my ass. I'm not that kind of girl."

And that struck the tone for the rest of the day. Rather
like rolling a bandage over a wound, the community
wrapped itself around the two Shadows, drawing them into
the billiards room, offering them food and drink.

It was clear that, in spite of that moment of levity, Trez
was hurting badly. He was wearing some kind of gray robe,
and his skin was nearly the same color as the cloth. But he
seemed determined to be present and participate.

iAm, on the other hand, appeared to have a serious case
of vertigo. Like a guy who'd just stepped off a boat that had
sustained heavy waves, he steadied himself on various
things . . . the pool table, the sofa, the bar.

He declined the offer of booze. Took Coke instead.

Rhage was so damned happy they were home in one

piece, but even so, he couldn't man up for too much inter-action. He told himself it was because of the raid on the Lessening Society they were going to do at that prep school with Assail and those two cousins.

It could well be a historic slaughter.

And then there was always the Band of Bastards on his mind. Even if he and his brothers killed off all the slayers and the Omega needed time to recoup the losses, there were still Xcor and his boys to worry about.

But the reality was, he still didn't feel right.

And after a time, he became aware that he wasn't the only one.

Layla was likewise standing on the periphery, one hand on her belly, her eyes straight ahead but not really focused on anything.

"You okay?" he asked as he went over to her. "You need Doc Jane or something?"

When she didn't reply, he leaned in, "Layla?"

She jumped, and he reached out to calm her, as she mumbled, "I'm sorry, what?"

"Are you all right?"

"Oh. Yes." She gave him the same sort of smile he'd given his Mary. "I'm fine."

He was tempted to call her on the bullshit, but he wouldn't have appreciated anyone doing that to him.

"You want me to call Qhuinn over?"

The male and Blay were talking with iAm, both of them nodding their heads . . . only to recoil in shock, as if they couldn't believe the story that had, up until now, been deliv-ered secondhand by Steve Wilkos's PR man over there with the phallic symbol on his forehead.

"Oh, no. No, thank you."

As Rhage took in her affect, he thought, man, he really was as selfish as he thought he was. She had lost her blooded sister Selena just days ago.

Of course she would look like some version of Trez.

Standing next to her, Rhage wished he could help some-how. But he worried that he was as incapable of doing any-thing for her . . . as he was defining this seismic shift that had somehow occurred under his skin.

Ostensibly, everything was the same and all was well.

He just felt like a different male for no good reason.

And that . . .

. . . that he found terrifying.

Across town, at Abalone's Tudor mansion, Paradise was sitting up in her own bed, in her own room, staring at the wall across the way.

She supposed she should have been happy. According to her father, the threat from the s'Hisbe had been neutralized, and everyone was safe . . . but she was completely unsettled.

Of course, she'd moved back home.

In spite of all her independent-streak posturing, the reality of living away from her father in uncertain times was just too dangerous. And this was a step back from her autonomy.

At least she still had her job—

The knock on her door was quiet.

"Yes?" she said.

As the panels swung wide, her father appeared in between the jambs. He was in his navy-blue silk bathrobe, the one that had the family crest stitched into the breast and the tie that was as long as the hem.

"You're still up?" she asked.

"I could not sleep."

"So much going on."

"Yes." He hesitated, looking around her room as if he were renewing himself with its acquaintance. "May I come in?"

"Of course, it is your house."

"Our home," he corrected gently.

When he only got as far as the edge of that needlepoint rug that covered the floor, she frowned. "Are you not feeling well?"

He opened his mouth to speak. Closed it. Tried again.

Failed.

Moving her legs over, she sat up. "Father?"

Her father finally came all the way forward, and that was when she saw that he had something in his hand. A piece of paper.

In lieu of an answer, he offered whatever it was to her.

"What is this?" she said as she took the thing.

Looking down, she frowned.

"Oh . . . my God," she breathed. "My *God* . . ."

It was the application to the Brotherhood's training program. And he had filled all of it out, in his own hand.

For her.

"Father!" Leaping up, she threw her arms around him. "Thank you! Thank you!"

He held on to her. "It's a safety issue," he said roughly. "I just . . . you're right. You need to learn how to fight. The idea that sometime you might be unprotected in some capacity . . ." He pulled back. "You're right. You need to learn."

He was clearly, in the words of Peyton, shitting Twinkies at the thought—but that was what made the gesture so grand. Even though he was scared . . . he was going to let her go anyway.

"Thank you," she said, grabbing onto him. "I'll be careful! I promise!"

Assuming she got in. Jeez, she'd better start working out if she was going to pass the physical-requirements test.

"I promise," she vowed, "I'll be careful."

"I shall be praying for that," he all but groaned. "Every single night."

"I love you, Father!"

He closed his eyes as if he were on a roller-coaster ride he wasn't sure he could handle. "And you, dearest Paradise, have my heart."

EIGHTY-SIX

Queen Catra vin SuLaneh etl MuLanen deh FonLer-ahn sat alone in her quarters, the silence around her one that she had created by asking her maids and servants to leave her.

She was not moving into the former Queen's suite of rooms.

No, she was having those turned into a nursery for the young of those who served in the palace. That way those precious little ones would be close to their parents, and for the first time, servants would not have to leave their sons and daughters with relatives or in the cold, dark jail-like facility near the poor housing area.

That had not been her first decree, however.

No, the first thing she had done, after accepting the mantle of leadership over her people, was to abolish the Anointed One curse.

She had set iAm free.

Not that he knew it. Everyone else in the s'Hisbe did, however, so at least he wouldn't ever have to worry about seeing her or the Territory again.

Every breath she drew in hurt.

Stars above, that so much damage had been done by one so greedy.

The good news, she supposed, was that she, in concert with s'Ex, whom she had elevated to a position equivalent to King—even though, obviously, they would not be mated—would see to it that no one else was ever treated so capriciously and carelessly.

And as she would never have young, she didn't need to worry about some kind of latent evil gene popping up.

Indeed, with iAm out of the picture, she was prepared to be celibate. Who else would she want, anyway? She had met her match—it was even decreed in the stars.

That he didn't want her?

Well, one's fate was not another's, no matter the emotions involved—

As the door slid open, and a waft of food smells preceded a servant, she frowned and looked at the time on the ancient windup clock by her dressing table. She had been sitting here for hours.

"I am not hungry," she said without looking over. "But I thank you."

When she sensed the figure had not moved from the doorway, she glanced over at the *farshi*-dressed male.

"Thank you," she repeated numbly. "But I am not as yet hungry. Please return it to the kitchen—no, wait, offer it to your fellow males and females?"

Instead of bowing and ducking out, the male came in farther, the door panel sliding shut behind him.

Then he slowly lowered himself to his knees, put the tray down in front of him, and stretched his torso out flat on the marble floor toward her.

And that was when she felt the echo of herself in his blood.

Unless she was mistaken?

Wait . . . was this truly—

"iAm?" she whispered hoarsely. "iAm, is that you?"

The male figure straightened and removed his hood. And as she clasped her hands to her face, she prayed she hadn't fallen asleep and was only dreaming.

Because his eyes, those almond-shaped, beautiful black eyes, were shining with love.

"So," he said in that wonderful voice of his. "I heard I got demoted."

"I'm sorry, what?"

"s'Ex called me. Told me I've been demoted. Guess I'm not the Anointed One anymore, huh."

iAm got to his feet and walked over to her, his big body causing the robes to shift, his scent that of dark spices.

When he was close to her, he lowered himself back to his

knees. "You saying you don't want this anymore?" he drawled, indicating himself. "Really?"

She closed her eyes, and turned away from him, the pain too great to bear. "Please . . . do not torture me."

He clasped her hands. "Look at me. Come on, look at me . . . *maichen*."

As he used the name she had first given him, she opened her lids and glanced over. Her vision was wavy from tears, and he brushed her cheeks with his knuckles.

"You saved my brother," he said.

"No, I didn't. I was too late."

"He survived."

"It nearly killed him. This whole nightmare . . . nearly killed him."

"You were not the cause, you were the solution I had been begging for."

"I lied to you."

"And I forgive you."

"How?" she choked out.

He leaned up and brushed her mouth with his. "You're easy to forgive. You risked your life to go find out the truth. You were the one who found the lies and turned everything around. You are the savior I've spent my whole life praying for, Your Highness."

She shook her head. "Do not call me that. Please. I picked *maichen* because I don't believe I'm better than anyone else. With beating hearts and open minds, we are all the same."

"See," he whispered. "You just keep getting more beautiful."

She looked at him for the longest time. Then, with a shaking hand, she reached out and touched his face. In response, he pressed his lips to her fingertips.

"This is real," he told her. "You can trust this. You aren't going to wake up and have this be over. You and I? This is our beginning."

"I love you," she said in a rough voice. "I want no one else but you."

iAm smiled and pushed in between her legs, bringing his body against hers. "And I feel the same way, my *maichen*. I love you, I love you . . . I love you. . . ."

As he started to kiss her, she found it hard to believe that it was really happening. That he had come back to her. That once parted asunder, they now were united as a single whole.

Pulling away a little, she asked, "You're sure this is real?"

He shrugged and smiled at her. "Of course it is. You and I were written in the stars. . . ."

With that, he kissed her lips again.

And she kissed him back.

EIGHTY-SEVEN

The meteor shower happened at midnight on the dot.

As Trez stepped free of the mansion's warmth, and walked some distance past the courtyard and onto the descending drive, he got out of the lee of the exterior security lights, and that was when he looked up and saw the sky clearly.

Against a dense, velvety black and among the pinpricks of bright white stars, a sprinkling of flashes was cast across the sky, like gold dust let loose from an open palm.

He smiled sadly. "Thank you, my queen. I needed this."

Watching the display, he felt both very alone and totally connected, especially as he reflected on that vastness above.

If anyone ever wanted to sense the infinity of time and existence, all they had to do was look at the night sky and feel their precious dead staring back at them. It was the great duality of union and separation.

It was just as his Selena had told him at the door to the Fade.

He wanted her beside him so badly that he'd woken up again with a wet face and a soggy pillow. But yet he was here, upright in his boots, prepared to somehow figure out how to breathe while the one who had made his lungs work was on the other side.

"I'm going to go now," he said. "Come with me—"

Trez jumped and spun around.

Sure as he knew there was no one behind him, he could have sworn a gentle hand had rested on his shoulder.

He prayed it was the ghost of his *shellan*. If it wasn't, he was probably losing his mind.

Short trip.

Wha-hey.

Closing his eyes, he had to wait a moment for the concentration to come . . . and then he was off, scattering his molecules through the cold, clear autumn night.

When he re-formed, it was in front of Sal's Restaurant.

He supposed he could have gone around to the back, but no. This was a big night, a kind of reintroduction for him. He would enter through the front.

Going over to the keypad by the glass doors, he entered the code and then opened his way in. Instantly, the old-school Rat Pack decor sank in for him, the red-and-black flocked wallpaper bleeding into his retinas, the he'd-been-here-a-thousand-times sense seemingly both accurate and a lie.

Walking forward, he mounted the couple of steps and went by the hostess stand; then headed past the dining rooms and into the bar area in the back. The flap doors to the kitchen were over on the right, and he took his leather jacket off as he went, leaving it on the bar.

The place was empty as usual on a Monday night.

His clubs were closed, too.

He was going to go to them tomorrow night, though. Because . . . well, that was just what he was going to do.

Unless the Brothers needed him.

Jesus, and he thought he'd owed Rehvenge before? It was nothing compared to what he felt for the Black Dagger Brotherhood and their King.

Anything, anytime for those males.

Forevermore.

He found himself hesitating at the kitchen's entrance, staring at the pair of doors, both of which had circular windows of Plexiglas in them so that the waitstaff didn't smack each other around as they carried trays of food in and out.

Putting his palm on the one on the right . . .

. . . he finally pushed in.

Right away, the smell of his brother's famous marinara sauce hit his nose—and actually, for the first time since his Selena passed, he felt a pang of hunger.

iAm was facing the stove, stirring a huge pot with a

spoon as long as an arm. ". . . proper amount of oregano. It's mission-critical."

Over on the left, at the far end of the stainless-steel counter, a small round table had been set up with a linen tablecloth, place settings, and flowers in the middle. And the Queen of the Shadows was sitting at the thing, her head and hair exposed, her beautiful, kind face tilted toward his brother . . . her eyes lit with such devotion and love, Trez took an instant adoration to the female.

She noticed his presence before iAm, Mr. Formerly Silent But Now Chatty Cathy, did.

With a quick flush, her face changed, tension tightening the features, squeezing out her smile.

iAm wheeled around. "Oh, hey, brother, you made it."

"Ah, yeah." Trez pushed his hands into the pockets of the jeans he'd worn. "I'm here."

"Well. Ah, good." iAm came around, and even though they weren't normally huggers, he gave a good, hard embrace. "Ah . . . so, yeah. Thanks for coming."

"Thanks for having me."

They both looked at the Queen. Who slowly rose to her feet and smoothed down the shimmering robe she wore.

Diamonds. It was covered with a fine mesh of diamonds.

And for a moment, panic fisted Trez's chest, the sight of those gems set in metal returning him to—

No, he thought. That was not necessary. That was no longer the reality they were all living in.

It was over. The nightmare was well and truly over, and he was going to need to trust that—because this female? She was going to be part of his family.

There was no way the two of them weren't getting mated ASAP.

He could smell the bonding scent riding on the air over all those Italian spices.

Trez broke off from his brother and went over to the tall, slender female.

It felt really fucking bizarre, but goddamn it, he sank to his knees and prostrated himself at her feet.

"Oh, please don't," she said as he began to recite the proper greeting. "No, please. I'm . . ."

When he looked up, she had actually gotten down on her own knees with him.

"Please," she said. "Call me *maichen*. That's what iAm calls me."

maichen. As in maid? Trez thought.

Huh. Now he had another reason to like her.

Sticking his palm out, he said, "Hi. I'm iAm's brother . . . Trez."

She started to smile. Then she laughed—and clasped what he'd offered back. "Hi. I'm iAm's—what's the word?"

"Wife. Well, soon to be," iAm said roughly as he came over. "But 'wife' is what you're going to be out here in Caldwell."

She squared her shoulders and tried it again. "Hi. I'm iAm's wife . . . *maichen*."

Trez smiled back at her. "Nice to meet you . . . *maichen*."

Some two hours later, the three of them were still around that little table. After an initial awkwardness, it was a shock how easy it was. Then again, even though she was a queen, iAm's *maichen* was down-to-earth, funny, sweet.

And man, oh man, was she in love with him. She couldn't seem to take her eyes off her man, and every time he looked at her in return, she blushed.

Jesus, if Trez could have picked someone for his brother? She would have been it.

"More cannoli?" iAm asked as he got up with his plate. "I need another."

"No, thank you," *maichen* said. "I'm so full, I think this robing is going to split."

"I wish you'd met my queen," Trez blurted to her.

As both of them froze, he shook his head. "No, don't freak out on me. I'm . . . I just wanted to say it. I think Selena would have thought the world of you."

maichen looked at iAm. Looked back at him. Then she put her hand over Trez's. "I know I would have adored her. iAm spent most of this afternoon talking about her."

"Really?" Trez said, glancing across to his brother. "You did?"

iAm came back with a couple of cannoli. "Yeah. I wanted *maichen* to know who her sister-in-law was."

Annnnnd cue the eye sting.

Shit.

Looking away to the stove, Trez cleared his throat a couple of times. "I think that's awesome. That's just ... really awesome. Thank you."

When he was able to shift his focus back, he found the pair of them staring into each other's eyes, as if they were so grateful to have one another, as if they knew just exactly how lucky they were ... as if they had every intention of cherishing each night they had together.

May it be a hundred thousand more.

As Trez looked at them both, he thought his queen had been right. If he had stayed up in the Fade with her? iAm would not have this moment, that female, these coming years.

Selena had been one hundred percent correct.

Painful as it was to be without her, agonizing as some nights were undoubtedly going to continue to be ... seeing his brother happy and in love gave him a sudden peace about it all.

Somehow, in the midst of the great infinite, and in spite of his mourning, he knew he was exactly where he was supposed to be at this point in time.

Guess it was fate.

As iAm leaned in to kiss his mate, Trez tilted his head back and mouthed, *Thank you, my queen. We needed this.*

New York Times bestselling author J. R. Ward
is coming out with a sexy spin-off series to
the Black Dagger Brotherhood.
Read on for a sneak peek at
the first novel in the Black Dagger Legacy series,

BLOOD KISS

Available from Signet on December 1, 2015.

THE KING'S AUDIENCE HOUSE, CALDWELL, NY

Some graduations happened in private.

Some of these important markers of the next stage of life had no caps and gowns, no orchestras playing the humans' "Pomp and Circumstance." There was no stage to walk across or diploma to hang on your wall. No witnesses, either.

Some graduations were marked by the simple and the everyday, the nothing-special—like a person reaching out to a Dell monitor and hitting the little blue button on the lower right corner of the computer screen. Such a mundane action, done many times in a week, a month, a year—but nonetheless, for one particular instance, a great division between before and after occurred.

As Paradise, blooded daughter of Abalone, First Adviser to Wrath, son of Wrath, sire of Wrath, King of all vampires, sat back in her office chair, she stared at the now-black screen in front of her. Amazing. The night she had been waiting for was almost here.

For most of the last eight weeks, time had been going at a crawl, but in these final couple of evenings it had switched things up and flipped into catapult mode. Suddenly, after having suffered through seven-thousand-hour waits for the moon to rise, she felt like she wanted to slow it all down again.

Her first job was now a thing of the past.

Looking across the desk, she moved the office phone over an inch—then switched the AT&T whatever it was back to where it had been. She straightened the stained-glass dragonfly shade on the Tiffany lamp. Made sure the blue pens were in one holder and the red ones in another. Smoothed her palm over the dust-free blotter and the top of the monitor.

The waiting room was empty, the silk chairs unoccupied, the magazines put in order on the side tables, the drinks that had been served by *doggen* to those who had come all cleaned up.

The last civilian had left about thirty minutes ago. Dawn was about two hours off. All in all, it was the normal end to a night of hard work, the time when she and her father would head back to the family estate to enjoy a meal full of talk and plans and mutual respect.

Paradise leaned forward and looked around the archway of the parlor. Across the foyer, the double doors that led into what had previously been the mansion's formal dining room were closed.

Yup, just a normal night except for the very un-normal meeting that was taking place in there: Right after the final appointment had left, her father had been called into the audience chamber and those doors had shut tight.

He was in there with the King, and two members of the Black Dagger Brotherhood.

"Don't you do this to me," she said. "Don't you take this away from me."

Paradise got up and walked around, re-straightening magazines, re-plumping throw pillows, stopping in front of the oil painting of a French king.

Heading back to the archway, she stared at the closed panels of the dining room and listened to the pounding of her heart.

Lifting her hands, she prodded the calluses on her palms.

They hadn't come from working here for her father and the Brotherhood for the last couple of months, organizing the schedule and tracking issues, resolutions and follow-ups. No, for the first time in her life she had been hitting the gym. Pumping iron. Running on treadmills. Working the Stair-Master. Pull-ups, push-ups, sit-ups. Erg machine.

Before now, she hadn't even known what an erg machine was.

And it was all in preparation for tomorrow night.

Assuming that group of males in the King's audience room wasn't taking it all away from her.

Tomorrow, at midnight, she was supposed to join the Scribe Virgin only knew how many males and females at a secret location—where she was going to try to make the cut for the Black Dagger Brotherhood's training program for soldiers.

It was a good plan—something she had decided to pursue, a chance to be independent and kick some ass and prove to herself she was more than her pedigree. The problem? Fully blooded daughters from the *glymera*, from one of the Founding Families no less, did not train to become soldiers. They didn't handle guns or knives. They didn't learn to fight or defend themselves. They didn't even know what a *lesser* was.

They didn't even *associate* with soldiers.

Daughters like her were trained in needlepoint, classical music and singing, manners, and running vast households filled with *doggen*. They were expected to know the complicated social calendar and the festival cycles, keep up with the wardrobe requirements of all of that, and know the difference between Van Cleef & Arpels, Boucheron and Cartier. They were cloistered, protected, and cherished as all jewels were.

The only dangerous thing they were permitted to do? Breed. With a *hellren* chosen by their family to ensure the sanctity of their bloodlines.

It was a miracle her father was letting her do this.

He had certainly not been on board when she'd first shown him the application—but he'd had a change of heart and let her apply to the program: The raids of a couple of years ago, when so many vampires had been killed by the Lessening Society, had proved what a dangerous place Caldwell, New York, could be. And she'd told him that she didn't want to go out and fight in the war. She just wanted to learn to defend herself.

Once she'd framed it in terms of her safety? That was when her father had changed his tune.

The real truth was that she just wanted something that was hers. An identity that came from a place other than what her birthright had forced on her.

Plus Peyton had told her she couldn't do it.

Because she was female.

Screw that.

Paradise checked those closed doors again. "Come on. . . ."

Pacing around, she eventually wandered out into the foyer, but she didn't want to get too close to where the males were meeting—as if that might jinx things.

God, what were they talking about in there?

Usually the King left right after the last audience of the night. If he and the Brotherhood had any private business or stuff about the war to deal with, it was handled back at the First Family's residence, a place so secret that not even her father had been invited to go there.

So yeah, this had to be about her.

Back in the waiting area, she went to the desk and counted the hours she had sat at it. She'd only had the job a couple of months, but she'd liked the work—to a point. In her absence, assuming she stayed in the BDB training program, a cousin of hers was taking over, and she'd spent the last seven nights showing the girl the ropes, clarifying the procedures Paradise had put into place, making sure that the transition was going to go smoothly.

Sitting back down in her chair, she opened the middle drawer and took out her application—as if that could somehow reassure her that this was all going to still happen.

As she held the paperwork in her hands, she wondered who else was going to be at the orientation tomorrow . . . and thought of the male who'd shown up here at the audience house, looking for a printed-out version of the application.

Tall, big shoulders, deep voiced. Wearing a Syracuse baseball cap, and jeans that had been worn out from what looked like actual work.

The community of vampires was a small one, and she'd never seen him before—but maybe he was just a civilian?

That was another change in the training program. Before now, only males from the aristocracy were invited to work with the Brotherhood.

He had given her his name, but refused to shake her hand.

Craeg. That was all she knew.

He hadn't been rude, though. In fact, he'd been supportive of her applying.

He'd also been ... captivating in a way that had shocked her—to the point where she'd waited for weeks to see if he brought the application back. He hadn't. Maybe he'd scanned it and sent the thing in that way.

Or maybe he'd decided not to try for the program after all.

It seemed crazy to be disappointed that she might never see him again.

As her phone went off with a chirp, she jumped and went for the thing. Peyton. Again.

She would see him at the orientation tomorrow night— and that would be soon enough. After that fight they'd had about her joining the program, she'd had to pull away from the friendship.

Then again, if the Brotherhood was putting their foot down in there with her father? That righteous indignation she felt toward the guy was going to be a moot point. But come on, females were allowed to apply.

The problem was, she was not a "normal" female.

FFS, she did not know what she was going to do if her father took it all back. Surely the Brotherhood wouldn't wait until the last minute to deny her a spot, though.

Right?

Across town, Marissa, mated *shellan* of the Black Dagger Brother *Dhestroyer*, a.k.a. Butch O'Neal, sat back in her desk chair at Safe Place. As the thing let out a creak, she tapped her Bic pen on the OfficeMax calendar blotter and shifted the phone receiver to her other ear.

Cutting into the stream of blabbering, she said, "Well, I certainly appreciate the invitation, but I can't—"

The female on the other end didn't miss a beat. She just kept on talking, her aristocratic intonation sucking up all the bandwidth—until it was a wonder that the entire zip code didn't suffer an electrical brownout. "... and you can understand why we need your help. This is the first Twelfth Month Festival Ball that has been held since the raids. As the *shellan* of a Brother, and a member of a Founding Family, you would be a perfect chair of the event—"

Giving her *no* another shot, Marissa cut in, "I'm not sure you're aware of this, but I work full-time as the director of Safe Place and—"

"... and your brother said that you would be a good choice."

Marissa fell silent.

Her first thought was that she found it highly unlikely that Havers, the race's physician and her very, very, very estranged next of kin, had recommended her for anything other than an early grave. Her second was more along the lines of a calculation ... how long had it been since she had spoken to him? Two years? Three? Not since he'd thrown her out of their house, about five minutes before dawn, when he'd found out she was interested in a mere human.

Who had actually turned out to be Wrath's cousin and the embodiment of the *Dhestroyer* legend.

How ya like me now, she heard in her head.

"So you just *have* to chair the event," the female concluded. As if it were a done deal.

"You must needs forgive me." Marissa cleared her throat. "But my brother is not in a position to proffer my name for anything, as he and I haven't seen each other for quite some time."

When a whole boatload of nothing-but-quiet came over the connection, she decided she should have aired her family's dirty laundry about ten minutes ago: Members of the *glymera* were supposed to observe rigid codes of behavior — and exposing the colossal rift in her bloodline, even though it was well-known, was something that was simply not done.

Far more appropriate for others to whisper about it behind your back.

Unfortunately, the female recovered and changed tactics. "At any rate, it is vitally important for all members of our class to resume the festivals—"

A knock on the door to her office brought Marissa's eyes around. "Yes?"

Over the phone, the female said, "Wonderful! You can come to my estate—"

"No, no. There's someone who needs me." She spoke up louder. "Come on in."

The moment she saw the expression on Mary's face, she cursed. Not good news. Rhage's *shellan* was a consummate professional, so for her to look like that? It was really a problem—

Was that *blood* on her shirt?

Marissa dropped her tone and cut the politeness. "My answer is no. My job requires all my time. Besides, if you're this passionate, you should take the job. Good-bye."

Dropping the phone back in the cradle, she got to her feet. "What's going on?"

"We've got an intake who needs medical assistance STAT. I can't reach Doc Jane or Ehlena anywhere. I don't know what to do."

Marissa rushed around the desk. "Where is she?"

"Downstairs."

The pair of them hit the stairwell at a run, Marissa in the lead. "How did she come to us?"

"I don't know. One of the security cameras picked her up out on the lawn, crawling."

"What?"

"My cell phone went off with an alert, and I ran out there with Rhym. We carried her into the parlor."

Rounding the corner at the bottom, Marissa skidded on one of the throw rugs. . . .

And stopped altogether.

When she saw the condition of the female on the sofa, she put one hand over her mouth. "Oh, dear God . . ." she whispered.

Blood. There was blood everywhere, on the floor in drips, soaking through white towels pressed to wounds, pooling under one of the female's feet on the carpet.

The girl had been beaten so badly there was no way to identify her, her features so swollen that, if she hadn't had long hair and a torn skirt, you wouldn't even have known what sex she was. One arm was clearly dislocated, the limb hanging badly from the shoulder . . . and she had only the left high-heeled shoe on, her stockings shredded.

Her breathing was bad, very bad. Nothing but a rattling in her chest, as if she were drowning in her own blood.

Rhym, the intake supervisor, looked up from where she had crouched by the couch. Through the tears in her eyes, she whispered, "I don't think she's going to live. How can she live . . . ?"

Marissa had to pull herself together. It was the only option. "Doc Jane and Ehlena are both unreachable?" she said in a hoarse voice.

"I've tried the mansion," Mary replied. "The clinic. Their cell phones. Two times in all places."

For a split second, Marissa was terrified about what that meant for her own life. Were the Brothers in medical trouble? Was Butch okay?

That lasted only a moment. "Give me your phone—and get the residents into the Wellsie annex. I want everyone there in case I have to bring a male in."

Mary tossed over her phone and nodded. "I'm on it."

Safe Place was exactly that—a safe place for female victims of domestic violence to come for shelter and rehabilitation with their young. And after Marissa had spent countless, useless centuries in the *glymera*, being nothing but the unclaimed betrothed of the King, she had found her calling here, in service to those who had been at best verbally abused, at worst, horrifically treated.

Males were not allowed inside.

But to save the life of this female here, she would break that rule.

Answer your phone, Manny, she thought as the first ring sounded. *Answer your damn phone. . . .*

It wasn't the whole Black Dagger Brotherhood.

In fact, there were only two Brothers with the King.

As Abalone, First Adviser to Wrath, son of Wrath, sire of Wrath, entered the audience room to stand before his ruler, he was acutely aware of the other males. He had never known any of those warriors to be aught than protective and civilized, but considering he was about to turn his only blooded offspring over to them, their more obvious attributes were like screams in the night.

The Brother Vishous was staring at him with diamond

eyes that didn't blink, those tattoos at his left temple seeming properly sinister, his muscle-roped body clad in leather and stung with weapons. By his side was Butch, a.k.a. the *Dhestroyer*—a former human with a Boston accent who had been infected by the Omega and left for dead—only to become one of the few to survive a jump-started transition.

The two of them were rarely apart, and it was tempting to assign them bad-cop, good-cop roles. Right now, though, the paradigm had shifted. Butch, the male who tended to smile and talk to people, seemed like the one it would be best to avoid in a dark alley: His hazel stare was narrow and unwavering.

"Yes?" Abalone asked his King. "May I be of service in some manner?"

Wrath stroked the boxy blond head of his guide dog, George. "My boys here need to talk to you."

Ah, Abalone thought. And he suspected what this was about.

Butch smiled for a split second. Like he wanted to preemptively take the sting from whatever was going to come out of his mouth. "We want to make sure you're aware of what's involved in the training program."

Abalone cleared his throat. "I know that this is very important to Paradise. And I'm hoping there are some self-defense courses offered. I should like her to be . . . safer."

That potential benefit had been the only thing that had helped him through the clash between what he had expected for her and her life, and what she seemed to be choosing to do.

When there was no response, Abalone looked back and forth between the Brothers. "What are you not telling me?"

Vishous opened his mouth, but the Brother Butch raised his palm and shut him up. "Your role here with Wrath comes first."

Abalone recoiled. "Are you saying that Paradise is ineligible because of my position here? Dearest Virgin Scribe, why didn't you tell us—"

"We need you to understand that what's going to happen is not all book learning. This is a preparation for war."

"But the candidates don't necessarily have to go fight down in the alleys during the program, correct?"

"What we're worried about is here." The Brother indicated the room. "We can't have anything affect your relationship with Wrath and what you do for the King. Paradise is as welcome as anyone else in the program, but not if the prospect of her dropping out or being cut could create tension between us."

Abalone exhaled in relief. "Do not worry about that. She succeeds or fails on her own merits. I expect no special treatment for her—and if she cannot keep up? Then she should be dismissed."

In fact, although he would never say it aloud, he both prayed for, and expected, that to be the case. He did not look forward to Paradise being disappointed in herself or her efforts, but . . . the last thing he wanted for his daughter was her being exposed to any ugliness—or, God forbid, actually trying to fight in the war.

He couldn't even fathom that last one.

"Worry not," he reiterated, glancing at the Brothers and at the King. "All shall be well."

The Brother Butch stared at Vishous. Then looked back. "You read the application, right?"

"She filled it out."

"So you didn't read it?"

"This is something she's doing independently—as her father and *ghardian*, was I supposed to sign it?"

Vishous lit a hand-rolled. "You might want to be prepared, true?"

Abalone nodded. "I am. I promise you, I am."

Paradise was a female gently raised in the proper traditions of the aristocracy. She'd been working on her physical conditioning for the last two months—quite diligently, actually—and he could feel the excitement rolling off of her as she wound up her duties here and prepared to exit her position. There was, however, a very good chance that after the orientation tomorrow evening, when the real work started, she would find herself either bowing out . . . or being asked to leave.

It was going to kill him to see her fail.

But better that than her dying out in the field just to prove the point that she was so much more than what her aristocratic station dictated.

As the pair of Brothers continued to look at him, Abalone lowered his head. "I know this is not going to go well for her. I am more than braced for that. I am not naive."

After a moment, Butch said, "Okay. Fair enough."

"Is there aught else, my lord?" Abalone asked the King.

When Wrath shook his head, Abalone bowed to each of them. "Thank you for your concern. Paradise is my most precious one—all that is left of my beloved *shellan*. I know she shall be in kind and fair hands on the morrow."

As he turned to leave, the Brothers remained grim, but then again, he was not privy to what was going on with the war—and there was always something. The fighting and the strategy were nothing he had ever been involved with, and for that he was grateful.

Just as he would be if Paradise left that program.

Verily, he wished her *mahmen* were still alive. Perhaps this all would be moot if his *shellan* had been present to talk some sense into the girl.

Opening the double doors, he heard a clattering in the waiting area. "Paradise?"

He strode across the foyer, and as he rounded the corner into the parlor, his daughter straightened from picking up red pens that had been knocked off the desk.

"Is all well?" he asked.

Her eyes met his. "Is it? Are you allowing me to go to-morrow night?"

Abalone smiled—and tried to keep the sadness out of his eyes, his voice. "Of course. You're in the program, that was decided months ago."

She ran over and embraced him, holding on tight, as if she had been convinced she was going to be denied what she wanted so badly.

Embracing his daughter, Abalone was vaguely aware of the Brothers and the King leaving out the front door. He paid them no mind.

He was too busy wishing he could save his daughter from any and all disappointment. That was not among the parenting skills he had been granted upon her birth, however.

Oh, how he wished his *shellan* were here with them instead of in the Fade.

She would have handled all of this better.

*   *   *

Standing over the horrifically injured female, Marissa closed her eyes as she got Manny's voice mail for the third time. What the *hell* was going on at the clinic?

Just as she was about to redial, her phone began to ring. "Thank God—Manny? Manny?"

Something about the tone of her voice caused the wounded female to stir, her bloody face moving against the sofa cushions. God, the sound of that wheezing rattle was enough to make the heart skip beats.

"No, it's Ehlena," said the voice in her ear. "Manny and Jane are doing emergency surgery on Tohr. He has a compound fracture of the femur and I have to head back into the OR. Is there something wrong?"

"How long are they going to be?" she asked.

"They just started."

Marissa closed her eyes. "Okay, please have them call me when they can? I've got a . . ." She turned away and dropped her voice. "I have a trauma case that's just come in here. I don't know if we have a lot of time."

Ehlena cursed. "We can't spare anyone here. Can you call Vishous? With his medical training, he may be able to stabilize things."

Marissa tried to imagine that Brother walking through the house. Not her first choice, and not because she didn't trust the male. Her *hellren*'s best friend was a stellar vampire all the way around.

His appearance was just terrifying.

Then again, if everyone was in the Wellsie Annex . . .

"Good idea. Thank you."

"I'll have them call you as soon as we're done."

"Please."

Cutting the connection, she hit up V. And got goddamn, frickin' voice mail. "*Shit.*"

Rhym spoke up from where she was pressing a towel to that leaking gash in the female's shoulder. "When are they coming?"

It was getting close to the end of the night. V could just be in transit between the alleys of downtown Caldwell and the mansion. Or . . . he could be stuck fighting whoever had injured Tohr like that.

As the female on the sofa began to cough and sputter, the calculation was done in a split second. The last thing she wanted to do was reach out to her brother, but she couldn't live with herself if her personal problems cost someone their life.

Marissa dialed Havers's cell phone number by heart, and hoped he hadn't changed it. One ring, two rings . . .

"Hello?" came his voice.

"It's me." Before there was some kind of awkward silence or hello, she said, "We have a medical emergency here at Safe Place. I need you to come right now—or send someone. The Brotherhood's physicians are in surgery and we don't have a lot of time."

There was a short pause, as if the race's primary healer were switching from a personal track to a professional one. "I shall be there in but a moment. Is it a trauma situation?"

"Yes." Marissa lowered her voice again. "She's been badly beaten and . . . brutalized. There's a lot of blood. I don't know. . . ."

"I'm bringing a nurse. Are you containing the other residents?"

"Already have."

"Unlock the front door."

"I'll meet you at it."

And that was that.

Guess the universe was determined to have her brother on her radar screen this evening. First that idiot call with the socialite, now . . .

Marissa nodded to Rhym. "Help is on the way."

Through the eye that was not swollen shut, the injured female seemed to try to focus.

Marissa leaned in and took a bloody hand. "My brother is going to take very good care of you."

For a split second, she worried whether she should have kept quiet about the fact that a male was going to treat her. But the female didn't seem to be tracking.

Dearest Virgin Scribe, what if she died before he got here?

Marissa crouched down, tucking her blond hair behind her ears. "You're safe, it's going to be all right." That one eye looped over to her face. "Do you have kin we can call? Is there someone who we can get for you?"

The female's head went back and forth.

"No? Are you sure?" The eye shut. "Can you tell me who did this to you?"

That face turned away.

Shit.

Backing off, Marissa went out to the shallow hall in the front of the house. There were long, thin windows on either side of the door, and she looked out to the lawn. The trees that had been so brilliantly colored just weeks before had molted their spectacular red and gold and yellow leaves, the spindly limbs underneath revealed like the bones of a too-thin dog.

It was impossible not to glance at the mirror next to the door and check to see that her hair was in place, and her makeup was holding up even after a ten-hour day.

Back when she had lived with her brother, she had worn silk gowns and heavy jewels, and had her hair styled up high on her head. Now? She had a pair of Ann Taylor slacks on, a blouse with a stand-up collar, and a pair of Cole Haan driving shoes on her feet because they were comfy. No jewelry other than a tiny gold cross that she wore because Butch's God was important to him and her *hellren* had given her the necklace during his last Christmas season. Oh, and she had a pair of pearl studs in her ears.

In spite of Butch's transition having been jump-started, and his status as a Brother and a relation of the King, her male remained fundamentally human, everything from his Catholic belief system to his taste in books and movies to his opinions on what he wanted in a "wife," a product of his upbringing among Homo sapiens.

Touching the gold chain on her neck, she frowned as she had to fight the urge to take the thing off because her brother wouldn't approve of it.

But come on, whether the symbol of her mating was on or off her throat, it wasn't as if that changed anything. In her brother's eyes, she had taken a rat without a tail as a *hellren*, and that fall from grace would never be forgiven.

A split second later, two shadows materialized out of thin air on the sidewalk: one taller and masculine, dressed in a white coat, the other smaller and feminine in a traditional nursing uniform.

As they approached and were illuminated in the security lights, Marissa rubbed her sweaty palms on the seat of her pants. Havers looked exactly the same as he always had, from the bow tie and the horn-rimmed glasses to the dark hair parted on the side and kept in *Mad Men* order.

At the last minute, Marissa switched the cross around to her nape and opened the door. Trying not to sound as if she were nervous, she announced, "She is in the parlor."

No "Hello, how are you?" or "Hey, have you stopped being a prejudicial asshole?"—but then again, this was a medical emergency, not a social call.

"Marissa," her brother said, nodding his head and stepping by her. "This is Cannest, my head nurse."

"My pleasure, I'm sure," the nurse murmured.

Marissa nodded at the female. "This way."

Her legs felt stiff as she led them deeper into the modest house with its common furnishings, and for some absurd reason she pictured herself as a flamingo, her knees facing the wrong way. Meanwhile, all manner of memories boiled under the surface of her conscious mind, only the psychic weight of the tragedy unfolding in the other room keeping a lid on her emotions.

Her brother stopped at the archway into the parlor and gave his doctor's bag to his assistant. "My nurse will do the triage, and advise me as to her condition. It will be better than having a male perform the examination."

Marissa glanced into Havers's eyes for the first time, and noted that his stare had remained the identical shade of blue that hers was. As if that would have changed, though?

"That is very considerate of you," she said before looking to his associate. "Come with me."

In the parlor, the nurse went directly to the sofa, and was kind to Rhym as she took the staffer's place. The victim stirred as if recognizing that there was a new presence before her, and then moaned as her pulse and blood pressure were taken.

Marissa stood off to the side, crossing her arms over her chest and putting her hand up to her mouth. The movements were good, she told herself. It meant that the poor girl was still alive.

"Be careful," she blurted as the nurse felt down that arm and tears mixed with the blood on that beaten face.

Dear God, who had done this? It had to be a member of the species—she couldn't catch the scent of anything human on her.

Marissa had to drop her eyes as the exam became more intimate, and she motioned for Rhym to join her by the archway, as if she were protecting the privacy her brother was already respecting.

After what felt like forever, the nurse spoke quietly with the female and then came back over, nodding for Marissa to follow her out to where Havers was standing with his hands clasped behind his back. He bowed his head as he listened to his nurse speak in a quiet tone.

"She has extensive internal injuries," the female reported. "She will have to be operated on immediately if she is going to survive. The arm is the least of the problems."

Havers nodded and glanced at Marissa. "I took the liberty of arranging for transport. It should arrive in approximately fifteen minutes."

"I'm going in the van with her." Marissa got ready for a fight. "Until her blood comes, I am her *ghardian*."

"But of course."

"And I will assume the cost of treatment."

"That will not be necessary."

"It is very necessary. Allow me to get my things."

Leaving them, she spoke to Rhym, and then she ran up to her office and got her phone, her purse, and her coat.

She thought about calling Butch, as there was some chance she wasn't going to be home for the day, but she wasn't going to know that for a little bit. And unfortunately, if she dialed up her *hellren* every time a crisis hit here at work? She would wear out his ringer.

Halfway down the stairs, she realized there was another reason she wasn't reaching out to him.

Too close to what had happened to his sister.

And there was a possibility things could be completely the same if this female died from her injuries.

No, she thought as she returned to the first floor. He had enough on his plate without having old triggers scatter his grey matter yet again.

"I'm ready," she told her brother, as if daring him to change his mind.

"The ambulance is two minutes out. I shall need to be in it with her as well—she is going to require a feeding if she has any chance of surviving."

Havers gave her a little bow and retraced his steps to the front door. As he turned the corner, Marissa shook her head.

The idea that he would give of his own blood to help some unknown female, who was probably naught but a civilian, was both amazing . . . and a source of frustration.

That the male could be so kind to his patients and so cruel to her personally seemed like an insupportable contradiction.

But that was the *glymera* for you. Double standards abounded.

And typically were used to screw daughters, sisters, and mothers.

FROM #1 *NEW YORK TIMES* BESTSELLING AUTHOR

J. R. WARD

An enthralling new series set amid the shifting dynamics of a Southern family defined by wealth and privilege—and compromised by secrets, deceit, and scandal....

THE BOURBON KINGS

For generations, the Bradford family has worn the mantle of kings of the bourbon capital of the world. Their sustained wealth has afforded them prestige and privilege—as well as a hard-won division of class on their sprawling estate, Easterly.

For Lizzie King, Easterly's head gardener, crossing that divide nearly ruined her life. Falling in love with Tulane, the prodigal son of the bourbon dynasty, was nothing that she intended or wanted—and their bitter breakup only served to prove her instincts were right. Now, after two years of staying away, Tulane is finally coming home and no one will be left unmarked: not Tulane's beautiful and ruthless wife; not his older brother, whose bitterness and bad blood know no bounds; and especially not the ironfisted Bradford patriarch, a man with few morals, fewer scruples, and many, many *terrible secrets*.

Available wherever books are sold or at
penguin.com

S0611